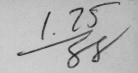
NO TURNING BACK . . .

She felt his hands running urgently over her shoulders and back, expertly untying her stays and sliding them away from her body.

"We shouldn't," she gasped.

But he cut off her words with his lips, and, her protest lost, she wildly returned his urgent kiss. All the emptiness, all the months of longing left her helpless before this onslaught of sensation. To be in the arms of a man who wanted her as badly as she did him—she could no more turn back than she could cease to breathe.

Something had caught fire between them, and willingly, gratefully, she allowed herself to be engulfed . . .

BEYOND THE SHINING RIVER

Maryhelen Clague

BERKLEY BOOKS, NEW YORK

This Berkley book contains the complete
text of the original hardcover edition.
It has been completely reset in a type face
designed for easy reading, and was printed
from new film.

BEYOND THE SHINING RIVER

A Berkley Book / published by arrangement with
Coward, McCann and Geoghegan

PRINTING HISTORY
Coward, McCann and Geoghegan edition / August 1980
Berkley edition / September 1981

ISBN: 0-425-05037-8

A BERKLEY BOOK ® TM 757,375
Berkley Books are published by Berkley Publishing Corporation,
200 Madison Avenue, New York, New York 10016.
PRINTED IN THE UNITED STATES OF AMERICA

for Bill—
because he believed in me

contents

author's note

Westchester County lies just north of New York City in a country of wooded hills, bordered on one side by the Hudson River and on the other by Long Island Sound and Connecticut. Until 1898 it included all of what is now the New York City borough of the Bronx, including Morrisania, Hunt's Point, King's Bridge, the town of Westchester, and West Farms, that area so important to this story. Because West Farms today lies partly within the southern portion of the Bronx Zoo it is still possible to appreciate the beauty of the Bronx River and the lovely surrounding fields of Bronxdale somewhat as Celia Deveroe knew them.

Beyond the Shining River is a work of fiction, but anyone who knows the history of Westchester County may recognize at once that the character of Ewan Deveroe is based upon the life of James De Lancey, the celebrated Colonel of the Westchester Refugees during the Revolutionary War, and that the Deveroe family is to some extent taken from the lives of the powerful De Lancey clan of West Farms and New York City. Samuel Deveroe, his children and Celia herself—that branch of the family which is central to the story—are all fictional characters who have been worked into the tapestry of actual events.

A character quickly becomes his own man, and Ewan Deveroe is in no way meant to be a biographical portrait of Colonel De Lancey even though many of the actual events from the life of one are depicted as happening to the other. The Colonel was a valiant, proud, typical eighteenth-century gentleman, and I like to hope that somewhere, as he rides his charger through the Elysian Fields, he will look down and forgive me for making so free with his life. I even like to hope he might be pleased.

Part I
Celia
1769

one

Celia Broussard had never ridden in a carriage before. She wanted desperately to savor the pleasure—the swaying motions, the pungent smell of leather and horse, the bounces that sent her slight body upward on the horsehair seat like a flower pod flying in the wind. Yet she could not enjoy it. All delight was overwhelmed by the suffocating grief that filled her chest. Watching the faces of her friends as they receded into the green of the forest hills, she felt as though her body were a raw wound. It was not that she minded going. With the blunt honesty of a ten-year-old she knew she had no alternative. But she had only a few days before seen her father's pine coffin lowered into the barren East Chester earth, and those decrepit shacks fading now into the distance were the only home she had ever known, those white faces the only people to whom she had ever belonged. It was hard to leave them.

Peering back around the window frame, she tried to catch one last glimpse of kind old Dominie Brec, but he was only a brown blur on the thick greenery around the clustered shacks. Actually, he was the one person she really regretted leaving. Leaning back against the seat, she pulled the neatly tied bundle of clothing—all she had carried away with her—tight against her chest. Her throat felt as though it had closed so no air could get through. Then, glancing up, she saw that next to her the large man in the resplendent green coat and the silver-white wig with its fat side curls was peering down into her face with grave intensity. He looked as though he was afraid she might burst into tears.

"Are you sorry to leave, Celia?" asked Samuel Deveroe gently, using the familiar Anglicized version of her name. "No doubt you will be seeing your friends again. Our summer home is not that far away."

3

She did not know how to answer him, so she simply stared back, her large eyes liquid with unshed tears.

"You will enjoy your new family," Samuel tried to reassure her. "My daughter, Hester, is near your age and will be a good friend to you. There will be much to do and many new things to learn." He reached out and lifted her arm, so thin that the bones protruded. "And we will have to put some flesh on you. I'll wager you will be eating better and dressing better than you ever dreamed possible. Won't that please you?"

Celia hesitated, then nodded slightly because the strange man seemed to expect it. Perhaps, if what he said was true, there would be enough coarse bread and gruel on his table that for once in her life she could lie down on her straw pallet without a gnawing ache in her stomach. As for her dress, she was proud of the drab brown homespun, for she had made it herself, from dyeing the wool in hickory bark to sewing the tight, careful stitches.

Samuel turned away to stare out of the window. Such a silent little thing, he thought. Perhaps in time she'll liven up a bit. It is still too soon after Gabriel's death.

Celia too was thinking of her father. In fact, he had seldom been out of her mind these last few days. She knew what death was, having seen it many times in her young life, and she knew the certainty of never seeing him again. In some vague way she supposed Papa was now with all the saints and with Mama, and that, no doubt, would make him happy. But, oh, it was hard for her, left behind to long for him, knowing he would never come home again to pull her up into his broad lap, his arms confortingly around her, his coarse wool coat reeking of tobacco, his beard rough against her cheek, his deep, rich voice weaving the old familiar tales of the wonderful places they would someday visit together.

Never again would he describe for her the beautiful home that had once been theirs in Grand Pré on the island of Acadia, a country of green fields rimmed by a silver ocean. No crust of boulders studded the verdant earth of that land as they did this inhospitable West Chester valley in the province of New York, and in that country there was always plenty to eat. Best of all, the emerald fields and sloping hills were their own, their land, their home. Papa had often told her about this wonderful Acadia, and there was always sadness in the telling because before she was born they had been forced to come as exiles to these foreign shores where there was never enough to eat, where the work was never done, and where they would never belong. Now the vision of that mystical country was gone forever. She would never be able to find it alone, for she had no idea where it was. It was a dream buried along with Papa in the coffin of white pine boards, raw to the sun and covered with the earth. And she must go and live with strangers.

Then she remembered Madame Peletaire. Shifting her weight against the seat to ease the pressure on her back, she thought ruefully, without Papa, even strangers might be preferable to living with Madame Peletaire. Her back was still sore from Madame's last caning. Celia could not remember a hand laid on her body until six months ago when her father had taken that ill-fated trip to Lake Champlain and she had been forced to stay at Madame's house. Knowing her for a cross, disagreeable old woman, she had tried hard at first to please her, but on her second day there, when she accidentally dropped and broke a cherished china bowl Madame had brought with her from Acadia, Celia realized she was in for a different kind of life than any she had known before.

"You wretched child," Madame had screamed, her thin lips drawn into one tight line, the wrinkles on her brown face pulled together like a dried apricot. "Your father has spoiled you beyond redemption." Her clawed fingers bit into Celia's shoulders, shaking them with such force that the girl's head rocked back and forth. Perhaps Madame might have been satisfied with a thorough rattling, but Celia in her outrage had twisted her head around until she managed to sink her teeth into the wiry arm, raising two bloody marks against the white linen sleeve.

That did it. Hardly a day passed after that but she committed some infraction of Madame's strict rules which had Celia bending over the back of a straight oak chair so that Madame could flail her narrow shoulders with a stout hickory switch. Bad as they were, the switchings were easier to bear than the poor table Madame kept. The memory of the never-ending hunger she had endured while under Madame Peletaire's roof was a searing scar across her mind.

Only once had she appealed for help to her friend Dominie Brec, teacher and pastor of the exile band. In his gentle, ineffectual way he had tried to talk to Madame while Celia stood outside, her ear pressed to the cracks in the door.

"The child is . . . is very thin, I've noticed of late," he stammered, not able to look Madame directly in the eye. "I fear

Gabriel will think she has been ill while he was away."

"Her only illness lies in her disposition," Madame answered without a qualm. "She has a frivolous nature and must be taught meekness and obedience. That is no easy task, I tell you, Père, with the way Gabriel has allowed her to grow unbridled. I am doing my best."

"I always found in her a sweetness of disposition—"

"You are a naïve man, Père. I am a better judge of what a young lady should be."

"She tells me that you have used a switch," he said, unwilling to back down without trying further.

"All children need punishment. It shapes their natural savagery into civilized behavior."

"That she must work from dawn to dark . . ."

"Hard work is good for the soul."

". . . and that she is always hungry," he blurted out the final complaint.

Madame looked down her thin nose, barely able to disguise her contempt. "We are all hungry in this detestable place, as you well know. Celié would be a better child to stop complaining and accept the conditions of our exile. For a man who has wisely led us since we were forced onto those British warships, Gabriel uses little judgment where his own daughter is concerned. Since her mother died she has been allowed to run wild. I intend to see that she is molded into a proper young lady before it is too late. Gabriel will thank me for it someday. You'll see. In fact," Madame went on, "I intend to convince Gabriel when he returns to allow her to live with me. She does not belong in a house with only her father and no woman to guide her."

Outside the door, Celia's heart turned over. Live with Madame! She would rather die. Her only hope was for her father to return and take her out of this hateful house. If only it could be soon.

But the months had dragged by before Gabriel reappeared on the dirt road before the dilapidated shacks. And to Celia's distress he was in no condition to stand up to Madame Peletaire, for he was so weakened by a fever and ague that he was already near death. How she had pleaded to be allowed to go home and nurse him, but for once the whole band of exiles had been solidly against her. Not an adult of the company but thought she was better off at Madame's house, and only a few times was she even permitted to visit her father, lying weakened and half out of his mind in his empty house.

She could still see so clearly that huddled group of people watching around the deathbed in the stifling cabin on the day Gabriel died, stepping aside to let through the large man in the satin coat who now sat beside her in the carriage. He had been sweating profusely, long rivulets of water streaming down the sides of his face from under his powdered wig. She had seen him before a few times but never paid much attention. And she did not pay it now, so filled was she with dumb despair. For when the last breath left Gabriel's wasted body she was gripped tightly by the hand and led firmly back to Madame's threshold which, like the portals of hell, she crossed leaving hope behind. Her soul shriveled within her. If only she could have died with Papa!

A jolt of the carriage threw her frail body against Samuel's sturdy one. Celia pulled herself back into her corner and shyly smiled up at him. She was not happy. She was terribly frightened. But whatever the future was, she had at least been delivered from Madame's house. She was at least grateful for that.

It was reassuring to Samuel Deveroe to see Celia give him that timid half-smile. In fact, as the coach lumbered and jerked its way down the rutted paths toward West Farms, he had begun to fear he had made a mistake in coming to take the girl into his home. But one does not lightly go back on one's word to a dying man.

He remembered how he had been sitting in the shade of the summerhouse in the rear of the garden trying to escape the hottest part of the day when word came that Gabriel Broussard was dying and had asked to see him. Without hesitation he had put on his coat, wig and gold-laced hat and turned his horse down the road to East Chester.

How many years had he and his late brother, James, struggled alongside Broussard to bring some decency and order into the lives of this ragtag, rootless, destitute band of exiles? It had to be nearly ten years. Ten years of retrieving them first from the East Chester jail where the Borough Assembly was perfectly content to have them stay, and into some kind of shelter, and then of attempting to assimilate fifty foreigners into a Colonial way of life. They were industrious and intelligent. They could have made a good life for themselves on this verdant New York soil, but no. They clung to the hope of returning to Acadia as they clung to their incomprehensible French language.

Samuel shook his head. Other exiles had made good lives for themselves in this rich country. Perhaps it was because they had come willingly, while these French people had been dragged bodily onto British transports and carried away by force. He could never have managed them at all without Gabriel. Broussard was the best of the lot. Strong, intelligent, a realist yet one who understood and sympathized with the longings of his people. When he was gone God only knew how the Assembly was ever going to resolve the problem.

He was back again in the sweltering room. "You came . . ." Gabriel whispered, his words barely audible. Samuel had to lean close to the dying man's lips, holding his scented square of blue silk against his nose to keep away the contagious humors.

"As soon as I got word. My dear friend. I'm so sorry."

Gabriel's fingers clawed at the lapel of Samuel's coat. "You help me now, Samuel, *mon ami*?"

"Of course I'll help. Don't worry about your people. I won't let the Assembly neglect them, I promise."

To his surprise Gabriel feebly shook his head. "No, no. You help *me*, monsieur? My Celié? You take her? She has no one now. I can . . ."

His voice trailed off, leaving Deveroe to sit back mystified. Celié? Who was she?

Looking around, he found himself staring directly into the large amber eyes of a child standing near the bed. Of course. Gabriel's daughter, the girl he had struggled to raise alone since his wife died five years before.

Gabriel struggled to raise his head. "I ask the great favor of you, monsieur. Take her from here. Let her grow up in a better place." Mistaking Samuel's startled silence for hesitation, he fought to speak louder. "She is not . . . poor. I have the deed to my land. It is hers now. Care for her, *mon ami*, and Gabriel will die content."

Samuel gently untwisted the fingers from his coat and helped the dying man to lie back. "Have no concern for the child, Broussard. I'll care for her myself, I promise you. She will never want for anything while I am able to help her."

Closing his eyes, Gabriel whispered a faint, "*Merci, mon ami* Samuel. *Merci* . . ."

He seemed to have slipped into a quiet sleep. Unable to

bear the oppressive heat any longer and filled with apprehension at what he had just promised, Samuel laid the man's hands across his chest and rose to leave. Before he turned from the bed he saw the old dominie put a large crucifix in Gabriel's hands. At least the priest had had the courtesy to remove the offensive thing while Samuel was in the room.

Outside, he felt a hand pulling on his coat and turned to see the dominie almost wringing his hands.

"Ay, monsieur, how will we manage?" he began in his broken English. "What will become of us now? *Mon Dieu, et après?*"

Deveroe hardly knew how to reassure him. There was really no one to take Gabriel's place. "You'll have to elect another delegate to represent you. I'll need someone to work with. You can handle that, can't you?"

Brec shrugged hopelessly. "We always looked so to Monsieur Broussard. He was our . . . *notre force*—our strength."

"I know. He cannot really be replaced, but we have to try. And, Dominie, please try to find someone who has learned to speak English!"

"*Oui*, monsieur. It will be done."

Deveroe had one foot on the mounting block when he turned back and called the dominie to him. "Was that the child there by the bed—Gabriel's daughter?"

"*Oui. La petite* Célie. *Pauvre enfante!* All alone now."

"I'll be back in a week or two to take her away with me. That will give me time to prepare Madam Deveroe as well as allow the child time to accustom herself to the idea of a new home. Can your people care for her in the meantime?"

"She has been living with Madame Peletaire."

Samuel looked up sharply. That unpleasant, tight-lipped shrew. No wonder Gabriel had asked him to take the girl.

"Tell Madame Peletaire to have her ready."

"*Oui, monsieur. Elle sera prête.*"

Vividly he could still see the old man stumbling back into the cabin, a black shawl already draped over the door. He had been about to add that the child should prepare to leave her Popish practices behind, but he decided against it. Gabriel had asked him to take her knowing better than most men that an English household would mean the English Church. No need to make an issue of it.

She was a pretty little thing, although thin and bony as a rail. Looking down at her pinched face, pensive in the shadows of the coach, he was struck once again by the thought that she must be about the same age as Hester, his daughter. She would make a good companion for her—fill in the gap left by his two other daughters dead in infancy. Hester had two strong brothers, but a little girl needs a sister. And this child certainly needed a good home.

He sighed. Pray God he had done the right thing.

Glancing up, Celia was suddenly aware that the big man in the white wig had been speaking to her.

"Excuse me, sir," she said quietly.

"Well, little one, so you have a voice after all. I said, how much do you know of grammar or arithmetic? Did you go to school at all back there? Did you ever study a primer?"

"Oh, yes, sir. My papa sent me to Dominie Brec with the other children for part of every day. I know a few sums and can write a decent hand."

"I see you do not mix up your speech with a lot of French words. Did your father not wish you to learn his language?"

"*Oui, monsieur. Je parle français mon berceau.*"

The little minx. Deveroe smiled to himself. So young and already bilingual. Perhaps she was a clever child after all.

By the time the coach rattled into West Farms, Celia's numbness had worn off sufficiently that she was able to take an interest in her surroundings. The road followed the curve of the Bronx River, wide at this point, and took them past a tall house of white-washed stone standing in front of a wooden mill whose sloping roof sank almost to the water's edge. Beyond were grain-heavy fields bordering outbuildings of stone, stretching away to the edge of the horizon where the forests began. Her eyes widened in disbelief as the carriage pulled to a stop before one of the largest and grandest houses she had ever seen.

The driver hopped down and stuck his head in at the window, giving Celia her first good look at him. He was a young black slave, with dark liquid eyes in a broad face. When he pulled the steps down and took Celia's hand to help her from the carriage she could hardly believe his size. Behind her, Deveroe hoisted his bulk out of the coach, sending it swaying on its springs.

"Vestal, carry Miss Broussard's, er, belongings into the hall," he said to the young black man.

Celia gripped the pitiful bundle of clothing to her chest.

"I'll keep it," she murmured, not really trusting this hulking African with her few treasured possessions.

Vestal looked at Samuel, the smile still on his face. "Well, I suppose you may carry it yourself if you wish. Come along, then, child, and meet Mrs. Deveroe."

There was no porch, just a small stoop, but the hall inside the doorway made Celia gasp. The wide plank floors were polished to a shade of old copper so that she hesitated to place her mud-encrusted wooden clogs on their shining surface. The afternoon sunshine filtered through the fanlight over the door, illuminating the brass sconces on the wall and the huge silver bowl overflowing with summer flowers on a cherry-wood table.

Celia's eyes widened again as another Negro servant, this one in shiny green silk livery and a wiry horsehair wig tied with a satin ribbon, stepped up to receive Samuel's hat.

"Where is Madam Elizabeth, Jess?"

"She be in the mornin' room, sir, and she looking for you to come home this day long," the servant replied, trying to ignore Celia's curious stare. Although she had seen black slaves from a distance, Celia had never been so close to one before. She was as fascinated with his lilting hybrid speech as she was with his clothes.

Embarrassed, Deveroe took her hand and pulled her away. She followed him docilely down the hall to a room liquid with sunshine, where sitting behind a tambour frame was the loveliest woman Celia had ever seen. From a high sweep of silver hair soft curls cascaded around her exquisite face. She was wearing a silver lace stomacher over a skirt of rose-colored brocade that fell in gentle folds over her softly curved figure, and though the dress must have been unbearably stiff, and hot, she looked as cool and contained as a queen.

"Samuel, my dear. Finally you have returned."

Elizabeth Deveroe offered her cheek to her husband, then turned to meet Celia's direct stare.

"And this must be Mistress Broussard. Come here, child, and let me look at you."

Celia stood rooted to the spot until Samuel gave her a gentle push forward. Then the beautiful lady reached out and took both her hands, turning them over in her own.

"My, she's a frail little thing, isn't she. But clean. That's important. Well, child, Mr. Deveroe tells me it was your father's wish that we should care for you. Would you like to come and live with us?"

Celia hesitated, then decisively shook her head no.

"Ha!" said a voice behind her. Turning, Celia saw a plump young man lounging on a sofa against the wall. His puffy face was red from the heat and his wig was pushed back high on his forehead to allow a little air against his polished pink skin. "She's an honest little urchin, isn't she," he said, and Celia blushed under the contempt in his voice.

Elizabeth Deveroe threw him an angry frown. "Be quiet, Henry. We must be patient, after all. Tell me, Celia, what *would* you like to do? Is there someone else you would prefer to live with?"

Something in her kind manner helped to relax the tightness in Celia's chest. "Please, ma'am. I wish to live with Papa."

Elizabeth gave her husband a wary glance. "Of course you do, child, we wish that you could. But your papa is dead now and it is best that you are cared for by my husband and myself. Can you understand that?"

For the first time Celia's eyes filled with tears. All the pain of Papa's burial washed over her again.

"Odd's death, I hope she's not going to cry!" said Henry Deveroe from the couch. "I can't stand wailing children."

"Henry," Samuel said sternly, "go out to the stable and see that Vestal takes proper care of Bonny. We don't need you here."

"Tom's the groom. Let him show Vestal what to do."

"Henry!"

Reluctantly the young man pulled himself out of his slouch and ambled to the door, muttering at his indignity. While Samuel eased his body into a wing chair nearly as large as himself, Elizabeth gently smoothed back the tendrils escaping from Celia's tight braids. She had not known what to expect when Samuel told her he was adopting Gabriel's orphan child. From her first dismay she had moved to grudging resignation, then to pleased anticipation. It might be very satisfying to transform an untutored urchin into a lady of quality. But now that the girl stood before her, some of her old doubts came rushing back. Still, the child was not completely hopeless. Though she wore her poverty like a second skin, her eyes seemed intelligent and she had a good face.

"Such lovely, golden-brown hair," she said soothingly. "And look, Samuel, her eyes match the color of her hair."

But Samuel was still grumbling over his oldest son. "That boy is just like all the Variens. He gets it from your side. I sometimes wonder what's to become of him."

Elizabeth ignored the familiar insult. It was typical of a proud Deveroe to lay every bad trait at the foot of the mother's family.

"Don't cry, little love," she went on. "You'll become used to us and then you may even grow to like your new home. We'll get you a new dress—that one is patched beyond repair. And you will learn to be a lady. It is a grand opportunity for you, Celia, if only you knew. You'll study penmanship and music, you'll learn to dance and sew. Do you have a sampler started yet, my child?"

Celia looked at her blankly.

"Can you make a cross stitch or embroider at all?"

"Oh, you mean my *exemplière*. Yes, it is half finished." And well done too, she knew. For once she was almost glad of those long hours bent over her frame with Madame Peletaire scrupulously checking every stitch.

"The little minx speaks French, Elizabeth," Deveroe said. "A proficiency that already puts her ahead of our Hester."

"French! Master Garver will be so pleased. Samuel dear, would you go to the window and call Hester? We might as well let the girls become acquainted right away, since they'll be so much together."

As Deveroe lifted the sash at the curtained window, Celia heard children laughing and calling to one another outside. Their voices had been there all the time, in the background like birds chattering, but she had not really heard them. Now there was something reassuring in the familiar sound. This was her world, one she knew and understood. These strange adults in their powdered wigs and elaborate clothes were aliens, their questions left her bewildered, uncertain how to respond. Surely other children would not be so different.

Flinging open the door, a bundle of dimity skirts and white-blond curls came bouncing into the room. Instinctively Celia stepped back before all this energy and brightness. The young girl, nearly two inches shorter than herself, peered up into her face, looking her over in frank appraisal.

"Hester dear, where are your manners?" Elizabeth said sharply. "Is that how you were taught to enter a room?"

Hester Deveroe bobbed a curtsy in her mother's direction. "I'm sorry, Mama. We were having a game. I outran John and Ben, both of them. Everyone but Ewan."

"And look at your dress! Decidedly unladylike. Ah, well,

come here and meet your new sister. This is Mistress Celia Broussard. You may wish her a good day."

Hester's eyes narrowed in surprise. When her mother had first used the word "sister," Hester had conjured up a vision of her second self—all blond curls, pink skin and dimity ruffles. This thin, tall, bony girl was as unlike that picture as possible. With her hair pulled back in tight country braids, her coarse dress quilted with patches and darns, her clumsy wooden clogs and worsted stockings, she looked more a peasant or a bound girl than a member of the proud Deveroe family. And this was to be her sister? Hester stared in horrified silence while the girl's golden-brown eyes, too large for her pinched pale face, stared frankly back at her.

"She's very tall."

"Hester!"

A clatter at the doorway interrupted Elizabeth's reprimand. Celia looked around to see a boy's wiry figure, all arms and legs too long for his torso, advancing upon her. He was older than Hester by several years and he had light-brown hair in place of her gold, yet there was an unmistakable similarity in their features.

"Is this the new girl?" the boy asked, giving Celia the same candid appraisal.

"Look at both of you. I declare, you must have been running like colts. Ewan, fix your shirt and stand up properly. Is this the way ladies and gentlemen behave?"

Hester brightened. "Ewan and John had a fight. You should have seen them, Mama, rolling around on the grass."

"Hester, straighten your kerchief. Where is your cap?"

Indignantly Hester pulled at her skirts. "But *she* doesn't look like a lady."

Elizabeth looked helplessly at her husband. "Samuel, speak to your daughter."

"Another Varien!" Samuel snorted from the depths of his chair.

Ewan stepped closer to Celia and looked hard into her face. "Yes, she *is* a lady. I can tell by her eyes, even if the rest of her is shabby."

"Oh, Ewan, that's ridiculous. You can't tell a lady by her eyes!"

"That'll be enough from both of you." Samuel's stern voice sent them both stepping back. "Mistress Broussard is our guest. She has only a few days ago seen her father laid in the earth and she now has no home but ours. I trust you to make her welcome and help her during the time it takes her to grow accustomed to us. Is that clear?"

"Yes, sir," Hester murmured reluctantly, sending Celia a withering glance.

Ewan was obviously moved by this explanation. "I am deeply sorry about your father, Mistress Broussard," he said kindly. "And I take it back. You're not shabby."

"Hester, dear," said Elizabeth, "take Celia upstairs and show her the room we prepared for her. You know where it is. And perhaps you could find one of your dresses that might fit her."

How that was going to be when the girl towered inches over her Hester could not imagine. But she could see that argument was useless. "Yes, ma'am," she said primly. "Come along, miss."

Bobbing a curtsy, she led Celia out of the room, into the hall and up the stairs, followed closely by Ewan. On the second landing she stopped suddenly and turned to face Celia.

"You *are* too tall, you know. And shabby, as Ewan said."

"Oh, I don't know. She looks all right. Perhaps I was a bit hasty."

"No, you were not. Come along, mistress. I suppose I must take you to your room, though why I should have to give you a dress when you are bigger than I am—well, I've no choice."

Ewan stayed on the landing looking after them as Hester briskly climbed the narrow stairs to the third floor. "Hurry back, Hester," he called, "or Richard will have left the game and gone to the stables."

"I'll only be a minute."

It was a small room under the eaves with a window that looked down on the garden below and beyond that to the fields sweeping toward a forested ridge. Celia barely glanced around, too hurt and furious to care about the thick woven mat on the floor and the real bed with its quilted coverlet.

"I don't suppose *you* ever had a room like this before," Hester said smugly.

Celia clutched her bundle against her chest. "You are a very rude girl, you know."

Hester's face flushed with anger. "Well, miss, that is not for you to say."

"I may not live in a grand house, but Madame Peletaire taught me manners when I was younger than you. I would not speak to you this way if you came into my house."

There was enough truth in Celia's comments to turn Hester's smug complacency to fury. Darting forward, she grabbed Celia's arm between her fingers and gave it a sharp pinch. Celia yanked her arm away and stepped back, trying to control her urge to slap that white face. Like quicksilver, Hester's fury turned to contrition. Both hands went to her mouth and she stood looking at Celia with fear in her pale-blue eyes.

"I shouldn't have done that! Please don't tell Mama. She'll be so angry at me."

Celia rubbed the red blotch on her arm and glared at the girl. It would serve her right if she ran right back to the parlor and showed it to Hester's parents.

"You won't tattle, will you? I'm sorry I was rude to you. Why don't you put your things away and come downstairs? We're playing a game."

"Will your brother mind?"

"My brother? Oh, you mean Ewan. He's not my brother, he is my cousin. Richard is my brother. But they won't mind if I don't. Do you know how to play stone-poison tag?"

Celia stared at her incredulously. Did she think she was half-witted? Every child knew how to play stone-poison. She nodded.

"Good, that's settled. Come on down, then." Tossing the words over her shoulder, Hester ran from the room, glad to escape a bad situation.

Celia watched after her, then, still clutching her clothes to her chest, walked over to the window to look down on the green garden below, where she recognized the top of Ewan's brown head as he raced around the flowerbeds. In a moment she caught sight of Hester's white dimity as she ran down the path to join him, shrieking with delight. Celia turned away and went quietly over and sat down on the bed, staring at the floor.

In the sun-filtered morning room Elizabeth Deveroe pulled the wool through her gummed-silk tapestry cloth and shook her head.

"I don't know, Samuel. She's such a ragged little thing. Would it not have been better to have her bound out? Or to take her into our house as a servant?"

"Appearances are deceiving in this case, my dear. I knew Gabriel Broussard well and worked with him for nearly ten years. He was a gentleman in every way despite his poverty. Had he been left in peace in Acadia no doubt he would be a prosperous squire right now instead of lying in an exile's grave. Besides, he once told me that his family was related to the d'Autricourts, one of the four great families of Lorraine. You cannot ask for more impeccable credentials than that for a Frenchman. It would not be right to treat his daughter as a servant."

"But will she be able to learn the manners of a lady after living so long in such reduced circumstances? It is one thing to speak French because you learned it in your cradle, quite another to learn wit, music, graces—everything that sets a lady apart from a countrywoman."

"She will learn. I think she is clever. We must at least give her a chance."

Elizabeth sighed. "Yes, I suppose we must."

It was nearly an hour later when Ewan and Hester bounded up on the porch of the pretty little outside summerhouse where tea was set out and where Samuel and Elizabeth had already taken their places at the table.

"Where are the others?" Elizabeth asked her daughter, brushing away the flies that hovered over a tray of cakes.

"Richard went up to change his shirt," Hester said, reaching for a pink-and-white confection.

"And Celia?"

Something in her mother's voice stopped Hester's hand in midair. "I don't know. She never came down to join us."

"Well, she must still be in her room. Go up and ask her to come down, Hester. I particularly want to have her here."

"Mama! Let Jess go and call her. He's a servant. Why should I have to do it?"

Samuel glared at his daughter. "Hester, you will not speak to your mother in that tone. Now go at once and call Celia."

"But I'm hot and tired!"

"Daughter! Do as your mother says this instant!"

"Oh . . . yes, Papa." With leaden feet Hester set off down the path to the house. Behind her she could hear Ben and John snickering, and her outrage grew in proportion. Who was this urchin, anyway, to so upset her life? The dislike she had felt for Celia when she first saw her standing in the morning room crystallized into near-hatred.

She found the girl sitting where she had left her. Her pathetic bundle of clothes had been laid out on the bed.

"Mama wants you to come down to tea," Hester said from

the doorway. Absently she walked over to examine the dresses. One of them was a lovely shade of vermillion, a color Hester liked above all others. But on seeing it close up she could tell at once that it was of an inferior quality and was crisscrossed with patches and darns. For a moment she was struck by the poverty of such a wardrobe. Perhaps if Celia had come as a servant she might have been moved to pity. It was the thought of accepting her as a sister that rankled.

"Well," she said brusquely.

"I'll come," Celia replied.

"Don't you want to comb your hair or wash you face? Your neck is dirty."

The eyes Celia turned on Hester were bleak, unreadable. She answered quietly, "I'll be down in a minute."

Hester shrugged. "Well, I'm going back down."

"Where—where do I go?"

"To the summerhouse. You can see it down there if you look out your window. We always have tea in the summerhouse on sunny days when we're in the country."

"Thank you," Celia replied with icy politeness. She watched Hester leave, then walked hesitantly over to a looking glass, small and round, whose wavy surface reflected a distorted image of the room. Yet it was clear enough to show the dark smear across her neck. Carefully she dipped her hem in a pitcher of water standing under the mirror and wiped off the worst of the smudge. Then she forced her feet to walk to the stairs. She got down the first and then the second before she lost her nerve and stopped dead, longing to run back to her room and close the door, blocking out this hateful house and its unknown inhabitants. But that would be such a cowardly thing to do, and, unable to go forward or back, she simply sat down on the stairs and buried her head on her knees, giving way to bitter tears. She really did not want to cry, but it was so hard not to when she could still hear the gray earth thumping against the boards of her father's raw pine coffin. If only he were not dead he would come and take her away from this awful place.

"Is something wrong, little girl?"

Celia's head shot up. At the bottom of the stairs a boy, tall and white-wigged, with the gawky look of adolescence, stood watching her intently.

"Why, you're crying. What's the matter?"

To Celia's horror he started up the stairs toward her. She jumped to her feet.

"No, I'm all right. Truly, I am. Go away."

He was standing a few steps below her now, smiling up at her with the gentlest, kindest eyes she had ever seen. He had a narrow, reflective face with heavy arched brows and a mouth as shapely as a girl's. Celia wiped at her eyes with her sleeve.

"Here, take this," he said, offering her a large square of blue silk that just matched the color of his satin coat. "It's mine, but you can use it. And it's perfectly clean—I just took it out of the press."

"Thank you, sir."

"You don't have to say 'sir' to me. I know who you are. You're Gabriel Broussard's daughter. Mama said you would be coming today. I'm Richard Deveroe."

"Did you know my father?" Celia asked hopefully.

Richard flipped up the bottom of his coat and sat down on the stairs below her. "No, not really, although I did see him once or twice when I accompanied Papa on his circuit to East Chester. He was a fine-looking man, I remember. I'm sorry he died."

"Thank you." Keeping a good distance between them, Celia resumed her seat on the stairs above and pretended not to notice how Richard's eyes looked her over, taking in every detail. Suddenly she was grateful that she had washed her neck.

"Why were you crying just now?"

"I wasn't! Well, maybe I was just a little, but I don't know why."

All at once the boy slapped his hand against his forehead. "What a silly question! Your father has only just died and here you are in a strange house among strangers. No wonder you cried. But don't be sad, Celia. You'll like it here when you get used to us, I promise you."

"Your sister said I was to come down to tea."

"Hester?" Richard had a sudden flash of intuition. "She hasn't been unkind to you, has she? If she has I shall box her ears. She is a silly girl and extremely spoiled."

"I—I don't know how to find the summerhouse."

Richard laughed. "So that's the problem. Well, Mistress Celia, you need worry no longer. I will escort you. I was just going there anyway."

Reaching for her hand, he lifted her to her feet. "Mademoiselle, will you do me the honor—"

As he bent forward in an exaggerated bow the red heel on his shoe slipped on the waxed stair. With a cry of surprise and with arms flying he went careening down on the seat of his satin breeches, thumping down each step, to end up in a heap at the bottom.

Crying out, Celia ran after him, sure that he had broken his neck. When he pulled himself up, unable to speak, she began to smile, partly in relief and partly at his ridiculous appearance.

"You're not hurt, are you?"

Richard brushed off the sleeve of his elegant coat and sat up. His white wig had fallen down on his head and was draped half over one eye. All at once, from deep within Celia laughter began to well. It was the kind of release she had not known for a long time, and it overflowed with the tears in her eyes.

"You beastly little girl," Richard said, trying not to laugh with her. "I might have been killed and you find me hilarious!"

She clapped her hand over her mouth. "I'm sorry, but you did look so—so—"

"All right, I'll try once more." Straightening his wig and pulling himself to his feet, he made her a deep bow, one hand over his heart and the other sweeping the air behind him. "Mademoiselle, will you do me the honor of allowing me to take you in to tea?"

She gave him a curtsy. "Thank you, kind sir."

"Now, that was better. And 'sir' was appropriate then. But please stop laughing or Ewan and Hester will demand to know why and then we'll have to tell them I fell down the stairs and Ewan will never let me forget it. You won't tell, will you?"

"Not a word," Celia answered, determined that nothing on earth would ever drag the secret from her.

"Good. Now let's go and have some tea or Hester will have eaten all the cakes."

two

In spite of her grief Celia soon began to enjoy her new home. There were so many delightful new things to enjoy— her lovely new clothes, a table covered with delicious food not just once in a while but every day, beautiful leather-tooled books, the joyful discovery of the world of music the first time she sat down before the yellow keys of the harpsichord. She soon got over her shyness with Samuel and Elizabeth and began to respond to their kind and gentle ways with a tentative, grateful affection, something she could not at all feel for their daughter.

She had recognized right from the beginning that Hester resented her presence. The girl grudgingly carried out every directive from her mother to "help Celia with this" or "show Celia how that is done," but whenever the two were alone she was quick to mock Celia's lack of education or to lay down angry rules that what belonged to her was not to be touched. Then, like quicksilver, her mood would change and she would offer to share a toy or a garment that only a few hours before she had declared off limits. Celia soon became accustomed to these rapid mood shifts, but it was a long time before she learned to take them in stride. Hester was a pincher, and Celia's arms were blue and discolored from her angry nips until she learned to pinch back.

Where Celia disliked and distrusted Hester, she soon learned to be wary of Ewan. He had a way of naturally dominating any group, and when there was something to be done or a game to set up, it was always at Ewan's bidding. He good-naturedly bossed everyone, and from the youngest to the oldest they accepted his leadership unquestioningly. Demanding as he was, he also had a kind way about him, and Celia never minded any more than the others that he manipulated them all. What she did learn to fear was his utter lack of regard for the consequences of his madcap schemes. More than once he brought down Samuel's wrath upon the heads of the entire group or saw some reckless prank of his devising end in cuts or bruises for someone other than himself. Yet the very next day they would all be back, allowing some crazy adventurous plan of Ewan's to land them all in trouble again.

Celia saw very little of Henry Deveroe, for he was already a young man who looked with contempt on the antics of children. What little she did see left her convinced he was fatuous, boring and self-centered and always smelled of horses, which were his single passion in life. On one occasion his fiancée appeared at the Manor House—as the Deveroes' West Farms home was called—and she turned out to be as silly and uninteresting as Henry himself. She had an unpronounceable name, Guinevere, and Celia's first impression of her was of a walking gushing mass of ruffles and curls—an image that never varied.

But Richard Deveroe—ah, that was a different matter altogether. Celia thought him by far the most kindhearted member of the family, while his natural elegance was a striking contrast to Ewan, who more often than not had a torn sleeve or mud-stained breeches. Though nearly the same age as Ewan, he was taller and lighter and had about him an air of quiet self-containment which was in direct contrast to his volatile cousin. He was just enough older than Celia to regard her devotion with a kind of amused tolerance. The kindness he had shown her on that first miserable day at West Farms had won him her absolute loyalty, and the gentle and considerate way he continued to treat her did nothing to alter it. He was her first friend and she felt sure she would love him for that until the day she died.

It did not take her long to sort out the rest of the people who made up the little colony at the Manor House. John Deveroe was only a little older than she, but his interests did not include anything pertaining to girls and she soon learned to stay out of his way. Ben was a great deal younger, and Celia learned to watch over him, carrying his chubby body when his short legs grew tired and washing away the cuts and scratches which inevitably resulted from wading in after the bigger boys. Their father, Peter, Samuel's older brother, was a taciturn man who only shook his head at the folly of his brother taking on another child. His wife had died several years earlier, and his preoccupation was his mill, the most active one in the area.

The farm was managed by Malachi Forbes, who lived with his rotund wife in a cottage near the stone bridge. Tom, the groom, however, was a genial Irishman who quickly became her friend, helping her to learn to ride a pony without falling off or letting it run away with her. He had a round, perpetually pink face, the result of his attachment to hard cider, and, though stern, was fond of all children.

There were three principal servants at the Manor House— Jess, his wife, Dinah, a housemaid, and their son, Vestal, the large, genial driver who had carried Celia from East Chester. Celia had assumed they were slaves, but they quickly let her know they were free blacks, not like those at the Mill House who had all been bought by Master Peter of the mill. She learned to like them all, for they accepted her immediately as one of the family. Because Samuel had made a point of giving them their freedom they were completely devoted to him. Gratitude had made each of them more of a slave to his family than slavery itself would ever have done.

In the oppressive heat of a late August afternoon, Celia and Hester sat at their tambour frames and looked longingly at the window, thrown wide on the airless garden outside the morning room. Across the green expanse of box hedges they could see Tom leading one of Mr. Deveroe's chestnut mares through the stable and out toward the pasture. The drone of a bluebottle fly blundering against the curtains mingled with the far-off voices of the men harvesting the barley fields beyond the barn.

Celia worked her bone needle into the tambour frame and stepped over to the window. A faint breeze laid its cool fingers on her face. "Look, there's Ewan. Out there in the garden."

"It can't be," Hester cried, throwing down her sewing. "I thought you said he was supposed to be working at the mill all day."

But Ewan it was, his waistcoat covered with the course yellow grain dust of the Mill. He was waving to them across the rows of fragrant southernwood, one of Elizabeth's favorite decorative hedges.

"Come on out," he called, "and we'll have a game."

"Can't," Hester called back, leaning over the wide sill. "Mama says we have to finish our four lines or we'll have six to do tomorrow."

In a few bounds Ewan was standing outside the window,

his eyes alight with mischief. "What good little Pamelas," he said sarcastically. "Staying inside sewing on such a beautiful day."

"Ewan Deveroe," Hester said, pouting, "how did you get away from Uncle? You sneaked off, didn't you, you rascally boy."

Ewan hoisted his thin hips up on the sill and leaned against the frame, pulling up his coarse cotton stockings. "Well, and if I did, what's the bother? Father has John to help him and plenty of outside men as well. He'll never miss me. And I've been working since dawn. I couldn't stand those four steep walls any longer. They're like a hot box!"

"So is this room," Hester replied. "I feel as you do—I want to be outside in the pasture just running and running."

"I want to ride, running is too slow. I ache to jump on Jezebel's back and fly across the swale, taking fences, brambles, trees—"

"And breaking your neck," Celia interposed.

Ewan laughed. "Cautious Celia. But you're right. I probably would."

"You can't ride Jezebel, anyway," Hester said, pulling herself up on the other end of the sill and flouncing her skirts. "She's a blooded mare and far too high-spirited."

Ewan's face flushed darkly. "I can ride any horse, anywhere, and you know it!"

Celia could not suppress a laugh at his boasting. "You know that's not true," she began, but Ewan, his face turning a shade darker, interrupted her.

"And I don't need any corrections from a penniless orphan!"

"I'm not penniless!" she responded angrily. "I have the deed to my father's land . . ."

"That's true," said Hester. "I saw it once. It's all in French and has a wax seal the size of a clamshell dangling from the bottom."

Ewan's anger faded as swiftly as it had come, leaving him a little abashed. "Yes but it's to land on a barren island halfway up the north sea. One you can't even return to."

"It is *still* land," Celia said stubbornly.

"All right, then, you're not penniless. I apologize. But I can bloody well ride Jezebel and I'd show you if I only had the chance."

"Well, you won't have," said Hester, "for I saw Tom taking her out to the back pasture just a while ago."

Ewan sat up, his eyes gleaming. "You did? That's perfect. No one would see us if we slipped around there. I could ride her and no one would be the wiser."

"Oh, Ewan, you know Papa has ordered us to ask permission if we want to ride one of his horses. Of course, he's never refused it," Hester added, thinking that it would be diverting on such a hot afternoon to see Ewan's pride brought down a peg or two.

"Of course he hasn't. And we can't ask him, for he's gone to White Plains for the day. Let's do it."

Hester's enthusiasm wavered only a moment. "Mama won't like it. I haven't finished my sampler. I don't know . . ."

"Oh, come along. You can slip back and finish your stitching before your mama even knows you've gone. And imagine what fun it will be. I'll even take you up behind me."

This was more than both girls could resist. "Do you really think Papa Deveroe will mind?" Celia added, her wariness fading.

"I'll tell you what," Ewan said before Hester could answer. "I'll ask Richard. Henry is not here, so Richard, as the second son, would be the man in charge of the household. We'll get his permission. I'll go get him. You two slip out the back door and meet me down by the stone fence in a quarter of an hour."

"We really shouldn't," Hester said lamely. "Proper girls wouldn't."

"Proper girls die of boredom. Come along and have some fun."

It was all Hester needed. Jumping down, she grabbed Celia's hand and pulled her, giggling, toward the door. After making sure Jess was not in the hall, they dashed out through the back doorway, down the piazza and through the garden, their pleasure at being outside heightened by a sense of intrigue.

Celia and Hester reached the stone fence that crossed the back pasture before Ewan showed up with Richard, sweaty and tired from the hot work in the grain fields, his shirt clamped to his back in damp patches. But he was as happy as the others at the prospect of adventure and had already made up his mind to ride Jezebel, too.

Far down the rolling green carpet of the pasture, the mare peacefully grazed, blissfully unaware of the approach of the marauding band.

"Do you think you can catch her!" Celia whispered.

"There never was a horse I couldn't catch," Ewan replied,

working his way quietly down the field.

"I ride her after Ewan," said Hester.

"Oh, no," her brother replied. "I'm next. You're only a girl."

Hester's protest was lost in admiration as she watched Ewan, with the intuition of a born horseman, ease up on the mare's back and canter her back toward them where they sat on the fence.

"Watch this," he called, and took the big horse leaping over the fence down from them and galloping up the path toward the house. Halfway he pulled her up, turned and came cantering back, smiling triumphantly. "I told you I could ride her."

Hopping down, Richard went running up to meet them. "Now it's my turn."

"No it isn't," Hester cried, running after him. "I get the next ride."

"You can't go alone, Hester," Ewan said, looking down on them. "There's no bridle and I have to hold onto her mane. I'll take you around the field and then Richard can take Celia."

"*After* I've had my turn," Richard added to save his pride.

"I can go by myself," Hester protested.

"So can I!" pride made Celia add.

"No, Celia," Richard said firmly. "Let Hester break her neck if she wants but you haven't been riding long enough to go alone. Ewan is right. You should go with me."

Celia suddenly realized that this was not such a displeasing idea, so she quietly surrendered. But Hester, who was not so easily persuaded, had her way in the end and sedately guided the mare twice around the field by herself, while Richard found himself half wishing the horse would throw her. It would serve her right.

Jezebel's red flanks were soon beginning to stream with sweat, and the girls began thinking it was time to slip back into the house. Then Ewan decided to have one last go at a wide jump over a candleberry thicket near the wood's edge.

"That barrier is cruel high, Ewan," Richard cautioned.

"Not so high *I* can't clear it," the boy called as he took Jezebel far back in order to get a long start.

It was a beautiful jump, perfectly cleared with a high arching flow of rider and beast.

"Marvelous, wonderful!" Richard was carried away with the ease and beauty of it. "Let me try."

Ewan, his face flushed with pleasure, brought the mare up

to the fence where the three sat watching.

"Do you think you can, Richard?"

"I'm as good a horseman as you," Richard said defensively, knowing full well it wasn't true.

"Perhaps you shouldn't," Hester said, confident it would egg him on.

"I wouldn't want you to get hurt," Celia added, still basking in the pleasure of sitting behind him, her arms wound tight around his waist.

"Oh, listen to her, Richard," Ewan simpered. "Your little shadow doesn't want you to get hurt."

Celia glared at him. "Well, I don't!"

"Pooh. I won't get hurt. Come on, Ewan—get down and let me up."

Swinging his leg across Jezebel's back, Ewan slid off and took Richard's place on the fence, thinking that the mare was sweating badly by now and it was time to get back to their chores before they were discovered. All three of them watched almost absently, preoccupied by the need to leave, as Richard turned the mare back along the track Ewan had taken. Celia heard the thudding of Jezebel's hoofs on the hard turf of the pasture and her blood began to race as the horse tore past toward the thicket. Holding her breath, she saw the chestnut blur as horse and rider rose to take the barrier. Then with growing horror she saw the mare fail to clear it and come crashing down into the shrubbery in a tangle of flailing hoofs, while Richard's body sailed over the horse's head to land in the grass in a crumpled heap, motionless.

"God's blood!" Ewan gasped as they scrambled down from the fence and went flying to the tangle of rider and horse. By the time they reached the spill, Jezebel was struggling back to her feet, at least able to stand. Both girls, frantic with apprehension, knelt over Richard's still body while Ewan quickly ran his hands down the mare's legs to make certain she wasn't badly hurt. Yet his relief over Jezebel's safety did nothing to calm the dreadful fear that stuck like a lump of dough in his throat as he knelt beside Richard. The boy was unconscious, one arm lying in a grotesque angle to his body. He was, at least, still breathing.

"Richard, Richard," Celia cried, a cold knot of terror congealing in her chest. "Wake up! Are you all right?"

"Oh, Ewan," said Hester, looking up at her cousin with panic in her eyes. "He's not dead, is he? Oh, dear heaven!"

Celia caught the word "dead," and hysteria clouded her mind. Richard had been her anchor in this strange new home. If she lost him as she had everything else . . .

"I don't think so." Ewan tried to sound calm though his heart was thumping. "His arm may be broken and I think he struck his head."

"His head!" Celia wailed, the tears beginning to spill down her cheeks. "He'll die, then, I know he will!"

"Calm down, Celia. Hester, go to the creek and bring some water. Dampen your apron and bring it back."

Hester raced off to the brook while Celia, pulling wildly on Richard's shoulder, cried out his name.

"Don't do that, you foolish girl!" Ewan shouted. "Don't shake his arm—it may be broken!"

"I don't care," Celia sobbed and turned a white stricken face on Ewan. "This is all your fault," she screamed. "You've killed him with your mad schemes and your wild jumps. I hate you, Ewan Deveroe! I hate you! I'll hate you forever!"

The blood drained from Ewan's face. Then, hearing a groan, he felt a great surge of relief sweep over him.

Hester ran up with her dripping apron. Ewan draped it over Richard's forehead and watched as his cousin opened his eyes. Sitting back on his haunches, he silently offered up a prayer of thanks.

"Oh, Richard," Celia said, bending over the boy. "We thought you were dead. Are you all right?"

"*You* thought he was dead," Ewan said with an edge of bitterness in his voice.

"My head . . . and my arm . . . hurts," Richard moaned.

"What are we going to do, Ewan?" Hester asked fearfully. "Now they'll have to know we were riding Jezebel."

"Don't move, Richard. I think your arm is broken. Hester, you will have to go back and get Tom. He'll know what to do."

"But—"

"There's no other way," Ewan answered sharply. "We'll have to take the consequences. Richard must have a surgeon."

Hester reluctantly got to her feet. "You come with me, Celia. You're as much to blame as I."

"No!" Celia grabbed for Richard's hand. "I'm not leaving Richard!"

Ewan groaned. "Oh, for God's sake. Richard, tell her to go with Hester. You're the only one she'll listen to."

The pain in his shoulder was almost unbearable and Richard was impatient to have the girl loose his hand. "Go on," he said curtly. "I don't need a little girl hanging about. Go with Hester!"

Celia dropped his hand and stepped back. Now that she knew he was all right her hysteria seemed a little silly. Yet her fear had been so strong, so real. It stung her that he would speak so sharply to her when all she wanted was to help him. Keeping her face averted to hide the hurt in her eyes, she ran after Hester.

"She was very upset," Ewan said quietly. "We all were. I thought you had been killed for sure."

"I feel as though I was," Richard muttered. "I'm never going to take another jump!"

"Better not talk too much or move around, Richard. Save your strength. You are going to need it when your father hears of this. *We* all are!" Ewan added grimly.

The storm that broke over their heads when Samuel discovered how Richard had been hurt effectively ended the carefree pleasures of the summer. Ewan received a thorough caning from his father as well as a furious reprimand from his uncle, who, once he knew his son would recover, gave vent to an almost uncontrollable rage.

"You knew your Uncle James gave me that mare!" he shouted at the boy. "She's a blooded, valuable animal and you might have crippled her. Where is your head, Ewan? What *could* you have been thinking of, a fine horseman like you! Sneaking away from your proper work and jeopardizing everyone—it's the work of a scoundrel, not a young gentleman. A caning's too good for you!"

Celia saw very little of the boys after that. Ewan was kept busy at the mill with enough work for three men, while Richard was confined to bed by the surgeon until that worthy felt sure the bump on the head had caused no permanent damage. When the two hot, slow weeks preceding the move back to New York finally dragged by, Celia was as happy as Hester to pack the endless sewing and embroidery into wicker boxes and climb into the coach for the drive to the city.

Samuel Deveroe's New York house, Wayside, stood on Corlaer's Hook—or Crown Point, as it was also called—not far from his brother James's estate on Bowery Lane. A box-

shaped house built of rubble stone, it was similar to the one
at West Farms but larger and filled with the English and French
furnishings that arrived daily at the harbor in the city below.
Behind the house a large formal garden laid out in the English
manner gave way to neat beds of vegetables and herbs. Beyond
that, bordering the Hook, was an orchard of apple, peach, pear
and cherry trees that blocked from view the salt meadows of
the Bowery, the Stuyvesant estate. Celia took an instant liking
to the house and to the city not far to the south. A half hour's
carriage ride down Division Street past the Rope Walk, skirting
the Fresh Water Pond with its pungent tanyards, brought them
to Broad Way, the wide, graceful thoroughfare whose elegant
houses and church spires enthralled her. From the first she was
caught up in the excitement of the city, an excitement growing
out of the grand stew of noisy traffic in the streets, ladies in
fashionable dresses gossiping along the walks, the melee of
horses, carriages, sedan chairs and vendors' carts that crowded
the cobbled alleyways, narrow once you left Broad Way, and
the shops with their amazing array of goods piled in the windows. Each sharp image stayed clear in her mind: the Dutch
roof fronts of faded brick marching upward in steps; the painted
signs swinging outside the taverns and coffeehouses; the Tea
Pump, crowded with a long line of slaves and servants filling
pitchers, buckets and barrels to carry back to their establish-
ments; the confusion and noise of the long harbor, where ships
arrived from all over the world to unload baskets, barrels and
crates of unimagined treasures on the wharf. The smell of the
sea was there, mingling with the briny odor of oysters, clams
and fish, adding its sharpness to the still stronger reek of garbage littering the streets and of the privies crowded behind the
jammed houses in the tangle of alleys which had grown haphazardly around the docks.

　　She learned to love the Fly Market with its long rows of
stalls filled with produce ferried across from Long Island, over
from the Jerseys or down from West Chester, its strong smells
heightened by the cacaphony of haggling voices. She learned
to identify all the myriad buildings—churches, meeting houses,
the Almshouse, the prison and even the college. She even
learned to enjoy the long, rather prosaic services at Trinity
Church, where the family worshiped. She was so caught up
in the fascinating new things there were to learn in this bright
world that she was only occasionally troubled by the old dark
dreams of poverty and pain.

One warm September afternoon, shortly after the Deveroes returned to New York, Celia sat in the garden playing with her new doll. It was the grandest toy she had ever owned—a foot-high replica of a London lady dressed in the mode of ten years before. Indeed, the doll had been sent originally on a ship out of Plymouth in order to show American ladies the latest trends in London fashions.

Celia was busily rearranging its ruched silk skirts over wide hoops when she looked up to see Richard rounding a hedge of high box. She had seen little of Richard since his accident and she fancied he was still angry with her for her childish behavior. She was already making her way down the path when she heard him call her.

"Celia! Don't run away. What were you doing?"

Reluctantly Celia turned back. "I was playing with a doll your mama gave me."

"I haven't seen you for such an age. Not really since I was able to get out of bed. Come and talk to me."

Richard made a place for her next to him on the bench, and hesitantly Celia sat down, secretly pleased that he had asked her to stay.

"Well, and how do you like New York town? And Wayside?"

"It's most agreeable."

"My, you *are* quiet. Why don't you talk to me as you used to in West Farms?"

"I thought you didn't like me anymore."

"Now, why on earth—silly little goose. Of *course* I like you."

"But you said—you told me you didn't need a little girl hanging about."

Richard shrugged. "Oh, that. That was only because Ewan was there, and after all I can't have boys like Ewan thinking I need a girl to fight my battles, can I? You do understand that?"

"No."

She looked at him with such earnestness that he could not suppress a laugh. "Well, never mind. But you must forget my hasty words and confide in me as you did before. Agreed?"

Curbing her impulse to throw her arms around Richard's neck and kiss his pale cheek, she gave him instead a broad smile.

"Now, that is more like it. Here, show me your doll."

Turning it over in his good hand, he gave it a cursory inspection. "It's all right, I suppose, for a doll."

"I think it is quite the prettiest doll there ever was."

"You would think that. But it's too fine a day to spend with dolls. Come with me and I'll show you some real sport."

"Not jumping a horse?" Celia said quickly.

"How could I with my arm in a splint? I can't do this alone, either, but you can help me. Come on."

Her heart swelling with happiness, Celia followed Richard down through the garden to the orchard below, past the fragrant trees to the river's edge, where the ground sloped sharply downward in a buttress of gravel and dirt. Sliding down this five-foot barrier, Celia watched curiously as Richard headed straight for the tall sea grass lining the shore, where, after rummaging around for a few minutes, he dislodged a small gray skiff.

"Are we going to ride in that!" she cried, dancing up and down with anticipation.

"We are indeed, if you will stop jumping about and help me get it unmoored. Come on, climb aboard."

Perched on one end of the small boat, watching Richard's lithe body as he skillfully worked one oar to maneuver the craft away from the grass, Celia thought to herself that this must be what heaven is like. The sun on the gray water sprinkled its sequined patterns like fairy steps all the way across to the Long Island shoreline on the far side. Because the currents in the East River tended to be treacherous, Richard kept close to the York Island or New York shore, working the craft leisurely past the rock-filled fields and wooded copses of fir and hemlock until they were almost opposite the long waving swards of the salt meadows of the Bowery.

"You were never in New York town before, were you?" he said as they quietly drifted on the incoming side.

"I've been in *three* times with Hester and your mama—once shopping and twice to church. It's wonderful! I want to go back as soon as I can."

"I'll go along with you next time and show you all the really interesting places. You'll have to see King's College. I'll be going to school there in two years."

"What's a college?"

Richard rested his good arm on the oar and leaned forward, his eyes alight. "A college is a grand school where young gentlemen learn the skills of their profession. I want to go there so that later on when I'm grown I can be elected to the Assembly like Uncle James."

"What's an Assembly?"

"My, you don't know anything, do you? The Provincial Assembly makes our laws. It takes the place of the Parliament in London because, naturally, some governing has to be done by the people on the spot. Uncle James was one of the most powerful men in the Assembly, and I want to be like him."

Abruptly Celia leaned forward, setting the boat rocking as she pointed out to the wide expanse of river.

"Look, Richard! Over there! A bird flew right down and landed on the water! Did you see it?"

"It was probably a blue bill or a sea tern. We're very near the ocean here—and *don't* ask me what an ocean is!"

Fascinated, Celia shielded her eyes with her hand and watched the bird sweep gracefully up toward the silver sky. The sun warmed her shoulders through the thin calico of her dress, and the clear air was pungent with salt. Huge billows of white clouds shifted against the cobalt blue of the sky, creating a serene beauty that made her want to cry out for joy. She had never felt so completely happy before.

Leaning forward, Richard fingered the worn brocade of the doll's skirt lying in Celia's lap. "That's a lovely color, isn't it? Just the shade that sometimes comes with the sunset over the North River. It's a very indifferent quality of cloth, however."

"I think it's beautiful," Celia said in defense of her treasured possession.

"Of course you would. I don't suppose you ever had a doll before, did you, Celia?"

"Dominie Brec carved me one once, but it wasn't half as nice as this."

Settling back, Richard watched her reflectively. She had filled out a lot, becoming rather pretty, in fact, not a bit like the frail, skinny child who had first come from East Chester. "You have a lot of things now that you never had before. Do they make you happy? Are you still sad that you came to live with us?"

"Oh, no. I still miss my papa, but I like it here. I like being with you."

"What was it like, Celia?" Richard asked, remembering how appalled he had been on his one visit to the French emigrants in the East Chester jail. "Sometimes I think you must learn how to look at life more realistically when you have so little than when you have so much. It gives you a better perspective."

He was musing to himself, and Celia did not understand what he was saying at all. But his words brought to mind two early impressions of the Deveroe home which had never left her. The first was of standing beside Hester as she opened the press in her room to reveal half a dozen dresses packed among the crushed sandalwood, each one more beautiful than the other. Celia had no way of knowing that four of the six had been cut down from Elizabeth's outgrown frocks of years before. She only stood transfixed at the richness of a luminous gold taffeta, the transparent sheen of a blue-green brocade, the heavenly softness of an indigo wool capuchin cloak trimmed in coffee-colored beaver. The second was of the Deveroe family sitting down before a table so crowded with dishes you could not see the linen cloth. Each day was a banquet where it was not uncommon to feast upon four meats, a fish, game birds, pastries and several different wines. At first she had picked at her food, overwhelmed by all the choices. Then she had gone to the other extreme, wolfing down as much as she could as though she feared it would not reappear tomorrow.

Time had not dimmed her awareness of the discrepancy between her life before and after the Deveroes. It was not so much that she consciously wished to possess what they had. She only knew that where her life before had been drab, this now was bright and full of color. That life had been ragged homespun, and this was the sumptuousness of silk and fur. That had been trying to appease her ever present hunger pangs with coarse bread and corn mush, and this was more delicacies than one could eat. She was not able to explain it to Richard or even fully to articulate it to herself, but deep within her the conviction had taken root and was sending forth its stubborn tendrils that whatever life had been then, this was better. No, she was never, never going to go back!

Best of all was sitting in this gently swaying boat, the warm sun on her back and across from her this kind, princely friend.

"Richard," she asked impulsively, "you are really not angry with me anymore, are you?"

"Of course not, silly," Richard answered. "I was never really angry with you. I was angry with myself for getting hurt so foolishly."

"And we'll always be friends?"

He sat forward, peering into her oval face. She was such a trusting little thing, so wistful and so easily bruised. He remembered vividly how poignant she had looked that day he discovered her crying on the stairs, and he found himself wanting to comfort her as he would an affectionate puppy.

"Of course we'll always be friends, Celia."

"Always and forever?"

Reaching over with his good hand, he squeezed her thin fingers. "Always and forever."

"I love you, Richard," Celia said in a burst of feeling. "Is it all right for me to love you? You don't mind?"

Settling back, Richard took up the oar. "It's all right, only don't ever say so in front of Ewan or Hester! Come on, now, take this other oar and help me turn the boat. We'd better get back and we'll be going against the tide now, so row heartily. We don't want to miss our dinner."

three

By the summer of 1772 when Celia turned thirteen, she had grown completely at home in the Deveroe household. Tall for her age, with good food and care she had filled out to a rosy, slender girl with the beginnings of a trim figure. Richard at fifteen had grown a head taller and had the uncoordinated gait of a puppet not quite properly put together. The family had just moved back up to the Manor House in West Farms for the summer, and already there was a lanquid carelessness to their days.

The crystal-clear morning gave promise of a warm day ahead. Celia and Richard were sitting on the front stoop enjoying the coolness of the early morning when Celia looked up to see Ewan riding up the road on his handsome sorrel mare. Ewan too had grown, and, nearly a year older than Richard, he had become a man in the year they had been away. Not quite so tall as his cousin, he nevertheless showed signs of being more athletic, and his walk betrayed a self-assurance his more introspective cousin would never possess.

"You're out early," Richard said.

"I've important business. Are you busy? It's rent day and it's a long circuit. Will you join me?"

"Certainly. I just have to get my horse saddled. I'll only be a minute."

"Richard, please let me come too," Celia asked hesitantly. "I've never seen a rent day before and I'd far rather be out riding than sitting around the house doing chores."

Richard hesitated, glancing at his cousin.

"God's life, Richard," Ewan broke in. "We won't have time to be looking after a child. I've work to do."

"You won't have to look after me," Celia said stubbornly.

"I can keep up with both of you with my eyes closed. Please, Richard."

"Oh, come along, then." Richard was unwilling to let Ewan have his way completely. Besides, he enjoyed Celia's company. To his surprise Ewan took it in good grace, muttering under his breath, "That child has you in her pocket, Cousin."

Celia was so delighted to be included that she vowed she would not even breathe loudly as she skipped behind Richard to the stable to saddle her pony. Stepping lightly on the mounting block, she straddled the dapple gray's back with her skirt billowing over her knees, her stockinged feet dangling.

Ewan could barely hide his contempt. "For heaven's sake, Celia. Don't you ride sidesaddle? Look at you with your ankles bare to the world!"

"She's only a girl," Richard answered as he brought his bay around. "Let her alone."

Throwing Ewan a smug glance, Celia fell in behind as they started off down the dirt trail toward the Lawrence farm.

That day would be etched clear in Celia's mind, partly for its peaceful beauty and partly for the contrasts they encountered along the way. At their first stop, the prosperous Lawrences', the mistress of the house sat them down at a polished plank table in the large gleaming kitchen before pewter mugs of homemade cider while Ewan and Mr. Lawrence briefly retired to a small office off the parlor to square accounts. Celia had met Mrs. Lawrence and her daughter, Mercy, when they called at the Manor House, and she knew the girl to be as shy and quiet as her mother was overbearing. Now, seated in their comfortable kitchen, she decided to try to draw Mercy out while her mother's concentration was on Richard. Mercy was only two or three years younger than herself, an astonishingly pretty child with a pale white face framed by thick black curls. Her pale skin blushed pink as Celia slid closer on the bench and spoke directly to her.

"We've just come out for the summer," she began. The child turned her face away to stare at the shelves of polished pewter on the far wall. "I have a gray pony," Celia continued, undaunted.

Mercy sidled farther away from her. "I know," she whispered.

"Do you have one, too? Maybe we could ride together sometime."

"No!" Mercy did not lift her eyes.

"Oh. Well, we will be at the Summer House for the next two months. Perhaps you could visit one day and we could play some games."

Looking away, the child twisted her fingers in her apron, clearly miserable. Celia gave up the struggle. She was beginning to think Mercy was not quite bright when abruptly the girl spoke up. "Are you like that other one?"

"What other one?" Celia asked in surprise.

"She pinched me."

"Oh, Hester. No, I won't pinch you. I'd like to be your friend. Would you like to be mine?"

"No." Mercy turned her exquisite face back to the other side of the room, apparently having used up her entire allotment of conversation. Well, she wasn't completely without spirit, Celia thought, thankful to see Ewan returning. As they were leaving, Mrs. Lawrence forced Mercy out from behind her skirts long enough to give an embarrassed curtsy to Ewan which he barely acknowledged.

The three rode for a long distance before reining in at the Trentons', a smaller, untidy version of the Lawrence farm. Celia had been in West Farms long enough now to know most of the families within a ten-mile radius by sight if not by name. So when they rode into the Trentons' cluttered farmyard her eyes were immediately drawn to two strangers standing by the sling well near the one-story whitewashed stone house. One was obviously an older man, dressed all in parson's gray, while the other, possibly his son, was thin and lanky, in a round hat and shirtsleeves with a long homespun waistcoat. Beside them a small donkey stood bowed under the weight of two huge bales strapped to its back.

"Look at that," Richard muttered angrily. "That poor beast is carrying twice as much as it should."

Celia averted her eyes from the unfortunate animal and concentrated on Ewan's conversation with Isaac Trenton, who stood leaning on the handle of a hoe.

"Can't pay ye in specie, Master Ewan," Trenton said apologetically. "Crops came in good, but the missus has took sick with the last bairn and it required all my extra dollars to care for her and finish up the barn."

"How many children do you have now, Trenton?" Ewan asked, glancing around the barren yard.

"Let's see—I believe it do be fourteen with this last, but he's only a mite of a fellow, not like to see the year out."

"Fourteen!"

The stranger in gray who had hovered on the outskirts of the conversation suddenly thrust himself between them. "The Lord says be fruitful and multiply!"

For a moment he had their full attention. His appearance was as formidable as his voice, Celia thought, for he had cold gray eyes and a face that looked as though it had been carved from flint.

"Well, sir. And who are you?" Ewan asked coldly.

"The Lord says—"

"Be quiet, Malachi!" Isaac Trenton interrupted nervously. "This here's Malachi Carne and over there's his son, Jaspar. Pay him no mind, Master Ewan. He's just passing through on his way to King's Bridge."

"Are you a preacher?"

"No preacher, but a believer in the stern righteousness of the Lord."

"Yes, sir, fourteen young ones now," Isacc Trenton tried to continue, turning his back on Carne. "The older ones be good workers and most because of them I've good flax and some bags of buckwheat for your pa. I killed a pig and there'll be a ham off that for ye, too."

Ewan shrugged. "That will be fine, Isaac. I'll explain to Father."

"A man should till his own land," Carne spoke up, waving a finger at Ewan. "'Tain't fit that the sweat of his brow should go to keep popinjays in pride and fancies. The Lord will see that justice comes—"

"I tole ye to be still!" Trenton hissed. "I'm doin' the best I can, and old Peter of the mill, he always understood. I'll bring those goods round tomorrow, Master Ewan, and meantime you give your father my best."

Clearly he was anxious for them to leave, so Ewan, without pressing a quarrel the old man seemed to expect, climbed back on his horse. Reluctantly, glaring at the three of them, Carne turned back to the well, where his son stood quietly observing the scene.

As they cantered away from the farm, Richard pulled up beside Ewan's mare. "What an unpleasant man! And yet he has a point. Think of it," he said reflectively, "grubbing your life away on fifty acres that belong to another man, using up all your strength to keep food in the bellies of a parcel of children that grows larger each year. God's blood, I'd sooner die than live out my life like that!"

"It happens often enough. It's what you bargain for when you marry. We'll both likely find ourselves in the same fix when we take a wife."

"Are you going to marry, then, Ewan?" Celia spoke up cautiously from behind them.

Ewan laughed as he skewed sideways in his saddle to look around at her. "You probably are wondering why anyone would marry me, aren't you, little Celia?"

"I never said that. It was just a question."

"And it deserves an answer. Yes, I am going to be married someday to that shy little girl you saw earlier at the Lawrence farm."

"To Mercy Lawrence! But she's only a child. And she hardly ever says a word!"

Ewan fell back to ride closer to Celia's gray. "She's young, that's true, but we've been promised since she was born. And I hope she continues to remain quiet. I cannot imagine anything worse than being wed to an argumentative woman."

"You don't *mind* having to marry her?"

"No, not really. I have to marry someone someday, so it might as well be Mercy Lawrence as anyone."

Celia shook her head over this pragmatism and secretly resolved that never would she be pushed into an arrangement so callous and unfeeling.

"What about you, Richard?" Ewan added. "Have you lost your heart yet?"

Richard shrugged. "No. I haven't really thought about it. I shall have to marry, of course, because I'm a younger son and Henry inherits everything. But I'm thankful my parents did not promise me to someone so much younger. Besides, I hope to love the woman I marry."

"You always were an idealist," Ewan called and cantered ahead of them on the road.

Following behind, Celia smiled to herself. How nice it was that Richard so often agreed with her on important matters.

As the day wore on, the various families they visited merged into a single blur. A few were highly prosperous, and those usually paid Ewan in coins. At the other extreme were one or two families who lived in slovenly houses little more than shacks and whose fields were unplowed and yards cluttered with debris and ragged children. Pleading poverty, these few put off paying anything at all, much to Ewan's disgust. But for the most part, the farmers of West Farms were somewhere in between—comfortable, earning enough from their animals and crops to feed and clothe themselves adequately if not in style. These people usually paid with the proceeds of their labors.

At the last house they stopped briefly to beg a cool drink from Theophilus Hunt, a freeholder who had grown up with Ewan's father, Peter, and had known the boys since their infancy. The afternoon sun was beginning its slow descent when the three started back toward the mill after making a wide circle of the West Farms area. Richard had been listening and watching all day, saying little, lost in his own thoughts. Now he spoke with an edge of bitterness.

"So this is rent day. I'm glad to finally see one firsthand."

"This is a very modest example, I hope you realize. When Mr. Philipse collects his accounts it is a two-day affair with free beer and food for all."

"Nevertheless, it doesn't seem right. These men work their farms, but the land is actually owned by the Deveroes. It smacks of feudalism to me."

"I don't know why you should say that. It happens to be the practice throughout West Chester—and the province of New York, for that matter."

"That is just what I mean," Richard said dryly. "Nowhere else in this country—save perhaps the South—would you find such a blatant example of the old English manorial system. It's not at all in keeping with the rest of the Colonies."

"But you must remember that New York was settled from the first by manorial grants and patents—it's a heritage from the Dutch. Besides, the Deveroe holdings are small indeed compared to those of the Philipses, the Van Cortlandts, the Van Rensselaers and the Schuylers. And the farmer *is* free to buy his holdings."

"If he can ever get enough money together—an unlikely prospect when all his extra earnings every year go to support the landlord."

"Why, Richard, you are beginning to sound like one of the Sons of Liberty. One would think you were a tenant farmer yourself rather than the son of a squire who lives very well off his land."

"Oh, I admit I live well and enjoy it. But at times my

conscience troubles me that I do nothing to earn my livelihood. That in fact it is earned for me by the sweat of other men's brows."

"Richard, I fear you are one of those unfortunate people who will never allow themselves to enjoy anything without making certain they suffer for it. Not I. I love the English system and I believe it is the finest ever devised for the nourishment of gentlemen."

"You only say that because you are one of the gentlemen!"

The three weary horses turned onto the tree-shaded stretch of road that would bring them back to the Bronx River and the mill, stepping up their pace now that they were headed for the barn. Celia shifted in the hard saddle. She had kept her bargain and said very little all day, either to comment or to complain. Even now she sighed wearily to herself rather than admit how tired she was. Every bone ached, and her back felt as though it would snap like a brittle branch if she did not soon sink into a supporting chair.

Abruptly Ewan pulled up his horse, nearly causing Richard and Celia to career into him. Before them the narrow trail was blocked by a young man wielding a long oak stick over the head of a hapless donkey staggering under the heavy weight of two panniers. At once Celia recognized Jaspar Carne, the boy in the round hat from the Trentons' well.

Richard recognized the donkey and was outraged to see the overburdened animal being beaten for what it could not help. In a fury he jumped down from his horse and ran to the startled young man, wresting the stick out of his hand. Angrily he brought it crashing down twice on the boy's shoulders.

"You villain!" he cried, all the Deveroe authority in his voice. "Don't you know that poor beast can't walk under such a load. You're going to kill the animal."

Suddenly, he was ashamed of letting his fury get the best of him, and, dropping the stick, he stepped back to find himself staring into the coldest gray eyes he had ever seen. The boy's face was as flinty and angular as his father's.

"You've a nerve minding other men's business," Carne said through clenched teeth, rubbing his arm.

"Cruelty is every man's business." Now that his first surge of anger had subsided Richard began to wonder how he was going to get out of this confrontation gracefully. Actually, suffering animals were commonplace in his life, but he hated to see a good piece of equipment so badly, stupidly used. And he was not going to apologize!

"You Deveroes must not only own men but you must tell them how to conduct themselves as well. Does your arrogance have no limit?"

This was too much for Ewan, who had been watching half amused from the sidelines. Sliding off his horse, his face dark with rage, he stalked over to Carne and with one swift swing knocked his hat into the dust. "Take off your hat in the presence of your betters!"

Celia held her breath, expecting the younger Carne to wade into a real fight. Instead he stood staring at Ewan, murderous hatred on his face but a furious self-control holding him back. Then he casually leaned down and picked up his hat without saying a word.

"And get that beast out of the road," Ewan went on. "You're blocking our passage."

Richard threw the stick into the underbrush. "If you had an ounce of common sense you'd relieve that animal of some of that weight just to keep from killing him. As it is, you'll probably end up carrying those bales to King's Bridge yourself. It will serve you right!"

Jaspar Carne glared at the two of them, weighing his choices. He was here alone—his father was still at a meeting of the Sons of Liberty at Trenton's farm. These two popinjays could beat him senseless and probably get away with it—such was the power of the Deveroe name.

"Someday you'll get what you deserve," he muttered. "Changes are coming. You won't be able to lord it over better men forever. Someday—"

"Oh, good God!" Ewan sneered. "Besides being rude and heartless he's one of those Liberty Boys as well. Come on, Richard. Leave him here. I'm tired and I want to get home."

Feeling unsettled by the whole incident, Richard climbed back on his horse and made his way around the weary donkey and the glaring young man, deliberately not looking back. As they cleared the trees, they saw the Manor House white in the distance. From a near field Vestal raised his big body from a hand plow and waved to them.

"I know those Carnes," Ewan growled. "Bible-thumping seditionists, every one of them."

"They're from Horseneck, up near Rye, aren't they?" Richard asked absently.

"Yes, thank God. They only come through West Farms now

and then. They're part of the rabble that's trying to force separation and rebellion down our throats. You see, Cousin," he said bitterly, "*that's* the kind of company you'll keep with your sympathy for independence."

"I never said I was for independence," Richard answered.

"No, but what you did say smacks of it. And men these days are getting very testy about semantics. Just remember to think whom you are speaking to before you say how you feel. It never hurts to be a little cautious."

"You're a fine one to say that, Ewan!" Richard snorted. "But I take what you say in the spirit of kindness. I'll remember."

four

By the time Celia was fifteen she had, to Elizabeth Deveroe's complete satisfaction, acquired the proper veneer of a lady of quality. She had slipped into the proprieties of good breeding as naturally as she would into a new dress, repeating the polite responses proper to each situation as easily as she would sing a new air by Master Hopkins, executing the correct steps of each social encounter with the same aplomb with which she moved through the intricate patterns of a gavotte.

Underneath she never lost the feeling that she wore a mask. The early years of her life in East Chester were always there below the surface, reminding her that once she had been part of a very different world—a world of exiles. As she grew into young womanhood she could look back and smile to herself at the stages she had gone through—first, clinging almost angrily to what she had left behind, then trying to obliterate it and become a Deveroe, inwardly as well as outwardly. While passing through that phase she had for a while become almost as much a snob as Hester Deveroe. But in the end, after feeling pulled between two distinct worlds, she had finally come to terms with herself. She could look almost objectively at the Deveroes and all they stood for and could assume the outward attitudes they expected of her. But she knew there was more to life than their comfortable, self-satisfied world, and as she grew older she became more determined both to never lose sight of that vision they could not share and to grasp at her own portion of the comforts they had been born to. Of all the Deveroes, only Richard seemed to have some inkling of this side of her. His own sensitivity helped him to appreciate the way other men lived, and he was somehow able to put himself in their shoes. Although he was now one of the two dozen or so young men enrolled in King's College and so was not often at home, he always seemed to understand the struggles she was going through in her effort to mesh both sides of her life. He listened sympathetically when she raved over some ridiculous restraint that society imposed on young ladies, and more than once when she was consciously outdoing Hester in putting on airs she would look up to see him trying to stifle a smile.

She had even learned to feel some sympathy for Hester Deveroe. The spoiled only daughter of the family, Hester had learned from her cradle to accept society's dictates, but underneath she fought constantly to force a willful spirit to conform to the lady she was supposed to be. After being thrown together for five years, Hester and Celia had achieved a détente. Celia never ceased to be amazed that the gentle, patrician Elizabeth and the kind, good-natured Samuel had produced such a volatile daughter. Hester's quick bright nature drew people like a flame, and there were moments, many of them, when Celia felt truly close to Hester and loved her like a sister. But Celia also knew that underneath that luminous vivacity Hester was essentially selfish, entirely incapable of putting someone else's concerns before her own. Time and again, after some unpleasant exchange, Hester would make an impulsively generous gesture toward her, and Celia always found herself forgetting the selfishness that motivated it, convinced that the girl's true good nature would win out in the end. After all, Hester accepted her now as one of the family and it was lovely to have a confidante and friend her own age.

Like most girls her age, Celia paid small attention to politics. Of course, it was common knowledge that there was a great deal of dissatisfaction with England in the Colonies, but she neither knew nor cared what had provoked it. When arguments erupted among the Deveroes and their friends at supper parties or between Richard and his colleagues from King's College, she and Hester either turned to their embroidery or left the room. Now and then when Samuel Deveroe ranted over some letter in Hugh Gaine's *Weekly Mercury* or, in a rage, threw an offending pamphlet across the room, she wondered idly what all the strong feeling was about, but it all seemed too complex to understand. There was much anger directed at "Boston," a city she knew dimly was northward on the New England coast, and that anger had something to do with threats to the port of New York, but precisely what the quarrel was she never bothered to learn. It was obvious that the sympathies of the other provinces, which were rallying to keep Boston going in spite of an English blockade, would find little support in the Deveroe household where they at once feared what a similar embargo would do to the port of New York and were more inclined to come down on the King's side than the rabble-rousers'.

Her little cocoon of indifference was shattered forever one sultry September afternoon at the corner of Pearl and Broad streets. She had gone with Hester to the city to look over some fabrics just arrived from London on the *Empress of Russia*. Elizabeth had entrusted them to the protective care of Vestal, whose massive shoulders were calculated to discourage any ruffians from bothering the girls. Scorning the fashionable silk livery of his father, he sat next to Tom on the box, massive arms folded over a chest swathed in new black broadcloth, a white horsehair wig under his tricorn hat, and glared around at the traffic as though daring anyone to speak so much as a rude word to his young mistresses.

When Celia and Hester came out of the shop, they decided to walk the three blocks to the King's Arms coffeehouse, where they could take a dish of tea and enjoy the admiring glances of the young men of the town. Though Vestal most emphatically did not approve of this, he dutifully fell in behind them on the crowded footpath, making sure his protective presence was obvious.

As they neared the corner they saw that a crowd had gathered to watch a group of men who were swarming down the middle of the road, forcing carriages and chairs aside. Hester gripped Celia's arm.

"What is it? Some kind of parade? I hear singing and laughing but no hautboys or drums."

"I don't know. Vestal, can you see?"

Tall enough to see over the heads of the people who had clustered on the curb, Vestal took one look down the street and wagged his head in alarm.

"An't fitten for young misses! We be better go back."

"No, no," Hester cried, jumping up and down in an effort to see around the wide straw hat of the lady in front of her. "I want to know what it is. Come on, Celia." And grabbing Celia's hand she began to push and shove her way through the crowd.

Vestal's eyes grew wide with alarm. "No, no, Misse Hester, you come back," he cried, seeing trouble descending on his own head. But Hester had managed to worm her way to the front of the crowd with Celia right behind her, and as the mob drew abreast they stared in horror at the grim spectacle.

Laughing and calling to the crowd, the men were carrying something unrecognizable between them. It took both girls a moment to realize that the hunched, miserable object before their eyes was actually a man. Patches of bare skin showed obscenely pink through the black sticky sludge that covered him from his clotted hair to his bare feet. Scattered in its surface were hundreds of white feathers.

"Merciful God!" Hester shuddered. "It's tar. Tar and feathers. I've heard of it."

Celia was too horror-struck to answer. The man was sitting stark naked on a sharp wooden rail, his hands tied behind him, trying vainly to shift his weight on the cutting edge of the plank. She got a brief glimpse of blotches of red on the rail and then, looking up, at the white, shocked eyes staring out of the encrusted black face. Abruptly, revulsion turned to fury. Reaching out, she grabbed the arm of one of the men passing before her and was pulled by him away from the curb and into the street.

"Why are you doing this? Who is this man?" she cried. Behind her she was conscious of the indignant howls of the mob as Vestal forced his way toward her.

"Let be, mistress," the man cried, trying to shake free of her grip. "That's a King's man. An English-lovin' Tory, and he's gettin' just what he deserves."

"But it's cruel and savage. You don't have the right."

"Stay out of what don't concern you, miss," he said, digging at her fingers on his arm. All at once his gaze was arrested by her large, intense eyes and her white face surrounded by walnut brown ringlets and pink ribbons. "Say, ye'r a right pretty lass to be bothering with men's work," he smirked, thrusting his thin face close to Celia's.

"Hey, Jeremy," a companion called as he came alongside. "What have you there? Bring the wench along to enjoy the fun."

"You don't have the right," Celia sputtered, trying to keep to her point. Stumbling into the middle of the street, she glanced back, to see Hester shrinking into the crowd and Vestal's head bobbing above them as he tried to fight his way through.

"Why don't ye come along with me?" the man said, grinning lewdly at her now. "I could show ye a right fine time this afternoon, I could."

"You ruffian!" she cried, jerking her arm away. "It's not a crime to stand for the King. And I'd rather die than go with you!"

"So I'm a ruffian, am I? Well, well, here's another one. We've a Tory in ribbons and laces this time and proud as Lucifer."

"Ah, come along," his friend called. "We're getting left behind."

"I'll come all right. But not before I give you somethin' to remember me by, little proud miss."

Backing away, Celia saw him swoop down and grab a hand-ful of damp horse dung from the gutter. Laughing, he threw it at her, splattering the front of her blue lutestring underskirt.

"That's scum for Tories!" he yelled, running down the road after the mob. "Be glad it's not what *he* got!"

Celia stood dumbfounded, looking down at her ruined skirt. Rage such as she had never known swept over her. She reached down to grab up her own handful of dung to sling at the man's retreating back, but Vestal had finally reached her and he caught her arm.

"Now't of that, Misse Celia. We don't wants no trouble. No, ma'am."

"Did you see him! He threw filth on my dress. The scoun-drel! The . . . the reprobate!" she spluttered as Vestal pulled her back toward the walk.

"Yes'm, Misse, he all them things. But we be better to leave off. We don't wants no part of they people. They be the Liberty Boys. They be trouble of the wost kind."

Hester stood grinning on the curb as the people who had gathered to watch the fun began drifting off. "You looked so funny, Celia. I wish you could have seen the look on your face staring down at that offal."

"I don't see anything funny about it. What savages they are. I never saw anything so beastly cruel in all my life."

"Please, Misses, we be goin' home. City's not fitten place for young misses," Vestal pleaded, anxious to avoid any more mishaps.

Celia shook out her dirty skirts. "Well, I certainly can't go into the King's Arms like this. I'd just as soon go back." The security of home and the Deveroes suddenly seemed most wel-come.

"I suppose I would too," Hester reluctantly added.

Without giving them time to change their minds, Vestal

lifted his eyes heavenward as he shepherded them back toward Tom and the waiting coach.

"Well, it has come to a pretty pass," said Elizabeth, "when young ladies of quality cannot cross a street without being slandered by a mob. I don't think it proper that you girls should go back into the city. You are safer here at home."

"Your mother's point is well taken," Samuel said quietly. He was more dismayed by this incident than he wanted to let on. "The times are difficult enough without courting trouble. Certainly, Celia, it would have been wiser to keep your indignation to yourself. From now on neither of you will be allowed into the city unless accompanied by Mrs. Deveroe or myself. Even I am sometimes surprised by the high feeling these debates are arousing. The animosity in the Assembly last week was more virulent than I can ever remember. There are a group of men who are determined that the province will send delegates to a Continental Congress no matter how strongly the rest of us oppose it. I can't see how it is all going to end."

"You know, my dear, that men like Isaac Sears talk openly of rebellion, even of war."

"I know it, but I hoped you had not heard. What a horrible thought—civil warfare between American Englishmen! Surely it will not come to such a pass."

Celia watched them both reflectively, keeping her own counsel and for the first time thinking seriously of the divisions abroad in the land. War meant little to her, and, while she loved the Deveroes, she could not really share their horror of defying the English government. The bitterness her father and his people felt for a King and an army who had ruthlessly uprooted them had been too well nurtured in her, and something of their despair had remained etched in her spirit. The mob that so cruelly turned on a helpless man was, of course, disgusting. But the principle of throwing off an English yoke—that was something else entirely, though it would never do to say so in this company.

five

"I must say, Miss Celia, that although your actions were a trifle foolhardy, yet they showed great courage. I mean, to openly defy one of those ruffian Liberty Boys . . ."

"Thank you, Mr. Barnett. You are too kind."

Celia bent her head to avoid the white glare from the window, intent on her embroidery hoop, stealing glances from under her lashes. Across from her, Cortlandt Barnett, his three chins hidden behind a huge billow of Valenciennes lace, tore his eyes off Hester long enough to nod her a bow.

"I don't know that courage was involved," Hester said petulantly, twining a ribbon around the neck of a kitten in her lap. "She didn't *know* they were Liberty Boys and she might have got us all mixed up in some terrible fracas."

"That would have indeed been too unfortunate for words," Cortlandt said quickly, afraid he had offended his deity. "I only meant—that is, why, I did say it was foolhardy, you know . . ."

"We know what you meant, Cortlandt dear," said his sister, Prudence, sitting beside him on the back-parlor sofa, and giving his pudgy hand a reassuring pat. "And you were right. You were both foolish and brave, Celia dear."

Celia concentrated fiercely on her sewing, knowing that if she caught Hester's eye they would burst into giggles. This difficult visit was aggravating a dull headache she had awakened with that morning. She wanted to laugh at Cortlandt, yet at the same time she felt sorry for him. A contemporary of Henry Deveroe's, like Henry he had always thought of Hester with contempt when he thought of her at all. But now that she was sixteen, pretty and engaging, he had got it in his mind that she was the love of his life, to her decided dismay. Taking advantage of every opportunity to visit Wayside, he had come today using the excuse that Henry was down from Hartford and he wished to see him. Also much to Celia and Hester's disgust he had brought along his plump sister, Prudence, as a means of keeping them captive in the room. Poor Cortlandt, Celia thought, had surely misjudged the way to Hester's heart, for his principal approach was to sit mooning like a lovestruck calf, devouring her with his heavy-lidded eyes and tripping on his tongue for fear of saying the wrong thing. Celia could not help but pity him.

"I say, Cort, are you going to the races at the Fresh Water Pond tomorrow?" Henry asked from a chair near the window. "I have twenty pounds riding on a liver chestnut. Prime cattle! You'd stand to win something."

"I might consider it," Cortlandt answered. "Would you be accompanying your brother, Miss Hester?"

Hester tossed her head. "La! I should hope not."

"Drag children to a first-class race!" Henry snorted. "God forbid. You must have been out in the sun too long."

"If you ever gave a thought to anything in life besides horses and cards, Henry, you might have noticed that I am nearly sixteen years old and not a child."

"Well, there really an't anything in life *worth* giving a thought to besides horses and cards," Henry said complacently.

"Oh, I don't know. You've got a very pretty wife," Cortlandt offered with what was meant for a leer. "Had I one I'm sure I wouldn't spend my time at the races and gaming tables." He smiled knowingly at Hester.

"She might wish that you did," Hester whispered so that only Celia could hear. Burying her face deeper in her embroidery hoop, Celia tried to suppress her laughter. How could the man be so obtuse not to see what Hester thought of him? Love must indeed be blind.

"The only thing that pretty wife of mine thinks about is what new mantua maker or milliner to visit next. If I don't spend my fortune on horses and games first she will certainly spend it for me decorating her person. She's a good-natured little thing, I'll grant you, but she's got nothing but cotton wool in her head."

Celia was surprised to hear that Henry's estimate of Guinevere tallied so completely with her own. Yet, watching the Deveroes' eldest son as he lounged half out of his chair, refilling his wineglass from a decanter of canary with the ease of long practice, she could not help but feel that he and his wife were well matched. There had probably never occurred one deep thought between the two of them.

"I had hoped Richard might be home today," Prudence spoke up. Short and bosomy, Prudence was a younger, feminine version of her brother, with the same pouting cherub lips and heavy-lidded eyes. Because they were heirs to the considerable fortune their father had made in the China trade, they held a place in society that no amount of grace would have provided.

"He is still in the city preparing for his graduation next week," Celia answered. "He will be home the week following."

"Oh, then we must pay a return call, Cortlandt. It does seem like such a long time since I've enjoyed the pleasure of an intelligent conversation. One can always count on Richard for that."

Hester and Celia exchanged glances before looking to the opposite ends of the room.

"What will he be doing after his matriculation?" Prudence went on.

"After his *graduation*," Hester answered, "he is going to be working with Mr. Jay in his law office. That gentleman has taken a shine to Richard and is going to take him on as a clerk."

"That Whig!" Cortlandt said, causing Hester to look indignantly down her nose at him.

"Mr. Jay is not a Whig," Celia said quietly. "Just because he was in partnership with one of the Livingstons does not make him a revolutionary. He is doing Richard a great service, because there are strict quotas about how many clerks a lawyer may hire."

"Egad! The canary's gone," Henry interrupted. "Ring that damned bell, Hester, and tell Jess to bring up another bottle."

"You seem to know a great deal about it." Prudence glared at Celia. She had always treated Celia as though she were a family retainer attempting to rise above her station, and now, for the first time, Celia recognized the hint of jealousy.

"I'll get it for you myself," Hester said, jumping to her feet. The kitten landed in a heap on the floor, howling indignantly. "Come, Celia, you can help."

Without giving her time to object, Hester grabbed Celia's hand and pulled her to the door. Once outside, they collapsed on each other, giggling hysterically.

"No wonder it's been such a long time since Prudence had

an intelligent conversation—living with Cortlandt!" Hester howled.

"I wonder if she even realized how insulting her remark sounded."

"Of course not. That would take a little sensitivity. Thank heaven Henry ran out of wine. I thought we would never have an excuse to leave."

They started at a slow pace down the cellar steps. "You know, don't you," Hester said, "that the odious Cortlandt has asked Papa for my hand? Imagine! And Papa wishes me to marry him because he is rich. I can think of nothing worse."

"Cortlandt is not odious," said Celia, lighting a flint for the lamp. "A trifle boring, perhaps..."

"Boring! He's deadly dull. He talks of nothing but money and horses and he looks at me as though he would like to eat me! I can't stand him."

Celia laughed. "Then you shouldn't flirt with him as you do. I suspect you are flattered to have him dangling after you."

"Oh, it's nice enough to have a beau." Hester shrugged. "The trouble is, I can't decide *whom* I want to marry. I mean, all the young men I know are so interesting and attractive that I lose my heart to a new one every week."

"I know." Celia smiled to herself. The truth was that Hester never really lost her heart to any of them. That was her dilemma.

"I don't suppose I shall ever know my own mind," Hester sighed, running her hand along the row of dark, dusty bottles. "I love them all."

"Except Cortlandt Barnett."

"Yes, and he, no doubt, is the one I shall have to marry in the end. Perhaps his purse shall make up for his lack of élan, but a merry dance I shall lead him, all the same."

"I can assure you, Hester, there is no virtue to being poor. A fat purse should compensate for all kinds of deficiencies."

"You are always so sensible, Celia. Why don't you ever lose your heart? You flirt and charm and never seem a bit bothered by which one shall eventually bed you. Yet I cannot imagine you giving yourself to a wrinkled old man with only half his teeth just because his pockets jingle! Ah, at last. Here it is."

Celia stood aside while Hester pulled out the squat green bottle. The truth was, she wondered herself why none of the attractive young men who visited Wayside seemed to awaken in her that mysterious warmth and excitement so prized in the poetry books, and romantic novels she devoured. Since she had known most of them for years, she supposed her indifference came from taking them for granted. Yet even that was not completely true. The one she had known the longest and felt closest to, the one who was like a brother to her, was still the only one she ran to with complete delight, always happy to see, always pleased to sit beside sharing confidences. Richard Deveroe had not been home much these last two years, since his studies at King's College kept him in the city most of the time. Now in just a few days he would graduate and come back to live at Wayside—her true friend, the person in the world she loved the most. The thought of it sent a swelling warmth all through her. Could it be that this was the kind of feeling which catapulted Hester into such raptures? She really did not know. She only knew that there was no one else who aroused any kindred feelings within her.

"What are you smiling at?" Hester asked, catching her glance in the candlelight.

"I was thinking that Richard would be home soon."

"Oh, bother Richard. He's only a brother, and a smug, conceited one at that. But then you and Richard were always a pair."

"Come, now, Hester. It is true we're friends, but I'm sure he thinks of me only as a second sister. Besides, I suspect Prudence has her eye on him."

As they started up the stairs Hester extinguished the lamp. "She probably does, for all the good it will do her."

At the door to the back parlor Celia hesitated.

"Do you think you could make my apologies, Hester? I've a terrible headache."

"What a capital idea! I shall have one, too."

"No, no. It's true. I don't feel at all myself. Some melancholy humors asserting themselves, no doubt. Besides, it was really you they came to see."

"All right. But I shall expect the favor returned someday."

Thankfully Celia turned away and started up to her room, keeping her hand over her eyes against the glare.

By the next day Celia was shivering under quilts and blankets while a high fever left pink spots on her cheeks and her throat dry as dust. When the time came for Richard's graduation the worst of the dreaded malaria was over, but the family was forced to leave her behind, weak and, in spite of the warm weather, propped up under a blanket in a chair near a small fire in her bedroom. Every ounce of strength seemed to have drained from her body, while disappointment was like ashes in her mouth as she watched through the curtained window the Deveroe coach roll down the drive.

Richard was almost as disappointed as Celia. When he finally stood in the pulpit of St. Paul's Church to give his speech, he knew it would have bolstered his courage if only he could have seen her smiling face among those of his teachers and the parents and friends of his seven fellow graduating students who sat expectantly looking up at him.

After the graduation the Deveroes did not come back to Wayside but spent nearly two weeks in the city, visiting friends and celebrating. When they finally turned their coach horses up Bowery Lane toward Corlear's Hook the house seemed strangely quiet after the busy clatter of New York's streets. Changing his clothes, Richard had just come back down to the center hall and was planning to go search out his boat when his father stepped out of the study and called to him.

"Richard, stop in for a moment. I want to talk to you."

Seeing the solemn look on his father's face as Samuel pulled out the chair in front of his secretary, Richard began to fear that something had gone wrong with his plan to enter Mr. Jay's law office.

"My son, it is time you thought about getting married."

"Married!" Richard sat forward in his chair, surprise and dismay clear on his face. This was the last thing he had expected. "Papa, I've only just turned eighteen and graduated. I haven't given a thought to marriage."

Samuel waved a hand reassuringly. "I know. And your mother and I are not trying to rush you into it. But the matter has come up and we wish to have it settled, if at all possible." He smiled a little at the crestfallen expression on his son's sensitive face. "We don't mean that you must cry the banns tomorrow, my boy. It's just that circumstances are such that we would prefer to settle your situation while it is advantageous to all concerned."

Richard sat back. Marriage! It was the last thing he wanted to think about. A sick feeling began to grow in his stomach.

Samuel seemed to read his thoughts. "As you know, we have been hopeful for some time now that Hester would announce her betrothal to Cortlandt Barnett. I confess I should feel some relief to see that flighty girl safely wed, and she could hardly make a better match. As it happened, I was talking to Mr. Barnett just the other day at the Merchants' Coffee House and he mentioned that his daughter, Prudence, would not look with distaste on an alliance with yourself."

"Prudence Barnett! I hardly know her." But he remembered her. She was a copy of her oafish brother, with the added disadvantage of a cloying, hypocritically sweet manner. Worse yet, she had the largest, plumpest bosom of any respectable girl he knew. A coldness stuck in his chest like a knife.

His father's damnably reasonable voice continued. "It would be a fine alliance, brother and sister to brother and sister. The Barnetts are a substantial family with large holdings in the Jerseys and extensive shipping interests. You'd be allying yourself to solid wealth and good breeding—not to be disdained, either of them."

Richard's fingers dug into the upholstered arms of his chair. Ships, land, wealth, breeding—he began to feel trapped.

"And when you have children . . ."

The rest of his father's words were lost as Richard suddenly pictured himself climbing into bed with a naked melon-breasted stranger whose hands groped for him. He felt nauseous. The truth was, he had never known a woman at all, had never even visited the bawdy houses near King's College. He had never seemed to feel the urge for one that consumed so much of the energy of his fellow students. They used to tease him about his innocence until he won their respect on other terms. Not that he was a prude, he hoped, or—worse yet!—one of those perverted *trikes* who preferred men to women. But friends, books, philosophy and government were enough for him. Besides, he was suddenly convinced, it was not the idea of physical contact with a woman that he found so repugnant. It was the idea of marrying a stranger, a woman he didn't know and who did not know him, a woman he had barely exchanged ten sentences with in his entire life.

He realized that his father had stopped speaking and was quietly studying him.

"I . . . I really hadn't thought seriously of marriage, Father. I was rather hoping to postpone it, at least until I got myself established and earned a place in the Assembly."

"I can understand that. And in the natural order of things I would agree. But this is a singular opportunity which has almost fallen into our laps, and I should hate to see you pass it up without consideration. Besides, things are so unsettled these days. There are a group of men in these Colonies who seem bent on forcing us into open hostilities with England. If war should come, I should like to think that the future of all my children was secure. God knows what you shall have to face."

"But would it not be better to have *no* obligations? I mean, if war should come, I should not like to leave a wife behind."

"Oh, I doubt it will come to that," Samuel said. He had expected some hesitation, but not this degree of dismay. He knew Richard was a very different kind of boy from his brother. There was none of Henry's lusty sensual greed for life in this reflective, serious young man. Yet he never thought the idea of marriage would have shaken him so. He walked over to Richard and laid his hand on his son's shoulder.

"I can see that this is a new notion to you, my boy. Don't worry over it now. Just allow it to wander about in your mind as you enjoy the next few weeks. I am sure you will come to see what a fine opportunity it is."

"Yes, Papa," Richard murmured miserably. "May I go now?"

"Of course. Oh, and, Richard, that was a fine oration you gave. I'm not sure I remembered to tell you, but it was most impressive. Logical, concise and eloquent."

Richard stopped with his hand on the doorknob. How proud he would have been to hear those words before this distressing talk of marriage. Now it was impossible to appreciate them.

"Thank you, Papa," he murmured. "I am gratified that you liked it."

He stepped into the hall.

Brooding, he stood beside the door for a moment, then looked up to see Celia coming down the stairs. He had not seen her for almost four months and he was shocked at her appearance. Thin and waiflike, she was sallow-skinned, her eyes larger and darker than he remembered. Yet, gradually, surprise gave way to admiration, for in the time they had been apart she had passed from the child he remembered into a startlingly lovely young woman. Her figure in her yellow print dress was taller and more finely molded than the girl he had known. Her golden-brown hair was pulled gently back to fall in curls around her shoulders, accentuating the new finely turned planes of her face.

For a moment he was afraid he *was* seeing a stranger, but

the bright smile she gave him as she ran to take his outstretched hands reassured him this was the same, sweet Celia he had always known.

"Richard! I'm so glad you've come home." Celia kissed his cheek lightly, then impulsively threw her arms around his neck and gave him a quick, heartfelt hug. When she stood back he noticed the brightness in her eyes. "Can you forgive me for not coming to your graduation? For not hearing your speech? I wanted to so badly, but I didn't have the strength."

"There is nothing to forgive. Of course you couldn't go. Mama told me how ill you've been. Should you be down here now? You must not overtax yourself."

"It's all right. I simply had to say hello and I'm not that much an invalid."

Richard drew her arm through his and started toward the door that opened onto the terrace. "Come and sit with me and tell me all about yourself. It's been ages since we've had a good visit."

"I shouldn't, but I will," Celia said, happily accompanying him. "Don't let Dinah know, though. She has decreed that the grave will claim me if I so much as sit in a draft."

He stopped by the door, looking intently into her face. "My poor girl. You do look tired and pale. If I had known you were this bad I could never have kept my mind on my Latin paragraphs. Yet even with your illness you look prettier than I've ever seen you. Why, you've become a young woman, Celia, in these months I've been away. A lovely young woman."

Celia colored at the compliment and laughed with embarrassment. "Oh, Richard, I do love you so."

It was said as a simple statement of fact, and it seemed the most natural thing in the world for the two of them to slip into each other's arms, holding each other close. Celia leaned her head against Richard's coat and felt completely at peace with the world, all unaware that he, resting his chin on her thick hair, was struck by a sudden inspiration.

"Celia!" he said, grasping her shoulders and putting her away from him. "Will you marry me?"

"Marry?"

"Yes, marry. Father wants to pack me off to the Barnett family heiress, but I don't want her. I want you, Celia. I've always loved you. We're friends and we suit. Say you will marry me, please, my darling Celia."

The idea seemed so absurd she came close to laughing. But

something of the earnestness on his face told her he was not teasing.

"But, Richard. I can't marry you. Your parents would never allow it. I'm—I have no dowry at all. All I have in the world is a worthless deed to land in Acadia and what your parents have given me. You must do better than me when you marry. Considerably better."

"Your blood is as good as anyone's and better than the Barnetts', who, after all, started out in trade. And I love you and you love me. That is what matters. You do love me, don't you?"

"Yes, but . . ."

"Then it's a wonderful idea. I don't know why I never thought of it before. It must have been somewhere in the back of my mind for years and finally rose to the surface now, just at the right moment. Oh, say you will, Celia, please."

His exuberant delight was contagious. There was a lot of sense in what he said. She could almost believe it had been ordained since that first day when she had been so grateful to him for his kindness on the stairs. They were already so close. To be married, to face life together, never to be parted by other loves—the thought sent Celia's heart soaring.

He studied her face anxiously, not reading the thoughts that raced behind her cryptic smile. "You haven't given your heart to another man, have you?" he asked, almost afraid now to hear her answer. "If you have, then of course . . ."

"Richard, I have loved you since I was ten years old, and to marry you would make my life complete. But *you* must stop and think. Your parents will not look kindly on such an attachment. They have high hopes for you, you said so yourself. Think of their disappointment."

Throwing up his hands, he turned his back on her, leaning against the terrace doors. "You sound like Father! Must I sacrifice my happiness all the rest of my life to please them? Must I tie myself to some twit of a girl to whom I can barely speak two sensible sentences, just because the alliance will please my parents? I won't do it! They have no right to ask it of me."

Although his words were angry, Celia recognized at once the fear that lay beneath his defiance. Richard was no lusty young rake, easily able to handle women. He would be helpless attempting to woo a girl he barely knew. Sensitive and shy, he revealed his better nature only when he was around people he knew and trusted. He would be no bargain to Miss Barnett, whereas to herself he would be the dearest possession of all her life. Against her better judgment Celia let herself imagine that it could really happen. How wonderful it would be! Slipping her arms around his waist, she leaned her head against his back.

"Perhaps we can find a way," she murmured.

He turned in her arms, holding her close in a way he never had before. "Is that what you want, Celia? Truly?"

She lifted her face to his and lightly kissed him on the lips. "With all my heart."

The long impassioned kiss he gave her was, in its earnest desperation, as different from the friendly pecks he had always dropped on her lips as night from day. For Celia to finally feel the surge of passion other girls seemed to know convinced her as nothing else could that here was her one true love. And the relief and joy it brought her was only a little less than that Richard himself experienced. He pulled her to him, hugging her and whirling her around so wildly her feet left the floor. Laughing, they stopped and fell naturally back into another long kiss. When she finally laid her head in the curve of his neck, Celia felt she was about to drown in happiness.

"Oh, Richard," she said wistfully. "How I wish it could be. I wish it so. But I can't believe your parents will ever give their consent."

"They will. They must. I'll speak to them today—no, better not today. Let Papa think I'm considering marriage with Prudence Barnett so that at least he can't accuse me of dismissing the match out of hand. Can you wait a few days?"

"Of course. My worst problem will be to make myself remember how unlikely it is they'll ever approve. I'll pray. I'll ask Saint Anne to intervene for us. Surely God would not be so cruel as to let them separate us."

He pulled her to him, crushing the breath from her. "Nothing will separate us, my dearest Celia. Nothing! Pray to your saint and to all the saints in heaven, and in the meantime I'll try to martial every argument in our favor. Between us we'll have all heaven and logic too on our side. Poor Father will never be able to stand up to all that!"

"Marry Celia!"

Automatically Samuel's eyes shifted to his wife sitting in quiet dignity on the sofa, and the long look they exchanged was full of unspoken amazement. Richard walked to the fireplace and leaned against the mantel, trying to look nonchalant though his heart was pounding. He plunged ahead.

"I'm excessively fond of her, Papa. There is no girl *any-where*"—special emphasis on that word—"that I would more wish to have for a wife."

"My boy, *I'm* fond of Celia, too. She is almost a daughter to your mother and me. But I confess I never gave a thought to her marrying you. I am . . . well, I'm quite taken aback."

"Please consider it, sir. We are very well suited, and if she seemed like a daughter before, then this marriage would make her truly one. A daughter you already love and respect."

Elizabeth nervously pulled out a clove-scented handkerchief that lay tucked inside her bodice and dabbed at her nose. "Why, Richard, it would almost be like marrying your sister!"

"But she's *not* my sister. We haven't a drop of blood in common between us. And as far as blood goes, hers is considerably better than the Barnetts'."

He could see at once by Samuel's sharp glance that that had been a mistake. "The Barnetts are a good enough family, Richard," his father said curtly, "and blood is not the issue here. Have you given any thought at all to the fact that Celia has no dowry? There would be no capital coming into the family through this marriage, dear as the girl is."

"There is her father's land in Acadia," Richard said weakly.

"Foolish thought! I would expect you of all people to realize how futile it is to hope that anything will ever come of that."

Richard conceded the point. "You're right, of course. I have no hope on that score, nor does she. I love Celia for herself. That is really all there is to my desire to marry her. Even without a dowry she's worth more to me than any girl I know."

"But she's so young," Elizabeth protested.

"Why, Mama, she is already older than you were at your marriage. Fourteen, wasn't it?"

Elizabeth made a show of replacing her handkerchief. "That was a long time ago," she murmured.

Richard could see he was never going to convince his parents by arguing with them. He had one good defense and he would win only by emphasizing it above all else.

"These arguments are not really important anyway, are they? Papa, I know you wish me to marry Prudence Barnett, but I can only tell you that the idea is repugnant to me. It's not her money or her family. It's that I hardly know her and little like what I do know. Celia, on the other hand, has been my friend for years. I am comfortable with her and I feel a great affection for her. I want her as my wife and I don't want Prudence. Doesn't that count for anything?"

Samuel sat down heavily at his secretary and drummed his fingers on its polished top. He had never been the kind of father who gave no thought to the feelings of his children, and he had small stomach for beginning now. Elizabeth waited expectantly for her husband to speak, then finally turned to her son.

"What does Celia say to all this? Have you asked her?"

"Yes. Not that I intended to. It just grew out of what we felt for each other. She loves me and wants to marry me as much as I do her. But she won't go against your wishes. Her affection and gratitude for you both prevent that."

Samuel could see how much this answer pleased his wife, and he began to feel that he had already lost. Damn the girl! Why couldn't she be less obliging!

"My boy," he said gently, "the truth is that in every respect save a practical one, I would welcome Celia as my true daughter. I have seen over the years the affection you bear for each other and I know her for a good, honest girl. It is only that I had hoped to see you comfortably settled. I'm not young anymore and I have less than my brothers to leave my children. Henry will inherit the bulk of my estate, as you know, and Hester will be comfortably off with Cortlandt. I would wish to see you as well placed as they, yet I have no way of establishing you myself."

"I understand your concern, Papa, but it doesn't bother me at all. I intend to make my way in the world with or without a handsome dowry from my wife."

Elizabeth spoke up shyly. "You know the land upriver, the land my father left me? It's not a large grant, but it does have some value. Henry and Hester will have no need of it and I've intended for years it should go to you, Richard, when you marry."

She was rewarded by the happiness on his face. "Then that's it! We'll develop the land and make our home there."

"But it's only forests now. It will take years to develop. How will you live until then?"

Samuel thoughtfully fingered the worked buttonholes of his brocade coat. "I suppose they could have the Manor House at

West Farms. I have often regretted that it stands empty so much of the time. Richard could put his experience in farming to good use there."

"You've forgotten, Papa, that I'm to start as clerk to Mr. Jay. Will I be able to manage both?"

"Oh, I think so. Mr. Forbes is a fine overseer and he can continue to do the real managing of the farm. And since Mr. Jay plans to have you help with his business in West Chester, it might work out very well. I could trust Celia to take better care of the house than it has been these last years. But we're talking of the future. When did you imagine this wedding taking place?"

"As soon as possible," Richard said, seeing the defenses begin to crumble. He didn't want to give them time to change their minds. "Next month."

"That is quite impossible," his startled mother answered. "Why, Celia would have too much to prepare."

"Two months, then."

"No," Samuel said. "If I agree to this match, Richard, it will only be on the condition that it take place next year. That will give you both time to make sure this is what you really want. And it will also allow you time to become established in Mr. Jay's office."

Jumping up, Richard pumped his father's hands delightedly. "Thank you, Father, thank you with all my heart. You won't regret it, and you've made two people who both love you very happy."

"I don't suppose there is any point in insisting you make an effort to get to know Miss Barnett during these months— no, I thought not. That substantial dowry! Dear, dear!"

Elizabeth, resigned to the idea of Celia as a daughter-in-law, was becoming more and more pleased with the romance of it all. Kissing her son lightly on his cheek, she drew his arm through hers and walked him to the door. "Now, go and find Celia and bring her to us. We may as well begin right now to make plans for the wedding."

six

As soon as Hester heard of Celia and Richard's engagement, she immediately accepted Cortlandt Barnett, making sure that her wedding was set for next February while Celia would have to wait until April. Thus they both had several months to finish up all the assorted household linens and woolens a bride was expected to bring to her new home.

Hester's wedding soon became one of the most important social events of the season, preceded by a round of parties and soirees that seemed to grow progressively larger as the date drew near. Celia was panic-stricken at the thought that she might have to endure the same kind of notoriety, and in order to avoid it she and Richard agreed to have a simple ceremony at the Manor House with only the family and their West Chester friends in attendance. Although it took a long time to get Elizabeth to agree to this, in the end they had their way.

While Celia fought to keep her wedding simple, Hester positively reveled in her new role as star of the social season of 1775. Along with her resignation to accepting Cortlandt Barnett as a husband had also come her determination to enjoy the enlarged privileges of wealth and status which he brought her, and enjoy them she did to the hilt. Celia watched her, a cryptic smile on her lips, for even now Cortlandt mooned after her while Hester flitted among her friends, giving him the barest of glances. He seemed immensely proud of capturing all this small, quick silver-gold brightness, and, shaking her head, Celia wondered if he knew what he was getting into. Still, one never knew. Perhaps once the wedding took place Cortlandt would assert himself. She hoped so, because Hester Deveroe was not the kind of girl to be so gently managed.

The worst thing about all these social occasions, Celia found, was that through them she was constantly thrown into

Prudence Barnett's path. She made every effort to avoid her, and when that was not possible she tried to be coolly polite. Prudence was always gushingly effusive, yet, underneath, the barely disguised resentment she felt for Celia was obvious.

"I really think she hates me," Celia confided to Hester after one particularly unpleasant confrontation.

"She'd like to tear out your eyes." Hester said gleefully.

"I thought as much. But it was not my doing. Richard never wanted to marry her at all. And *he* asked *me*!"

"Well, you can't expect her to believe that when it is so much more flattering to think a wicked wanton lured him away, now, can you? Besides, she is as foolish as her brother. I don't know how I shall bear either of them."

"Oh, Hester. Are you sure you should be going through with this?"

Hester shrugged and turned the hem of the petticoat she was finishing. "Why not?"

"It's just that I'm so happy and I want you to be happy, too. Richard and I, we almost seem like one person already— I feel he is so much a part of me and I of him. Surely marriage should be like that."

With an uncompromising eye Hester studied Celia's ruffled cap bent over her sewing, the gently smiling mouth, the innocent amber eyes. "Oh, Celia, you are such a sentimental goose!"

Celia's head shot up. "Why, what do you mean?"

Exasperated, Hester threw down her sewing and flounced to the window. "*Nobody* lives like that! Two parts of one person, indeed! What claptrap! At least I'm going into marriage with my eyes open. I already see Cortlandt for what he is, his bad and his good points—yes, there *are* a few good ones there, too. But you! You have a romantic notion of Richard, and he is not that way at all. He's self-centered, withdrawn and cold. He is as unlike you as possible, and I don't understand why you've never seen it."

Celia fought to hold her temper. "I don't believe you. That is not the man I know. He's never been anything but warm and affectionate to me. Perhaps because I love him I see a different side of him than you do."

"You see what you want to see. Oh, I know I am not blinded by love for anyone but myself, but perhaps that is not such a bad thing. Underneath all that affection, I tell you, he is a very cold-blooded young man, and someday you are going to come crashing to earth if you don't begin to see it, too."

Jumping to her feet, Celia gathered up her silks and threw them into the sewing table. "That's quite enough. Look at your future any way you please, Hester Deveroe, but don't try to spoil mine for me."

Hester laid a hand on her arm. "Oh, don't run away. I'm sorry if I offended you. I should have known you could never take any criticism of my brother. Perhaps in some small way I envy him your adoration. I could never admire anyone that unreservedly."

Celia hesitated. This was a familiar scene—hasty words followed by contrition. This time she was not sure she could forgive her.

"Hester, I am truly fond of you, but I don't understand you."

Hester laughed. "Sometimes I don't understand myself."

Although Celia tried to shrug off Hester's chilling words they kept echoing in her mind. Hester had always taken a jaundiced view of people, but to call Richard "cold" was absurd. There was no more warm, kindly person anywhere than Richard Deveroe. Who should know that better than Celia herself, who for more than seven years had been closer to him than anyone in the family? Could she be so wrong about anyone she knew so well? And Hester was no judge of character.

Yet when Richard came home from West Chester for his sister's wedding Celia found herself watching him—judging evaluating, holding Hester's assessment up to him like a suit of clothes to see if it fit or fell short. By the time he left she was completely reassured. Richard's gentle, loving ways were as apparent to her as they had ever been. They spent many tender moments together when they could manage to be alone. Together they dreamed and planned—first, the changes they would make in the Manor House and, then, looking years ahead, their development someday of the land upriver. In the quiet times when the household had settled down, he sat with his arms around her, staring contentedly into the last of the firelight. In those moments Celia was supremely happy and convinced that it was because Hester lacked this closeness with Cortlandt that she called Richard "cold."

Yet in spite of her confidence Celia was a realist, and she had to admit Richard had certain traits which might lead someone like Hester to view him differently. He was a person who kept his feelings under tight rein, who had a positive abhorrence of giving way to strong passions. Even his response to the violent political questions of the day was reasoned and objective and revealed none of the raw partisan emotion so easily aroused in other men.

Yet, she told herself, she was glad he was that kind of man. He would stand back, analyze and conclude, not rush in wildly swinging sword or pistol, regretting later when someone got hurt. And they were well suited to each other, his reasoned judgment balancing her tendency to be led by her emotions.

Besides, had she not loved his kind, gentle ways since she was ten years old? Hester had to be wrong!

She was never more convinced of this than on that raw February day when Hester Deveroe, her silver-gilt hair shimmering in the wavering lights of more than sixty candles, stood under a red velvet canopy next to Cortlandt Barnett and became his wife. Not even the glittering diamond-and-gold parure he had given her could enliven the dullness of her eyes. Hester's shoulders were back and she carried herself proudly, but there was no joy, no sense of beginning a new and delightful existence. When Hester turned to greet the fashionable crowd around them, Celia saw with a terrible clarity the icy, resigned emptiness in her eyes, and she wanted to weep. It was the only time Hester allowed her true feelings to show. Ten minutes later, surrounded by laughing well-wishers and friends, she was smiling and vivacious, charming them all, and Celia knew that by the time they returned from their long four months' wedding trip down South, she would be her old self, slipping easily into the trappings of a wealthy young matron. But in that terrible brief glance, Celia had grasped Richard's warm hand in her own, and savored the closeness of his body as she leaned against him for reassurance, thanking God fervently that when this moment came for her she would belong to a man she loved above all others.

While the preparations and celebrations of the two Deveroe weddings went on, the world around Wayside grew increasingly uneasy. It seemed to the inhabitants that mankind was infected with a plague of lunacy. Tories and Whigs, Liberty Boys and King's Men, Patriots and Loyalists—daily the hatreds between them led to violence and reprisals of violence, riots and the burning of effigies, anarchy and the tyranny that tried to control anarchy.

The arguments raged in the coffeehouses, in the newspapers, pamphlets and handbills and in the political bodies that attempted to govern in spite of the growing turmoil. In January of 1775, a month before Hester's wedding, the New York Assembly absolutely refused to appoint delegates to a Second Continental Congress. The radicals of the city took the issue to the freeholders—men who owned at least forty pounds unencumbered by debt. This group proposed a totally new legislative body, a Provincial Convention to be called for the following April 20. The choice for delegates to this convention, for New York at least, drew the lines dramatically between King's Men and Separatists. By this time, if you were a man of consequence, you had to choose which side you were on—Congress or Parliament. Both sides ran the risk of being branded traitors and suffering for it, but to remain neutral was now almost impossible.

For Celia it was becoming increasingly difficult to keep her own counsel, and she was grateful that the concerns of her wedding took her mind off politics. Almost to a man, the Deveroes were pro-English. Their religion, their inherited wealth, their family's long involvement in the political and power structure of the province all conspired to make them Loyalists. Celia was not half so inclined to love and honor England, but she did love and respect the Deveroes and she was resolved to do nothing that would hurt them. It helped that she was not particularly drawn to the Patriot cause either—perhaps because of that old Acadian sense of exile deep in her blood. She worked diligently to prepare her new home, trying to shut out the arguments raging around her, and praying fervently that they might be settled without disrupting her wedding.

In early April when the family moved to the Manor Farm to prepare for the wedding, Celia felt a great relief at leaving the city. Yet, if she hoped to find peace in the rural atmosphere of West Chester, she was immediately disappointed. Although there were no newspapers in the country, information had a way of getting around and the population there had become as clearly divided as in the city.

She learned the extent of this opposition on April 11, the day that Richard came home from White Plains after a meeting to elect delegates to the Second Continental Congress which was set to open the following month in Philadelphia.

"It was terrible," he told her, looking drawn and white and still showing signs of fatigue after the long ride back to West Farms. "If ever I had a hope of a compromise between the radicals and the Loyalists, it's gone forever now."

Celia took a hot poker from the hearth and thrust it into a mug of cider, handing it to him where he sat sprawling in his chair, still wearing his riding boots.

"Tell me everything that happened," she said, leaning back against his chair. "Surely there was no bloodshed?"

"No, nothing as bad as that. Five hundred people came. From all sides of the county. Everyone went to his own camp—the Loyalists to Hatfield's tavern and the Patriots to Miles Oakley's. When the Patriots moved across to the courthouse, the other group followed. Isaac Wilkins spoke eloquently against the election, but it did him no good. Finally the Loyalists withdrew and Chairman Morris got on with the business of electing the six delegates. Just to make everything more divisionary, the committee also passed resolutions endorsing the actions of the first Congress and praising the members of the Assembly who supported them."

"And did the Loyalists try to disrupt them?"

"No, they went back to Hatfield's and passed a resolution of their own protesting both Congress *and* committee."

"But, Richard, it sounds very orderly to me."

"Can't you see, my dear, they are creating a situation in which we will all be forced to take sides. Oh, the so-called Patriots keep saying they are only against Parliament—they even cheered the King before dispersing. But I really fear in such a volatile atmosphere it will take only one small careless incident to lead to open war. That's what some of the more hotheaded really want, though they won't say so publicly."

"Not war! Surely it won't come to that."

"I wish I shared your optimism. I think, though I won't say it to anyone else—I think war is almost inevitable."

Celia laid her hand on his. "If it does come, Richard, what will you do? What did you do today?"

"I was torn in two. All my family feel that to go against England is nothing short of treason. Yet I have spent almost a year now working with men like Mr. Jay—who is certainly a man of great integrity and no radical. He has come to the strong conviction that this country would be better off apart from British domination. It should be free to try its wings, to find its own way. It can only be hampered by remaining a colony—even a British colony.

"Today I was attending at Mr. Jay's request, so I stayed near the Whigs. But I could see my father, my Uncle Peter, Ewan, John, my relatives, many of my old friends, all in the other camp. It was painful, Celia. Terribly painful. I feel I am going to have to sort out my loyalties and go where honor leads me, but right now I'm not sure which way that will be."

Reaching out, he laid his hand on her hair, stroking the glossy curls. "How do you feel? What would you have me do?"

She smiled up at him. "I too would have you go where honor takes you. But, to be practical, I don't think it hurts to have a foot in the radical camp at the same time that your family is staunchly Loyalist. Perhaps it will never come to choosing sides, but, if it does, so much is at stake."

"Our country itself is at stake."

"More than that. Your home, this house, your livelihood."

He shrugged. "Our wealth, you mean. I think I can make my way without my father's money."

"No, I don't mean just that. I mean your land. *That* is the only thing that really matters, Richard. That is the only thing that endures. I have no partisan feelings about either side in this conflict, but I would keep my eyes open and do anything to protect my holdings. Because when it is over, if you have land, you can always begin again."

Richard sat forward in his chair, surprise and dismay clear on his face. "Are you suggesting I play both sides? Would you have me an opportunist?"

"Of course I'm not suggesting that. I know you for too fine a person. I'm only saying that perhaps you should delay taking sides for as long as you can."

"And see which one is likely to win! I'm surprised at you, Celia."

She looked at him, a burning earnestness in her eyes. "Richard, I have been poor and my parents were exiles from their own land. I know what that is like. I intend never to be poor again!"

She said it lightly, but there was something in her voice that startled him. Smiling, he leaned forward and gently kissed her forehead.

"My dear, it is hardly likely to come to so desperate a point.

Put your fears behind you. You will never want for anything so long as I am here to care for you. Now, what about another glass of that mulled cider?"

He sat back, watching her as she turned to the fire, amazed that after all these years she still remembered the terrible poverty of her childhood. Yet there was a soundness to her words, and he knew he would give them careful thought. No need to rush into committing himself. He would take his time. All the time he could manage.

Staring into the flames, he reflected that it had been a disturbing day all round, and never more so than toward the end when he was leaving Oakley's Tavern and found his way blocked by a tall figure dressed severely in a black serge coat and gray hose.

"Mr. Deveroe?"

Richard stopped, removing his hat and placing his riding crop under one arm, "Your servant, sir."

The face was vaguely familiar and Richard searched his memory for a name. The narrow cheeks, the thick overhanging brows, the thin lips—where had he seen them before?

"I believe, sir, you are in the wrong company."

"I beg your pardon."

"My friends and I"—the man gestured to two men standing close behind him—"deeply resent your presence here today among patriots of good standing."

Taken aback, Richard thought perhaps he hadn't heard the man correctly. "And who may I ask are you, sir?"

"My name is Jaspar Carne, secretary to the Committee of Safety."

Pieces of a picture began drifting back. A boy in a round hat applying a stick to the head of an overburdened donkey.

"I remember you."

"I well remember you, too, sir."

"Where is your father?" Richard said, half in jest and looking around. "Shouldn't he be here among this assembly? He was one of the early instigators of its business."

Carne's lips drew into a tight line. "My father is dead. I count myself privileged to carry on his work."

Embarrassed, Richard dropped his eyes. "My apologies, Mr. Carne." What a strange fellow. He couldn't be more than a year or two older than Richard himself, yet already he seemed as old as his father had that distant afternoon in West Farms.

"It's of no consequence. What matters more is *your* presence here among men committed to the overthrow of tyranny. It seems strange indeed that you should stand against your entire family, especially when its interests are so closely allied to the preservation of the colonial system."

"Aye, that's right," one of the men behind Carne spoke up. Richard recognized the blunt, roughhewn features of Shubel Merritt, a well-known agitator and troublemaker from New Rochelle. His resentment began to grow.

"Are you questioning my motives?" he asked coldly.

Carne stared at him without answering. For an instant Richard's Deveroe pride flared and he came close to slapping the haughty fellow. Controlling his temper, he replaced his hat and took his riding crop carefully from under his arm.

"I do not owe you or your committee any explanations, Mr. Carne. I am here today acting as clerk for Mr. Jay, who was one of the delegates to the First Continental Congress. If you have any questions about my honor I suggest you apply to him."

Abruptly turning away, he started back across the common, but not before he heard Merritt call out, "Spy!" behind him.

The whole incident was profoundly disturbing. He hardly knew this Jaspar Carne, and what he saw he little liked. Probably the man had never forgiven him for that drubbing on the road so long ago. If this was the kind of person he was going to have to join forces with...

Yet his association with men like Jay had helped him to understand the idealism and the dreams of a true republican government that fueled this quarrel with Parliament. More than anything in the world Richard wanted to be a part of that new and emerging order.

Celia shifted her head against his and rubbed her cheek along his high leather boot. His hand stroked her lovely hair. Well, almost more than anything. . . .

seven

It was Celia who had insisted that her wedding should take place at the Manor House. She had loved it since that first day when Samuel Deveroe had brought her there from East Chester. The house in New York, undeniably grander, had never held the same associations. More than anything she wanted to avoid the ostentatious display of Hester's marriage, and she felt it was only appropriate that she should. After all, Hester was the Deveroes' daughter, while she was only their ward, and Cortlandt Barnett represented the cream of city society—something she and Richard did not even care about. The smaller, more intimate society of West Farms seemed perfectly suited to the two of them, while the house itself had the special distinction of being the place where they had first met. Now it would be their home—their first home. She thought it wonderfully apt that they begin their life together there.

She was never to regret that decision. Their wedding took place on a beautiful day in late April. The house had been decorated with the new greens of spring and all the early flowering blossoms of lilac and dogwood. Everyone agreed that Celia had never looked more beautiful. The white satin of her gown trimmed in lace edged with silver set off the perfect creaminess of her skin. She had piled her hair high, and Dinah had twined a spiral of artificial rosebuds amid her powdered curls. Her only jewelry was a gift from Richard, given him by his mother for this occasion. It was a flawless topaz set in an ornate scrollwork of gold and hung on a golden chain. It was the first really valuable jewel Celia had ever owned, and the fact that it was a Deveroe heirloom and given her by her new husband made it all the more precious.

Her husband almost outshone her in splendor, for Richard had always enjoyed wearing stylish clothes, not to impress others as so many men did, but simply for the pleasure they gave him. His coat was a pale-blue satin worked with silver, set against a white waistcoat embroidered with pale pastel flowers. Ruffles of Valenciennes lace at his throat and wrists, silver buckles on his shoes, white satin breeches and silk hose, and an immaculately powdered silver wig made him a striking figure. Together they were a handsome pair. Watching the obvious happiness on both their faces, Elizabeth Deveroe sighed to herself. Samuel, she knew, was still thinking of that lost Barnett dowry, but she felt sure this marriage was the right thing for both her children.

They had wanted the wedding feast to be held outdoors, but evenings in April were still too cool for an affair which promised to go on for many hours. Instead, Jess had thrown open the doors between the rooms on one side of the house, turning parlor and morning room into one large hall. A lavish supper was laid across the way in the dining room, and those who could not find a place there carried their plates back to the hall, where sofas and chairs had been pushed against the wall to allow for dancing later.

Once the simple ceremony was over, Celia began to enjoy herself. Everyone crowded around her at once—Mr. Forbes, the overseer, standing beside his wife, who looked like a tent in a huge green satin overskirt, Tom, the groom, who had run Samuel's stables for years, Jess, Vestal and Dinah, hovering on the edges of the crowd, smiling broadly. John and Ben, Richard's cousins from the mill, rushed forward to press their hands, and Celia hardly recognized them, they had grown so. The tenants and the freeholders of the area had all come bringing their wives and, in many cases, their children. They came out of respect and friendship for Samuel, but also out of fondness for Richard and Celia, whom they had watched grow to maturity. She glimpsed the Trenton family, looking threadbare as always, standing about uncomfortably, and she recognized the Lawrences, handsome in their best dress, their daughter, now a darkly lovely girl of about fourteen, hovering close to her mother. The poor child looked as though she had to force herself to step forward and take Celia's hand.

"Congratulations, Miss Cel—I mean, Madam Richard. I wish you joy."

"Why, thank you, Mercy. We are going to be neighbors now, and I hope we will also be friends. Won't you come and visit with me one day soon?"

Blushing pink, Mercy looked helplessly at her mother.

"Why, she'd love to," Mrs. Lawrence responded hurriedly. "It would be most appropriate for Mercy to see how a young bride settles into her new home, for she may be doing the same one day soon."

Poor Mercy looked as though she wished the floor would open and swallow her. From pink she went to scarlet staring down at the polished parquet, too miserable to speak. Celia felt a great pity for her.

"I'll tell you what," Celia said, speaking directly to the girl. "As soon as I'm settled I intend to have a spinning frolic for all the ladies of West Farms. Will you come? I've seen some of your woolen coverlets, and they are beautiful. I'd love to watch you make your patterns."

Mercy smiled shyly at her, obviously pleased. "Yes, I'll come," she murmured while her mother beamed.

"Good. Then that's settled."

And a minor victory won, Celia thought as she turned away to take Henry Deveroe's outstretched hand. Henry was beginning to mirror his father's corpulence. He and Guinevere had come down from Hartford especially for Richard's wedding, and now he stepped up to lay one large arm around Celia's shoulders and give her a hug that crushed the breath from her lungs.

"Now you are a true sister indeed," he said enthusiastically. Even in his best clothes Henry had a lingering odor of horses about him.

"Thank you, Brother. Richard and I were both so pleased that you and Gwen could come down for the ceremony."

"Wouldn't have missed it, would we Gwennie?"

Henry's wife simpered and gave Celia a wet kiss on her cheek. "Miss dear Richard's marriage? La, I never heard of anything so foolish. You look absolutely gorgeous, my dear. I myself would prefer a little more trim on that gown, but it suits you, yes, it does."

Celia covered her smile with her fan. Guinevere clearly preferred more trim than gown. She was so laden with bow-knots, seed pearls, flounces and artificial flowers she looked like a walking shop. Try as she would, Celia could feel no affection for Henry and his wife. But, with their home in Hartford and hers in West Farms, they were not likely to be thrown together often.

Hearing a familiar voice, she looked up to see the crowd

part to allow a tall striking figure in brown velvet to approach, walking with a natural authority that the people around him automatically acknowledged. Celia was impressed.

"Ewan!" she smiled warmly, extending her hands. "I haven't seen you this age. How grand that you could be here."

He raised both her hands to his lips, then made her an elaborately polite bow which was completely belied by the mischievous gleam in his eyes.

"Dear Cousin Celia. So you finally caught him."

Celia's laughter was crystal glass touched by the wind. "Nothing you can say will make me angry today, Ewan. Come, now. Aren't you happy for us?"

"Happy indeed, when I can forget how envious I am of the joy on both your faces. You look radiantly beautiful today, by the way."

"Thank you, sir. I feel beautiful."

"Richard looks beautiful, too."

"He does look grand, doesn't he? This is such a happy day for us both."

"You were always a pair, you two. I cannot imagine a better fate for either of you."

"We are going to be neighbors now, did you know?"

"Yes. Father told me you will be living at the Manor House. I'm very glad because I have often wished Richard was nearer, even though I'm not often in residence myself. I was recently elected sheriff of the county, and that keeps me on my horse a good deal of the time."

"Sheriff? Why, you must be the youngest ever. What a triumph for you, Ewan. I am so pleased."

"I should be more pleased if it required a little less of my time. But yes, it was an honor and I take it very seriously. Now I must offer my congratulations to your husband. 'Your husband'—have you become accustomed to hearing that yet?"

"It gives me a delicious tingle. Go and speak to him. I know he'll want to see you."

She watched him cross the room, almost unable to tear her eyes away. Ewan would always be like that, she supposed. It was that same presence he had used to keep them in thrall when they were children. Small wonder he had already been elected sheriff.

She spent the rest of the evening beside her new husband, first at dinner, then in the ballroom for dancing. She danced only once with Ewan, a lilting country reel which left her breathless, and only one other time did she notice him. That incident was a small masque, played to Celia's eyes only against the indifference of the crowd. For most of the evening Mercy Lawrence had sat primly against the wall, not joining in the dances. Celia's attention was caught when she absently noticed Ewan's brown velvet coat as he crossed the room to speak to the girl. Suddenly she remembered that Mercy was his intended, and he was, of course, the object of that sly remark Mrs. Lawrence had made earlier. That shy little creature and this handsome, self-confident man—what an intriguing pair.

Her attention was riveted on Ewan's back as he leaned toward Mercy. Celia could hear nothing of their words, but since Mercy was facing her she had a good view of the girl's reactions. As usual, Mercy kept her eyes glued to the floor, her skin flushing pink and her lips barely moving in response to Ewan's remarks. But when he turned and strode away, the downcast eyes shunted quickly to his retreating figure and the naked adoration in her gaze was a veil suddenly lifting. Celia smiled to herself. Ewan has made his usual conquest, she thought dryly, and he isn't even aware of it.

She was enjoying the evening so much that it took her a while to realize that something was wrong. Suddenly the men were off in groups, talking and gesturing with an animation that had nothing to do with the wedding. With a stab of irritation Celia assumed that they must be back to their eternal politics, but on second glance she saw there was more to it than that. Leading Richard aside, she asked what had happened.

"There's been a skirmish at Boston, and several militiamen are killed."

Celia's heart sank. "Oh, no. Not Boston again."

"Where else? A British regiment marched out of the city to one of the nearby towns to confiscate some powder. They met a band of American militia, someone fired a shot and that set it off. The rumor is ten or fifteen killed."

"Americans? Dear heaven! What does it mean?"

"It means the worst, I'm afraid. It means it has actually come to bloodshed. There can be no reconciliation after this, I'm sure."

Celia grasped at a faint hope. "But Boston is such a long way from New York. Perhaps we can avoid involvement."

Richard smiled bitterly. "As we did after the Non-Importation Act. You must know by now, my dear, that a stone thrown in Boston lands on all our heads."

"Oh, I hate those Yankees!" Celia exploded. "They are just what your father calls them, hotheaded radicals and renegades. They are going to bring war down on us all no matter what we do."

"Give some credit for it to the British. After all, they've not shown exceptional judgment in handling all this. But come, we mustn't let it spoil our wedding party."

"Look around you, Richard. It already has."

It was true. Some of the gaiety and lightheartedness had gone out of the celebration. Even as the fiddles and the flutes kept up their sprightly tunes, the men drifted away from the dance floor to stand talking in earnest groups. Word spread quickly among the women, and they too gathered on the chairs around the room, whispering. Perhaps it was time to call it a night. Several people, Ewan among them, had already made their goodbyes and moved to the door, where Jess was helping with the hats and cloaks.

She took Richard's hand. "Do you think we can slip away without all the usual 'bedding down' fuss?"

"God, I hope so. You go ahead and I'll send Mama after you. Papa will see everyone out tactfully. I'll be up in a little while."

Grateful for the time to herself, Celia quietly picked up her skirts and took the back stairs to the second floor. She had redecorated Henry's old room, which was larger than either hers or Richard's, and it was wonderfully warm and inviting. The windows, which were at the front of the house, were closed, their blinds drawn, and Dinah had a fire crackling in the hearth. The large feather bed, covered with its blue-and-white resist quilt which she had made with her own hands, looked soft and cozy. There was a full decanter on the table, and the soft candle glow from the lamps sent long shadows across the flocked wallpaper. Elizabeth followed her and helped her to change her tight stays and hoops for a soft flowing brocade dressing gown and to let down her hair—no mean feat with its heavy pomponade. By the time she heard her husband's step in the hall she was sitting alone before the fire, a glass of claret in her hand, looking as cool and relaxed as the flowing gown around her.

Yet she was not cool inside, and she knew instantly by his face that neither was Richard. She was both looking forward to and dreading their first night together. Elizabeth had carefully instructed her in what to expect, but it seemed like something that other people experienced. How they would manage she could not imagine. Yet she knew this was something she wanted desperately, both because it would consecrate their love for each other and because it would bring them children. And, in some strange way, it would mean she was truly a woman. A warm glow spread through her at the thought.

Her husband was in so little hurry that they sat before the fire talking long into the night, well after the household had settled into sleepy quiet. Only once did Celia try to hurry him a little, but his answer, "I can wait," was so obviously made out of what he thought was consideration for her that she said no more. Now that he was here holding her close, she grew more anxious for his lovemaking but it seemed somehow wanton to tell him so when he felt no urgency.

Eventually the fire died, the house grew very still, and joyfully she felt Richard's hands begin to drift over her body. Without another word they moved to the warm enveloping darkness of the high curtained bed.

Later, in the early-morning hours, she woke to hear the first faint murmur of the birds outside her window. Beside her, Richard's level breathing told her how soundly he slept. She stretched and smiled to herself, reveling in the thought of her gown on the floor beside the bed and the smooth feel of the sheets against her bare skin.

Now she was truly married. She belonged to Richard and he to her. She was no longer a virgin, she was a woman. Oh, it was marvelous!

She knew they had a way to go, but that would come with time. There had been a lot of fumbling last night, and Richard in his concern for her had been so careful she had almost taken to urging him on. She blushed a little at the thought. What kind of woman was she that had enjoyed his lovemaking so much? But enjoyed it she had, even with the pain it brought. This was a new side to life, one she had not known before, and she welcomed it with outstretched arms. Now her body belonged to this man and she longed for him to caress and fondle it, sometimes in the hot blood of passion and sometimes just as two lonely people holding each other against the dark. And there would be years and years ahead to explore all these new and grand dimensions.

Oh, it was wonderful to be married!

eight

Celia wakened to soft movements about the room. It took a moment for her to remember where she was, to recall last night's supper party, the first in her new home. What a success it had been, she thought, and how she had enjoyed her new role as lady of the house. It was a congenial company—Ewan, John, the Lawrences—for once without their uncomfortable daughter—and Dr. Sayre, the new physician in the town of West Chester who with his quiet young wife promised to become a good friend to the Deveroes.

She had been married for two months now and except for Richard's long absences she was perfectly content.

Richard's long absences—

Barely opening her eyes in the gray dawn light she could just make out her husband putting on his clothes. Coming abruptly awake, Celia stretched and sat up.

"I was trying not to wake you," Richard said a little guiltily from across the room.

"Must you go out so early? You've only had one day at home."

"I know. But I promised Mr. Jay I would ride up to Bedford before Thursday, and today is the only time I will have to do it. Can't be helped."

She propped up the pillows and leaned back, watching him, trying not to give way to disappointment. "Mr. Jay again! Sometimes I think you should have married him!"

Richard looked up from where he was bent over, pulling on his boots. "What?"

"Oh, nothing. The weather doesn't look at all promising for such a long ride. Couldn't you put it off at least until later in the day?"

"And get caught up-country by nightfall? No, my dear.

Someday when I'm admitted to the bar, I'll be released from the tyranny Mr. Jay holds over both our lives, but not until I've served my apprenticeship."

You are hardly an apprentice, Celia thought dryly. This tyranny, she was beginning to realize, meant more to Richard than her company, and, try as she might, that sat badly with her.

Glancing up, Richard was struck by how lovely she looked, her tawny hair fanned out against the stark white of the embroidered pillow slip. He went to sit on the edge of the bed, taking her hands. "You look so beautiful lying there I regret my duties more than ever."

Celia felt a surge of hope. She slipped her arms around his neck and kissed him. "Then don't go, please, Richard. Stay with me for just a little while."

His skin flushed as he understood her meaning.

"I waited for you last night, but you were so long coming to bed that I fell asleep in spite of myself."

"I'm sorry. I had so much reading to do to prepare for this court session today. And I thought you would be worn out from the party."

"Tired, but very much wanting you in spite of it."

"I wish I had known." His lips nuzzled her neck, and his hands on her back sent warm waves of delight all through her. Then, abruptly he reached up and disentangled her arms from around his neck. "No, darling. Pleasant as it is, I cannot linger here any longer if I expect to report back by Thursday. Keep my place warm for me."

Celia sank back, dust in her mouth. "I'll put a light in the window," she said, her voice edged with sarcasm. He didn't seem to notice.

"Goodbye, my dear. I hope to be back on Saturday." Picking up his cloak, he gave her a light kiss on the forehead and opened the door. "Try to go back to sleep."

Celia smiled back wanly. She tried to tell herself she should have expected nothing else. Richard had a single-minded compulsion to work, and no seductive wife was going to interfere with it. His passion, like his temper, was kept under a tight rein. He also had a lot on his mind these days—truly desperate problems. Besides, it wasn't as though he never wanted her. He was an ardent enough lover when the moment was right. If only the moment could be right a little more often!

She threw herself into the day's activities with a vengeance, hoping to work off her frustration in hard work. With Vestal's help, she attempted to hang new curtains in the parlor but damask was a hot fabric for late June and they were difficult to manage on the rods. Celia was almost to the point of hurling them through the open window when she heard a carriage drive up to the front door.

"Who is it, Vestal?" she said, delighted to have company.

"Why, bless me, Misse Celia," the big Negro said, poking his head through the window. "It's Misse Hester. Misse Hester, herself!"

Hester! Never had Celia been so delighted to see anyone. Throwing the curtains aside, she ran to the front door, not even bothering to let down her pinned-up skirts. She darted down the steps just in time to see Hester alighting from the coach in a swirl of scarlet muslin, the feathers of a huge hat completely eclipsing her curls.

"Hester! Hester! I'm so happy to see you," Celia cried, throwing her arms around the petite figure while Hester clutched at her hat.

"Celia, dear, you are crushing my straw! And look at you. Already you are the perfect picture of a country housewife."

"And you the fashionable city matron. When did you get back? Come in and we'll have a cold drink. I've never been so glad for company."

Hester chatted without a break as they made their way to the morning room.

"We got back last week and I could not wait to come and see you. Oh, Celia, you don't know how starved I've been for a friend to talk to. Four months—four interminable months alone with Cortlandt! We exhausted every common topic of conversation in the first two days, and after that—annihilating boredom!"

"Come, now," Celia laughed. "You could not have found Charleston boring. I hear it is a very gay city. Confess that you enjoyed it."

"Oh, *it* is gay enough, at least when the gentlemen forget their damnable politics long enough to think about their pleasures."

"Well, that is just as true here."

"And the gentlemen are extremely courtly. I enjoyed that. I had great fun making dear Cortlandt jealous."

Celia refused to take all this at face value. "Now, Hester, I can't believe you don't like being married. You are enjoying yourself hugely, tell the truth."

Hester's pixie smile was the first honest look she had given Celia since their warm embrace at the door. "You know me too well, Celia dear. All right. I confess I do enjoy some things about it. Cortlandt never begrudges me anything. I'll give him that. But he is such a bear of a man, sometimes I think he will drive me mad with his clumsy ways."

Celia shook her head. Poor Cortlandt, he was certainly not the man to tame Hester. "You should learn to be patient with him. If he is so good to you and loves you so much, that is worth some appreciation."

"Spoken like the little 'Tommy Truelove' you are! I sometimes feel a monster that I cannot like him more. However, I'm doing my duty. I make him a gorgeous wife to show off and—," she leaned forward, tapping Celia's arm with her fingers—"and I am already in the family way. After only four months!"

Celia beamed with pleasure. "Hester, how wonderful! I'm so happy for you. A child of your own, just think. What a joy for you both."

"What a bother, don't you mean. Dear Cortlandt already treats me as though I was made of cut glass, which makes me quite want to jump out of my skin. Not to mention the dreadful dangers I face when my time comes for lying-in."

"But a baby, Hester. Doesn't it make you melt with happiness? I want a baby so much. I hope we have a houseful."

"That's what you say now. Wait until you've had one or two. Here I've gotten with child the very first thing. It probably means I will have a pregnancy every year. Do you realize how quickly that can ruin the figure?"

"Well, I don't think I would mind at all if I got with child right away. But since we've only been married a month, I don't worry about it yet."

"And how is my dear brother?" Hester asked, glancing around the shabby room, so rustic compared to the elegance of Queen's Street.

"He is very busy, half the time scribbling away in a stuffy law office in New York and the other half running errands for Mr. Jay all over West Chester County. And he's worried about the bad feeling which seems to be everywhere. He is in the unique position of working for a so-called Patriot while belonging to a family of avowed Loyalists. I don't think he quite knows what to do about it yet."

"I understand John Jay had to do a little soul-searching of his own before he decided to join the Whigs. I just hope he doesn't sweep Richard along with him."

"No one sweeps Richard along. He'll make up his own mind in time. The sad thing is that he has to choose at all."

"I don't see how there can even *be* a choice. Imagine turning your back on your King and following in the wake of those scallywag rabble-rousers. Remember that afternoon in New York?"

"How could I ever forget? But Mr. Jay is not rabble, nor is Lewis Morris or any number of others I could name. It is a difficult decision, Hester, you must see that."

Hester tossed her curls. "Well, I'm glad Richard is not here, or it would only be something else we should argue over. For I can tell you, Celia, I would have no trouble choosing. Do you know that Cortlandt has promised to take me to England to meet his relation Lord Lamberton? And he has assured me that when we go I might be presented to the King and Queen. Imagine, Celia. Hester Deveroe making her cursty to the Queen of England!"

"I can think of no one who could do it more prettily or enjoy it more." That was true. Such a scene would be Hester's fondest dream come true. And with such a dream, how could she ever really understand what made men become revolutionaries?

"Enough of politics," Celia said, suddenly shivering. "I want to hear all about Charleston. Tell me everything."

Hester spent two days visiting Celia at the Manor House, then returned to her new house in fashionable Queen Street. Celia saw little of her after that, for she was more content to stay in her country home than to make the long trip to a city which was becoming more turbulent every day. Only once in late August did she accompany Richard to Wayside. She found that even the shady walks and Georgian houses of Queen Street could not disguise the signs of tension, from the liberty pole on Bowery Lane to the new breastworks around Fort George facing the harbor. The few ugly incidents which had occurred around West Farms were nothing in comparison to the extravagances of the city mobs. A man had only to raise a glass to the King's health, it was said, or to mutter a carelessly unpatriotic oath, and he was like as not have the Sons of Liberty breaking down his door. Celia breathed a sigh of relief when their visit was over and they drove up the Bloomingdale Road toward King's Bridge and home.

October was beautiful that fall of 1775, and Celia found that with Richard away so much of the time she was more than ever involved in bringing in the harvest and preserving a sufficient food supply for the coming winter. She welcomed the activity, for it kept her mind off her increasing loneliness. She longed for Richard to discuss the problems of his work with her as he used to when he came home from college full of some new theory. Or to make a point of taking time just to go riding with her on the fields around the Manor Farm, or to take the chaise into West Chester village, or simply to reach out and hold her when she was so desperate for his touch.

But she was beginning to realize that this was not Richard's way, and it was a bitter pill to swallow. He truly felt that he was doing her a favor by encouraging her to go alone on these little excursions or by not bothering her when his mind was so full. And when he was tired and discouraged, he had more need to be alone than to be held, even by a sympathetic wife. Of course, there were the good times, the close times when she felt they were as near to each other as two people could be. It was just that they happened so seldom.

The fact that, so far, there had been no sign of pregnancy did not help to ease her distress. She threw herself into any useful work she could find, and when it was done and she was alone she learned to find other entertainments. She became a familiar figure riding the roads of West Farms on her old gentle horse, Bonny. In the evenings when the time seemed most tedious, she learned to escape into a book or one of the popular political pamphlets.

She made regular calls at the mill to see Richard's Uncle Peter, who, in the last few months, was beginning to show signs of senility, and to make sure that young Ben was being well cared for by Ewan's house slaves. Occasionally she met Ewan himself on the road, traveling out on the business of his office. It was one day in late November as she was heading back down a road already tinged with frost that she saw him waiting for her on the bridge ahead.

"I thought I recognized that decrepit animal," he called, falling in beside her.

Celia patted the mare's dark mane. "Please don't speak disrespectfully of Bonny. She's been a faithful servant of the Deveroes for a long time."

"Twenty years at least."

"More like ten. But she still gets about and she suits me. After all, we can't all go in for the blooded animals you raise."

Ewan beamed. "I've always had a passion for good horses. My Uncle James taught me that. It was he who helped me get a worthwhile stable started. I'm surprised Richard hasn't given more thought to one."

"He will someday when things are settled. Right now he's so busy with his practice he's content to let Tom and Mr. Forbes handle the stock."

He rode with her as far as the house, entertaining her with the latest gossip making the county rounds. Ewan could always make her laugh, Celia thought, watching him with sideways glances. Yet, in spite of his lighthearted manner, his handsome face looked drawn and tired under his tricorn hat and he wore that same troubled look she had seen so often on Richard's face. Though he shrugged off any references to persecutions around the county, she was not fooled into thinking he had avoided them. Like her husband, he was just attempting to shield her. Foolish men, she thought, waving to him as he galloped on toward the mill.

Three days later Tom came running up from the stable to call her from the house.

"Miss Celia, come quick. Hurry now, do."

Tom's ruddy Irish face was alight. Curiously Celia left the loom where she was weaving a new coverlet and threw a shawl around her shoulders. Even from the terrace she recognized old Diamond, one of Ewan's slaves from the mill, standing beside a beautiful young blond horse with a black stripe down its back and a black mane and tail. Celia walked around the filly admiring it while Diamond, his face deadly serious, repeated word for word what he had been made to memorize.

"Massa Ewan 'specially wants you to know he not can 'ford to have he kinsman ridin' 'bout on poor ten-year-old cattle. He have no reputation left!"

Celia laughed in spite of herself. "He sent this for me? This beautiful animal?"

"He say, this fine hos' a Deveroe gift for a Deveroe."

"But I can't accept it. I'm not sure my husband would approve." As she ran her hand over the sleek neck she caught a glimpse of growing disappointment in Tom's eyes. The horse nuzzled her hand in a manner so friendly it might also have been coached by her cousin.

"We've not had an animal like this on the place for some time, Miss Celia," Tom said hopefully.

Celia felt her resolve weaken. "Well, we might at least care for her until Mr. Deveroe comes home, mightn't we, Tom. And Ewan did say it was a 'family' gift, did he not?"

"Oh, yes, ma'am," the groom responded, smiling broadly. "He was most precise about it being in the family."

Celia walked around the filly's handsome flanks and stroked her silky sides. She was very young, probably only a little more than a two-year-old. How like Ewan to make this impetuous gift.

"She looks a little frisky, Tom. Do you think I'll be able to manage her?"

"Miss Celia, you ride now better than Miss Hester ever did. And she's young enough to train. I think she'll be just to your liking."

"Massa Ewan say she a gentle thing, for all she young," Diamond spoke up. "An' good-natur'd too."

"How grand. I could never mount those spirited brutes your master rides. And we can train her to the chaise so she'll be truly a family horse. What a lovely gift."

"She is that, Misses. I raises all Massa's hoss's, and this a fine beast."

"Tom, lead her to the stable and we'll care for her until Mr. Richard gets back. He'll have to make the final decision."

Tom took the halter from Diamond's hand and led the horse away, nearly dancing with delight. Even Celia could not suppress a smile. Now if only Richard wouldn't mind.

By the time Richard arrived home two weeks later she had grown so fond of the blond horse that she could hardly bear the thought of returning her. To her relief, he was as pleased with Ewan's gift as she was.

"I wish I had thought of it first," he said, pulling off his boots before the bedroom fire. "I should have offered to buy one of Ewan's horses for you. It just never occurred to me that we needed one."

"That's because you neglect me so shamefully," she teased him, pulling a brush through her long hair. In the glass before her she could catch his wavering reflection across the room.

"You're sure you don't mind? That it's, well, proper and everything?"

"Of course it's proper. Ewan is our cousin, isn't he? Perhaps he is trying to make amends for that escapade when I broke my arm."

"But that was years ago." Her glossy hair cascaded under the strokes of the brush and caught the golden highlights from the lamplight.

"Yes," he said, "but it's like him to remember. Besides, right now Ewan needs all the friends he can get."

"Why do you say that?"

"Because as sheriff he is more and more reluctant to carry off to jail the men who have been committed there by the Committee of Safety. It has earned him a good deal of suspicion."

Watching him in the glass, she saw him pull away his neckcloth and settle back, loosening the buttons of his waistcoat. "These men sentenced to jail—they're Tories, aren't they?"

"Usually. They refuse to turn over their arms and they indulge in careless talk about 'unlawful' congresses and committees. If Ewan isn't careful he is going to brand himself as one of them. It is unfortunate, my dear, but the majority of towns in West Chester County are Whig, no matter that many disagree."

"Well, I think Ewan was only trying to be neighborly. I know that Vestal has asked him for permission to marry Diamond's granddaughter, Betsy, and he gave that readily enough."

"Hmmm, that means I shall have to pay a manumission fee. All Ewan's blacks are slaves, you know. That is another point of difference between his father and mine."

Celia smiled mischievously. "Perhaps he means to ask you for a fee that will cover Betsy and the horse too."

"We all know Ewan's strong affection for the British way of life," Richard went on thoughtfully, ignoring her small jest. "Nor is any man less given to compromise. I worry that he may involve himself in real trouble if he isn't more circumspect."

Laying down her brush, she went to sit on the rug beside his chair. "And you, Richard? Are you keeping out of trouble?"

Smiling, he ran his finger lightly down the curve of her cheek. "I find that my association with a notable Patriot like Mr. Jay is a kind of protection. Even though the committee distrusts my family, they have so far given no sign of distrusting me." With the conspicuous exception of Jaspar Carne, he thought, whom he carefully avoided.

"But how long can you put them off? Aren't you going eventually to have to declare your convictions one way or the other?"

"I've walked very carefully so far, while giving the matter a great amount of thought. And, truth to tell, Celia, I cannot completely disagree with the motives of the Congress. I've read Locke and Rousseau and Blake. I've studied the pamphlets and I've heard the orators. They have a fine concept in their idea of a republican government, one that I believe might even be superior to the English colonial system we've known all these years."

"Your father believes that a democratic government would only allow the dregs of society to rise to power."

"I know, and many agree with him. But these men also fear, and with good reason, that with democracy their class-ridden society would be confounded. Look at Ewan himself— how often has he extolled the country gentleman as the highest form of civilized life! Yet you know that I have never felt that way."

She rubbed her cheek against his knee. "I know. And my own sentiments lie closer to yours than to your cousin's and parents'."

"You won't be angry, then, if I should throw in my lot with the rebels?"

"Never. Only, Richard, I do hope and pray it will not cause bad feelings within the family."

"I don't think so. We have enough affection for one another to prevent that. But I am relieved you support me. I confess that it worried me somewhat as to how you would feel."

"I love you, Richard, you know that. And I am your wife. I'll stand by you whatever you decide."

Looking up at him, her face framed by her hair, her night-dress falling away from the white swell of her breasts, she struck him anew with how beautiful and mature she had become in his absence. He leaned forward and kissed her warmly.

"Thank you, my dear. And now, I have been away too long. I think it is time we got to bed."

A winter quiet descended on West Farms with the heavy January snows. It was a time for sitting by great warm fires, or hurrying across frosted crusts of ground between cellar and barn and kitchen. The roads were so deep in snow that little traffic could get through, and, with Richard and Ewan both in New York most of the time, Celia found the solitude of the farm very peaceful. Occasionally she put on her ice creepers and crossed the road to visit Ben and John at the mill. And when the snow cleared a little, Vestal took out the sleigh and put on the bell harness so that she could drive to the Lawrences' for an afternoon's strained conversation with Mercy and her mother.

The only real break in the monotony came one day when Jess appeared at her door, having come out from Wayside to pick up provisions and bearing a note from Elizabeth with the news that Hester had been safely delivered of a baby boy. Celia was thrilled for Hester and tried valiantly to ignore the ache this news sent coursing through her. If only she could have a child, her life would be complete. She felt sure that the joy of being a mother would satisfy the emptiness within her and ease the restlessness in her heart.

nine

There was a cheerful expectancy to the jangling of the bell as Celia opened the latticed door to the apothecary shop and walked inside. No one stood behind the counter that ran across one side of the small room, and one glance told her she was alone. Row upon row of amber glass bottles, all neatly labeled, covered three of the four dark walls, the other given over to stacks of drawers all with the same neat markings.

"Quite an assortment, isn't it?" She recognized Jonas Sayre's voice and turned almost guiltily to where he stood in a doorway leading to a room behind the shop, pulling his coat on over his striped waistcoat.

"I had no idea there was such a variety of medicines any-where outside New York," she said, smiling and extending her hand.

He bowed over it. "I was fortunate enough to receive a shipment on one of the last merchantmen allowed to unload her cargo at the Whitehall docks. My dear Mrs. Deveroe, how nice it is to have you visit my establishment."

"I was in the village to do a little shopping and happened to be passing by. The violets along the path to your door looked so inviting I impulsively decided to stop in and wish you good day."

"How fortunate that you found me in. I am often out visiting my patients. Perhaps you would be so good as to share a glass of claret with me."

"Why, thank you, yes, I will," she said, preceding him into his office. It was slightly larger and just as dark as the shop but comfortable enough if one ignored the metal surgical tools and brass clyster laid neatly on the shelf near a large bookcase. Celia eyed the diplomas framed on the wall as she settled prettily on a leather chair near the window.

"My wife will be sorry not to greet you," Dr. Sayre said, handing her a small cup. "We often speak of our pleasant evenings at your hospitable table."

Celia nodded and sipped the wine while the doctor perched on the edge of the table, one thread-hosed leg dangling. His eyes twinkled above his spectacles as he watched her attempting to cover her nervousness.

"I suspect you are not accustomed to finding yourself in a surgeon's office."

Celia laughed nervously. "No, I am not. Is it so obvious, then? The truth is . . . well, I did not just happen to stop by today. I was especially hoping to talk to you." She plunged on. "You have a diploma there on your wall that says you are qualified in midwifery."

Jonas Sayre nodded his graying head. He had suspected as much. "Yes, I am. And you are expecting. How grand."

"No, no. I am not expecting."

"Oh, I see. And *that* is the problem, is it?"

Celia's eyes shunted to her glass. "Yes," she admitted softly. Something in his kind manner reassured her that perhaps this would not be as terrible as she had feared.

"It is not a disgrace to be without child, Mrs. Deveroe," he said gently. Pulling up a chair, he sat down before her. "Now, how long have you been married?"

"Over a year."

"And have there been no indications during this year that you might be pregnant? No missed courses? No unusual patterns?"

"None." She was grateful for his matter-of-factness. She could not have borne any embarrassment, so great was her own.

"I see. Now, Mrs. Deveroe, I must ask you some intimate questions and you must be honest with me. Otherwise I will not be able to help you."

"All right. I'll try."

For nearly ten minutes he explored some personal aspects of her relationship with Richard, the nature of her family and the nature of her husband's. The fact that Mr. Deveroe was frequently away from home did not seem to bother him as much as the fact that she was an only child, something Celia herself had never considered. Then he stood up, his hands behind his back under his coat.

"Will you allow me to examine you?" he said guardedly.

Though Celia was not overly modest, she had never submitted to an examination by a male doctor in her life. She blushed deep red in spite of her determination to be blasé.

"Oh, dear." She took a deep breath. "I feared as much. It is a measure of how much I want a child that I am willing to go through with this."

Smiling, Dr. Sayre replaced his spectacles on his nose. "Good. Is your woman outside?"

"Betsy? Yes." Vestal's new young wife was now her maid.

"Then call her in. You shall merely have to stand quietly. It is all done by touch, very modestly. And remember, I am a man of science. I pride myself on that."

It turned out to be not so bad, though neither she nor the doctor met each other's eyes during the entire ritual. Afterward, when she once more took her place on the chair by the window after sending a scandalized Betsy back outside, she felt more sure than ever that it had been wise to come. Jonas Sayre was competent and professional and he showed a consideration for her feelings which she greatly appreciated.

"I cannot really see any reason why you have not got with child," he said, rubbing his chin thoughtfully. "You are small-built for child bearing—though one would never know it under those hoops—and no doubt you will have a hard time of it when you do have a baby. Yet there are no obstructions that I can tell and nothing that indicates an abnormality. But—of course, we know so little."

"Does that mean I will have a child?" she asked hopefully.

"Not necessarily. I cannot guarantee such a thing. I only wish I could. Some doctors would have you bled regularly, others would dose you on a concoction of southernwood or calamus root. I don't favor either. Go on as you have. Keep busy. Who knows? One year is not a long time."

Celia sighed and picked up her hat. "But so many women have their first baby within a year. All my friends and family."

He stared at her, impressed with her youth, her loveliness, her warmth. She would make a good mother, he felt instinctively. He tried to choose his words carefully.

"Have you considered, Mrs. Deveroe—that is, has it occurred to you that you might be barren?"

"Barren!" The word was ashes in her throat. The day went gray around her.

He attempted nonchalance. "Occasionally women are, for what reasons we don't know. It is a possibility that you might be wise to accustom yourself to—just in case."

Celia stared unseeing out the window. "Oh, Dr. Sayre . . ."

"I am not saying that you *are* barren, you understand," his quiet voice went on. "I'm only trying to prepare you for any eventuality."

This was no good. She threw off her pain, set her hat on her head and briskly tied the ribbons under her chin. "Thank you," she said, rising and giving him her hand. "I know what you mean and, yes, it has occurred to me. But I don't like to think on it."

"Of course not. The best thing is to relax and let matters take their natural course. You are young and healthy. There is no reason at all for despair."

He went before her to open a door from the office that let out onto a path along the side of the building.

"I do hope we shall see you and your good wife soon at the Manor House, Dr. Sayre. You will stop by when you are in our neighborhood?"

"It will be our pleasure."

Moving lightly down the few short steps, she opened her sunshade and gave him a smile and a wave where he stood at the door looking after her. Did he realize how utterly desolate she felt behind her jaunty posturing? she wondered. No matter.

After all the courage it had taken to come here she really knew no more now than she had before.

Celia never told her husband about her visit to Jonas Sayre, and in time it drifted to the back of her mind, a thing to be taken out and inspected when she was alone or particularly depressed. There was little time for either solitude or self-pity, as events in the county began to move so fast that she was swept up in their ferment.

General Washington's Continental Army was now ensconced in the town of New York, giving rise to more restlessness and high feelings among the populace than ever before. Since it was almost certain that the British Army intended to invade New York in order to force a battle which might well end the rebellion forever, the Provincial Congress prudently adjourned to White Plains. As the summer opened and the city prepared for the onslaught, Celia suffered the first recurrence of the malaria fever which had plagued her two years before. She was just beginning to feel well again when Richard was scheduled to attend the congressional sessions at White Plains and insisted that this time she come with him. She packed a few things in a portmanteau and, riding Kit, went to White Plains, where Richard had managed to obtain a comfortable room for them at the large home of the well-to-do Chatterton family outside town.

Thus it was that she was among the small group of people assembled before the courthouse on the morning of July 11 to hear the first reading of a declaration from the Congress at Philadelphia in which the American Colonies were proclaimed independent of both King and mother country. When she heard the call to the people of the newly proclaimed "state" of New York that they risk their lives and fortunes to support this declaration, something cold and fierce struck like a knife within her. She could see by Richard's face how impressed he was with both the logic and the high ideals of the beautifully worded document. But, looking around at the other faces—some fired with the glow of patriotism, some struggling against fury, and some curious but indifferent—she had a sudden sense of utter helplessness. They were all being swept along by events they could no longer control. They were asked to risk everything that made life supportable in a contest they barely understood. How had this happened? Without any strong feelings for or against the new government, Celia could only swear to herself that, come what may, she would do anything to keep from risking her fortune in this mad contest. Richard might sympathize all he liked with this rebel cause, but she would lie, cheat, or swear an oath to any congress in the world just so long as she could keep their livelihood intact.

Her sense of helplessness increased as events moved swiftly from that hour. By the end of the month word came that Lord Howe's fleet bearing the magnificent British army commanded by his brother, Sir William Howe, had entered the Narrows and anchored off Staten Island. Richard immediately hurried her back to West Farms and, for once putting his own concerns above those of the new United States, went with her to keep watch on his property.

He was nearly frantic with worry about his family at Wayside, and it was only Celia's urgent pleas that kept him from riding down to check on them. "Suppose that instead of attacking the city the British decide to sail up the East River and march through West Farms. We'd be completely alone. We need you here."

"You could come with me."

"And leave this place to the mercy of a marauding army? Never! This is our *home*, Richard. The only home we have. We cannot abandon it."

"But they are my family. Can I abandon them?"

"Everyone knows your family is sympathetic to the Royal cause. The British won't hurt them. And they have so many people around to protect them, while we have so few. We need you here, Richard, with us."

Reluctantly he agreed to stay, but when the distant sound of thunder became instead the echo of cannon around the city, Celia was almost sorry she had kept him. He had always been so poised and cool, so in control. She had never seen him so distracted.

It was almost a week before a hastily scrawled note from Hester arrived, reassuring them that the family was safe, though they had not got through the battle of New York unscathed. Many of the trees in Wayside's orchards had been left jagged and broken by cannonfire. The corn and barley fields had been stripped by the soldiers, fences had been wrecked, livestock had disappeared, and they had had to bury the body of a young American soldier who had ventured into the open meadow and been killed by a shot fired from one of the British ships in the East River.

The British now have New York [Hester wrote] and that blundering rebel army is somewhere in the north of the Island. So it seems for the present that we shall have peace and a chance to repair the damage. However, I fear for you because the storm seems likely to move across King's Bridge and into West Chester. Pray, keep to yourselves and watch your stock and grain carefully. The Americans think nothing of freely taking what they need, and it is our experience that the German allies of the British do the same. They say the whole city of New York was burned to the ground in the fire which the rebel army set before abandoning it, so for the present we will all stay here at Wayside. Papa is very ill and the calamities of the past days have done nothing to help him regain his strength. May God keep you safe and may He have mercy on our troubled and unhappy country.

Your worried and affectionate sister,
H.B.

Although it was impossible to know exactly what was happening on York Island, enough information filtered into West

Chester to inform the anxious people at the Manor how bad
things actually were. General Howe had made a great tactical
error in allowing Washington's army to escape from Brooklyn,
where it had been boxed in, but rumors that New York had
been destroyed were exaggerated. Only a fourth of the houses
had been burned, in one long swath along Broad Way and the
North River. It saddened Celia to learn that Trinity Church had
been one of the buildings demolished, as the dear old frame
building had been one of her first familiar landmarks. General
Washington's pitiful army, already proving itself as inept at
fighting as it was ingenious at getting away, had entrenched
in the Harlem Heights around impregnable Fort Washington.
The British had complete control of the city and the rivers on
both sides of the island, and their ships roamed freely from the
Narrows to Spuyten Duyvil on one side, and up the East River
to Throgg's Neck on the other. King's Bridge was for the
moment in the hands of the Americans under General Greene,
all of them camped close enough that Celia could hear the
sounds of their musket practice in the distance when she stood
on the flagstone piazza at the back of her house.

In this unsettled situation they sat and waited, attempting
valiantly to go about the daily business of farming, with nerves
raw from straining to hear the terrible sounds that signified a
clash of arms. Only once did Richard suggest sending her to
safety in the northern part of the county. Her absolute refusal
to leave the house convinced him it was useless. At least they
were there together. If war came their way they would handle
it together. Until then, he would do his best to protect his home
and maintain a posture of neutrality. This last was the hardest
of all, for not an hour went by that he did not have to hold
himself back from riding over to Harlem and volunteering his
services. Everything in him urged him to it—his ideals, his
sense of adventure, his youth, his manhood and his growing
conviction that the cause of revolution was just. But he simply
could not bring himself to make the decisive break, the one
action his family would brand as treason. And every time his
wife looked at him he saw fear in her eyes—not a fear that
showed a lack of courage but a desperate worry that he would
leave her to defend their home alone. And once more he would
put off doing what he wanted most to do.

The loud banging on their front door brought them both
forward in their chairs. It was late and the house had settled

into the quiet of evening. While Celia sewed, Richard had been sitting smoking a pipe and reading a slim volume of Pope's poems. With the sudden noise their eyes met, filled with dread and questions. When they recognized Ewan's voice in the hall they settled back with relief.

The moment he walked into the room Richard knew he had brought trouble with him. "What is it, Ewan? You look as though the devil himself were after you."

Ewan waved aside the glass of wine Celia offered him and sat on the edge of a chair, his arms on his knees. "The devil is after me, I fear. You know that I was detained last week by the Provincial Congress?"

"Yes, I heard. I also heard you had been released to live peacefully at the mills."

"That's correct. I gave my parole." His head shot up. "God's blood! I had to or rot in some damned rebel jail."

"It's no disgrace, Ewan," Richard said levelly. "Many other men have done the same. Mr. Philipse right at this moment is on parole in Connecticut. He was not even allowed to return to his home, so you were more fortunate than he."

"Fortunate! God damn these radicals. What *right* have they to confine me to my home! They represent an illegal Congress and are themselves an illegal committee. How dare they arrest and detain me!"

"Ewan, Ewan. Calm down. They represent the only government in the country right now. Mr. Philipse tried to form a countergovernment among the men who support the Crown, and he failed. Unfortunately these 'radicals,' as you call them, have the only power there is, legal or not. I hope you will restrain yourself and do nothing to alienate them any further."

Jumping from his chair, Ewan turned on his cousin. "They hold it against me that I refused to arrest the men they wanted put away. My God, Richard, you know they care nothing at all about criminals. Their only concern is political. If they had their way every upstanding Tory in the county would be in jail."

"Be fair. Had they been a Tory committee, would it not be the Whigs who were condemned? Would you have carried out the sentences then?"

In his anger Ewan's face went dark. Impulsively Celia moved between them. "Is there not enough bad feeling in this county already without kinsmen going for each other's throats? Please, both of you, try to listen and help each other."

To her surprise her words seemed to make a difference. Once again Ewan took his chair. "Perhaps I will have that wine, Celia."

With careful deliberation she poured and handed him a glass.

"Little peacemaker." He smiled up at her, then turned back to Richard. "We have been friends for many years, Cousin, and I value your good opinion. Even though I believe you are dead wrong in sympathizing with these revolutionaries, the bond that has been between our families, even more so since your marriage, has been of great personal satisfaction to me."

He paused, waving Richard down when he attempted to speak. "No, hear me out. That is why I wanted to explain to you what I am about to do. There is a British tender lying in the East River at this very moment. I intend to board it and ask for passage to the city." He paused, watching the horrified expression on their faces as his words sank in. "I intend to offer my services to the Crown."

"Ewan!" Celia cried. This was worse than anything she had imagined.

"Furthermore, John is going with me."

"You gave your oath!" Richard's voice had a steely evenness. "You're on parole. Your word . . ."

"I know. Believe me, Richard, I do not take this step lightly."

"To break your parole! Ewan, you might as well be committing suicide. You compromise yourself and your whole family."

"No!" Ewan answered angrily. "It is true that I swore an oath, but to whom? I do not consider that an oath which was coerced to begin with, made to an irregular body, can be truly binding. They claim they speak for our country. Well, I feel that I am defending our country by defying them."

"What will you do?" Celia asked, feeling sick inside.

"I don't know. I would like to join the British dragoons and fight this rebel army, but I doubt that is possible for a Colonial. There are too many regulations involved. But there are some Loyalist units. I feel sure I can get a commission in one of them."

"Ewan, have you really thought this through?" Richard asked quietly. "What about your home at West Farms? Who will protect it while Uncle Peter grows more childlike every day? What about the enmity this will bring you in the county? It's bad enough to join the Loyalists. To break your parole in order to do so is going to seem unforgivable to a good many of our friends."

Ewan's face went hard. "One cannot worry about friends in a civil strife. And that is what this is, Richard. You have been so carried away with all the fine phrases that you haven't faced that fact. Many of us consider this rebellion treason, I more than most. Former friendships are likely to be swept away, have already been swept away, in the discord and hatred men are beginning to feel. Besides—" he tried to smile—"when have I worried about what men thought of me?"

"But your good name!"

"If the British will take me I shall fight for them with as much honor as ever I would have given these rebels, had I thought their way."

Richard shook his head. "I know you think you are doing the right thing. But I fear for you. What repercussions will it have?"

Quietly Celia rose and refilled her cousin's glass. She took some for herself as well, and its burning warmth helped steady her. "Perhaps we can help you by keeping a watch on the mill," she suggested.

"Ben will be there, and a number of my slaves. And, who knows. I know this county better than most, so perhaps the British will find a place for me close to home. Of course, everything depends on what happens next in New York."

A large gray moth worked its way around the gauze curtain and flew triumphantly at the glass cover over the candle on the table. Its mindless, self-destructive obsession burned an image into Celia's mind of fluttering dark wings silhouetted against the yellow light. Beyond the lamp, Ewan's face, always so boyish and mischievous, looked now as though it had been sculpted in stone. In the shadows beyond she could see her husband, something of the turmoil he felt for once reflected in his cool, self-contained aesthetic face. What was happening to them all? Like the pitiful moth, they were all being drawn to a mindless destruction by forces they could neither stop nor control.

Ewan slowly turned his glass in his long fingers. "It is possible, Cousin," he said, "that we may end up on opposing sides. I came here tonight because I want you to understand that no matter how our beliefs may differ, I bear you no ill will. I hope you feel the same."

"You know that I do," Richard answered. "But is there

nothing I can say that will at least convince you to postpone this rash decision until we see the outcome of the next battle?"

"No! I should go mad sitting around the mill, trying to live up to the terms of that enforced parole. A man must go where his conscience leads him. Surely you above all can understand that."

"Yes."

"The time has come for me now and I can delay no longer." He downed the wine in two quick gulps and rose, extending his hand to Richard. "Will you wish me good fortune?"

"Of course," Richard said, grasping his cousin's hand. "Whatever our disagreements, we must never let them stand in the way of family loyalty. I never will if you won't."

Ewan laid an arm around Richard's shoulder and walked with him to the door. "Nor shall I. Pray for me and try to understand."

Celia followed him into the hall. "I too wish you Godspeed, Ewan," she said, laying her hand on his arm. "Be careful."

Tipping her chin upward, he kissed her lightly on the forehead. "Dear Celia, you always worried over my impulsiveness. I hope you will both keep safe here. If Howe's army can destroy Washington's rebels on York Island, the war will be over and none of this will matter. But should he come this way to attack from the rear, well, be careful not to venture too far from your door."

"We'll be careful. Just remember to reserve some of that caution for yourself."

Setting his hat at a jaunty angle, Ewan draped his cloak around his shoulders, looked back as though he feared never to see them again, then was gone into the night. Celia saw the door close, then moved into her husband's arms. There was a terrible coldness in her chest, a bleak, numbing despair that cried for things to go back to normal again, to reassemble into the old, comfortable patterns. But they were shattered now—shattered forever.

Holding her close, Richard had to struggle with his own demons. Ewan had been part of his life for as long as he could remember, and the thought that someday he might have to face him musket to musket, across a battlefield, was too bleak even to consider.

"How like him this is," he said bitterly. "We should have known he was the least likely of men to sit out the war quietly. Anyone but Ewan!"

"But he truly believes he is doing what is right. I am sure that's why he came here—he probably could not bear the thought that you might hear of it secondhand and think he had simply gone back on his parole."

"I can assure you, my dear, that is what other men will think. He is going to be soundly condemned for breaking his word, no matter how right it seems to him."

She leaned against him, clasping her arms around his thin body. "Oh, Richard! I hate these times. I hate your revolution! Why can't we live in peace as we used to?"

He smiled down on her like an affectionate father patiently indulging a petulant child. What was the use of trying to explain to a woman the complex reasons behind a great patriotic movement?

"Come my dear. It's time to call it a day."

It was nearly a month before they learned what had happened to Ewan. By that time the war had indeed moved to their doorstep, and if they thought of him at all it was only with the certainty that he was somewhere with Howe's British forces. General Washington had abandoned New York, leaving behind only a large garrison at Fort Washington, and was leading his ragged army up the middle of West Chester County to take a stand at the central village of White Plains. Opposite him the British were moving the best-trained and -equipped army in the world to come at the village from the east. Yet, with all the anxiety of the impending battle, in the taverns, kitchens and parlors of rebel sympathizers men still took time to curse that turncoat Ewan Deveroe.

ten

Washington's army was three days in passing through West Chester on its way to White Plains. Although West Farms was below King's Bridge and thus not in the path of the army, Celia knew at once that there had been an influx of men into the area. She looked up one morning to the hills beside her house and spotted the bobbing bright colors of checked barlicorn shirts as soldiers began to move through her cornfields stripping what was left of the harvest. Firewood began to disappear and fences were dismantled and carried off. Officers with cockades in their hats and a patriotic fire on their youthful faces appeared at her door regularly to requisition grain, cheeses, flour, vegetables, livestock and hay—all of which Richard readily supplied.

"You sympathize with these robbers because they are Continentals," she raged at her husband. "Suppose they were the Royal army? Would you be so generous then? It's not fair. Everything we've worked so hard for—all our winter supplies!"

"Of course it's not fair. As for the Royal army, they might well be along next. Can't you get it through your head that we are sitting between two opposing armies and we stand to lose a lot more than firewood? Soldiers have always lived off the land. Besides, what we don't give them they'll take anyway." He grinned at the anxious frown on her face. "Don't worry, Celia, they won't leave us destitute. I'll make sure of that."

Early on the third day she rode with Richard up to Williams Bridge to watch the last of General Heath's division heading north. Though she knew she was watching only a part of the army that had lately occupied York Island, she was still amazed at the size and variety of this one division. What seemed like miles and miles of men trudged by, most of them dressed in civilian homespun or fringed leather shirts rather than the vari-colored military coats prescribed by the Congress. Wagons and carts lumbered along loaded with kegs, sacks of grain, bundles of hay. Oxen laborously dragged a few fieldpieces down the rutted road, followed by wagons and litters of the sick and wounded. She was startled to see a number of women—soldiers' trulls and soldiers' wives, some carrying kettles and sacks of meal, others with canvas harnesses slung on their backs for their infants.

When the last of the army had disappeared on the road north she sighed with relief and turned home to survey the damage it had left in its wake. And it was appalling. Fields stripped, her garden plundered, the orchard nearly plucked bare, fences broken and burned, woodpile decimated and stock stolen.

Yet later when Celia stood in the wreck that was Ewan's house and looked around at the devastation there, she could only give thanks that at least her house had been spared. Many of Ewan's fine furnishings had disappeared. Mattresses and blankets were gone, the cellar of wine and cider was completely depleted. About the only thing left untouched was old Peter Deveroe himself, who had survived under the care of the American doctor who had turned the house into a hospital. And, of course, most of Ewan's fine horses, who had been safely hidden far away. She turned back to her own home praying that this would be the only time the war would touch them all so directly.

"I'm going to follow the army!"

She was conscious of her hand clenched against her apron. "You can't!" she said stiffly. "You can't leave me like this."

"Celia, now, please don't take on. I won't be gone long. I shall be back as soon as I see which way this confrontation with the British turns out."

He watched her, not really wanting to see the hurt in her eyes. She had no right to hold him here against every leaning of his heart. Her amber eyes looked yellow with anger and stubbornness against the white of her face.

"You are in no danger here now," Richard went on evenly. "We've survived the Americans, the British fleet has moved off Throgg's Neck toward the Sound, and Vestal, Tom and Forbes will remain behind to support you in case any stragglers should happen by."

She stared unseeing at him. Deep within her, her distress was slowly congealing into cold fury.

Richard looked everywhere in the room but at her. "Really,

Celia, you must see that I have to know which way this thing is going to go. It may well be decided once and for all at White Plains. And it's not as though you will be unprotected."

She could not trust herself to speak. Richard drummed his fingers along the leather side of a book lying on the table beside him, then suddenly sent it crashing to the floor. "I can't just sit here!" he shouted, jumping up from his chair.

"Go, then! Go ahead. Follow your precious Mr. Jay and all the rest of the men that brought this trouble down on our heads! What does it matter what happens to our home and our land? Go carry a musket and dash about in a cocked hat, brandishing a saber! Have a wonderful time playing soldier."

"For God's sake, Celia. I have no intention of *joining* the army. I simply want to know the outcome of this battle, if there is one. If there seems any likelihood of one or the other of these armies turning back this way I shall get home as swiftly as possible."

"If you can!"

This was hopeless. Her unbridled fury brought a surging response in him which he fought down. "Celia, sometimes you can be so stubborn," he said, turning away. Whatever had happened to that soft, pliant creature he thought he knew so well when they were married?

"I will *never* leave our home," she said through clenched teeth. "Go ahead and make your observations or whatever it is you intend to do. I shall stay here and see that this place is protected, even if you won't."

Retreating into his usual frustrating emotional insulation, he turned his back on her and stalked from the room.

Celia watched the door slam, then sank onto the sofa to give way to her tears. *Damn him*! Just when she thought he was going to put her and their home first he must go gallivanting after this accursed rebel cause once more. It was no use trying to turn him from it. She knew that well enough. But to leave her alone when danger was so near! How could the man who had vowed to love her always do such a thing?

She unbent long enough the next morning to give him a grudgingly light kiss, then watched him ride away. To her chagrin she had to watch Forbes, the farm overseer, ride away with him. Like Richard, he could not bear the thought of being left behind by the excitement of the war, and he had the added inducement of relatives living in White Plains. He had already made up his mind to move his wife there if they would take her in. The Deveroes were leaning a little too close to the Loyalist way of thinking for Forbes, who, though he was no flaming Patriot, had more to gain in an independent America than one under the heel of Parliament and King.

Several days passed quietly. Celia was almost too busy with the work of the farm to wonder what was happening in the middle reaches of the county, and no messenger came clattering through West Farms with any news of victory or defeat.

Then one cold early November afternoon, she was working alongside Vestal, Betsy and Tom sorting what was left of the apples when a platoon of British horse rode right into her yard. Celia could barely believe her eyes, while her servants, awed at the gorgeous accouterments of horses and men, immediately jumped to the conclusion that their throats were going to be cut. Seeing them beside the barn, the men drifted over in a line, their fine mounts blowing steam, the sun glinting on the brass studs of their harness and reflecting silver shafts of light off the bright metal plates of their caps.

The officer in charge, although he treated Celia with a kind of condescending politeness which he considered respect, made it clear that they were there to purchase forage and would take what they needed regardless of her feelings in the matter.

"We are prepared to pay for everything and in good Spanish dollars, too."

"I don't want your money," Celia exclaimed, her alarm growing with the mental inventory of their dwindling supplies. "We need everything we have to get through the coming winter. You cannot just ride in here and carry away our provisions."

"I regret the necessity, madam, but such are the exigencies of war."

"That is just what the Continentals said before they stripped us bare!"

"That is hardly my problem. The Royal troops are taking over those forts on the Harlem River, and we will to a great extent be dependent upon the area for support. It is the way of armies, madam."

For all his fine words, Celia knew he felt not the slightest regret as he sent his troopers scouring her outbuildings and barn. Helplessly she watched as they carried out bags of grain and seed, the last of the apples, casks of cider and all the potatoes she had managed to save from the American occupation. Then, hearing a cry, she looked around to see one of the men returning from the lower pasture leading Kit. Her heart turned over.

The captain straightened up in his saddle and looked admiringly over the yellow-and-black filly. Nausea rose in Celia's throat. Running to the trooper, she tried to grasp the bridle from his hand.

"No, no! She is *not* for sale. She belongs to *me*. You cannot have her."

Ignoring her, the captain ran his hand down Kit's sleek yellow neck. "A capital mount. What an unusual coloring with that black tail and mane and that dark streak along her back! And good trim legs. I'll wager she's fleet as the wind. Excellent, excellent! What will you take for her, ma'am? Twenty guineas?"

"I tell you she is not for sale. You can't have her." Frantically Celia turned to Tom and Vestal, pleading silently for their help, but in a glance she could see they were both too overawed by the dragoons to interfere. They hung back silently near the barn wall.

"Twenty guineas it shall be, then. I'll add it to the total sum."

"This is outrageous," Celia sputtered. "Where is your sense of honor? Your decency? I had thought better of British officers!"

That seemed to reach the man. He looked at her for the first time directly. "Come, come, madam, remember we are paying you in coin. That, I understand, is more than the Americans did when they swept through this country recently. Since we'll be stationed in this area it might be politic of you to cooperate with us. Otherwise you run the risk of becoming branded one of those damned rebels, in which case you will find that our behavior today is civilized indeed."

"That has nothing to do with this and you know it. You can take our food and firewood, but to carry off my horse against my express opposition—that is outright theft!"

"Madam, I must remind you that good horseflesh is the first prize of war. Your servant, ma'am."

Motioning to his trooper to lead Kit by her bridle, he turned his horse to lead the group away. Celia fought down a sick outrage. Kit. It was so unfair! So cruel!

The captain had circled his mount back to the head of his troop when he caught sight of Vestal standing in the shadows under the eaves of the barn and cantered closer. "You there. You look like a fine strapping buck. Do you know that you slaves can be free men if you join the King's troops?"

"He is not a slave," Celia exclaimed, her panic rising anew. If this despicable thief lured away her most able-bodied servant, what in the world would she do? "Don't listen to him, Vestal."

The captain never looked in her direction. "We've a fine fort near Williams Bridge manned by black fellows like yourself. You'll have a few coins in your pockets for once and your soul to call your own. Why don't you ride along with us?"

"Vestal," Celia said desperately. "You're needed here. *I* need you."

Vestal stood quietly for a moment, weighing the captain's words. He understood enough of them to know that what was being offered was a kind of independence he had never had before. But then he had never wanted it either. Lines of stubborness settled over his dark features.

"Vestal don't be no slave. Massa Richard, he good 'a me always. Don't fancy no thieves!"

Celia sighed with relief as the captain pulled his mount around. "Have it your way, then. But if you change your mind you know where to find us."

Tossing its head, his horse picked up its legs daintily as a dancer and walked nearer where Celia stood. The captain, leaning down from his saddle, attempted to hand her a leather purse. Stubbornly she refused it, scowling up at him. He shrugged and dropped it at her feet, then called to his troop as they went clattering out of the yard. Celia fought to keep from bursting into tears. Her beautiful Kit's flying black tail was the last thing she saw as they rounded the curve toward the stone bridge. The bleakness in her heart was as gray as the day when she finally turned back to the barn.

Tom hurried over to her, all sympathy. "Oh, dear, Miss Celia, your beautiful filly. But there was nothing to do. I've been in raids before when I was a boy in Ireland. The poor farmer is helpless. Completely helpless."

"We'd better take inventory," Celia said listlessly. "We have to get some idea if anything is left. Thank goodness they didn't bring a wagon or we'd have been stripped bare."

"You want these dollar," Vestal asked, picking up the purse from the ground and handing it to her. "These dollar, him all you got now." She took it as if it were a rattlesnake.

"I suppose I'd better put it away. Mister Deveroe would

count it complete folly not to salvage something from all this."

He started to turn away, but she laid her hand on his sleeve to stop him. "Vestal, thank you for not following those men. It is a great comfort for me to have you here. I would have been desolate to have lost you too."

His large face creased into a smile that was pleased and proud all at once. "All right, Misse Celia. You knows you always 'a count on Vestal."

"*Why* did you have to be away? Perhaps you could have convinced them not to take our stores. Now we're going to have a difficult time before this winter is out."

"I think you handled yourself very well, certainly as well as could be expected under the circumstances," Richard said. He still wore his dust-covered coat and hat from his ride from the White Plains. Celia had barely given him time to climb out of the saddle before she descended on him with her distraught account of the dragoons' visit. He gulped down a second glass of porter he had brought back from the village.

"As soon as Forbes gives me an idea of how much was taken we can make a better assessment of what the winter will be like."

"I told you exactly how much it was! How *can* you be so nonchalant when English soldiers came right into your home and carried off your stores, and your livestock. You make it sound like a tea party!"

"Come, now, Celia. Did they manhandle anyone, threaten to rape you? All they did was to cause us a little winter hardship. I think you are overreacting."

Furious, she gripped the back of the chair and dug her fingers into its creweled upholstery. She had expected at least a little sympathy.

"They took Kit!" she began and burst into tears. He watched her throw herself sobbing into the chair and quietly came over and laid a hand on her shoulder.

"My dear, I know how frightened you must have been. And the loss of your filly is a keen disappointment to you, I realize. But try to be a little more objective. The British will be posted at those forts the Americans abandoned for at least as long as General Howe holds New York. They are only a few miles from here and we will probably see more of them than just this one raid. We had better get used to selling them our supplies, don't you think? Now drink a little of this porter and let me tell you about what I've been through."

The ale felt warm and comforting all the way down. "How did it go in White Plains?"

"A stalemate at best. There was a battle, and the regulars took Chatterton Hill, but General Howe delayed striking at Washington's army so long that they were able to reform and entrench in the hills behind the village. At length the British simply withdrew back toward New York. We don't know what will happen next. There's a large division of American forces at Peekskill, one at White Plains and one in the Jerseys, so we are surrounded on three sides by the Continental Army, while the British sit below us nearly on our doorstep."

"Oh, dear. That means we probably shall see more of the dragoons. I shall never get used to it."

Richard sat down opposite her and brushed the dust from one knee. "You know, I never told you, my dear, but the Americans went through the lower part of the county last month with requisitions to take straw and hay from the farmers. They left us alone that time because of my relationship with Mr. Jay, but they are not likely to the next."

"You mean we may have to provide for the rebel army too!"

"It is certainly possible."

"But how will *we* live? It's not fair."

He laughed, yet there was little humor in it. "Fairness has little to do with war. I saw something of real fighting myself last week and I think we will be fortunate if all we lose are a few bales of hay."

We have already lost more than that, Celia thought bitterly, thinking of her beloved Kit.

"Was there any news of Ewan?" she asked, trying gamely to change her mood.

"No. But the British are most assuredly using men who know this county as guides. He may well be among them."

Silently studying his face, she searched for the courage to say what was uppermost in her heart. "Richard, stay home awhile. Stay here with me. It will give you space to think and it will certainly make my spirit easier. We need you here."

His dark eyes bored through her, yet she knew he was considering what she said.

"Vestal is big and strong," she went on, "but he needs guidance. Tom, well, Tom is an Irishman who's seen years of raiding. He believes in standing by and letting the soldiers have anything they want. I was frightened—truly frightened—by what happened. I would be so grateful if you would not go back into service with Mr. Jay."

For a long moment he was silent studying the glass he turned in his fingers. "Very well, my dear. Perhaps you are right and time is needed to stay quietly at home. And though I think you exaggerate the dangers from these dragoons, as well as my ability to control them, still if it will comfort you to have me here, then here I shall stay."

Flinging herself from the chair, she threw her arms around his neck. "Oh, thank you, Richard. Thank you!"

"For a time at least. Agreed?"

"Agreed."

eleven

For a while the world around the Manor Farm grew quiet, giving Celia and Richard time to restore some of their depleted resources. After General Washington's astounding victories in the Jerseys at Christmastime, both armies retired to winter quarters—the British to New York and the Americans to the hills around Morris Town. There they passed the bitter cold of January and February without incident. There would, of course, be another major campaign in the summer, and rumor had it that it might be directed at Philadelphia, where the Congress sat. If only it would, Celia thought wistfully. Perhaps the war might then move away from West Chester completely, leaving them free to go back to an ordered existence. It was almost too much to hope for.

She was in the milk room washing down the last two of her nearly ripe cheeses when she heard the ominously familiar chink of harness and thudding of horses' hoofs on the road. Her heart sank as she hid the wrapped wheels behind a disguising wall of old bricks and ran to the window. Reining up in front of the house in a cloud of dust was a group of dragoons, the sun glinting on their metal-studded harnesses and the wind lifting the black plumes on their caps.

"Oh no, not again!" Celia cried, barring the door in hope of preventing the theft of the last of her carefully nurtured cheeses. Then one of the figures at the head of the column turned in his saddle, gesturing to his men, and she recognized him at once. Who else would throw out orders so cavalierly?

"Ewan!"

Lifting her skirts, she ran out toward the road just as Richard came sprinting from the front door. They both reached Ewan at the same time. He had vaulted from the saddle to throw an

arm around each of them and hug them to his chest, his eyes
bright above his broad smile.

"Ewan, look at you," Celia cried, stepping back. "How
dashing you are."

He preened under her admiration. "Do you like my scarlet
coat?" he asked, smoothing down the black lapels. In his powdered military wig, with one silver epaulette at his shoulder
and the pewter buttons glinting, he had never looked so handsome.

"They gave you a commission, after all," Richard said, half
asking. "What is your rank? How are they going to use you?
Come in and tell us everything."

"Hold, Cousin. Be patient and I will explain it all in a
moment, but first I must accomplish the purpose of my mission.
Bring up that mount!"

"Oh, Ewan," Celia cried in a delighted surprise. "It's Kit!
You've brought her back. My beautiful Kit." She rubbed her
cheek along the velvet neck. "How did you manage it?"

"It took a little finesse, Cousin, but I won her in a game
of cards. I knew the minute I saw her with Connell that she
was your Kit, and I determined right there and then to return
her to you." He was obviously delighted at the joy that lit
Celia's face. "Are you pleased?"

"Pleased! How can I ever thank you enough? I think I
grieved more over losing her than over all the food the soldiers
carried away."

Richard took his cousin's hand. "You have my gratitude as
well, Ewan. Celia was terribly depressed over the loss of her
horse, and, though I tried to make inquiries, I was never able
to trace her. We are both very grateful. Come and have a glass
with us to cut the dust in your throat."

Ewan turned back to his good-looking private and handed
him the bridle of his own horse, then followed Richard into
the parlor, where Celia poured out the last of the French brandy.
After carefully closing the door, Ewan settled back into a chair
with his old assurance. Celia could not help but remember the
distraught young man who had sat there the last time, telling
them how he was about to break his parole and go over to the
British. Nothing remained of that uncertain, half-guilty figure
now. He crossed one booted leg over the other and fussed with
the lace below his black leather stock.

"They've made me a captain to raise a troop of horse," he
began, "but I have the promise of higher rank later on. Right

now I'm suffering under the command of that idiot Bearmore from Throgg's Neck. Technically we are part of his division of Queen's Rangers, but I must allow that we have a great deal of autonomy."

"Are you posted at Morrisania?" Richard asked politely, his eyes even more veiled than usual. He was fighting down a terrible surge of envy—not for the side Ewan espoused but simply for the excitement and glory of a military life.

"Yes, among the Yagers and Emericks' light troops and the Seventeenth Dragoons. Our purpose is to keep the King's Bridge open for supplies entering the city, but I see much more advantage in scouring the countryside to obtain the forage itself. Since most of us know the area so well, we have advantages the British and Hessian troops lack."

"I noticed familiar faces among your troops out there. Gilbert Totten and Kipp—and young Cleary from the farm on the Mill Road. You're not going to rob your own people, surely?"

"I am not the only person in West Chester, Cousin, who feels that these rebels are wrong. As for robbing—give me an alternative. I am trying very hard to build proper discipline in my corps, but it's no easy task, Cousin, because at times old animosities get confused with the need to supply the troops. Even I catch myself thinking it would be easy to take out an old grudge on the farmer who has the most cows and grain, but I have so far managed to avoid going to that extreme."

"Oh, Ewan, you're not going to take my last two cheeses, are you?" Celia asked, trying to lighten a conversation that her husband threatened to turn deadly serious.

"No," he laughed. "I promise not to rob my family. But I cannot promise the same for the other troops stationed nearby. I thought to warn you to find a good out-of-the-way spot to hide your horses, at least Kit and your fine gelding, Richard. You will certainly lose them otherwise, for good mounts are taken first. If you turn them out to pasture, be sure to post a guard."

"That is an excellent black you are riding, Ewan," Richard said, gamely putting animosities aside. "Did you win him at cards as well?"

"Goliah? No, I bought him from an English dragoon. Took almost my last guinea, but he was worth it." Ewan's face went grim. "I suppose you've seen the house."

"Yes," Celia answered. "I'm so sorry, but there was nothing anyone could do. First it was taken over by the Americans and later by the Hessians who passed through last December. They carried off everything of value, even the shutters and doors."

"Have you seen Uncle Peter yet?" Richard asked. "We tried to bring him here, but he refuses to leave his home, so we content ourselves with looking in on him regularly. I don't know how much longer he can survive these raids."

"I've seen him, yes. And I keep in close touch with Ben. Since I shall be in the area now, I expect to be able to stop in more frequently and keep an eye on him."

"But, Ewan," Celia said, "suppose the Continentals come back this way. You couldn't possibly show your face around them."

"No, but it's not likely they will. General Washington has left a division at White Plains and another at Peekskill, but both those places are a good distance north of Morrisania. With our strong outposts at King's Bridge it isn't likely the whole American army would come down this far. But small rebel patrols have already ventured down looking for trouble and will probably continue to."

"Do you mean you have fought battles with these patrols?"

Ewan smiled at her naïveté. "More like skirmishes. We spend a good part of our time either seeking them out or fending them off."

"Seeking them out! You venture up there seeking skirmishes? How rash!"

"Why, my troops have been up as far as Pinesbridge on the Croton River, not to mention North Castle and Crompound. It's dangerous, of course, but that's why we are here. We frequently return with a few casualties but more often with prisoners to be sent into New York. And in all fairness, I must confess they sometimes carry off some of us as well. But I'm proud of the way this troop is shaping up. They'll be a crack fighting unit in time, I believe, and a real protection to the city."

"The city," Celia echoed wistfully. "In her last note from Wayside Mama Deveroe reports that New York is quite a gay place these days. It's changed almost beyond recognition."

"Oh, that reminds me." Ewan reached inside his coat and drew out a folded paper, handing it to Celia. "I stopped in at Wayside last week and this was entrusted to me for you. It nearly slipped my mind."

"From Hester," Celia said, breaking the seal. "Will you excuse me if I read it now?"

"Please do," her husband answered. "I'm anxious to know how they are."

"They are safe enough at Wayside as long as the British hold New York, Cousin. And the shortages in the town have not yet affected them too severely. I should not worry over them too much."

"As a matter of fact, I worry more over Celia here at the Manor House. I've tried my best to convince her to go in to Wayside and stay with Mama and Hester, but she refuses to leave."

Ewan studied Celia's golden-brown hair as she bent over her letter. "She really should leave, you know. This is not a safe place to live anymore—almost nowhere in West Chester is. And more than likely it will get worse before it gets better."

"I know. I know. But try to persuade her!"

Celia handed her letter to her husband. "Hester is distraught because Cortlandt is planning to take her to England. I don't think she wants to go now that New York is so lively. She wants us to come in and see her before she leaves, Richard. Do you think we might?"

Richard turned the letter over in his hand. "Of course. We must. A voyage like that is perilous enough at any time, and now, with warships on the high seas, even more so. England is a long way off, and who knows when we shall meet again. Yes, we must go in."

Ewan set down his glass and rose to leave, pulling down the tabs of his white waistcoat. "It's a little precipitate of Cortlandt to fly to England at this time, wouldn't you say, Richard? The game's not half up yet, and if it continues along the same lines it has this past autumn, Sir William has only to make one good stroke to destroy Washington's army. Then this rebellion will be over for good."

"Oh, Cortlandt needs little excuse. He is a snob with a titled relation in Surrey. He has always wanted to move there, and this war gives him good reason. And for all Hester's tears, she is doubtless the one who drove him to it. My sister can be as grand a snob as Cortlandt any day of the week."

"You wrong her, Richard, you've always been too critical of Hester." Celia took Ewan's arm and walked with him toward the door. "Please stop in and see us any time you can. It's a comfort to know you're nearby. And thank you again for returning my beautiful Kit to me. I can't express how grateful I am to you."

Ewan stopped and extended his hand to Richard. "You are going to need a pass, Cousin, if you plan to go in to New York. I'll send one around by Ned Carne. And while you are at Wayside, see if you cannot convince this headstrong wife of yours to stay. She would be far better off."

"Must I do battle with you too, Ewan?" Celia shook her head. "Someone must keep watch over our home, and who better than those who care most passionately about it? I will not leave it to all you destructive military men."

"Madame, you cut me to the quick!"

"You see now what I have to put up with," Richard said, and Ewan noticed that his smile was forced. There was something in Richard's sad, sensitive eyes that Ewan had not seen before—a concern or worry that hid the good-humored kindness which had always been there. How much of it was real fear for his wife's safety, Ewan wondered, and how much chagrin that she refused to obey him? He saw Richard glance wistfully out the door to where the troop stood patiently calming their horses in the road, and in that instant he realized that his scholarly cousin would like nothing more than to be there himself, wearing the proud uniform and carrying the saber. Add to all that the high calling of honor and patriotism—even when it set them on opposing sides—and it was a hard beacon to resist. This slender, lovely girl at Richard's side, as dear as she was, was like a chain fastening him to a place where he really did not want to be. Ewan set his cap firmly on his head and silently thanked God he wasn't married.

"Cousins, God keep you. I shall stop in when next I visit my father. Meanwhile, don't forget to hide your horses. I don't know if I could win Kit back a second time!"

He bounded down the steps, leaving them standing in the doorway watching after him.

"If I lose her again I'll consider her gone for good," Celia called. Then, looking up at her husband as he watched Ewan and his company gallop down the road, she felt that familiar sinking sensation. She too recognized the look in Richard's eyes as one of wistful longing.

"Richard, come inside. We must begin making plans if we are going to go in to New York."

To her relief he turned and followed her silently back into the house.

Crashing noises dragged her unwillingly out of a dreamlike lethargy. With a start Celia came awake, conscious of the darkness of her bed, the shadowed sentinels of the bedposts shrouded in the dark around her. Fear rose in her throat as she heard the distinct calls of men and the blowing of horses outside the house, the night punctuated by crashing blows against her door. Richard was already over the side of the bed pulling on his clothes.

"What is it?" she said fearfully. "Who could it be? Dragoons again?"

"Possibly. You stay here. I'll handle them."

"Richard, don't leave me!"

"Now, Celia, don't panic. You said yourself the British had no thought of hurting you. They probably only want a bottle or two." With hasty, fumbling gestures he struck a light from a tinderbox and thrust the candle into the lid, setting shadows writhing on the wall.

"But in the middle of the night . . ."

Richard pulled his buckled shoes over his hose and moved quickly to the window, pulling back the shuttered drapes to look down on his front yard.

"Who are you? What do you want?" he shouted.

The banging stopped abruptly. In the light of several bobbing pine-knot torches he could make out the dark outline of a body of nearly ten men on horseback grouped around the front stoop.

"Open up at once, you damned Tory!"

The dim light was enough to comfirm his worst fears. These were not dragoons from the Harlem forts. Not a uniform among them. Worriedly he glanced back at Celia huddled on the bed, her face white in the flickering candle glow. He tried not to let his voice show his concern.

"What do you want? This is not a Tory home. Go away and leave us in peace."

"Either you open this door or we'll burn your fine house down around it."

"Aye, aye," the group called, laughing. "For God and Congress!"

"Oh, Richard," Celia cried, running in bare feet to stand at the window behind him.

Grim-faced, he turned and gripped her shoulders. "I'll have to go down and deal with them. I'd tell you to hide, but they'd only drag you out. Get your clothes on in a hurry."

"But what will they do?"

"I don't know. Nothing, I hope. Now get dressed and stay quietly in the background. Don't protest at anything I give them, do you understand? I can't deal with them and you at the same time."

He was already half out of the room, taking the light with him. Groping in the darkness, Celia pulled on her dress, stockings and shoes and bundled her hair into a cap. Then she slipped quietly to the top of the stairs. Below she could see the hallway fill with men, rough men in seaman-style jackets and trousers, their faces blackened with soot that gave them a diabolical cast and set the whites of their eyes in stark relief. One whose heavyset, loutish-looking figure was faintly familiar had Richard pinned against the wall, his face right up against his.

"Where's your specie? We know you got plenty—you Tory gentry always do."

A second man flicked the point of a glinting saber in the heavy folds of Richard's shirt. "And you'd better give it over or we have ways of making you. Ways you won't find none too pleasant!"

The point disappeared into the cloth at Richard's neck, and Celia could almost feel it pricking her own skin. Surely she knew that voice and that face. Then it came to her. Lester Hunnicut, a ne'er-do-well known in the lower county for his violent ways. She could not remember the name of the other man, but she recognized his voice—he was a friend of Hunnicut's, both of them criminals and thieves. Slipping down the stairs toward Richard, she could make out the other figures in the group moving in and out of the rooms off the hall. Her anger rose as she realized they were stalking her parlor and dining room, heedless of their mudstained boots on her fine carpets, pulling out drawers and stuffing the contents into their pockets then dumping what was left onto the floor. And, though she could not see them, she could hear at the end of the hallway another two or three rifling her kitchen.

Richard had heard of these lawless gangs who were taking advantage of the chaos of the war to plunder and steal. "Skinners," they were called, because of their habit of skinning the clothes and valuables right off their victims. They were easily provoked to cruelty. He had been told only last week that they had tied old Wesley Knight in New Castle to a chair, torn out the seat and built a fire under it, all in an effort to get him to reveal where his money was hidden. Richard made up his mind not be heroic.

Hunnicut was losing patience. "Come on, then," he cried. The sharp point of the saber dug painfully into Richard's throat.

"Do you want us to play rough? It's all the same with us, a little sport will help to pass the time."

"No," Richard said quietly. "There is no need for that. I'll give you what specie I have."

The saber swung downward. "That's better, then."

Standing above them in the shadows of the stairs, Celia, white-faced, fought back an urge to protest. One of the men came stalking from her dining room carrying her fine silver sconces which he had pulled right off the wall. They still had vestiges of plaster clinging to them. With dismay she saw Elizabeth's heirloom silver teapot protruding from a saddlebag that one had slung over his shoulder. Shrinking against the wall, she closed her eyes, determined not to look, and gritted her teeth in silence.

Richard moved with dignified despair into his study, followed by the group leaders. From a secret drawer in his secretary he produced a long tin box. The skinner grabbed it eagerly, tearing it open and upending the contents on a table.

"Is this all? It don't look like enough for such a swell as yourself."

"It's all I have in the house. I swear it."

"You'd better be tellin' the truth. We have little patience with Tory scum and if we find you were lyin' to us, we'll come back and make you pay for it. Make no bones about that."

"Odd's life, man," Richard exploded, "haven't I cooperated? I tell you this is all the money I have."

Stuffing the case into his pockets, the skinner moved quickly from the room back into the hall. Glancing up the stairway, he caught sight of Celia shrinking in the shadows. He gave her a long appraising look while she held her breath, more terrified than she had ever been in her life.

"Mayhap we ought to fire this house anyway, Capt'n," one of the blackened faces said, stepping up beside Hunnicut. "She'd make a bonny blaze!"

The man pulled his eyes away from Celia and back to Richard, smiling evilly. "Aye, it'd make a sight all right." He seemed to be weighing the thought. Richard looked directly into the cunning white eyes, trying silently to convey what he had already determined in his mind. If this damned bunch of villains burned his house he would personally seek out every one of them and kill them.

Perhaps Hunnicut read his look. He dropped his eyes and snickered through missing teeth. "And it'd bring those dragoons from Number Eight down on us before we could make Morrell's Tavern. No," he said, turning away, "we've got enough, boys. Let's save a little for next time."

In only a few moments they disappeared, clattering their horses out of the yard and down the road, with cries of "For God and Congress" echoing behind them.

Celia collapsed on the stair, almost afraid to breathe, hardly daring to believe they were really gone. When she opened her eyes she could see her husband leaning stiffly against the newel post. For the first time she recognized that he had been as worried as she. Because she couldn't stop herself, she began to cry.

Startled to realize she was there, Richard walked up the stairs and sat beside her, putting his arm around her shoulders.

"It might have been worse," he said grimly.

"It was bad enough! You gave them all our money."

"That's because I've known them to cut a man up to find it. I thought in this case wisdom seemed the better part of valor. Besides, we can replace the money. Some of it, anyway."

"Would they really have burned our house?"

"Yes, they would. *And* the stable, *and* the barn—whatever might strike their fancy."

"I recognized that Hunnicut and that other villain—I forget his name. They were always worthless creatures."

"Exactly," Richard answered, finally beginning to allow himself to relax. "Renegades and rascals, every one. They see the poor citizens of the county being stripped bare by both armies and think to get in on the looting. If truth were told they don't give a damned fig for God *or* Congress. And the worst of it is, there's little we can do about it. I could complain to the committees in White Plains, but I doubt it would do any good."

"Will they come back?" she cried, clinging to him.

"Probably. Since you are resolved to live here, you'd better become accustomed to this sort of thing. Perhaps the fact that we are so near the Harlem forts will discourage them from venturing down this far, but I doubt it. Celia, I cannot urge you strongly enough to leave this place. Get out of West Chester and go to New York. You *must* go!"

Her only answer was to bury her face against his chest and fight back her tears. She was trembling so that he put his arms around her and held her like a child. She knew he was right. Every instinct told her to leave this war zone of marauding bands of violent men, but she could not bring herself to do it. What was the use of living safely if you had nothing to call your own?

Gently Richard rubbed her shoulders. "In any case, I think tomorrow I will ride down to Fort Number Eight and ask them to keep a watch on this area. With British patrols around, perhaps these scoundrels will stay away from West Farms. As for now, my dear, we'd better try to get some sleep."

Celia raised her tear-stained face. "Sleep! I won't be able to close my eyes for the rest of the night. Suppose they come back?"

"I don't think they will, but perhaps you are right. Let's make a fire in the kitchen and then I'll wake Vestal and we'll prime Papa's dueling pistols and sit there with them. Meanwhile, see if you can hunt up any strong drink from the cellar. Anything will do. We both need it."

By late spring Celia's spirits had revived and she was looking forward to the trip to the city. There were times in the dark of night when the noise of horses on the road or voices calling near the stone bridge would wake her in terror, but gradually the horror of that Skinner raid began to lessen and she found the tightness within her easing. Her determination to stay in West Farms was as strong as ever, but she could not deny she felt a sense of relief as they started early one morning on the path toward Hunt's Point and the East River, where a British tender waited to carry them to that stronghold of Royal occupation, New York City.

Once past the treacherous whirlpool called Hell's Gate, it proved to be a leisurely trip downriver. Without touching the city docks at all they left the ship at Corlear's Hook and were rowed to Wayside, where Jess handed them up, full of smiles. Jess had aged, Celia noted, and his ebony skin had a chalky look under his grizzled wig. The house showed signs of decay, as well. Celia was startled to see the stripped, stump-filled flats around it where once trees and fences had gentled the landscape.

Elizabeth met them at the door, pink and delicate as ever, her patrician face still unlined. Hester, flying down the stairs, gave Celia a warm embrace, and even Cortlandt and Henry pumped Richard's hand and Guinevere kissed his cheek as though they were all grateful to see them.

The real shock came when they were ushered into the dining

room. At first, Celia did not recognize the frail old man slumped in an armchair at the head of the table as Samuel Deveroe. Disease had wasted his large frame to a shadow. These months they had been apart Celia had kept an image in her mind of the robust man she had always known, vibrant and controlling the world in which he moved. Now the world controlled him. He was too weak to stand, but he took her hand in his cold, limp grasp and smiled.

"How good to see you again, Celia. We've missed you."

"Dear Papa Deveroe," she said, kissing his forehead and trying not to show her dismay.

Richard pulled out a chair beside his father and spoke in a very matter-of-fact voice, which he hoped hid his own distress. "I had a devil of a time getting her out of West Farms, Papa. I think she fears that if she's not there to protect it, the Manor House will be confiscated either by the rebels or by the Royal troops. Or burned by the Skinners."

Celia bit back a reply as they settled around the table. Across from her, Cortlandt Barnett heaped food upon his plate. He had grown portly, and as Celia watched him she began to understand why.

"That is no idle concern, Richard," he said without lifting his eyes from his plate. "The best estates in America belong to the Tories, and those Bible-thumping, liberty-crying despots of committees all over New York would like nothing better than to get their avaricious hands on them. They'll do it, too. Why do you think I'm going to England? You'd best have an eye out for your own security."

"But surely you don't need to worry about losing your patrimony, surrounded as you are with the whole might of Britain."

"That is true, my son," Samuel roused himself to answer, his voice reflecting some of the old authority. "But suppose, God forbid, the Colonies should actually sever their ties with Great Britain and become independent. What do you suppose then will be the fate of those who have remained loyal? Damned as Tories and Episcopalians, to a man!"

"That is absolutely unthinkable!" Guinevere said prissily.

Cortlandt waved his knife in her direction. "Perhaps so, but I have not been overly impressed with the British performance so far. The mightiest army in the world, and they cannot even do away with a bunch of ragtag upstarts who don't even have proper boots on their feet. Time and again Sir William Howe has delayed striking the blow that would destroy Washington. One might almost suppose he was actually on the side of the Whigs!"

"Perhaps it is providence that is on their side," Richard muttered. He turned to his brother. "And do you feel this way, too, Henry? Are you for taking ship to England?"

Henry could not resist puffing himself up a little. "Not at this time. The fact is, I have a deal of influence with Commandant Robertson, here in the city. He relies on my knowledge of the area, and I have hopes of an appointment as the hay inspector for the Commissioner of Forage—there are great profits to be made in that direction, Richard. Great profits."

Hester laid a hand on Celia's arm. "Well, whatever they say about the British generals, Celia, there is one field upon which they excel. New York is now the most entertaining place in the world. Balls, soirees, horseraces, even a theater! And you will not *believe* the number of handsome officers on the streets. I declare, one cannot walk half a block without some courtly proposal."

Cortlandt stopped chewing long enough to scowl at his wife across the table. "Of course to Hester that is the most important function of an army. You never saw an ugly officer, did you, my dear?"

"Never! It must be the uniform."

"Well, as for me, I've finished with New York. I'm for England, and America can go to hell itself if she pleases."

"This dreadful civil war," Elizabeth said, passing a small silver tray to Celia. "Here, my dear, have some of this West Indian preserved ginger. It is a great luxury in these spartan times. We saved it especially for your visit."

Samuel leaned toward Richard and tugged weakly at his coat sleeve. "We know you have different sympathies, my son, and we don't question them. I only say to you, hold on to whatever influence you have with these mule-headed Whigs. It may stand you well in the end. I for one don't see how you can stomach them, but since you seem able to, and since there are some men of integrity who feel as you do, then I say hang on to any associations that might bring you through this unscathed. You know we stand behind you."

Richard gripped his father's hand. "Thank you, Papa. I know too well that there are many men in the country right now who while crying 'liberty' at the top of their breath are roaring despots when it comes to dealing with those who don't agree with them. God forbid I should ever go that way. But there are also moderate men who deplore the excesses of the mob yet feel the cause is a just one. If I stand with them, it is because I feel as they do, not because I want to stay wealthy by political expediency."

"I know you too well, Richard, to think that of you."

"That may be, Brother," Henry exclaimed, "but you cannot deny that many good men have been condemned as Tories, beaten, hanged, stripped of their estates, run out of the towns, brought to utter ruin."

Cortlandt pounded his fist on the table. "What more can you expect from rule by rabble!"

And so the conversation went until the end of the difficult meal. At the first sign that it was finally over, Hester jumped up from the table, grabbed Celia's hand and drew her to her feet.

"Enough of politics. Come along, Celia, you and I are going to leave these men to their port while we have a good old-fashioned girl chat. Excuse us, Mama?"

"Of course, dear. Why don't you take Celia upstairs to her old room? She would probably welcome an opportunity to rest."

It did not take much urging for Celia to leave the stuffy room. Her old bedroom at Wayside was a welcome sight, and thankfully she loosened her stays and sank onto the dark-blue woolen coverlet. Hester plumped down at the foot of the bed and curled her tiny feet under her skirts.

"Oh, my dearest Celia, I can't tell you how happy I am that you are here. This terrible trip! I am frightened half to death already. I do think it is dreadful of Cortlandt to drag me away from New York just when the city is at its gayest. Really, he is the most selfish, insensitive creature living!"

Celia listened patiently while Hester ran on, but it did not take her long to realize that in spite of Hester's professed distress she was looking forward to London.

"And there is this too," Hester said, looking up from under her pale-yellow lashes. "I am with child again. Just imagine! Carrying me off across an ocean in such a delicate condition."

Celia fought down the lump in her throat. "How wonderful for you," she heard herself saying lamely.

"It's not wonderful at all, it's dreadful. With Tyler only a year old! I'm sure I shall miscarry, probably in some horrid cabin below decks where no doubt the child and I shall both die!"

"Nonsense, Hester. You are as strong as one of our West Farm horses. By the time you are making your curtsy to the Queen you will have two fine children. Stop complaining and think how fortunate you are."

Hester smiled at her obliquely. "Celia, you are the only person I know who talks frankly to me. And you are probably right. However, even though I agree with what you say, I shall never stop complaining about it. Where would be the fun in that!"

"No fun at all. Now tell me all about the changes in the town. All the parties and assemblies. I want to hear every detail."

They stayed at Wayside for a week, and Celia found she enjoyed herself more than she had ever anticipated. She was grateful for the chance to visit with Samuel and Elizabeth Deveroe, the one so changed, the other so worried about losing her daughter, and both still so very dear to her. She enjoyed the hours of playing with Hester's toddler. After his first shyness, Tyler learned to waddle into her arms whenever he spotted her entering a room. She found the city endlessly fascinating, the streets filled with every color and variety of uniform from Highland plaids to Hessian blue—and, of course, everywhere the scarlet coats and gold and silver laces of the British. She even enjoyed the flamboyance of the harlots on Trinity Walk, who were, some of them, very beautiful. And it was glorious fun to dress up once again in finery and jewels and dance until dawn at the balls and assemblies, or to attend the races at the Fresh Water Pond or sit in a box at the John Street Theatre and watch British officers display their acting skills.

Yet the city bore the marks of war: on the streets where shabby refugees with their starving children begged for their suppers in spite of the imported delicacies crowding the grocers' shelves; in the cries and groans of the prisoners that assaulted the ears of passersby on the streets around the improvised jails in the Provost, the churches and the sugar houses; in the bleakness of burned-out flats where the great fire had destroyed homes and warehouses that even the efficient British Army had not found the resources to rebuild. Celia knew that for every brazen and expensively dressed prostitute parading on Trinity

Walk there were ten scrawny, diseased trollops in the "Holy Ground" around the college hospital. New York under British occupation was as paradoxical as ever it had been as a Colonial city—exciting, diverting, gay, bleak, cruel, hardened, fascinating and mysterious. Celia warmed to it just as she had years before when she first came there as a child. Yet, in her deepest heart, she was thankful when the time came to take the boat back upriver to the Manor. For, even surrounded by the rigors of war, West Farms was her home and there was no place on earth she wished more to be.

She knew that their final parting would be difficult and she dreaded it. Yet when they finally stood on the Wayside dock in the wet blue early-morning fog, waiting for the tender that would carry them up the East River, it was not Celia but Hester who lost control, sobbing as though her heart would break.

"I may never see you again," she cried, throwing her arms around Celia's neck, for once without the least trace of artifice.

Celia tried to smile through her own tears. "Don't say so, my dear Hester. You may come back. Or, who knows, when this rebellion is settled perhaps we can sail to England and visit you. You can introduce us to London society."

Even Richard was a little moved at his sister's grief. He laid an arm comfortingly around her shoulder and kissed the top of her golden head. "God keep you safe, Hester. Write to us. Let us know how you get on."

It was one of the few times Hester forgot her long-standing irritation with her brother. "You will watch over Mama and Papa, Richard? Henry is so obsessed with trying to rise in Commandant Robertson's esteem that he neglects them terribly. And Papa is very ill. You will see they want for nothing?"

"I promise I shall do everything I can to care for them."

Kneeling down, Celia crushed Tyler to her and covered his pink face with her kisses. "Oh, I wish he were not going so far away. I should so like to watch him grow up." The little boy struggled to get back behind Dinah's skirts. Giving him a last squeeze, Celia turned back to Hester and embraced her. "God keep you, Hester. I shall miss you terribly."

"And Ewan," Hester sobbed against Celia's neck. "Tell Ewan goodbye for me. And tell him to . . . to take care of himself."

"We shall tell him. And when the war is over he shall come with us to pay you a visit. You'll see."

Wiping at her eyes, Hester scoffed with a little of her normal petulance. "Oh, Celia, you were always such a sentimental goose. But this time I hope you are right."

As the long boat pulled away into the river Celia watched through the wispy shrouds of fog, straining to see Hester's drooping blue figure standing on the dock until all that was left was a bright shimmer where a limp shaft of sunlight touched her silvery hair. Then she turned and leaned against her husband, her heart like a stone in her chest. Confound the war! This pointless, damnable war!

twelve

It was nearly ten o'clock in the evening before Celia left the little house at the back of the garden where Betsy had just given birth to her first child, a boy they named Luther. Holding the lamp high to light the frosted path to the piazza, she hurried along, every muscle aching with fatigue, for it had been a long and difficult lying-in. Without her help and that of several neighbor women, both Betsy and her child might have died this night. It was a grim consolation to Celia that if she could not bring a child of her own into the world, she might at least assist others to have theirs.

She ducked inside the dark, empty hallway, wishing desperately that Richard were here with her to share her sense of accomplishment. Wearily making her way upstairs to her bedroom, she poured herself a glass of marigold wine—a homemade variety which was all that was left in Richard's cellar—and sank into a chair before the bedroom hearth. There was no fire in any of the other rooms now, since firewood was so precious, but at least Vestal had had the foresight to keep this one going for her, and she was grateful for its warmth against the autumn chill.

She was almost too tired to go to bed, yet the cold, dark shadows of her room were so depressing as to make its escape inviting. She was incredibly, terribly lonely, and she ached for the companionship of her husband, the warmth of his body and the comfort of his concern. Why must he always leave her like this? Why must she always miss him so!

Leaning her head back against the chair, she forced herself to look at the problem squarely. After all, it was not as though she were without protection. True, Forbes was away almost as often as Richard himself, but Vestal's strength and fierce loyalty were a constant support. With Uncle Peter's death last spring the last of his slaves had come to live at the Manor Farm, so she had more servants around her than ever before. Diamond and Plato were old and Jim had a crippled foot, but the fact that there were four men defending the house could not help but give second thoughts to the armed patrols which harried the area.

She had almost drifted asleep when the noise of a horse galloping into the front yard and a loud banging at the door brought her suddenly awake. Grabbing the lamp from the table, she hurried into the hall, and down the stairs, fighting down panic. Then she heard Ewan's voice whispering loudly through the door.

"Celia! Let me in. Hurry!"

Setting down the lamp, Celia raised the bar to allow him to slip inside. Pushing past her, he quickly closed and barred the door behind him and then blew out the candle.

"Is there a place I can hide?" he said, gripping her arm. "They are right on my heels."

"They? Who?"

"An American patrol. Freddie Stephenson. We were surprised at Lawrence's house. I managed to get away, but not before I was recognized. Where can I go? They'll be here any moment."

"I don't know . . ."

"Anywhere, Celia," he said, looking around wildly. "Think. It's only me they want. No one else."

Her thoughts raced. "My bedroom upstairs. Surely they won't dare to barge in there."

The muffled sounds of horses on the road told them there was no time to wait. "I'll have to risk it," Ewan muttered and was off up the stairs. Celia started to follow when the loud banging on the door stopped her.

"Ewan, your horse?" she whispered loudly.

"I sent it on . . ."

She waited long enough to hear the door close behind him on the upstairs landing, then slipped to the front door, her heart pounding.

"Who is it? What do you want?" she called.

"Lieutenant Frederick Stephenson, ma'am, of the West Chester Rangers," the answer came briskly. "Open this door at once or we shall be forced to knock it in!"

"My husband is not at home, I'm alone and defenseless here. If you are gentlemen, you'll go away."

"You're wasting our time, Mrs. Deveroe. If you hope to keep your door intact, you had better open it."

When she hesitated the pounding began in earnest. "No, no, wait," Celia called. "Don't break it down. I'll open it for you."

She tried to take as long as possible, but at the first slip of the lock the officer outside forced the heavy oak door and the hallway filled with men. Quickly the lamp was lit, the long shadows reflecting on faces of young men she had seen often enough to recognize. Lieutenant Stephenson looked especially fierce and intensely angry.

"Search the house," he barked, sending his men scurrying through the halls and up the stairs.

"How dare you burst into my house like this," Celia said, trying to brazen it out.

He brushed her aside as though she were a servant. "You'd best be quiet, madam, for your own good. We know you are harboring a known Tory and a damned traitor and we intend to find him. If you don't care to go to prison with him, just keep out of this."

"You—you unprincipled knave! My husband works for Mr. Jay. The Committee of Safety shall hear of this."

"Lieutenant," came a voice from the upstairs landing, "come see this. It's worth all this night's discomfort."

A grim smile lit the lieutenant's features. "The Committee of Safety will be so delighted to know that Ewan Deveroe has been taken, your complaints won't matter a fig." Grabbing her arm, he pulled her with him up the stairs. "Where is he, Dykeman? Have you discovered him?"

Celia's heart sank as she was pulled to the door of her bedroom. The soldiers, laughing and gesticulating, were grouped around her high double bed. Lieutenant Stephenson released her and, smiling broadly, leaned against the door jam. He was beginning to enjoy this night's work.

"Come on out, Ewan," he said, and Celia watched miserably as they dragged her cousin from under the bed ruffle. Her heart went out to him, for she had never seen him more crestfallen. To be captured at all was bad enough, but to be dragged out of hiding from under a bed—it was one of the few times in his life that Ewan had found himself standing in mortal man's shoes, and the humiliation on his face wounded her almost as much as him.

"Well, well," Stephenson smirked. "The distinguished

Colonel Deveroe. And hiding under a lady's bed! Tsk, tsk!"

Celia felt her cheeks blaze as the soldiers grinned lewdly at each other.

"Watch your tongue, Freddie," Ewan snapped. "My cousin had nothing to do with this. I forced myself in here against her wishes."

Lieutenant Stephenson made Celia a mocking bow. "We have no reason to tarnish your reputation, Mrs. Deveroe. The truth is, we were so close on Colonel Deveroe's heels we know he only arrived a moment before us." He turned back to Ewan. "But under a bed—that's not up to your usual flair, Ewan."

"Shut your mouth!"

The lieutenant's eyes narrowed. "No, you shut yours! You're under arrest. And you're coming with us."

Although he had known him for years, Ewan looked through Freddie Stephenson as though he could not recall his name. "How? On foot?"

"Oh, you are much too fine a prize for that. You're the most wanted man in West Chester County."

"You flatter me."

"Not a bit. Had you not made such a profession of stealing from your neighbours, perhaps your reputation would not have made you so infamous. As it is, you and your band of so-called Cowboys have more than won the name traitor and coward. Truss him up, boys."

Celia saw Ewan flinch as his arms were pulled behind and tied. "I might consider that worth a challenge under different circumstances, Freddie, except that it comes from the lips of a damned rebel!"

Stephenson started forward, and Celia thought for a moment he would strike his prisoner. Instead he held his arm back and turned to go downstairs, ordering his men to bring the Colonel along.

Ewan passed her in the doorway without so much as a glance. She wanted to stop him and say how sorry she was, but he carefully avoided her eyes. Meekly she followed the troops downstairs. The door stood open, and from outside she heard one of the soldiers call to the lieutenant, "We found his horse, sir."

Celia again recognized Garret Dykeman, one of a family well known for their rebel sympathies. Behind them she could just make out Ewan's big black stallion, Goliah.

"We're not going on foot, Colonel," Stephenson said,

pleased with himself. "We're going to ride your excellent
mount. You always kept the best horses in West Chester. Throw
him up, boys!"

Like a trussed pig Ewan was tossed up into the saddle while
Stephenson climbed up behind him, and the troop thundered
out of the yard without a backward glance. Celia stood in the
doorway watching them, filled with the most terrible distress
she could ever remember. Ewan, the strong, the self-assured,
always totally in command—carried away tied to a saddle, to
be thrown into some dark, stinking jail, or even, God forbid,
to be hanged like a common criminal.

Richard! She must let Richard know at once. She would
send Vestal to White Plains first thing come morning. Richard
knew all the right people among the rebels. If anyone could
help Ewan he could.

She went back to her bedroom, cold now from the drafts
the soldiers had let in. Sleep was impossible, so she took a
quilt from the bed, wrapped it around her shoulders and sat in
the chair before the embers of the fire, trying to compose her
letter to Richard but seeing only Ewan's white face in her mind,
his tense lips and angry, wounded eyes, fighting for composure
while his pride lay in shards around him. Why wouldn't he
look at her? Was she afraid she would laugh just as those uncouth
louts they called soldiers were laughing to see the proud Colonel
Deveroe brought so low? How little he knew her. Far from
enjoying his embarrassment, she wanted to comfort him. She
wanted to reassure him that this glimpse of vulnerability only
made him dearer to her. If only she could have told him so
just with a single glance. It might have made the whole thing
less bitter.

A brief note arrived from Richard the second week in October explaining that he had moved with the New York Legislature up to Kingston, a place Celia only dimly remembered
as a Hudson River town somewhere north of Peekskill. His
letter told her that Ewan had been carried away to prison in
Connecticut and that he was moving cautiously to see if his
hotheaded cousin might obtain another parole. It was not until
several days later that Celia learned of the momentous events
behind the move to Kingston. The Americans had won a great
victory in upstate New York, forcing the surrender of a huge
British army of nearly five thousand regulars under the command of General Burgoyne. Burgoyne's push down from Can-

ada had been part of the strongest effort yet by the British to
end the rebellion. In Pennsylvania General Howe was moving
solidly to take the capital city of Philadelphia, while in New
York General Clinton had sailed his forces up the Hudson to
capture the forts guarding the Highlands near Peekskill, forcing
the State Legislature to move before them to Kingston. West
Chester County was now completely under the control of the
British and the Loyalists, and Richard was farther away from
her and their home than ever before.

Yet as the weeks wore on it became obvious that nothing
had been achieved to bring an end to the war. In Pennsylvania
both armies retired to winter quarters—the British to the glittering society of Philadelphia and the Americans to the bitter
miseries of Valley Forge—while General Clinton abandoned
the outposts he had won on the Hudson and sailed his troops
back downriver to New York.

The Whigs, who quickly swept their influence back over
the county, were jubilant, assured by their stupendous victory
over Burgoyne that they could defeat the so-far-invincible British army, and cheered by the thought that Saratoga and Free-
man's Farm had encouraged the French to support their revolution.

For Celia there was only bitterness in the growing realization
that the raids would go on as before, resolving nothing. Over
and over she debated leaving the Manor Farm for the safety
of Wayside. She well knew that if she abandoned their home
while Richard was so involved in the problems of the government, there would be nothing left but a shell when they finally
returned. Farming had already dwindled to the bare necessities—there was no use trying to grow crops which would only
be stolen. Now there was no end of the war in sight, Uncle
Peter was dead, Ewan was lying in prison, and it would please
Richard no end if she followed his advice and moved into New
York. Why not? What was the use of staying now? Reluctantly
she decided to give in and close up the farm. She would tell
him so the next time he was home.

Richard came home for Christmas, an unusually warm and
mild one. They took Christmas dinner at the Lawrences',
where, by combining the meager resources of two families,
they managed to put together a suggestion of a feast. When
the last tart had been consumed and the ladies rose to leave,
Mrs. Lawrence excused herself to see to affairs in the kitchen

while Celia went to sit with Mercy in the drafty parlor waiting for the men to finish their port.

Celia had been around Mercy long enough now to accept her quietness. In fact, she had long ago given up trying to draw her out. Since she could never get beyond that wall of icy reserve, she had begun to suspect that in addition to a natural shyness Mercy simply didn't like her very much. So she sat watching the dancing flames, her thoughts wandering absently. She was startled when Mercy herself broke the silence.

"Has Mr. Deveroe had any news of your cousin, the Colonel?" she said, looking as though every word had to be wrenched from her lips.

"Why, yes. He is still in prison right now, but we are very hopeful of an exchange. The Whigs, of course, are making a determined effort to keep him jailed, but the Legislature is most anxious to exchange him for a certain rebel Major Key. So with any luck he will soon be back at his command."

"He will not have to break another parole, then."

"I don't suppose anyone would ever expect him to keep one. He's far too involved with his troop of Refugees, and Ewan is not the man to let others fight this war. As you probably know."

"He is far too valiant."

Celia smiled to herself as she watched Mercy keeping her eyes demurely on her hands in her lap, her long black lashes stark against the whiteness of her face. The girl was amazingly pretty, she thought, with that dark hair and those rose lips and fair complexion. If only there were some animation behind that exquisite façade.

"I heard that he was taken in your bed."

If Mercy had suddenly slapped her face she could not have been more startled or outraged. How dare this chit of a girl suggest such a thing, she thought angrily, then was surprised to see Mercy's usual bland expression turn sullen. Good God, she thought, the girl is jealous. Of me!

"Did you hear also that he only arrived a bare three minutes ahead of the pursuing rebels? Hardly time for an assignation. As a matter of fact, he was caught *under* the bed, not in it!"

Mercy had the decency to look embarrassed. "Of course, I never suspected . . ."

"How very kind of you."

"I mean . . ."

Celia sighed. "I know what you mean. It is unfortunate that my cousin Ewan was taken as he was, but not half so unfortunate as that he was taken at all."

"I only meant to suggest that I wish he had come here. We have several excellent hiding places where he might not have been discovered at all."

"I'm sure," Celia answered dryly. She was remembering the adoring look Mercy had cast at Ewan's retreating figure at her wedding so long ago. Obviously the girl's feelings had not altered. And they were promised to each other, strange as the union seemed.

"The bed was Ewan's choice, made in desperate haste. Not a very wise one, I fear."

She noted with satisfaction that her words brought a flash of anger to Mercy's eyes. "I am sure Colonel Deveroe knew exactly what he was doing," the girl said through tight lips.

Celia smiled to herself, savoring her opportunity to crack Mercy's reserve. It served her right. "You really care for him, don't you?" she said smugly.

Mercy blushed and turned away. "He is a most—a most agreeable gentleman."

"Agreeable" was hardly an apt description of Ewan, Celia thought, trying to suppress a giggle. "He is so caught up in this rebellion that I don't suppose he will be giving any thought to mundane things like marriage and home until it is over." It was a nasty jibe, but Celia could not resist.

For the first time Mercy's black eyes met hers directly and she was surprised at the steely conviction she saw there. "I shall wait," Mercy said quietly. "I have been waiting for him for years."

Celia tried not to laugh at the seriousness on the girl's face. All this adoring devotion—and for Ewan, a man who, dear as he was, seldom did anything except to please himself.

"He is worth waiting for," she said obliquely, then heard Mrs. Lawrence's red-heeled shoes tripping down the hall toward them. In a way she was sorry to be interrupted, for this was the first direct conversation she had ever shared with this enigmatic girl. Yet in another way she was relieved. Somehow she was not comfortable discussing Ewan in these circumstances and with his intended wife. She did not even like to think about the two of them together. Someday, when she had fewer problems of her own, she must ask herself why.

On the way home they stopped the chaise by the banks of the Bronx River to sit there in the mild weather. Richard spread a wool coverlet on the brown earth and Celia drew her thick shawl close around her face and shoulders, delighted to have this time together.

From where they sat near the river she could clearly see Ewan's house, pockmarked by last year's devastation, looking sad and lonely in the twilight.

Celia felt Richard's arm around her shoulders and she nestled against him. "Isn't it strange how an empty house seems almost to cry?" she said.

"That house has reason to cry. With Ewan's reputation he is fortunate it has not yet been razed to the ground. I can't think why it's been spared except that the rebels know he isn't there."

"Poor Ewan," she said, remembering her conversation with Mercy. "That Lawrence girl he is promised to is actually very much in love with him. I can't really take to her, but she is lovely to look at. I hope someday she gets over her excessive shyness, especially with Ewan for a husband."

"Mmmm," he murmured.

Celia sat up. "Richard, are you listening to me?"

"Of course, my dear."

"No, you were not. Confess it. What is preoccupying you so? You've been wool-gathering all day."

His gray eyes turned to slate, like the river before them. Then he smiled and pulled her back into his arms, nestling her head against his chest. After a long silence he plunged into the conversation he had been waiting all day to begin.

"Mr. Jay is likely to be leaving soon to join the Congress. He has asked me to go ahead of him to Lancaster as an observer, to send back firsthand reports. I'm to be his liaison, so to speak."

He felt her body stiffen in his arms. "He has just been appointed chief justice of the state, you know, and so is not certain when he can get down there himself. I'd be able to see the Continental Congress in action, Celia. I would be right at the center of this new government."

She sat up abruptly, filled with disappointment and a growing anger. "Lancaster! But that is wilderness." Actually she was not sure where it was except that it lay in the western section of Pennsylvania and on the edge of that vast unexplored Indian territory that no one knew anything about.

"Not quite wilderness," he began, as disappointed as she that their close moment had been lost. "It is much farther to the west than West Chester, of course, but the Congress will probably continue to meet there as long as General Howe occupies Philadelphia." He paused, studying her profile as she looked unseeing at the gray river. "I suppose it is pointless to urge you to move down to Wayside."

All her good intentions vanished into thin air. "Yes. Pointless."

"Then I shall trust in your uncommon ability to handle things here as well as you have in the past. There is not much more that I can do."

"You could stay at home!"

He gritted his teeth silently. How he dreaded the old, familiar quarrel. "We've been over this ground so many times, Celia . . ."

Impulsively she jumped to her feet, staring down at him with a wildness in her eyes. "It's because I'm barren, isn't it?" she said in a voice as cold as the air around them. Stunned, he could only stare at her incredulously.

"It's because I've never given you a child, isn't it, Richard. If you had a son—if you had children—you'd never go away like this and leave us to the mercy of marauders. You wouldn't! I know it. It is all my fault!"

"Celia," he said, jumping to his feet and trying to grab her hands as she wrenched them away. "Celia, my dearest wife. Childlessness has nothing to do with it. Have I ever, ever reproached you because God has not given us children? I had no idea you felt this way."

Her tears came flooding and she covered her face with her hands as he pulled her into his arms. "Oh, Richard," she sobbed, "I want a baby so badly. I don't have the comfort of a family and now, because of this war, I don't have your comfort either. If you loved me, really loved me, you'd stay by me."

This time she felt him stiffen. "And if you loved me you would either be an obedient wife and go away from here as I ask or at least freely allow me to follow my profession. Love moves both ways, Celia."

She slumped in his arms. In his quiet, rational way he would always beat down her arguments, ignore her feelings.

"Celia," he said, looking intently into her eyes, "no two people ever married more from love than we did. So many marriages are business arrangements, but we were allowed to follow our hearts. I care for you more than anyone in the world, but, Celia, you know I never wanted to be a farmer. I care nothing for agriculture, not now and not ever. Government, law, philosophy—almost anything you can name interests me more than crops and soil and breeding a better grade of wool. This new-hatched democracy is fighting for its life and I want to be in on its survival and evolution. That means everything to me. Everything."

It was an impassioned speech for Richard, and it moved her in a way she had never felt before. Everything he said was true and if she was honest with herself she must admit that she had known it all for years. Without her at the Manor House he would probably never have come back to care for it at all. It would have decayed and stood ravaged and empty just as Ewan's house now stood. Yet she could not give in.

"But, Richard, this land is all we have. It is our equity, our future."

Something of his quiet resolve finally broke and he turned angrily away from her. "Must I suffer all my life because you are so afraid of being poor!"

His words cut deeply. The chill air of the dusk stirred through her bones and she pulled her shawl tighter around her. Before she could answer he turned back, his anger gone as swiftly as it had come.

"I know," he said, trying to smile. "I've never *been* poor. But Celia, my love, the land is not going to go away. Even though it has become a battleground, it will still be here when the war is over." He laid his gloved hand against her cheek. There were no tears there now, but her face was flushed and angry. Drawing her hand through his arm, he started up the bank.

"Come, let's not spoil our Christmas Day with quarreling. Whatever happens, it will not be until next April or May, so we have many months to discuss the matter. Let's go in. It is getting cold out here."

She followed him silently up the bank and into the road, where the frost crunched under her iron creepers.

Not as cold as it will be inside the house, she thought bitterly.

It was well into January before Celia learned that Ewan was back in West Chester at his old command. Though Richard visited him at Morrisania, Ewan carefully avoided the Manor House, and it was not until she accidentally met a mounted patrol on the road near the Lawrences' that she saw him again,

sitting astride his beautiful black stallion with his silver epau-
lettes shining in the weak sunlight, every bit as haughty as
before. Her pleasure at seeing him free and active once more
was quickly soured by his brusqueness. He greeted her politely
enough, even warned her against riding the roads of West
Farms alone in these unsettled times, but she could not help
but notice the way he avoided her eyes and spoke with cold
civility. Celia rode home, her cheeks burning, both sorry and
angry at this cavalier treatment. All the sympathy and affection
she had always borne him carried no weight at all against his
hurt pride, he had made that obvious. So be it, then! She would
not look for concern or friendship from him again.

She saw Ewan only two or three times the whole of that
tumultuous spring, and each time his polite indifference only
reinforced her anger.

And what a terrible spring it was. With the coming of the
warm weather the raiding back and forth across the county
intensified, leaving the poor civilians in the path of the armed
patrols with barely enough on which to subsist. The Deveroes
managed to keep only a few horses and one cow by hiding
them in the woods. What crops they put in were in enclosed,
protected areas that would grow only enough to feed the oc-
cupants of the farm. What was the use of doing more when
anything extra was requisitioned? Celia hid everything of value
in her house, even their best clothes, and lived with the barest
of necessities.

In March Richard took a boat downriver to visit Wayside
and returned with a letter from Hester. Celia broke the seal and
settled back to read of Hester's life in England with an inner
excitement she had not felt for a long time.

"She was presented to the Queen," she read excitedly to
Richard, who sat puffing on his clay pipe and warming his feet
on the brass fender.

"She says Queen Charlotte is ugly and plump but excep-
tionally gracious. And the gorgeous gowns at the court are like
nothing we could even imagine, not to mention the diamonds
and rubies around everyone's neck. She loves London and says
it must be the most fascinating city in the world. Beside it,
New York is a country town. 'But,' she writes, 'you would
not believe the great contrasts here between the most wretched
squalor on the one hand and the most abundant luxury on the
other. Fine gentlemen strut in laces and velvet, but the streets
are full of thieves and beggars. The houses of the rich are

decorated in gold leaf and rich damask, but the mean, winding, dirty warrens of the poor make one despair.' "

"The poor of London must make a strong impression indeed for my sister to notice them, never mind despair."

"She says she met the famous Dr. Johnson at a supper party and he quite captivated her. He is the only man she ever saw who could insult every person present yet still have them go away thinking he was capital company."

"Yes, that is the sort of man who *would* appeal to Hester."

Celia looked up from her letter long enough to frown at her husband. "Now she writes that they have visited Cortlandt's titled relation, but they received a cool reception. However, they were invited for a visit to his stately home—a great pile of brick so filled with servants that if one but wants a glass of wine one has only to extend a hand."

"An exaggeration, I'm sure."

"Then she says—oh, but this is personal."

She read on to herself, reluctant to share with her husband the last of Hester's scrawled news. It seemed that all was not well for the Barnetts, as London was a frightfully expensive place to live in and they had not received the hoped-for preferment from their titled relation which had been the reason for making the trip. Besides that, the pleasures of the city were 'not such as would enhance family life,' being in effect, heavy drink, gambling at pharoah and whist, and loose women. Unfortunately, Cortlandt Barnett had taken to all three like a man born to debauchery. Underneath all Hester's enthusiasm for the sights and fashions of the city there was an undercurrent of real anxiety. Celia folded the foolscap to put it away and sighed.

"It must be wonderful to see a great city like London."

"Why, you won't even leave West Farms for New York. How do you imagine you will ever see any of the grander sights of this world?"

It rained the morning Richard left for Pennsylvania—a cold, dismal drizzle that turned the spring of May back to winter's frigidness. With dry eyes Celia kissed her husband, wrapped a knitted scarf she had made for him around his neck and wished him Godspeed. He was fastidiously dressed for such a long journey, in a plain brown coat with top boots and with a meticulously powdered wig under his tricorn hat. His thin face looked younger than ever, the darkly etched brows were drawn together and his gray eyes with their long lashes held depths of sadness and bewilderment she had never seen before.

"You know that I love you," he said self-consciously, fidgeting nervously with his hat. Beside him his horse stirred, restless to be away.

"I know. And I love you too. You are my dear husband and friend."

He blurted out, "I fear for you, leaving you here in this place, Celia."

"Richard, this is where I want to be. You are going where you want to be. Perhaps we have simply to accept that for each other."

He kissed her quickly, then bounded into the saddle. "I'll write you as often as I can."

Grasping his hand, she pressed it to her lips. "You must, you must."

Leaning down, he tipped up her chin and ran his gloved fingers along the line of her cheek. "Goodbye, my dearest wife."

Before she could answer he was off clattering down the road, his cloak billowing out over the horse's rump. Celia watched until a bend in the road took him from her sight. Then she drew her cloak tightly around her and started back inside the house.

Now, and only now, would she allow herself to cry.

It was more than a month before she heard from Richard, and by that time other concerns had driven resentment and hurt pride from her mind. She would look up from hoeing the garden to see a formation of red-coated infantry marching across the bridge, their boots rattling a tattoo on the planks. Or, hearing the thudding of horses on the road, she would pull away the linen curtains at the window to see sixty or more dragoons in green hussar coats and plumed hats galloping toward West Chester village. One day it would be the blue coats of the Hessians, the next the Loyalist Refugees in their tricolored uniforms. And almost every day there passed a troop of British regulars in their scarlet jackets and white gaiters, their Brown Bess muskets bouncing on their shoulders as they loped along.

Vestal managed to purloin her a copy of Rivington's *Royal Gazette* (that gentleman had returned to New York now that it was occupied by the King's forces and was back printing his newspaper) from a tavern near Hunt's Point. As she smoothed out the worn pages and read the tiny print, she began to realize the reasons for this sudden influx of British and Loyalist military units into lower West Chester.

These were the men, of course, of the army just returned from Pennsylvania. General Howe had been relieved of his command and had been replaced by General Clinton, who had abandoned Philadelphia and once again made New York City the base of British operations. In order to keep the supply lines to West Chester open an army of three thousand Hessians had been sent to the forts along the Harlem River, in addition to the Loyalist and hussar units.

Celia crumpled the paper in her lap and had a moment of serious reappraisal of her position. This was not exactly catastrophic news, by any means, for with all these regulars around her, surely the American patrols and the lawless Skinners would not be likely to venture down this far. But how safe could a woman alone be, without a husband to protect her and surrounded by hordes of armed men from differing cultures and countries? Even now she could see the beginnings of a blockhouse not half a mile from her door. What should she do?

"Misse Celia," Betsy called, poking her turbaned head around the doorjamb. "There's this gen'leman standin' in the yard . . ."

Oh, dear, Celia thought, another traveler on the road? Hopefully he was only a traveler and not the harbinger of one more disastrous visit by a mounted patrol.

Glancing quickly through the window, she was relieved to see a small man in a round hat, dressed completely in black, standing under the linden tree studying her door as though reluctant to knock.

"You don't 'pose he be one of them thieven' Skinners, ma'am?" Betsy slipped anxiously up behind Celia as she moved to the hall.

"No, no. He's a Quaker gentleman." That was bad enough. The Whigs held Quakers in greater contempt than Tories. "Let's see what he wants, and just in case I ask him in, you go into the kitchen and fix us some lemonade."

"Don't ask him in, Misse Celia! Not safe takin' in strangers off'n the road these wicked times." Her almond eyes widened in fear and her brown hands twisted in her apron.

Putting an arm around the girl's shoulders, Celia pushed her gently down the hallway toward the kitchen. "Go along, Betsy. I'll be all right."

"I send up Vestal. He be out weed'n in the garden. He don't mind."

"All right. It probably would not hurt to have him in the house, just in case." Celia looked back to see Betsy scurrying off through the kitchen, then carefully opened the front door just wide enough to see through.

"Who are you?" she called, dispensing with the polite formalities that might have been second nature in another time.

Startled, the little man moved toward the steps, stopping before the first one.

"Be this the home of the Deveroes? Art Mr. Deveroe to home?"

"Yes, it is. I am Mrs. Deveroe. Who are you? What do you want? My husband is not here at the moment." She opened the door a little wider.

"Ah, it was thee I hoped to see, madam. Would thee have a moment to speak with me?"

His round face looked so mild that Celia decided to risk opening the door.

"Oh, yes." He smiled when he saw her tall slim figure. "Thou art very young. Thee must be the one I wish to see."

Celia rested her hands at her waist and studied him. "You seem to know who I am, sir, but I do not have the same honor."

Without removing his hat he made her an elaborate bow. "Forgive me, mistress. I have been standing here so long wondering if I should approach that I have quite forgot my manners. Thou art speaking to Friend Elijah Lister, a member of the Society of Friends near Tuckahoe village. Perhaps I should also inform thee that I am just now returned from a visit with a mutual friend—the medical practitioner Jonas Sayre in West Chester village. Perhaps that good gentleman's name will offer thee some corroboration that I am who I say I am."

Celia felt herself relax. The man was obviously a genuine Quaker, and Dr. Sayre's name banished the last of her apprehension. "Forgive my poor manners, Friend Lister, but I have grown so accustomed to suspicion that I too forget the niceties of polite society. Won't you come in and take a glass of lemonade with me? I should be pleased to know how Dr. Sayre and his family get on."

She directed him into a morning room, where a still suspicious Betsy soon appeared with a tray and two small glasses, all that was left unhidden of Celia's fine crystal. Lister eagerly gulped down the welcome drink then came directly to the purpose of his visit.

"Thee once lived in East Chester, I believe, Mrs. Deveroe. Is that not so?"

"Yes. I was born there and lived there until I came here as a ward of the Deveroe family. But that was long ago."

"Madame, God has entrusted these last few years a poor, unfortunate soul to my keeping. He is the purpose of my seeking thee out. He is an old man and failing, who long ago knew and loved a little girl and watched her go off in a grand coach to live the life of a princess. He never forgot thee, Mrs. Deveroe."

Something stirred deep within her. It was as though a ghost from years past was suddenly recalled to stand before her, a brown figure with a shock of white hair and a gentle face.

"Oh, Friend Lister," she cried, sitting forward in her chair, "not Dominie Brec?"

"Exactly." He beamed, bouncing his fingertips together. "That good old man is exactly the one I speak of."

"He's still alive? But I thought they were all gone. I went through East Chester some time ago and I was told they had all moved to Lake Champlain. No one told me he stayed behind."

"Perhaps no one realized it. When these unfortunate civil divisions started, most of your French compatriots felt the need to be away, and, receiving a parcel of land from the new Congress, they went upstate to begin homesteading anew. But good Brother Brec even then was too infirm to start a new life in the wilderness, and he chose to stay behind. For some time he lived alone, but eventually, with his growing frailty, my wife and I took him to live with us. I need not tell thee, my dear, that it bothered us at first that he was of the Popish persuasion, yet we have found in knowing him that the sweetness of his disposition and the Christian piety he displays have overcome all other considerations. We are indeed deeply fond of him and it grieves us that he must soon be taken from us."

"He is dying, then? If only I had known before. I could have been of some help, I'm sure of it."

"There is little that he desires beyond setting his tired eyes once more on thy face. I think that all he has left of worldly wishes is to see thee once more and to know that thou hast grown to a fine young woman. I thought long and hard before approaching thee, wondering if perhaps like so many well-established young ladies thou wouldst not wish to be troubled by an old man's concerns. I even stood outside thy door asking our Lord which way should I go—back or forward."

"How could I not care about Dominie Brec? He was so very good to me. Of course I must go to him."

Frowning, Elijah Lister leaned forward, resting his arms on his knees. "I must tell thee, Mrs. Deveroe, that though such a visit would mean the world to this old man, it could involve direct dangers to thyself. We are right in the heart of the 'Neutral Ground,' and our lives are fraught with marauding soldiers by day and raids by night. It is not a safe journey I am proposing to thee."

"I have been up that way before. My husband took me to White Plains in '76 for the convening of the state Congress. And I have servants to go along. No, I will not keep away because of the risks. This is a small enough thing to do for a person whom I remember as a dear and loving friend."

Lister coughed, looking uncomfortable. "We have, of course, heard much of thy kinsman Colonel Deveroe's mounted horse up our way. Might I suggest that thou ask the Colonel for an escort. It would put my fears much to rest."

Celia looked quickly away. She could, of course, approach Ewan. It was not at all unreasonable, considering the dangers of the road. But no. He had grown so cool and distant to her of late—and all because of something that was in no way her fault. No, she would not swallow her pride to ask such a favor of him.

"I shall consider your request, Friend Lister. But now tell me exactly where your house is. I will not be able to start north until the first of next week, and by then I shall have worked out all the details."

"Excellent. If thou can furnish me with pen and ink I shall draw thee a little map. That should make it easier."

"Of course. I'll just be a moment." Quickly she ran up to the bedroom to bring down her writing box. She was filled with excitement. So Dominie Brec was still alive and wished to see her. The dear old man—it would warm her heart to kiss him again and receive his blessing as she had on that long-ago-day when as a frightened child she left her old life behind.

thirteen

She met opposition head on. Tom was furious at the idea of her venturing out on the roads on such a foolhardy errand, and to his objections were added the more subtle but equally adamant disapproval of her servants. When they finally concluded she had resolved on going and would surely carry out her threat to set out alone, they turned their minds to working out the safest way for her to make the trip. The duties of the farm were so demanding at this season that only one of them could be spared, but that must be the largest and strongest of all. Accordingly, Vestal combed his grizzled wig, brushed his best black suit and brought the chaise from its hiding place in a haysack to be washed down and have its axles greased with lard. Celia packed up what spare food they could afford to give away. Then, armed with her map and Richard's old but serviceable dueling pistol, she climbed aboard early one morning as the sun was expanding into a red rim above the trees, to set off down the road north toward White Plains.

A lurching, swaying, exhausting journey of many miles over rutted roads finally brought them up the old York Road past Mile Square and Tuckahoe village to a small, almost undefined track leading due west into the hills bordering the Saw Mill River. It was a lonely region of small domestic farms and thick wooded hillocks; only with difficulty did they finally stumble on Elijah Lister's run-down little homestead just as the noon sun reached its zenith.

Yet, for Celia, the rigors of the trip were all worthwhile when she saw the joy on the face of the frail old man who struggled to stand on his feet when she entered the farmhouse kitchen. Her dream of bringing him back to live with her in West Farms quickly fled, for he was much too fragile ever to survive the journey. In his archaic French, which she now found difficult to understand, he assured her he was ready to give up the struggle entirely since his eyes had once more rested on her lovely face and seen what a fine lady she had grown to be.

She lingered far too long, seeking news of the people she remembered from East Chester and recalling the happy memories of her father. Even Madame Peletaire, whom she still remembered with loathing, was the subject of long reminiscences. Mrs. Lister, a thin, nondescript, silent woman, had put together a poor dinner of salt pork and peas, and, because she knew what a feast it was for them, Celia purposely stayed to enjoy it. But it meant setting out later than she had planned, and Vestal's worried frown told her he suspected they might not reach home until after dark. Anxiously she kissed the old man, promising to return when she could and to send up some real wheat flour for the family when the harvest came in.

She twisted in the chaise, looking back to watch the dilapidated farmhouse until the overhanging trees masked it from view, then settled back to endure the long trip home to West Farms. After the intense heat of the day the skies were beginning to darken with thunderclouds. The chaise was rolling briskly down a long stretch of road shadowed by a canopy of tall trees, and Celia was congratulating herself for insisting she could make the trip safely, when suddenly a wheel lurched into a pot hole and broke away, sending the cab flying. Celia went tumbling with the chaise down into a heap on the road as Vestal jumped quickly off the seat and ran to grab the bridle of the rearing horse.

"Hold still, hoss!" Vestal called, struggling to calm the frightened animal. "Misse Celia, be you all right?"

Shaken, Celia crawled out from the frame of the chaise and stood up, slapping the dirt and dust from her skirts. "I think so, Vestal. Yes, I'm all right, thank goodness. But look—" her hand swept the upturned hood of the cab with its wheel lying off to one side—"what are we going to do about this? It could hardly be worse. Here, give me those reins and you look at that wheel and see if you can fix it. This is no place to be stranded."

They had, worse luck, been caught in an isolated section of the old York Road, thick with overhanging trees and the loud whisperings of the forest around them. Far to the north she remembered passing the small Clark farm, and she guessed that the substantial Willett house was nearly as far south. But here there was nothing.

"This wheel, he need but little fixin'," Vestal finally pronounced. "Blacksmith he do it, no time."

"Yes, but we don't happen to have a blacksmith at hand!"

"Misse Celia, I believe it right you mount that hoss, I lead him, and we walk to blacksmith. What say you?"

Celia rubbed a finger across her lip. Vestal had hit on what was probably the most sensible way out of this catastrophe, but it meant abandoning the chaise here, and any kind of vehicle these days was too prized a possession to leave unguarded. Her chaise meant not only convenience but status. Did she really want to lose it?

"No, Vestal," she answered. "I want you to unhitch the horse and ride him to Willett's place up ahead. Get the wheel fixed there—they'll help you, I'm sure. Then come straight back with it. That is the quickest way to repair the damage and get back on the road."

She could see the stubborn lines settle on his dark face. "Misse Celia, I don't hole with leavin' you here by you'self. It be too dang'rous."

"I know it's dangerous, but I'll be all right. Look..." She rummaged under the chaise and drew out her basket with the pistol. "I have a gun, and, besides, what do I have to fear? I know most of the farmers in these parts, and they have always treated me with courtesy."

"But supposin' them soldiers come ridin' by? Or them debbil Skinners! Misse Celia, it the wrong way. Massa Richard, he skin my hide, I leave you here alone!"

"He won't know anything about it. And if more than one person rides by, I'll hide in the woods. As soon as I hear their horses I promise I'll run for cover. Come, now, Vestal, you're wasting precious time."

"Please, Misse."

But Celia had had enough. "Vestal, I order you to mount that horse and get that wheel fixed. Get along at once. I'll be all right."

What could he do? With a terrible foreboding in his heart, he climbed aboard the horse and, hanging tightly on to the wheel, went hurrying off down the road, not even daring to look back. When she could no longer hear him or see him, Celia spread her light cloak on the grassy bank and sat down to prime her pistol as the heavy silence of the woods closed around her. She was not even sure she could fire the gun, though Richard, the first time he left home, had made sure she practiced it. Perhaps she would be lucky and no one at all would come along the road. She strained for the slightest sound that might indicate a horse treading the packed earth, but all she could hear were the chatterings of the insects, the rustlings of the trees in the woods around her, and, over the hills toward the river, the first deep rumblings of thunder from the Catskills.

Ewan shifted his weight in the saddle, cursing the fierce July heat that kept his wet shirt clamped to his back under his heavy military coat. For the hundredth time he waved away the flies that buzzed around his hair, lured by the pomade on his wig. Far down below he could see the Willett house peaceful in the growing dusk, the only movement a figure that now and then crossed between the outbuildings, small as an ant in the distance.

The silence around him was broken by the constant swishing of Goliah's thick tail and the drone of the fat bluebottle flies. Then he caught from the trees behind him the sharp laughter of the men of Tarleton's platoon.

To hell with this! he thought. I've been watching that house for half an hour and if there's an ambuscade down there I'll eat my hat. I'll be damned if I'll give up my supper for some arrogant puppy of an Englishman, even if he is a lieutenant colonel!

Turning Goliah toward the trees, he picked his way slowly through the brush to a natural clearing deep inside the woods, where several soldiers in short green jackets leaned against tree trunks, passing around a canteen. Judging by their hilarity, it contained something more potent than water. Their commanding officer, handsome, arrogant and very young to be a lieutenant colonel, sat on a stump off to the side fingering a silver filigreed canteen of his own. He barely gave Colonel Deveroe a glance when Ewan dismounted and strolled over.

"Colonel Tarleton," Ewan said briskly, "that Willet house is as peaceful as I've ever seen it. I take it you've no more need for me, so, if you've no objection, I think I will ride down there and beg a little supper."

Tarleton barely lifted one shapely eyebrow. "Have you abandoned hope of surprising our rebel patrol today, Colonel Deveroe?"

"Isn't it obvious that either they've eluded us or they were never there? We've been thrashing around in these woods long enough to know it by now."

Tarleton's fine black eyes narrowed. "I don't recall asking your advice, Colonel. I make the decisions in this platoon."

Ewan bristled at the man's arrogance. Damned stripling, strutting it over better men because General Clinton had favored him with a promotion in the King's dragoons. Hadn't Ewan himself grown up riding these roads? He'd known hours ago there was no American patrol in this area. A damned wild-goose chase, this whole thing!

He shrugged and moved away, nearly colliding with a horse-man from one of Tarleton's scouting platoons who had just ridden in.

"No sign of any rebels, Colonel Tarleton," the man said, wiping his arm across his wet brow. "But I found something else almost as interesting. There's a young lady on the road a few miles back with a chaise that sprung a wheel."

"A lady! Alone on the road?" Tarleton's attention immediately picked up.

"That's right, sir. Her slave went ahead with the wheel to fix it. He's down there now at that farmhouse over the hill while she's waiting back there alone for him to return."

Tarleton lowered his voice. "Now, that is the first diverting development in this entire day. Tell me about her. Is she really a lady or could she, perhaps, be a lady's maid?"

"Why, I don't know—" The soldier flinched at the look his superior threw at him. Lieutenant Colonel Tarleton was known for his willingness to strike a man on slight provocation. "She might be a lady's maid, sir. She's not fancy dressed, that's for sure."

"Now, that sounds very interesting indeed." Picking up his fur hat Tarleton set it jauntily on his handsome head. "I think we should help this damsel in distress. It is not at all safe for a woman to be out alone on deserted roads, especially with darkness falling."

Ewan walked up in time to hear this last comment. "So you've found a lady to assist, Colonel? Well, that should at least make your day worthwhile."

The sarcasm was ignored. Tarleton had a reputation as a womanizer that would do credit to a much older man. "Colonel Deveroe," the Englishman called. "You have my permission to go along to that farmhouse and divest them of a meal."

"I'm not at all sure I need your permission, Colonel."

Tarleton shrugged. "You Refugees are so touchy about protocol. Very well, then. You have my leave to go searching for your dinner while I shall go after my 'dessert.'"

Ignoring the crude jest, Ewan turned Goliah's nose west while behind him he could hear Tarleton issuing orders: "Private Hanson, bring up my horse. Lieutenant Rogers, take all the patrol except Subaltern Rutgers and ride down to the Morrell Tavern. Rutgers and I will rescue this lady and join you there."

The lieutenant hesitated but finally spoke up. "Are you sure you won't want a few more troopers to accompany you, Colonel? Suppose this is a rebel trap and that woman is the bait?"

Tarleton was already in the saddle. "I'll risk it. Such a plan would require far more finesse than these rustics have shown so far."

By the time Celia heard the horses approaching, the first light drops of rain were beginning to fall, and the thick trees had grown so dense she was almost relieved to know someone was coming down the lonely road. Perhaps it was Vestal returning with another horse for her. If so, she would willingly go along with him this time. It had not taken her long, alone in this secluded spot, to decide that perhaps a chaise was not so precious a possession after all. All the same, she moved back to the shelter of the first trees and kept her primed pistol ready at her waist.

The green coats of the dragoons merged so well with the forest that she almost didn't recognize them until they were nearly upon her. Then, when she tried to shrink farther into the shadows, to her dismay she heard them call her out. Somehow they had learned she was there, and she could only hope that Vestal had sent them back for her.

She knew enough about British uniforms by now to recognize an officer's gold braid and feathered hat in the dusk, and she could tell that the stylish young man who dismounted and approached her was one of the most dashing officers she had ever seen. Cautiously she stepped from the shelter of the trees.

Tarleton sized her up in one glance. She was naïvely young and dressed in the simple country garb of these rebel farmers—no doubt some virtuous country girl. If he played his cards properly this little lass might provide him with a diverting evening after all.

"Mistress," he said, sweeping off his fancy fur hat, "may

I introduce myself. Lieutenant Colonel Banastre Tarleton of the British Legion. My scout saw that you were stranded here, told me of it and we came at once to assist you."

Celia sighed with relief and, lowering her pistol, offered him her hand. "Madam Celia Deveroe, sir. And I am indeed stranded. The wheel to my chaise came off and my servant has gone forward to the Willet house to repair it. I am so very relieved to have your assistance, Colonel."

"Madam," Tarleton said silkily, bending over her fingers. He barely caught her name, he was so busy calculating. Married, was she? All the better. At least his harmless seduction would not be ruining a young virgin for life. And this was a very pretty woman with her glossy curls and amber eyes.

"So happy to be of service, madam. My subaltern will see that your chaise is repaired and returned to you. In the meantime, may I carry you to the Willett house myself? It would be a far more appropriate place for you to wait than this lonely road."

"That is very true, Colonel, and I confess that after the time I have spent here I would be relieved to wait among friends. Thank you."

Casually Tarleton reached out and took her pistol, grinning as he turned it over in his hands. "I very much doubt if this ancient weapon could be fired. Was this the extent of your protection?"

Celia smiled. "Yes. Pitiful as it is, I doubt I would have ever had the courage to fire it, but my husband insisted I carry it while traveling."

"In these perilous times, madam, the safest protection is simply to stay at home. Allow me."

Handing her up, he vaulted up behind her on his magnificent English stallion. With a few orders to Rutgers, he was off down the road. Even with the two of them astride, Celia had not had such a smooth, swift ride since the last time she had mounted her own Kit. She cast one last lingering look at her broken chaise, certain she would never see it again, then settled back in relief.

Her first apprehension came when Tarleton, with his arm tightly around her, cantered right past the entrance to the Willett farm. Celia struggled to turn in the saddle and tell him his mistake, watching with a sinking heart as the whitewashed buildings faded into the misty rain behind her. When they were well past the entrance, Tarleton pulled up his horse and she turned on him, angry and incredulous.

"Colonel, I cannot believe you did not realize when we passed Master Willett's. Why didn't you turn in?"

Tarleton's smile was condescending. "Now, don't concern yourself, Madam ... Celia? That was your name was it not? A very pretty one too. I only had the thought that instead of putting up at the Willetts', which must be unprepared for company, we would go a little further and stop at Morrell's Tavern down the road, where my own troop awaits me. That should suit you better, I should think."

"On the contrary, Morrell's is not suitable at all. It is a disreputable place and will probably be filled with soldiers. I cannot believe you would wish to carry me there against my wishes."

"Perhaps it is not elegant, but, madam, you must admit that for a British officer to ride into a rebel stronghold like Willett's farm might be a trifle risky. You will be perfectly safe at Morrell's, and I personally shall see that you have the very best accommodations."

"Mr. Willett tries very hard to remain a neutralist," she said lamely, sensing the iron will beneath the Colonel's gentlemanly facade.

"Perhaps I was mistakenly informed. But please do not be concerned. You shall be completely under my protection."

There was little she could do, pinned against him on his horse, yet she was not at all sure now that she wanted this officer's protection. There was something in his manner that suggested she should be highly pleased to be carried away by him. Celia began to wish she were back on the empty road beside her upturned chaise.

The first sight of Mr. Morrell's run-down tavern did not reassure her, yet when Tarleton handed her down and hurriedly led her through the hot, crowded, smoke-filled room to a secluded nook at the rear, she began to feel a little better. He spoke to the tavernkeeper, then stepped in beside her and yanked across the mud-colored curtain that hung over a rope across the doorway. Celia sat down at the tiny table and looked around nervously, noting that there was not another door in the room and that the one window was fastened tight by its outside shutters.

Setting a green bottle on the plank table, the Colonel poured out two cups of a poor grade of claret. Downing his in a long swallow, he hung his hat on a wall peg and pulled up a chair across from her, the very picture of a proper gentleman. Celia sipped her wine, which felt deliciously warm going down, and relaxed enough to sit back in her chair, studying the young man opposite her. His fine features were drawn with fatigue and in the dim light she could tell that he had already had a lot to drink. In spite of that, he kept up a light, bantering, polite conversation. Yet there was a nagging worry in the back of her mind all through the simple supper the landlord laid before them. The small room was stifling hot with the window shuttered, but the Colonel made no move to open it, and the homespun curtain did nothing to close out the roars of laughter and the rowdy singing from the other room that increased with each round of porter.

"Is it not somewhat dangerous, Colonel, for your troop to be enjoying themselves so freely this far above your lines?" she asked hesitantly.

Tarleton shrugged. "We've covered enough of the territory around this tavern today to know there are no Americans down this far. And if some should come along, thinking to surprise us, our pickets will give us ample warning. Besides, by daybreak we'll be back at Morrisania."

That was a relief. Perhaps after supper he would be on his way, leaving her to spend the night here and ride back to West Farms tomorrow. It was silly of her to worry. Yet, as she idly picked at her salted cod and biscuit she wished that the Colonel would take more of his supper from his plate and less from his bottle.

"Are you sure you won't have a second piece of pie, Colonel Deveroe? Our Mindy makes the very best berry pie in these parts, as you well know."

Ewan propped his feet against the brass fender before the empty hearth and settled back in his chair. He had not felt so contented and well fed for many a day.

"No, thank you, Mrs. Willett. Excellent as it was, one is enough. I certainly am grateful for that meal. It was a proper feast."

Martha Willett beamed under the handsome Colonel's praise and arched her back a little in her straight chair the better to show off her full, shapely breasts under her low-cut, ruffled neckline. Outside she could still hear the sounds of the hammer on the iron in Mr. Willet's shed and she calculated there would still be a good half hour before her husband left off helping that slave to fix a wheel and joined them in the kitchen. Artfully she leaned forward and picked up a clay pipe, handing it to Ewan. She could feel his eyes on her. Well, why not? Mr. Willett was old and she was still young. And the Colonel was a fine-looking man with a knowing gleam in his eye. His visits were rare enough these days and she intended to savor every minute of this one.

"Won't you take a pipe, Colonel?" she said, giving Ewan her brightest smile as she twirled a long curl that fell from under her cap.

"Why, thank you, yes. Just the thing to set off such a supper."

"Here," she cried, jumping up and lighting a spill from a candle. "Let me strike it for you." She bent forward to put the taper to the bowl, giving Ewan a good view of her décolletage while he puffed away at the clay pipe.

By God, here would be a fine romp in the hay, he thought to himself, then settled back and trained his gaze on the beamed ceiling. No. She was tempting and she was certainly willing, but he had no intention of courting disaster. Old Avery Willett would beat her black and blue and shoot him besides. And he would lose one of the most excellent spots in the county to drop in for a meal or spend a quiet night. Since his disastrous capture he had made it a habit never to sleep in the same place twice. Never again did he intend to be dragged shamefully out from under a bed, and to prevent it he had cultivated a whole string of hideaways. He never stayed with his men if he could avoid it, and where he did stay no one but he ever knew.

Glancing over at young Mrs. Willett with her pretty curls and white throat, he sighed, regretting that safety was more important than a delightful interlude. Then he noticed that the hammer blows from the shed had finally stopped.

"Sounds as though that visitor has his wheel fixed."

"Yes, I suppose he does by now," she said, touching her ringlets. If the Colonel only knew that that Negro out there belonged to his kinsman he would be out of his chair and in his saddle in a flash. But she had carefully avoided mentioning that a Deveroe black had come to their door earlier, and though it caused her to feel some slight guilt, that was more than compensated by the pleasures of flirtation. All at once, to her consternation, she heard her husband's heavy boots on the stone steps before the kitchen door. 'S death! He was coming in much earlier than she had hoped.

"Here, now, Ewan," Avery Willett spoke gruffly from a washbasin near the door.

"How've you been?" he asked, drying his hands and extending one to the Colonel. "It's been some time since we're seen you."

"I've kept busy, Avery. Your mistress here has given me a fine supper and I'm grateful to you both."

"Will you be stayin' the night?"

"No, I must get along, thanks all the same. I'm only lingering now to finish this excellent pipe."

"Aye, enjoy it. Come on, mistress, get my supper. Such a woman, wants to sit and gossip instead of waiting on her man."

Annoyed that her tête-á-tête was over, Martha Willett let her temper get the best of her. "I've worked all day," she exclaimed testily. "A lady is entitled to sit for a while after supper. And genteel conversation is not gossip, though *you'd* never know the difference!"

"Woman," Willett shouted, and launched into a tirade as loud as her own.

Tuning out their noisy accusations and amused at them both, Ewan settled back to enjoy his pipe. Whoever that had been with the broken wheel, he must have gone on or Willett would not have come inside. Unless, that is, he mistrusted his young wife enough to worry over leaving her alone with a younger man. Oh, well, Willett's problems were none of his concern. He would leave soon now before this squabble turned vicious. At least he had got a good supper.

In spite of all the wine he had drunk, when Colonel Tarleton got to his feet and picked up the tin candleholder he was as steady as when he had taken Celia down from his horse.

"Come, now, my dear, and I'll show you to your night's bed," he said smoothly. He knew without seeing it what that meant—rope springs, straw, corn husks or horsehair in the mattress, clammy sheets which had been used by God knows whom before them, and an assortment of vermin happily at home, ready to receive visitors. But he had no intention of sleeping in such a bed, and for what he did propose to use it, it would suit perfectly.

Celia stirred uneasily. Tarleton was looking her up and down suggestively. She was beginning to feel terribly afraid.

"I'm sure I could find it myself, thank you, Colonel."

He laughed. "Come, now, Madam Celia, do you really want to thread your way through those men out there alone?"

Celia made a valiant effort to keep her hold on reality in a situation which was taking on more and more of the texture of a nightmare.

"My experience of the British army, Colonel, is that they have always acted as gentlemen and treated me with courtesy, the regulars as well as the officers."

"Perhaps so, but I wonder if you have ever been alone in a place like this without the helpful presence of husband or servants. My men are tired and a long way from the discipline of their billets. They have also had a great deal to drink. It would not be to their discredit if they perhaps got, shall we say, the wrong idea of your situation."

He might as well be describing himself, Celia thought, yet there was some truth in what he said. Better to have to fight off one man than several, even if right now that one seemed the most dangerous of them all.

"Very well, Colonel. I shall appreciate your assistance."

Tarleton bowed and motioned her toward the curtain. Then in one quick movement taking a grip on her arm, he steered her through the crowded room toward the stairs. Ignoring the smirks of the men, she tried to summon all the dignity she possessed, but once she was at the top of the stairs her courage almost failed her. How had she come to be here in this dingy tavern with this man almost pushing her toward what she felt in her bones was going to be an unpleasant confrontation?

Glancing sideways at the Colonel, she took in the fine lines of his lusty, youthful face. She well knew that there were plenty of girls who would dance up these stairs at the idea of bedding such a man. What was wrong with her that she felt only anger and foreboding? It was surely not because she didn't welcome lovemaking itself. During Richard's long absence there had been nights when she felt she would die for the want of a man. But not like this! Not with this arrogant officer who treated her like a servant there for the taking. She was a lady, accustomed to consideration and respect. Besides, under Tarleton's gentlemanly façade there was the suggestion of something disturbing—something cruel and hard. She would have given almost anything she possessed at that moment to be back in her safe, shabby bedroom at the Manor House.

The larger hall was filled with beds, listing at all angles and covered with tattered quilts. At one end was the only room

Morrell kept for travlers who could afford a little privacy, and it was into this room that Tarleton half pulled her, closing the door behind him.

With a sinking heart, Celia turned to face him, trying to brazen it out.

"Colonel, thank you for your help," she said in her most ladylike manner. "I shall always be grateful."

He smiled and moved to set the candle on the table beside the bed. Then, to her chagrin, he began pulling off his green jacket.

There was no use pretending now. Celia stepped away from him and felt the rough splintered wood of the door pressing into her back.

"Colonel Tarleton, I think you forget yourself. If you are truly a gentleman, you will leave me alone here."

"Madam," Tarleton smirked, "let us forget all this talk of gentlemen and ladies. You are a woman and I, as you have no doubt noticed, am very much a man."

In his waistcoat and fine linen shirt dripping Alençon lace, he moved against her, pinning her to the door with his lean body. Bracing one arm against the wood frame, he dropped his head and kissed her long and hard. Shrinking from under him, she experienced a myriad of impressions—his bony hips pressing against her skirt, the hard bulge in his tight breeches, his lips cold and insistent, the door biting into the thin fabric of her summer frock as she twisted to get free. And then, an upsurge of the most searing, all-consuming fury she had ever known. How dare this cad force himself upon her! Was she some kind of loose woman that he thought he could take as he wished? No one in all her life had treated her with such callous contempt. Her rage drove out all other feelings.

When he finally lifted his head, she twisted out of his grip and slapped his face with all the power she could summon. He was startled by the blow, and she took advantage of his surprise to tear frantically at the door, almost wrenching it free. But Tarleton recovered quickly, and with a yelp he slammed it shut and, brutally grabbing her shoulder, pulled her away from the door and across the room. Furious, Celia locked her arms around the solid oak bedpost and clung frantically. Suddenly he stopped, his whole tone changed and he stepped away, trying to regain control of his temper.

"Forgive me, madam," he said, visibly subduing his anger.

"I am not accustomed to having my face slapped by young ladies and I quite forgot myself."

"If you treat other young ladies as you have me, I should think you would be *thoroughly* accustomed to it," Celia said in clipped tones, distrusting his new politeness just as deeply as she did his old ruthlessness.

Tarleton stepped up and lightly ran one hand across her shoulder. His face was so near her own she turned away to avoid his heavy claret-scented breath.

"You are a lovely woman, Mrs.—Madam Celia. I find myself quite distracted by your beauty."

"Get away from me!"

Silkily he got one arm around her neck in spite of the heavy bedpost while with the other he began working his way up her bodice. Celia writhed but found she was pinned against the post just as firmly as she had been against the door. She was never going to get away from this man without submitting to the indignity of his lust, and the thought of it sent tremors of fear through her. Tarleton felt them and, assuming that his hot hands were warming her cool blood, renewed his seduction with a vengeance.

"My husband will kill you for this," Celia muttered through clenched teeth.

He pictured some fat country farmer. "Perhaps he will find that he has bitten off more than he can chew!"

Covering her face with his kisses, he found her mouth and this time tried to force his tongue through her stubborn lips. Celia twisted furiously under his grip until she was able to force him off balance and break away. He was past finesse now, and, lunging at her, he caught the thin fabric of her dress, tearing it down the back where the laces were weakest. Celia grabbed at her dress to hold it together with one hand while reaching out with the other for the first thing she could find— a large tin flint striker. Turning, she threw it across the small space, catching him on the forehead.

He gasped, "Well, I'm damned!" and dabbed his hand at the trickles of blood that the sharp edge of the flint had raised.

"You little she-devil. So *that's* the way it's to be, is it?"

"Don't you touch me," Celia cried. "I'll scream my head off. I'll bring them all up here."

He only laughed. "Do you really think they would hear you? Or that if they did, anyone of them would dare to interrupt?

Oh, no, my girl. You belong to me for the time being, so you might as well give in and enjoy it. Enough others of your sex have."

"Then go and find one who likes to be treated that way and leave me alone."

"Ah, but you are here and they are not. Besides, there is nothing I like better than a woman who gives me a fight, unless it's a horse that does the same. Subduing both is the best sport in the world!"

Grabbing her arm, he pulled her to him and she felt her dress slipping. Pummeling him with her fists, she heard him laugh as he caught her hands while her dress fell around her feet, leaving her in her petticoat and chemise. Without bothering to strip her of those, he lifted her easily and carried her to the bed, throwing her down on the lumpy mattress. Celia scrambled toward the top of the bed as he dug at his own clothes. She tried to scream, but his hand closed over her mouth and she felt herself slipping, falling under this body, this force that crushed both body and spirit in its debasing assault.

"No, no, please . . ." she heard herself crying and, from the dim reaches of a suffocating blackness, recognized the despair in her own voice.

fourteen

The angry scene with his wife left Avery Willett immersed in an aggrieved silence that neither of his two companions bothered to break, one out of a fury of her own and the other from bored disinterest. Finally, Ewan broke off the end of the pipe he had been smoking, rose to replace it on the mantel and adjusted his coat.

"I'll be off now, Avery. My thanks once more for the fine supper."

"No trouble, Ewan. Come again." Willett's polite words almost but not quite overcame his surly manner.

With a bow to the wife of the house, now sitting across the room with two furious pink spots on her white cheeks, Ewan left them to their bad humors and, with a sigh of relief, headed out back to the smokehouse where he had hidden his horse.

He was gone only a few minutes before the clatter of a rider in the yard brought both ill-tempered Willetts to their feet. The mistress, hoping that perhaps the dampness had changed Colonel Deveroe's mind and he was returning to spend the night, anxiously peeked through the kitchen window.

"Oh, it's only that black servant again," she muttered, as Vestal, his haste overcoming his training, banged on the door, then threw it open to step inside.

"Massa Willett!"

"What is it, man?" Willett growled, barely noticing the fright on the Negro's face. "Did the wheel break again?"

"No, sur. She be gone! Misse Celia, she not be there when I returns."

"You mean she was not waiting by the shay?"

"No, sur. I look everywhere, but she not there. I calls and calls, but she not answer. What I do, Massa Willett? I fear somethin' terrible bad happen! What I do?"

"Why, I'm sure I don't know what to tell you. Anyone could have come down that road and carried her off. The foolish woman should never have stayed there alone."

Vestal's long fingers crushed the wet brim of his round hat. "I gots to find her, Massa Willett, and I doesn't know where to look! Jesus Lord . . ."

"Now, calm down, calm down. I'll get my hat and help you, at least until it gets too dark to see. Martha," Willett said, turning to his wife, "would you be so good as to light a lantern for us?"

"Light it for yourself, Mr. Willett," she snapped and flounced from the room.

"I light him," Vestal cried, springing up to the hearth.

Willett stood looking after his wife. That woman needed a good thrashing, she did, and now was the time to give it to her. The nerve of her refusing his command, and in front of a servant, too. Damned harridan. He'd show her who ran this household. Let Mrs. Deveroe solve her own problems, for they were surely of her own making.

"Vestal, you go ahead and I'll join you in a while," he said through pursed lips. Poor Vestal felt his best help slipping from his grasp.

"But Massa Willett, Misse Celia she might be in bad trouble."

"I'll come soon enough. Take the lantern and go on ahead."

The pitiful look Vestal gave him caused him a moment of guilt, but, looking back at the stairs, he quickly threw it off. Just as the huge black was nearly out of the doorway he thought of Ewan and called him back. Why hadn't this occurred to him before?

"Vestal, Colonel Deveroe was here just now. He must be only a short distance down the road. If you hurry you'll catch up with him. He'll help you. After all, she's his kinswoman. You can borrow the lantern."

Vestal felt his first glimmer of hope. "Massa Ewan? He here? Which way he go?"

"I don't know. He never tells anyone where he's headed. But you'll find him, I'm sure. If not, come back and get me. Good luck."

Willett was already fingering a hickory switch from the kindling basket as Vestal, swinging his lantern, bounded out the door, slamming it closed behind him. He took one quick circle around the yard on his mount, but there was no sign of any horseman, so he headed toward the road, black in the gathering dusk and stretching away empty in both directions. *Which way to go?* He prayed a silent prayer to his forefather's dark god of the forest, and dropped off his horse to study the tracks in the mud. Yes, one looked new, and the deep hoofprints certainly fit the kind of horse the Colonel rode. Repeating an ancient singsong African incantation, he climbed back aboard the horse's back and started as fast as he dared down the lonely road in the darkness.

He caught up with Ewan only a few miles away from the Willett farm, not on the road at all but in a field stretching away to the east. Had he not had the lantern he would never have found him. Quickly he told the startled Colonel, who could scarcely believe his eyes to see a family servant this far north of West Farms, how Celia had been left by the road and had disappeared. It took Ewan only a few mental leaps to put the woman whom Tarleton had dashed off to "rescue" together with his cousin's wife, and then his mingled fury and fear knew no bounds. For the first time in Vestal's life he saw the Colonel nearly speechless.

"I can't believe it. I can't believe she would be so stupid!"

"We gots to find her, Massa Ewan. She be frightened out in this night, him so dark."

"Ha! It would serve her right if she got the fright of her life, and if I know Tarleton, she probably will. I'd bet everything I own he took her to Morrell's, and that's where we'll look first. Come along, Vestal, make that horse move."

Their mounts were nearly blown by the time they raced up to the bend in the road where the black shape of the tavern loomed in the darkness. Instead of riding to the front, where several horses stood nodding at a hitching post, Ewan left Vestal to cool off the horses and went to reconnoiter the building. He had no intention of dashing in half cocked to fight off a platoon of British dragoons.

Just above the lilac-shrouded necessary house Ewan could see dim chinks of light showing through the shutters. He knew the tavern well enough to know that that light was coming from the only private room, and likely if Celia was here at all she was in that bedroom. Then he went back to the front of the tavern and spoke sternly to Vestal before they climbed the low steps to the porch.

"We'll go in together and I'll slip upstairs while you stay

down in the taproom where everyone can see you. Beg a meal or offer to work—do anything that will keep you there."

"I don't know, Massa Ewan. I don't thinks too good some-times . . ."

"You don't have to think, you have to be seen! As long as they see you they'll think I'm upstairs as well. If I don't come down in, say, half an hour, just stay there a while and then leave. Go back to the Manor House. If I do find Mrs. Deveroe, I'll get her home myself. Do you understand?"

Vestal nodded. He didn't like this at all, but if it helped get Miss Celia home safely, then he supposed he had to do it.

One look around the stifling, smoky taproom and Ewan knew that Tarleton was not among the lounging soldiers en-joying their drink. Spotting the young dragoon who had earlier that day brought the news of Celia's broken chaise, he sauntered over and asked a few questions, quickly confirming his fears that the Colonel was upstairs sporting with the rescued lady. The obscene jokes and comments the soldiers threw around about Colonel Tarleton's favorite kind of recreation made his skin turn dark under his military wig, but he controlled his anger. Then, settling Vestal near the hearth, he cautiously worked his way to the stairs and, as soon as he felt that no one was paying any attention to him, vanished up to the second floor. In the large room above there were already one or two soldiers passed out on the blue-and-white patched coverlets. He stood outside the door of the private room, listening only long enough to hear the sounds of the struggle inside and Celia's muffled cries. At that he burst into the room, keeping enough presence of mind to drop the bar into the slots behind him.

In the creamy glow of the candlelight he could make out only the shape of the bodies struggling together on the bed.

"Tarleton, you blackguard," he shouted, "take your hands off my cousin!"

The Colonel's sword belt was lying on the floor near his feet. Quickly Ewan grabbed it up and drew out the ornate sword. He'd kill the bastard if he had to! Run him through with his own blade and enjoy it.

Ewan's roar was like a pitcher of freezing water thrown over Tarleton's ardor. Jumping back more from instinct than thought, Tarleton leaped for his sword and saw it glinting in Deveroe's hand. He stared at Ewan, rage, bewilderment and disappointed hopes all written on his face. Slowly the word "cousin" began to sink through his lust-clouded consciousness.

Behind him Ewan had an impression of Celia's white, shocked face framed by her tangled hair, watching him through stricken eyes. And in her shift too, damn the bloody rake!

Tarleton had the grace to look flustered. "Cousin? Why, I had no idea..." Several disjointed pieces began to fall together. Damn, he should have known, though. Now that he remembered, she did say her name was Deveroe, and all these colonial families were related!

"Look here, Colonel Deveroe," he said, backing away from Ewan's black face and murderous eyes. "It was a mistake. I did not realize that the lady was your kinswoman. It was just a...a romp."

"Did you ask?" Ewan's voice was cold as ice. "Was it a romp for her as well? Damn you, Tarleton. I know you for a ravisher of women, but I know my cousin too, and I'll wager there was more of rape than romp in this night's work. I ought to run you through."

Tarleton's outrage was beginning to get the better of his momentary guilt. "Now, wait a minute. I stand here unarmed. You'd be bringing a lot of trouble down on your head, Colonel, if you kill me."

"Ewan!" Celia managed to get the words out. "Don't kill him, please. He's not worth ruining yourself."

Some glimmer of the sense in her words broke through his icy fury. Throwing the sword point into the plank floor, he lunged for Tarleton's throat, catching him off guard long enough to send him crashing to the floor. Grasping his hands tightly around his neck, he banged his head up and down against the floor.

"Ewan!" Celia screamed, scrambling to her knees on the bed. "Stop it! You'll kill him. Stop!"

He heard her finally, and, grabbing Tarleton by his ruffled stock, he raised his head far enough from the floor to crash his fist against the elegant chin. Tarleton fell in a heap, unconscious, and Ewan, drained now of his rage, stood over him, rubbing his bruised knuckles.

Then he remembered that they had very little time. Once the Colonel came to, there would be hell to pay. He looked up to see Celia still sitting motionless on the bed, her hands covering her face.

"Get up," he barked. "We've got to get out of here before he wakes up."

He expected an argument, but she only looked at him

blankly. "Get up!" he cried again, yanking her off the bed. "Where is your dress?"

"There on the floor. But I can't wear it. It's torn."

"Here," he said brusquely, taking off his sweaty coat and forcing her arms into the sleeves. "Put this on and hurry. We'll go out the window."

Like someone in a daze Celia let him lead her. With one good thrust he broke the ancient catch to throw the shutters open and handed her out onto the roof of the shed. A short slide brought them to the ground, where, lifting her up into his saddle, he jumped up behind her, gripping one arm around her waist. Guiding Goliah with his other hand, Ewan made a fast sprint through the woods to some hidden paths that quickly left the noise and confusion of the tavern far behind. Darkness and silence closed around them, only Goliah's thudding hoofs breaking the pattern of the night. Never once did she ask where they were going.

It seemed to Celia that they rode for hours. A gentle rain began falling, and before long they were both thoroughly wet and chilled in spite of the hot day just past. She accepted the thumping ride, grateful for the strong grip at her waist which was almost her only contact with reality in what had become some unreal world holding her suspended in an awful dream. She kept herself numb, clamping down fiercely on any stray thought that might take her back to that horrible upstairs room. When Ewan finally stopped she did not even look around. She had no idea where they were, but neither did she care.

Celia did not recognize the mound of dark earth they were approaching as a shelter until Ewan led Goliah inside and they were blessedly out of the rain. It was a simple structure built into a hillside, the kind which in another country would be called a crofter's hut. One side, almost a cave, formed a small stable with straw scattered on the earth floor and a crude wooden box serving as a manger at one end. That Ewan had not stumbled on this place accidentally became quickly apparent as she numbly watched him remove stones from a well-concealed hole in the wall and pull out a wooden water bucket stuffed with some blankets and grain. With skilled practice he pulled the harness off Goliah, rubbed his hide down with some of the straw and threw a blanket across his back. Only then did he remove several planks from a wooden panel in the wall and lead her into a small room on the other side. It was hardly larger than the adjoining shed but showed signs of the same careful preparation. In place of the stable door, this room contained one window, nearly concealed by the earth that banked it, but conveniently placed for a quick exit. Ewan rummaged once again among the stones and produced a second blanket, a flint and a candle stub, and a small brown bulb-shaped bottle. The flickering candlelight threw dancing shadows on the low ceiling. Celia sank wearily onto the straw while Ewan set about striking a light to the small bundle of kindling stacked in a tiny circular hearth. Above it a hole in the ceiling provided a chimney.

The fire's warmth, small as it was, steamed the damp clothes that lay plastered to her clammy skin. Her cap had gone long ago and her wet hair streamed down her back and around her face. She crouched nearer the flames, staring into them unseeing while Ewan struggled to remove his wet boots and hung his soaked coat and waistcoat on a peg. With the part of her mind that was not still back in that room in the tavern, she was aware of him moving about in his shirtsleeves as he poured out some of the rum from the brown bottle into a tin cup and sat it near the fire to heat. Only when it began to give off a thin wisp of smoke did he hand it to her and sit back on his haunches resting his arms on his knees and staring angrily into the fire.

The hot liquid burned all the way down, but it revived the numb feelings she had been attempting to repress. Her hand began to shake, and she gripped it with the other to prevent the rum from spilling. That would be the moment he picked to launch into his lecture.

"You little fool," he said bitterly. "When are you going to accept the fact that this is a bloody war we're waging, not an afternoon tea party!"

Celia gripped the cup tighter as she felt her body begin to shudder.

"You got just what you asked for," he went on in his cold, contained voice. "Tarleton is a rake, but what else was he to think, finding you sitting alone by the roadside? Richard would thrash you if he knew of this, and I've half a mind to do it for him."

The shudders were becoming violent. She stiffened her spine to bring them under control and her whole brittle body rocked back and forth. Picking up one of the unlit sticks near the hearth, Ewan poked at the fire.

"I cannot imagine how any woman would be so addlebrained as to be out on the roads in these times. I have always thought you had good sense, Celia but . . ."

Drawing up her knees under her petticoats, Celia laid her head on her arms and, in spite of all she could do to prevent it, began to cry. The first silent tears quickly gave way to great racking sobs which brought her cousin around, startled.

"Oh, good God, Celia! You're not going to weep!"

But his impatience quickly gave way to a true concern as he watched her shoulders heave under the thin chemise. Her long damp hair spilled down over her arms, catching bright sparks of light from the fire.

"Come, now," he said, half-consciously but more gently, putting an arm around her. "It can't have been that bad."

That was all she needed. Falling against him, she gave full vent to the fear, rage and self-disgust that were the residue of this ghastly night. Patiently he let her cry it out, holding her and rocking her back and forth, stroking her soft hair and cursing himself for an insensitive clod.

"Poor girl. You've had a bad time and all you get for it is a tongue-lashing. I'm sorry, Celia. I should at least have waited."

"No, no," she sobbed against his wet hair. "Everything you say is true. I *was* a fool!"

He smiled grimly, "Well, I won't disagree with that, but perhaps the matter is best discussed when you've recovered." He waited while the shaking of her shoulders subsided, listening to the gently burning twigs in the hearth snapping. "Damn that Tarleton! He didn't hurt you, did he?"

"I don't think so," she sniffed. "But if you hadn't come when you did . . ."

"Hush," he answered, tightening his arms around her. "We won't talk any more about it now. Let's rest, and as soon as the rain lets up I'll take you home."

Celia pulled away and wiped at her eyes. Gently he put the cup to her lips, and the warm liquid seemed to revive her. Hearing her teeth chattering against the metal rim, Ewan draped one end of the blanket around her shoulders and the other around his own, leaving the front open to the fire. The rain kept up a gentle patter on the sod roof, sending damp drafts through the chinks between the rocks in the walls.

"Where are we?" Celia asked, leaning her head on his shoulder and letting the comfort and warmth of the moment flow through her. "Where is this place?"

"Oh, it's just one of my hideways." His fingers idly stroked her arm, though he was not even aware of it. "I have them scattered all over. I try never to be where any rebel patrol would expect to find me."

Without his mentioning the episode of his capture it flashed into both their minds. Celia nestled closer to him and quickly changed the subject.

"Though I shall always detest that Tarleton, I must say that I don't understand him. He cuts a dashing figure. Why does he think he must force himself upon a woman when with a little finesse he might make many conquests?" It was difficult for her to talk of Colonel Tarleton, but she did it deliberately, remembering all too well how Ewan had avoided her after she witnessed his disgrace and capture. If she could share her shame with him, then perhaps he might feel more comfortable facing his with her.

"He is a man of high ambition and no small talent. Very brave in action. But he can be brutal. I once saw him break a truly magnificent stallion using cruel spurs and a stick. He's known as a ravisher of women, but, if truth were told, most of them seem to welcome it."

"This one certainly did not!" A shudder went through her again as she remembered the scene on the bed, and he drew her closer under the blanket. A comfortable languor settled over them both—an aura mingling many emotions: peace after violence and rest after a hard and demanding ride; warmth and shelter from the cold rain; the comfort of the hot, stimulating rum; and the pleasant reassurance of their bodies closely touching. The world ceased to exist outside this tiny room, itself suspended in the middle of a vast, empty darkness. Only here was reality, the soft light, the heat, the comfort wrapping them together in an isolation where they existed only for themselves.

Almost automatically Ewan's hand resting on her shoulder began to move lightly up and down her neck. Waves of sensuous delight went through her. She raised her head, meeting his eyes, and suddenly saw before her a man she had never really seen before. The dark shapely brows, the heavily lashed eyes that looked out at her with such a steady intensity, the full, sensuous mouth, so beautifully sculpted that she suddenly ached to trace the outline of the lips with her finger.

The shock of physical longing that went through her was like a blow. "Ewan," she whispered in amazement, seeing in the dawning amazement in his eyes that he was held as fast as she in the grip of a transformation. Astounded, yet almost expecting it, she felt his lips brush her own, lightly at first, then hungrily.

How could she know that in that moment, from one instant to the next, she became a different person? That in the space of a single kiss her whole world shifted and rearranged itself into an entirely new order?

It was a shattering moment for them both. Like blinders falling away, Ewan too saw before him a person he had never seen before. Long ago he had known her, first as Richard's little ally, then as Richard's wife. Now he saw her for the first time as herself, a being of utter loveliness in whose beauty all the beauty of women merged and in whose womanliness all that was feminine in the earth coalesced. He was startled at first by the unexpected ardor of her response, then, like her, he was swept from conscious amazement to a plateau of pure feeling.

They were both consumed with an urgent need for each other, as exciting and demanding as it was new and unknown. The blanket fell away as they scrambled to their knees, clutching hotly at each other. She felt his hands running urgently over her shoulders and back, expertly untying her stays and sliding them away from her body.

"Ewan," she gasped, "we shouldn't . . ." But he cut off her words with his lips, and, her protest lost, she wildly returned his urgent kisses. All the emptiness, all the months of longing left her helpless before this onslaught of sensation. To be in the arms of a man who wanted her as badly as she did him— she could no more turn back than she could cease to breathe. Something had caught fire between them, and willingly, gratefully she allowed herself to be engulfed. She knew when he laid her gently back on the blanket and she no longer cared.

They lost all awareness of what was happening until it was over and they lay panting and sated in each other's arms. Even then, the wonder and joy that filled them both left no room for guilt or recrimination. Only later did she wonder if she was some kind of wanton to go so willingly from that terrible scene with Tarleton to this complete physical abandon with Ewan. Yet the two events were somehow related. Ewan brought her joy and a reaffirmation of love and life that helped dispel the degradation of Tarleton's lust. So unlike Richard, with his reasoned, controlled appetites, Ewan awakened her body to depths of feeling she had never known were in her, while offering her at the same time healing for her bruised spirit in the tender and eloquent way of his lovemaking.

For a long time they did not speak, afraid that words might break the spell and restore them to the old patterns. To Celia it seemed there were no words adequate.

"Ewan," she whispered, holding his lean face between her hands. "I can't believe this. I've known you for years and never thought of you this way. How is it possible to know someone and not be aware that they can be so precious to you?"

"God!" he moaned, covering her face with his lips. "Don't talk. Just hush!"

And she did. It was enough to express all she felt with her body.

Like two people who have suddenly discovered a whole new world, they spent the hours of that dark night learning of each other. After their first exquisite burst of passion, they could not get enough of each other. Celia reveled in this new freedom. To be so open with a man was a delight which only made her love him all the more. They talked finally, made love again, dozed and loved again until the rain stopped and the first far-off sounds of morning told them that the world had not been suspended but was waiting outside with all its old disorder and triviality.

It was still dark when they left the small hut, but by the time Ewan lifted her off his saddle at the Manor House the gray dawn was stretching its arms sluggishly and the birds were about their morning chatter in the trees.

He led her around to the piazza at the back of the house, where they stood in the shadows of the huge ragged lilac bushes so as not to be noticed by Betsy or Diamond stirring in their cottages far down the empty path.

She had managed to get her dress back together well enough to make the ride, but she still wore his coat around her shoulders. He caught the collar in his strong hands and pulled her face to his, kissing her long and thirstily as though he could never have enough of her lips.

Celia clung to him, dreading the moment he would turn away. "You'll come back soon?"

"Tonight if I can."

"Oh, Ewan, this is all so strange. I've known you for years and suddenly I don't know you at all and I love you terribly."

He stroked her hair back from her brow. "I know. I know. It is the same for me."

"We—we will have to be careful."

"Yes. And we will be. I have no wish to hurt you, Celia. Not you, nor Richard."

There it was, the name they had both avoided mentioning during all these wonder-filled hours.

"But we are hurting Richard, aren't we. We can't help but hurt him."

He laid his finger on her lips. "We won't talk of that now."

"But—"

"No, Celia. I don't quite know how this happened, but it certainly happened without our seeking it. For me, I have never known anything so strong as what I feel now for you, and I think you feel the same for me. Don't ask me to stay away for Richard's sake, for I'm not going to be able to. What we are, we are, and this attraction—love, whatever you call it, it just *is*. Let us take joy in it and in each other while we can."

As appealing as his words were, she knew he was only putting off what must be faced eventually. Yet she did not argue. Take the joy while you can, she reasoned. The reckoning will come soon enough.

Throwing her arms around his neck, she pressed her face to his. "Oh, I love you, I love you. I don't know if I can live until tonight!" she said breathlessly.

Reaching down, he broke off a long, lacy branch from one of the overgrown bushes that bordered the garden, entwining it like a rose in her hair. Celia recognized the pungent, lemony smell of one of Elizabeth's favorite border herbs.

"Southernwood," she smiled up at him.

"'Lad's love,' 'maiden's ruin.' A symbol of love. Keep it nearby, and when you think of me today hold it in your hand to remind you that I shall be back."

"It will help me to know that last night truly happened. Already it seems like a dream. A magical, wonderful, beautiful dream."

"It is no dream, my dear. It's almost more reality than I can handle." He raised her hands and kissed her palms. "Until tonight." Catching her face between his hands, he kissed her one last time, then disappeared into the gray dawn.

Celia stood on the piazza for a long time watching after him, leaning against the post, her arms crossed at her waist. Was it years ago or only yesterday that a foolish young girl had valued a chaise above her life and safety? To the woman who watched longingly after her lover, hugging her joy to herself, that girl was less than a memory. She was a stranger.

Part II
West Farms
1778

fifteen

"I think Ned Carne is the handsomest young man I ever saw," Celia said, leaning back against Ewan's chair, her head against his knee.

"You and half the women of West Chester! He has a string of conquests that would stretch the length of York Island." His hand caressed her hair and, under it, the long planes of her neck, sending waves of pleasure rippling down her back.

"The way you keep him dancing attendance on you one would think he had you too under his spell."

Ewan laughed. "I like him well enough. He's an engaging young man of many accomplishments—he sings, plays the violin, dances divinely and, most of all, is dependable. I can count on him doing what he is told."

"Is he one of the Carnes from Horseneck? I thought I knew them all."

"He's from the wrong side of the blanket but of that family nonetheless." Reaching down, he slipped his arms around her and kissed the nape of her neck. "And why are we discussing Ned Carne, my love, when there are better things to do? I'll have to leave soon. Come, sit with me and give me a last kiss to hold in memory until I can return."

Willingly she allowed herself to be pulled into his lap, where she nestled against him, entirely content. The only sounds in the quiet room were the popping of the fire in the hearth and an occasional cry of an owl outside. Ewan was not often in her bedroom, for they were far too likely to be discovered there even though none of the servants slept in the house. Since their return from the crofter's hut most of their brief, hurried meetings had been snatched in out-of-the-way places, and for Celia the comfort and warmth of her own bedroom was a delight. It had rained that day, so she had good reason to draw the heavy drapes and light a fire in the hearth, creating a warm cocoon around them which shut out the rest of the world. From the high fourposter bed they had moved to the fire, drinking the madeira Ewan had brought with him and savoring the pleasure of being close. Her lips drifted along his cheek, happiness swelling within her.

"Don't go. You've plenty of time till daylight."

Nuzzling her ear, he murmured, "Mmmm. But this is not the place to be caught unawares."

Deliberately she let her night robe fall away from her shoulders, and a thrill of utter delight went through her as his hands closed over her breasts and his lips moved downward.

"At this rate, my love, I won't be able to go," he muttered, not fighting the excitement which engulfed them both.

Celia threw back her head, arching her breast against his mouth, and laughed deliciously and with complete abandon as the robe fell away from her body.

The wonder of it still left her amazed and incredulous. It was not just that Ewan himself was her lover—that was still difficult to believe. The boy and later the man whom she had thought of with an affectionate complacency seemed now to be another person entirely. That that face, those hands, that body could be to her the most treasured thing in life was still utterly preposterous. But more than her love for Ewan was her complete delight at the openness and freedom between them. She had tried not to think of Richard, for she knew that if she remembered the consideration her husband had always shown her, her guilt would drive her to despair. So instead she thought of him only in contrast to his magnetic, sensual cousin. Richard would never allow himself to be so abandoned as to sit half naked before a fire, consumed with sexual passion. Instead of taking a frank pleasure in her supple body, with the firelight on her skin, he would make sure that their lovemaking was in the dark, on the bed with the hangings closed. More than that, he would always be certain that sensual abandon was neatly balanced by rational thought, and, more often than not, the second would be more on his mind than the first. When she remembered how starved she had felt at times for her husband's love, she reasoned that it was partly his fault that she now threw herself so passionately into this intensely fulfilling relationship.

And yet . . .

She pushed the "and yet" from her mind. It would have to

be faced sometime, but not now, Never now when, as they slipped from the chair onto the floor, thought and reason were all but drowned in ecstasy.

"Oh, Ewan, I love you so," she murmured, lying on the rug before the fire.

Completely spent and completely contented, he held her without speaking, without thinking, without caring for anything or anyone else in the world but this one soft, yielding, perfect body.

For Ewan too had learned to push Richard from his mind. If Richard had stayed at home where he belonged, all of this would never have happened. In some ways this affair was of his making. If he did not appreciate this passionate woman who was his wife enough to hold her to him, then he must expect her affections to stray.

Yet Ewan was realist enough to know how unfair an argument this was. Richard would never dream that his cousin would take advantage of his wife in his absence. And was he taking advantage? He did not think so. What had drawn him to Celia was something so strong that neither of them could have denied it even had they wanted to. He was sure it would have come about someday, somehow, whatever the circumstances. Never had a woman captivated him so thoroughly. There had been plenty of other women and some he had fancied he was quite fond of. But this was love such as he had never dreamed to experience. He was drawn almost against his will to her side. Thoughts of her face and body intruded on his waking hours. Dreams of her tortured him on the nights when he could not get to her side. Even if he wanted to leave her out of honor or guilt, he was powerless to do so. She had obsessed him, and the only time he felt alive these past weeks was when he was holding her in his arms.

The first sleepy twitter of the birds outside her window broke the silence of the dark. Sighing, he forced himself to sit up.

"My darling, my love, I must go. It won't do to be letting myself out of your window in the first light of day. Help me to leave, for I don't want to go at all."

With an effort Celia rose and pulled her discarded robe about her body. "Let me help you dress," she offered.

"No! One touch of your hands and I'll never get my clothes back on. You stay here and pour me a last glass of wine."

She sat by the fire, her glass in her hands, enjoying the

sight of his strong, lithe body as he pulled on his clothes.

"I shall probably see you today," she said absently. "I'm goint down to Morrisania to deliver some grain which Captain Terrell asked to purchase as soon as it was ready."

"You'd better not go alone. I won't have you traipsing recklessly about these roads ever again."

"Vestal is going with me, and it's only to Morrisania, after all. We can easily do it in a few hours. Will you be there?"

Idly he buttoned his waistcoat and pulled his scarlet miiitary coat over his full sleeves. "Yes, for there is to be a horserace early this afternoon and I wouldn't miss it. In fact, I have several guineas riding on the outcome."

"A race," Celia exclaimed, rising to help him adjust his coat. "How exciting. I should love to see it."

He kissed her lightly. "How I am going to be able to pretend you are only my cousin's wife, I simply don't know. Do you think we can fool anyone or will the whole Refugee corps see through our charade?"

"We must dissemble and do it well. I shall be distant and aloof, barely civil, but underneath you will know that my heart is pounding out your name."

"If you are aloof it will drive me to distraction. All the time I'm making a valiant effort to ignore you, I shall be fighting the urge to carry you away to the nearest bed."

She tried to smile. "Oh, Ewan, whatever are we going to do?"

Holding her close, he kissed the thick, rich hair. "I don't know, my love. I don't know." Then, putting her away, he reached for his sword belt and pulled it over his shoulder. "But in the meantime, I'll be back as soon as I can. Don't go down with me. It will be easier if I let myself out while it is still good and dark."

She watched him leave the room, miserable and happy at the same time. Standing by the shrouded window, she listened for the faint sounds of the door closing downstairs and the muted thuddings of his horse on the road.

Whatever were they going to do?

She rode into Morrisania that noon astride Kit with Vestal plodding behind on old Bonny, loaded before and aft with sacks of grain. Celia was astounded all over again at how the area had changed. Once a place of open fields bordered by woods along the banks of the Harlem River, it had been transformed by hordes of Refugees from the upper country into a bustling settlement of log huts, congested with milling throngs of soldiers, horses, women and children, wagons and livestock. It had all the urban turbulence of lower Broad Way in New York, magically transferred to the quiet banks of the once peaceful river. Even the Harlem itself was crowded, with sloops, barges, tenders and warships plying the narrow water roadway from Spuyten Duyvil to the city's docks.

The dusty trails between the rows of huts was churned by the traffic of men and beasts into a choking miasma. Celia quickly found the quartermaster's office, deposited her cornmeal and carefully concealed the valuable English pound she was paid for it. Then, trailing a staring, fascinated Vestal, she went in search of Ewan.

He was sitting on the small porch of one of the Refugee cabins, obviously waiting for her. Recognizing her yellow straw hat and familiar walk, he was quickly on his feet and down the steps, taking her hands with none of the aloofness they had agreed upon. Then he remembered.

"Mrs Deveroe," he said carefully and loudly.

"Cousin . . ." She hoped the curved brim of her hat hid the joy in her eyes.

"Come along inside and give me news of the family."

He led her into his office, where with the open windows he could do no more than kiss her hand.

"I don't think I can bear it."

She snatched her hands away. "We must, Ewan. Come, let me sit here and you sit over there and tell me about the race. I'm very anxious to see it. It's been such a long time since I enjoyed anything so diverting. Who is racing? What horses?"

"Totten, Kipp, Jeffreys . . . I think you'll remember them all. And they're using their own mounts. Each one thinks he sits the best saddle in the county."

"But surely you're entering one of your horses. You've the best horses in camp."

Ewan smiled and leaned back with one booted foot against the rough plank table that served as a desk.

"Of course. I couldn't let such an opportunity go by. Ned is racing one of my mares. She's a swift one and I'm betting on her to beat even Kipp's roan gelding. It should be a good race."

"Oh, Ewan, let me put something on your mount. Here, I just was paid this pound note for the cornmeal. Put it on your horse for me."

He did not reach for the money. "Do you really think you should? You might lose, after all."

"Oh, I know. And if Richard knew about it he'd be furious. But everyone else will have something riding on the outcome, and I should like to, too. It makes it so much more exciting."

He had to agree. The wagers on cockfights and horseraces that flew back and forth through the camp would do justice to a London gaming house.

"All right," he said, rising. "Let's go over to the field and I'll place it for you."

The race was held in a bare stretch of road bordering a barley field on the camp outskirts. Lifting her up to a high perch on a stile, he stood below and worked out the betting. Celia knew most of the faces of the principal riders as men who before the war had passed through West Farms from the upper reaches of the county. Ned Carne cantered up on Ewan's fine bay mare, her coat sleek in the warm sun. He looked very impressive in a figured silk wasitcoat and fine linen shirt-sleeves, and, as he stopped to exchange a few words with her, she was struck once again by what a personable young man he was.

"I hope you have a stake on the Colonel's mare, Mrs. Deveroe," he said, his engaging smile showing even white teeth.

"I certainly do, Ned. And I'm counting on you to make it pay for me."

"I'll do my best." Doffing his hat to her, he turned the mare and with an easy grace cantered her off toward the starting line. Celia felt her excitement mount.

She leaned down to whisper to Ewan, "Do you really think your horse will win?"

"She'd better," he answered grimly, "or I'm a poor man. I don't like the look of Kipp's roan, though. He's going to be hard to beat."

Clutching at her hat, Celia rose up on the stile as the saber dropped and the first three horses thundered down the road. They were running so closely together that it was difficult to see which one was ahead. With loud cheering the spectators along the fence urged them on. As they neared the end of the half-mile stretch of track, she could see Ned pulling away before the other two horses. Surely he had it, she thought, cheering loudly and jumping up and down in excitement on the narrow stile. Then just as the mare neared the finish, Kipp's gelding made a surge of speed and passed Ewan's horse to cross the line a head before the others.

"Oh, no," Celia moaned, sinking back down on her perch. A whole pound gone for nothing! What would Richard say? Somehow she'd have to find a way to keep it from him.

She was cursing herself for a fool when she saw Ewan's face going black. Oh dear, she thought. He's taking it worse than I. She tried to pass it off lightly. Laying a hand on his shoulder, she said quietly, "You nearly had it, Ewan. There'll be other races."

"Nearly is not good enough, my dear," he answered grimly. Then, seeing her soft face near his own, he made an effort to throw off his bad humor.

"Well, perhaps the second race will be better for me. What about you? Do you want to hazard another wager?"

"No! One is quite enough, thank you. I'll just sit here and enjoy watching the horses run."

There were several more races of three horses each, and since Ewan won one of them, his losses turned out to be not very great after all. Still, when the men who had won from him hurried over to collect, they could not help needling the Colonel a little as he dropped the gold guineas into their hands.

Captain Kipp was especially galling. "I told you, Colonel, I had the swiftest mount in West Chester. That's a prime animal, that is, admit it now."

"Come, now, Kipp," said Totten, a small, well-made young man from North Castle. "You beat the Colonel's mare, but you'd never beat Goliah. There's the best horse in West Chester and you know it!"

"How can I know it when he never races Goliah?" Kipp answered, pocketing the guineas. "He's a beautiful animal, I admit, but he wouldn't beat my Valiant."

"Come on, Colonel Deveroe," Totten prodded. "How about it? A race between Kipp's roan and your black—that would be capital sport. What do you say?"

"Nobody rides Goliah but me," Ewan said firmly, but Celia could tell the prospect was one that interested him.

"Let me ride him this once," Ned pleaded. "I'll handle him with the greatest care. Wouldn't you like to win back that stake?"

Ewan's resistance was crumbling under the lure of seeing

his horse puncture Kipp's vanity and win back some of his money. Against his better judgment he made a quick decision.

"All right. Vestal, run to the stable and bring my black. Can that mount of yours run another race, Kipp? Or is he winded?"

"Winded! Colonel, my Valiant could run six races and still have your Goliah eating his dust."

"Ha! We'll see about that. Your Valiant ought to have been named Vanity."

Vestal was off in a flash, delighted to be a part of the challenge, and soon he was back leading the beautiful English horse, saddled and ready. With obvious relish Ned Carne jumped into the saddle, cantering back and forth in front of the crowd to get the feel of the horse under him. Stroking the sleek neck, he spoke softly to the magnificent animal, his delight in handling such a horse almost as great as his pride in being the only other man in camp whom the Colonel had ever allowed to mount Goliah. When Kipp brought his mount around, looking not the least the worse for wear in having already won one race, they moved off together toward the well-churned roadway for the start.

"Don't enjoy Goliah too much, Ned," Ewan called, as he watched them walk away. As much as he wanted to win this race, it was disturbing to him to see another man astride his favorite horse.

The saber fell and the two animals thundered past Celia, neck and neck, sending the dirt flying around them. As they neared the finish, so close it looked to be a tie, she found herself jumping up and down again and urging Goliah on. The great horse, with a little prodding from its rider, gathered his strength and began to forge ahead as they reached the finish, outdistancing Valiant by almost a length.

"What about that!" Ewan cried, all smiles now, and lifted her up and swung her down. Throwing her arms around his neck, she hugged and kissed him before she remembered protocol. Then quickly she moved away, adjusting her hat and hoping that her enthusiasm looked to be only part of the natural excitement of the race.

When Ned brought Goliah around to the Colonel, it was with the greatest reluctance that he made himself get down. "He's the finest mount I've ever ridden," he said enthusiastically, handing the reins to Ewan.

"He's the finest I've ever ridden, too," Ewan echoed, rubbing the horse's nose. "You'll get a share, Ned, when Kipp has paid up."

"I'd almost ride this horse for nothing, Colonel," the young man answered.

With the races over, Ewan reluctantly escorted Celia back to where her own filly waited in the shed.

"You should have raced Kit," Ewan commented idly, handing her up.

"No, thank you. Oh, she's swift enough. I know that from one day when she ran away with me. But I'd just as soon these men didn't know it."

"You're wise to keep that kind of knowledge to yourself. Good mounts are soon stolen. In fact, that is one reason I hesitate to put Goliah on exhibition. But I couldn't stand that Kipp lording it over me with his inferior cattle. Serves him right to lose to a better horse."

They were hidden in the shadows inside the shed, waiting for Vestal to walk back from the stable where he had returned Goliah. She leaned down and laid her palm against his cheek.

"This has been so pleasant. Thank you, Ewan."

He turned her palm to press it to his lips. "I don't want you to leave."

"And I don't want to go. You'll come to me soon?"

"Yes, but not tonight. We may be going up into the neutral ground either tonight or tomorrow. One of our spies tells us there's to be a herd of cattle coming through Bedford intended for the camp at Peekskill. We think they could be of more use to the army in New York."

"Then you'll be fighting again."

"That is generally what soldiers do, my love. It is what makes our lives exciting."

"Exciting! You men! Don't you know that if anything happened to you I would die? Promise me you'll be careful."

Outside they could hear Vestal approaching, humming a little tune as he ambled along.

He reached up and kissed her once, hard. "I can't promise that, but I do promise to come to you as soon afterward as possible. I'll let you know where."

"I'll try to live until then," she whispered as Vestal came round the door.

Autumn was almost gone when, weeks later, Ewan made his way through the cantonment at King's Bridge toward the stable where Goliah waited. He hated to ride into this place with its acres of huts and tents and its haughty English officers. For Celia's sake as well as for the sake of his own reputation he had avoided Tarleton, knowing that to meet him would mean a challenge or a duel instigated by one or both of them. Although part of him would welcome such a confrontation, another saner part knew it would ruin him in the eyes of the military. Tarleton wasn't worth that.

Stalking through the compound, he debated stopping at the sutler's wagon for a quick draft when he saw the first of von Donop's Hessian chasseurs straggling back into camp. They had been gone nearly a month, scouring the neutral ground as far north as White Plains, and from the look of them they had found good pickings. Though their uniforms were clotted with dust and their black snakeskin pigtails almost as stiff from grime as from pomade, each one was carrying a huge amount of booty. Several pairs carried long sticks between them with pigs and chickens dangling below. Clothes and bedding, household goods, all kinds of animals, some walking but most dead, produce and equipment—all the things Ewan recognized as the everyday paraphernalia of a well-equipped farmhouse—were carted into camp on the shoulders of the troops. Pity the poor households, he thought grimly; they probably did not leave them enough for a week's rations.

He ignored their coarse jokes and raucous laughter as the men in the camp began to cluster around the returning soldiers, anxious to barter what they could. Ewan really couldn't blame them for stealing, it was the only way they knew for an army to sustain itself. But it was just this kind of lawless thievery which was earning him a black name in the county, for whenever it happened it was blamed on the "Cowboys," as men had taken to calling his Refugees.

Scowling, he remembered the countless times he had attempted to be fair when one of the countrymen came in to protest the theft of his cattle or horses. How many times had he forced some poor private to pay full value for the animals he had stolen? How many times had he returned an animal to its owner? How often had he issued permits allowing countless farmers to keep one cow or horse for their own use even though they were expected to turn over the others for the supply of the army? Did that count for nothing? The rebels stole and plundered, too, but it was the Loyalists who earned the bitterness. And the most despised of all was Colonel Ewan Deveroe! By his own friends and countrymen. It was a bitter reward for loyal and true service to one's King.

Then he thought of Celia. Her warm body and her adoration

were waiting for him in the shell of a burned-out house they had discovered abandoned by its owner, who had fled West Chester for more peaceful parts. It had become a haven for them, isolated and quiet, where the bitterness of war could be temporarily forgotten. Spurring Goliah forward, he galloped down the road, anxious now only to reach her.

"A penny for your thoughts," Celia said quietly, watching him from under the narrow brim of her riding hat as their horses plodded lazily back toward the Manor House. When he didn't answer she wisely kept silent, brushing away the small pieces of straw that still clung to her skirts from their long sojourn on the floor of the empty farmhouse. As always, she was filled with a sense of perfect contentment, yet she knew that something was troubling Ewan—something he had not been able to lose even in the high excitement of their lovemaking. There had even been a fierceness, a wildness, in the way he had taken her this afternoon, terribly satisfying but different somehow from the man she knew so well.

He looked across at her now and smiled ruefully. "They would not be of interest to you, my love."

"Don't you know that everything about you is of interest to me?"

Their mounts ambled along the shaded road. It was getting cool now that the last of summer had gone and fall was upon them. She pulled the collar of her old riding habit closer around her neck and shivered. "Soon we'll not be able to meet like this without building a fire that might betray us. You'll have to go back to scaling the wall to my room."

But he could not throw off his malaise. "Celia, do you ever wonder what would happen if you should conceive? That would betray us as nothing else, what with Richard so long away."

"That's nothing to worry about," she said lightly. "I'm barren." Looking straight at him, she was relieved to see not pity in his eyes but only a mirroring of the pain in her own.

"How do you know that?"

"Dr. Sayre told me. That is, he all but told me."

"He would have to be a seer to know such a thing."

"Is it not enough proof that I have never conceived, even when I wanted to so badly? And should such a miracle happen now, I would still welcome it. But it won't."

He reached across and gripped her hand where it lay on the indigo velvet of her riding habit. There was nothing really that he could say, so he did not try. It was enough to know that she too had her moments of despair.

"Let's not be glum, my love," Celia cried, determined to preserve the happy mood of the afternoon. "Soon there will be snow, and hot mulled cider by the fire, and Christmas. The winter is ours to shut out the world and love each other."

"The world has a way of intruding."

"We won't let it! We'll forget the war and Congress and arrogant British officers and live to ourselves. We'll pretend there is no such person as the 'outlaw of the Bronx'—oh, yes, Ned Carne told me they call you that—and we'll worship and admire the Ewan Deveroe whose steadfast loyalty is an example to all men."

He nearly laughed at that. "Celia, I love your irrepressible spirits. Whatever would I do without you?"

She started to lean from her saddle for his kiss, filled to overflowing with warmth and love for this man who had become the most precious person in all the world to her. But just as she moved toward him she saw him pull up Goliah, staring down the rutted trail to where it bent to cross the bridge into West Farms.

"Why, that's Vestal, isn't it? Whatever could he be waiting there for?"

Vestal had seen them and, wildly waving his hat, started running toward them down the road. Ewan cantered forward with Celia following, sensing that something of the brightness had gone out of her afternoon.

"Misse Celia! Misse Celia!" She heard Vestal calling. Oh, dear, she thought, what could have happened? One of the servants hurt? A raid that carried off the last of their supplies? Then from the distance she made out his broad smile as he ran toward them, and something of the words he was calling.

"Massa Richard, he home! He come home!"

Celia pulled Kit up short and stared at Ewan.

Richard!

Their eyes met as Vestal came running closer, joy and excitement in every long stride. "I try to find you. Went to Lawrence's, and Hunt's, all over. Then I see that yellar hoss. Massa Richard, he waitin' for you at Manor House, right now. He home, Misse Celia."

All her lovely visions of moments before fell in shards at her feet.

"Ewan," she said softly. "Oh, Ewan, what shall I do?"

Their eyes locked across a great void that had opened between them. When he spoke, it was stiffly, as though the words stuck in his throat.

"What else is there, Celia? You are going to welcome back your husband."

sixteen

Take the joy while you can. The payment will come later. Her own words echoed in her mind, throbbing like some painful wound. She was paying now. Not with any overt punishment—that might have been easier to bear. It was in the thousand daily reminders: trying to dissemble a delighted welcome she did not really feel and she was sure was transparent to her husband; trying to remember not to give herself away by a slip of the tongue which might betray her feelings for Ewan; trying not to turn away in revulsion when her husband drew the bed curtains; trying to be the girl she used to be when that girl had somehow fled, leaving only a complex and guilt-ridden woman in her place.

Richard knew something was wrong, but nothing in his experience led him to imagine what it actually was. Celia had changed. That had been apparent from the first day when she returned from her ride with Ewan to offer him a startled and almost cool welcome in place of the effusive one he had come to expect. Of course, his arrival was a surprise. He had not known himself that he was coming until the very last moment, and by then there was no time to get off a letter. Perhaps she is still angry because I went away, he thought, wondering at the ways of women. Yet, with his usual rational way of looking at things, he decided it was best to not worry about it. She would come round in time, or, if not, she would certainly come out with whatever was weighing on her mind. So he went on, as constant and steady and detached as always.

It was the worst thing he could have done, had he only known it. Celia almost wished that he would confront, question, rage against and castigate her. She would welcome confession and fury, and with them the hope of forgiveness. But this polite pretense that all was as it had been nearly drove her to distraction. Her body as well as her spirit longed for her lover, and in that longing she suffered such pangs of guilt as she had never known existed. It seemed there were always tears standing in her eyes ready to overflow. She contemplated riding away on Kit, somewhere, anywhere, into the vast wilderness, never to return. She pictured her body floating lifeless on the gray waters of the Bronx, no longer a trial to herself or others. That picture usually brought her good sense surging back, and she would laugh at her melodramatic imaginings. But it was a difficult situation and daily she grew more confused, wondering how to resolve it.

"I may have to go away for a few days, Celia."

Richard studied his wife's white-capped head where she bent over the basket of sheared oily wool, separating the tufts for washing and skeining.

"Oh?" she said, without looking up.

Was it the weak afternoon sun that made her look so pale? He sat down, tapping the heavy paper against his knee, and waited for the usual angry reaction.

"I've had a letter from Mr. Jay. He is preparing to take his seat in Congress early next month and wishes to know more in detail what my stay there was like. He's asked me to visit him at his home in Rye for a few days. I should not have to be gone more than a week."

"If you must go, you must. That was the reason he sent you to Philadelphia in the first place, wasn't it?"

At this unexpected response, Richard reached out and tipped her chin up to look into her face. Her amber eyes were huge against her thin cheeks.

"Celia, are you ill?"

"Why, no. What makes you ask such a foolish question?"

"You have hardly seemed yourself since I got back last week. I am very worried about you. Even now—this new trip. Once you would have stormed from the room and not spoken to me for days."

She tried to smile up at him. "You should be grateful that I can accept it at last."

Deliberately she turned back to her sorting, hoping he would leave, but he sat quietly reflective.

"Did anything happen while I was away to upset you?"

Her hand pushed over the wool "What do you mean?"

"I'm not blind, my dear. I can see how ravaged the farm

has been in my absence. How many raids were there? Did any of those rough men hurt you?"

"No, no, Richard. It's nothing like that. I told you just what happened in every case. We've been robbed—sometimes politely, and brazenly at others—but never were we mistreated brutally or harmed in any way."

"Thank God for that. The tales I hear from the Neutral Ground are enough to raise your hair. The Skinners in particular take some kind of delight in torturing their poor victims. Shube Merritt has earned a name of such villainy that he will be lucky if he isn't cut down on the street."

"He always was a worthless person. I never could bear him with that horrible stump of an arm and his vicious face. As for the Skinners, we've only had that single visit—I suppose because we're close to the cantonments on the Harlem River and, besides, I make sure I never have any money in the house. What we do have is buried in the field, while I give it out that you took it all south with you."

"That's wise." He rubbed one long finger across his chin. "I went away so confident you could manage in my absence, but now . . . I don't know."

Celia shrugged, avoiding his eyes. "I managed satisfactorily, didn't I?"

In a sudden warm gesture he put an arm around her shoulders and kissed her pale cheek. "You've been magnificent. But now I wonder if it is not time your husband took care of you. Perhaps when I come back from this trip I should make up my mind to stay home and watch over our farm."

She looked sharply away, leaving him mystified at her cool response, remembering how once she would have thrown her arms around him and covered his face with kisses at such news. Would he ever come to understand her?

The most direct route to Mr. Jay's estate in Rye was straight north from West Farms right through the middle of the county. But Richard, on a sudden impulse, decided to go far out of his way and follow the old King's Highway that twisted along the Hudson River toward Albany, in order to take a first look at the land his mother had deeded over to him. He was never sure if the land he located was really his, but it bore so much resemblance to the rest of the topography that it did not matter. It was enough to learn that this was not farming country. From the river's edge the land sloped steeply up and inward for at least a mile, reaching a great height that must easily overlook Teller's Point and on beyond to the Highlands. Those hilly, rocky, perpendicular steeps were probably fit only for grazing sheep. The timber on them was thick and valuable, but whatever else he was to do with them he couldn't guess. Still, land was land, and Celia was right in urging him to hold on to it. At least, he would keep the taxes paid up until he decided what to do. Perhaps after the war he might even sell out and use the money to restore the Manor Farm.

He stayed that evening in a shabby rustic tavern just south of the tiny village of Sing Sing on the Hudson. After a light supper, he inquired of the landlord—a tall, thick fellow who still bore traces of a Scottish burr—how he might walk to the river.

"There's a path right outside that winds through yon trees. Just follow it and ye'll touch the water. It's a steep climb back up, though, sir, I warn ye."

"I don't mind," Richard answered absently, anxious to stretch his legs after sitting astride a horse all day.

"When ye reach the shore if ye'll follow the path north I'll wager ye'll come to the old silver mine. 'Tis about the only thin' of interest in these parts."

Richard's interest was caught at once. "A silver mine? Is there ore, then, in these rocks?"

"Oh, aye. Just pick up a few of 'em and ye can see it, right in yer hand. It's a rich country, right enough."

"Is this mine still in operation?" he asked politely, almost sure that if it had been he would certainly have heard of it before now.

"No, more's the pity. The devil English tried to run it for a while, but the war's put a stop to all that. They claimed it's played out, but we as live round here knows that's just their lyin' rumors to keep other investors away. There's riches lyin' under yon rock—I'll bet my life on't."

It would bear looking at. Doffing his hat, Richard stepped from the dingy tavern and started down the path, his knowledgeable eye taking in every detail of the rough contours of the land. The path to the shore wound almost straight downhill and there were no cleared areas or small homes anywhere along it, though when he stood on the shore itself he could see a few fishermen's huts both up and down the river. Kneeling, he ran some of the coarse, gravelly soil through his fingers. It likely had a high mineral content. The small rocks he had picked up

along the way showed a silver iridescence even in the deepening
dusk, though he suspected there was more of mica than of
actual silver in their makeup. At the beach he walked a way
back from the sandy shoreline to take in the wide view of the
Tappan Sea, looking around him thoughtfully. Silver might not
be the wealth here, but there were riches nonetheless. He had
recognized the whitish chalk that revealed great quantities of
limestone—very valuable indeed if it could be quarried. The
river itself was a treasury of fish, both fresh and salt-water in
this particular stretch of estuary. More than that, he had noticed
on his ride up how the feeder streams had run to it like veins
along a mighty artery. How many had he crossed this very
day? For years past Mr. Philipse had operated the only mill
allowed in this area, but if this revolution was successful that
would surely change. Dam up just a few of those streams at
intervals, and valuable mills—someday perhaps even factories—would be cheaply available. Then there was the river
itself. When the war was over it would go back to being a
major roadway for carrying supplies and produce between New
York and Albany. Goods grown in the fertile reaches of the
upper counties could be cheaply and efficiently transported to
the city by river. Timber along its shores was there for the
taking to build sloops and barges. Without the stranglehold
which the great landowners along its banks had long used to
keep its riches to themselves, there was no limit to the opportunities this area offered an enterprising man.

   Reluctantly, Richard turned to go back to the tavern. It was
all very interesting, but it was not for him. First and foremost
he wanted a life in government. And after that, there was still
the Manor Farm, so dear to Celia and so much a part of his
life since the day he was born. If he was honest with himself
he would admit that it was like a millstone around his neck,
but, given the passion his wife felt for it, he had little choice
but to save whatever energies he had left after politics to run
his farm. No, what lay here was for other men to plow, sow
and harvest. Yet he was not sorry he had come. The land was
worth seeing if only to know what it was he would be selling
when the time came.

   A late-afternoon sun threw long shadows on the tents that
surrounded the common in the White Plains village as Richard
rode in. He might have gone directly home and saved a day
or two, but he decided that as long as he was traveling through

the country anyway he would visit the camp where for the time being General Washington had his main headquarters.

There was more than mere curiosity involved in the way Richard's knowledgeable eyes took in even the smallest details of the encampment. How many times he had seen the business of the army mishandled by a Congress whose members never seemed able to put the needs of the military they themselves had created above their own petty concerns. How many pleading letters had come to their attention, everything from the carefully written missles of Washington or Heath to the scrawled notes from a half-educated general like Putnam, all begging for the same things—uniforms, flour, meat and guns. He knew that the soldiers went without pay while many of the men who were paid to supply clothing or ammunition were in fact lining their own pockets. Great sums were allocated for flour and bread to be sent by nonexistent wagons from the New England or Southern states while the paid-for supplies either never materialized or rotted by the wayside. What he did not know firsthand was the actual situation of the army, and here was his chance to see it for himself. He stabled his horse at Odel's Ordinary, hired a bed for the night and strolled down the common to the camp, pulling his cloak close around his shoulders against the cool air of dusk.

It was good dark by the time he returned to the tavern, having seen enough during the course of his short walk to confirm his worst fears. Sitting in the small dining room, he picked listlessly at his dinner of rabbit stew and beaten biscuits, trying to tune out the tipsy racket from the taproom beyond. Both rooms were full of soldiers, mostly officers in blue-and-buff uniforms, sleek leather boots, and yards of silver laee. They bore little resemblance to the men he had just seen huddled near pitiful fires in the cantonment, many of them in makeshift moccasins or oversize boots obviously stripped from some hapless corpse, and too many with no shoes at all. How many had he counted without coats who had only their threadbare homespun shirts to keep off the cold November night air? A fringed leather countryman's tunic was a rarity, while here and there a ragged, worn civilian gentleman's coat showed some enterprising soldier's quick hand. Tents were scarce and even straw to cushion the cold ground seemed a luxury. And the winter had barely started.

His concentration was broken by a voice at his elbow.

"Excuse me, sir, but are you not Richard Deveroe?"

Richard looked up to see a short handsome officer in a spotlessly groomed white military wig smiling down at him. At once he recognized the pleasant face with the closely placed eyes, and he sought to put a name to it as he glanced over the man's shoulder at a vaguely familiar tall black-coated figure standing behind.

"Yes, I am. And I remember you. Young Mr. Hamilton, isn't it?" Rising, he offered his hand to the short young man standing almost a head beneath him.

"I was sure it was you. I still remember with awe your Latin dissertations at King's College. You were two years ahead of me and I felt sure I could never match such erudition."

"I think you more than matched it. I read your letters, you see, in answer to the famous 'Westchester Farmer.'"

"My one claim to fame! That and the fact that I now have the great honor to be adjutant to General Washington," Hamilton replied, shaking his hand warmly.

"I can see it is Colonel Hamilton now. Won't you do me the honor of joining me in a draft?"

Eagerly the Colonel pulled up a chair. "I have only a moment, but I would not let go this opportunity to renew an old acquaintance. Oh, and let me present to you the Honorable Mr. Jaspar Carne," he added, indicating the tall man in black.

"Sir." Richard nodded politely, a sinking sensation in his chest as he watched Carne draw up a third chair to the table. Twice before he had confronted this man, and both encounters had been as unpleasant as hell.

"I've met Mr. Deveroe," Carne said stiffly. "One occasion, on the Hunt's Point road, I am not likely ever to forget."

God's blood, Richard thought, the man still bears me a grudge for that childish incident. "That was a long time ago," he said, looking directly into Carne's eyes. An image unaccountably came to his mind of the Fresh Water Pond deeply frozen, icy gray, its banks white and snowy, where they used to skate in the winter long ago.

"What brings you to White Plains?" Hamilton broke in before Carne could reply. "Oh, of course, I forgot. Your family is from West Chester, aren't they? West Farms, isn't it?" and he launched into a long, brilliant discussion of his impressions of the war and the county. Richard remembered Alexander Hamilton as an intelligent, ambitious youth, and now it seemed he had found his ladder to the top of the heap. Carne was another matter altogether. He tried to sum him up while he half-listened to Hamilton, amused at the same time to see how Carne was coldly scrutinizing him in return. A natty dresser in neat black coat and breeches, gray stockings, steel buckles on his shoes and a grizzled gray bag wig covering his hair, he looked as enigmatic as a cat staring through the branches of a tree at some unsuspecting prey. Richard was struck once again by the fact that though Carne was a young man, perhaps a year or two older than himself, he somehow had nothing of youth about him. When Carne finally broke in impatiently on Hamilton's good-natured wanderings, Richard knew he had read the man correctly.

"Mr. Deveroe's name is well known in West Chester. I might even say notorious." There was a challenge in the way Carne spoke the word.

Hamilton caught his breath at such an open breach of etiquette, but Richard only stared back, smiling into the cold eyes.

"I am aware that my cousin Ewan has something of a questionable reputation," he answered lightly.

Jaspar Carne's thin lips lifted at the corners. "'The Scourge of West Chester' is one of the more polite epithets his neighbors have given him."

"Tell me, Mr. Carne, are not you one of the Carnes of Horseneck?"

"Yes, I am."

"I believe, then, there are one or two members of your family who are now serving with my cousin's Refugees. Does that mark you a Loyalist?"

"Hardly! However, I do not find the comparison apt. One or two misguided members of my family are hardly to be compared with the Deveroes, who, if I am correct, have only yourself to dissemble an allegiance to patriotic zeal."

Hamilton started up. "Now, see her, Carne . . ." But Richard waved him down, carefully controlling his own anger.

"I do not appreciate your use of the word 'dissemble,'" Richard answered coldly. "In times like these many families have divided loyalties. I believe each man should be judged on his own convictions, not those of his family."

"A noble sentiment, Mr. Deveroe, but one perhaps a bit too luxurious. May I remind you that many men move through this very camp claiming patriotic sentiments when their true motive is to pick up information which they then pass along to the enemy."

Richard's fury showed only in the quiet lowering of his voice. "Are you suggesting that I am a spy, Mr. Carne?"

Jaspar Carne smiled back, obviously pleased to see that he had penetrated that Deveroe composure. "I suggest nothing. I merely relate a well-known fact of wartime life."

"For God's sake, Carne," Hamilton exploded, "I've known Richard Deveroe for years. He is an honorable man and comes of a fine family in spite of their misguided loyalties. You overreach yourself, sir!"

Effortlessly Carne rose to his feet, giving Richard a barely perceptible bow. "My apologies, Mr. Deveroe. Evidentally your family's reputation for honor is strong enough to overcome your cousin's treason and rapine. If Colonel Hamilton vouches for you, who am I to question? Good evening, gentlemen."

Richard watched the slim back weave smoothly across the room. "What a damned peculiar man. Is he a friend of yours, Colonel?"

"I should hope not! He's a charter member of that overly zealous Committee of Safety that sees a Tory lurking behind every tree. They make our job ten times more difficult. Lord deliver us from self-righteous piety!"

"It concerns me very much," Richard said thoughtfully, "that my cousin Ewan's name is becoming difficult to live down. Is he such a devil? I don't know him for one at all."

"Perhaps it is because he preys upon his own people. I think that is the real basis of the resentment against him."

Shrugging, Richard lifted the brown bottle on the table, holding it over Hamilton's glass. "Will you join me in a toast?"

"Just a quick one for liberty, then tell me what you've been about. I heard you were with the Congress and I'm anxious to know if they are truly as hopeless as my good General is beginning to believe."

"More hopeless from what I've seen here today." Richard poured the amber liquid into their tin cups. "Is his Excellency so discouraged, then?"

Hamilton's face darkened. "He believes we are on the brink of utter ruin. If something isn't done soon to bring order out of this chaos, he doesn't think the army can hold together much longer."

Richard lifted his glass. "Let's pray that God will save us from the incompetence of men and guide our country safely into liberty."

"To liberty!" the Colonel answered and downed his drink in a few quick swallows.

Outside the tavern Jaspar Carne stopped and leaned against the door, drinking deeply of the cold night air. He had done it again. For a third time he had let this Deveroe cub loose the tight rein he kept on his emotions. For a man who prided himself on his rational approach to life, it was unforgivable that the sight of one man could unleash such deep-seated resentment.

With careful deliberation he set his round hat on his head and started off down the common, pulling his coat around his neck. What was it about Richard Deveroe, he thought, that made him want to strike that aristocratic face? Of course, there was that old incident on the Hunt's Point road. He was never going to forgive that fancy upstart for striking him as though he were a common servant. He had known from the moment it had happened that someday he would wreak vengeance for that blow.

But this involved more than a personal vendetta. The sight of a wealthy, land-rich Deveroe walking among patriotic men was almost more than he could bear. This Richard Deveroe pretended to care for a republic which was set on making him equal with other men. Surely he was dissembling. Worse than that, Carne thought, he was almost certainly there to spy for the British. It was the only answer that made sense, and Jaspar Carne valued sensible solutions above all things. Richard Deveroe had powerful friends in Congress and the army, so it would not be easy to prove him false. But it could be done if he, Jaspar Carne, pursued it patiently enough. His thin lips lifted in a grim smile. He knew himself to be, more than most men, stubborn to a fault where justice was concerned. Like the prophets of old, he would bide God's good time, keeping the faith and waiting for the mighty to fall under the righteous rod. And Deveroe would fall. Of that he was as sure as he was of the tiny stars he could see twinkling in the night sky over the dark outline of the North Castle hills.

How satisfying it was to have God on your side!

Celia wandered aimlessly into the old milk room, not really conscious of where she was or why she had come. Idly she set about rearranging the crocks of drying herbs and checking behind the paneling where what was left of their cheese and butter was carefully hidden. It was her common state now to seem to be two people—one moving methodically through the familiar chores, the other watching and grieving from the side. Richard had been home from his trip north for two weeks now, and each day seemed harder to bear than the last. She was all too conscious of her failure to do any more than carry out the letter of her resolution. She had not seen Ewan and she would not. She would not give her body to her lover again. But she sometimes wondered what the use was of being true with your body when your heart was so faithless. She had failed even to give her husband a polite civility, much less the love he expected of her. She saw the grimly determined way he threw himself into carting timber and sawing lathes with which to repair the barn—chores she knew he despised but which had to be done. He had borne it with his usual maddening grace, keeping his quiet temper, returning her clipped words with hurt glances, respecting the cold distance she managed to create in their narrow bed. She caught the anxious, mystified looks with which he studied her when he thought she wasn't watching. She knew she was being unfair and cruel to this man who was only asking that she be the wife he had always known, and she hated herself the more for it. God forgive her, she even hated Richard, while with every fiber and nerve of her body she longed for Ewan's arms around her, his lips against her breasts.

The thought itself brought a searing pain. With a groan, she shoved a section of the paneling back into place, throwing out her arm and knocking her elbow against one of the large earthenware crocks Betsy had placed on the shelf. The jar wavered for a moment, then fell to the floor, crashing into pieces and scattering the herbs Betsy had saved to make medicinal water.

"Oh, bother!" she groaned, and fell to her knees to pick up the drying plants and the pieces of the jar in her apron. As her hand reached for a frilly collection of lacy stems, she found herself staring down at a clump of southernwood. The room faded, she was back in the garden at daybreak and Ewan was weaving the plant into her hair. The tears started, soft at first, then in a flood of great racking sobs.

Richard found her there, kneeling on the floor, weeping as though her heart would break. In an instant he had her in his arms, rocking her back and forth like a parent comforting a hurt child. It was all he had wanted to do for a long time.

"My poor dear girl. Don't carry on so. It's only a jar.

Perhaps I can mend it, or if not there are plenty more. Please don't cry so."

She almost laughed, miserable as she was, yet there was a solace in his arms around her, the closeness of his familiar body and willingly she leaned against him.

"That settles it," he said firmly. "I'm not going away again. I've wondered if I should and now I know that leaving you would not be wise. You've borne too much alone too long. I'll write tonight to Mr. Jay and tell him I cannot accompany him when he takes his seat in Congress next month."

How was she going to hide her dismay? "Are you sure?" she finally murmured.

"Never more sure. You've gone away from me too far already. I don't want to lose you completely."

Celia cringed, not daring to think how much she had already become lost to him. "Yes, Richard. I want you to stay. Stay, please, for my sake. Help me."

"We'll do it together. I can run a farm, I know I can. Somehow we'll keep the place intact until this war is over. I'll save it for you, Celia, I promise. Will that relieve your sadness?"

She stopped, laying her hand against his thin cheek. "You are such a good man, Richard. You deserve a better wife."

Celia hoped the worst was now behind her, but of course the closeness of that moment did not last. Each day was a renewed struggle to force Ewan from her mind and keep herself from shrinking from her husband's touch. Sometimes she succeeded, but more often not, leaving Richard confused, impatient and, finally, irritable. They moved around the house, two polite strangers, the gulf between them widening all the time. When, in the dark of their bed, her longing finally drove her into her husband's arms, the wildness of her passion and the desperate weeping it provoked left him mystified and helpless. He took refuge in hard work, driving himself to do with the inadequate help of their three servants what had been left undone for two years.

In all that time she saw Ewan only once. After a sleepless night, she climbed from the bed in the gray light of early morning, hugging a counterpane close around her against the bitter, bone-chilling cold of their room. She never knew what led her to the window, but there she was, pulling back the curtain to look out on the misty dawn, the ground glazed by frost. She almost failed to recognize the man sitting on the great black horse in the road, staring up at her window, until in the dim light it seemed their eyes met. She could barely make out his red coat underneath a heavy black cloak, but she knew Goliah at once, pawing the ground with one hoof and blowing against the cold in his impatience to be off. She never knew if he saw her or not, he turned so quickly and galloped down the road south, but she knew it was Ewan. He must have spent the night at his house and paused there by her door before continuing his journey. Somehow it reassured her to know he longed for her as much as she did for him, and for a few hours she was happy again.

But that too passed, and gradually Celia took some kind of strength from merely living her day-to-day existence, trying to recapture the life she had once found so satisfying as Madam Deveroe of the Manor House Farm. Christmas brought a welcome hamper of exotic imports from Wayside, straight out of the New York shops, and a terse little letter from Hester that sounded as though England had failed still to meet the Barnetts' expectations. There were also small gifts left occasionally at their door accompanied by a brief scrawl from Ewan. Bottles of hard-to-obtain wine, a bolt of superfine cloth, two yards of exquisite Mechlin lace and a tooled leather copy of Rousseau's *La Nouvelle Héloïse*, gifts which remembered both the Deveroes and so could not be misconstrued.

By early February the weather had effectively ended all but indoor chores. On one sparkling sunny day when the snow lay so deep that fences and rails had disappeared beneath its depths, Richard and Vestal brought out an ancient family sleigh and hitched up the bell harness to one of the three horses they still had left. Bundling her up in all the robes they could find, with a warm soapstone at her feet, Richard drove her off across the fields to visit their neighbors, enjoying the cold, brisk, invigorating air after the closeness of the house.

It turned out to be a pleasant afternoon, and Celia was beginning to feel almost her old self as they started along the silver-sequined path home. When she saw the men on horseback waiting by the bridge, panic rose in her throat and even Richard slowed the horse, taking stock of the scene. Then a smile lit up his thin face.

"Why, I believe it is Ewan." he said, jingling the harness. "I haven't seen him since I got back. What good luck!"

By then she had recognized him too. Slipping down into

the rugs, she drew her hood around her face, afraid to look for fear of rekindling all the old longings, yet unable to keep her eyes away. As they neared the small group of horsemen, Ewan broke away and rode to meet them, his face as dark as the gray dusk.

He never glanced in Celia's direction, but rode directly up to Richard, shoving a handbill at him.

"Do you know anything of this, Cousin?" he said rudely.

"That is not a very warm welcome, Ewan, after so long a time. Let me see it." Not smiling now, Richard took the paper and read it quickly. "So they did it after all," he muttered under his breath.

"You did know, then. You might have told me."

"No, I did not know for certain, although I had heard rumors that this was coming." He turned, handing the bill to Celia, assuming that she would be curious.

"The New York Provincial Congress has passed an act of attainder," he explained quietly. "All the lands belonging to men who are loyal to the Crown now become forfeit to the state."

Ewan glared at them both. "And prominent among them is the Deveroe name. I suppose you noticed, Cousin, that your father and brother are there, and, naturally, myself as well. But I notice that your name is conspicuously missing. How very providential for you."

Richard had not seen Ewan for some months. Seeing him now in such a state of contained fury, he noticed for the first time how hard his cousin's face had become. The war had changed him, and not, it seemed, for the better.

"I had nothing to do with this, Ewan, surely you know that. As for my name not being on this list, no doubt that is due to my association with Mr. Jay. I certainly pulled no strings on my own behalf, and I resent your implication that I would do such a thing."

Ewan looked away from his cousin's steady gaze. It was just so damnably infuriating that these arrogant rebels could, with a stroke of the pen, proclaim that his home, his lands, his livelihood were forfeit. That they could legally brand him a traitor.

He pulled himself up in the saddle. "My apologies, Richard. My outrage over this thing was so great that I misjudged you. They have a nerve, you must admit."

Richard folded the paper and handed it back to his cousin.

"You're in good company, you know. Frederick Philipse, Beverly Robinson, Judge Thomas—some of the best men in the province." And very shrewd of the Provincial Congress, he thought. All the great landowners and wealthy men of property, Episcopalians and gentry, almost to a man. This act should break forever the power of the land barons in New York.

"This war is not over yet," Ewan said bitterly, looking out over the frozen Bronx River. "Let's see them enforce their little acts—this extralegal declaration by an unlawful group!"

"A lot will depend on the outcome. If the rebellion should be successful—"

Ewan pulled Goliah's head around. "It won't be! I trust that when next we meet, Cousin, it will be under more pleasant circumstances."

Richard watched him join the men on the bridge and canter down the road toward old Hunt's farm. Glancing over at his wife, he noted her intense stare following the retreating horsemen and put it down to affront.

"I don't think I've ever seen Ewan so upset," he said, flicking the reins over his horse's back. The sleigh slid smoothly forward, setting the bells jangling. "He so far forgot his manners as to not even greet you."

"Oh," Celia replied lightly, trying to ignore the misery knotting itself around her chest. "Did he? I didn't notice."

Two weeks later Richard deliberately made the trip to Morrisania to visit Ewan and try to restore their severed friendship. He was gone most of the day, returning in the early dusk, tired and cold, but much satisfied. He brought with him a gift for Celia sent by their cousin, an exquisite hair ornament of tiny seed pearls sewn on a green velvet ribbon.

"I suppose it is a peace offering," Richard said, watching his wife run her fingers along the cool creamy jewels, "to make amends for his ignoring you the last time we met."

"It's very beautiful."

"He told me he picked it up on a visit to the city, but, knowning Ewan, he is more likely to have won it from some British officer in a card game or a cockfight." He poked at the fire, then leaned back in his chair, resting his boots on the fender.

"I shall have to bury it, I suppose, until the war is over. There is no place to wear it now and I should hate to have it stolen."

"Put it away for now, but mark the place, for by next spring, as soon as the ice thaws, I would like to take you with me to visit Wayside. I'm anxious to see my parents, and surely that close to the city there will be some kind of society. You will need a little finery then and I notice there is little left. What happened to your topaz? Was it stolen?"

"No. It is buried in the field. I'll put this with it."

"Such times these are," he said, shaking his head. "Even our best food is buried out there in holes in the ground to be dug up when there is an important visitor. We live like squirrels!"

"Be glad you have the food to bury. Many people don't have even that much."

"I suppose."

Silence sat heavy in the room. The flickering light from the fireplace and the candle on the table sent dancing shadows on the walls.

"And how was Ewan?" Celia asked quietly.

"In much better spirits than when I saw him last. He is quite the king down there, you know. It suits him, this running a brigade. He does an excellent job of it."

"Did you reconcile your differences?"

"Oh yes. The act of attainder still rankles, but he has other things on his mind now. His impatience with me was forgotten in his anger over some young trooper of his who had deserted and gone back up-county. It happens every day, of course, but this fellow was a special favorite and Ewan felt he had been betrayed."

Celia looked sharply at her husband. "Not Ned Carne?"

"Yes, I think that was his name. Do you know him?"

"I met him once or twice last summer. He is an exceptional young man and everyone likes him. I'm surprised he would desert."

"So was Ewan. I gathered he never expected it from this particular fellow." He looked up suspiciously. "I met one of the Carnes when I was in White Plains, but there was nothing attractive about that gentleman. I wonder if it was the same family."

"Ned was from Horseneck."

"It is the same, then. They're probably related in the way so many of our people are in the county. Ah, well, even members of the same family can be very different. Look at Henry and myself."

Celia held the soft ribbon to her cheek and rubbed its velvet surface along her skin. It said so much, this impractical, frivolous, feminine gift. It told her more clearly than words that, with all Ewan's concern over Carne's desertion, the attainder of his lands and the problems of his Refugees, he had not forgotten her.

seventeen

"You've a very bad cut there, Colonel, and you've lost a lot of blood. You're going to have to lie up for a few days if you want to go back to doing this kind of thing again anytime soon."

Dr. Sayre tied the last of the linen strips around the lint bandages on Ewan's arm and sat back to survey his work. A neat job, if he did say so himself.

"Damn my eyes if you haven't ruined my coat!" Ewan commented testily. "Do you realize how difficult it is to find a proper military coat these days, Sayre? You might have been more careful."

"I didn't ruin your coat, Deveroe. Here, have another draft of this brandy. It'll put some strength back into you. How did you get such a wound, anyway?"

"A skirmish with a Continental patrol on Pell's Point. Two Connecticut rebels rode out on the ice after me swinging their sabers for all they were worth. I caught one of them right across the face, but the other managed to slice my arm before my horse could get away."

Dr. Sayre shook his head. "Folly! Utter folly! You might have been killed—and for what? A few rebel prisoners and a little plunder, neither of which will bring the resolution of this civil war one day closer."

Ewan hardly heard him, "How are the others?"

"All fine except the fellow with the musket ball. I removed it and dressed the wound, but putrefication is almost certain to set in. I'll keep him here awhile until we see how he does."

Gingerly Ewan moved his arm back and forth. "God's blood, it would be my sword arm! It will heal, won't it?"

"Give it a little rest and it should be good as new. Now..." Dr. Sayre rose to remove a basin of bloodied water. "Where can you go where you'll be cared for? And don't say back to camp, for I know you'll have no rest there."

Ewan slumped in the chair and leaned his head against the high upholstered back to still the spinning of the room. "I don't know. Does it matter?"

"What about your cousin Richard? I feel sure his missus would take good care of you; they're your kin, after all."

"No. I won't bother them with my troubles. Besides, that would be too obvious. I like to be where no one would think of looking for me."

"Is there anyone else?"

Ewan thought a moment. "Yes, I know the very place. The Lawrences are friends of mine; in fact, I'm promised to their daughter. They would put me up for a while, I feel sure, and they know how to be quiet about it, too. That ought to serve until I can get over being dizzy every time I sit up."

"If you want to use that arm again you'd better plan on staying there at least as long as it takes that wound to heal. Those are doctor's orders."

It was nearly three weeks later that Celia and Richard learned that their cousin was at the Lawrences; recovering from a wound. Richard went at once to check on the progress of his convalescence. He found him propped up in the warm kitchen, smoking a pipe and, in spite of the fact that his presence here was supposed to be a secret, holding court with a constant stream of orderlies from Morrisania bearing papers, letters, requisitions and orders from British headquarters. Mrs. Lawrence, pleased to have her daughter's fiancé as a house guest, fussed over him with all the solicitousness of a mother, while, Richard noted, the real care of the invalid was carried on quietly and efficiently by her darkly pretty daughter, who had grown several inches since Richard saw her last. Ewan was in good hands, he reported back to Celia, thinking she would be relieved to hear it. To his disappointment the news hardly rippled her languid composure.

"Was he badly hurt?" she asked listlessly.

"No, only a saber cut on the wrist and arm. He's tending it carefully so as not to lose the use of it, but I suspect that he'll be back at the camp very soon now. He feels the loss of his horse more keenly than the wound on his arm."

Celia sat up at that. "Goliah? He's lost Goliah?"

"Is that the name of his big English black? Then that's the

one. It was stolen last week, along with a valuable mare. Ewan was livid."

"How? Who could have taken him? Ewan would never have left him unguarded!"

He noticed with some surprise that this was the most consternation she had shown in days. "Evidently it was a well-planned foray made by some of the men from the upper party—Thomas Ferris, you remember him, he's always up to some kind of mischief, Carpenter and that Carne fellow again. They watched the field where the horses were pastured until a rainstorm drove off the boy who was supposed to be guarding them, then rode away, two of them on one horse and one on the other. Nearly made it scot-free, too."

"Not Ned Carne?"

"That's the one—the fellow who deserted not long ago. Anyway, they had nearly got past a patrol of Refugees when someone recognized the Colonel's horse and took off after them. They chased them all the way to New Castle, but couldn't catch up. I doubt he'll ever get the horse back now."

Celia stared into the fire, seeing the dusty track at Fort No. 8 with Ned Carne proudly cantering Goliah before the admiring crowd. How could he have paid Ewan in such poor coin? No wonder the Colonel was so furious. Poor Ewan. His young protégé first a deserter, then a horsethief, his favorite mount stolen, and now he himself wounded and at the mercy of the Lawrence family! How she ached to care for him, and instead he must make do with that painfully shy, tongue-tied little Lawrence mouse.

"I told Ewan I would stop in again in a few days to bring him some of Betsy's medicinal water," Richard said in an attempt to bring her out of her reverie. "Would you like to go with me? It might be good for you to get out and visit people for a change."

"No!" she exclaimed, looking at him with startled eyes. "No, you go without me. I don't really want to see anyone, especially Mercy Lawrence."

Leaning forward, Richard placed his hand gently over her long fingers lying on the arm of her chair. He said in his most conciliatory voice, "It would do you good. You work too hard here, my dear. And Ewan has always been able to make you laugh."

Anger broke through the surface of her composure, an anger born of the terrible grief that filled her heart. Hardly able to bear the touch of her husband's hand, she quickly snatched her own away. "I told you I don't want to go! Why must you badger me? Leave me alone!"

He watched her rise and leave the room, too astonished at first to call her back. Then, after a moment, such burning rage consumed him that he would not have called her back anyway. Whatever was bothering her was making her impossible to live with. God knows he had tried everything—patience, kindness in the face of her irritability, and the difficult effort of not allowing himself to become angry over her rejection of him. Nothing helped to dispel this baffling black cloud she carried around with her.

And why was she so touchy about Ewan? They had always been the best of friends.

The idea touched his consciousness and suspicion flared in spite of all he could do to force it from his mind. It was absurd, foolish, ridiculous! And yet . . .

Hadn't Ewan been found hiding under her bed? But that was innocent, of course. Why did they behave so strangely together, avoiding each other's eyes, never speaking directly? There could be any number of explanations. Why did she never talk about Ewan anymore, show no interest in anything that concerned him? Once she would have insisted on being the one to care for his wounds. Why was she so changed?

Richard stood up impatiently and, grasping the fire tongs, poked up the fire. Somewhere deep inside he felt ill. He had nothing, not one shred of evidence, to back up his suspicions, yet something in him sensed they were all too possible.

His wife—his cousin? Angrily he kicked at the logs.

It was absurd!

As winter gave way to spring Richard worked out his frustration and disappointment in tending the farm. Keeping busy until he dropped from exhaustion, he plowed and sowed the fields they had put under cultivation, cleared off a few new acres of woodlands to put in a new barley field next to the old one which had worn itself out, repaired the outbuildings, brought in straggling stock and devised new, more prudent hiding places for their horses and valuables. It was a constructive outlet for his restlessness although it did not in the least make up for his unhappiness.

As the weather cleared they began to fear new attacks both by the soldiers and by the guerrilla bands that freely roamed the countryside. Richard devised a system of watches for himself and the servants over the ripening grain in the hope that he might be able to harvest, grind it and hide it away before it could be stolen or requisitioned by the army. His hard work paid off, and as spring wore on the farm began to be in better shape than it had for two years. His vigilance was a deterrent to the lawless raiders, who left them alone for a longer period than at any time since the war started, and Richard began to feel hopeful about his land if not his marriage. In late April a letter came from Mr. Jay urging him to make the trip to Philadelphia, but he reluctantly laid it aside. Then in early May something happened that changed everything.

A second letter had come only the day before informing him that this time Mr. Jay had managed to wangle a place on a committee. The temptation was almost more than Richard could resist. Now he would really have a foot in the door. It was not too much to think that this might be the first steppingstone to his ultimate goal of congressman, and to refuse it for the sake of an unresponsive and depressed wife was very hard for him to do. Yet it was his duty to his marriage to do just that. He was trying to frame the difficult words to write Mr. Jay another rejection when he heard a horseman ride into the yard.

It was his young cousin, Ben, so upset he was almost incoherent. It took Richard several minutes to get the story, but when he understood what the boy wanted he went immediately to get his hat. Celia walked into the hallway from the kitchen, a question in her eyes, watching as he hurriedly threw on his black broadcloth coat.

"What's the matter?" she finally asked when he did not volunteer the information.

"It's Ewan. His Refugees took that Carne boy prisoner and Ewan is threatening to hang him. Ben wants me to see if I can stop it."

Her face went white. "He wouldn't do that!"

With deft movements Richard fastened his spurs to his boots. "I don't think he would, either, but I don't intend to take a chance on it. Ewan has a black temper and he bears this young man a grudge."

She grabbed at his arm, digging her nails into his sleeve. "Let me come with you. Perhaps I can help."

"Come with me? Have you completely lost your senses! This is man's work. It's no place for a woman."

"He'll listen to me, I know he will."

He looked up sharply. "Why should he listen to you if he won't to me? What nonsense. You stay here, Celia, and let me handle this. I don't want you involved."

He was already out the door, but she followed him, pulling on his arm. "Richard, please. Take me with you."

"No!" For once his anger got the better of him, and he shook off her arm. "I tell you I do not want a wife of mine mixed up in such an ugly business. You stay here, Celia, I insist. In fact, I order you to stay inside this house."

She stepped back, her eyes as cool and steely as his. Without answering she watched him hurry down the piazza steps and run down the path to the wooded copse behind the barn where his horse was tethered. A few minutes later he rode furiously out of the yard, Ben clattering behind him. Celia gave them just enough time to get out of sight, then, throwing off her house slippers and going barefoot, she ran to the barn and grabbed a bridle, lured Kit in from the secluded pasture where she had been grazing, and galloped bareback down the road toward Hunt's farm behind her husband, not caring what he was going to feel when he saw her there.

There was already a small crowd gathered around the open door to Theophilus Hunt's stable. So intent were they on what was happening inside that Celia was able to fasten Kit's reins to a bush and slip up to the edge of the group unobserved. She recognized most of them—old Theophilus, of course, his heavy white brows knit in concern, Ben and Richard, an old slave named Lunnon, well known around West Farms for his ability to play the fiddle, several troopers from Ewan's Refugee corps, and Ned Carne, with his hands tied behind his back but looking as handsome and debonair as the last time she had seen him. Only the paleness of his skin and the restless shifting of his eyes betrayed his concern. Standing before him was Ewan, his face dark with anger, brandishing his saber in his hand.

"I've known ye since ye were a lad," she heard Hunt saying in his level, reasonable voice, "and this is not the kind of work I'd expect of Ewan Deveroe. Come, now, Colonel, don't be rash. Think on it awhile."

"Bring me that rope, Lunnon," Ewan barked in response.

The old Negro looked around as though seeking a way to escape, then handed the rope to Ewan as he asked.

"You can be the executioner, Lunnon," Ewan said as he slipped the rope into a noose and knotted it. "Here, put this around the horsethief's neck."

"Oh, Lawd, Massa Ewan. Not me! I wants no part o' this."

"Do as I tell you!"

Richard's hand shot out for the rope, but Ewan grabbed it away.

"For God's sake, Ewan, there's been no trial. You can't make yourself judge and jury over this boy. Send him back to the jail and cool down before you punish him."

Ewan shoved Lunnon up beside Carne and looked around at the group, glaring, his saber raised.

"I'll cut the first damned rascal who tries to stop me," he said in a voice Celia had never heard before, "and that includes you, Richard. This is my affair and I'll handle it my way. Now get back, all of you, and stay back. Bring up that barrel, Lunnon, and slip the noose around this deserter's neck!"

"Gawd Almighty, Massa Ewan..."

Near tears, the old servant put the noose around Ned's neck and dragged up the small barrel beside him. Ewan threw the other end over a rafter and prodded Carne with the edge of his saber to stand on the upturned end. Celia saw Hunt start to speak, then draw back. It was useless, they could all see. In all the years she had known Ewan she had never seen such stubborn madness in his eyes before. She could see it reflected on Carne's pale face as he looked around the group.

"If you were to hang every man in your company, Colonel, for stealing a horse, who would be left?" he asked quietly.

Without answering, Ewan turned furiously on the slave. "Knock away the barrel!"

"Oh, Gawd, Colonel, I cain't! I cain't do dat. Don't ast me to."

"I told you to knock away that barrel," he cried, slapping the man on the ear.

"No, no, I won't do dat. I jus' cain't! You asts too much o' this ole slave!"

Ewan looked coldly around the group. "Which one of you will bring this renegade to his just reward, eh? Is there no man here with enough gumption to pay a foul deserter and thief in kind? Not one of you?"

"Ewan, in God's name, I beg you to reconsider," Richard desperately tried again, afraid to get too near his cousin's restless saber. "Let the boy down. You'll think better of it later, I know you will."

"What do you know about anything!" Ewan yelled, turning on him. "Stay out of what does not concern you, Richard. This is my business."

Over the heads of the crowd Ned Carne's blue eyes caught
Celia's and she shrank from what she saw in them. All the
group began speaking at once, nearly on the point of rushing
the Colonel to stop him.

Sensing it, he lashed out at them all in a fury, "A bunch
of damned cowards, all of you," and he rushed at the prisoner,
kicking the barrel, which went spinning, sending the helpless
man plunging down until the rope caught his neck and jerked
him upward. Celia screamed and covered her face with her
hands as a horrified silence fell on the group. When she looked
up it was to see the grotesque figure of Carne swinging slowly
from side to side, his head at a crazy angle and his boyishly
handsome face growing black as coal. It was all she could take.
Running blindly from the barn, she caught at Kit's reins and
clambered on her back, to clatter off down the road. She had
no idea where she was going. It didn't matter. All that mattered
was to get away from that place as fast as possible.

Behind her, Richard, who had heard her scream, saw her
disappear. It was all part of the nightmare that had begun when
he first walked into this barn. This could not be happening.
These could not be the people he had known all his life, the
people he had been closest to of any in the world. He watched
Ewan staring at the boy's body and saw only a stranger.

"You can have his clothes, Lunnon," Ewan said, stiffly
sheathing his sword. "See that he's proper buried."

No one spoke as he walked among them, not lifting his eyes
to meet the accusations of his young brother or his cousin, the
men who served under him or the old man who had been his
friend since childhood. He went straight to his horse and left
them all, riding back toward West Farms, more alone than he
had ever been in his life.

Celia did not return to the Manor House until dark had just
fallen. In the hours she was riding the roads and fields of West
Farms she barely knew where she was, seeing over and over
the look of bemused hopelessness on Ned Carne's face as his
eyes met hers. Whenever she stopped to rest Kit she would
slump to the ground, her head on her arms, groaning and crying
until there were no more tears left. It seemed as though all the
misery of the last few months, the desperate, hopeless longing
for Ewan, had been unleashed in one great tide that threatened
to overwhelm her.

As she was riding slowly back down the road that skirted

the river she passed the Mill House and noticed a tiny light between the closed wooden shutters inside the windows of the east parlor. A whinny from the woods behind her led her toward the rear, where she recognized one of Ewan's horses tethered just inside the fringe of the trees. She stared at the house, torn between her desire to rush inside and her commonsense resolution to stay away from Ewan forever.

He was inside that house, she knew, probably alone, and he needed her, somehow she knew that too. And for the last, grimly resolute time she turned away and rode across the bridge to her own home.

Just inside the door were her slippers with her worsted stockings thrown carelessly down beside them. It was almost with surprise that she looked down at her feet and saw she was barefoot. Sinking into a chair, she began to pull one of the stockings up over her leg when a muffled noise brought her head up and she saw her husband standing in the doorway of the morning room. The lamp he held in his hand threw ghostly shadows on his face, setting it in crevices. Even in the dim light the anger in his eyes was like a blow.

"Where have you been!"

It was more accusation than question. For a long moment she didn't answer.

"I've been riding," she said in a darkly level voice.

Moving rapidly, Richard reached down to grab her arm, jerking her to her feet. "What the devil do you mean going off like that, roaming the countryside alone without telling anyone where you were!"

His words were like a lighted match to her own anger. Snatching her arm away, she said furiously, "Take your hands off me. I don't have to tell anyone where I go. I'll go where I please."

"Oh, that is obvious, isn't it. Look at you, bare feet, hair flying, like a country trollop!"

Celia gasped. "How dare you speak to me that way!"

"I saw you riding away from that place today, your skirts up around your knees. And after I forbade you to go down there! Who's to say, 'How dare you?' I have more right to those words than you!"

What was the use of this? Celia started to turn away and leave him, but he seized her arm, twisting it and pulling her around to confront him.

"Yes, like a country trollop, that's exactly how you looked.

My wife, the lady of the manor, the dutiful, aristocratic Celia. My orders meant nothing, did they? After all, I'm only your husband! When I give my wife an order I might as well be talking to the wind. That's all it means to you."

"Richard, you're hurting my arm," she cried.

Quickly he dropped her wrist and stepped back, trying to control his fury. "I ought to beat you as other husbands do their disobedient wives. Perhaps that is the answer."

She rubbed at her arm, glaring back at him. "You're acting as crazy as Ewan!"

Furiously he turned to her. "*I'm* crazy! Look at you and look at him and then call *me* crazy! You've dragged around here in a black melancholy for weeks, barely speaking a civil word, cold as ice, ignoring everything I say, barely tolerating my presence. I'm not blind, you know."

"That's not true—"

"It is the gospel truth and you know it! And then to throw your reputation to the winds..."

"I've done no such thing."

"...and go galloping off to a despicable, grotesque hanging like some campfollower."

"I don't have to listen to this!"

"Oh, yes you do! You'll hear me out for once and you'll pay attention to what I say. Never, never again as long as we both live will you disobey me as you did this day!"

Grabbing up her shoes, Celia began furiously to pull on her stockings. "I'm not your possession, Richard Deveroe! You can't order me about as though you owned me body and soul, like some kind of slave."

She had her stockings on and she jammed her feet into her buckled shoes, reaching for her shawl that hung on a peg near the door. He grabbed at her arm again.

"Oh, but you *are* my possession. You became that when you married me, and I demand that you respect me as a husband!"

Celia jerked her arm away and with a swirl of the crocheted wool threw the shawl around her shoulders, gripping the ends against her chest.

"Demand all you want," she answered between clenched teeth. "But demand it to the air, because I won't stay to hear it."

"Celia!"

Her hand was on the iron latch when the coldness of his voice stopped her.

"What has happened to you? You're a stranger. I don't know you anymore. What's happened to Ewan? He killed that boy down there today in cold blood. What is this madness, this insanity that has distorted the whole world around here into something I don't recognize? I don't understand any of it and especially I don't understand you."

She gripped the latch, fighting back the tears. If she was ever going to turn back, this was the moment. He was giving her this single chance to work through their anger and grief and perhaps find something of what they had lost. Then she remembered Ewan sitting in his empty house alone. Lifting the latch, she pulled the heavy door open.

Richard spoke once more behind her, not in anger now but in a ruthless quiet. "Celia, I know where you're going and to whom. If you go through that door you should do so knowing that I will not be here when you return."

She never turned round, though she hesitated a moment more before flinging back the door and running out into the night. Her own resolution carried her down the road across the bridge to the Mill House. Her marriage was wrecked now, she knew, and she no longer cared. If there was anyone to see her going into Ewan's house her reputation would be shattered, too, but she did not care about that either. Only one thing mattered—she was going to the man she loved, leaving everything broken behind her. Out of her need and out of his she was going and she did not even know if he would welcome her. Her breath was tearing at her chest as she neared the house and worked her way around to the window. It took several minutes before her light tapping on the windowpane brought him to the shutters, and even then he did not speak and she knew only from the flickering shadows of the light that he was there.

"Ewan," she whispered. "It's Celia. Please let me in."

There was no movement or sound from inside the room, and she began to fear he did not want to see her.

"Please, Ewan . . ."

The light faded and, hoping for the best, Celia slipped to the front of the house, where after a few moments she heard the quiet lifting of the lock. She waited for the door to open, and when it did not she tentatively tried the latch. It creaked on its hinges as she slipped into the darkened hall. Far down at the end she could see the light from the parlor where he had already returned. There was no furniture at all in the hallway or any other room, and the plaster had gaping holes where the fixtures and the usable wood had been stripped away. Celia moved quietly down the hallway to the back parlor, once the most elegant room in the house, now furnished with only a rough plank table and a turned chair in the center and a narrow camp bed against one corner wall. There were two bottles on the table, one with the stub of a candle in its mouth, the other open and half empty. By the wavering light of the candle she could see him sitting, staring down at his hands lying on the table, his red coat like dark blood in the gutted room. She stood in the doorway waiting until he finally looked up at her, his face haggard, his eyes dark holes in his skull.

There was nothing to say. She held out her arms and he came into them, leaning his head against her shoulder, and she felt his tears through the thin fabric of her dress.

A pale sun rose the next morning, obscured by dark, threatening clouds and a hazy, misty rain. In the gray dawn of the Mill House parlor Celia stirred in her sleep and turned over, waking only long enough to feel Ewan's arm go protectively around her as she nestled close against him in the narrow bed.

Outside, unseen and unheeded, Richard rode past the house, his saddlebags packed with such of his belongings as he could carry and, tucked among them, part of the hard specie he had dug up from the field to pay for his trip. He left nothing behind but one portmanteau with instructions to Vestal that it be put on board a ship for Philadelphia. He left no note or memento, carried with him nothing to remind him of West Farms or the wife he was leaving behind. He was not a man to weep— indeed, he had not cried since his boyhood. And now the bitter, unshed tears were a weight pressing him down. His head ached and his eyes smarted and somewhere inside a knife was twisting into his vital organs. Yet without a backward glance he turned his horse's head westward and rode away from his home, telling himself he did not really care if he ever saw it again.

eighteen

It was more than a year before Celia saw her husband again. The farm quickly reverted to the same kind of casual husbandry it had known before Richard's return. Caterpillars invaded the apple trees, leaving huge white webs on the branches and destroying both blossoms and leaves so that the crop that fall was the poorest ever brought in. During that summer of 1779 the fighting in and across the country never ceased. Tryon raided up and down Long Island Sound while Tarleton led a daring raid on Pound Ridge and burned the town of Bedford. On the Hudson the British took Verplanck and Stony Point in an effort to close King's Ferry, but thanks to a daring retaliation led by the rebel General Anthony Wayne, they lost both before a month was out. In August Celia, recuperating from another bout with the malaria fever, stood behind shuttered windows and watched as nearly one hundred and fifty Continental soldiers marched down the Bronx River banks to make a surprise attack on Morrisania. Later she watched them sweeping back, carrying prisoners—both military and civilian Tories—along with them. Refugee soldiers bent on revenge followed on their heels, and the running fight that ensued lasted as far as the Connecticut border.

What concerned her more was that after the American retreat through West Farms she discovered that Jim, the Deveroes' lame slave, had followed the army, taking advantage of the laxity and confusion at her house finally to run off in pursuit of his freedom. Celia did not even bother to advertise for his return, although Ewan threatened to administer the standard military punishment of one thousand lashes if he was ever caught. As far as she was concerned he could have his freedom with her blessing even though it meant more work for the remaining servants and herself as well. Ah well, she thought, shrugging, they would do what they could and the rest would just have to go to seed.

Yet she was not uncaring. In the long months after Richard's departure she took cold, quiet stock of her life. She would not, could not give Ewan up—yet neither would she sacrifice her future or her livelihood to her passion for him.

Her good name, her husband's honor, their home and land were not to be lightly thrown away, for, once gone, they could never be brought back again. She did not intend to bring scandal down on herself or Richard if it could in any way be avoided. Although she could not tear herself from Ewan's arms, she made very sure that when she went into them no one knew of it. She was not being hypocritical. She knew this did nothing to alter her guilt or her sin. It was simply the only thing left she could do for her husband.

Without Richard her life revolved around her farm and her lover. The one took every measure of her strength and energy, while the other continued to be her solace, comfort and joy.

Richard himself, as the months went by and no hint of scandal concerning his wife reached his ears in Philadelphia, was profoundly relieved, for he knew that if Celia openly defied convention he would hear of it sooner or later. He told himself that perhaps his suspicions were wrong and the separation between them was simply the result of the stress of the war. Finally he sat down and wrote her a terse, polite note that inquired after her health and informed her of his. She answered in the same vein, and after that politely formal communications passed between them infrequently, with just enough news to let each other know that the breach was not irreversible. Only once did Celia realize how much she had hurt her husband. A letter from Elizabeth told her that Samuel Deveroe was failing badly and Richard had briefly come up from Philadelphia to see him. It hurt her a little to think that her husband had been at Wayside without bothering to come to West Farms to see her, yet on reflection she saw the wisdom of his action. His presence there would only force the issue once again, while without it they could both pretend their marriage was not a complete failure.

One beautiful fall day in late September, Vestal brought news that a miller from the camp was at the Deveroe mill and that anyone who wished grain ground should take it there. The weather was so lovely that Celia took the sacks of grain herself, leading old Bonny, who was nearly blind now but still had good legs. While she was waiting with the crowd around the dilapidated worn porch of the building she felt a hand on her shoulder and looked around to see Ewan behind her.

"Leave that for now and come out on the river with me," he said, slipping her arm through his.

"Dare I? Flour is as precious as gold these days."

"Murpheson here will see that it gets ground for you, won't you, Elijah? As a favor to me."

"Aye, Colonel, all right. Its a good day to take a lady out on the water even if she do be yer cousin."

"Thank you, Mr. Murpheson," Celia called over her shoulder as she followed Ewan down the dirt path toward the river. She had not thought to see him at all this day, and her heart was singing as they walked beside the whitewashed walls of Ewan's house.

A small oak bateau was pulled up on the grass and in only a few minutes Ewan had it pushed to the water's edge, where he handed her in. Dipping the oars into the quiet water, he pulled away from the shore and sent the boat gliding between the tall pines and oaks that shadowed the water downstream from the mill. It was a narrow river and on a sparkling day like this its surface was a mirror of the still blue sky above it. Celia pulled off her housewife's cap and shook out her hair to let the slim breeze touch her neck.

"You look like a wanton with your hair falling down that way," Ewan said, studying her from under his arched brows.

She smiled up at him. "I thought you liked me to be wanton."

"I do, but not here in public with all of West Farms to see. I like the unladylike side of your nature to be my secret and my treasure."

"And so it is," she said, lightly squeezing his hand where it rested on the oar. Reluctantly she piled her hair back inside the cap.

"I had not thought to see you here today. It was a pleasant surprise."

"I came down with the men who are running the mill because I was hoping to meet you. I planned to drop in at the house until I saw you sitting on the porch with the rest of the yeomen."

"Why not? When we are all scratching to keep enough to eat on the table it seems foolish to play lady of the manor. I never felt quite so at one with my neighbors as I have these last two years. Even the Trentons are not so different from the rest of us now."

"Yes, and that is because you all live now as they used to!"

"I know of no other way, Ewan. We have all been reduced to poverty, so we may as well share in it as brothers."

"A fine republican speech for a Deveroe! You should join the upper party, since you talk like one of them."

"I am only half jesting," she said lightly, "so let's not quarrel about it. It is too fine a day to be unhappy."

He picked up the oars, "I wanted to tell you that I will be away for a time. The British are opening a front in the Southern colonies and most of the regiments in West Chester will be sailing soon for the Carolinas. No one knows yet just where the Refugees will end up, though I suspect we will be back here very soon. They plan to raze some of the lesser forts on the Harlem, but I feel sure they'll leave Morrisania and Number Eight intact."

"They won't send you so far away, will they?"

"I doubt it. I'm of more use to them right here. After all, those people in the city must still have food, and who knows better how to scout the countryside to deliver it to them than one who grew up here?"

"It causes you some pain, doesn't it?"

"It pains me that the good people of the county see only my crimes and not my reasons. And that they ascribe every criminal act to me personally, even when I am helpless to prevent it. You know the lengths I go to in order to elude another capture. It is not only because I fear the humiliation. It's because I know I would be their prisoner only so long as it took to hang me. But I won't quit—not while there is a hope of putting down this rebellion and restoring the King's peace."

"*Is* there any hope, Ewan?" Celia sighed. "The war seems to drag on so. Rumor has it that the rebel army has never been so demoralized. Why doesn't General Clinton strike one strong blow to end it all? I don't understand."

"You are not alone, my love. And this ragged rebel army always seems to come up with some encouraging action just when things are the worst for them. Like Wayne's brilliant coup at Stony Point last July—curse his black heart!"

"I hope you won't be gone long," she said quietly. Their eyes locked across the length of the boat.

"I hope the same."

A redwing blackbird gliding above them cast a thin shadow on the water. Ewan studied the lines of Celia's long, graceful neck and the swelling of her breasts in the close-fitting bodice of her worn calico gown. He knew every line, every curve, and it gave him a sense of warm pride to know how familiar her body was to him. She had come a long way from the young girl with the wide brown eyes he had always taken for granted. She was a woman now, with long lashes on the pale cheeks she lifted to the sun, a smile on her wide, sensuous, finely shaped mouth. And she was his. It almost frightened him to think how dear she had become to him.

Opening her eyes, she caught him watching her and, smiling, reached for his hand. It was the only gesture allowed them on the open river where anyone could see.

"Where have you been staying the nights?" she asked lightly.

"In places you would not believe. Why, I even spent the better part of two days up in a pine tree! One of Hull's advance patrols refused to move from a very inconvenient camp nearby."

"That must have been uncomfortable."

"Not in the least. I even had supper brought to me—secretly, of course."

"I wish I had known you were there. I would have brought it to you myself."

"Mercy Lawrence did as well."

Celia sat forward, sending the boat rocking. "Mercy Lawrence! You're jesting. That spiritless little child dared a rebel patrol to bring you a meal? I don't believe it."

"Oh, Mercy has spirit enough once you get past her reserve. She's been a help to me more than once, in fact. I was pleasantly surprised to find she has both intelligence and initiative, and, God knows, I can't have too many friends with both."

"She has certainly kept them well hidden."

"Perhaps that is because you never had the opportunity to need them."

Celia felt the unpleasant stirrings of jealousy. "Please, in the future when you have need of friends, remember me. You know there is nothing I would not brave to help you."

He smiled, lifting her hand to his lips. "My love, you help me with the most important needs I have, those no one else is so well qualified to serve. Isn't that enough?"

Removing her hand, Celia dabbled her fingers in the water, rippling its calm surface. She was annoyed with herself for feeling so distressed that this snippy girl could have been of such invaluable assistance to Ewan.

"Have you heard from Richard?" he asked, jarring her out of her reverie.

"Yes, once, briefly. He is busy as ever and not a little upset that the Patriots distrust him so. He'd expected to head a committee by now, but it seems opposition to his family has prevented it."

"Did he mention when he might come home?"

"No. I don't think he wants to return, and certainly I don't want him to. Let him stay down there where he loves to be. It is the only way you and I can be together."

Ewan picked up the oar and pushed it through the water, turning the bow of the boat back toward the mill.

"You *do* want us to be together?" she asked softly.

"I don't have to leave for New York until tomorrow. I'll be at your window tonight."

For two summers the British had virtually occupied West Chester County, their strong bases in the southern section allowing them to roam the upper reaches at will. The American forces at White Plains and Peekskill, though they made frequent forays into the Royalist strongholds, still kept their main army securely above the Croton River. All this changed when in the fall of 1779 most of the King's forces were shipped to Charleston in the Carolinas, and West Chester once more became an open territory, "neutral" in name only. As Ewan had suspected, the partisan corps on the Harlem River were left there to keep the supply routes across King's Bridge open, and if they thought this was going to be an easy job they were quick to learn otherwise. The British force had barely sailed out of New York Harbor before the Continental Army began making bold raids down as far as Morrisania itself, evincing a new spirit of self-confidence earned slowly and painfully through four years of guerrilla warfare. Then, as if the war were not bad enough, the weather also turned against the county's suffering inhabitants.

It was the coldest winter anyone could ever remember, worse than the famed 1697. The harbor between New York and Staten Island was frozen so solid that supplies were carried back and forth across it by sleigh. Rumors from the city told of severe suffering due to a great shortage of fuel and overcrowding in a city filled with homeless refugees. It was bad enough in West Farms, and Celia had all she could do to bring herself and her servants through it alive. She moved into a single room, the kitchen, and would have brought them in also but that their small cabins were easier to keep warm. The two horses she had left were stabled out of necessity, even though that made it all the easier for them to be stolen. Every morning left dead birds and the frozen bodies of animals scattered on the icy meadows surrounding the farm. In November she had a letter from Richard saying he would try to get home by the first of the year, but the winter months went by without his appearing, probably because the weather prohibited travel. Yet the cold did nothing to halt the fighting and bring respite to the civilians in its path. Raid and reprisal, vengeance and plunder were the order of the times.

Spring finally thawed the mountains of snow into rivers of mud and roads were made impassable for weeks at a time. When the warm weather finally came, Celia looked over her ruined fields and wept. She simply did not have the strength to begin again, though this was usually the busiest time of the year for sowing and planting. Gradually as she talked to her neighbors who had talked to their neighbors, she learned that she was not alone in her lethargy. The people of the county were worn out. Everywhere was a sense of ruin and hopelessness. Half the farmhouses of any given district stood abandoned and empty, if not stripped and burned. Fields that should have been green with new buds of growing grain were choked instead with weeds and grass. The herds of cattle, horses and sheep which once foraged freely through the forests and meadows were not to be seen, for where they existed at all they were kept carefully concealed.

At the end of June word came that Samuel Deveroe had died two months before, another casualty of the winter. Celia closed herself up in her room and wept silently and alone. Though these last years of illness had reduced his huge frame to a gaunt shadow of what he had been, she still saw him as the large, kind, grandly dressed stranger who sat beside her in the coach that day he brought her from East Chester to West Farms. All the years of kindness now weighed her down. He had taken her out of a life dark with poverty and misery and set her in his family almost as a daughter. He had even allowed her to marry his son. And what had she given in return? For the first time in two years her guilt and remorse almost eclipsed her obsession with Ewan.

Richard returned to Wayside to comfort his mother and visit his father's grave, and then, warily but determined, took the boat up the East River to his home. It was good that he did, for it was only because of his presence there that a pitiful crop of barley and oats was harvested and the buckwheat seeded. He was appalled, not only at Celia's paralyzing apathy, but at the way that same slipshod attitude had communicated itself to the servants. Simply by his energy and enthusiasm he soon had Celia and Vestal, Betsy and Diamond back at work.

Celia was grateful that he had come, for only then did she realize how deeply the depressing condition of the county had affected her. During the time they spent alone together he was coolly polite but never the least hostile, and though they shared their old bed he never made a move toward her. She let him set the tone and she followed it completely, knowing now that she could never keep this place going without him. It was only by a few suggestions and hints that she guessed how disappointed he was with his work in Philadelphia, yet he also made it clear that he expected to resume it again. What he did not tell her was that Mr. Jay had been appointed minister plenipotentiary to Spain and was going abroad, and that when he, Richard, went back to attempt to carry on his duties with the Congress, it was going to be without his mentor's protection.

He was off again in the fall, just before the startling news broke that rocked the county, the army and the Congress. One of the most famous and zealous Continental generals, Benedict Arnold, had turned traitor and attempted to sell out the garrison at the new fort on West Point. Because the hapless British officer, Major John André, who was the liaison between Arnold and General Clinton in New York, was taken prisoner in nearby Tarry Town all West Chester talked of nothing else for weeks. Argument raged: Arnold was a blackhearted traitor or he was a man who simply saw the error of his ways; André should be hanged as a spy, as indeed he was, or he should have been exchanged as the innocent victim in a tangled web of intrigue. The three men who had taken André prisoner in Tarry Town were all local residents, acclaimed by many as heroes and castigated by others as greedy bounty hunters who accidentally happened on a stroke of luck.

The danger so providentially averted had the effect of moving the state assemblies to action against the Loyalists in the county. Whole families who were suspected of being friends to the British were evicted from the middle ground and moved south to the British camps. Taxes were levied on any family who had a father, son or brother serving with the British, and also on the Quakers, who did not believe in any kind of fighting. A "Black Rate" was levied on resident Loyalists in order to raise sums to cover losses brought about by enemy raids, adding more hardship to people who already were barely able to survive. Small wonder, Celia thought, that so many families of the county picked up and moved to other provinces not so sorely affected by the war.

As the year wore on, the American forces were reduced to a minimum of several regiments stationed above the Croton River, leaving the entire middle and lower county at the mercy of partisan troops. There were rumors that the French were sending ships and men to help the rebels, and rumors too that the British were winning great victories in the South. Now and then Celia read of them in an old copy of Rivington's *Royal Gazette* which Ewan brought back from New York, and she would look out over her empty fields—not snow-covered now, for this winter was as mild as the one before had been severe— and hope would rise anew that an end to war would come. At times she was not sure whether she really wanted the conflict over, for if peace would improve life in one way, it would complicate it in another. What was she to do when her husband returned to live at the Manor Farm and Ewan returned to the Mill House? If she had learned one thing from those few months of trying to be a faithful wife, it was that she could not do it. It would have to be one or the other, completely and finally, and she herself did not know what decision to make. With Richard came respect, honor, a good life, security, and the land she loved so deeply. With Ewan came her heart, her passion and nothing else. There could never be a divorce—it was impossible. So long as Richard lived she would be able to have only half a life with the man she loved above all others. Was it worth it? Was Ewan more to her than this earth which now had become almost a part of her life's blood? She did not know.

Terrible as the war was, at least as long as it continued she would not have to choose.

The mildness of that winter of 1780–81 brought a measure of hope to the weary people of West Chester, and with the beginning of spring those who were left once again tilled the fields, broadcast the seed and repaired what fences and out-buildings they had left. Celia urged her servants to new efforts so that when Richard came home in the summer he would not find the farm reduced to the dilapidated state of the year before.

It was on a mild day in early April that the woman appeared. Celia looked up to see her walking wearily across the old bridge straight toward the house. She was barefoot and her stooped shoulders and shuffling walk suggested a beggar of some sort. Reluctantly Celia put aside her carding comb and went to see what she wanted.

One look at the lined, leathery face and she knew she had seen her before, though where she could not remember.

"Madam Deveroe?" the woman asked timidly, shifting her sore feet on the soft grass.

"I am Madam Deveroe. And I know you from somewhere . . ."

"Yes, Madam met me when she came to visit Dominie Brec nigh on two years ago. I am Mrs. Lister, Elijah Lister's wife."

Celia recalled the shadowy woman who had moved in the background of the Lister house near Tuckahoe. She smiled. "Of course, I remember now. Come and sit beside me and tell me about my friend the dominie. You look as though you are about to drop from fatigue. Surely you did not walk all this way?"

Gratefully Mrs. Lister sank onto the bench, rubbing her dusty feet with a gnarled hand.

"Yes, ma'am, that I did. 'Twas the only way I had to get here—shank's mare, so to speak." She pushed some long strands of graying hair back under her cap and sat working her hands in her lap, obviously ill at ease.

"Are you hungry?" Celia asked.

"Oh, no ma'am. Not a bit. I don't want to burden you none. I'm fine."

"When did you eat last?"

"Somewheres along the road, I forget where."

That was obviously a lie. "Look, you rest here and I'll go and tell Betsy to fix you some dinner. Wait here for me."

Celia hurried off to speak to Betsy and when she returned she found Mrs. Lister leaning against the thick trunk of the tree, her eyes closed. In repose her face had a quiet prettiness about it that vanished when she opened her haunted eyes.

"Betsy will bring us out some refreshment soon," Celia said, sitting down beside her. "Meantime, tell me about my friend Dominie Brec and your husband. Are they well?"

Mrs. Lister looked down and her hands began to work again in her lap.

"No, ma'am. They an't well at all. That is, well, Dominie Brec, he is dead, and Mr. Lister, I don't know how he is. You see, the Committeemen came and arrested 'em both. Took 'em to jail without trial nor mercy of any kind. I went to visit 'em once there and it was a terrible place—dark, gloomy, with fevers and sickness. They wouldn't even let me bring 'em sustenance enough to keep body and soul together."

Celia turned away as the woman's eyes filled with tears. Dominie Brec dead! And not once had she gone to see him again as she had promised. Her experience on the road that fateful day and all the turmoil it had led to had put from her mind any possibility of venturing north again. And now he was gone forever.

"Why would they arrest that good old man? And your husband too? They could not possibly do harm to anyone."

"They was called Quakers and cowards and damned papists, and a danger to the district." Mrs. Lister dabbed at her eyes with the sleeve of her dress. "It wasn't true. Mr. Lister, he's a true Christian gentleman, and even if he was a Friend, he wasn't no enemy to the Congress. And poor old Dominie, he was too sick and old to harm anybody. But they was accused and that was all that was needed."

Why had she come? Celia wondered. Perhaps she thought Richard could do something about moving the Committee to mercy. She was going to be disappointed to learn that he was not even here.

"You see, ma'am," the woman went on, "when Mr. Lister was carried off I had very little left. My only consolation and support was old Gretchen, my brown-and-white cow. I figured as long as I could keep her I'd get by. With milk and just a little meal a body can make do for quite a time. When she was taken off, too, I thought to die."

"You mean the Committeemen took your cow too? Is there no limit to their arrogance?"

Mrs. Lister worked her hands and looked away, hesitating. "No, madam, it wasn't them as took old Gretchen. 'Twas them Cowboys. 'Twas that devil Deveroe's Refugees as heard there was a poor old woman with one cow left and swooped down and took her off, bold as brass in plain daylight. I couldn't do nothin' at all about it. Then I thought of you and remembered how kind you were when you come to see the old dominie."

Celia sat back, stunned.

"I remembered, madam, as how Colonel Deveroe, he's your

cousin. I thought if maybe I could get down here fast, before Gretchen was carried on to York Island to be butchered, maybe you could ask him to return her to me. It would mean the difference between living and dying."

"My God," Celia exclaimed, appalled at the woman's story as well as her simple request. Why had she come to her for help? For a horrible moment she feared it was because it was known throughout the county that she had a special relationship with the infamous Refugee leader. Yet, studying Mrs. Lister's worn face, she could see no duplicity there.

"My dear woman, you have indeed suffered from both parties in this dreadful war. Of course I will ask Colonel Deveroe to return your cow. He is not the monster that report has made him. He probably does not even know about the theft."

For the first time the woman smiled. "Oh, thank ye, madam. I knew you was a good woman the first time I set eyes on you kneeling by the old dominie's chair. Such a pretty lady, I says to myself, and with the sweetness of heaven on her fair face. I shall always be grateful to you."

"Where is Friend Lister now?"

"They carried him off up to Kingston jail. I don't even know if he's alive or dead."

"When Mr. Deveroe comes home I shall ask him to inquire into the matter for you. But now come, I want you to have some dinner and then a rest. Then we shall take a ride down to the Archer house, where my cousin has his headquarters for the moment. With good luck we'll bring your Gretchen back with us when we return."

To her horror Mrs. Lister grabbed her hand and pressed it to her lips. "God bless you, madam. In truth you're an angel!"

Firmly Celia pulled her hand away. If this woman only knew how far from angelic she actually was! Here at least was one small deed with which to compensate for the enormity of her sins.

As it turned out, Gretchen had not yet made the trek across King's Bridge toward the slaughter pens, and Ewan was able to single her out of the drover's herd and return her to Mrs. Lister. He also provided the lady with the loan of a mount and a small escort for her return to Tuckahoe, as well as a permit allowing her to keep one cow for her personal use.

"However," he told her, "If I were you I'd keep that paper well concealed. It will mean nothing at all to the Skinners, and if the Committeemen learn that you have it, it will bring even more suspicion down on you and your husband."

Celia watched her ride happily off, leading the lean brown spotted cow, and felt that she and Ewan between them had done someone a good turn in a world where more often than not evil seemed to compound upon evil. Gradually the incident slipped from her mind as her days became increasingly busy with the spring chores.

A letter from Richard informed her that he would be home in late June. She showed it to Ewan one warm summer evening as he stopped by for supper, which Vestal served them on the piazza. His eyes read quickly down the page, then he sat back in his chair, loosening the lace at his throat.

"He is very formal, isn't he?"

Celia shrugged. "Can I expect more? I am happy that we have achieved this polite distance. Any alternative would be intolerable."

"If he arrives in July, at least I won't be here. That should spare you some inconvenience."

Celia glanced up at him. "Ewan! You make it sound as though I enjoy balancing between wife and mistress. I hate it! It is just that I don't know any other way. You know I would only be an encumbrance to you if I left him, besides ruining my own reputation. He asks very little of me when he is here. Can I begrudge him that much?"

Ewan looked around to make sure Vestal had gone back down to the kitchen, then leaned forward across the table and took her hands.

"Forgive me, my love. It is my own misery that makes me speak so bitterly. I can hardly bear it when I know he is here with you, seldom as that is. I see no other solution, either, though God knows I wish I did. But you know, Celia, that someday this war will be over. He'll be back then for good and you will have to make a choice. It will be impossible to go on like this when I am living only a few rods away."

"I know. But I put the thought from my mind. Surely we'll find a solution before then. Sometimes I feel as though this war will never end."

"Oh, it will be over and soon, I think. We're having some great successes in the South—Savannah, Charleston, Ninety-six. With just a little more luck we'll have Virginia, and that should break the rebels' backs for good. There is a large French army which has been cooling its heels at Newport these many months. British headquarters believe it will move soon to join

Washington here in West Chester in order to attack New York. If that happenes we will probably have to pull our forces back across the Harlem River onto York Island."

Celia threw up her hands. "Merciful heavens! We've had the British, the Germans, the rebels, the Loyalists and now the French! Is there no end to this?"

Ewan laughed. "With Richard at home you may be entertaining Generals Washington and Rochambeau to dinner. That should be a diversion for you."

"I hope they enjoy tansy pudding more than you. You haven't eaten a bite."

Throwing down his spoon, he rose and pulled her up beside him. "The weather is too hot for food, and besides, I'm really not hungry. Come, my love. Let's take a walk. I see you've replanted the borders of southernwood. Does it still remind you of me?"

She slipped her arm through his as they started down the narrow brick paths where the pungent scent of the new flowers and plants perfumed the evening air.

"It will always remind me of you."

By the time Richard returned to the Manor Farm, Ewan, as he had predicted, had pulled his Refugees across the Harlem River to the comparative safety of York Island. Although he was obviously pleased with Celia's hard work and the signs of improved husbandry that showed everywhere he turned, Richard was preoccupied and more distant then ever before, concerned over his own affairs and especially over his inability to make his way in the circles of government where he most wanted to succeed. As hard as he worked to prove his devotion to the new republic it was never enough to overcome the obstacle of distrust of the Deveroes. Rumors, innuendos, unproved allegations he could never trace to their source—they constantly undermined whatever reputation he built up based on his abilities and convictions. And now that Mr. Jay was in Spain it was even worse. Even though men in responsible positions of the Congress privately offered him the greatest courtesy, when it came to actually placing him in a position of responsibility they always balked. It was confusing and frustrating, but Richard was determined to overcome their distrust. Nothing else mattered anymore to him but a future in politics.

Richard heard the men ride into the yard as he was at his

desk in the morning room going over the farm's logbooks. He heard Vestal show them into the parlor, and, pulling on his coat, he went to see who at this hour of the morning would be visiting the Manor House. Entering the room, he had a quick impression of four men. Two were civilians, one tall and severe, dressed all in black, who stood with his back to the room, the other familiar—Clarence Oakley of White Plains. Beside them stood a resplendent officer in white, one of the new arrivals of General Rochambeau's army, and beside him an American colonel in blue and buff. Then the tall man in black turned around, and with a sinking heart Richard recognized him.

"Mr. Carne, I believe," Richard said coolly, wondering what could possibly bring this disagreeable man into his house. "Won't you take a chair, gentlemen, and make yourselves comfortable."

"We prefer to stand," Carne said officiously. "This is no social call, Mr. Deveroe. We are here on business—the official business of the Committee of Safety."

With a nonchalance he did not really feel Richard leaned one arm carelessly against the marble mantel. "I find it difficult to imagine what business the Committee of Safety would have with me. I have not even been in West Farms for nearly a year. And in fact, as I am sure you know, during that time I was about the business of the Congress in Philadelphia."

Mr. Oakley started to speak, but Carne broke in. "We are quite aware of your work with the Congress," he said in a voice that sounded to Richard as though filled with regret. "We came down to West Farms this morning to look over the forfeited Deveroe estates, and it seemed opportune to inquire into another matter of importance at the same time."

"Forfeited estates? Just what do you mean by that?"

"Mr. Oakley here, as chairman of the Committee of Safety, should perhaps explain."

"Well, well now," Clarence Oakley, obviously more uncomfortable than his fellow Committeeman, sputtered. "You must know, Richard, that your cousin's lands have all been laid under attainder. Mr. Carne here, who has been appointed the Commissioner for Forfeited Estates, thought to look over the acreage involved. It is a valuable piece of property, you well know, being on the river and involving both a house and a mill."

Richard did not take his eyes off Jaspar Carne. "Perhaps

Mr. Carne intends to go into New York and look over my brother's estate as well. It too is under attainder."

The American colonel, Wells, stepped forward. "No need for sarcasm, Mr. Deveroe. It is only because the British have abandoned this country that we feel secure enough to roam it freely. Surely you can understand that. With the Continental Army occupying this part of West Chester along with our welcome allies"—he nodded to the French officer, who bowed back—"it becomes possible to put into force these resolutions which were passed long ago."

"I imagine there are a number of men who would like nothing better than to get their hands on my cousin's estates. However, since Colonel Deveroe is only a short way away, just over the Harlem River in fact, I would suggest that it might be the better part of valor to wait a while longer. Ewan is not one to accept incursion into his property lightly."

With studied control, Carne fingered the lapels of his elegant broadcloth coat. "We are quite aware of the violent nature of your outlaw relatives, particularly Colonel Deveroe."

Richard's face went white. "You go too far, Mr. Carne," he said icily.

"Come, gentlemen," Oakley interjected. "This is not the matter upon which we came at all. It was only incidental that we were examining Ewan's farm, anyway."

"Can one go too far who has felt personally the temper of your cousin in the cruel and wanton murder of one of his own kinsmen? I think not."

The scene in Hunt's barn sprang vividly into Richard's mind. "Ewan was wrong to hang that unfortunate boy. I told him so then and I believe it now. But surely your compatriots were no better when they strung up poor old Barnett for no other reason than revenge."

"You keep abreast of what happens in the county, Mr. Deveroe, for one who is so seldom here. Perhaps in that case you can guess the reason for our interview this morning."

"I haven't the slightest idea why you are here. *My* estates are not forfeit. It will do you little good to look them over."

"Now it is you who go too far!"

Reluctantly Richard moved to the hall, where he called to Celia to bring out a bottle of whatever was left in their cellar. An uneasy quiet settled over the room when the two officers excused themselves to stroll outside. Jaspar Carne and Richard glared at each other while Mr. Oakley sat down heavily near the window and wiped his handkerchief across his brow, wishing devoutly that he was back in his own kitchen.

When Celia glided into the room looking fresh and pretty in a blue-and-white muslin gown trimmed in white ruching, Richard introduced her to the gentlemen. She spoke a brief word to each, then was starting to leave when Carne spoke up.

"It might be appropriate for Madam Deveroe to stay, since our business concerns her specifically."

Celia looked up in surprise.

"What possible concern could you have with my wife?" Richard asked.

Carne stared Oakley into answering from where he stood uneasily by the window.

"As a matter of fact, Richard, we have it on good information that Mrs. Deveroe had been offering aid and comfort to the enemy. On very good information, I might add."

"That is hardly surprising when we live so close to the British forts. Celia, my dear," Richard said quietly, taking her arm. "Do you know what these gentlemen are talking about?"

She was glad enough to have his support. "I haven't an idea. In the past year I have hardly stirred from the bounds of this farm. How could I have given aid to any enemy that you gentlemen would care about?"

"Come now, madam," said Carne, "can you deny that you took in a woman from the neutral ground whose husband is a convicted Loyalist lying at this moment in prison? That you aided her to regain some property stolen by the infamous Cowboys and, further, helped her to obtain a worthless extralegal document given by the enemy which allowed her to keep that property in the face of the urgent needs of the Continental Army?"

"Mrs. Lister!" Celia whispered the words, more to herself than to anyone in the room.

"I see that you do remember."

Celia looked up to see her husband questioning her with his eyes. "The woman was a friend," she began haltingly. "She came here in desperate need. Her husband was the kind gentleman who took in Dominie Brec and I met them when I went to visit the old man. She asked my help..."

Richard hesitated, unsure how to handle this. There appeared to be some truth in the allegation against his wife, yet it sounded like an innocent, kind deed which these fanatics were turning into a criminal act. Then he saw the thin smile on Jaspar Carne's face. The man was relishing this small triumph over a helpless woman. All the dislike Richard had felt for Carne from the first moment he met him years before crystallized into sheer loathing. That he also used this power in the name of liberty and had managed to get Celia underneath his thumb were the crowning insults to an already festering dislike. Yet before he could speak Celia turned on the two civilians angrily.

"You castigate me for helping that poor destitute woman, but what about your own sins! Can you deny that you threw her husband into prison for no reason whatever and that you brought to a pitiful end the life of that good man Dominie Brec who never did harm to anyone in all his saintly life. I think you have very little room, gentlemen, to accuse me when you yourselves showed so little mercy."

"Mr. Lister is a contentious Quaker, one of those pretended conscientious, nonfighting, Torified fellows who mask their cowardice behind a creed."

"And for that you taxed him into poverty and threw him into a stinking jail to starve. If this is what you call liberty—"

"Celia!" Richard's stern voice interrupted her. "That will be quite enough."

With difficulty she bit back her words. This was neither the place nor the time to challenge her husband.

"Well, Oakley," Richard finally said, refilling the man's glass. "What *did* you come here for? Are you proposing to carry my wife back to jail with you?"

"Why . . . why, of course not, Richard. No such thought ever entered our minds, did it, Jaspar?"

"I do feel that a fine is in order. The expenses of the county, incurred in part by the depredations of your notorious cousin, are staggering. Taxes and levies do not begin to cover the cost."

"I pay my taxes, Mr. Carne, and all levies the assemblies ask of me. But I will pay no fine for a deed of kindness my wife made in Christian charity. You can take that any way you will. Not a penny will you take back with you from this house."

He had the satisfaction of seeing a slight flush on Carne's gaunt cheeks.

"That is hardly the proper attitude for a so-called patriot, Mr. Deveroe."

"Especially one whose relatives come down mainly on the King's side, eh, Carne? Let us not mince words. You made it clear in White Plains that my family's loyalty was an affront to you. You'd like nothing better than to prove me as much a King's man as they, would you not? Well, you cannot do it, because I believe as strongly in liberty as you and I have worked as tirelessly to bring about a republican government for this country."

"Richard," began Clarence Oakley, but he was stopped by Richard's uplifted hand.

"No, I will speak my mind. I think you came here today, Mr. Carne, with no purpose other than to embarrass me and humiliate my wife. I think you are an ambitious, greedy sponger who is using your patriotic fervor to bring down better men and to grasp at the spoils of their ruin. I have seen too many like you, both here and in Philadelphia, men whose sole aim in serving our cause is to add riches to their coffers. Justice, mercy, compassion—they have no part in your single-minded avarice. And this you do in the name of liberty! You disgust me!"

To his surprise, where most men would have advanced with gloves raised, Jaspar Carne stood smiling placidly at him, only his eyes betraying his fury.

"Richard," Oakley said, nearly wringing his hands, "for mercy's sake, man, retract those words. No man has served our cause more loyally than Carne here."

"I retract nothing," Richard answered. "My only regret is that I was moved by anger and to insult a guest in my house. But my every word was true."

Carne reached for his hat. "You have spoken your mind, Mr. Deveroe. Very well. I am not a dueling man or I should have to call you out. But I promise you this, you will one day regret this conversation. Regret it very much indeed." He turned on his heel and started for the door. "Come along, Clarence. There is nothing to be gained here."

Oakley followed, whispering to Richard as he went out shaking his head. "You should not have spoken so harshly, my boy. That is a bad man to make an enemy of."

Celia called to him before he was through the door. "Mr. Oakley, what happened to Mrs. Lister? Did she keep her cow?"

"Why, no, I believe it was appropriated for the army in Peekskill as part of the forfeiture for her husband's crimes. The last I heard she had moved away."

Halfheartedly Richard followed him to the door to let him out. Carne had already disappeared. When Richard came back into the room he found Celia staring at her hands, sunk in the chair.

"All for nothing," she cried. "Everything we did to help that poor woman. And now it has caused you to make an enemy of that zealot Carne. Good God! Is there no way to make things right?"

He laid a hand on her shoulder. "No matter, Celia. I think Jaspar Carne has been my enemy since the day I knocked him down for beating that poor donkey. He resents all the Deveroes. And Ned Carne's death was the seal on his hatred. Somehow our lives seem to cross and there is little we can do to prevent it."

"But it was my fault. When I tried to help that woman I never, never thought to bring trouble on your head. I am so sorry, Richard."

Abruptly he left her and walked over to the window. "Please don't worry about it. If the Continental Army had not come so far down into the county they would never have had the nerve to appear here and accuse you. I blame you for nothing."

She could not find the words to answer him, so isolated was he in his own concerns. Even his words, intended to be reassuring, closed her out. Well, what more could she expect?

"Can I . . . can I get you something? Some wine perhaps, or a . . ."

"No," he said without looking at her. "I should go back and finish the books, but I don't feel like it. I'll just go saddle up my horse. Don't worry about me if I don't return for dinner."

She sat in her chair and watched him leave, knowing he would not be back for hours. Alone and isolated, he would wander the fields until his composure was reestablished. There was no way she could help him—she who was the cause of his distress and the one person he once would have turned to. For two years past she had nurtured her anger at Richard for what she thought he had done to her, but now, all at once, she hated herself for what she had done to him.

nineteen

With careful deliberation Hester Barnett folded the letter from Henry and wrapped it together with the others she had received from America, tying them up in a packet with a ribbon. All the while she was seething inside. Why was it that letters from home always left her so disgruntled? She received them with such excited anticipation, yet once she read them she wanted to tear them into shreds.

Outside, the square windowpanes streamed with the drizzling rain. Wet again! It was always raining in this damnable country, Hester thought dismally, and pulled her wrapper closer around her shoulders. Dampness and drafts were her constant companions since they had been forced to move to this shabby flat on Watling Street. If only they could have stayed in the lovely house on Chatham Square. It was all Cortlandt's fault. Everything was Cortlandt's fault!

"Excuse me, madam, there is a man outside the door who wishes to see the master."

Hester looked up to see her timid serving girl standing at the door. Scarcely more than a child, the girl had the pallor of children from the London streets. How humiliating it was to be reduced to employing titmice like these.

"It's probably another creditor. Good God, I cannot face one more of those ugly, demanding leeches. Tell him Mr. Barnett is not at home."

"But he's terrible insistent. He says he wants to see you if he can't see the master."

"Then tell him I'm not here either."

The girl hung her head. "But I already told him the Madam was inside."

"You stupid child! Just get rid of him any way you can.

241

Tell him I'm asleep, I'm ill—anything you please. I will *not* see him."

"But, madam—"

"Out of here before I box your ears!" Hester exclaimed, starting toward the girl.

The girl fled down the hallway, pushing the door closed behind her. Venting her frustration, Hester picked up the nearest book from the table and threw it against the door.

"What's all the racket about?" said a sleepy voice from the bedroom. Rubbing his eyes, Cortlandt Barnett wobbled into the room, swathed in a huge brocade banian with a wilted turban around his head. Hester looked him over disdainfully. He had grown heavier than ever, and had a large paunch. His face was blotched with too much wine and in his hung-over state now looked more puffy and gross than ever.

She did not even try to hide her contempt. "One of your creditors is outside. Why don't you handle him yourself for once? They're your debts."

Cortlandt groaned and headed straight for the brandy decanter. "Always *my* debts, aren't they? What about your mantua makers, milliners, drapers and grocers? I'm not the only one in this house who knows how to spend."

"Perhaps you would prefer that Tyler and I give up eating and go about in society with rags on our backs. You'd like that, wouldn't you? It would give you more to spend at the gaming tables and on your whores!"

"Please, Hester, not first thing in the morning."

"If you suffer in the morning you should try not taking so much to drink at night."

Cortlandt raised his glass to her in a mock toast. "Thank you, m'dear, for the free advice."

"You know very well, Cortlandt, that most of these men who come here are looking for you. Yet you continue to borrow vast sums at huge rates of interest. What do you expect the end to be? If you were only as good at making money as you are at throwing it away."

Draining his glass, Cortlandt refilled it and turned away. He had not been able to tell her yet that he was being threatened with debtor's prison. Surely he would find a way out before it came to that.

"If only Lord Lamberton had given us the preference he promised we'd never be in these straits," he said lamely.

"He never promised anything. That was a lie you used to

lure me away from America. Even then he might have relented, but you bungled the whole thing so badly he refused to bother with you. Just as you do everything."

"Your devotion is so touching," Cortlandt said sarcastically. His head was splitting and his eyes refused to focus clearly, yet he was beginning to feel the familiar urge to get out of this house at all costs. How blind he had been not to see the scold under all that petite, golden prettiness. Well, he'd paid for *that* mistake in full.

"You might as well know," Hester said, "that I've had a letter from Henry and he plans to emigrate to London. He's fed up with the Colonies and the war and thinks he can live better here, more fool he!"

"Henry in London. Why, that'll be like old times. Perhaps he might be just the answer for us."

Hester threw up her hands. "You idiot! He expects *you* to help *him* get established. Little does he realize that the only places where you will introduce him are the gaming halls and brothels! Meanwhile I shall have the care of Mama and Guinevere and all her brats! We can barely manage now. What are we going to do when we have the whole family to care for?"

Cortlandt sighed. "Now, calm yourself, m'love. We'll find a way."

"That's just the point," Hester flared. "There *is* no way. I want you to sit down right now and write Henry not to come. He must not think he can move in here with us."

"I don't think it will do any good. Now that the war is all but over all the Tories are fleeing to England."

"The war is not over yet."

"You know as well as I that the King is expected to sign a peace treaty very soon. And since that fiasco at Yorktown over a year ago, there's been no fighting of any importance. You can't blame Henry for wanting out."

"Can't I get you to understand, Mr. Barnett, that Henry is counting on *our* help? All the Deveroe inheritance has been confiscated by this rebel government. If the British pull out they will take everything. Henry will come here in worse straits than we are, if such a thing is possible. You must write at once."

Grasping the neck of the bottle, Cortlandt headed back toward the bedroom. "All right, Hester. I'll write to him today, I promise. Later, when my head's clear."

"Your head will be more muddled later than it is now," Hester screamed after him, watching the door slam between them. "Oh—!" she said, gritting her teeth and flouncing back into her chair. He was never going to be of any help. If she wanted this handled she must do it herself. Drumming her fingers on the table, she weighed her options. There was Richard, of course. But he was always off with that silly Congress, and besides, she was reluctant to confess to Richard the extent of their predicament.

Celia? Hester's lips narrowed into a straight line. She had a mental picture of Celia that never altered—Celia living in West Farms in the gracious comfort of the Manor House, tending to the gentle household chores, playing the virginals in her spare time, untouched by the vicissitudes of life. How unfair it was! Celia living in style and comfort while she, the true Deveroe daughter, was forced into poverty, disgrace and exile. No, she would never ask Celia for anything.

Then she remembered Ewan. Of course. If anybody could talk sense to Henry it was their strong, sensible cousin. He had nothing to do anyway but ride around West Chester on his flashy horses showing off his fancy uniform. He could easily take the time to go down to Wayside and talk Henry out of this disastrous notion.

Yes, she would write to Ewan this very afternoon.

The Mill House was beginning to look like a home again. Over the past year Ewan had replaced the shutters and doors, repaired the broken planks, and restored some of the furniture. It had none of the elegance it had possessed before the Revolution, of course, but neither did it resemble the ravaged shell which had stood abandoned for the past seven years.

The front door was open and Celia could see soldiers moving about inside as she walked up the steps. Evidently her cousin had brought a detachment of his own men to work on the house while he was there. She found him at a handsome table in one of the front rooms, surrounded by stacks of books and several Queen Anne side chairs.

"You have made some improvements here, Ewan," she said, looking around the room. "They almost make me remember your father's house as it used to be. Are you planning to move back here permanently?"

"Yes, I am. Not without some trepidation, of course. We expect word to come with each new packet sailing into the harbor that the peace treaty with the King has been signed. So, my brigade is slowly dispersing. I want to do all I can to furnish and repair the house before I lose my men entirely."

"Do you really think it will be safe for you here?" she asked quietly. She did not want to face that issue any more than he, but it was a fact that was not going to go away by wishful thinking.

Pushing back his chair, he drummed his fingers nervously on the desk. "Probably not. In fact, there is so much hostility to me I probably should not live in West Chester County at all. But, damn it, I will not quietly give up my heritage. They will have to kill me to get it."

Her heart sank. "Oh, Ewan, don't say such things. Surely there must be some better solution. Could you not ask for amnesty?"

"Celia, you must know me better than that. Ask those God-damned rebels for their forgiveness! I'd sooner die. And they'd sooner hang me than give it. No, that is no answer. I could make an armed camp of this place, but one hates to live that way. Yet the only other option is to move away completely, to England or Nova Scotia as many others are doing."

"Move away! For good?"

He shrugged. "It may be my only choice, though, God knows, I hope not. This damned independent republic that so believes in liberty has passed a law which lays claim to every blade of grass and every shilling I own. The farm and the mill, the estate my father poured his life's blood into building so he could leave it to his sons—with a stroke of the pen all this is snatched from my hands, leaving me with nothing. And in the name of democracy!"

"Oh, my dear. Is the feeling against you so strong that you could not work through it somehow? You still have many old friends here and many people who served the King as well as you."

"Yes, but more and more of them are choosing exile. It will not be a charitable enemy one faces here. Why, in Bedford just a few weeks ago the town council established a committee to run every Loyalist straight out of town. And I am probably the one Loyalist they would most like to hang. Sometimes I think it would be the better part of wisdom to take the next ship myself, then I get angry all over again and swear I'll make them fight for every inch of ground they take from me."

Outside the room Celia could hear two men laughing and

talking as they tried to work a large sofa through the doorway to the parlor. Every part of her ached to move into his arms, to hold him with all the force she possessed, to keep him from leaving her. Yet she could not even touch his hand. She looked miserably down where her hands twisted in her lap.

"Come, my love," Ewan said so gently that only she could hear. "I did not ask you down here today to depress you. There will be time enough to talk of this when we are alone, though it is probably good that you know of it, since, if my heart tells me correctly, you will have to be making some decisions, too. We are both going to be put to the test now that the war is really over."

"Yes. I knew that once peace came this would have to be faced. But, somehow, I never thought of you leaving..."

"Well, perhaps I won't. We shall see. What about Richard, though? Have you heard if or when he is coming back? Whatever decision you and I make, he will of necessity be involved in it."

"He says only that he will be home probably next month, but not for how long. He is very discouraged about his work with the Congress, but more than that he never says."

"You may not know, then, that his family is planning to join Hester in England. They are set to sail on May eighteenth."

Celia sat forward in her chair. "Mama Deveroe is going to England? Why, I can hardly believe it. It is such a perilous voyage and she is so old."

"Nonetheless, that is their plan. The estate at Wayside is under attainder, so Henry has decided to sell everything while he can and take the family where the climate is more sympathetic."

"I wonder why Richard did not tell me." Yet she knew the answer. This was how far they had grown apart, that his family who had once been hers too now made such a decision without her knowledge or advice. Without realizing it she had let her estrangement from her husband also estrange her from the only family she possessed.

"That is why I wanted to see you," Ewan went on. "I've had a few letters from Hester over these years of war and she has probably been more honest with me than anyone else in her family. I happen to know that Henry is counting very strongly on Cortlandt Barnett's support when he arrives in London, and somehow we have got to convince him that there isn't going to be any help at all from that quarter."

"What do you mean? I thought Hester was living well. Her letters suggest a style of life that is far gayer and more luxurious than any she had here."

"That is what she wants *you* to think. The truth is Cortlandt has gambled away most of his inheritance. He is being threatened with debtor's prison and she is expecting another child. She writes me that between trying to keep up appearances and at the same time put enough to eat into their mouths, she is becoming old before her time."

"Do you believe her? You know Hester sometimes likes to make an effect."

"I don't think so. Hester never played those games with me, because I could see through her too well. Perhaps I was the only one in whom she felt she could confide the truth. At any rate, Henry would never listen to me, because he knows I see him for the ass he is, but he might listen to Richard. For God's sake, get Richard to point out the facts to him so that he doesn't sail away half-cocked, expecting to live in the lap of luxury at Barnett's expense."

"Poor Hester. It must be a terrible comedown for her."

"Will you explain all this to Richard? Even though Henry is a boor I should hate to have Aunt Elizabeth suffer when they arrive there. They are family, you know."

She felt the flush on her cheeks and looked quickly down at her hands lying in her lap. "Of course I shall, Ewan. After all, they are my family too."

True to her promise, she got off an urgent letter to Richard the very next day. Only a few days later the news reached West Chester that the British had signed the peace treaty which ended the war, though it was to be almost another month before that news was formally given to the American Army by proclamation at their camp at New Windsor. By that time Richard himself was on his way home, leaving the sloop which brought him up the East River at Hunt's Point to ride up the familiar road toward West Farms. He felt weighed down by hopelessness. He had no future in politics and government, he knew that now with a terrible certainty. Yet he felt no enthusiasm about anything else. He hated farming, but what other way could he keep the Manor Farm for Celia? *If* he kept Celia. That was the most hopeless cause of all. He was not sure of his own feelings for her and he did not know what to expect from her now that he would be home permanently. The whole world seemed to have fallen into disjointed pieces and he did not have the heart to pick them up and put enough of them together to go on.

He was nearly past Hunt's farm when he saw the body of horsemen coming toward him and recognized their scarlet-and-green coats. Relieved that they were not Skinners, nevertheless he had a bad moment when he recognized Ewan riding at their head. He had not set eyes on his cousin for more than two years, and, suspecting what he did of him, he did not really wish to see him now. But there was no place to go but ahead.

It was something of a shock to see how Ewan had aged. His face was thinner and more flinty, yet he still rode the most splendid horse in the troop. He appeared to be just as startled to have run into Richard, and there was a wariness in their greeting. They exchanged a few pleasantries while in the back reaches of his mind Richard found the old warmth returning. This was the boy, the man, he had been closer to than any other. He simply could not believe Ewan would play him such a bad trick as to steal his wife.

Abruptly Ewan turned his mount and motioned Richard to accompany him a short distance apart from the rest of the company.

"Did you stop at Wayside?" he asked, wondering how effective Celia's warning had been.

"Yes, but it made no difference at all. Henry is convinced the future lies in England and he has Mama agreeing with him. Who knows? Perhaps he is right. Certainly there is nothing left for them in New York."

While he listened to him speak, Ewan carefully assessed his cousin. Richard still had that soft, sensitive poetic look, and he was as carefully dressed as ever. Only the lines around his eyes and the somber expression deep within them suggested any depths of pain. Yet he knew his cousin too well not to remember that there was a toughness of fiber within him, little as you might expect it from his appearance.

Their horses stood neck against neck, swishing their tails and nodding their heads impatiently. "Why don't you bring your mother up here? She could live out her remaining years with you and save herself the agony of this readjustment."

"I tried to convince her of that, but she refused even to consider it. Perhaps she wants to see London before she dies. But I don't think so. I think that the feeling among all the people who tried to remain loyal to the Crown is that they no longer want to live in a country that has taken everything they owned. They are bitter. As bitter as I have ever seen anyone."

Ewan laughed sharply. "That is not difficult to understand, surely."

Richard smoothed his mount's sleek neck. "What do you intend to do, Ewan? Is it England or Canada?"

"Neither. I intend to stay and rebuild. This is my land as it was my father's before me. I want to hold on to it."

Richard gasped. "You must be mad! Why, you can't stay here. You would be shot down within a week, and if not that, your house and mill would be fired. Don't you realize the extent of the hostility to you?"

Ewan's face darkened. "Yes, I realize it, but I feel that a great part of it is unfounded. After all, why should I be held responsible for every crime my men committed, when many times, even if I had known about it, I could not have stopped them?"

But Richard pushed on relentlessly. "That comes with command. You know that as well as I. Good God, Ewan, your lands were sold four years ago."

Ewan looked away, stubborn anger in every line of his face. "Unlawfully sold."

"Sold, nonetheless. If the King had kept these Colonies, then under his law that sale would stand as invalid. But with independence a fact, the law of the land is now that of the United States of America. And under that law that sale is valid indeed. Face it, Ewan, every inch of ground you claim is owned by John and Comfort Sands."

His face went dark. "God damn you, Richard—"

"It does no good to damn me. I don't like it any more than you. But I do care about you and your safety, and I don't want to see you killed."

"Is that all you think about?" Ewan cried, losing all control. "Are you also afraid my reputation might be a threat to your own lands and safety? Afraid of losing your own precious acreage, maybe, or perhaps something more valuable!"

"Now see here, Ewan..."

Ewan angrily turned his horse in the narrow roadway. "A thousand thanks for your advice, Cousin," he called, and cantered back to his men, leaving Richard to stare after him, his cheeks flushed with surprised anger. The group thundered away, stirring up the dust on the road's surface and startling a flock of kingbirds squawking out of the treetops. In spite of

everything Richard understood his cousin's response. Ewan
was a fighter, a man used to quick, decisive action. He didn't
want to face the fact that seven years' effort had ended in
defeat—that like so many others he was going to have to pull
up stakes and move as a stranger to a new and unfamiliar land.
He had tried to avoid the decision by deluding himself that he
could hang on here. Then he, Richard, had come along and
confounded that delusion. No wonder his reaction was so swift
and so angry.

And yet, Richard thought as he rode on along the road,
probably there was no one else who could say those words to
Ewan. And no one else he would take them from.

But if he did sail away, would Celia go with him? That
thought brought with it an ache Richard tried hard not to feel.
Straightening his spine, he gave his mount a little kick to get
her moving. All these years he had avoided facing this terrible,
wrenching issue. But with every step toward the Manor House
he knew more clearly than ever that this time there would be
no evasion. He was coming home to stay. There would be no
more war, no more trips to Philadelphia, no more pretending
he and his wife could live separate lives. Ewan was not the
only one who faced a choice.

Richard stayed at West Farms only a few days before he
went back down to Wayside to try to talk his family out of
their move to England. In this he failed, and when word came
that Henry, his wife and children and Elizabeth were actually
set to sail on the *Argonot* within a week, Celia hurriedly followed his suggestion to go and wish them farewell. She planned
for Vestal and Betsy to accompany her, but at the last minute
Ewan arrived at the house and insisted that he would go with
her instead.

"You needn't worry that I'll make it uncomfortable for you,"
he said lightly, though he had obviously thought it all through
long before. "I'll see you to the dock at Wayside, then go on
down to stay at one of my mother's houses in the city. It may
be that I can help Henry handle the bureaucracy of the British
command, otherwise I'll only be around to wish them Godspeed. As for the boat, Betsy will be with you, so it won't
appear anything more than your cousin providing an escort."

She could not look at him. The words were clamoring behind
her lips, but she refused to speak them. Would it always be
like this? Observing the formalities so that the world would not

know what they really meant to each other? Was this all that the future held for them? She could see nothing more. Yet to say it, to face the issue squarely, somehow held a terrible danger and the possibility of a rift. So she kept silent. And he, studying the silent struggle within her, followed suit.

She enjoyed the boat trip to the city. Once they were past the dangerous tides of Hell Gate, she stood at the rail and watched with pleasure as the land unfolded before her. When the distant spires and tiled roofs came into sight it gave her a warm feeling of nostalgia.

As early as Kips Bay she began to notice the ravages of the war. New York had changed beyond recognition, even as West Chester. She expected the burned flats left from the fire of '76, but now to those shantytown areas had been added others risen from the ashes of the fire of '79. The beautiful trees lining the streets from the expansive Broad Way to the smaller meandering alleyways were all of them gone. Anything that could be cut down and used for fuel had been hauled away, leaving a melancholy barrenness.

And she had never seen such crowds of people on the streets. British and Hessian soldiers still filled the walkways, but they were nearly crowded out by the civilians, refugees whose Tory sympathies now left them with only one direction in which to go—the sea. Men, women and children, most in ragged clothes, filled the wharves where the ships loaded them daily or clamored in the courtyard of the Commandant's offices to plead for compensations and pensions in return for their confiscated properties. New York was a city in transition, a city in turmoil, tinged with sadness and defeat that could be sensed in taverns and coffeehouses. Only in the shops and in the homes of the older residents did one sense that there waited an expectation of new life, biding its time until these despairing refugees moved out and others could move in with a new vitality.

She stood with the Deveroes in the middle of the teeming crowd on Coenties Slip the day of their sailing, and her heart hurt with the finality of it all. A tearful Guinevere clung to her brood of children. Elizabeth, white-haired and frail, with only a few lines in that lovely patrician face, embraced Celia for a few silent moments. They had grown apart these long years of the war and she could see that the young girl she had welcomed as a daughter had matured and saddened with these years.

"Now, Mama, no long tearful farewells," Henry said, bustling around them with his old officiousness. "We must get aboard or the ship will take the tide and leave us standing here."

Celia kissed Elizabeth's translucent cheek. "You will give Hester my love, won't you? And write to us when you are settled."

"Yes, yes, I promise."

Richard gave his mother a warm embrace, then turned quickly away to help a sobbing Guinevere get her children into the launch. Henry had already climbed down the rope ladder and was standing in the boat calling to Elizabeth to hurry. She turned back to Celia, who caught her hand and pressed it to her lips.

"My dear girl," Elizabeth began, her voice faltering, "promise me you will take care of my son. He appears so self-sufficient, but in truth he needs you so much."

"Oh, Mama..."

Elizabeth leaned her earnest face closer to Celia's. "When you came to us, homeless and orphaned, we gladly took you to our hearts. We gave you all we had, including our son, when that was what you both wanted. Do this for me now, Celia, and I shall know God has rewarded me for that kindness. Promise me you will give Richard the care that I cannot."

"I..." Celia faltered.

Elizabeth's pale eyes seemed to bore into her. All the memories of the tenderness, the care and teaching, the warm acceptance this good woman had always shown her came crowding back.

"Yes, yes. I promise."

"Mother, come! Don't you hear the bell!" Henry's voice roared out over the heads of the people filling the wharf.

"Thank you, my dearest girl. Now I can sail with a clear heart."

After throwing her arms around Celia one last time, Elizabeth hurried toward the end of the dock, leaving Celia stunned and miserable behind her. Men and women jostled her roughly as she stood in the crowd, dimly aware of the overpowering odors of human sweat and of the stagnant waters of the dock basin. She felt as though one more strand had been overlaid on the net of circumstances which pinned her down and kept her struggling. Would she ever be able to disentangle them, to know her own heart and to be sure what she must do? Even as she watched the launch pull away from the dock and move out into the harbor waters where the ship waited, one thing became ever clearer in her mind. She had put it off long enough. It must be faced. A choice must be made. Henry and Elizabeth had made theirs, Richard had made his when he abandoned the political career he had always longed for. Now it was time that she made hers.

twenty

When Celia alighted from the boat at Hunt's Point the next day she noticed that a large crate was being unloaded. Inquiring about it, she was even more surprised to learn that it belonged to Richard and was marked for delivery to the Manor Farm. All the way up the narrow trail to West Farms she wondered what Richard could be sending home that required such a huge, strangely shaped crate, and when it was finally carried through the front door to be set down in the hall she was almost as eager as Vestal and Betsy to crowd around it and see the slats removed.

Vestal had lifted off only one or two boards before she recognized underneath the familiar painted design of Elizabeth's harpsichord. With a cry of sheer delight she hurried Vestal on to get it unpacked so that it could be moved into the parlor and set upon its beveled legs. It was barely in place in the middle of the room before she was running her fingers over its yellowed ivory keys. Of course it was hopelessly, horribly out of tune and her fingers were stiff from the years of not playing, yet she could already begin to recall in the lilting chords of Byrde's "Lord of Salisbury, Pavane" the great pleasure her music had once brought her. It was Vestal who found the note in the packing crate and brought it to her.

CELIA,
   I was not able to salvage very many of Mama's possessions but this I felt was meant for you. A few more items will follow on next week's packet. I hope this instrument will give you great pleasure. You used to play so beautifully.
                                                              RICHARD

She was strangely moved by the brief words. Leaning her arms on the broad frame, she rested her head against them, full of feelings she could not sort out. The familiar old instrument brought back poignant memories of years full of lighthearted happiness. The elegance of that life was only a dim memory now. All the people who had made it so significant were gone. Samuel dead, Elizabeth and Hester gone to England, Richard and Ewan and herself so lost and confused by what war and their emotions had brought them. No words could have said more eloquently than this instrument how much he still cared for her in spite of the pain she had caused him.

Suddenly conscious of a presence in the doorway behind her, she turned and saw Ewan standing there, watching her quietly.

"I didn't hear you come in," she said, smiling him a welcome.

Quietly closing the door behind him, he came to stand near her, running his hand over the painted wood.

"Do you recognize it? It was Mama Deveroe's. Richard was able to save it from the clutches of Wayside's new owner and send it up here for me. Is it not a lovely gift?"

"I can tell by the expression on your face how much it means to you." His fingers traced the line of her cheek and lips. She rose to go into his arms, holding him tightly, feeling the familiar hard lines of his body against her own.

"My love," Ewan said gently, smoothing back her hair from her forehead. "We must talk. Come, sit with me here on the sofa."

Her heart suddenly a stone within her, she let him take her hands and lead her to the small sofa against the wall, where the shadows kept them from the window's view. She knew instinctively that this was the moment she had dreaded—now it was going to have to be faced.

"Celia." Releasing her hands, he sat forward, leaning his arms on his knees. "When I was in the city I had a talk with General Carleton. He feels sure that if I send in a memorial for the services I have rendered the King in this war I will be eligible for a very substantial pension. With that and with what I have managed to salvage from the past seven years I should be able to make a good start."

"Ewan!"

"Oh, yes, I know that I said I would never leave. But the truth is, I cannot stay here. Richard tried to tell me and I refused to listen, yet in my heart I knew he was right. Though it galls me to leave this land which belonged to my family long before this rebellion was ever dreamed of, I really have no choice. I have so many enemies here that they will either kill me outright the first month or systematically destroy everything I try to rebuild. It's not worth the risk."

"Where will you go?"

"To Canada, of course. Hester's example is enough to keep me out of England. There is land to be had near the St. John— great tracts of it. I shall do what my ancestors did, build a new dynasty in a new country. Someday my sons shall have a great estate to inherit, and God forbid that they should have to see it stripped away by scurvy bastards as I have!"

"Oh, Ewan." Her hands covered her face. Pulling them away, he forced her to look at him.

"Celia, you know that I love you more than I ever loved any woman in my life. If you will go with me—"

"No, no . . ."

"If you will go with me we can build this life together. We will not be completely destitute. Have you not heard the rumor that I have fully six barrels of gold pieces gleaned from my plunder of the county these past years? Like most rumors, that one is highly exaggerated, but still I am not a poor man. And I will receive some compensation from the Crown both for my services and for confiscated properties. You will only have to trust me."

Taking her hands again in his own, he faced her, looking deep into her eyes. "Celia, the only real question is whether or not you will go with me. I love you, I need you, but I must leave this country forever, with or without you. Will you come?"

Every instinct urged her to cling to him, but she knew that nothing would be gained by that. When she finally spoke it was with a grim quietness. "I want to go with you, Ewan, because without you I am not sure life would be worth living at all. But there are other considerations, and you must examine them as well as I. You spoke of sons. In these years that we have been, in effect, living together, have I ever become with child? No. Nor did I when I lived with Richard. If you really want sons, the heritage of children, you must not count on me. Dearly as I want to give them to you, God has not seen fit to grant me that gift."

"Celia . . ."

"No, no. Please let me finish. Even more important is the hard fact that I am Richard's wife, and nothing is going to change that. You know as well as I that English law—which is as strong in Canada as here—will never grant us a divorce except by an act of Parliament. And Richard will never petition them. The disgrace it would bring upon us all would be too great. We would have to live openly as man and mistress among the very exiles from this country who know us both. I don't know if I can face such a life. Can you? How would you ever build your 'new dynasty' with me at your side? You could never live down the dishonor."

She could see that her words were reaching him in spite of the stubborn lines still etched in his face. Relentlessly she went on. "And to tell the truth, I don't know if I could leave West Farms. I stayed and held on to it throughout all these terrible years because I could never bear to be landless and poor. I love you so much, yet I don't know if my love for you could overcome the terrible fear I have of being poor again. Forgive me, my dearest love, but it's true!"

Ewan got up and walked to the window, staring through it without seeing the bright day outside. He knew she was beginning to cry, yet he could not face her.

"Everything you say is true, Celia. And if I look honestly into my own heart I must admit that I too do not wish to live down a dishonorable alliance. My only consolation in going away is that I can rebuild a measure of what I am leaving behind, and that will be twenty times harder if my reputation and integrity are lost on the way. But . . . but I would do it for you. As for children—there too for you I would take my chances."

"I will destroy everything you want to create. My love will ruin you, can't you see?"

"As for being poor, yes, we will be poor, for a time at least. But my strong conviction is that it will not last. The point is this: you must choose between Richard and myself. If you love me you will take these risks with me. If not, then you must stay and try to rebuild a life with my cousin."

"What kind of love is it which destroys its lover just by its existence?"

"Which of us is it to be?"

"Ewan . . . Ewan, give me time. I don't know what to do. Let me think on it for a little while, I beg you."

"When does Richard return?"

"I don't know. Within the month, I suppose."

"And I must leave within the month. So, once and for all,

these next few weeks will settle the matter."

She saw his back stiffen. He was angry with her, she was sure. Angry that he was willing to accept these terrible consequences as the risk of taking her with him and she was so unwilling to come.

"If I do not come with you, will you hate me?"

"I could never hate you, you must know that."

"You will be so alone!"

"No, I shall not go alone. If you won't go, I suppose I shall marry Mercy and take her with me. She at least is eager to go."

Celia's head shot up. "Mercy? Do you know her that well, then?"

"Yes. Since the time I was an invalid in her house she has been something of a friend to me. After all, we were promised long ago."

He turned then to see her sitting in the shadows of the sofa, despair and torment in every line of her supple body. What a child little Mercy was compared to this beautiful mature woman who had come to fill every fiber of his body and spirit. How could he leave her, never to see her again? Moving quickly, he went to kneel before her, taking her in his arms. Her cheeks were streaked with the silent tears she could not stem. He kissed them away. Her arms went around his neck and she sobbed against him.

"Ewan, my dearest, dearest love. What should I do? If I don't go with you, you'll marry that snip of a girl and my heart shall break."

"Try to remember that Mercy will be small consolation for me trying to live with the knowledge that you belong irrevocably to Richard."

"We cannot win either way!"

A few days later the small box containing the last of the items from Wayside arrived at the Manor Farm, and ten days after that Richard himself rode in. It was not an auspicious homecoming. A pervasive atmosphere of impending change dampened everything, from Celia's quietly restrained welcome to the weed-choked fields, only a quarter of them recovering from the ravages of the war. Immediately Richard set about making a detailed survey of his property, riding over every inch of the fields and the woods, counting the depleted stock and listing their every liability and asset.

In the long evenings he sat reading silently in the parlor while his wife sewed or practiced her music on the harpsichord. He knew Celia was preoccupied and distressed, and guessed from her distracted manner that she still did not know her own mind. He would look up from the stiff pages of one of the books from his father's library to watch the copper glow of the candlelight on her golden-brown hair, stirred by the sadness of her profile so white against the shadows of the room. Sometimes he ached to take her into his arms, to sit beside her and openly discuss the issues they so carefully avoided. But the estrangement and hurt between them was like a wall, and he had never been a man to reach out until someone first reached out to him. So he would once again lay the book aside and quietly step from the room, leaving her to the solace of her music.

After two days of constant rain, he woke one morning to a sparkling crystal world where even the noisy chatter of the birds seemed a hymn to beauty. Saddling his mare, he started out to explore the larger area around West Farms in the same detailed way he had now surveyed his own lands. It was astonishing, he thought, how growth and maturity and change could enable you to see familiar sights with new eyes. These old well-loved fields and farms, dotted here and there with a burned barn, a shell of a house, fields covered with briers and nettles, even the scattered remains of the blockhouse seemed as poised for change as the people who moved through them. The war was done and a new order was about to begin. Knowing this better than either Celia or Ewan, and knowing better what to expect, Richard resolved anew that he would not be left a helpless victim of the changing times. He was not sure yet how he would manage, but he was determined to build something for himself from the wreckage of the past. With Celia or without her.

It was past noon when he realized with a start that he had let his horse carry him nearly to the docks at Hunt's Point. He had left the house without breaking the night's fast, so it seemed sensible to stop at a small tavern which the Murphesons had taken over near the fork where the road branched off. It was not much of a place, small and shabby, but Richard knew that old Mother Murpheson had a reputation as a cook, and a good plate of Brunswick stew would not be unwelcome right now.

Stabling his horse, he walked into the one room which served as dining room and taproom. At a table near the window

where he could sit alone, he was dipping a wooden spoon into
a bowl of the steaming fragrant stew when he heard his name
called and looked up to see Ewan standing beside the table.

Abruptly Richard set his spoon on the table. The two men
looked at each other for a long moment without speaking, then
Richard rose and extended his hand.

"Will I be imposing on you if I join you, Richard?" Ewan
asked.

"No imposition at all, Ewan. Please sit down. This stew is
uncommon good if you'll have some."

"No, thank you. This will be enough dinner for me right
now," Ewan said, placing a bottle of porter on the table. "Did
Celia tell you I am emigrating to Canada?"

Richard's eyebrow moved upward. "No. No, she did not.
You changed your mind, then?"

Ewan shrugged. "It seemed the better part of wisdom. You
see, I did listen to what you were saying when we met on the
road that day, much as I wanted to run you through for saying
it."

Richard pushed his plate from him. Somehow the stew had
lost its savor. "It's a wise decision, even though I know it must
be a difficult one."

With his face stark as flint Ewan looked up at Richard from
under drawn brows. "I've asked Celia to go with me," he said
quietly.

Only the tightening of Richard's cheek betrayed his effort
to remain calm, and when he finally answered his voice was
bitter.

"Now it becomes my turn to want to run you through! You
have a nerve to sit there and tell me to my face how I have
been cuckolded."

"Cousin, you know that was not my intent. My God, Richard, of all men you are probably my closest friend."

"So it seems!"

"Celia and I did not wish this to happen and we certainly
did not seek it out. Perhaps if you had been more at home . . . I
am not trying to excuse our behavior, because it was dishonorable and we have all suffered for it. But neither of us wanted
to hurt you. Surely you must realize that."

All at once the anger left him and Richard sat forward,
leaning his elbows on the table and rubbing his long fingers
against his forehead. "I had hoped never to speak openly of
this—" he began.

"We *must* speak of it now. There are decisions to make—important ones."

"I should have stayed at home," Richard went on, almost to himself. "I thought to make a future for myself and for her too, and all I've done is to destroy both my public and private lives. How the gods must be laughing!"

"Is there no future for you with the Congress, then?"

"No." He looked directly into Ewan's taut face. "There was, perhaps, while Mr. Jay was there, but since he left I have been pushed more and more to the back of the bench. They don't trust me enough, and without credibility I shall never rise."

"I don't suppose my reputation helped any, either."

"No, it certainly did not. Nor Henry's, nor Uncle James's. But that's all past now. As for Celia, what happened between the two of you would probably have occurred sometime anyway. We seem not to be able to understand each other. We were very young when we married and now she is a different person, as I am. We don't know each other anymore."

Abruptly Ewan poured himself another glass and drank it down. Keeping his voice low, he leaned across the table. "Do you know what she plans to do?"

"No. But look here, Ewan. I talked facts to you once before and now I feel I must presume to do so once again—perhaps for the last time. Have you really thought this through? If Celia wants to go with you, naturally I shall not try to stop her, but you must realize what disastrous consequences you shall be bringing on yourselves. The scandal, the disgrace. *You* might well outlive the ruin of your reputation, but can she? And Celia is a woman to whom appearances are important. She clings to respectability because it offers her security. More than anything in the world I think she fears the specter of poverty. Will it be fair to her to ask her to risk all that to go with you?"

"You say all this because you want to keep her."

Richard looked up sharply. "Yes, I do. But I have said nothing of it to her, nor will I. She shall have to make up her own mind. Perhaps she has no feeling left for me, but I think that whatever she feels for you, it will be sorely tried to survive the strains you will put upon it."

"It might all be set in order if you would divorce her."

Lines of stubbornness settled on Richard's aesthetic face. "I can bend a good deal, Ewan, but don't ask me to go that far. It would ruin the three of us, and I fancy I have not earned that."

Ewan slumped forward, suddenly defeated. "I confess, Richard, that I have said all these same things to myself. I love Celia and I want to take her with me. But to what future? It is going to be hard enough to build something new in this barren land I am forced to adopt. If she comes, circumstances being what they are, it will be ten times harder."

"I know you don't wish to go alone—"

"Oh, I shan't be alone. Mercy Lawrence will marry me in a minute, and, ironically enough, she *wants* to help me resettle. She'll make a decent enough wife, but . . ." His fingers gripped the neck of the green bottle. "What should I do, Richard?"

"I can't answer that for you, Ewan," Richard said, his voice bitter. "I feel that in spite of our problems Celia will have a better life with me here than she will if she throws her hat over the windmill and goes off with you. But," his voice dropped off, "of course, I *would* think that."

"No. No, Cousin. You have always been a fair man." Ewan laughed dryly. "How has it happened that you are the one who is always showing me the hard truth, when as children I was the one always giving directions? How have we come to such a pass that our lives are in such disorder? I had thought to live out my days at the mill, a gentleman on his estates, his heart, or as much as he cared to give of it, in the hands of his wife and children. Now I find myself in exile, branded a scourge and an outlaw, stripped of the land I love, and my heart helpless in the hands of my revered cousin's wife. Dear God! How did it happen?"

Richard reached out and took the bottle out of Ewan's hands. "You have had too much of this, Cousin, and these troubles become overpowering when the senses are dulled by spirits. Come, now. We can't solve these things today. Put them aside for a while and ride back with me."

Ewan managed a wry smile. "I have just enough clearness of head left to know that you are right once again."

Leisurely turning their horses toward West Farms, they ambled the narrow paths that skirted the fields, waded through rocky creeks and threaded their way through clusters of oaks and ash trees, many of them holding some familiar memory.

"Do you imagine these fields will ever bear again?" Richard asked absently as they passed a long clear slope once thick with grain, now covered with the stubble of vines and creepers.

"I hear the soil in Nova Scotia is barren and rocky," Ewan answered bitterly.

There was such despair in Ewan's voice that Richard made an effort to answer lightly. "Well, you won't starve at least, not with all that water around you."

"I was never overfond of fish, but I suppose now I shall have to learn to be."

"Will you take any of your livestock along?"

"Oh, some, I suppose. As many of my good horses as I can and some cattle and sheep." He looked sharply over at Richard. "I am not exactly penniless, you know, and what I will need to start over I can purchase in New York before I sail. I intend to carry along anything that will ease the burden of living like a savage."

They emerged from under a shadowy canopy of newly green maples and birches into the bright sunshine of open fields. Far off in the distance a familiar barn stood in stages of decay next to a white clapboard house—Theophilus Hunt's barn of haunted memory. Hunt himself was working dispiritedly at hoeing a large plot of newly turned earth this side of his house and barn.

"Old Theophilus is putting in some corn," Richard said. From the distance Hunt looked up and saw the two riders approaching. Grateful for the chance to rest, he propped his hoe in the soft earth and came toward the road, wiping at his brow with his arm.

"Good morrow, Richard, Ewan," Hunt said nodding his white-crowned head. "It's a fine day, ain't it, but hot. We've not seen you about here for many a day, Richard. Are you come home to stay now the war's over?"

"Yes, I'm home to stay," Richard answered without enthusiasm. "In a day or two I'll be out plying my hoe just like you, worse luck!"

"Why, you still have that big black to help you. I saw him myself not long ago riding right down this road behind your madam. Put him to the hoe and you'll have a crop soon enough."

"Vestal works hard, Theophilus, but the farm is large. It's more than either of us can handle now that old Diamond is too infirm to do heavy work."

Ewan looked from one to the other and gave a bitter laugh. "Neither of you has cause for complaint. I only wish I had the welcome task of bringing my lands back under cultivation. Instead I must leave them for another man's hand!"

Theophilus Hunt shifted his eyes away from Ewan, obviously uncomfortable at his words. "I'm that sorry, Ewan, ye have to leave this country. Can't see what else you *could* do, though."

"Nor I," Ewan replied, looking bleakly around at the lovely vistas of Bronxdale spread out around them. "Was it a mistake? I was so sure that what I did was right. I was so certain we would outlast this rebellion, that this revolution was only the wild imaginings of a rabble mob."

"A man has to follow his convictions," Richard answered quietly.

"Ewan," Hunt broke it, "I've known ye since ye were only a little lad. You chose your side and you did your best to bring it success. But ye lost. Now ye have to face the consequences of that choice."

Ewan looked down into pale old eyes. "That is just the kind of thing my father would say." He tried to smile at Richard. "Everyone seems to be forcing me to face facts today."

Turning back to Hunt, Richard made a stab at changing subject. "You are going to have a job here trying to bring your farm back to what it used to be," he said lightly.

The old man responded with great feeling. "I don't know how I'm going to manage it!" he said, waving his arm around. "My fences are in ruins, my Negroes have run off, my fields are weed-choked. My barn needs overhauling and my livestock is all stolen or lost. God alone knows how I'll ever be able to handle it!"

Ewan stared at him with bitterness in his eyes. "Bad as it is, your distress is nothing compared to mine. All my life has been spent here among these fields and hills, and now I must leave them forever. Sometimes I think . . . I can't bear . . ."

To Richard's horror his cousin's voice broke and in a sudden rush of feeling the tears began to stream down his cheeks. Embarrassed and unable to help, he and Hunt watched numbly as Ewan fought for control. Finally Ewan said in a choked voice, "Farewell, Theophilus," and, spurring his horse forward, galloped furiously down the road toward his home.

"That's a tormented man," Hunt said, looking after him. "There's plenty who'd say it was no more than he deserved, but . . . I don't know."

Richard sat in silence as Hunt went on. "Ewan was always one to let his feelings master his judgment. I recollect how he hanged young Carne that day, right here on this very spot. 'Twas always my feeling he meant more to scare that boy than to kill him."

"Unfortunately that doesn't give Ned Carne back his life."

"No. And that's the tragedy Ewan has to live with the rest of his life. He'll carry it with him to New Scotland too, or any other place he goes. I don't envy him."

Making a halfhearted farewell, Richard left the old man standing by his broken fence and started off slowly in Ewan's wake. What Hunt had pointed out about his cousin's emotional weaknesses was all too true. Richard felt he would be able to forgive Ewan more easily if only Celia had not been caught up in them, too. Like Ewan, she had allowed her feelings to cloud her judgment, possibly because he, Richard, had always been so careful that his never should. They were all of them to blame when you came right down to it. What mattered now was that some element of good sense should prevail to bring order out of the chaos they had created.

As the days passed, Celia waited for Ewan to come to her to learn her decision. A hundred times she went over the words she would say. The trouble was that no two rehearsals were the same.

Yet over the long dragging hours one side gradually won a slight ascendancy over the other, and she finally knew that, much as she loved this man, she would not sacrifice her life—and Richard's and his own—to her passion. Carefully, painstakingly, she memorized the words that would leave her heart in pieces but her life intact.

But as the days passed and still Ewan did not appear, her resolve began to grow less firm. Tentatively, with only questions filling her mind, she began walking each day toward the Mill House hoping to see him. She found the house deserted, a few crates standing on the shaggy front lawn waiting to be carted away to Hunt's Point for the boat to New York. Once or twice she saw a strange servant clearing out the bare rooms, but her hesitant inquiry brought no clear response.

Questions gave way to confusion, confusion to hurt, and hurt at last to anger as she began to fear that she meant less to him than she had thought. She tried to question Richard, who was keeping very busy about the farm, but if he knew anything of Ewan's plans he was certainly not sharing them with her. And then, just when she thought she could bear the indecisions and agony no longer, his letter came.

She knew it had come from Ewan's hand even before she turned it over to see the Deveroe arms impressed on the wax

seal. Some sixth sense told her he was reaching out to her,
though nothing prepared her for what she read when she opened
the page and spread it out before her.

MY BELOVED,
    By the time you read this I will have been married to
Mercy Lawrence...

"No!" Celia cried aloud, the strangled sound catching in her
throat. The walls of the room seemed to sway around her. She
forced her eyes back to the page.

...for nearly a week. We are sailing on the *Empress of
Russia* with the first tide on the morning of the 25th inst.
The desolation I feel at leaving my native land is second
only to that which afflicts my soul at the thought of leaving
you. Yet it must be and I pray that you too will see as I do
that this is the best way for us both. That you can find it
in your heart to forgive me is all I can ask. In return I can
only assure you that your memory will be the cherished
treasure this heart carries with it into exile. Adieu, my
beloved. God bless and keep you.

                                        Your devoted
                                        EWAN

"No, no, no, no, no!" she cried, crumpling the letter in her
hand. How could he marry that girl and leave her without even
so much as a last goodbye? How could he take the initiative
from her, her cherished resolve to be firm and sacrifice herself
for him? It was not fair! It was not loving! All she was left
with was this terrible letter. She looked back at the neatly
formed lines—"...the first tide on the 25th inst...."—and
suddenly her anger gave way to sick despair. He was sailing
away and she would never see him again. He would be gone,
even now was gone, and she had not even spoken a last word,
exchanged a last kiss, burned the image of his face into her
memory. How was she going to be able to go on living?
    Throwing the crumpled paper to the floor, she rushed across
to the desk and threw it open, searching wildly among the
stacks of papers for a newspaper. What day was it anyway?
Perhaps he had not yet left. Perhaps it was not too late. Catching
up a wrinkled copy of Gaine's *Weekly Mercury*, she quickly
calculated from the date at the top. The twenty-fourth! To-

morrow morning he would sail. If she hurried there was still time.

Running out into the field nearest the house, she pulled a startled Vestal away from his hand plow and ordered him to saddle Kit and one of the farm horses for himself, for he was going to accompany her into the city.

"But Massa Richard, he say nothin'."

"Don't be impertinent!" Celia said angrily. "Do as I say! I don't even know where Richard is." With her hair flying and her eyes wild, Vestal could hardly believe this was his usually easygoing mistress.

"He be up lookin' at that burned lan', near Williams Bridge. I go bring him back, Misse Celia. Don't take but a minute."

"No!" she demanded in a voice he had never heard before. "There's no time for that. I want to leave at once. Go and do as I tell you, now!"

"But Misse Celia..."

Celia grabbed his arm and pushed him toward the house. "I'm going to ride to York Island this afternoon, Vestal, with or without you. Now go this minute and saddle Kit!"

Shaking his head, Vestal hurried to get the horses ready. He stopped by the kitchen long enough to order Betsy to somehow get word to Richard that his wife had lost her wits and was flying for New York, then, despairing at the folly of starting out on such a journey when the afternoon was half over and the plow left standing in an unfinished field, he dutifully followed her breakneck pace down the road to King's Bridge.

They rode until dark made the lanes impassable, pushing the horses too hard and taking risks on the dangerous Harlem Heights roads. He was finally able to convince her to put up at the Blue Bell Tavern on the King's Bridge Road by threatening to let her ride on alone, killing her mount in the process. Celia, distraught and weary, had no wish to be left alone beside a dead horse on a dark highway, so she grudgingly agreed. As luck would have it there were two other women staying the night, traveling with their husbands. She shared a lumpy, damp bed with them, listening to the snores of one and the coughing of the other as she tossed and turned through the long dark hours. At first light she was back on the road, her eyes burning from sleeplessness and her body driven by sheer nervous energy.

Once they reached the city Celia went straight to the White-

hall wharf where the passengers were to board the launch for
the *Empress of Russia* standing out in the harbor, her sails half
unfurled. The dock was already thick with people, crates, animals and farm implements. In the confusion she could see that
a launch had just pushed away, dipping its oars as it shoved
its way out toward the ship. A light misty rain had begun with
the sun's rising and it picked up a little, dampening Celia's
face as she searched frantically for Ewan's familiar tall figure.
She had nearly despaired of finding him when she suddenly
saw him standing at the ladder, talking to a group of people
clustered around him and with a large sheaf of papers in his
hand. Frantically Celia fought her way through the crowd,
calling his name. Through the din something of her voice carried and he looked quickly up to see her on the edge near the
street, trying to work her way to him. Even in the grayness of
the day she could see the color leave his face when he recognized her. Quickly handing the papers to a man standing
near him, he hurried through the groups of people until he
reached her, then grabbed her elbow and steered her across the
cobbled street to the dim recess of an alley lying between ths
stained brick walls of two warehouses. She hardly knew where
she was, or cared. She only knew that as quickly as they were
out of sight of the mob on the wharf his arms were around her
and he was covering her face with his lips and her heart felt
as though it would burst. Clinging to him, the tears on her
cheeks mingled with the rain, she clutched at his body, sobbing
bitterly.

"You little fool," he said at last. "Coming down here like
this! Oh God, God, Celia! How am I going to be able to leave
you?"

"Take me with you, please, please, Ewan. I don't want to
live without you. I'll die, I know I will. Take me with you . . ."

"I can't! You know I can't. It's not only Richard that stands
between us now. I'm married as well. There is nothing for us
together, you know it as well as I."

"You were going to go without even saying goodbye! You
were going away, leaving me with nothing but one cruel letter
to last the rest of my life. Is that all my love meant to you?"

He pulled her away from the edge of the damp bricks where
a thin waterfall of rain fell from a gutter on the roof above.
Crooking his arm around her neck, he bent his head to afford
her some of the shelter of his hat and smoothed back the wet
hair that lay in long clinging strands on her drenched face.

"You're soaked through, and you didn't even wear a hood or pattens. My foolish girl."

"It doesn't matter," Celia answered, nuzzling into his coat. "Nothing mattered but seeing you again."

"Where is your horse? God, Celia, you didn't come alone?"

"No, no. I remembered there was a stable near the Queen's Head, so I made Vestal take Kit around there."

"And Richard? Did he come with you?"

"No. I didn't see him at all. I just left the minute I realized there might be time to reach you before you sailed. Oh, Ewan, take me with you. Don't leave me here alone!"

For a moment he held her close. Then he heard the sharp ringing of the launch bell sounding over the noise of the crowd on the wharf.

"That's for me," he said in a voice full of grief. "It's the last dinghy out to the schooner and I must be on it." Grasping her shoulders, he put her away and looked into her eyes, veiled with utter misery. The hollows of her face were streaked by the rain and her own tears.

"Celia, listen to me. You won't be alone. You'll have Richard and you'll have what you really care most about—your home at West Farms."

"Ewan, please . . ."

"Look at me. You know me better than anyone in the world. I am a selfish man, Celia, and I have done some harsh and cruel things in my life. This once, I am giving up the person who means the most to me because I truly believe it is the right thing for her. I've steeled myself to this for you, for your sake. That was why I married Mercy without telling you and why I was going to leave without saying goodbye. Don't break my resolve now. Every thing in me wants to stay with you, but I know, I *know*, it would not be the right thing, the 'loving' thing, to do. Accept it as a measure of my love for you. Accept it, please."

"Ewan, you will break my heart!"

The bell began to clang in irritation. Glancing nervously toward the end of the wharf, Ewan dug his fingers into her shoulders.

"Hearts mend. I know my cousin for a good man. Lean on him and let him help you."

One last time he looked deeply into her face, burning the memory of every line and plane into his mind. Then, grasping her tightly to him, he kissed her fiercely and hard, bruising her

lips with the intensity of his own. When he let her go she sank
back against the wall, her trembling legs unable to support her,
her eyes closed.

"Goodbye, Celia. God keep you always," she heard him
whisper, and then she heard his steps on the damp cobbles
hurrying away and lost in the crowd.

How many minutes did she lean there, trying to etch the
impression of his lips into her own memory? When she finally
opened her eyes it was to see the narrow walkway empty and
the crowd on the wharf beginning to turn back toward their
homes. She made her way through the stragglers to the end of
the dock, where, looking out over the slate water, she could
make out the shape of the dinghy with its oars like a giant
beetle on the water, carrying the last of the passengers to the
schooners. Surely that was he in the end of the boat, almost
the last one to climb the rope ladder to the deck above. She
stared so hard at the indistinct figure that it became a blur and
she had to shift her eyes to bring it back into focus. Sinking
onto one of the ends of the piers, Celia watched numbly as the
ship's sails unfurled and slowly, creakingly it began to slide
through the dark waters. The rain began to fall harder in a
heavy mist, and still she sat watching as the ship grew smaller
and inched its way around the sister vessels at anchor, moving
gracefully at full sail to begin its trip toward the Narrows.
Though the sloping fields and occasional rooftops of Gover-
nor's Island blocked her view, she fancied she could see it
moving majestically past the Watering Place on Staten Island
to pass through the Narrows and from there on toward the open
sea. She fancied that Ewan was standing on the deck looking
back as the city faded into the mist and that his eyes met hers.
It never occurred to her to leave, for where was there for her
to go, and besides, she could not leave those other eyes burning
toward hers across the waters. So she sat, drenched by the rain,
staring out to sea. And when there was no longer a question
of seeing the ship, she saw it in her mind's eyes, sailing past
Sandy Hook and breaking through the whitecaps of the rolling
ocean to catch the current north.

How ironic that before her birth her parents had left Nova
Scotia to travel along the identical path to their new home on
these shores. She had always fancied she might retrace their
voyage someday and see Acadia for herself. And now it was
not she but Ewan who was going back to the nearly forgotten
homeland. Yet, she thought, perhaps it was not so ironic after

all. She might not go herself, but her heart was going back.
It was returning with the man she loved, never, never to come
back to her again.

It was nearly dark when Richard found her still slumped on
the pier, soaked to her skin, already beginning to burn with
the early signs of fever. He had located Vestal at the stables
on Broad Street, and the two of them, beginning their search
at Whitehall Slip, managed to get her into a carriage and back
to the Queen's Head Tavern.

In a private room upstairs, Richard put her to bed, piling
on all the blankets he could get from a reluctant landlord and
calling for a posset. Then he sent Vestal for a doctor and with
a slip of paper to the apothecary for some powdered Jesuit's
bark. Alternately he cursed Celia and fretted over her. How
stupid of her to sit for hours in a rain when she had always
been subject to this dreadful and dangerous recurring ague.
Already her mind was wandering and it looked to be a bad bout
coming on. It may have already been starting when she dashed
off on this fool's errand, and she had made it ten times worse
by her recklessness.

Yet in his heart as he watched her toss and turn on the
feather mattress, he knew that that very recklessness was a
measure of her grief. He remembered how when Betsy told
him she had left, his anger was so great that he had made up
his mind not to follow her. Then he found Ewan's note crumpled on the parlor floor, and, reading it and knowing his wife,
he realized in his heart the pain it must have caused. Perhaps
there was no other way, but it was severe and cruel of Ewan
to cut her off so abruptly.

This was not a bad tavern bedroom as such rooms usually
went, but for Richard, who seldom left it, it grew steadily more
depressing as the first days of Celia's illness became a fright-
ening mixture of long hours of delirium and frantic efforts to
lower her raging fever. There was a time midway through when
he almost gave up hope, so high was her fever and so pitiful
her will to fight it.

For Celia herself, there were only dim floating memories
of faces barely recognized. A woman, whose shadowy face
materialized first into the patrician features of Elizabeth Deveroe, then reassembled itself into a scowling, angry Madame
Peletaire. And a man, kind and considerate, who never seemed
to stay the same person, jumping around like a Punch-and-Judy

figure and becoming first her father, then Dominie Brec, Samuel Deveroe and Richard. Time and again she called Ewan's name. Finally a day came when she realized with a sharp sense of recognition that it was Richard who was supporting her with his arm around her shoulders and forcing a bitter draft down her unwilling throat. After that, she would wake at all hours of the day and night to see him sitting by her bed, sometimes worriedly studying her face, or slumped wearily, sleeping in an uncomfortable straight-backed chair, or quietly reading a book by a dim single sputtering betty lamp. She did not realize how much she had grown used to his being there until one morning she opened her eyes and he was gone. Filled with an unreasoning panic, she tried to rise but was too weak. She sank back into the pillows and felt absurd tears pour down her cheeks. Only a few minutes later the door opened and he entered, carrying a tray with a bowl of some steaming liquid. Celia buried her face in the linen pillowcase so he would not see how foolish and upset she had been, but the relief and the sense of safety which swept over her at the sound of his voice and the light touch of his hand upon her shoulder were profound. Without his presence she knew she surely would have died—from the lack of anything to live for, if not from the fever.

When Celia was strong enough, Richard brought her to a sunny, comfortably furnished bedroom in a rented house on Cherry Street. In this more relaxed, quiet atmosphere, where the house was run by a serving girl and a cook, she soon worked her way out of her physical debilitation, though the spiritual depression lingered. In the warm June sunshine she sat in the small garden behind the house listening to the cries of street vendors and the low rumbling of traffic, enjoying the exquisite warmth of the sun on her pale skin and the fragrant aroma of flowering trees and shrubs. When thoughts of Ewan or West Farms or questions of the future broke her quiet repose she fiercely forced them from her mind. The future was a void. West Farms was a painful reminder of the past, and Ewan—she would never see him again. Even Richard, the person who had sustained her during her illness, could he ever forgive or want her again after all she had done to hurt him? There was no future for her.

Near the end of June Richard went back to West Chester to look over his property while Celia remained in the house on Cherry Street. It was a measure of how much better she was, she thought, that she could accept his absence. Whatever their future would be, she began to think that her own strength of will would return and she would be able to manage. It was a healing thought and one which was like a buttress to her weakness.

He returned one quiet afternoon to find her stretched out on the sofa in the drawing room, a light quilt over her legs. Her color was much better, he noticed, though the shadows under her large eyes were still dark against it. She had pulled her hair back and tied it with a grosgrain ribbon so that the long strands fell over her shoulders. Watching her from the doorway, the edges of her sculptured lips lifting slightly at a book she was reading, he felt his heart give a sudden lurch. She looked up and smiled at him, laying the book in her lap, and he forced down the rush of feeling that overcame him.

"I'm glad you're back," Celia said, catching back the hand which she had almost automatically extended. He came over to her, throwing his hat on a table, and pulled up a chair beside the sofa, facing her. Once he would have kissed her, lightly and quickly but warmly nonetheless, and for the first time in many months she missed the affectionate gesture.

"You are looking very well. Do you feel better?"

"Much better, thank you. Another week and I should be good as new."

"Just the same you must go slowly. This fever drains the strength."

He sat, staring at the hand on his knee, with a thoughtful hesitancy on his face. Celia waited while he struggled. It had been better between them when she was so desperately ill, she thought ironically. She needed him then and he had been so willing to reach out and help her. That was all gone now.

"Do you feel like discussing . . . discussing the . . . our . . . future?"

Her hands gripped the book so tightly that its sharp edges cut into her flesh. "Of course, Richard. If you wish it."

He was loath to face the subject as she, she realized.

"I am up to it," she said quietly, hoping it was true. "Richard—"

"No. No, let me say first what I want to say. I have been thinking very hard, Celia, not only about us but also about the future and what to make of it. When I was in West Chester I listened and watched and explored. I've come to some conclusions. You won't like them, so you should know that I feel very strongly they are the right thing to do."

He hesitated while she waited for the blow. What else could he have determined but that they must separate?

"I have decided to sell the Manor Farm," he declared. Celia looked up, startled.

"What?" she asked, surprised and relieved all at once.

His words came in a rush. "I know you will object strongly after all you did during the war to save it, but I'm convinced it would be the wisest thing to do. Land speculation is going to be the thing, with all the big estates on the market now that the great landlords are gone. The state will sell confiscated lands first, of course, but after that it's the best price a man can get to resell what he bought from the state. The land rush has already started and I believe it will grow even bigger these next few years. There are fortunes to be made, I'm sure of it."

She was so stunned she could not answer, and he misread the shock on her face. "Now, before you absolutely refuse, listen further, and think about it, I beg you. I propose to keep the land Mother gave us over near the river. Someday it will be valuable for its mining deposits and its closeness to the Hudson. The river is going to be a very important highway between Albany and New York and as the country recovers its importance will grow."

He was leaning forward now, his arms on his knees, engrossed in his plans. "With the money from the farm—and I propose to get every penny I can for it—I'll set up a law office, somewhere, it doesn't matter where. Perhaps in one of the towns on the Sound. I don't know yet. My practice should support us while I use the capital to invest in whatever I feel will make it grow. West Chester is going to grow, too, I'm convinced of it, and there will be plenty of need for all kinds of things—everything from lumber and grain and cloth to nails and ship timbers and limestone. With capital behind him an enterprising man should be able to make a tidy fortune."

She finally found her voice. "Richard, this is so . . . so unlike you! What has happened?"

He shrugged. "I'm not really sure," he said softly. "Perhaps I learned the wrong lesson from my experience with the Congress. I went there feeling I had some political talents to offer, and they refused to let me develop them. I watched other men growing fat on money for requisitions while the army starved and froze. Perhaps it has made me bitter."

Celia threw aside her book and swung her legs to the floor. "I do not think you are bitter. A bitter man could not have cared for a wife such as I have been, even through an illness."

A flush spread over his light skin. She went resolutely on.

"What do you want to do with me, Richard? I've caused you nothing but pain and trouble. You have every right to put me out of your life."

He turned, looking startled. "I have no wish for that. I only tell you of these speculations of mine because I hope you will share them with me."

"Why? You know what I've done—what an unfaithful wife I've been to you. Why should you even want me near you?"

"Celia!" Quickly he came and knelt before her, taking her hands.

"Listen to me, Richard," she went on. "I loved Ewan very much. Wrong as it was, I loved him. In my heart I knew how foolish it would have been to follow him to Nova Scotia, yet that day on the wharf I begged him to take me. If he had agreed I would have gladly gone away with him. You must understand that."

He gripped her hands, hurting them. "We won't talk of this again. Ewan has gone."

"Yes, he's gone now forever and we won't talk of it again. But if you take me back, you must accept the fact that what I felt for him was that strong. You must accept it in order to forgive me for feeling it. Can you forgive me?"

"Forgive? I'm not sure I know what it means. I was angry and hurt, so much so that I nearly refused to come after you when you dashed off to the city that day. Yet something in my mind told me Ewan would not let you smash all our lives. And I knew that when he was gone you would need someone to lean on. You *are* my wife, Celia, though for these many years we have not really lived together. What future does either of us have now if *not* together? I can't hate you. Nor can I hate Ewan. It's going to be a different world now from the one we've known. Can't we put the old one behind us and begin to build something new?"

She did not have the physical or emotional strength to hold back the great rush of feeling that overwhelmed her. Covering her face with her hands, she wanted to weep but there were no tears left.

He hesitated for a moment, then slowly put his arms around

her and drew her to him, resting his head against her soft hair. No words of love came from his lips—they would not be appropriate now. But for the first time he felt sure they would come again, sometime. There was hope for them now. Ewan had given them that much by refusing to take her with him. Now it was up to them to nurture that hope back into a marriage. He realized more clearly now than ever before that he was not a passionate, emotional man. But he still loved Celia as he had always loved her. Somehow he would find a way to show her that love.

"What about the farm, Celia? You haven't yet told me how you feel about selling it. I expected that to be my greatest obstacle."

She rubbed her fingers across her eyes. "I never thought I could leave it, Richard, but now . . . now it represents to me all my failures. The war, Ewan, my failure as a wife. I never thought to say these words, but perhaps we would be better to start afresh somewhere else."

"You're sure?"

"Yes, I'm sure." She gave him a suspicious sidelong glance. "You did say we would get a large sum of money for it, didn't you?"

He smiled at her affectionately. "Yes, my dear. And I'll be very slow about reinvesting it, so you won't have to fear that bankruptcy is around the corner. Then, too, we will always have Mother's land."

"A new home in a new place—perhaps that is what *is* needed now. You never did want to be a farmer, did you?"

"No! And that has not changed. You know that my true wish was to be involved in public affairs, but since I cannot have that, I will put my energies into building you a fortune. Will you trust me?"

She laid her palm against his cheek. There was little left in that thin face of the boy she had once adored and the young man she had married. He was harder now, forged by suffering, disappointment and adversity. With a start she realized she did not really know this man who sat with his arm around her, any more than he knew the woman she now was. So, let it be, then. They would start over, begin again to get to know each other and possibly, eventually, to love each other a little once more. Not as she loved Ewan—never the same as that—but a love and an affection nonetheless.

"As you have given me your forgiveness, I will give you my trust. It's as you said—what else do we have if not each other?"

That would be enough for now.

Part III
Josh
1784

twenty-one

Almost a year passed before the house at West Farms was sold and Celia packed up the last of the family's possessions for the move to her new home. During those long months she tried not to notice the new family in the Mill House and the changes they made there. She worked endlessly to force from her mind the memories associated with every vista of field and river and to push down the terrible emptiness that overcame her when she walked among them. Driving herself tirelessly, she faced each day determined not to give way to thoughts of Ewan. Where was he now? What was he doing at this moment? How had life worked out for him in his new country? She dropped wearily into bed each night, her unshed tears trapped within her aching heart.

For all these years she had believed the farm to be her greatest security, but now, in a complete turnabout, she knew that her only hope of putting her old life behind her lay in leaving this place forever. Her hopes were dashed several times when Richard refused to sell for what he felt was not the best price. When he finally did accept an offer, there was no question but that his waiting had paid off handsomely. With a large sum of money as security he methodically set about searching for the best place to resettle, and after many weeks of riding about West Chester County he at length decided on the old Huguenot town of New Rochelle.

"It has several advantages," he told Celia as he removed his coat, still clouded with the dust of the road. "It will give me the opportunity to explore the area up and down the Sound for opportunities of development. It is large enough and central enough to sustain my small law practice, and—" he glanced at her sideways to see her reaction—"there are still many people of French extraction living there. I thought you might enjoy that."

Celia took the coat from him and began to brush at it halfheartedly. New Rochelle meant nothing to her, and now one place was as good as another.

"Where will we live?" she asked quietly.

"I thought we might take a ride up there next week to have a look around. There are some houses for sale whose owners have either moved away or been forced out for their Loyalist sympathies. I don't wish to make a decision until you've seen them. It's a pleasant little village."

"It will be a new experience to live in a town."

He reached across and gave her hand a light squeeze, "Perhaps you will find you prefer it."

She attempted a smile. "Perhaps."

Celia's first impression of New Rochelle was one that never changed in all the time they lived there—a kind of objective indifference. It was a pleasant little town, as Richard had said— a village of nearly seven hundred people, one main street, a small stone church, a few scattered stores along High Street and pretty white farmhouses lining the roads that led out like spokes on a wheel to the surrounding countryside. From the first she loved the Sound, whose sparkling waters were visible from the upper windows of the house they finally selected and from where she could watch the boats docking at the tiny wharf at the bottom of the hill. Their new home was on Myer's Point, a shingled house with a sloping roof and dormer windows in the bedrooms off the long hall in the upper floor. It was much smaller than the Manor House, but Celia soon came to appreciate its coziness. There was a small barn at one end of the property with fenced pens for livestock and one tiny cottage which Richard quickly turned over to Vestal, Betsy and their two children. He made a halfhearted effort to convince Vestal that this was the time to start out on his own, but although Betsy was anxious to try it, Vestal with his strong sense of family loyalty was outraged.

"I has been a Deveroe man all my life, Massa Richard," he said stubbornly, "an' I don't wants to start be'in somebody else's now."

Old Diamond was too infirm now to make the move from West Farms, the only home he had known since he was first bought as a slave for the Mill House, so Richard arranged for him to remain with the new owners. He clutched at Celia's hand the day they left, and his tears fell warm on her skin. It was the hardest moment of her leave-taking. She pressed an ornate silver spoon into his hands and fought back her own tears, climbing into the carriage to roll down the road past the ruined blockhouse without ever once looking back, feeling as though the very heart was being torn out of her.

Perhaps it was that grief that caused her to take so little interest in the new house. With Betsy's help, and the haphazard efforts of Betsy's two small children, she cleaned and scrubbed and placed the furniture around the rooms so that the house was livable. Beyond that she found she did not really care what was done to it. At first she made a halfhearted attempt to respond to the friendly overtures of her new neighbors, who politely came to call in spite of the Deveroes' Loyalist reputation, but she could not bring herself to leave the house and try to get to know them better. She knew she was earning a reputation as a snob and a recluse, but she did not really care. In fact, there was very little in life that she did care about.

Then one day she stood on the back porch of her house and looked out over the long yard stretching toward the edge of the hill. Beneath the overgrown weeds and vines she caught a glimpse of an old brick path and a few bright petals of wild portulaca—all that was left to suggest the rows of neat beds from former days.

Hitching up her skirts and tying a turban around her hair, she went with a spirited step to the barn and dragged Vestal away from where he sat mending harnesses.

"Go and fetch a hoe and a scythe," she demanded. "You and I are going to get to work!"

With more enthusiasm than she had felt in over a year, she threw herself into clearing away the overgrowth, breaking up the verdant soil, planting new vegetable beds in neat rows and nurturing the young plants into respectable plots of carrots, peas, onions, beets, beans and squash. She was delighted to find the remains of an old asparagus bed, which she gradually brought back under cultivation. With Vestal's help she trimmed the wild gray gooseberry and currant bushes, put in an herb garden of sorrel, savory, parsley and sage, and planted borders of sweet william, phlox, larkspur, alyssum and honeysuckle. She restored the brier roses and pruned the patriarchal apple, cherry and quince trees. She set up a bench of wooden beehives, put in a sundial and even had Vestal construct a small dovecote.

In another year's time the large garden behind the Deveroe home was a wealth of beauty that furnished the house with flowers and the kitchen with all the vegetables and herbs they needed.

She did not realize how therapeutic her garden had been for her until one day after it was well established when, looking around at its symmetrical patterns, she thought how lovely and nostalgic it would be to have a border of southernwood lining some of the beds. From that day she found that she could once again hold the lacy plant in her hand without her heart breaking; that she could think of the love and the passion she had shared with Ewan as a thing of the past; that the fragrant plant was only a reminder of a bittersweet time now gone instead of the painful memory of love lost. She vowed to herself then that she would never be without it around her again. To hold it in her hand and against her cheek, drinking in its fragrant aroma— that was all she had now to make him real again, to remind her he had not been just a dream.

"And how is Madam Deveroe?" Dr. Sayre asked, settling back in his leather chair and brushing the lint from his black worsted hose. Across from him Richard sat leaning against the table, turning the brim of his hat slowly in his long fingers.

"Her health is good, but her spirit, I fear, is sorely vexed. It was partly on her account that I stopped in to see you today."

Sayre rubbed a long finger across his broad chin, thinking to himself that if Mrs. Deveroe was poorly, her husband was looking better than he had ever seen him. Long hours in the saddle had given Richard's fair skin a welcome tan and put a lean, hard edge on his slim figure. Though his clothes were not cut from the elegant fabrics of earlier years, they still had his characteristic flair.

"Perhaps she is working too hard trying to settle in her new home," the doctor offered.

"I wish that were the problem. No, she does not take the interest in her house that I fancy most women would. All her efforts go into her garden. She works long hours there, she takes walks, occasionally she accompanies me to Sunday service at the church in the village. Other than that, I fear she is becoming a recluse."

"My, that hardly sounds like the woman I recall. But you must remember, my good sir, the war has left many people of the county with melancholy dispositions. Suffering and privation must take their toll. And you know as well as I, Richard, there is as much hatred and revenge at work now as there was during the war years."

He watched the young man as he stared through the window into the yard that connected Sayre's office with his home at the rear. Glancing out, the doctor saw several of his children running and laughing around the walk where his wife sat on a bench sewing. "I know what you are thinking, my friend," he said kindly. "And you are right. If your good wife had a houseful of children to care for she would not be such easy prey to these melancholy humors. It's unfortunate."

Richard's eyes came swiftly away from the window. "It's not only that," he answered quietly. "If she just had a friend, another woman she could confide in, a sister or a mother. She has no one and she makes no effort to cultivate anyone. I confess it worries me a good deal."

"Perhaps I could stop in and see her when next I'm up that way. I have patients in New Rochelle and I often include them in my rounds."

"I would appreciate that, Jonas. Why not stay the night with us? In fact, bring your wife along. She might be just the female companionship Celia needs."

"Thank you, Richard. I shall try to work it out. Now tell me something about yourself. How does the law practice go?"

Richard shrugged. "Well enough. I stay busy between my clients in New Rochelle and my duties with the courts at Bedford and White Plains. I've also got quite a deal of work here in your town of West Chester. But my practice is not my real interest. Did you know I've purchased a sloop? I'm convinced a valuable business is going to grow up carrying farm supplies between the Connecticut towns and New York City, and I intend to get in on it. If this boat turns a profit I intend to buy another as soon as possible."

Dr. Sayre did not miss the enthusiasm that lit up Richard's face as he launched into his plans. It was the most animation he had shown in the entire visit.

"If you would like a word from a medical man who has only his opinions to back him, I would suggest you forget the Sound and look instead to Hudson's River. I did a lot of sailing on that water in my youth, and if there is to be a highway connecting the city with the valuable farmlands to the north, that will be it. You might explore it a little more thoroughly before you commit yourself to the Sound."

In the last two years Richard had learned never to let any information pass him by which might be turned to a useful profit someday. Now he leaned forward, suddenly alert.

"Why?"

"Because, well, the farmlands of Dutchess, Orange and West Chester Counties are all extremely rich. Because it is a straight link north with Albany, and has a deep channel for larger boats. As an inland river it is not as subject to the terrible storms and vagaries of weather as the Sound. And because it is lined with valuable forests and rock deposits."

"But Connecticut is already growing in the direction of manufactured goods. Its rivers have proved excellent for the establishment of mills and even factories."

"True, but its farmland is not as fertile as the land in the Hudson Valley."

"Yet look at West Chester. It's almost devastated. It will be years before it comes back to the kind of productivity we used to know."

"My friend, it will come back and more. Surely you know that, having once farmed its land yourself."

Richard smiled sheepishly. "Yes. You are right. The land recovers before the people do! I shall remember your suggestion, Jonas," he said as he rose to shake Dr. Sayre's hand. Mentally he made a note to ride through the Hudson Valley soon.

"Let me know when we may expect you in New Rochelle."

"I shall. And with any luck we shall have your good wife smiling and enjoying life once again. But I think I'll bring along some of my Bostock's Elixir, just in case."

There was a brisk wind off the Sound which had Celia gripping the wide brim of her straw hat to keep it from being blown away. As she hurried down the dirt track that led by a back path toward the water, she thought over the events of the last two days, smiling to herself. The Sayres had left that morning after spending a difficult two days in her house, and it had been with a great feeling of relief that she saw them ride down High Street and out of her life. Jonas Sayre had been pleasant enough to have around, but his wife, Martha, who had obviously been brought along to keep her company, had proved tiresome.

Richard, of course, would never understand, but the truth was that she was not interested in *any* companion right now.

Perhaps she did spend too much time in melancholy reflection, but she was not unhappy in it. In fact, she much preferred the company of her plants and herbs to a woman whose conversation was completely limited to one subject—her children and their reactions to everyone who touched their lives. In fact, Celia thought, clutching at her hat in the sharp breeze, she now knew more about the Sayre brood than she had ever really cared to know. It had been a relief to get back to her garden.

A large rock half hidden in the weeds nearly caused her to stumble down the sloping path. Below her she could see the tiny house, its sagging shingled roof worn with the constant ravages of the weather off the Sound. Going almost sideways down the hill, she finally came to even ground, where she hesitated, looking toward the shabby cabin in the distance. Should she go in? Celia wondered. It had been an almost casual reference of Jonas Sayre's which had brought her here, and now she was uncertain whether she should have come at all. Well, why not? Holding tightly to her hat, she moved briskly along the sandy path toward the cabin door.

That evening, with her face more animated than Richard had seen it in two years, she leaned intensely across the supper table.

"You would not believe it, Richard! The poverty, the squalor! There was hardly a crust in the house, and those poor children in rags. The stench was overpowering. I could see that the older girl had tried, really tried, to bring some kind of order to the place, but it was simply too much for her."

Richard found his horror growing with every detail.

"Good God, Celia, you can't go into such a place. Think of the diseases you are exposed to. I won't have it!"

She gripped his hands across the table. "But you don't understand. These children have no parents now that their mother has died. There is the girl not even fourteen years old to look after them and only the alms of the town to support them. They are in desperate need, Richard."

"Send Betsy, then. I never thought when Jonas Sayre was describing their situation that you would take it into your head to go down there." He stopped as he saw that the brightness on her face of a moment before had fled completely. He said more genlty, "How many children did you say there were?"

"Six—and the youngest only a child of three. She is a beautiful baby, too, Richard, with yellow hair and big green eyes. She was frightened of me at first, but by the time I left she was cuddling against me. I think she misses her mother."

Richard grimaced, trying not to think of the deadly contagions of that destitute household. Damn Jonas Sayre!

"What did you do for them?" He was almost afraid to ask.

"I helped them clean up the two rooms a little. I got the older ones washing clothes with some poor soap which was all they had, and kicked up a fire and got a little gruel going for them. There are so many things they need and some I'm sure we can spare. Medicines, sheets, bread, some shirts to cut down . . ."

"Oh, Celia!"

Her eyes narrowed. "Do you mind so much?"

As he looked into those topaz depths, a great tenderness came over him. "No, I don't mind. I only fear that you will expose youself to some illness."

"But, Richard, I'm strong. It is only that recurring fever that ever affects me, and that has not come for two years now. And I want so much to help them."

He tried to smile. If it meant so much to her, how could he stand in her way? "You won't be bringing all six of them here to live?"

"No," she answered, laughing. "I promise not to go that far. Though I would have loved to bring that darling little girl home with me. She and I are going to be very good friends, I just know it."

Maybe Jonas Sayre knew what he was doing after all, Richard thought.

Though Celia kept her promise not to bring the six Grover children to live with them, Richard sometimes felt in the weeks that followed that she had all but done so. He grew accustomed to seeing them sitting around the kitchen table, doing chores in the garden and even joining them for meals. The smallest girl, Hannah, became Celia's shadow, following her around and clinging to her skirts almost as though Celia were a surrogate mother. She was a thin, frail child whose sallow skin had probably borne the cast of ill health from her birth, but her devotion to Celia brought such a glow of happiness to his wife's eyes that he suppressed all his apprehensions. The town fathers wanted very much either to parcel out the children to neighbors or to pack them off to an orphanage, but because of Celia's support and the children's desire they decided not to carry out that plan.

Celia was indefatigable in her efforts. She wrote letter after letter to the children's relatives in other states in an effort to find one who would take on their permanent care, all to no avail. She helped work out a plan by which the older boy of twelve would be hired out to the town farrier and talked Richard into standing surety for him. She taught the eldest girl better methods of hygiene and home care, and she saw that the other children had chores to do and some basic schooling.

On the frail Hannah she lavished all the devotion she had never been able to give a child of her own, embroidering dresses, aprons and caps for her, dressing her hair, telling her stories, rocking her to sleep, holding her frail little hand as they walked along the beach looking for sand crabs, and sitting against a sandy dune with the child in her lap, the newly cropped fine yellow hair tucked underneath her chin. Something told her this was a transitory and fragile relationship, but she was too filled with joy to listen. At last she had a child of her own! It was a healing thing.

At last a letter arrived from a woman calling herself a cousin who lived in New Hampshire and who was willing to send her husband down to New Rochelle to look over the situation. Richard waited to give the letter to Celia until early one morning, just before he was to set out on a trip to New York. She was looking so very cheerful that day, sitting at the table with the gold of the sun turning her hair to bronze, that he impulsively broached the subject.

For Celia it seemed some of the brightness went out of the morning as she read the letter.

"She sounds terribly abrupt, doesn't she? And so . . . well, ignorant. If you read between the lines it sounds as though she has some ulterior motive. Perhaps she only wants cheap labor for her farm."

"Celia, that is unfair. Come, now, we don't know that the children will go to live with them. Let's at least keep an open mind until we meet her husband."

Celia tried to smile. "You're right, I know. It's just that I don't think I can bear to give them up, especially Hannah. Will you answer her right away?"

"Oh, no. I must make this trip first. I want to see Comfort Sands about a valuable piece of property he has for sale just above Rye which might be a suitable place to build a dock on the Sound. Our little *Venture* is doing very well, but I think having our own landing would be even more worthwhile. It might well be the first step in building up a whole fleet of sloops."

"I thought Comfort Sands was a merchant," Celia said absently, her thoughts still on the letter.

"He is, but he is also one of the more successful land speculators in West Chester County. Celia, are you listening to me?"

Her eyes shifted from her lap, where the letter lay in her hands. "Yes, yes. A land speculator. Will he sell, do you think?"

"Oh, I think so. I've written him my offer, which is a fair one. I told him I hoped to visit his office this afternoon to get his agreement. Why don't you ride in with me?"

"I promised Hannah I would take her to Mr. Ferris's store for a string of rock candy. I don't want to disappoint her."

Impulsively he leaned across the table and kissed her lightly. "All right, then. Next time."

Richard worried over the Grover family troubles all the long way into New York. The break must come and the sooner the better. Each day was going to make it more difficult for Celia to part with these children. He would have some time this evening in his room at the Golden Hill tavern. Perhaps he would answer that letter right away after all.

The streets of New York seemed busier and dirtier than ever. After brushing the dust from his clothes at the Golden Hill, he made his way on foot down Broad Way to Sands's establishment. Climbing the two flights of stairs leading to several small rooms under the roof that served for storage and offices, he was led by an officious clerk with ink-stained fingers into a tiny sitting room and told to wait.

The room was comfortable enough and had a fascinating bird's-eye view of the busy harbor. When Richard heard the door open he pulled his gaze away from the window and turned, expecting to greet the affluent Sands. One look at the tall, stern figure standing in the doorway and his smile faded to a scowl.

"Mr. Deveroe, your servant."

Jaspar Carne! Merciful God, this gentleman was always turning up when he was least expected. "I have an appointment with Mr. Sands," Richard said unceremoniously. "Surely this is a mistake."

Jaspar Carne smiled his thin smile and sauntered into the room. "No mistake, Mr. Sands sends his regrets. He is unfortunately preoccupied this afternoon and has asked me to stand in for him."

"You must forgive my surprise, Mr. Carne. I did not expect to see you in the city, much less in this office."

"I have made my home in this town since not long after the British Army made their welcome departure. I happen to be Mr. Sands's chief representative and thus the logical person to handle this matter. You are interested in a parcel of waterfront near Rye, I understand." There was no trace of cordiality on Carne's lean face, and his eyes were as cold as Richard remembered them.

Richard picked up his glazed leather hat from the table. "I really do not wish to discuss this with you, Mr. Carne. Perhaps you will ask Mr. Sands to inform me when he is available."

"It will do you no good to wait," Carne replied in a level voice. "Mr. Sands employs me to handle all his dealing in real estate. Land is my business, Mr. Deveroe. I'm very good at it. So if you refuse to deal with me you will not deal with anyone."

Richard was conscious of his tight grip on the brim of his hat. Reluctantly he turned back and sat down.

"Since you know so much about Mr. Sands's business I presume you know the parcel of land I am interested in."

"Oh, yes, indeed I do."

"And you know my offer."

"Yes, sir, I do."

Richard waited while Carne sat impassively studying the tips of his fingers.

"Well, sir?"

Not a muscle moved in Carne's enigmatic face. "You cannot have it."

Startled, Richard thought for a moment he had misunderstood the man. "I beg your pardon?"

"The land is not for sale."

"But I understood it was. I am prepared to meet Mr. Sands's price as long as it is fair."

"You cannot have it at any price."

"If this is a jest . . ."

"You must know me better than that, Mr. Deveroe. That land is not for sale—to you."

Richard fought down an impulse to jump to his feet. "I find

this most insulting, Mr. Carne. I have come here in good faith prepared to make a reasonable offer, and you will not even name a price. Is this the way you handle Comfort Sands's business? If it is I wonder that he is not a poorer man than he is rumored to be."

Carne hesitated without moving his eyes from Richard's face. "Very well, I'll name a figure. One hundred thousand pounds."

Richard gasped, sitting forward in his chair. "You are joking, of course."

"That is the price."

"For sixty acres of salt marsh! Why, you could buy all West Chester County for that. I know these are speculative times, but, God's blood, sir, that is preposterous!"

For the first time the ghost of a smile played about Jaspar Carne's thin lips. "Come now, Mr. Deveroe. Of course it is preposterous. Let us not continue these foolish games. That property is not for sale to you at any price and it never will be as long as I am Mr. Sands's agent. When he does sell it, he has already agreed that I shall have the first offer. And I shall buy it, if only to keep it out of your hands. That is the truth of the matter and you would do well to accept it."

Furious, Richard sat back and stared the man down. Carne was bringing it all out into the open, all the years of resentment and dislike. It seemed that now he must pay for his own rash words to Jaspar Carne that day in the Manor House and for Ewan's ruthlessness in hanging Ned Carne, a young man he barely remembered.

"I know why you want that land," Carne went on as though he could read Richard's mind. "I know of your boat, the *Venture*, Mr. Deveroe, and I can surmise that those sixty acres of salt marsh, situated as they are, would make an excellent landing." He paused, letting his careful words sink in. "The blood of good men was not spilled on their native soil, Mr. Deveroe, so that treasonable Loyalists could grow rich on the spoils after their death. I consider it my patriotic duty to prevent people like you from building a fortune on the bones of better men."

With a cold fury Richard stared back at him. "People like me, or just me, Mr. Carne. You have always hated my family, haven't you? Well, in spite of what you think, I was never a Loyalist."

"No? That is a matter of conjecture, at best. Certainly every other member of the Deveroe clan proved a traitor to the Revolution. I find it difficult to believe that one would go against the entire sympathies of the others. I *always* found it difficult to believe."

"You have a nerve, Mr. Carne, branding me a traitor," Richard said icily. "I worked long and diligently for the Congress throughout most of the years we were struggling for independence, suffering the breach my commitment caused in my own family."

"I could never see that there was any breach in your family, Mr. Deveroe. As for the Congress, they seemed to have felt some hesitancy about entrusting their important work to you. I notice you have left politics behind now."

"You seem to know a great deal about me, Mr. Carne."

For the first time, Jaspar Carne's eyes shifted away from his guest, and Richard knew he had hit a nerve.

"Why?" he asked in genuine bewilderment. "We've had one or two unpleasant confrontations, and other than that I barely know you. I don't understand how you can turn an old grudge into a vindictive crusade. What have you possibly to gain by it?"

A very cool, contained man, Jaspar Carne sat without moving a finger, but his eyes were black with self-satisfied zeal.

"If it was the death of your young kinsman—" Richard went on.

A hand lifted, interrupting him. "Though I have not forgotten that unfortunate young man, you must not make the mistake of thinking his death is the motive for my actions now. No, on the contrary, I make it a matter of policy never to sell one inch of confiscated land to anyone with the slightest hint of disloyalty or opportunism. As long as I have the power, no Tory will profit by his treason. Your family, Mr. Deveroe, was always overbearing and power-hungry, playing at lords of the manor while better men worked to keep you in luxuries. Well, we have a better system now. The land belongs to a free people, and their liberties will never again be placed in jeopardy if I have any way to prevent it."

"I find it difficult to see how my purchasing this public land puts anyone's liberties in jeopardy."

"Ah, yes. But having been denied a power base in politics, don't you think I can recognize that you now intend to build one in trade? If a free society takes away the Deveroe grip on the land, you replace it with an empire built on business. Very enterprising, but *not* while I am alive to prevent it."

Abruptly, Richard rose. He felt that if he stayed longer he was certain to strike this infuriating man.

"It seems there is no more to be said between us," he said angrily, setting his hat on his head.

"Good day, Mr. Deveroe," Jaspar Carne rose as though they had just concluded a most amiable conversation. "I trust we shall meet again."

"Not if it can be avoided, sir," Richard replied in clipped tones.

He stalked through the door, hurried down the steep stairway to the street and took off up Broad Street with long strides. He was standing on Wall Street looking across at the ruins of old Trinity Church before he realized he was trembling with rage.

Damn the scurvy bastard! A common farmhand giving himself airs because he had been able to grasp power from the struggles of the Revolution. A sanctimonious, long-nosed patriot using the new order to work out old resentments. What satisfaction it must have given him to thwart Richard Deveroe's business enterprises.

Only then did it occur to Richard to wonder how it was that Jaspar Carne knew so much about his experience with the Congress. He started sedately walking up Broad Way, the very picture of a gentleman of ease out for a pleasant stroll, but deep within him a grim determination was taking root. From that moment on he would set about trying to learn as much about the enigmatic Mr. Carne as that gentleman seemed to know of Richard Deveroe.

Celia walked down the path beside New Rochelle's High Street, Hannah's hand clasped tightly in her own. She looked down at the child, feeling a sense of pride and affection. Only that morning she had put the finishing stitches to a green cambric cloak and matching wide hat trimmed with ruching, which she fancied made the little girl look as though she had stepped out of a picture book. Celia slowed her stride to keep up with the child's short legs, trying at the same time to wave out of their path the assorted chickens, pigs and dogs which strayed into the village from the nearby homes. She was so absorbed in shooing the obstacles from the walkway that she nearly collided with a tall young woman just ahead of her.

"Good morrow, Mrs. Deveroe," a smooth voice said over her head.

Celia looked up into the warm brown eyes of a young woman

she recognized as one of the neighbors with whom she had exchanged calls when she first moved to New Rochelle. Before she could search her memory for a name the woman smiled and said, "Are you celebrating this fine morning with a walk into town?"

"Good morning, Mrs. Wister," Celia said briskly, thankfully recalling the lady's name. "I promised Hannah we would buy some rock candy in Ferris's store. I never realized, however, just how many obstructions there are for little people on the town paths."

Mrs. Wister looked kindly down at Hannah. "You have done wonders for that child, my dear lady. She has more color in her cheeks than I have ever seen before. They are all sickly children, those Grovers."

"They had such poor care," Celia answered.

Rosalind Wister knelt in front of Hannah to look directly into the child's sallow face, oblivious to the dust of the road on the folds of her fine cambric skirt. She was a handsome woman with black hair artfully arranged under her wide straw bonnet and the creamy complexion of perfect health. There was a directness in her manner, yet there was warmth there, too. Celia wondered why she had been so quick to refuse to know her better.

Rosalind reached out to twist one gold ringlet around her finger. "You have such pretty hair, my dear. And such a lovely cloak. It matches your eyes."

Hannah shrank back against Celia's skirts and looked up at her for reassurance. Reaching down, Celia lifted her into her arms, where the child nestled her head against her.

"She's very shy."

"She seems to have warmed to you," Rosalind said, smiling. "I wish my youngest, Jenny, would show some signs of that shyness. She is so active she quite drives me to distraction. Perhaps you would like to visit me some afternoon and bring little Hannah with you. They might be very good for each other."

Celia was surprised to find that the idea of a visit was a welcome one. The Wisters lived only a few houses away. Yes, it would be very nice to pay her a call and take Hannah along.

"We should both like that very much, Mrs. Wister," she said, setting the child back on her feet.

"Please—Rosalind. Though I've borne my husband's name for a long time now and am quite proud of it, yet I have never become used to the formality of 'Mrs. Wister.'"

"And I'm 'Celia.'"

"Good. Shall we say next Monday about teatime?"

"I shall look forward to it." It occurred to Celia then that she had not really had a woman friend since Hester went away to England, all those years ago. And the prospect of having Rosalind Wister to confide in seemed suddenly delightful.

Hannah pulled at her skirts. "May we go now? Sweet. Sweet."

"Yes, darling," Celia said, retrieving the thin little hand. "Right away."

She was so full of her anticipated visit to the Wisters and so happy at the prospect that when Richard returned home the next evening he decided not to mention his unsettling conversation with Jaspar Carne. The Carne name raised too many specters for both of them. He shrugged off the matter of the land with a brief explanation that it had not been for sale after all and let her run on about her new friend.

He watched his wife, sitting in the candlelight, her tawny hair reflecting tiny golden lights. Though still too thin, she was looking far lovelier than she had in months. There was an animation about her that had almost erased the old melancholy. Richard folded and sanded the letter he had finished and laid it away, closing the lid on the writing box.

"Did I see Hannah asleep upstairs?" he asked gently.

"Yes. She was very tired and had the first sniffles of a cold coming on, so I put her to bed in one of our spare rooms. You don't mind, do you?"

"No, of course not. You are becoming quite the little mother to her, aren't you?"

Celia laid her sewing in her lap. "I suppose I am. But, oh, Richard, I do enjoy it so. She needs mothering so badly, and I, well, perhaps I need to give it as much as she needs to receive it. She has made me happy, I confess."

"Then that is all that really matters. Only, please, Celia, remember that she may have to go away soon to live with her relatives. Also, she is not strong."

"I know. I try to remember, but the prospect is so painful that I simply put it out of my mind."

Impulsively he went to stand behind her, putting his arms around her shoulders and laying his cheek against hers. "I just don't want you to be hurt," he said quietly.

She laid her palm against his cheek, grateful for the affectionate gesture. "Thank you, Richard. You are very good to put up with all this, you know."

All at once he was aware that the events of the last two days had shaken something of his innermost tranquility and that his wife's arms would be a comfort he had not enjoyed for a long time. "Coming to bed?" he asked.

Celia lifted the lid of the sewing table and, laying her work inside, rose to move into his arms. "Yes," she whispered against his cheek. "I think it long past time."

During the next two months two events occurred which were to have far-reaching effects on both Celia and Richard. The first was the arrival of Jonathan Strep, the husband of the Grover cousin. In spite of herself, Celia liked the man for his quiet, kindly manner, and after only an hour with the big taciturn New Hampshire farmer, she felt her earlier suspicions vanish. After much discussion, not only with the Deveroes but with the town fathers, arrangements were made for Jonathan Strep to take five of the children back with him. Hannah, who could not seem to throw off her colds and lingering cough, would be allowed to stay with Celia until her health improved sufficiently for the trip north.

In the midst of all these arrangements, Richard took time to ride across the county and pass several days on the shores of the Hudson River near his mother's property. His encounter with Jaspar Carne was never far from his mind, and, recalling Dr. Sayre's comments about the development of the Hudson River, he decided to turn his attentions to the western side of the county, where perhaps he would be less likely to run into the man.

His journey proved to him that everything Dr. Sayre had said was true. There was already a tiny growing fleet of sloops specially designed to carry freight up and down the Hudson's challenging waters. The farmland was showing dramatic signs of a recovery. People were moving back to homes abandoned during the war years, and new immigrants were arriving from Europe almost daily to settle the acres of uncultivated land. Striking up an acquaintance with one of the sloop captains, he arranged to come aboard for a trip as far north as Albany, and he came back convinced that the land bordering the river was as fertile as any he had ever seen. Furthermore, near his property, in Mount Pleasant, there was already a small dock where some of the sloops were making stops. Everything pointed in the direction of the river for future growth, and with enthusiasm he turned his hopes away from the Sound and toward the Hudson. For the time being the house and the law office in New Rochelle would remain his home base, but with a strange certainty in his heart he felt that in looking to the magnificent river he was beginning to build the basis for his future, his and Celia's. Perhaps even Hannah's, he thought ruefully, and smiled at the thought.

twenty-two

As the weeks went by not even the good fresh food from Celia's garden seemed to add any weight to Hannah's fragile frame. Richard was certain she was consumptive until Dr. Sayre finally convinced him she was not suffering from that dreaded ailment. She simply was not strong, perhaps as a result of her early years of malnourishment, and hover over her as she would, Celia could not reverse the trend.

In spite of it, Celia enjoyed her new role as a mother to the fullest. Even her friendship with Rosalind Wister blossomed under the shared concerns of child-rearing. With a healthy brood of four children of her own, Rosalind was a walking textbook on the care and feeding of children.

"I'd try molasses and sulfur on that cough if I were you," she suggested as they sat together sewing in the Wister garden, while Hannah and Jenny romped around the brick paths.

"I might as well," Celia sighed. "I've tried everything else from Daffy's Elixir to boneset tea. I even was almost persuaded to let Betsy tie a dirty stocking around her neck—that is supposed to keep the evil humors from sinking lower into her chest."

"Sounds a typical slave remedy."

Hannah, suddenly fatigued with running, moved across the grass and laid her head in Celia's lap. "Home, Cea'l. I want to go home."

Stroking her yellow hair, Celia smiled down at her. "Of course, dear. It's time we were getting back anyway. Here, let me tie your bonnet and we'll walk home. Then you can have a nice drink of cider and a rest before supper."

"Have you heard anything further from the Streps?" Rosalind asked, wondering if the bond between these two was not becoming too strong.

"No, but Richard has written them that we would like to keep Hannah to raise as our own. I'm hopeful they won't object. They have such a houseful already."

"That's very generous of you both."

Celia lifted the child's slight body and set her in her lap. "I think he only goes along because he knows I want to keep her so badly. Every day I feel she is more like my own child."

Rosalind studied the child's white face with the yellow lashes lying on her skin like soft downy feathers. She recognized the signs so well. Even if Celia was able to keep Hannah she would be lucky to raise her. Impulsively she laid her hand on Celia's arm in a gesture of reassurance. "I'm sure it will all work out for the best."

Yet, with the passing of time, Celia found that even the comfort of Hannah's presence could not keep off the old black dogs of melancholy. For one thing, Richard, absorbed in his new plans, was away more now than at any time since he had returned from the Congress. She found she missed him very much. It was a measure of how much she had come to depend on his quiet, undemanding support. In spite of all she could do, her thoughts would stray to Nova Scotia and Ewan. There had never been any word of the emigrants, but something in her heart told her that Ewan could not be dead or she would have sensed it. When thoughts of Mercy or their possible children intruded, she suppressed them ruthlessly. When memories of the times she had lain in his arms sharing a heedless passion she had not known since he left sent her body reeling, she fled to the garden and worked herself into numb exhaustion. These terrible moments grew more infrequent with time, giving her hope that someday they would lose their power over her altogether.

It came as a shock to her one day to realize that her mental decline was only a reflection of a physical state, that something was not right inside her body. It was, at least, some reassurance to think that her lingering depression might be the symptom of a sickness rather than the cause of it.

It was on the day the whale was brought in that she finally made up her mind to seek help. Their faces shining with excitement, two of Rosalind's older children came running to her door to tell her that a large whale had been beached and she must climb down the hill at once to see it. It was a blustery fall day with a brisk salt breeze off the Sound, so she left Hannah warm inside with Betsy and, wrapping her fur-lined cloak around her shoulders, went down the path toward the beach.

The whale was nearly thirty feet in length, larger certainly than any sea creature the enthralled residents of Myer's Point had ever seen before. One of the schooners had spotted it swimming in the bay near Throgg's Neck and had driven it up the Sound. By the time Celia reached the shore it was quite dead and the adults were trying vainly to keep the children from clambering over the slippery mountain it made on the sand.

Celia sat down near a rustling, dancing cluster of sea oats and watched the scene absently. There was something almost obscene about the great whale's white underbelly lying exposed to the thin gray sunlight, its unseeing eye staring at the whooping children. A cold breeze fringed the fur around her face. She felt chilled right through to her very soul. Drawing her knees up under her skirt, she wrapped her arms around them and laid her head down, overcome with a deep despair such as she had not felt since that day on the Whitehall dock when Ewan's ship sailed out of the harbor. She knew suddenly with a terrible certainty that she was sick and she was going to die. Whatever this thing was that was taking over her body—and she knew enough to suspect it was a tumor of some sort—she saw clearly that it would soon consume her. People would grieve awhile, then go on about the business of living and she would be forgotten, all her hopes, longings and dreams gone to dust.

In one way, she wouldn't mind. At least there would be no more remembering, no more yearning. Yet, on the breath of that thought came a terrible sadness that she must leave this world before she had really learned what it was about. Suddenly she wanted desperately to know so many things—to find the answer to the riddle of their lives, the answer that had eluded her everywhere she looked. How could she so willingly accept going down into the dark before she had even known the light?

No! Even if there was no hope of arresting the growth within her, she must try. Dr. Sayre might know some way to identify the malignancy and perhaps even some way to keep it from destroying her life.

Deliberately she turned away from the specter of death on the beach and started back up the hill. She would not give in so easily. Even if there was nothing she could do to stop it, she would fight it every step of the way.

"How long has this been going on?" Jonas Sayre asked, studying Celia's tense thin figure in the chair across from him.

"I'm not sure. Many weeks."

"And you never came to me in all this time? Don't you realize how foolish that was?"

She could not look him in the eye. "I was afraid to. Afraid of what you would tell me. It seemed better not to know, so I put it off, hoping each day that it would improve. Now I know it isn't going to go away, ever. In fact, it is getting worse." She raised her large eyes fearfully to his round face. "Is there anything you can do to help me? Any hope you can offer?"

To her surprise he laughed. "Hope! My dear lady, what did you think was wrong?"

"I don't know," Celia said, startled. "But I'm terribly afraid it is some kind of growth. A tumor..."

He leaned forward to take both her hands, and she braced herself for the worst. Small brown freckles stood out against the pink skin on the back of his hands softened by feathery blond hairs. She seemed to see them starkly, clearly, where she had never even noticed them before.

"Yes, my dear Celia, it is a growth. But unless I am very much mistaken, your mysterious 'growth' has a heartbeat. You are going to have a baby, dear lady!"

Her heart seemed to stop beating. "A baby..." she whispered.

"Yes," he said, laughing. "You are with child. You are going to be a mother."

Her voice was strangled in her throat. "No! It can't be. I'm barren. I've been barren all these years."

"Yes, you have. But it can happen that the barren conceive—we don't really know why. And that, by God's good grace, seems to be what has happened to you."

She gripped his hands. "You are sure you're not mistaken?"

"As certain as a doctor can be. What did you think when your courses ceased? I am surprised that it did not occur to you that there was a perfectly natural explanation."

"I thought it was the tumor. I'd given up hope. I had accepted the fact that I would never have a child."

His voice went gentle. "I know. And what a miraculous, wonderful, heavenly surprise this is. Congratulations, my dear Mrs. Deveroe."

Then she began to laugh. Small, effervescent giggles that

became waves of euphoria. Somewhere from the back of her mind came the echo of the biblical Sarah laughing behind the tent while Abraham heard the news that they would one day conceive a child.

A child! A baby! A son for Richard. It brought with it all the deepest yearning of her soul and body. In spite of her mistakes, in spite of her sins, her prayers had been heard. God was good indeed!

As Celia rode home from West Chester village in a state of bemused delight, Richard was near his own land, climbing down a steep dirt track that ran from the Albany Post Road toward the Hudson, wondering what mad impulse had brought him here. There were only a few houses along the river at this point, and one, even from a distance, fit perfectly the image of the run-down cabin which had been described to him. There was no sign of life anywhere around it, a distinction it did not share with its distant neighbors, where children played noisily and men worked at the nets spread on their circular revolving frames. The place had an air of abandonment hanging over it, house and yard. Signs of decay and lack of care fairly shouted, and he nearly turned back. But he'd come this far, he might as well see it through.

The door was hung badly and it sagged under his heavy knocking. When no response came he tried again, then was starting to move toward a cloudy window when he heard a noise inside. Someone was there all right. Pushing open the door, he stepped into a room which for sheer filth he had never seen equaled. A table covered with the leavings of several meals stood in the center, and around it, in a chaotic jumble, were chairs, clothes, a half-filled chamber pot, broken barrels, countless empty bottles and half-filled sacks of flour and beans. The place reeked of fish and the effluvia of the close stool. Revulsion nearly drove him back out the door before he spotted thrown in among the jumble of trash a recognizable chart of the river and a few well-thumbed books. On a shelf above them stood a wooden compass box, a sextant and a captain's logbook showing at least some sign that the owner had not completely lost touch with the world.

With a soot-darkened iron poker, Richard stirred up the near-dead embers in the hearth and set a half-filled kettle to boil on the trivet. A can of bohea tea lying on its side on the cluttered mantel told him this was not a house which lacked money, miserable as it looked. Throwing a handful of the tea leaves into the bubbling water, he searched around for a reasonably clean cup. Only then did he walk to the bed in the corner and lean down to shake the heavyset man snoring away there in an alcoholic stupor. When no response came, Richard looked around for a cistern and, finding none, went outside to the river's edge, where he filled one of the empty green bottles. This done, he forced himself back inside and calmly poured the water into the face of the snoring owner.

"What the . . . what the . . . God damn it!" the outraged man came up sputtering. "What the hell do ye think ye're doin'!" he shouted, trying to scramble away.

Dumping the last of the river water on the sheets, Richard threw the bottle back onto the heap near the table. "Do I have the honor of addressing Captain Yancy?" he asked with exaggerated politeness.

"Ye might." The blurred eyes struggled to focus, trying to take in the fashionably cut blue coat with its shining pewter buttons, the light hair smoothed back into a queue under a felt hat, the expensive lace at the throat and wrists, the high gloss of the riding boots, the shiny silk of the striped waistcoat.

"Captain Elisha Yancy?" Richard went on.

"Aye. The same. Ye'll excuse me starin', but I never expected to see such a vision standin' by me bed."

Richard went over to the small fire, poured out a cup of tea and handed it to the captain.

"Here. Drink this. It'll help you recover your senses."

Captain Yancy took the cup and watched in befuddled amazement as his guest set up a chair, drew a lace handkerchief from the cuff of his sleeve and gave it a swipe, then sat down facing the bed. He might have been in a duke's drawing room! Captain Yancy took a swig of the tea before he realized what he was doing, then spat it out in disgust.

"Ugh! Take this swill and give it to the gulls," he said, wiping his sleeve across his wide mouth. "If ye're as polite as ye seem, ye'll just hand me that there bottle standin' by yer foot. The yellow one, that is."

Picking up the bottle Richard set it down between his legs and, keeping one hand firmly on its neck, stared down the surprised anger in Elisha Yancy's eyes. It was not a pretty sight. The features, which once might have been handsome in a rugged, virile way, had sunk into putty. The black eyes were red and weepy, and the heavy lower jaw was covered with the stubble of several days' growth.

"Oh, no, Captain. You don't get any more of this devil's water until you and I have had a chat. I've gone considerably out of my way to come to this rat's nest of yours and I don't want to have to say everything twenty times in an effort to get through your fogged brain. Do I make myself clear?"

"Who the hell do you think ye are comin' in my house like this and tellin' me what I can and can't have? Bloody nerve, ye've got. I ought'er throw ye right into Hudson's River!"

"I doubt you could make it to the door. Allow me to introduce myself—Richard Deveroe of New Rochelle."

"Deveroe!"

The name obviously registered. "Yes, Deveroe. My father was Samuel Deveroe and my cousin is Ewan Deveroe. You have heard of us, I see."

"Bloody Tories! Well, 'Sir' Deveroe, since I can't make it to the door, ye'll excuse me not makin' ye a bloody bow, or whatever it is you fine gentlemen do to greet each other."

"*Mister* Deveroe. And I didn't come for polite exchanges. This is hardly the place for that, anyway."

Captain Yancy pulled up a worn blanket pitted with moth holes from the bottom of the bed and wadded it behind him against the cabin wall. Half sitting, he looked sideways at Richard, undecided whether he should be outraged or amused. Finally he gave a short laugh. "All right, *Mister* Deveroe. Ye see me at my worst. Say what ye want and get out, leavin' the bottle, if ye please."

Richard thought for a moment how he should proceed. This was a ruin of a man, but there was enough left of the captain who used to be to suggest the character of the man underneath.

"How much of your time do you spend like this?"

"I can't see as how that is any of yer business."

"A day, a week, ten weeks?"

"How should I know? When I'm ashore, I drink, and I don't usually bother to count the days."

"But not when you're on board ship?"

"No. Never." Resting his elbows on his knees, Captain Yancy leaned his head against the wall. "I'm like one of those river sturgeons who leaps out of the water and lands on the deck of a boat. Neither of us knows what to do with ourselves on land. He dies and I drink. Someday I'll die, too. It can't be too soon."

"Come, now, Captain Yancy. You don't strike me as a man given to self-pity."

"What do you know about anythin'! Ye asked me how long .I keep to spirits and I'm tellin' ye. While I'm on land I drink. When I get the feel of a deck under me, I get my spirits from the water. That's the way it is, sir—*Mister* Deveroe."

Suddenly he was alert, turning on Richard. "What are ye doin' here anyway? Comin' into my house, throwing water in my face, then sittin' there like the grand inquisitor, askin' me about my life. Who the hell are you? A magistrate? A sheriff?"

"Neither, though I am a lawyer by trade. I know a good deal about you, Captain, because I have taken the trouble to ask. For one thing, I know you're not the uneducated drunk you try to sound—louts don't make conversational references to 'grand inquisitors.' For another, I know you have a great weakness for drink. And I also know that you are the best damn captain running a boat on the Hudson."

"That's true, at least."

"I want to make you a proposition."

"Now we come to it."

"I have a small sloop, the *Venture*, which has been working the Sound back and forth between Connecticut and New York. I'm interested in putting a boat on the Hudson—one now, perhaps more in time—and I think you may be the man to help me. I don't know the Hudson, you see, while you, on the other hand, know it intimately."

Although Captain Yancy's eyes were still bleary, behind them the quick mind was taking in every word. "You have capital, I assume," he said, running a hand through his thick unkempt hair.

"Some. Enough to start. I'd like to put a sloop on the Albany–New York run right away, and I'd like you to captain her. If it proves profitable, I'll bring the *Venture* over to make a team. With enough encouragement I may even put three or four on the line."

"Or five or six, or maybe twenty! Eh?"

Richard shrugged. "Perhaps."

"And what's in it for me, aside from being master of my own boat?"

"That's a fair question. If I'm able to build up enough of

an enterprise, I'll offer you a generous share. I'm prepared to deal fairly with you, Captain Yancy. I need your expertise, the best there is available, I'm convinced. In return, I plan to make of myself a very substantial businessman. I think the river is the key to the county's future and I intend to get an edge on others who may get the same idea."

"Think to build yourself a fortune, don't you?"

"I do."

Elisha Yancy gave a short harsh laugh, but he was clearly impressed with Richard's open, honest answer. In spite of his fancy clothes and gentlemanly airs he sensed something steely underneath that fashionable exterior.

But he was still wary. "Why not buy up land like all the others are doing? That's where the fortunes lie. Sink your capital in a few of these Loyalist farms that are there for the taking, then sell them off again at three times the price. It's far safer than trusting to the wanton winds and currents of Hudson's River."

"I've considered that, of course, but I don't think it's what I want. It's too risky and too slow. I want profits fast and sure. Real profits. Not mortgages and bonds. What do you say?"

For a long minute the captain didn't answer. Then he leaned forward, arms resting on his drawn-up knees. "Aye, there's money to be made on the river, and not just in transporting lumber and grain between Albany and New York. The sloops'll grow, there's no doubt of that. There may be twenty now, but there'll be a hundred before the century's turned, mark my words. And where there's boats, there's industry. Shipyards, sawmills, rope walks, iron foundries, cloth mills. There's a small yard at Poughkeepsie now—has been for years—but it'll need more than that to outfit the river transports. And it's not only the farmlands along the banks that are valuable, it's timber, ore, creeks and waterfalls to power the mills." He rubbed a hand sprouting soft dark hairs back and forth across his chin. "If you've been sailing your sloop on the Sound you may want to re-rig her when you bring her over."

"You talk as though you are certain I shall want to," Richard said smiling.

Captain Yancy's rheumy eyes took on a faraway look. "Aye, the Hudson sloop, with her heavy rigging and square bottom is the trimmest little boat you could ever want for river traffic— perfectly suited to the smoother water and lighter winds of the river. Those old Dutch knew what they were about when they adapted her for these waters. Add to that a captain who knows the shoals and can handle the winds and there's nothing can beat her."

Leaning forward, Richard forgot for a moment the bottle grasped in his hands. "That's exactly what I foresaw. If I can build up enough capital through trade I intend to put it back into the industries it takes to build and outfit the sloops themselves. How much do you know of likely places to build these mills and foundries and factories?"

"I know every inch of that river, Mr. Deveroe. I ran a pettiauger on it when I was no more than a lad. All my life— all but for two years in prison in our late lamented mother country—has been spent plowing up and down the Hudson. I know it better than I know myself."

"That's exactly why I want your help, Captain Yancy. Between us we might build up a very tidy—"

He stopped as he suddenly realized that Captain Yancy's eyes were arrested on the bottle he had carelessly thrust almost under his nose. Restraining his first impulse to push it out of sight underneath his chair, he sat without moving and watched the captain devour it with his eyes. But he did not reach out to take it. When he finally looked up Richard thought he had never seen such emptiness in a man's face.

"Now we come to it. With all yer grand plans for the future, why come to a rummy like me—a slave to John Barleycorn? You know so much about me, Mr. Deveroe, ye must know what I am. I'll be no help to ye. Go find a sober captain for yer great enterprise."

"A lot of men drink hard, Yancy. And you have a reputation for never touching spirits when you're running a boat."

"Aye, but I more than make up for it when I make shore. It's been this way a long time now and gets worse as the years build up on me. Ye'd be takin' a terrible chance, puttin' yer hopes on this frail back."

Very carefully Richard placed the bottle on a table beside the bed. "I'll not try to argue with you, Captain Yancy. If you do agree to go into partnership with me, I'll expect you to run your life ashore as well as you do your ship. You'll be too busy to drink much, I suspect, and I would expect you to give all your energies to the job. What you do with yourself afterwards is your own business, as long as it doesn't interfere. If you cannot agree to that, then yes, I will have to seek someone else."

Angrily Yancy's hand shot out, and, pulling the bottle to his lips, he drank from it greedily. "God damn ye, ye smug fancy gentleman, comin' in here like some bloody archangel nearly drownin' me in me sleep and layin' down the law. Go on, get out. Go find some other river rat who'll play lackey. Elisha Yancy is 'is own man!"

"Make no mistake, Captain," Richard said carefully. "I'm offering you a good *reason* not to drink, not merely taking away your pleasure."

"What do I want with a bloody fortune?"

"It buys a lot of ships, Captain." Richard rose, looking down at the man sulking on the bed. "Think it over at least before you say no. I have a home and a law office in New Rochelle, on Myer's Point. If you change your mind, come and see me. I'll wait a week before looking for someone else."

Taking another swig from the jug, Yancy wiped his sleeve across his mouth. "Go back to New Rochelle. Go to hell! With all the rest of the damned Tories."

At the door Richard paused. "When were you in a British prison, Captain Yancy?"

"What's it to ye?"

"Merely a formality. I heard you had a schooner on the river during the war."

"I did. She was one of the ones they burned off Fort Montgomery when Clinton outfoxed old Putnam. Made a pretty sight, she did, flamin' on the water in the dark. After that I went with Captain Paul to tackle the British shipping in the Channel. Got took prisoner and spent some unwelcome time as a guest of old King George."

"Do you have a ship now?"

The black eyes looked through him. "You know damned well I don't."

"Well, while you are thinking over my proposition, Captain, just remember what a pretty little sloop a few hundred pounds will put under your feet again. We might be able to help each other more than you think."

"Like hell!"

Richard made him a bow worthy of a drawing room. "Good day, Captain Yancy."

As he trudged back up the hill, Richard felt satisfied with

the interview. There was enough left of the old captain, he hoped, to rise to this challenge. He was betting on it. It was the first real gamble in his well-laid plans. The first dice were thrown. Now to see how his luck would run.

It was dark by the time Richard rode his weary mare into the barn on Myer's Point. He had just sat down to enjoy a late supper in the kitchen when he looked up to see Calie framed in the doorway, her long hair streaming down over the shoulders of her blue night robe.

"Why, Celia. Did I wake you? I was trying to be quiet, but I forgot I had on my spurs until too late. Forgive me, my dear."

She went to sit opposite him at the table. "I was not asleep. I heard you come in. Richard, I'm so glad you were able to get back tonight."

"Yes, I had a good trip, but a wearying one. I met a fascinating man, Celia, one I hope will become a partner in my Hudson River enterprises."

"Oh?"

"He is not what you would expect in a partner. In fact, I had to wake him up out of a drunken stupor even to put him my proposition."

Celia tried to appear interested. "He's given to spirits?"

"Ashore, yes. It is a weakness I'll be gambling that he can overcome. But his reputation as a captain is second to none. He knows the Hudson better than any man alive. If I can keep him sober long enough I'm sure he'll be an asset to our future."

"Richard..." She stopped, wondering how to go on. How to tell a man after all these barren years that he was going to be a father at last? All day she had been hugging the joyful knowledge to herself, and now she was bursting to share it with him. His joy surely would be as great as her own. It simply had to be.

"You should have seen the shambles Captain Elisha Yancy calls home. God! I've seen slave quarters more livable..."

"Richard..."

"Yet he is not an uneducated man. He even has some of the qualities of a gentleman, though they are so buried by years of neglect that they are barely visible."

"Richard! I really don't care about your Captain Yancy right now. There is something I have to tell you."

Surprised, he looked more closely at her shadowed face. The tawny eyes were dancing with delight. Certainly she was full of some great news. "Forgive me, my dear. I was so absorbed in Captain Yancy and our possible partnership that I could think of nothing else. Obviously you are bursting to tell me something. You look like the cat who fell into the cream barrel. What is it? Is Hannah's cold better? Is Rosalind Wister with child again? Out with it."

She caught her breath. "Rosalind Wister? No—not Rosalind. But I went to see Dr. Sayre today and—oh, Richard, *I* am!"

"You're what? You're not ill?"

She threw up her hands in exasperation. "No, no. I am with child. Me! Us! We're going to have a baby, Richard. A child!"

His jaw dropped. She heard herself laughing.

"Well, can't you say anything?"

"Celia!"

"It's true. Dr. Sayre says it is a miracle, a freak accident. He doesn't know how or why it would happen to me now after all these years when I could not conceive, but what does that matter? It *did* happen."

"But when?"

She broke into a cascade of giggles. "I don't know when except that for the past four months I have thought I was ill. In fact, I was afraid I was dying. That was what finally drove me to Dr. Sayre. Oh, Richard. I'm so happy."

He finally found the strength to move, to believe what she was telling him. Moving quickly around the table, he knelt before her chair, placing his arms around her waist. She clasped her arms around his shoulders, leaning her head against his, her long glossy hair falling forward like a veil around him. For a long moment they stayed there, too moved to speak. When he finally pulled away he was not really startled to see tears in her eyes.

"Are you glad?" she said softly, stroking back the wavy hair from his temples.

"Of course. It's what we both wanted and had given up hope of having. Could Sayre give you any idea as to a date?"

"He says sometime next March, as near as he can guess."

"He is not worried about you, is he?"

"No. He says I am in excellent health. There are some things I can no longer do—like go galloping on the beach—but that's no problem. I don't mind doing anything to keep this baby safe. What shall we name him? I thought perhaps 'Samuel' after your father."

"It may turn out to be a girl."

"I don't think so. I have a feeling that it is going to be a boy."

Richard hugged her impulsively. "Oh, my dear, accidents do happen. Don't dream too much or you'll break your heart if something goes wrong."

Placing her hands on either side of his head, she leaned down and kissed him full on the lips. "Dear, cautious Richard. I know what you say is true, but I just don't think that will happen now. This is a good, strong baby I have within me, I know it. I felt its strength consuming me even when I thought it was an illness. Now that I know it is actually a baby, I feel a wonderful sense of wholeness with it. My baby. Our child, Richard."

When he rose from the flagstone floor it was as though the world had shifted and rearranged itself during the time he had knelt there. He was going to be a father. They would be a real family now. There would be a son or daughter to build and plan for in the years ahead. He was caught up in her intoxication.

"Come, my love. I am going to break out a bottle of Mr. Shedden's finest London port and we are going to drink a toast together. We have never had quite so much to celebrate before."

twenty-three

Before the week was out Elisha Yancy appeared at the house in New Rochelle to throw in his lot with Richard.

"I'll tell ye frankly, Mr. Deveroe, that I don't know if I can stay away from the drink long enough to do what you ask. I can only say I will give it a try. It's certain there's money to be made on the river, and if I can stay sober long enough, between us we should certainly get our share."

Richard was delighted. "That is all I want, Captain Yancy. We'll start with one small boat, one of the Hudson sloops you recommended, and we'll give it a few months to a year. If it turns a profit, then we'll invest in several more. I intend to build up a transport business before I branch out into the trades that will support a fleet."

Yancy, smiling in spite of himself, settled back and crossed his legs. "I take it, then, that we're in business."

"Business it is, Captain Yancy. Here's my hand on it. Now why don't you join my wife and me for supper."

To Richard, establishing himself in business with Elisha Yancy seemed at times like trying to grasp the tail of a tornado. With great energy, and with grim determination to stay off the bottle, the captain threw himself into the search for a sound sloop at a reasonable price. He found the boat he wanted at Newburgh—a sleek, well-built vessel that had been damaged by an inexperienced captain. With a minimum of work, he was sure she could be made seaworthy again, while the price was very fair. He had her towed to Poughkeepsie, where she was repaired, mostly by himself, and rechristened the *Elizabeth* after Richard's mother. Richard went along on her first voyage, inspecting docks and landings, overseeing cargoes of timber, apples and grain, personally meeting the farmers up-county who entrusted their produce to him and spending hours by the rail, avidly studying the ever-changing shoreline, and watching the playful antics of the dolphins who accompanied the boat along the majestic waterway all the way to Albany and back.

The small profit from the first run and, later on, from the second was immediately put back into commissioning bigger and more varied cargoes. By the end of two months larger profits had begun to accumulate, so large that Richard decided to bring the *Venture* over from the Sound to ply the river trade. In four months he was looking around for a third sloop.

So much of his enthusiasm was centered on his fledgling business that Celia sometimes wondered if her husband was as eager for a son or daughter as he had seemed at first. Even when he was at home she found him reluctant to discuss the coming baby beyond listening indulgently to her grandiose plans. What she could not see behind his reluctance was his very real fear for her safety. Aside from the burden of carrying an increasing weight, she had never felt better in her life. Richard, on the other hand, could not forget that one out of five women brought to childbed never rose from it again. Not only was her life at stake, but if one of the frequent accidents of birth should rob her of this child he feared for her mind as well.

It was on a cold, rainy afternoon that Celia felt the first mild symptoms that suggested her baby had reached its term. Hurriedly Richard sent Vestal for Rosalind Wister, who, with Betsy, set up a vigil in the upstairs bedroom. They quickly banished him to the parlor, where he sat going over Yancy's requisitions and tried to keep his mind off what was happening upstairs. It's foolish to worry, he told himself; women have babies every day.

He had nearly managed to concentrate all his attention on the papers he was reading when Rosalind appeared in the doorway, a worried frown on her face.

"Mr. Deveroe, I think perhaps you should send for Dr. Sayre," she said hesitantly.

"Why, I understood you women were accustomed to handling these things yourselves," he began lightly, then quickly changed his tone. "What's the matter? Nothing is wrong, is it?"

"I'm not sure, but, yes, I think something may be wrong. There has been a great deal of blood, you see. Too much at this early stage. I'm not sure how to stop it or what it means."

Richard was already out of his chair. "I'll send Tom to West

Chester village at once to bring Sayre back." He stopped briefly at the door. "You never had this happen?"

"No."

"Does it . . . is there a chance she will lose the child?"

"I don't know. Perhaps not. I've been told it is not such an unusual thing, but I would feel better to hear Dr. Sayre say that."

Richard nodded silently and hurried down the hall to the rear of the house. Sayre would not be happy to have his Sabbath interrupted, but he would come. He had known the Deveroes too long not to, and besides, no one knew better how much Celia wanted this baby.

Afterward he went upstairs long enough to speak to Celia and was reassured by her confidence. There were dark circles around her eyes, and her face was wan and pale, yet she appeared less worried than he. He felt better when he left her.

The hours seemed endless until Sayre finally stomped through the kitchen door, dripping rain from his old, serviceable cloak. Richard felt more at ease just knowing he was upstairs, even though the long hours dragged on. By dawn Monday, while the icy rain poured outside from a black-molasses sky, nothing had changed and Richard was exhausted with waiting. Occasionally during the long night he had ventured up the creaking stairway to sit by Celia's bed, but it seemed that each time he saw her she looked more wilted, the circles under her eyes darker, her lovely face more strained.

A dim sun was just struggling to fight through the gray fog when Jonas Sayre came down to the small parlor. Richard was dozing in one of Celia's upholstered chairs, but he came instantly awake as he watched the doctor walk to the sideboard and pour himself a glass of madeira.

"Well," the doctor said solemnly, "we have a problem."

A terrible numbness began spreading through Richard's chest. "What is wrong?"

"I remember this happening once before, when I was only starting out. A woman in Philadelphia. It's no one's fault, it just happens."

"What? What?" Richard cried impatiently.

"She's had a lot of hemorrhaging. I think it means that the afterbirth is in the wrong place—too low, and the contractions cause it to pull away. It should be higher, up above the baby's position. Unfortunately where it is, as the mouth of the womb opens, it is torn away, causing more bleeding."

"What does that mean? Can't you do something?"

Sayre's lined face looked diabolical in the flickering shadows from the candleglow. "There is nothing I can do. I think that eventually, when the baby's head gets low enough, it will close off the hemorrhage, but in the meantime she's losing a devil of a lot of blood."

"But isn't that good? You doctors are always taking blood—it's supposed to get rid of the evil humors. Why isn't this true for Celia?"

"Bloodletting is a common remedy, but there is a point where the loss of too much blood can be very dangerous. Besides, the real problem is one I feared all along. Underneath all those wide hoops many women are actually quite small. Celia is one of those, I'm afraid, and she's carrying a very large baby. Also, this is her first childbirth. The combination . . ."

Suddenly Richard felt his strength draining away. He sank into a chair, running his long fingers through his hair. "My God," he muttered, and Sayre recognized all the anguish, panic and fear that those poor words contained. How many times he had heard them.

"I am very sorry, Richard, but the plain fact is you may be forced to make a choice. It may be Celia's life or the child's."

"Has it come to that?"

"No, not yet. But if the bleeding does not stop soon, it will. I just want you to be prepared." Sayre sat his glass down angrily. "I may not be able to save either one of them, for that matter!"

"God knows, Jonas, I don't want to lose Celia. But this baby is so important to her. I don't know what to say."

"Well, we have another hour or so of grace. Why don't we wait a little longer? Perhaps the hemorrhaging will have stopped by then."

"Is it safe to wait?"

"I think so. Her pulse, though weak, is still steady. If the bleeding stops soon and the baby comes quickly everything will be to rights. That's worth holding off a little for, don't you think?"

"Yes, yes, I do." Richard hesitated. "Is she in discomfort?"

"Well, of course she's in discomfort. In fact, she's in great pain. What else did you expect?"

"I'd hoped it would be easy for her," Richard answered, his eyes moving involuntarily toward the ceiling.

"My friend, no one has ever found a way to bring a man into the world without suffering. However, Celia is strong and healthy. And no woman ever wanted a baby more. All of this is in her favor. We may yet see everything turn out well."

"I'll hold you to that, Sayre."

The doctor almost groaned as he started upstairs again. "No you won't. I'll do my best, but I am not responsible for accidents of fate. Just remember that."

The room seemed empty after he left, cold and forbidding. Richard started to pick up the wine decanter again, then put it back. He had better keep his head clear this day.

It was around ten o'clock when Sayre found him walking the wet paths of Celia's garden like a man lost.

"I had hoped things would move along," the doctor said, fatigue and worry creasing his face. "The hemorrhaging has stopped, but it's going to be long and hard. I thought I should warn you."

"Can't you do anything to help her?"

"Not much. Laudanum would suppress the labor and we don't want that. I have to fight off that Betsy with her knives under the bed and her other folk medicines. I finally banished her to the kitchen to stir up some breakfast. Mrs. Wister's help is invaluable. We're doing all we can."

"Let me go up and talk to Celia."

"No, not now." Sayre knew that if Richard saw his wife after all these hours of difficult labor and loss of blood, he might have two patients instead of one. "She's working very hard and there's nothing you can do to help her. Just keep praying."

For the rest of the day Richard sat in the parlor memorizing every detail of its paneled walls and molded ceilings, counting the creaks and groans in the floorboards. Apart from a few strangled moans there was little to hear. He kept waiting for the painful screams that he had always heard accompanied childbirth, and he dreaded the hurried shuffling that might indicate a crisis. He could not stop himself from mentally totaling the hours. How long had it been now? Twenty-six, twenty-seven hours in labor. Even he knew that was not normal.

He finally abandoned the parlor for a chair in the hall outside the bedroom, where through a window on the opposite wall he could just make out the red-gold of the sun sinking behind the dark hills.

As the long, dark day died away to midnight, Celia's baby finally pushed its way into the world. A large, husky boy, he was almost as worn out as his poor mother and, like her, was pale and weak from loss of blood. His large head was misshapen from the rigors of his birth, but the weak wail he gave when Sayre, working furiously, got his lungs going, rang like a hosanna to the three people in the room. To Richard, listening in the hall, it was the most beautiful sound he had ever heard. He rushed to the door in time to see Rosalind take the infant from the doctor's arms and wrap it in a soft blanket, then started toward his wife's bed. Sayre waved him back.

"She's all right, but we're not through yet. Go have a look at your son."

Weak from relief and fatigue, Richard almost did not have the strength to take the bundle Rosalind handed him. Yet when he pulled away the blanket and saw the tiny wrinkled face enclosed there, the long hours of worry began to fade. For a moment his son's eyes opened and looked directly into his, and surely that grimace of the tiny lips formed a smile. Was there any feeling on earth to equal what he felt? He had been so carefully detached about having a child, trying not to give way as Celia had done to high hopes which a capricious fate might snatch away. But now here he was, his son. With a finger that seemed giant-sized against the tiny face, he gently pushed away the edges of the blanket. All his life he had kept his distance from people, but one look at this miracle of creation, this beautiful little creature, and Richard Deveroe fell hopelessly in love.

"Don't be alarmed at his head," Sayre called from the bed-side. "It will straighten out. And those red marks on his temple were caused by the forceps."

"His head can stay just the way it is. He's perfectly beautiful."

Lying on her bed, Celia was barely aware of what was happening. She heard the voices in the room, and dimly she recognized all of them, yet they never seemed to stay put very long but faded and rose as though carried on the wind. For what had seemed a lifetime her poor body had alternated between the most cruel, ripping pains she had ever known to the most terrible, debilitating fatigue. Time after time she had come back to face the effort and the hurt, only to slide farther away, almost, to a point where it became too difficult to come back at all. She remembered hearing a baby's faint wail just before the weariness engulfed her completely and she drifted away from the confines of the room and the body that had become her prison. Faintly she heard Richard's voice calling to her, telling her to look at their son. Was she dreaming? With a great effort she forced herself to open her eyes long enough to see a tiny pink wrinkled face and with a surge of joy she realized it was over and she had her reward. Then the room went dark.

Sayre turned from the bed to hand Betsy a basin filled with bloodied towels and tainted water. "She'll be all right now, I think," he said to Celia's husband, who was looking a little pale himself. "She'll need to rest for a long time. If there are no further complications, both of them will need to take a long easy time to get their strength back. I don't mind telling you, Richard, there were moments this night when I never thought we'd have so much to be thankful for."

Richard grinned at him. "Come, Mrs. Wister, take this child and put him in his cradle where he can rest. Then you and Dr. Sayre and I have some very important business. We're going to open a bottle of the finest French brandy I could buy in New York and drink every single drop."

"Why not send up a bottle of claret for your wife, Mr. Deveroe?" Rosalind said wearily as she laid the baby in his cradle draped with embroidered batiste. "She'll need a draft when she wakes. It will help restore her blood."

They were all of them worn out and a little giddy. "I intend to get quite drunk," Sayre said dryly, reaching for his coat.

"And I," Richard added.

"I'd like to," Rosalind said thoughtfully, "but I'd better save some strength to get home and see to my own brood. Would you like me to keep Hannah a while longer, Mr. Deveroe?"

"Please, until Celia is a little stronger at least. She'll be anxious to see her by then. But we owe the happiness of this moment to your encouragement as much as anyone's. I'm not going to let you go home until you drink a toast with us."

Rosalind smiled, weary but grateful. "Agreed."

Celia recovered quickly, finding in the joy of her son all the motivation she needed to return to the world. Within the week she was sitting up in bed, doing her best to supply enough milk for her son's enormous appetite, keeping him beside her for hours until her strength gave out and Betsy took him back to his cradle. Richard, visiting her one morning before he walked into the village, thought she had never looked more radiantly beautiful.

"I've decided on a name for the baby," she said, reaching out her hands to take his.

"I thought that was decided months ago," he said, sitting down beside her. "Samuel and Gabriel—both our fathers' names."

"Yes, but I thought he should have something distinctly his own, perhaps a good Biblical name which isn't either French or English."

"Heavens, not something like Malachi or Hezekiah, I hope."

"No, I rather like Joshua. What do you think of it?"

"It's an agreeable name. Very masculine, somehow. But I'm surprised you aren't following the current fashion and naming him Liberty or States or even Congress."

"No," she said, smiling up at him. "I was never that much of a patriot, although I dare not say so except in the privacy of this room. Besides, Biblical names are still very fashionable and extremely American. I think Joshua would be a fine name for him, and we could call him 'Josh.'"

"Whatever you want, my dear. Joshua Samuel Gabriel Deveroe. Such a big name for such a tiny baby. Let's hope he lives up to it."

"Oh, he will. He's going to be rich and famous and noble and great. A real child of light. I'm certain of it."

Richard laughed indulgently. "Quite the most unusual, miraculous infant that was ever born, eh? I must remind you, my dear, that all new mothers feel that way about their first child. He will probably be a very ordinary individual who drinks too many spirits and beats his wife—just like his father."

"He could do worse than be just like his father." She laid her hand against his lean cheek. "Oh, Richard, I'm so happy."

Leaning forward, he kissed her warmly. "And I too, my dearest wife. We've been truly blessed. Now you lie back and get some rest while I'm in the village. Perhaps this evening we will try to get you back on your feet for a few minutes."

As he was descending the stairs he met Hannah coming up, carefully taking one step at a time. When she looked up and saw him towering above her, she pulled shyly back, looking down at her shoes. Richard impulsively picked her up in his arms. The startled child smiled with delight.

"And how are you today, Mistress Hannah? Do you like your new little brother?"

"Ceil . . ." Hannah said falteringly.

"She's waiting for you now. You may go in and give her a kiss, and the baby too, if you like."

"The baby, he cries," Hannah said quite seriously. "He cries a lot."

"That's because he's very small. But one day he'll be bigger and can play games with you. Would you like that?"

Her round eyes narrowed. "No."

Richard laughed and set her back on her feet. "Go on up, you little minx," he said as he watched her flounce up the stairs, her lace petticoats bouncing under the rim of her skirt like foam on the ocean waves. Even Hannah looked beautiful today.

Walking into New Rochelle, he thought back over his conversation with Celia. If anything could have saved his marriage it was the gift of this child. Both of them had already completely lost their hearts to their tiny son—in fact, he thought wryly, it was going to be very difficult to prevent him from growing up entirely spoiled.

A group of startled bluebirds flew from the low branches of a locust tree as he walked underneath its gray limbs. Strangely enough, he could think of Ewan at last without the old searing pain and jealousy. He and Celia now shared something she had never had with Ewan, something which drew them together into the bond of a real family. No, even if Ewan should walk into his house that afternoon and beg Celia to go away with him, she would never leave now. He need never regard Ewan as a threat again. Not only had he gained a wonderful son, he had regained a wife. And with it he had regained his own happiness as well.

What a fine, good, beautiful world it was!

Richard's heightened sense of well-being lasted only until the routine events of the day brought their usual distractions. By early afternoon when Captain Yancy appeared with copies of the *Elizabeth*'s first six months' receipts, life had become its usual round of trivia.

"This looks very good," Richard said, scanning the marginal-profits column. "Evidently she holds more than we anticipated."

"Aye. And there were elements in our favor. We had good weather and favorable winds most of the time except for January, when ice closed the river completely. Of the weeks we could sail I think we were only forced to use the sweeps three or four times. That won't last, of course, but it was a big help in getting started." Yancy ran a calloused hand across his wide chin just beginning to be fringed with a grizzled beard. "My biggest problem was to convince those farmers upstate I was sober. They know me too well up and down the river, ye see. But after the first couple of times I dropped their profits in their pockets the word spread, and I have more customers knocking on my cabin door than I have room on deck to accommodate."

Richard smiled to himself. "It's your reputation as one of the finest captains on the river paying off."

"*One* of the best! *The* best, I'll have ye know."

"What about the drink?" Richard said cautiously. Yet he knew the answer. Captain Yancy looked better than he had ever seen him. Gone was the unkempt, yellow, decaying ruin of that first day in the cabin. The man before him now, eyes alert, huge frame exuding vitality, possessed a kind of inner strength and purpose that had been completely missing before.

"Well, I won't tell ye I haven't been tempted," Yancy answered, "especially at the end of the runs in Albany or New York. But so far I've kept myself so busy there hasn't been time to waste taking drams ashore. I knew ye was anxious to make as many runs these first months as I was to see how the boat managed herself. So I stayed aboard most of the time."

"Were you satisfied?"

"Oh, aye. She's a bonny craft, all right. And I like having a deck under my feet again. Mark ye, I'm makin' no promises, but I'm pleased so far the drink hasn't lured me back from the river."

"I'm pleased, too, Elisha. I'd wager there's not another captain on the Hudson who could have carried as much cargo in as many runs as you have this first half year. Or got such shrewd prices for it."

Yancy beamed. "Some of that's knowing the cartmen in New York personally. I can get the best prices for firewood and timber of any man trading with 'em. One or two are former boatmen like myself, for that matter." He watched Richard's aesthetic face as he studied the papers. "Ye don't look as pleased as I thought ye would. Is something the matter?"

"No, no. The profits are excellent." Richard looked up warily. "I suppose they are as much as we can expect?"

"Aye. I'd say so. What's wrong with that?"

"Nothing, only . . ." Richard sat back fingering the worked

buttonholes of his coat. "You may think me foolish, Elisha, but the truth is I am a greedy man. I wanted to take the capital from the sale of my farm and turn it into a fortune."

Yancy gave a quick snort. "Aye, a fortune. That's the rub, isn't it?"

"Exactly. We can make a good business of transporting produce—a very good business. Enough to keep us both comfortable. But . . ."

"But it is not a fortune."

"Exactly. And it will take years to build it into one. Many of our profist will of necessity have to go back into the business. For the kind of profits I want, I need more outlay."

"What's wrong with being a successful small businessman?"

"Nothing. But it is not what I want. I want—it sounds like sheer avarice—I want *real* wealth and the power it brings. And I'm resolved to get it. For myself, for my wife, and someday for our son. How, I don't know, but I'll find a way or die in the attempt."

Surprisingly Yancy did not laugh. "Aye, you are resolved. I could see that the first time we met. Maybe that's why I'm going along with you. I'd like the free life that money brings, too, but I think I'd settle for comfortable, since that is more likely to be what we'll get."

"No, I won't settle. I have to find a way to get more capital. That's the key, I feel certain of it."

Leaning forward, Yancy rested his heavy chin in his hand. "Well, ye won't get it in the river trade. Especially not now with money depreciating the way it is. Why, ye wouldn't believe the number of men I had to turn away because they were not able to trade in hard cash—wanted to pay with those worthless securities issued during the war. You should be thankful, Richard, that ye've got real capital, when you see those poor fellows whose only assets are tied up in those worthless scraps of paper."

"They're not worthless," Richard said absently.

"Almost as well be. Five shillings on the pound they go for—even sometimes as low as two. Imagine if that was all you owned and count yourself lucky."

In the silence that fell between them Yancy stirred restlessly. "I don't like the look on your face, Richard Deveroe! What scheme are you hatchin' now?"

Richard smiled sheepishly. "I was thinking—if those securities are ever backed by the government—"

"Pshaw! What a harebrained idea. When the thirteen states don't even trust each other enough to recognize a common currency, what makes you think they'd ever get enough of a government together to back each other's securities?"

"Only my experience in the Congress. While there are a lot of mediocre men in Congress, there are some giants there, too. I think perhaps it might be to our advantage to renew some of my former friendships. Perhaps I can get an indication of the way things are tending. Meanwhile, why don't you just quietly begin accepting some of these securities in payment? Especially where you can get them for two or three shillings to the pound."

He could see from the frown on Yancy's face that the captain did not share his confidence. "Ye'll be taking a fearful risk. You know that, don't you?"

"Yes. I don't wish you to be hurt by it. I'll back up any loss with what's left of my capital now."

"But it might be years before these securities are paid off— if ever. If you tie up too much in them, you stand to lose everything. What becomes of our enterprise then?"

Richard took a long, thoughtful time to answer. He appreciated Yancy's point. There was more at stake for the captain here than for himself, for he had put his personal and emotional well-being on the line to build their river trade into a successful business.

"I shouldn't stand to lose everything," he said with quiet logic. "At the least I should get back what I put in, especially if we get them at the bottom price. On the other hand, if they do become backed at full value, think of the profits. It would be just the windfall we need."

"But it is such a shaky institution ye'll be bankin' on. To entrust your whole future to it—"

"That's true. But it's also true that if there is ever going to be a real United States government it must be formed within the next few years. Otherwise the entire Union will fall apart and we'll have another collection of sovereign countries like Europe. I'm betting that will not happen."

Yancy shook his head. "I hope ye're right. I've never been much of a gambling man myself, and the stakes here are steep enough to make me sweat."

"No fortune was ever made without risk, Elisha."

The captain shrugged and reached across the table for the

receipts. "All right. I'll go along and accept those scraps of paper in lieu of specie, though it goes against the grain to do so. But if I were you, Richard Deveroe, I'd start prayin' for the Congress this very minute!"

twenty-four

From where she sat in the open carriage, Celia could see over the heads of the crowd to the balcony of the Federal Building across Wall Street. Beside her, seven-year-old Hannah squirmed in excitement, wrinkling the starched muslin of her white dress.

"Oh, look, Celia!" she cried, pointing toward the crowded street. "There's a man over there with a monkey on his shoulder. A real monkey and with a collar around its neck."

Celia pulled the long ribbons of the child's green sash from under her and smoothed them out.

"It's probably one of those pet monkeys that do tricks for a penny."

Leaning forward from his father's lap, three-year-old Josh yanked the velvet cap off his blond curls and thrust it toward his mother.

"Here, Ce'il," he said, slapping at her hand.

"It's 'Mother,' darling," Celia said impatiently. "'Ma-ma.' Oh, dear, it does upset me so to hear him calling me 'Celia.'"

Richard set the cap firmly on his son's head, then went back to scanning the crowd. "He has heard Hannah calling you that. He'll outgrow it soon enough. I would just ignore it if I were you."

"Papa, Papa!" Josh cried, pulling at his father's neckcloth.

"I can just imagine how you would ignore it if he took to calling you 'Richard.'" She could not help but admire how handsome the pair of them looked, father and son.

"Stop it, Josh!" Hannah pushed away the squirming stocky body of her foster brother. "You're crushing my dress. Make him stop, Celia."

Celia tucked her arm around the girl's slight body and pulled her closer. "It's all right, Hannah. In this crowd no one will notice if your dress looks a small bit untidy. The important thing is to keep your eyes on that balcony over there, the one with the banner draped across it."

"Is that where the General is going to stand?"

"Yes. You'll know him by his height. He's a very tall man, and very dignified."

Hannah giggled at the antics of the monkey, who had perched on top of the hat of a portly gentleman standing in front of them. There was barely enough room in the crush of the crowd for the outraged man to turn and protest.

"Oh, I wish the dear little thing could come over here. I should love to hold him."

"The crowd is far too thick, my love. I don't think I have ever seen so many people pressed together in one street before."

"And so many flags, and soliders, and flowers and evergreen branches. And the General's white horses—they were so shiny. Their sides looked like marble."

"Their coats are covered with a paste of whiting," Richard said dryly, "then rubbed to a high gloss. I understand the General even insists that their teeth be scrubbed."

Hannah smiled up at him. "I should love to ride a white horse like that someday," she said wistfully.

Celia tucked a few wisps of the girl's feathery hair back inside her cap. "Perhaps you shall."

Richard's gaze moved from the pale thin girl to his restless stocky son. "I am still not convinced it was wise to bring the children into this mob. No telling what they'll be exposed to."

"But you said yourself it is a great occasion and one they should remember all their lives—well, Hannah, at least. It's really the beginning of the United States in a way. Can you see any sign of activity on the balcony yet?"

"No. But since Mr. Washington has entered the building it shouldn't be too long now."

Across from her, Betsy, in a new white spotless kerchief and calico dress, craned her neck round for a look at the great General she had come to idolize. Her third son, born only a year after Josh, had been christened George Washington in the General's honor. Now she and Vestal, who stood holding the horse's head against the milling crowd, were more excited than the Deveroes to see the Father of the Revolution inaugurated as the first President under the newly ratified Constitution.

The heavens had blessed the event with a beautiful late April day. Celia looked around, catching the excitement of the crowd.

Behind them, down Broad Street and along both sides of Wall
Street, people thronged the broad roadway, vying for space
with carriages and sedan chairs. Men hung down from the
rooftops, perched on the slanting cedar shingles like monkeys
in trees. Since Richard's carriage directly faced the Federal
Building and they had the height of the cab to elevate them,
they had an excellent view. Celia was conscious of taking part
in a historic occasion, but Richard was far more pragmatic. In
the two years since he had talked Captain Yancy into accepting
government securities, he had purchased many more of them
than he originally planned and without a shred of hope that
Congress would do anything to guarantee their value. Now that
New York had finally become the eleventh state to ratify the
Constitution, and now that this respected man had agreed to
become the first President, there was a real hope that something
would be done to solve the problem once and for all. He dared
not think of the consequences if the government refused to
honor its debts—he would be ruined. On the other hand . . .

He glanced across at Celia's flushed, excited face under the
wide brim of her fashionable leghorn hat. At least she was not
aware of how much they stood to gain or lose. She could enjoy
the drama of the occasion for itself alone.

A great roar went up as a group of men stepped out onto
the balcony. It was not difficult to recognize Washington, he
was so tall and carried himself with such stateliness. He was
also wearing, Celia noted, a plain suit of dark brown, made,
it was rumored, from all-American broadcloth, in honor of his
country's home industries.

"Oh, la, Misse Celia," Betsy almost moaned. "It's himself.
I'd of knowed that man anytime!"

Although Celia smiled at Betsy's vapors, she felt stirred
herself, and eagerly joined in the clapping and cheering of the
crowd.

It took several minutes for quiet to settle, and even then,
the voices of Chancellor Robert Livingston, who administered
the oath of office, and George Washington, though both spoke
loudly, could not carry very far down the jammed streets. Celia
heard enough, however, to feel that a sense of destiny carried
on the fragile voices. This federation of states might still fall—
after all, it had taken six long years just to get this far—but
she hoped it would not. The British were almost a memory to
her now. This country was what mattered. For better or for

worse, it was her home and she hoped God would give it His blessings in the years ahead.

The ceremony was over quickly and wild cheering went up again from the streets and the rooftops. Bells from all the churches in the city began to ring with a deafening clamour. Bands played from vantage points up and down the streets, and the boom of cannon in the Battery fort shattered the air. The chief actors in the drama moved quickly back inside Federal Hall, where President Washington was to address Congress. Only after they had disappeared behind the balcony doors and Richard was busy mentally checking off the number of familiar faces he had recognized, did it occur to him that, had things gone as he had planned, he might have been among them. Yet, looking at his handsome family, he had no regrets. Perhaps it was what God intended for him all along. One thing was sure. Had he pursued his career in politics he would not have Celia here by his side, and without her he would not have this beautiful young son squirming on his lap. No, he was satisified he had done the right thing. Only time would tell for sure.

Celia had been back to New York only twice in the years since that day she had followed Ewan to Whitehall wharf, and she was pleased this time to feel once again the old excitement of its varied and demanding pace.

Her first surprise came on the drive into the city when she saw that new houses had been built right up into the old property where Uncle James used to have his elegant estate. Wayside still remained untouched, but it was obvious that the spread of the city northward would soon devour its fields and orchards. The old almshouse and jail had their familiar grim look, but the gallows between had been encased in a gaudily painted Chinese pagoda, no doubt to lessen the barbarity of its savage work. The new Federal Building was probably the finest example of architecture in the city, but Celia found herself more nostalgic about the old worn Dutch brick houses with their steepled roofs and neat white-washed stoops. She revisited every familiar haunt from former days and made sure she took in each new attraction. They had tea at the Tontine Coffee House, New York's finest new addition; she scoured the Fly Market for produce from the country and the Catharine Market for clams and oysters from the waters surrounding the island; they saw a performance of *Richard III*—and not too badly

done—at the John Street Theatre and spent hours shopping for
the exotic foods, luxurious fabrics and fine wines which only
a great port town like New York could offer.

For their visit to the city, Richard rented a new house in
Oyster Pasty Lane near the burned-out ruins of Trinity Church.
The Deveroe house, like its neighbors, was tall and thin and
made of wood with a simple brick facade and with kitchen,
pantry and breakfast room on the ground floor, a parlor and
a dining room on the main floor, and three tiny bedrooms on
the top floor. A courtyard in the rear with young trees and
grass and a cistern to catch water offered some respite from
the busy traffic of the street, and provided a safe place for the
children to play on warm afternoons.

A week after the inauguration Celia was sitting in this courtyard watching the children romp with a ball when Betsy announced a visitor. She looked up to see a heavyset man with
a red beard, a blue master's coat and the unmistakable rolling
walk of a sailor approach her.

"Madam Deveroe?" he asked. "I'm Captain Brundy of the
merchant *Charlotte*. I've just returned from London and I bring
letters with me for you and your husband."

Excitedly, Celia took the package tied with a thin grosgrain
ribbon. At a glance, she recognized the ornate handwriting.

"Oh, it's from Hester! How grand. We've not heard from
her in more than a year and then only a brief note. Did she
give you these herself?"

"Aye. Put them into my own hand."

"How is she? Did she seem well? Dear me, I'm forgetting
my manners Captain Brundy. Won't you sit and take some
refreshment?"

"No, thank you, madam. I've just this moment come ashore
and I've much to do. When I learned you were in the city I
thought to bring these by and to tell you that we sail for Cork
again in two weeks. If you have any letters to return to Mrs.
Barnett, I'll be happy to carry them. I'll call next Tuesday for
your return letters."

"Thank you, Captain."

As her eager fingers tore at the ribbons she heard Hannah
give way to a fit of coughing near the water cistern at the foot
of the enclosed garden. Hurrying to her, she picked up the
slight body and, cupping some of the rainwater in her hand,
tried to get a little down the child's throat.

"My poor dear, you've been running too hard again. You must be more careful, Hannah."

The girl nestled her head on Celia's neck. "We were playing a game," she murmured. "It was fun."

"I'm sure it was, but you know how it tires you."

Josh, whose strong constitution left him with more energy than he could consume, could not understand why his sister gave out so quickly. He pulled at Celia's skirts. "Come on, 'Anna, play fox and farmer."

"No, Josh." Celia pulled him around and spoke to him severely. "Hannah must rest. Perhaps later." She set the girl on her feet and looked into her white strained face. "Are you all right now?"

"Yes."

"Then go along to the kitchen and get Cook to give you some buttermilk. You too, Josh. After that, you may go upstairs to the nursery and play quietly."

Hannah groaned a protest, but she knew from experience that Celia was right. Josh grabbed at her hand and began to pull her to the kitchen. "Hurry, 'Anna. Hurry up!"

"I'm coming. Slow down a little."

Celia watched them, the slight figure of the girl and the stocky little boy bouncing on fat legs ahead of her. As she had done many times, once again she fought down a cold knife thrust of panic at Hannah's fragility. She had come to love the child so. In every way she was like her own daughter.

With quiet restored, she turned back to the packet of letters and eagerly opened the one Hester had addressed to her.

MY DEAR CELIA:

Many times these last years I have sat down to write you and deliberately put on paper many untruths about our lives here in England. But no more. This last year has been so terrible that I can no longer pretend that life has become anything but a burden. . . .

Oh, dear, Celia thought, remembering Ewan's words so long ago at the Mill House. Up to this very moment she had hoped he was wrong.

. . . For the past year Cortlandt has been in the Fleet, imprisoned for his inability to pay his debts which amount to hundreds of pounds. I have tried everything to obtain his

release but to no avail and, of course, I cannot raise the
huge amount of money it would take to set him free. That
wretched Henry has moved Mama to a house in Suffolk
where I can never see her and where she is so frail as to
be near death. He absolutely refuses to give me another
penny, even though what he has given me amounts to a
pittance. My only hope is to cast myself and my poor destitute children on Richard's generosity and I beg and beseech
you, dearest Celia, to intercede for us. If he could send us
250 pounds it would make our lives sunshine again where
there has so long been darkness. Please, please, dear sister,
use your grace to our advantage and press him to help us
in our adversity.

If I can ever get my husband out of prison and find
enough money to pay for our passage I intend to return to
America and leave this wicked, degenerate country forever.
My fondest hope is to set sail at the least by next Spring,
with or without Cortlandt. Pray for us, dear Celia.

                    Your fond and most distressed sister,
                        HESTER BARNETT

Later in the evening when Celia sat alone with Richard in
the front parlor, she showed him the letter. He read it in silence,
thoughtfully.

"She says much the same thing to me in my letter. Two
hundred and fifty pounds! It's out of the question."

"She doesn't say how she is living, but I notice that her
address is Watling Street. Is that an impoverished neighborhood?"

"I don't believe so, but I shall have to ask. If I know Hester,
she'll survive."

"Oh, but, Richard, she sounds genuinely distressed. Can't
we send her something? I thought we were doing so well."

"We are, but you must realize that most of my assets are
tied up in goods and materials." And government securities,
he added to himself with a twinge. "I can get together possibly
as much as fifty pounds for her, but that is my limit. Besides,
even if I could afford more it would only encourage her to
depend on us, and God knows I cannot be expected to discharge
Cortlandt Barnett's debts! Can't you imagine how he ran up
such a sum? If we think gambling fever is rampant over here
it is nothing compared to the London scene. Great estates
change hands over the outcome of a hand of faro or whist in
those infamous gaming halls. No, I don't wish Hester to think

I am ready to shoulder all her problems simply because her husband turned out a wastrel"

"She has five children now," Celia said quietly. "I should hate to think they might suffer—"

Richard shifted uncomfortably in his chair. "They will not. I know of no more resourceful person in the world than my sister. She'll see that they are cared for. Now write her a pleasant, gossipy letter to counterbalance the cold, practical one I shall pen. Then I'll send them around to Captain Brundy's lodgings in the morning."

"Poor Hester," Celia sighed. "She always took adversity so personally."

"I should think fifty pounds would go a long way toward softening the blow," Richard answered laconically.

Years later, Richard would look back on the next eighteen months as the darkest of his life. It was not that his life was actually so bleak—in fact, it was just the opposite. True, Celia's every waking moment revolved around the children, but he did not really resent that, for he was as lost in wonder as she at the developing personality of their son. From infancy Josh showed a kind of joyful delight at the world around him, and if anything worried Richard about the boy it was the thought that he might grow up giddy and not take the world seriously enough.

His business too went along well, building up steady if unspectacular profits. Captain Yancy had taken on an apprentice, a young man of twenty whom he hoped to make into as fine a riverman as himself. Richard looked forward to the eventual purchase of a fourth sloop, which this young man, Robert Manning, would command for him.

No, it was neither home nor business which caused him his worst moments of panic and alarm. It was the thought of that steadily growing pile of securities locked in a lacquered tin box in the small room that served as his private office. He had not invested all his capital in these notes, but he had risked enough to cause him almost to break out in a sweat at the thought that they might turn out worthless in the end.

His answer was to cultivate anew his old friendships with the men who now stood high in the government. Of them all, he found that as he came to know him better Alexander Hamilton's shrewd mind and high ideals won more and more his admiration. As the possible new Secretary of the Treasury,

with ties of warm friendship to Washington, Hamilton stood
in the best position to work through a system of finance that
would put the fledgling country on a firm financial footing,
and Richard knew that crucial to his plan was the assumption
of public securities by the national government. The trouble
was that Congress had too many men who opposed Hamilton
and his concept of a strong national government, and if they
prevailed, not only would Richard's future be lost but, many
men felt, the future of the United States as well.

Hamilton finally put his financial plans before Congress in
December 1790, and for four anxious months Richard waited
to hear the outcome. By the spring the Congress had moved
back to Philadelphia, so he sent Elisha Yancy down with the
Venture to bring back news of the vote as swiftly as possible.

On a rainy day in April Yancy showed up at his office, his
face as stormy as the weather outside.

"Well," he said glumly, settling heavily in the familiar
wooden chair across the table from Richard, "the House voted
it down."

Richard made an effort to keep his face composed, but in
his chest a terrible commotion began to grow.

"It was those states that weren't so hurt by the war that did
it. Didn't see why they should carry the burden of the ones
who suffered. *Their* debts were paid! Let Massachusetts and
New York and South Carolina take care of their own! Bunch
of selfish, narrow-minded provincials!"

"What was Mr. Hamilton's reaction?" Richard asked,
amazed that his voice was so steady.

"I've no idea. He don't exactly confide in me, ye know.
But I tell you, Richard, I think we should start getting rid of
those securities as soon as possible. Sell 'em off now before
the word spreads, so that at least you get back what you put
into them. It's the only way."

Richard stood up and walked to the window, staring at the
rain that ran down the glass like silver tears. Though he looked
composed, his mind was working furiously.

"No," he finally said, turning back to Yancy. "No, I don't
think so. Not yet."

"God's death, Richard!"

"Now, Elisha, listen for a moment. I know something of
government from the days when I saw it firsthand. And I have
a great deal of faith in Mr. Hamilton. Remember how he con-
trived to get the State Assembly to ratify the Constitution? He

has had worse setbacks than this and I don't think he's beaten yet, in spite of the states' narrow provincialism. Besides, I believe as he does, that this measure must pass if the confederation of a United States is going to survive. Without some kind of national government with credit and financial integrity, we will only go back to the fragile confederation of squabbling states, and eventually—who knows?—another monarchy, anarchy, each state a separate sovereignty. Hamilton's is the only way to make a United States really work, and I'll bet he's not given up yet."

Yancy slumped in his chair and sighed. "Well, you have more faith in men and Mr. Hamilton than I do. And in governments too, for that matter. I just hope you—we—don't lose our shirt."

"Look, let me have a little time. I'll go straight down to New York and see what I can learn and I'll get a letter off to Hamilton right away. I'll do everything I can to find out the way the land lies. If by then it looks as though the assumption bill is truly defeated, we'll start selling the bonds to anyone who'll buy them."

"*If* anyone will by then. Ye're taking a fearful risk, Richard, but it seems I've said this before."

"I know, I'm risking my future in business, that's true. But I like to think I'm risking it on nothing less than the future of the republican government we fought a war to win!"

In the end Richard had to trust more to his judgment of the situation than to any inside information. He did discover that he was correct in thinking Hamilton would not be defeated by the failure of the assumption bill in the House. That indefatigable fighter simply turned to the one man who could bring the measure off for him, his old antagonist Thomas Jefferson. And in return for helping Jefferson to win a place on the Potomac River for the future capital, he enlisted his aid in passing the assumption bill.

It was August 4 by the time the measure actually became law, and by that time Richard's head was nearly swimming with the success of his gamble. Once the bill had been passed there was a mad scramble by speculators on all sides. Many raced to the frontier to buy up as many of the notes from old soldiers of the Revolution as they could before word came through that the script was now worth its face value. A great hue and cry went up against "jackals" and this "sordid tribe" of speculators—and not a little of it was leveled against Richard himself when it became obvious to his neighbors that he had so great an amount of the now valuable bonds.

But it did not bother him. He knew he had taken a terrible chance, and as he would have accepted the disaster which might have swept him under he likewise enjoyed the triumph which came from playing his hunch correctly. He stood to make a fantastic amount of money on his gamble—money that would once and for all set him on his way to becoming a rich man. Now the future was his, to make beautiful for his wife and son, and he gloried in it.

But he also took great satisfaction in the thought that with it he and his country both were now on a more secure footing. It pleased him to identify his concerns with those of the struggling government. They had both come through a dark time.

twenty-five

"Mama! Mama! There's a carriage stopping outside. They're here, they're here!"

Josh turned excitedly from the curtained window of the front room in the house on Oyster Pasty Lane and ran to where Celia stood in the hall nervously fingering the gauze kerchief around her shoulders.

"Oh, dear. Betsy," she called up the stairs as she hurried to the window. "Hurry with Hannah's hair. I think they've arrived. Are you sure it's them, my darling?" she said, pulling back the curtain.

"Yes, there's Vestal getting down from the box, and I see Papa now coming out of the carriage."

"Here, Josh, straighten your collar, and, oh dear, I should have combed your hair myself. It looks half done. Well, too late now." She knelt down beside her five-year-old and fussed with his jacket. "Don't forget, now, you've never met Aunt Hester before and you must show her your very best manners. Don't talk out of turn, take her hand, make her a proper bow—be a gentleman. Will you do that for Mama?"

"Are my cousins with her? Do you think perhaps she brought me a present from London?"

"Did you hear *anything* I said?"

"Yes, yes, Mama. I'll be good. There's the door."

He broke away and ran toward the hall while Celia stood and took a deep breath. She was more nervous than she had ever imagined she would be. Now that Hester was really here her feelings were so mixed and she felt herself so changed since the last time they had been together that she barely knew what to expect. Hurrying to the hall just in time to take Hannah's hand as she tripped down the stairs, she pulled her son back from the front door and held tightly to the two of them.

"You look lovely, Hannah," she said softly, smoothing the ruffles around the neck of the child's high-waisted dress.

Hannah twisted her mouth and scrunched up her nose in a self-deprecating frown. "I wish my hair looked better. No matter what Betsy does to it, it refuses to stay in a curl. I hate it!"

"Don't worry about it. It looks fine. I think you look very pretty."

Scowling, the child accepted Celia's judgment without for a moment believing it. She was beginning to be very conscious of what she saw in her looking glass, and she knew she wasn't pretty. Yet the idea of meeting Aunt Hester's children—one of them a girl only a little younger than herself—was too exciting to spoil for long with worry over her appearance. After all, they had been born in London, and they had just crossed the ocean in a great ship. They should have wonderful adventures to share. If they didn't like the way she looked—well, too bad!

Holding tightly to Celia's other hand, Josh danced in excitement, his brown velvet suit looking incongruously fussy on his stocky, exuberant body. He had his mother's honey-colored hair and it curled like a halo around his face, although no one would ever mistake those mischievous, dancing eyes for anything resembling an angel.

Suddenly the narrow hall was filled with people—Richard, children of assorted sizes, and then Hester herself, swathed in a worn red perriot with a huge Siberian wolfskin muff on her arm. Celia found her breath caught in her throat as she dropped her children's hands and threw her arms around her sister-in-law in a sudden burst of affection.

"Hester! How wonderful to have you home again. Welcome back."

She stood back, looking into Hester's face, startled at the changes the years had brought.

"Thank you, Celia, it *is* good to be back in America."

Celia had forgotten how small Hester was. It brought back old memories of how she so often used to feel that she towered over her. Hester was still tiny, compact and very neat, and her small face framed with its bright white-blond curls still had that fine delicacy. But the years had added hardness to it and her eyes looked more faded and empty than Celia remembered. And there was little warmth in her response.

"Come here, children," Hester said briskly, "and meet your

Aunt Celia." She pulled forward a tall thin boy of twelve whose pink face was marred with pimples. "This is Dexter, my second son, Celia. He lookes exactly as Tyler did at this age."

Celia found herself glancing around the hallway for the tall young man Tyler Barnett should now be.

"Oh, I left Tyler and my eldest daughter, Charlotte, in London." Hester explained, catching her questioned look. "Lord Lamberton finally unbent enough to take them under his wing—a great relief, I can tell you, though it quite broke my heart to part with them. But he can give them all the advantages I cannot—introduce them into society, that kind of thing. Come here, Dexter, and make your aunt a proper bow."

Embarrassed, the boy took Celia's hand in his limp grasp and dipped forward in so deep a bow that his hat fell at her feet. Turning bright red, he reached down and grasped at it, then ducked back behind his mother. Beside Celia, Josh erupted in a cascade of giggles.

"Oaf!" Hester spat out the word. "Can't you do anything correctly?"

Reaching behind Celia, Hannah gave Josh a pinch, and he clasped his fat hand over his mouth in a vain attempt to stifle his laughter.

"And this is Agatha." Hester pulled a very pale child of nine up to Celia and pushed her shoulders down in a curtsy. The girl appeared too shy to raise her eyes, but mumbled some politeness while staring into her kid shoes. As soon as Hester released her, she faded back behind her brother.

"And this little minx is Christabel, my youngest." She was a petite child, the same age as Josh, with long straight bright hair and blue eyes like her mother. She showed none of the shy self-consciousness of her sister. This is a spunky little one, Celia thought. She probably leads Hester a merry dance. She gave each of the children a warm smile.

"And now you must meet my family," Celia said, drawing her children forward. "Hannah, our daughter, and Joshua, our son." She was pleased with Hannah's curtsy and her well-spoken "Your servant, ma'am." Josh stepped up and looked into his aunt's pale face with a five-year-old's frank appraisal. Glancing at his mother, he gave Hester a polite bow and shook her hand.

"Did you bring me a present from London?"

Celia gasped and, grasping his shoulder, pushed him toward Hannah.

"Dear little fellow," Hester commented dryly. "I am happy for you, Celia, that you finally had a child. He's quite beautiful."

"Betsy, these children look exhausted. Take them down to the kitchen and ask Cook to give them something warm to drink. You too, Josh, go along, now, and get acquainted with your new cousins. Hannah, dear, see that he stays with you, will you?"

"Yes, Mama," Hannah answered, and, taking Josh by one hand and Christabel by the other, she shepherded them both toward the stairs. She glanced shyly at Agatha, sure that she was going to like her even though the girl seemed so quiet and retiring. Perhaps later she might show her the beautiful dollhouse Richard had brought her for her birthday. With any luck they might even become friends. It would be lovely to have a friend her own age.

Hester dropped her coat and muff carelessly on the hall table. "Where did you find that little girl?" she asked, looking after the children. "She must be a great help to you in watching your boy. How convenient."

Celia and Richard exchanged glances. "I wrote you about Hannah years ago," Celia answered. "Don't you remember?"

"Oh, yes. I seem to recall something about a pauper child. It was very generous of you, but then, of course, you can afford to be generous, you and Richard. However, you really should not allow her to call you 'Mama.' Very bad form, you know."

Taking Hester's arm, Richard pushed his sister toward the parlor, darting a warning look at Celia. It was enough to help her to bite back an outraged response, but her jaw was tight as she followed them into the parlor and sat down next to Hester on a tufted velvet sofa.

"Would you like some tea, Hester?" she managed to mutter.

"I should love that. I feel chilled to the bone."

"Let me look at you, Hester," Celia said, throwing off her irritation. "It's been so many years! What an unusual dress. Is that the latest fashion in Europe? We're nearly a year behind you, you know."

"I could see that on our ride here. Yes, it is quite remarkable, isn't it? Slimmer skirts, straighter lines, higher waists and the only padding at the back. And the more bosom you show, the better. This dress is actually very discreet compared to what you see in the London salons."

Celia masked her surprise. Above the low-cut décolletage

of Hester's striped silk dress, her ample figure was barely concealed by the flimsiest layer of Italian gauze. If Hester were to walk into a soiree in New York in that dress it would certainly set the cat among the pigeons.

"How was your crossing?" Richard was beginning to feel somewhat depressed.

Hester settled back, fussing with her kerchief. "As good as any crossing can be, I suppose. The girls were sick the entire voyage, and I myself would probably have perished but for Dexter's care. However, I didn't mind. With the push forward of every wave I thanked God that I was being carried farther from the coast of England!"

"Why, it's the dream of everyone in New York to visit London," Celia said. "How can it be as bad as you say?"

Hester laughed dryly. "Then everyone in New York should have to live there as I have these past fifteen years. Oh, we did well enough at first and I admit that I did enjoy London society then. Then Cortlandt started gaming and drinking and wasting his livelihood with those—those London jades who lie in wait on every corner, and we were hounded by creditors for years before he finally ended up in the Fleet—it is all too terrible to remember! When he finally died last fall, I made up my mind nothing was going to keep me from America. I shall never, never go back!"

Richard sat watching her over his hands crossed under his chin. "Have you thought how you are going to live here, Hester? Were you able to bring anything with you?"

"How could I when I had to sell everything we owned in order to get here? Richard, I'm throwing myself on your mercy. You are simply going to have to take care of us. You are doing very well now, I believe. Your reputation has even crossed the ocean. Surely you can spare a little for the support of your destitute sister."

Richard stirred uncomfortably in his chair. "I'll help you all I can—" he began before Celia blurted out:

"Now, let's not talk business at this happy time. Let us at least have a few moments for a pleasant reunion. You must come and stay with us in New Rochelle," she said politely, pouring the tea. "It's a pleasant little town and I have several friends whom you might enjoy meeting."

Hester looked up over the rim of her cup. "Certainly not! I did not cross an ocean to bury myself in a provincial backwater. Now that I am free at last of Cortlandt Barnett and his odious debts, I intend to enjoy life a little. I must have a house in New York, Richard, for my children and myself. Surely that is not too much to ask."

Richard exchanged an astonished glance with his wife.

"And I suppose Dexter ought to have a tutor. Thank goodness my other children are all girls and I don't have to bother with educating them. And we should have some kind of servant. Why don't you let me have Vestal and Betsy, Celia? They are family retainers, after all. Besides, that Vestal was always the slowest-witted Negro in the world, and the woman looks like she's not much better. You'll be needing more accomplished servants for your larger establishment. Yes, I think they should suit very well."

Deliberately Celia set her cup down on the tray with a clink. "You may as well forget that idea, Hester, because you are not going to have them. Nothing will make me part with Vestal and Betsy. They have served me too well for too long and their home is with me."

Hester gave her a sharp appraising look, then shrugged. "Oh, very well. You always *were* so sentimental."

"We'll say no more about your future right now, Hester," Richard broke in. "After tea you and I can take some time in my study to work out your plans. They don't involve Celia in any way, so I see no need to discuss them now."

"A little more tea, Hester?" Celia asked to break the uncomfortable silence. "Tell me, how are Henry and Guinevere? Since Mama Deveroe died two years ago we have completely lost touch with them."

"You could not have lost touch with them any more than I. Henry completely cut me off, unnatural brother that he is! Not a sou would he offer. Never did he once invite me down to stay with them in Suffolk, though my poor little family was living in the direst distress. I hope never to hear his name again!"

Wildly Celia cast around in her mind for a neutral subject. She looked searchingly at her husband, who set down his cup and rose from his chair.

"I think we've had enough refreshment for now. Come along, Hester. Let's get this finished and then I'm sure you would welcome an opportunity to rest a while after your long journey."

Willingly Hester rose. "Yes, I would. The room sways under my feet as though I were still on board that creaking, stinking ship. My, but it's good to be back on solid land again."

Celia watched as they left the room, feeling as though a minor storm had swept through the calm of her peaceful parlor. And this was only the beginning! She tried to picture the young girl she had known so many years ago, that bright, lively creature so captivating to her family and friends. Whatever sparkle Hester had possessed was gone now, leaving only the brittle, self-centered hardness which had always been underneath. Adversity had made this of her. Yet Celia recalled that she herself had lived through adversity. She hoped the desolation of those terrible war years had not left her as angry and bitter as her sister-in-law. Of course, their experiences were very different. Celia could not really imagine how it felt to be alone and penniless, responsible for the welfare of five young children, with a wastrel for a husband. Who was to say but that the experience might have twisted and warped her just as it had Hester? No, it was not scorn she should feel for her sister, but pity.

Yet as she carefully stacked the cups and the plates upon the tray she could not help thinking that it was going to be very difficult at times to remember that.

She woke in the dark hours of the early morning and, reaching out her hand, realized that Richard had not come to bed. The house was still, with only the scurrying in the walls of the inescapable mice. Far away she could hear the faint sound of the watchman crying the hour. She swung her legs down from the high fourposter and, slipping on a robe, lit a candle to walk downstairs.

She found him still sitting in his study reading by the dim light of a candelabra, nearly burned down to its wells. He looked up and smiled wearily at her.

"You're up very late," she said, taking a chair opposite him.

"Yes. After the memorable events of the evening I found I was in no mood for repose, and besides, I have been anxious to read over this report for several days now. This seemed an ideal time."

"Was your talk with Hester productive?" she asked hesitantly. "I thought she seemed particularly ill-humored at supper."

"It was ghastly! My sister would try the patience of a saint. I had hoped that perhaps marriage and adversity might have mellowed her, but, on the contrary, she is worse than ever.

She came back to this country convinced that I would naturally assume the entire burden of her establishment and care. And this without any assurance from me. Without even asking me, in fact! No wonder Henry put her aside. She probably tried the same thing with him."

Celia was not surprised. "What *will* you do for her, Richard? She is quite alone, you know."

"And is that my responsibility? Oh, I know—filial affection and all that. All right, I shall certainly try to help her as much as I can, but there have to be limits set. Otherwise she will ruin me in a year as I suspect she ruined Cortlandt. No wonder he turned to gambling and drink."

"Merciful heavens, I hope that won't be your fate."

For a moment he took her seriously, until, glancing up, he saw the mischievous smile playing on her lips.

"Thank heaven I have a different kind of wife. The truth is, Celia, I have done well and I intend to do even better. But I am building this wealth for you, for Josh and Hannah and myself, and not in order that Hester can live among the quality."

"Oh, dear. It sounds as though you must have had a terrible fight."

"Yes, I'm very much afraid we did. But she must understand clearly how things are." He hesitated, running his fingers through his long hair. "I agreed to help her find a rented house of respectable but not fashionable proportions, and I will make her a modest allowance. But that cannot go on forever."

"But, Richard, what else can she do? There is nothing left of your father's estate and she has no one else to turn to."

"Why, the solution is simple. She must marry again."

Celia stared at his face, tired and drawn in the shadows of the candlelight. It was a long minute before she could answer. "Did you tell her this?"

"Of course."

"For heaven's sake, Richard, no wonder she was so irritable. Of all things that must be the last solution Hester would want. She never cared a fig for Cortlandt Barnett, never wanted all those children, and look what marriage has brought her. Why, I should think she would resent such an idea more than anything you could have proposed."

"Be that as it may," he said crisply. "it *is* the only solution. Besides, if she married Cortlandt without caring for him simply because he was wealthy, she can marry someone else for the same reason. Hester is far too selfish ever to lose her heart under any circumstances."

Celia's thoughts flew upstairs to where her sister lay in the small guest room, her children on trundles around her. Perhaps Richard was right. Hester would never put up with that kind of life any longer than it took her to find a remedy, and if marriage was the only way to get out of poverty she would make use of it. But what an unfortunate reason.

"I think I shall go back to bed," she said wearily. "Hester's problems are too burdensome for the middle of the night. Are you coming?"

"Yes, I'll be up shortly." He ruffled through the sheaf of papers spread on the table. "Unsettling as it was, I'm glad it afforded me the time to read this. It is a report that Mr. Hamilton sent to Congress last winter on manufacturing. With his usual vision he may offer a real insight into the way the future is tending."

Celia smiled at him indulgently. "I suppose that means you now intend to invest in factories."

"Exactly. Farming, and trade—they are too slow and the profits too small. Transportation and industry—I think that is where the real money is to be made. This country is rich in natural resources—all the basic materials you need to build and operate factories. And he feels that immigrant labor will be coming here from Europe in increasing numbers to supply manpower. I think it holds a real promise to those of us who have the capital to invest. I intend to try, anyway."

"With all that 'capital' there must be a little left over for a poor relation."

His unsmiling eyes met hers across the dark void of the room. "Hester will never starve," he answered lightly. "But I intend to make sure she doesn't make us starve, either."

John Street was a milling confusion of carriages, sedan chairs, men in beaver felt hats, and ladies in feathers and gauze as Richard's one-horse chaise finally worked its way to the curb in front of the lantern-hung theater. Pushing his way into the crowd, Richard handed down Celia, resplendent in pale-rose satin, and Hester, in her fashionable but worn blue ball gown.

They had an eight-shilling box which looked directly down on the wide apron of the stage. For more than a week Celia had been anticipating this evening's entertainment, and when they finally forced their way to the box, where Vestal had been waiting since early afternoon to hold their seats, she was filled with a delicious excitement.

Hester settled in a spindly chair, her eyes moving scathingly up from the pit below past the rows of boxes to the upper gallery.

"I had forgotten how provincial New York is," she sniffed. "Look at that riffraff in the gallery. They brought their supper with them and are throwing the scraps down on the heads of the gentry below! And the mildewed painting and dim candlelight! The whole place needs refurbishing."

"You must remember," Celia said evenly, "there was great opposition to any theater at all in New York after the Revolution. This one has been struggling along now for seven years against the strong disapproval of the city fathers."

"How typical. Well, my dear, when one has been to Covent Garden and Drury Lane, not to mention the Royal Opera in the Haymarket, one is not much impressed by these secondrate enterprises."

To distract her, Celia pushed a playbill into her hand. "It is a varied evening. The first performance is a drama called *The Deserter*—very moving, I understand. Following that, a farce called *Darby's Return*, by an American author named Dunlap. It is famous in New York for being the only play which ever drew a laugh from our distinguished President."

Richard leaned forward. "That was such an auspicious occasion it was written up in the newspapers that General Washington actually gave a 'full, hearty laugh.' It made the play's reputation, you may well believe."

"Well, I hope it draws a laugh from me, for I could use one."

"Is Mr. Durang to dance his hornpipe between the play and the farce?" Celia asked, peering over Hester's arm at the playbill. "Now, you musn't laugh then, Hester, though if it is like his last performance you will be hard put not to. I fear Mr. Durang's best dancing days are well behind him."

"My, it sounds like a capital evening," Hester said dryly as she leaned toward the edge of the box and draped the soft folds of her embroidered silk shawl provocatively around her shoulders. She scanned the nearby boxes for any faces which might look familiar from former days and, to her delight, actually recognized one or two.

The orchestra struck up a squawking of fiddles which did nothing to lower the hissing and stamping in the hall as the prologue stepped out from behind the great green curtain.

Although Richard and Celia entered into the spirit of the performance, Hester had seen enough of the theater in London to recognize how shoddy the production actually was. Still it was diverting enough to help her forget her own problems and disappointments, for by now she was well aware that her expectations of generous aid from her brother were not to be met.

After Mr. Durang's halting dance there was time left for strolling when the men could move out of the building and enjoy a Spanish seegar and the women had a chance to sedately walk the halls or visit the coffee rooms. Richard was off at once, and Hester too, eagerly looking to renew old acquaintances.

Celia sat comfortably alone in her box, watching the people milling about in the pit and listening to the groans and creaks on the stage as the factotum moved the sliding wings and flats around to set the scene for the farce.

"Mrs. Deveroe, I believe," said a voice behind her. "May I wish you a good evening."

Startled, she looked around to see a tall, thin, severe gentleman standing in the curtained doorway.

"We have met before, sir?"

"Yes, we have. Long ago and under far less pleasant circumstances."

"Now I remember," she said, her smile fading. "You are the gentleman who wanted to carry me away to jail for helping poor Mrs. Lister."

"Jaspar Carne, madam. Your servant. That was an unfortunate incident, best forgotten. May I sit down?"

"Why, yes. Please do, Mr. Carne."

"I trust you are enjoying the performance," he said, settling himself stiffly on the edge of the chair opposite her.

"Yes, I am. Very much," she answered, recognizing at a glance that he was even more ill-at-ease than she. "As I trust you are."

"No, I cannot say that I am," Jaspar Carne replied gravely. "I do not care for the theater, you see. In fact, I believe it to be the devil's drawing room, a wicked instrument that encourages a waste of time and money by people who have neither. If I had my way this place would be closed down tomorrow."

Celia shifted uncomfortably in her chair. "I am surprised, then, that you bother to come."

"Although I am one of the town officials who would prefer to have no theater in New York, still I believe one must know the facts about what one is judging. It would not be honest for me to oppose the theater without knowing firsthand exactly what it is that I distrust about it, would it, now?"

"I suppose not," Celia murmured.

"As a matter of fact, I was invited by the Mayor to attend this evening's performance, so I took advantage of the opportunity to make sure my fears are justified. Unfortunately, they have been, every one."

"Yes, I suppose they would be. I must tell you, though, Mr. Carne, that I find the theater a diverting consolation when the day's work is finished."

"Ah, yes, but you, madam, are not typical. What about those poor folk up there in the gallery who spend their hard-earned two or three shillings here when they should be buying bread for their children? Should we, the custodians of the city, allow such temptations to exist?"

"But are there not often benefit performances for the relief of the poor?"

"I fear such benefits go more toward the relief of the actors—a scurvy lot if ever there was one!"

Celia made a valiant attempt to change the subject. "I believe I noticed your name in the *Packet*, Mr. Carne. You were recently elected an assistant alderman, were you not? Please accept my congratulations."

A thin smile darted across Carne's narrow lips. "Thank you," he answered, obviously pleased at her mentioning the honor. "From the Seventh Ward—the one that used to be called the Outer Ward."

A flush brightened Celia's pale cheeks. "I know that ward. It is where my adopted father once had his estate."

"Yes, Wayside. I know it well. In fact, I now own a piece of the land there. The house had to be torn down, of course, to make way for the building of the Belvedere Club. And the orchard as well. There were a few fine old trees left, but they too had to make way for progress. In a year or two we will fill in the salt marsh and build on that too. I daresay you would not know the place."

"I daresay," Celia replied, looking down at the floor and trying to blot from her mind the familiar picture of the warm, welcoming house and gardens where she had spent so many happy years. All gone now, to be covered over with bricks and cobbles. Narrow straight houses would march across the land in long blocks with hardly a speck of green grass to fight its way to the surface between them. All that fine long vista of fields and meadows, the thick salt grass where Ricahrd pushed his boat out into the river to drift under the circling bluebills and the warm sun. All gone, sacrificed to progress!

"It saddens you," Carne said simply.

She looked swiftly up into that narrow, oblique face. "Yes, I had so many happy memories of the place."

He stood up, reaching politely for her hand. "Please give my regards to your husband, Mrs. Deveroe. I shall wish you a good evening now."

Celia had the feeling he was trying in his stiff way to be kind. Perhaps he had mellowed since the last time she saw him. Or perhaps it was just that without Richard around he was not such a difficult person after all. She gave him her hand and smiled up at him.

"Thank you for stopping by, Mr. Carne."

Before he could answer, the curtain was drawn back and Hester swept into the box, her face shining. "Oh, Celia," she cried, "you'll never guess who I just saw—" She careened into Carne, who moved quickly back, smoothing his coat. "Oh, dear, excuse me." Hester fussed with her shawl, slyly observing the widening of Carne's eyes at the revelation of her white bosom, exposed under the thin muslin of her low-cut gown.

"Hester," said Celia, "may I present Mr. Jaspar Carne. Or perhaps I should say Alderman Carne. My sister-in-law, Mrs. Barnett."

"Your servant, madam." Carne bowed over her hand.

"I'm pleased to meet you, Mr. Carne. Are you part of the family at Horseneck? I remember them so well from our summers at West Farms. They were always trooping through on their way to King's Bridge carrying produce into the city."

Celia caught the sudden whitening of Carne's cheeks, though Hester, arranging herself prettily in the chair near the railing was completely unaware of the effect of her remark.

"I used to live in Horseneck—or, rather, Greenwich, as it is now called—but I have for the past several years made my home in the city." His words were clipped. With a nod at Celia and another short bow in Hester's direction, he slipped through the curtain.

"My goodness, what a severe man," said Hester, bobbing her curls at her friend across the way. "Does he never smile?"

"I don't think so. I haven't seen him in years, although I understand Richard has had one or two unpleasant experiences with him."

"Those Carnes were always riffraff. Putting on airs and lording it over their betters when everybody knew they were rustics. He looks one of the pack."

"Well, I am thankful he left before Richard returned. They don't get along at all!"

Making his way back down the hall and the stairs to the level below, Jaspar Carne hardly noticed the people around him. He hardly knew whether or not he was satisified that he had followed that impulse and stepped into Madam Deveroe's box. He rarely got a chance at her and she looked so soft and vulnerable in her dignified observation of the house. It was too good an opportunity to pass up, this chance to observe close at hand the woman who stood closest to the man he detested above all others. And in fact, it had probably been worth the risk. She was a pretty woman with a naïve warmth about her which might prove a means of getting at her husband.

Methodically he took out an enameled snuffbox and applied a pinch to his long thin nostrils, giving a little snort as he remembered her downcast appearance when he described the changes at Wayside. How typical! The landed gentry mourning their lost acres when they were given over to the use of better citizens. How many more people now enjoyed that vast countryside where before a few children and their parents played at being country squire. No, the republic was better off without these spongers. Yet how it galled him that Richard Deveroe should still be able to accumulate wealth while other men must scrape and struggle merely to exist. That he had survived the Revolution unscathed was bad enough. That he should be rebuilding the fortunes of the Deveroe family to what they had once been before the war was almost unbearable to Carne's strict sense of justice. Besides, had not the man insulted him to his face on two different occasions? If he was a dueling man he would have faced him across a field long ago.

The fiddles were scraping away as he entered the box and took his seat in the rear, nodding to the Mayor and his lady, already smiling in anticipation of the comedy. In the dim light he could look between the silhouetted shoulders of the figures in the box to see the Deveroes across the hall. Richard had returned and was just distinguishable in the shadows behind his wife. And flagrantly flaunting herself for all the pit to see was that sister of his in her shocking dress and crimped curls. What a wanton! He remembered hearing some rumor about her—husband died in debtor's prison, several children, returning penniless from jaded London. How typical of a Deveroe!

Next to him Alderman Bayard leaned forward to make a quiet comment. Carne nodded, then sat back, his eyes shifting again to the two women in the box—Celia, smiling delightedly toward the bright stage, and beside her Hester in repose, contempt lightly settling on her countenance. Startled, his gaze arrested, he looked closer at that patrician face with its pale pursed lips, its porcelain skin, its crimped white-gold hair, its eyes, so knowledgeable, so cynical and so angry. So there *was* something hard and brittle underneath that frivolous exterior. Something which, if he played his cards right, might prove useful in bringing down Richard Deveroe.

twenty-six

Richard stood on the deck of the *Venture* and watched with growing excitement as the schooner steered through a sea of masts to lay anchor near the Water Street dock in Philadelphia. The weather had held fine, Captain Yancy had proved good company on the sail down from New York, and now, with the spires, brick houses and wide streets of the city coming into view, he had the further expectation of renewing some old friendships and visiting some familiar haunts. Perhaps he would even be invited to observe sessions of the Congress. Enough time had passed that the thought gave him no pain. He came now with the credentials of a wealthy and established businessman, and aside from an occasional wistful regret, politics no longer interested him.

Near the prow of the boat the wharf was thick with rubbish dumped from the ships—rotting cabbages, onions, potatoes, even coffee, all in various stages of decay and clouding the air with an overpowering miasma. Garbage drifted on the waves around the sides of the boat. Looking around him, Richard recognized flags from ports up and down the eastern seaboard and from the islands of the West Indies. The din from the crowds milling about on shore, added to the stagnant and malodorous water, made him anxious to disembark. Philadelphia, with its Quaker heritage and neat, rectangular streets, was one of the cleanest cities he had ever visited, once you put the dock behind you.

Stepping up beside him, Elisha Yancy leaned on the rail, looking out over the heads of the crowds.

"She's a handsome city, this," he said casually. "How long do you expect to stay?"

"A fortnight or so. No longer. I've a few contracts to sniff out, a few friends to see—it shouldn't take too long."

"I could take ye back, you know. It's easy enough to make the run down, especially now I'm not really needed on the market sloops."

"No, no. I prefer to go back overland. It'll give me a chance to cast an eye around New Jersey again."

"By God, Richard, ye're not thinking of nosing about there too? We've got fifteen sloops on the Hudson, sawmills, nail factories, hemp and sailcloth interests—what more can ye want?"

"What else? I want to consolidate them into a single shipyard works. We already supply most of the materials for the boats—we might as well build them."

Elisha good-naturedly clamped a large hand on his shoulder. "Ye're never satisfied. We're both richer than we'd ever dreamed of being, and ye must have more."

"Now, you know you would enjoy experimenting with those ship designs you doodle about with. We might even be able to come up with an original idea for a crow's-nest model. Or follow through on one of your other pet projects."

Yancy's eyes narrowed beneath the heavy graying brows. "Aye, I'd like that. Did you know that a fellow named John Hicks only a few years back sailed a boat up this very river with three oars powered by steam? Sixty strokes a minute. If only I was of an inventive cast of mind, that's the way I'd go. As it is, the only thing I really know is wind power, but I think I might be able to shape a hull better for that than some of the tugs we have now."

He pulled out a heavy leather tobacco pouch and broke off a plug with his teeth, spitting a long stream of amber juice into the water below. "But I still say, Richard, if you want a yard, Hudson's River is the place to build it. Ye're wasting your time looking through the Jerseys or on the Delaware."

"Probably. But the competition is stiffer near New York, and besides, I'm not convinced that we should only build sloops, though certainly the Hudson is ideal for that."

A babble of excited voices drew his attention to a group of people standing around in confusion on the dock near the *Venture*. Looking up in surprise, Richard peered more closely at the group. They clung together as though lost amid their packing cases and bundles tied with hemp. Their clothes were obviously French and of light texture—he recognized a fine glazed cotton available only from Martinique. Negro servants in bright, garishly loud kerchiefs held tightly to the hands of the children or followed their mistresses with portmanteaus under their arms. Several held exotic birds, a cockatoo and a parrot, in wicker cages.

"Aren't those people speaking French? If they were not so obviously from the tropics I'd assume they were refugees from the Terror in Paris."

"No, they're from San Domingo. The first mate told me they only arrived ahead of us. There is some kind of slave rebellion going on down there, and the Frenchy whites are pouring into Philadelphia."

"Too bad Celia did not come with us. She might have been able to help them with their language problems."

"It's probably just as well that she didn't come. The mate told me those Frenchies have brought the influenza with them. You wouldn't want to risk that."

The small launch was lowered and ready to carry them ashore. Stretching in the sunshine, Richard turned away from the rail to go below and bring up his portmanteau.

"No, I wouldn't. And the sooner I get away from this Water Street area the better I'll feel. Have a good trip, Elisha."

Yancy waved a farewell at his retreating figure. "Aye, I will."

It was the glimpse of Hester's lovely profile through the window that brought him into Hugh Gaine's "Sign of the Bible." Jaspar Carne had not really meant to go inside Hanover Square's fashionable bookshop until he saw her standing there looking over a row of leather and doeskin-bound new arrivals, their horizontal ridges uplifted to the sun streaming through the window. That was enough to turn his steps momentarily from his appointment with Mr. Bayard at Federal Hall. She was wearing a pert yellow hat, her back very straight, her thin lips pursed in concentration. Behind and around her stood her patient court, a spindly, big-eared boy of twelve and two smaller girls. Carne passed them over with the barest of glances.

"Good afternoon, Mrs. Barnett."

Hester looked up to see the tall, severe man she recognized at once as the visitor to their box at the theater. He towered nearly a foot above her, and she had to stretch her neck to see his slate-gray eyes.

"Why, it's . . . it's . . ."

"Jaspar Carne."

"Of course. Mr. Carne, I remember well." With all the

attractive men she had met at the theater that night, this *would* be the one who turned up.

Carne shifted his weight a little self-consciously. "I see that Mr. Gaine has some new arrivals," he said.

"And some interesting ones. Dexter, here, take this copy of *Werther* over to the counter and tell them to wrap it for me. I've been that anxious to read it since it was the rage of London."

Dexter Barnett blushed a shade deeper. "But . . ." He sidled up closer to his mother. "But, Mama . . ."

"Just tell them to charge it to your uncle's account. His credit is good, I've no doubt," Hester said sharply.

"But shouldn't we . . ."

Flinging out her gloved hand, Hester boxed her son solidly on his ear. "Go do as you are told, you naughty boy. And hold those packages carefully."

His face a deep magenta, Dexter shifted the boxes and propped the book under his arm. Carne watched him weave his way toward the counter. "Ah, madam, I see you are a disciplinarian," he commented with admiration in his eyes. "Allow me to commend you. Nothing does children more good than to learn early in life to hold their tongue and be obedient to their duty."

"I fear my son has a deplorable tendency to question my word," Hester said petulantly, "though I've tried every way known to man to turn him from it."

"Mama, are we going home now?" the smallest girl, Christabel, asked in a whispery voice, clutching a handful of her mother's skirt.

"Hush, child, or you will get the same as your brother. Pestering me all the time, first to go out, then to go home. Agatha, take this naughty child over to the door and wait for me there. I declare, it's too much for a poor widowed woman to bear," she sighed, deliberately assuming her most pathetic posture.

Carne had to suppress a smile at her obvious theatrics. "My deepest condolences to you, madam. It must be grievous indeed to bear the burden of so large a family on such . . . such delicate shoulders."

"Oh, sir. It is." Hester sighed again.

"May I presume to say that you bear them most gracefully?"

Hester's faded blue eyes widened. "You flatter me, I fear, Mr. Carne."

"May I have the honor of accompanying you to your carriage?"

"Well, as to that . . . I did not bring the carriage out today. No, I thought the weather was too fine to ride, so I dismissed the coachman when we got to the square and decided to walk back. The children need the exercise, you see."

Carne saw all right. He knew Hester was living at the Deveroes' house in Oyster Pasty Lane and that was much too long a walk in the sun for a lady with the pastel complexion Mrs. Barnett obviously cultivated.

"Of course," Hester added quickly, "I did promise the children I would stop with them at the Merchant's Coffee House."

"Excellent. I would be honored to accompany you there, as I am just on my way to Federal Hall."

"You are too kind, Mr. Carne."

Though she did not really care for this stern, unsmiling man, Hester felt a sense of pride in walking down the brick sidewalk with her hand on his arm, followed by her train of meek, silent children. He was constantly doffing his hat and nodding to acquaintances. Obviously he was a man well known in New York and much respected. It could do her no harm to be seen with him.

"Yes, poor Dexter, I fear, simply has no grace at all. He is so gauche, just as his father was. I never know what he's going to knock into or break apart next. It is quite distressing, as I'm sure I can't imagine what his future will be with so little to recommend him."

"But surely," Carne said guardedly, "your brother will care for his future. He is a wallthy man, is he not? And you being without a husband, why, it should be an honor for him to subsidize his nephew's education and establish him in the proper station in life."

He was immediately rewarded with the blackest look Hester had cast him yet. Gone were the subterfuge and the play-acting, replaced by the bitterness he had seen in her unguarded expression at the theater. He smiled inwardly as she ranted away.

"Richard! Why, Mr. Carne you would be shocked, *shocked*, if I should tell you the ingratitude my brother has shown me and my poor little family. His own sister in distress, his nieces and nephews practically orphaned and condemned to the almshouse, yet do you imagine he will take on their care? Why, we might as well cast ourselves on the mercy of the Commissioner of Charities. He doles out barely enough to keep body and soul together and expects that we shall thank him for it. I am dreadfully disappointed in him, I declare I am."

"Why, I should think that you would be," Carne added, sympathetically, "especially since the two of you shared such a refined upbringing yourselves."

Hester was clearly devouring every word.

"And now while he continues to enjoy a style of life suitable to his former station, he allows you . . ." His voice trailed off. "But come, it is not my place to say such things. I am sure your brother has excellent reasons for withholding his help."

"Well, if he does, I'm sure I don't know what they are. However, I must not allow you to think he has not benefited us at all. As a matter of fact, he's taking his family back to New Rochelle next week and I am to have the house on Oyster Pasty Lane for my complete use, rent free. I must say I'm grateful for that. Dexter will have a tutor, and I an allowance. Not a large one, mind you, but something at least."

"Oh, yes indeed." His voice dripped sarcasm. "That is most generous. Your brother is all heart."

For the first time she flashed a genuine smile up at him. "Mr. Carne, I see that you at least are able to understand my position. That is very comforting."

He lightly touched the little gloved hand resting on his arm. "I understand it completely, Mrs. Barnett. Completely."

"What do you know about Jaspar Carne, Celia?" Hester asked the question lightly as the two of them bent over, straining to see their darning by the trembling light of a pewter lamp that stood between them on the parlor table. The house was quiet, with Richard still away and the children asleep upstairs. Through the open window they could just make out the rattle of carriages on the cobbles and the muffled cries of a hot-corn vendor up on Broad Way.

Celia looked up thoughtfully. "Not very much. He can be polite, as he was at the theater that evening, yet I remember once in West Farms when he was very cruel. He is a stern patriot who cannot abide former Tories or neutrals."

"But is he well off?"

"Why, I don't know. He is not ostentatious, as you can see by his dress. He was a commissioner during the war, and is an assistant alderman in the city now. He told me he owns some of the land where Wayside used to be. Yes, I would imagine he has been able to accumulate money." She smiled over Hester's studied concentration on her needle. "Why do you want to know?"

"Oh, no reason. I met him today in the Bible and Crown and he walked me to the Coffee House."

"Were you impressed?"

"Impressed? I should hope not. He is not half so attractive as our friend Mr. Long. No, 'impressed' is certainly not the word."

Celia's eyes lifted to the molded ceiling of the room as she became aware of Hannah coughing upstairs. "Oh, dear," she said, rising and setting aside her sewing. "I'd better put a hot flannel cloth on her chest. And camphor salve. The poor child just cannot shake off that cough."

Hester watched her skirts swirl as she swept from the room. No, "impressed" was not really the word. Carne was not handsome or young, and even if he was well-to-do he was rather too cool a customer for her liking. But he had seemed to understand her as no one else since she left London. It was pleasant, she thought, smiling to herself, to have someone sympathize with her in her troubles. He would do for a friend, and she needed friends. Yes, Jaspar Carne would do very well.

It was nearly a year before Richard found the right property for his shipyard, and, as it turned out, it was on the Hudson above the land his mother had given him near Teller's Point and the Croton River inlet. He visited it twice, then sent Yancy up for his opinion. The captain came back enthusiastic over the site but appalled at the slipshod operation going on there. "The location is perfect. Near enough to the sawmill and the iron foundry, easy enough to float logs down from upriver, and plenty of fresh water. I tell you, Richard, I couldn't believe that a man could take such an ideal spot to build boats and then turn them out so shoddily. That owner ought to be horsewhipped! Who is the owner, anyway?"

"A certain Jonas Stewart. His father began the yard as a small enterprise before the war. He has tried to carry on, but the debts accumulated during the Confederation have dragged him down. Since he just managed to stave off foreclosure last month, I think we can get it for a reasonable price."

Elisha rubbed his beard reflectively. "Well, it's a fine site with plenty of room for expansion. If ye're really set on doing this I'd rather see ye buy there than anywhere else. What will ye call it? Deveroe Shipyard?"

"No. I'd thought to call it Deveroe-Yancy, but on reflection it seemed better to have a name that has no personal connotations at all. I thought perhaps Dolphin, since I enjoyed so watching them play in the river all the way to Albany that first voyage I took with you."

"Dolphin Shipyards. Aye, it sounds good. You're the principal owner, Richard, but for whatever it's worth, you've got my approval."

Jonas Stewart proved to be a portly, graying man in his late forties with the ruddy complexion of a Scot who enjoyed his drink. He placed Richard in a chair covered with threadbare Turkey work and settled opposite him. The first sign of surprise showed on his face when Richard came directly to the point with an offer to buy the Stewart yards for a generous twelve hundred pounds.

"I don't know, Mr. Deveroe . . ." he began, looking away from Richard, his bushy brows creased over his tiny pink eyes like a petulant spaniel. "I don't know. My father began this yard and it was always his hope to keep it in the family. I have a son of my own . . ."

Richard settled back, crossed one black-silk-hosed leg over the other and gave up all attempts at subtlety. "Come, now, Mr. Stewart. I have made some discreet inquiries and I know that your son is of a tender age. I also know that you are in arrears of nearly five thousand pounds to various banks and associates. I propose to assume your debts relating to the operation of the yards, and in addition give you a clear purchase sum of twelve hundred pounds. Without that I seriously doubt your business will be around long enough for your son to inherit."

Stewart shot him an angry glance. "I have friends—" he began.

"Yes, but your friends have helped you in the past. How much longer do you expect them to subsidize your family business? Every time you borrow more you add to the interest on your total and drive yourself farther under the weight of near-bankruptcy. I propose to relieve you of all that."

"It's the times! The times were so difficult after the war. Currency was worth nothing. Nobody building."

"Nonsense. The commercial traffic of the river only began in earnest after the war. You should have been turning out six or seven boats a year. Instead, out of four contracts this past year you actually completed two."

"Couldn't get joiners, smiths, shipwrights, nor the where-withal to pay 'em. Maybe it was different down in your fancy cities where the merchants had cash, but up this way nobody has anything but depreciated currency. Why, the states won't even accept that for taxes. How can a man finance a boat with it?"

"I'll grant you that was true up until three years ago, but certainly it is not so now. Mr. Hamilton's proposals have put the national currency on a sounder footing than it has been since before the Revolution."

"You talk like a damned Federalist!"

"As for workers," Richard went on, "new arrivals step off the ships from Europe every day eager for jobs. I fancy there are some among them who are skilled shipwrights."

"Hire those devil Irish! Never."

"You're asking forty-two dollars a ton to build a two-masted schooner of one-hundred-ninety burthen. That's far too high. Thirty-four dollars is average, and if you can lower that you'll get even more contracts."

"And make no profit!"

All at once Richard became aware he was drumming his fingers impatiently on his knee. "Look, Mr. Stewart, I am making you a fair offer for a yard which is, in my opinion, in a very bad way through what I believe is sheer mismanagement. Do you wish to consider it or not?"

Stewart's narrow eyes darkened, but he let the remark pass. "I shouldn't want to consider less than twenty-five hundred. Plus a share in the company, and the family name must, of course, be kept."

"Fifteen hundred pounds. The majority of shares belong to me and Captain Yancy, with all final decisions made by us. And the family name will certainly *not* be kept." Richard knew already too well the local reputation that went with the Stewart yards.

Jonas Stewart shook his head. How he hated the thought of signing over his father's business to this popinjay simply because he was quality and had money while better men had none. But the old man was dead now, and with fifteen hundred pounds free and clear he could start over, get into something he enjoyed. On the other hand, all he knew was this business and it was very satisfying to see his name on the big sign over the gate.

"I don't know. I'll have to think on it."

"Of course." Richard rose easily and picked up his velvety black beaver hat, sure that ultimately Stewart would accept his offer. What options did he have?

"Suppose I return in two weeks? Will that be sufficient time?"

Heaving his girth out of the chiar, Stewart shrugged, "All right. Let's say a fortnight. I'll have an answer then."

"I shall bring along the necessary papers in the hope that we shall need them. Until then, sir, good day."

"Good day, sir." And be damned to you, he thought, watching Richard move through the door. Sinking back into his chair, he stared glumly through the clouded window. Below him a two-man team worked listlessly over the pit saw. Nearby a single keel, stretched over the tracks between stem and stern posts, supported several widely spaced curved frames, resembling the rib cage of a decaying skeleton. Drying timbers were lying haphazardly everywhere. Hadn't he told the foreman to move them inside the storage shop? Did he have to see to everything himself? God! How he hated the thought of selling. The ghost of his father would be walking the earth, crying into the wind! But what choice was there? In two months another magistrate would be knocking at his door, and whom could he turn to then for help? There was nobody left. Fifteen hundred pounds was a fair price, though he never intended to let that fox Deveroe know it. And it was the only offer he had. Foolish not to take it—fifteen hundred, free and clear. . . .

While Richard was mounting his horse for the ride to the dock and a boat downriver, Hester sat in the front parlor of the house on Oyster Pasty Lane, searching desperately for words to keep a dispirited conversation going with her unexpected guest.

If Jaspar Carne was more silent than usual, it was because just as he entered the house he had encountered that dandy Lawrence Long going out the door. While Jaspar's interest in the widow Barnett was more calculated than genuine, he still did not like the idea of having Lawrence Long as competition. A widower himself, Long had money, poise and family connections. Of course, he was insipid and silly and never had a thought that rose above his rotund stomach, but some women liked that kind of thing. Searchingly Carne studied Hester's pale, taut face for some sign that she was one of them.

Hester herself did not know what to think of this taciturn

man who seemed to turn up just often enough to force her to make something of him. He was certainly not easy to engage in frivolous, witty or diverting conversation—or any conversation at all, for that matter.

"I hear there is a dread pestilence in Philadelphia," she said hopefully after exhausting several other topics.

"Yes, there is," Carne said dryly, balancing his cup on his knee and staring through her with those cold piercing eyes.

"The newspapers are full of the most ghastly details. Children left homeless, people dying alone in solitary rooms because no one, not even their relatives, will stay to nurse them. Parents shoved out on the walkways at the first sign of a headache. So dreadful!"

"The yellow fever is a contagious disease, madam—it spreads like wildfire."

"I am so frightfully afraid that it will reach New York, and then what should I do to protect my little ones?"

"Leave the city at once, as every sensible person has already left Philadelphia. It is not likely to spread here, however, as the greatest precautions are being taken. Stages are stopped outside the city and people are not allowed in until they have been quarantined for at least a month to make sure they have not brought the disease with them."

"I am told it is spread through the decaying vegetables left on the docks. It started, you know, with damaged coffee putrefying on one of the wharves. But I am taking all precautions that I can, even though so far it has not got out of Philadelphia. Look."

She leaned forward, drawing a narrow ribbon out of the bodice of her dress. Carne was appalled to find his eyes riveted on the ruffled neckline that curved tantalizingly over the cleavage between her swelling breasts.

Quickly he sat back, tearing his eyes away and fastening his gaze over her head.

"Look," Hester went on, preoccupied with the ribbon. "I wear this bag of camphor constantly. It is supposed to have superb powers against any kind of pestilence."

Carne glanced furtively at the satin bag swinging on the end of the ribbon. "I have also heard that coffee grounds between the toes . . ."

Hester looked up quizzically. "Really. That never occurred to me."

He nearly laughed. This absurd woman did not even know when she was being ridiculed.

"Truly, madam, I would suggest that if there is any sign of pestilence you move your family immediately into the pure air of the country. That is your best prevention, I feel sure."

Hester shoved the camphor bag back inside her bodice. "I suppose you are right and if the fever did come we could always go and stay with Celia and Richard in New Rochelle. But I don't look forward to such an arrangement, I tell you that."

Only the lifting of an eyebrow betrayed Carne's sudden interest. "Why, I should imagine your brother would be happy to welcome you in the event of such a calamity. It would be the mark of a Christian gentleman to do so."

"You would think so, Mr. Carne, for I'm sure that is what you are. But my brother..."

"Yes?"

"Well, you know how he is. However, he would not likely be there anyway, he is so busy these days with his elaborate plans for a shipyard."

Carne found himself leaning forward in his chair. "Oh, and is Mr. Deveroe expanding his interests, then?"

"He is *always* expanding his interests. All he thinks of is how to make more money, never how to enjoy it or let others enjoy it. Now it is some run-down yard on Hudson's River that he intends to buy so he can build his own boats, or some such foolishness. I wish he would turn some of his expertise toward helping his struggling relations."

Slowly Carne stirred his tea with a thin silver spoon. "There are several yards on the Hudson, most of them run-down. I know of one near Albany, for example—"

"No, no, this one was much closer to New York. Somewhere around the Croton River, I believe. However, they don't share their plans with me, you know, so I only know what I happened to overhear the last time I saw them. Anyway—" she pouted prettily, aware of her effect—"I shouldn't mind staying with Celia. She always makes one feel welcome."

He was going to get no more out of her on that subject, Carne thought, and said absently, "You seem obsessively fond of your sister-in-law."

There was a long moment of silence, and, looking up quickly, he saw that Hester had turned away, staring pensively out the window.

"I am fond of her," she finally answered. "Yes, very fond. We are like sisters. In fact, I suppose we *were* sisters before I went away."

"Oh. How was that?"

"Well, you see, when Celia was only a child she came to live with us. Mama called me into the parlor one day and said, 'here is your new sister.' And since I had only Richard and Henry for brothers and no sister at all, I was very happy to suddenly be given one."

Jaspar Carne saw through her in a glance. There was more here than he had thought. Mentally he filed it away.

Hester shrugged and assumed her bright vivacity. "But come, now, we are always talking of me and my family. Tell me about yourself, Mr. Carne. Celia tells me you now own the land where Wayside once stood. Do you have much property in the city, or is that not a question a woman should ask?"

Carne coughed discreetly. So he was not the only one who knew how to probe. "Why, as a matter of fact, I am the happy proprietor of nearly forty lots scattered among the various wards. Most, however, are in the outer ward, as that was, of course, the area opened for expansion after the war." He did not miss the glint that came into Hester's eyes. "You see, Mrs. Barnett, I believe strongly in the value of real estate. In a true democracy such as ours, land should be available for the many, never limited to the enjoyment of a few."

"Why, Mr. Carne, I do believe you are an anti-Federalist." Hester laughed, cocking her head prettily.

He knew she did not have the faintest notion of what that meant, but he smiled condescendingly. "Yes, madam. I am."

"Another reason you and my brother don't see eye to eye. Why, he thinks Mr. Hamilton practically placed the moon in the sky."

"The aristocrats and landed rich will always protect their own interests, but it is to the common man that this republic belongs. Their interests will prevail, mark my words."

"Now you have become *too* serious, Mr. Carne. Frankly, I can't abide politics, and that is all you men ever want to discuss. It is not half so interesting a subject as fashion, music or the latest performance at the theater."

Carne set down his cup and rose stiffly. This was all he could take of the woman, yet his visit had not been in vain. He had learned one or two things—things it might be wise to follow up.

"I regret to tell you, Mr. Deveroe, but I've decided not to sell."

Richard exchanged a long look with Elisha Yancy. He had suspected this since they first entered the room and faced a very different, self-assured Jonas Stewart. This man was a far cry from the cowed, near-desperate man he had talked with only a few weeks ago.

Stewart seemed uncomfortable with the long silence and rushed in. "The truth of the matter is, I've come into some more money. I've a friend who assures me I can get new loans at a reasonable rate of interest. Under the circumstances I would prefer to hold on to my father's business."

"You're fortunate in your choice of friends, Mr. Stewart," Richard said, a hint of acid in his voice.

"Don't you feel you'll be pouring good money after bad, Stewart?" Yancy added. "You haven't been able to make this yard pay for any number of years. Why get yourself deeper into debt when you could be free and clear?"

"I'll give you twenty-five hundred to buy you out," Richard said.

Both men gasped. Yancy barely managed to stifle an obscene oath.

"You and I both know this yard is not worth so much, Mr. Stewart," Richard went on levelly, "but I feel it might have a future and I'm willing to invest in that. Now, assuming you borrow from you new 'friend,' how much of it can you actually put into building up your property? Most of any capital you can scrape together will have to go to your creditors. Were I one I would insist that I received my share before I'd allow one new keel to be laid. Twenty-five hundred pounds, Mr. Stewart."

He could almost see the man lick his lips. The small eyes in Stewart's pudgy face darted back and forth between the two of them.

"Three thousand," he said quietly.

"Twenty-seven," Richard answered, avoiding Yancy's eyes.

"Twenty-nine. And you keep the family name."

"Twenty-eight, and the name will be changed."

"Done!"

Yancy turned away to look out the dirty window as Richard rose to lay the papers before Stewart. Quickly he went over them, pointing out the important points and writing in with a turkey-quill pen the altered numbers. His lean body did not relax perceptibly until Jonas Stewart scrawled his signature at the bottom.

"Good," Richard commented, signing his own name and handing the quill to Elisha.

"I suppose this calls for some kind of libation," Stewart said ungraciously. It turned out to be the strong, throat-searing whiskey which was commonly hauled in from the Alleghenies, and Richard had to fight back a cough. Elisha, he noticed, downed his in a single swallow. Once the drink was done they left quickly.

"That was a close call," Richard said as they walked toward the dock. He didn't like his partner's uncharacteristic silence.

"I don't understand why you went so high. Mind, now, it's your business—I have no strong feelings one way or the other. But you must want this broken-down yard pretty badly to invest so much more in it than it's worth."

"I do want it badly. Perhaps because I had already settled my mind on having it, but also because I am convinced it will be worth the money someday. There is going to be a growing demand for sloops and schooners, you know. Packet boats are the future as much as market transports. At least this way we can meet the opportunities when they come."

"I'll not argue that, and certainly I've come to trust yer judgement. But twenty-eight hundred pounds! God Almighty, that'd buy the whole British Navy!"

With a sigh of relief Richard smiled at him. "Not quite."

On his way home Richard stopped in New York to confront Hester with the unpleasant problems created by her extravagant spending.

"Eight hundred pounds! How could you possibly have run up such a debt? What did you do? What did you buy?"

"I'm very frugal, Richard—"

"Frugal! I give you an allowance any widowed sister would be happy to live on. I think it unconscionable of you, Hester, to incur such bills over and above what you already have."

"You don't know *what* it takes to live in this town! How could you, stuck out in the provinces? I must keep up appearances. I must entertain."

"I understand that. But you are not living in London now. Appearances and entertainment are both managed here on a far less lavish scale. You have to learn to do it, Hester, or I promise you, I'll cut your allowance."

Her eyes narrowed. "How dare you! You would threaten me with poverty merely because I overspent a little in one month."

"Five months running. Scents, drapes, milliners, mantilla makers, wines—my God, where does it end! Celia doesn't spend half this much on our entire household in ten months' time!"

That brought a flush to Hester's pale complexion. "Why should she, with you off most of the time buying shipyards and factories? I have to cultivate friends here, especially gentlemen friends if I hope to remarry—as you have so indelicately insisted that I do."

Richard struggled with his temper. "If I am not at home it is because I am out working to protect my family's interests, yours as well as Celia's and mine."

"Oh, yes, it's just as Mr. Carne said, the landed rich will always protect their own interests. What about *my* interest!"

Richard shot forward in his chair. "Carne? Jaspar Carne?"

"As a matter of fact, yes. He calls now and then. He's been very attentive to me. A true friend."

There was a long silence while Richard's mind went leaping ahead. "You saw him recently?" he asked.

"A few weeks ago."

"Did you by chance mention to Carne that I was buying a shipyard?"

"How should I remember that? I just make conversation and seldom bother to remember what it is about."

She glanced up and a shock went through her. All Richard's self-containment was gone, submerged in a black fury she hadn't seen for years.

"You will not see that man again," he said icily. "Ever!"

Hester sat back, stunned. "I beg your pardon."

"You will not receive that man into this house again. And never, *never*, do you understand, will you ever speak to him of anything that has to do with my business dealings. If you do, Hester, I promise you—"

This was too much.

"Richard Deveroe, you may be my brother and I may be dependent on you, but you will *not* order me about like a willful child. You have no right to tell me whom I can receive and whom I can't. As long as I live in this house, even if it is by your leave, I will receive whom I damned well please!"

Deliberately Richard made his voice calm.

"Let me try to put it a better way. Jaspar Carne has tried in several ways to frustrate every effort I've made to expand my business. So far I have been able to circumvent him. But he is dangerous, and I do not wish to give him any leverage over me that can possibly be avoided."

"Celia said you hated each other, but I declare I can't understand why."

"He dislikes me because once long ago I humiliated him, because he is convinced that I was secretly a Loyalist during the war, because I am part of the Deveroe family of landed gentry which the republic swept away, and because Ewan hanged a young kinsman of his once in cold blood. He is my enemy, Hester, and you would do me a favor by considering him yours as well."

Hester resumed her seat, tossing her silver-blond curls. "Nonsense. He has shown me more understanding than anyone I have met so far in this standoffish town. I don't see why I should have to consider him a rascal simply because you cannot get along with him."

"You are as much a Deveroe as I. I am suspicious of his interest in you."

She looked quickly up at him, her eyes narrowing. "How you do flatter me, Richard."

"I mean you no discredit, but Carne is a shrewd, calculating man."

She shrugged. "Oh, all right. I'll watch my tongue. But I will not turn him away from the door." She thought of Jaspar Carne's stiff figure balanced on a chair in her parlor. "He's not really very good company anyway. I don't know why we should have a falling out over such a disagreeable person."

Richard breathed a little easier. "Exactly. Now let's get back to these bills."

twenty-seven

"I'm tired, Dexter. I want to go home."

Christabel Barnett, as if to reinforce her words, pulled her skirts around her and plopped her small body on the first resting place that came to hand—the edge of a stone watering trough. With a quick, angry gesture her brother reached out and pinched her arm, only to see his cap fall into the green slime in the trough.

"Ow!"

"Get up, you little brat. You're always tired. All you've done is whine since we left the house."

Josh watched miserably as Dexter jerked Christy to her feet and as fat tears began to roll down her cheeks.

"I'll tell Mama," she cried, angrily snuffing back the tears.

"Go ahead and tell her. I don't care. It's bad enough that I have to play nanny to the whole bunch of you and drag you around wherever I want to go. I'll be damned if I'll let you ruin my free time."

Hannah put her arm around the child's shoulders protectively. "You needn't be so nasty," she said, glaring at Dexter. "We didn't want to come. Your mama made us. We don't want to be with you any more than you want to be with us."

Wiping the dirty water off his cap, Dexter rubbed at it furiously with his arm. "She always makes you come. I can't go anywhere or do anything without a bunch of snot-nosed brats tagging along behind me. No other fifteen-year-old boy has to put up with this. It isn't fair!"

"Tell *her* that," Hannah grumbled, straightening Christy's dress.

"Don't think I haven't, but she never listens to me."

"I'm tired, Hannah," Christy murmured into the older girl's skirts. "My feet hurt. I want to go home."

"Hush. Come on, I'll carry you a little way. Here, Agatha, take my reticule."

Agatha, the silent one, took her friend's purse and fell into step behind them as they followed Dexter's retreating form down the street. Though she was thirteen now, Hannah was too small to carry a nine-year-old far, and in half a block's time she was gasping for breath and had to set Christy back on her feet. When Dexter finally turned around from the distance of two houses away, he saw them grouped on the walkway again. Christy sitting on the bricks in a heap and Agatha, Josh and Hannah sullenly standing around her.

"Not again! Come on, you little heathens, or I promise I'll go off and leave you here alone!"

"You can't, Dexter. We don't even know where we are. Aunt Hester will box your ears!"

Josh looked warily around him, realizing suddenly just how true Hannah's words were. This was a part of the city he had never seen before, rows of narrow, squalid houses and garbage-cluttered alleys and rookeries. Far down at the end were several boxlike buildings that looked like the warehouses near Coenties Slip. With a quick stir of excitement he spotted a familiar sight—the narrow pencil-shaped spars of several ships lying in the harbor, just visible through the curve of the street. If they were near the East River they could not be too badly lost. But his feet hurt as much as Christy's and his legs were just as tired. He too wished that Dexter would turn back, though he would die before saying so.

Impatiently, Dexter Barnett stalked back to the children clustered on the walk.

"Why won't you let us rest?" Agatha said plaintively. "Just a few minutes."

Fighting back his fury, he sank down beside them. "Oh, all right. But it had better only be a few minutes. You can rest longer at the wharf at the end of the street."

"Why are we going there, Dexter?" Josh asked, crossing his legs and sitting on the cold bricks.

"Because I want to. It's interesting. There are all kinds of things to see down there that you never see around our house. If you behave yourselves, maybe I'll buy you a pasty."

"It looks grubby and dirty to me,' said Hannah, wrinkling her nose. "And it doesn't look a bit safe. I bet Mama wouldn't like you to bring us here."

"Mama, Mama! That's all you ever say. There's never any

fun to be had with such prim little sissies. I'd like to see any
of my friends have to drag such a parcel of ninnies around.
It's disgusting!"

"I'm not a sissy," Josh said belligerently and quickly darted
out of the range of his cousin's fingers. He wondered why his
mama, usually so understanding, was so blind about sending
her children off with this unpleasant cousin. How he wished
that he and Hannah were back in New Rochelle, exploring the
beaches of Myer's Point for shells and arrowheads.

Dexter looked toward the end of the street just in time to
spot two boys nearly his age crossing the tiny open space where
the road curved. "That's enough rest," he cried, pulling his
sisters to their feet. "Come on. I'm going to have some fun
out of this if it's the last thing I do."

With a growing feeling of unease Josh looked around him.
He did not know what there was about this place, but something
made him feel sure they shouldn't be here. He had visited the
docks often enough with his father and Captain Elisha, but
never had he been to such a sinister area. Even Hannah and
the girls seemed to feel it and huddled closer to him, with eyes
that flitted back and forth between the rows of dirty, decaying
houses and the rotting debris that littered the wooden dock. Off
to one side Dexter stood talking with two other boys as big as
he was. One of them eyed the small huddled group of children
with disdain.

"Why'd you bring along the nursery, for God's sake?"

"Had to. Mama made me. They won't get in the way."

"Mama's boy!"

"Come on," Dexter answered nevrously. "I got the money,
didn't I? I'll see they keep out of the way."

Below where Josh stood the stagnant water trapped in a log
enclosure gave off odors that reminded him of the necessary
house in back of his home. Wrinkling his nose, he moved away
from the edge of the pier and sat down on a barrel near a huge
beehive of coiled rope.

"Hannah, I don't like it here," Christy moaned. "Can't we
go home?"

"Hush," Hannah answered, looking around for Josh. "We'll
have to wait for Dexter. We can't go back by ourselves. Just
be quiet, now, and you and Agatha stay near me."

"Is that the place?" Dexter motioned to a grubby doorway
across the street below a rusty sign. The picture was barely

discernible but underneath it the letters TAVERN were plain enough. Just beyond its darkened entrance a man slumped in a stupor, half in, half out of the gutter.

"Yes. They'll serve you all the grog you want as long as you can pay. Come on, we'll show you."

"And is the girl—that Jenny—is she there?"

"Oh, she's there all right."

Dexter hesitated. "Do you think she will like me?"

"Listen, like I say, if you have the brass she don't care what you grab. Come on, now."

Dexter was almost licking his lips as he started to follow the boys into the darkened doorway. Abruptly he turned back. "Now, listen, you brats. Don't you move from this spot or I'll pinch you black and blue and box your ears with it!"

"But, Dexter, it's not nice here," Agatha said.

"It's nice enough. All you have to do is not move till I come out, and mind your own business."

"You hurry, then!" Hannah called angrily after him. She was near tears herself. There were only a few people on the dock, but the ships anchored nearby had men working on them who eyed her in a way that made her uncomfortable, and the houses lining the streets had a constant flow of people in and out. Too many looked over their little group with more than casual interest.

They sat for nearly ten minutes before a gang of street boys approached, looking very tough. For a long time they only stood watching them with darting, shifting eyes and grins on their lean faces, but as the girls' nervousness grew they became bolder and finally grouped around them. One, a fat boy in clothes that looked two sizes too small, reached out a swift hand and grabbed Hannah's reticule.

"You give that back," Josh cried, lunging for the purse. His arm was roughly brushed aside.

"Let's have a look." The boy laughed, upending the bag. "Yoicks, there's not a bob here. Nothin' but fluff. Girl's fluff."

"Come on, then, give us your brass," another smaller boy said, sticking his face into Hannah's. She shrank back.

"We don't have any money. Honest. Dexter has it all, and he's in there."

"You're a pretty one," the boy said, grinning, and, reaching out, pulled a strand of her straight yellow hair.

"Leave her alone, you bully," said Josh, amazed at his own

words. He knew these boys were rowdies and toughs, and they frightened him a little. But his hackles rose at the thought of letting them push him around. Besides, who else was there to protect the girls?

"Hey, look at the little gentleman in his fancy suit," the fat boy said, and, reaching swiftly out, he gripped Josh's collar, twisting it against his neck. With one motion he lifted the lighter boy off the ground, dangling him by the throat. Coughing and sputtering, Josh swung his arms vainly through the air.

"Put him down!" Hannah cried indignantly, grabbing at the bully's arm. Behind her Agatha stood white-faced while Christy clung to her sister's skirts and set up a loud wailing.

With his free arm swinging, the fat boy knocked Hannah reeling and dropped Josh in a heap on the dock, then stood over him laughing. To his surprise both Josh and Hannah rose up as one and tore into him, fists pummeling.

"Two against one ain't fair," said a spindly companion, rushing in to grab Hannah around the waist and pull her away.

"Let me go, let me go!" she screamed, while at her feet Josh and the heavier boy went down on the dock, rolling and punching.

"Stop it," Hannah screamed. "You'll kill him!" Josh was giving it the best he had, but the other boy had two inches and several pounds advantage over him. People were running up around them now, but most were standing there laughing and urging them on. A third boy stood on the edge waiting for his chance to plow in at the first sign the leader was wearing down.

Then suddenly a hulk of a man in a cap and a blue master's coat pushed through the crowd to stand over the fighting boys. One huge hand reached out and grabbed the shirt of the fat boy and threw him off to one side.

"What's this all about? Carrying on like the hoodlums you are from the Dublin stews. My God, Josh Deveroe!"

Pulling himself up, Josh looked up into the startled eyes of Captain Yancy. His body sagged in relief at the sight of the familiar face and he had to fight to keep back the tears.

"What in God's name are ye doing down here fightin' with these . . ."

Josh rubbed at his chin. His jacket was torn and covered with the filth of the dock floor—the evil-smelling gunk was even in his hair. But he didn't answer.

Elisha looked around him. The boys from the dock area had

slipped off into the crowd, which, now the fun was over, was drifting away. He lifted Josh to his feet, noticing the bruises swelling on one side of his face.

"I'm ashamed of ye. If your mother knew . . ." Then, seeing the girls standing to one side, his voice grew more gentle. "Are you hurt?"

"No, I don't think so."

"What about you, Hannah? All right?"

Breathless, pale and fighting to keep back a suffocating cough, Hannah managed to murmur, "I'm all right, thank you, Captain Yancy."

Brushing the flaked debris of rotting vegetables from Josh's back, Yancy felt the boy's slight body for any sign of battered bones. Apart from his clothes and the bruise on his cheek he seemed little the worse for his experience. "What are you children doing down here?" he added quietly. "Surely ye didn't come alone?"

None of them answered, but he noticed Hannah's eyes fly to the tavern across the street.

"I'll just have a look in there," he said. "You brush yourself off and stay right here till I get back."

In a matter of minutes he emerged from the grog shop half dragging an indignant Dexter Barnett by the collar. Once across the street, he nearly threw him against the pier.

"Listen to me, young man. I'm only going to say this once. In a half an hour I will appear on your doorstep. I'll take these children with me in a hackney cab, but you will walk back. If you are not in your house by the time I arrive, I will immediately sit down and tell the whole sorry story of this morning's escapade."

"Half an hour! That's not enough time to walk back!"

"Then run the whole way, but you'd better get there fast. If you are there, I'll say nothing. But I warn you, if you ever bring these little ones back into such a place as this again, I'll break every bone in your body."

Dexter thought fast. What if Uncle Richard learned what he'd done and furiously refused to send him to college? Then, too, there was his mother. If she thought he had made his uncle angry at both of them, it would be his head on a platter. Without answering, he grabbed up his hat and tore off down the street. Elisha watched him contemptuously.

"Come along, children. I don't know how we're going to

explain the state ye're in, Josh, to your mother, but we'll think of something."

"I'll tell her I got in a fight with some bullies who tried to steal Hannah's reticule."

"That would be all right as long as she don't ask you where. We may have to do a little prevaricating, but I guess the Lord will forgive us this once." Lifting Christy with one arm, Elisha felt a soft hand slip inside his other. He looked down to see Agatha shyly glancing up at him. What a sweet little face, he thought, and tightened his hand over hers. He was rewarded with a timid smile.

With the children clinging closely around him he set off to hail a cab back to Oyster Pasty Lane.

By the time Celia got back to New Rochelle four days later Josh was already complaining of a headache and looking flushed and feverish. With a cold knot of fear congealing deep inside her chest she put him to bed and watched him anxiously, expecting to see one of the usual summer ailments that ran their course in a week. By the end of the second day, he was so sick she sent Vestal tearing to West Chester village to bring Dr. Sayre, while she sat fighting down her panic and dipping cold cloths to lay on his burning forehead.

The look on Sayre's face five minutes after he walked into the child's room confirmed her worst fears.

"It's the bilious, remitting fever. I'm sure of it."

Fighting for calm, Celia managed to mutter, "What can I do?"

"I wish I knew," Sayre answered. "Oh, there are a few things we can try, but I don't know how much they will help. First, let's get these blankets soaked in warm vinegar and wrap them around him."

"I'll call Betsy," Celia said, darting to the door. Sayre went on, talking almost as much to himself as to her. "In Philadelphia, during the plague, Dr. Rush used a combination of blood-letting and purgatives. However, I think he killed as many as he cured and I'm not sure we should use such stringent remedies on a child. Let's try the vinegar first and if that doesn't help, well, then, I'll see."

Staring at her feverish son lying so small and vulnerable on the bed Celia could not answer. Josh's eyes when he opened them were two coals in his white face. All the details she had

heard of the epidemic in Philadelphia that terrible summer of
'93 came rushing back. So many children had died. She winced
as Sayre laid a lancet and a cup on the linen coverlet.

"How did he pick this up?" Sayre asked, turning to her.
"Have you been out of the village recently?"

"We just arrived back from New York town last week."

Sayre shook his head sadly. "Oh, my dear Celia. Didn't
you know the yellow fever has spread to the city in spite of
everything they could do to prevent it? And to other cities as
well. You should have been more careful."

"But that was three years ago!"

"Yes, but it has never really gone away and has slowly
reached its tentacles up and down the coast. Every summer we
dread the thought of facing the terror Philadelphia suffered
when it began there. I suggest you send for Richard and keep
this room closed off. It is a highly contagious fever, you know.
In fact, you would do well to stay away yourself and let Betsy
care for the boy."

Celia grabbed at Josh's hot hand. "Never! If he should die,
I won't care if I live or not. No one else is going to care for
him!"

The next few days were like living in a black void for the
anxious parents of Joshua Deveroe. Hovering over him, watching for any variation in the inflamed eyes, the dusky, suffused
face, the pounding head, they watched for any sign that he
might be slipping into the dreaded coma that preceded death.
To Dr. Sayre's cautious remedies Betsy added a few of her
own, and the house reeked of burning tobacco, garlic and tarred
rope, all, she was convinced, powerful preventives of the
spread of the disease.

Celia found that she could not even pray, so numb was her
every feeling. In the back of her mind she kept saying that
surely God would not take her precious child from her when
he had given her only the one, and the one so beloved. Yet
some throbbing practical voice of reality kept clamoring at her
mind reminding her that fevers were dreadfully impersonal and
carried away young and old alike without thought to life's grand
design. Somehow to pray so hard that God would spare this
one child seemed irrational and selfish, even though she asked
it with all the strength within her.

For six days and nights she barely left her son's bedside,
trying to hold on to Sayre's reassurances that he was a strong,
healthy little boy who had seldom been ill, and keeping up her

constant flow of silent numb prayers. On the morning of the sixth day she was aware of a subtle change. His skin felt cool to her touch and his body broke out in a soaking perspiration. For the first time in days his sleep was quiet, more like normal repose. Celia and Richard looked through their utter weariness at each other and for a moment dared to let loose the all-consuming fear which had enveloped them since the fever struck.

After an hour, when Sayre stopped in, he confirmed their feeble hopes. "He's out of the woods. He'll be weak for a time, but he should recover now. Thank a merciful heaven."

Celia could not have felt more relieved if she herself had received a reprieve from death. With a lightness of heart she went downstairs to find Hannah, who had been for almost a week kept as far away from her sick foster brother as possible. Now it was time to comfort and reassure her daughter, who surely had been neglected while the household revolved around a desperately ill son.

She found the girl lying on a bench in a shady section of the garden. A half-completed drawing of Hannah's kitten lay on the grass next to her feet alongside a set of scattered pastels. At first Celia thought she was sleeping.

"Hannah, dear. I have such good news," Celia said, taking her in her arms. Tall and rangy at thirteen, Hannah's small head fell as naturally into the curve of Celia's neck as it had when she was a toddler.

"Oh, Mama. My head hurts so dreadfully."

So it was not over. One look at the girl's flushed face and Celia's short-lived relief fled, replaced once again by the terrible anxiety, the cold knife thrust of fear in her chest.

She put her to bed right away and once again started the round of warm vinegar and diuretics that had helped bring Josh through. By the afternoon Hannah's fever had soared and Richard had taken to his bed with the same complaints. The next day Betsy's youngest, George Washington, came down with it. Life began to seem unreal, a walking void, as Celia forced her body to stay busy in order to keep from thinking, from feeling.

She kept vigil beside Hannah's bedside as she had by Josh's. Richard's manservant, Thorpe, a quiet, unassuming little man who for two years had been a faithful valet, took over as much of his care as possible. Betsy gave her whole anxious attention to her youngest, and the cook from the village was set to watching over Josh's convalescence.

Somehow Celia sensed from the beginning that Hannah's illness was going to be different. Her frail body seemed to have no resources to fight back, and the fever consumed her like a flame. She said little, but when she opened her eyes, red as coals in a face as white as the pillow on which it lay, she seemed to always look for Celia. Tightening her grip on the small burning hand, Celia would lean over her, wipe her brow with a vinegar-soaked cloth and reassure her she was there. By the second day the eyes no longer opened, and quietly and peacefully Hannah slipped into a coma. Sayre knew then that it was over, but Celia refused to believe it. Moving numbly through a gray world, she would leave the child's bed only long enough to look in on Richard and Josh, then return to sit holding the inert little hand that since that first day in the dilapidated cottage on the beach had clung so tightly to her own.

By the evening of the third day Hannah's frail spirit slid gently away, as quietly and easily as the tide which outside her window was drifting toward a different shore.

Celia lit two candles beside her bed and covered her thin body, now turned a dark yellow in death, with a clean cloth, trying to do in simple actions what she could not bring herself to face within. She could not cry. Something dead lay inside her own chest and she could not give in to it or wrench it out because there was still too much care needed for her husband. Somehow she kept going, transferring her bedside vigil to Richard's room. She heard the wailing from the cottage at the rear of the garden the next morning which told her Betsy's youngest had followed Hannah, and she was told later that both Vestal and another one of his children had come down with the fever. Someone—later she found it had been Rosalind Wister—made the funeral arrangements for the two children to be buried, Hannah in the small churchyard of Trinity Church and George Washington she was never quite sure where. There was a Negro cemetery in New York, but New Rochelle?

Though Richard was hot and at times delirious, he never seemed in danger of succumbing to the fever. As ill as he was, she sensed he would come through, and, like Josh, after the sixth day of his illness he turned toward recovery. By then it had been almost three weeks since Josh had first become sick. Richard, Vestal and his oldest son were recovering, Josh was almost back to his former exuberance. Only then could Celia allow herself to rest; only then would she allow herself to feel, to weep.

And the tears, when they came, threatened to carry her away on such waves of grief as she had never experienced, not even when Ewan sailed away leaving her broken and miserable on the Whitehall dock. She had never known such pain before, such bone-wrenching, blood-draining, body-twisting, spirit-crunching agony. She walked the paths of the garden like a dazed person and came upon the dampened half-scrawled drawing Hannah had dropped there two weeks before; the searing pain of that moment came near to driving the very life out of her body.

Richard tried to comfort her as much as he was able with what little strength he had. Somehow she kept going, somehow she got through the worst early days. When the danger of infection seemed past, her friend Rosalind Wister was there to help her, and it was she who wisely packed up everything of Hannah's and either gave it away or put it where Celia would not be likely to stumble over it.

By the end of the summer a letter came from Hester in the city describing the particular hell they had been suffering while Celia's household lay ill:

> . . . the fever has taken the wind and has spread through town like a forest blaze. You would not believe the changes that have come over the city. There are bonfires on every corner, incessant musket and gunfire all day. Bells toll so constantly for the dead that finally the town fathers stopped them ringing altogether. Men, women and children go about smoking segars which is supposed to keep the fever away. No one in his right mind will touch the dead so the streets are filled with carts carrying the poor corpses, driven by a single negro. So far, at least, we have not had the ill carried out to the common as they did in Philadelphia, but that is all we have missed. There is not a street in New York but has had several homes touched by the plague. My own house reeks of the smell of gunpowder, burned tobacco, miter and sprinkled vinegar. Daily we pray for rain and an end to this insufferable heat which will bring us relief from the contagion.

"Does she say how her own children fared?" Richard asked, propped on his pillows with his face as sallow as the yellow wallpaper beside his bed.

"She says Agatha was dreadfully ill and came near to dying. Christy was nearly as bad, while she and Dexter escaped altogether. She was fortunate," Celia said, the tears welling up in her eyes.

He reached for her hand. "Yes, she was. Many children have been left orphans and certainly many parents have only their grief for comfort."

"Grief is no comfort," Celia said bitterly, seeing Hannah's thin quiet face. "Sometimes I don't think I can bear it."

"Find your comfort in Josh," he said with tenderness. "And in me."

She slid her arms around his neck and laid her head against his chest, hearing the pulsing of his heart through the fine linen night rail. "Oh, I do, Richard. I do. I thank God with every breath that you and Joshua came through alive. But she was so frail and she had depended on me for so long. I keep remembering that little hand in mine!"

He did not have the strength to do more than lay his arms comfortingly around her shoulders and let her cry. He could not admit even to himself how profoundly relieved he was that if God had to take one of his children, it was the maverick Hannah and not his trueborn son, Josh. The soft-spoken, fragile girl had always turned all her love on Celia, sharing with her a special empathy she had never offered him. Though he was truly sorry she had died, especially since it caused Celia so much pain, he knew in his heart that had it been Josh he would not have wanted to go on living himself. God forgive him, but that was the way it was.

It was a long, slow, difficult six weeks before Richard was up and about. By that time the October frosts had broken the long heat and diminished the ferocity of the plague. New York was safe to visit, and after repeated hysterical notes from Hester he finally felt he had regained enough inner fiber to go and see her, although he almost would have preferred another case of the yellow fever.

Hester had been badly shaken. There was a time when she thought she was going to lose both her younger daughters, and the fact that, looking around, there was no one to turn to for strength or support had brought home to her what a shaky foundation it was to have do depend solely on yourself. Dexter had been a terrible disappointment, being terrified of catching the contagion himself. It was as much as she could do to force him out into the streets to fetch a doctor or to call at the apothecary's. She was more convinced than ever that her only hope of attracting a substantial husband was to have a suitably impressive dowry, and when Richard finally walked into her parlor she went at him with a desperate fury.

It was the worst possible way to handle him. He missed the desperation completely and heard only the fury, which acted on him like a match to tinder. He was as stubbornly determined as ever not to give in to her manipulating ways. He hated these scenes, and when he finally stalked out of the house, leaving his sister in noisy tears to slam the door behind him, he felt as though his convalescence had slipped back three weeks in time.

Hester threw herself on her couch and sobbed without caring who heard. Her brother was never going to give up any of his precious money to help her get on in the world. She would always be dependent, always be poor, always be alone!

Through her loud tears she finally heard the osft voice of her servant bending over her.

"Excuse me, ma'am, but there is a Mr. Carne to see you."

"What? Who?" Sitting up, Hester dabbed at her burning, swollen eyes. "Jaspar Carne. Oh, good God. I can't see him now. I'm much too upset. Tell him I'm ill or something. Anything. Just get him to go away."

"Very well, ma'am."

The girl was nearly through the door when Hester stopped her. What was she doing? Well-to-do suitors were not that easy to come by, even unpleasant ones like Mr. Carne.

"Wait, Lucy," she called, rising to straighten her dress. "Never mind about that. I'll see him. Show him in—but give me a minute to make myself presentable."

Running to the mirror, she was appalled—her whole face looked bloated. Not the best of impressions to make on an available man. Hurriedly she splashed a little jasmine water on her handkerchief and dabbed at her eyes, smoothing back her hair and twisting one bright curl over her ear.

When Jaspar Carne walked into the room, his familiar, angular, black-clad figure as unprepossessing as ever, Hester almost regretted her impulsive gesture. But here he was. She might as well make the best of it.

"Mr. Carne," she said, extending her hand with a practiced graciousness, and fighting back a sob that rose spontaneously in her throat.

"Why, madam," Carne said, raising her hand to his lips and looking genuinely concerned. "Are you ill? Have I come at a bad time?"

"No, no." Hester waved him to the sofa. "I am very pleased that you did come. I was just feeling the want of some— pleasant company."

"Are your children well? Forgive me, Mrs. Barnett, I do not mean to pry, but it is obvious you have been in some distress. I could come back tomorrow."

"Please, please stay." Hester found herself meaning every word. "You are very perceptive, my dear Mr. Carne, for the truth is I was a trifle upset just before you arrived. But I am quite all right now. I would so much rather have a pleasant conversation with you than lie here weeping for myself."

"I admire your courage, madam. Self-pity is so defeating, I have always felt. But I do hope that whatever has brought you to it is not of a serious nature. One misses your customary brightness." Some deep chord of unaccustomed sympathy had been touched inside Jaspar Carne by the sight of the dainty Hester in tears. She was always so much the woman in control. Suddenly she seemed vulnerable, small and delicate. It was not unattractive.

"As you might suppose, it is my selfish brother once again who has brought me so low," Hester said, dabbing at her eyes, suddenly anxious to share her misery. "How long I shall have to endure his grudging charity I simply don't know. I shall probably die of it before he relents."

Jaspar's ears picked up. For once it had not occurred to him that Richard Deveroe was the source of Hester's grief. With all the fever the city had seen during the past two months he had supposed the plague had cut down one of her children. With a tinge of excitement he realized that Hester was so upset at her brother that she was not likely to remember discretion. He decided to be his most sympathetic.

"Your brother. Yes, I remember well how he has misused you in the past. So he is still up to his old tricks?"

"Even more so! He treats me as though I am a poor relation when the truth is I am as entitled to a portion of the family fortune as he is. Why won't he see it!"

Carne could tell at once that Hester had no idea how much of Richard's fortune he had built up by himself. But he was not about to enlighten her.

"Esau's birthright," he mumbled, lowering his chin into his cravat.

"What? What?"

"Oh, I was only remarking upon the similarity of your situation to the Biblical story of Jacob, who cheated his poor brother, Esau, out of his birthright. Naturally, I can understand perfectly how deprived you must feel."

Hester's eyes darkened. "Oh, Mr. Carne. A man of your sensibilities and knowledge is such a comfort to a poor defenseless woman like myself. I *do* feel cheated—I do indeed. You put your finger directly on it."

"Of course you must," he said warming to his subject. "To have your own brother deny you your rights is bad enough, but your sister as well!"

"She's *not* my sister!" Hester cried, allowing her old resentment free rein. "She was dragged in, a dirty child from the gutter without a copper to her name. Mama simply called me in one day and announced, 'Here is your new sister'—as though that could make such an urchin a member of my family!"

"My dear lady, you have indeed been cheated. I had no idea."

"And now she lives in all the comfort which was mine by right of birth while I—I must struggle and plead and beg to keep my poor children from starving. The injustice of it! The wrong!"

"Dreadfully unjust."

"Cruel."

"Iniquitous."

In a sudden burst of feeling Hester flew to the sofa and took Carne's hand. He sat back in surprise, but did not pull it away.

"Dear Mr. Carne, tell me what to do? How shall I manage? How can I retrieve my rightful portion?"

"Well, I—I'll help you. Yes, let me help you. I'll make your cause my own. Together we can bring your proud brother to account, I'm sure of it."

"You will? You'll do that for me?"

From his first surprise Jaspar Carne recovered quickly, catching some of the excitement of a sanctioned crusade against Richard Deveroe. "It will be my greatest satisfaction."

"Together?" Hester added cautiously.

"Yes, yes. Together."

"Do you mean you would willingly take on the burden of

a poor widow, be a father to her pitifully orphaned children, share your hearth and home with my destitute family?" Without waiting for an answer from her startled guest, Hester went on. "Oh, Mr. Carne. You are truly a Christian gentleman!"

Some glimmer of anxiety began to work its way into Carne's consciousness. Good heavens, what did this silly woman think he was proposing? What had he said? His mind raced back over his words.

Then Hester took both his hands and sat back, once more in control. "I accept your offer, Mr. Carne."

"Offer?" What offer? The words strangled in his throat.

Hester turned her provocative blue eyes full on him. Some instinct told her that although she had backed this eligible gentleman into a corner, he was a man who was susceptible to reason, never emotion, and it would add the right touch now to present her case in that light.

"I know that I am not a young woman, Mr. Carne, but I fancy I am not yet unattractive. I know how to run an orderly household and I am an entertaining hostess. I can keep my children from burdening you and I can assure you a comfortable home. I can bring you a good name and I have excellent health. Perhaps, with your help, I may even be able to obtain for you a portion of my father's estate. Not such a bad bargain, is it?"

He stared at her without comprehending much of what she had said until she mentioned her father's estate, and that sank in quickly. When you came to think about it, what a prize that would be. It was what he most wanted. Searching her face, he saw her almost for the first time. She was a handsome woman, that was true. And although she had a parcel of children, yet he had seen the way she kept them under her tiny thumb. She was headstrong, yes, but he sensed that she was capable too. And in the last analysis, he was impressed by the cool rationality behind her words.

But marriage! Jaspar Carne was nearly forty and he had managed very well without a wife. Somewhere in the back of his mind he had assumed that one day he would marry, but it was sure to be a woman with substantial assets. Hester Barnett had none.

Yet, she *was* a Deveroe. If he stalked out now, would he ever again be given such a glorious opportunity to bring about the ruin of Richard Deveroe and his little kingdom? Hester's brother would be livid at the thought of his sister marrying Jaspar Carne—not an unsatisfying thought.

He sat there with all these arguments flashing through his mind, realizing that he had better say something soon. Already he could detect the beginnings of distress in Hester's face. In a rare, impulsive acceptance of fate, he gave her hand a warm squeeze.

"Madam, you have made me the happiest man in New York."

He could almost see the weight lift from Hester's body. She smiled at him, a strange, enigmatic little grimace.

"Why, thank you, Mr. Carne. I am indeed honored and . . . and happy too." She knew she had trapped him into this, yet she knew also he was not the man to accept manipulation. He had come very close to leaving her sitting alone on the sofa, and the fact that he hadn't meant he had weighed all the options and accepted her. She felt a moderate sense of triumph. No, not triumph. They had struck a cold and calculating bargain between them. He was giving her security and she would be bringing him the Deveroe prestige—a prestige she fancied meant more to Jaspar Carne than he himself realized.

Ah, well. It was worth it. Even the best of marriages were often built on less.

"And now, let's discuss when the banns should be published," Hester said, patting his hand.

Playing her intuition, Hester did not write Richard and Celia about her marriage plans until the banns had already been cried twice. Although in her letter she asked Richard to stand up with her at the ceremony, she felt sure he would refuse and went ahead with plans to have her second son beside her. If she could have been an observer in the east parlor of the house in New Rochelle when Richard read her letter she would have complimented herself on her good judgment.

"Of all the ungrateful, selfish, treacherous things to do!" Richard raged, tearing the letter in pieces and throwing it into the empty grate. "After all I've done for her and her parcel of children, to use me in such a way!"

Celia could not remember the last time she had seen her husband give way to such unreasoning rage. "I certainly don't like the man," she said in her level voice, "but remember, you *were* anxious to have Hester married."

"To a man who hates me? Who for years has used every device to stop me from getting ahead and for no other reason than an old grudge against my family? I tell you here and now, he is only using Hester to get at me."

"Come, now, Richard. That is certainly not very flattering to Hester. Perhaps he cares for her."

"A man like Jaspar Carne knows exactly what Hester is. Besides, I don't think he has ever cared for another human being in his life. He's too crafty and too self-righteous. I tell you, no good will come of this—especially for us. Nothing!"

"Shall we go to the wedding?" she asked hesitantly.

"Never!" He paused, catching sight of his white face in the mirror over the mantel. Making an effort to get control of his temper, he hammered the wood lightly with his fist and lowered his voice. "You might as well send her a gift. A nice one. And I'll make her some kind of settlement. But I will not watch her give herself to that sneaking bastard who has made no secret of what he thinks of me."

"A settlement is very generous of you, Richard."

"It is as much as I will do for her ever again. She's made her bed, now let her lie in it. And a cold one it will be, I have no doubt."

He turned and stalked from the room, never seeing the long look she gave him.

Part IV
Southernwood
1805

twenty-eight

In the elegant bedroom of her New York house Celia stood looking at herself in the long framed mirror, smoothing down the glossy silk fabric of her dress. Her lips lifted in a smile as she remembered how fashions had swung nearly a 180-degree angle in the past twenty years, from farthingales and hoops, high headdresses and powder to the figure-clinging diaphanous creation she was so admiring. From a high waist below a very low-cut wisp of breast-emphasizing bodice, her pale-pink skirt fell in narrow graceful folds that clung to her hips and legs. She ran her finger around the provocative curls that framed both sides of her face below the high knot on the top of her head, where tucked between the wisps of curls lay the velvet band of pears Ewan had given her so long ago.

Could she really be almost forty-six? It must be impossible! She didn't *feel* forty-six. She still really thought of herself as the young girl who had ridden the fields at West Farms with such abandon and had assumed that life had been invented only for her to live.

Putting her face close to the mirrored surface, she pinched both cheeks to bring up the color. It was almost as difficult to believe that Josh was nineteen as it was to accept her own age. So much had happened both in their lives and in the world beyond them. Bonaparte had turned Europe on its ear and the repercussions were reaching into the very waters around New York. Richard had built up such a fleet of sloops and schooners in these last years that any threat to shipping must, of course, affect him. He was certainly secure enough in his business ventures to be no more than marginally affected by political problems, but they worried him just the same. They worried her, for that matter, with her son just on the point of sailing off to Nova Scotia.

Her sense of contentment vanished. Turning away, she sat down at her dressing table and picked up a brush, touching up her carefully coiffed hair. It was such a foolish journey. She had tried every way to talk him out of it, but nothing would do but he must go to look up his long-lost relatives who had left America after the Revolution. Bad enough that this trip should bring back memories of Ewan, though of course Josh couldn't know that. Even worse was her despair over ever weaning her son away from the sea. Was not even this trip merely an excuse to make another voyage, and this one longer and farther than any he had taken before? Perhaps if the British and the French had not become flagrant about stopping ships and impressing American seamen she would not be so concerned. But no, she would worry in any case because it was Josh, her precious son, who was sailing away.

The light from the lamp caught the translucent white creaminess of the band of pearls in her still-tawny hair. She had almost learned never to think of Ewan at all, but every time she thought she had succeeded, something conjured up his memory. Now Josh would return with real news of him. Perhaps he would even see him. Could she bear bringing alive his ghost in her heart once more?

"Madam," Betsy called, from the doorway. "Miss Hester is downstairs."

"Thank you, Betsy," Celia said, looking up almost guiltily. "I'll be right down. Tell her to wait for me in the morning room."

She watched Betsy waddle away, thinking how grossly fat her servant had grown. And Vestal, though still as large and broad as before, had become stooped and gray. Age was catching up with all of them. All but Richard. He still looked as fit and debonair as ever. And he still dressed more smartly than any other man she knew.

Her large eyes stared back at her, their amber depths echoing flecks of gold from the steady white light of an Argand lamp.

"Oh, Ewan," she sighed, barely audibly. Then, shrugging, she threw off the specters of the past and briskly turned down the lamp, winding a length of spangled pink gauze around her shoulders as she started downstairs.

Hester jumped to her feet as Celia entered the room. "I just knew we would be late," she said, grabbing up her shawl and gloves, "I hate to be late. Everybody stares at you as though you were the plague arriving."

"But to be late is fashionable, Hester," Celia replied, helping her arrange the shawl around her shoulders.

"Jaspar won't like it. Mark my words, someone will report it to him and he'll accuse me of deliberately putting myself forward. He's very sensitive about anything that reflects on him, you know."

Celia hurried her out the front door to the waiting carriage. "I am sorry, Hester, if I've caused you any trouble with Mr. Carne. It never occurred to me. But don't worry. This new groom of Richard's is a very fine driver—he'll have us there in no time."

"Well, I certainly hope so," Hester said, settling back against the cushions.

The coach clattered off, its iron wheels setting up an ear-splitting cacophony on the cobbles. Like the Park Theatre which had replaced the decaying John Street structure, the house on Oyster Pasty Lane had long since been sold off for a large three-story brick town house on James Street, in one of New York's growing fashionable neighborhoods. Celia watched with bored disinterest the traffic on the streets around her casting long shadows in the flickering light of the street lamps.

"I thought perhaps *your* husband might accompany us," she said, turning to see the profile of her sister-in-law.

"Jaspar disapproves of the theater. He claims it is licentious and an immoral influence on society. It was as much as I could do to get him to allow me to go."

"But this is the celebrated Mr. Cooper, and doing Hamlet too. Surely he can have no objection to that."

"That remark reveals considerable ignorance on your part, Celia. Shakespeare is certainly one of the most violent and immoral of all writers. He has a great deal to show of human foibles and almost never anything to say of edifying comment upon them. As a matter of fact, I went to some lengths to convince Jaspar I was going to see something more worthwhile, so please don't let out that we've seen Shakespeare."

"That's hardly likely," Celia murmured, "since I never see him anyway."

An uneasy silence settled between them as Celia turned back to staring out the window. It was so difficult to talk to Hester these days.

She was back sitting in front of her mirror late that evening, drawing the band of pearls out of her hair, when Richard came in wearing a brocade dressing gown. The golden light of the lamp danced on his wavy hair and emphasized the narrow planes of his face.

"How was the renowned Mr. Cooper?" he said lightly, coming to stand behind her.

"Very good, though I suspect his leading lady was there on sufferance. She forgot her lines and overplayed something fierce."

"She's probably his mistress. Theater folk are like that."

Celia shrugged. "Perhaps. But it was a pleasant way to spend an evening and it gave me a chance to visit with Hester, which I don't often do anymore."

"I hope you kept the conversation away from my business affairs. Every word goes straight back to Jaspar Carne and he uses it against me. I never know what to expect from him next."

"No, we did not discuss anything pertaining to your affairs. In fact, we barely mentioned you. We did see Josh, though. He was there with his young friend George Croker, and they escorted us to Vauxhall afterward. He is so full of excitement over his trip to Nova Scotia."

At the tone in her voice he moved away, pouring himself a glass of wine from a decanter that stood on a table near her bed. "I don't suppose that can hurt anything."

"Oh, Richard, sometimes I think you are becoming obsessed with this business of Jaspar Carne. It is all you ever think of—that and what new venture you can take up next. Surely we have enough money now and enough diverse interests that we can afford to think of something else once in a while."

"That's easy for you to say—you are the one I am trying to make secure. I wonder what your reaction would be if Carne succeeded in confounding my investments and bringing me to bankruptcy."

"Surely he could not do such a thing."

"How can you say that? He has tried through his political influence in New York to block my every attempt at expansion. He underhandedly attempted to buy three properties I was interested in right out from under me. He has seen that I did not get bids to which I was entitled, and he even brought a suit in Hester's name against me for my father's estate. You sit there and tell me I overreact to him. Frankly, I would prefer you did not see Hester at all, Celia."

She could see an argument developing, and this was one

evening she did not want anything to come between them. Some deep unrest within her drove her to go to him where he stood, and she slipped her arms around him and kissed him lightly.

"I'm sorry, Richard. I promise you I am guarded in what I say. I know Carne is a difficult man, but it is you I am concerned about. You worry about him, about your business, you think more of it than anything or anyone. I need you to think of me sometimes, Richard, and Josh does, too."

He stroked the long hair away from her forehead. Through the thin fabric of her dress he could feel her nipples pressing hard against his chest. "Everything I do is for you," he said, his voice more gentle. "You know that. Besides, Josh is doing very well without me. He's having a good life right now, feeling his oats, learning about the world. Yet he seems steady and sensible with it all. Josh will be all right."

"You should have seen him tonight—so handsome in his newfangled trousers and blue velvet coat. Even Hester remarked on what a fine-looking young man he had grown into. He charms everyone with his fine figure, his youthful optimism and his irrepressible spirits. What a satisfactory son he is!"

She reached up to touch his cheek, still holding the green band in her fingers. Looking down, he took it from her and turned it over in his hand.

"I remember this. You wear it a lot, don't you?"

"Yes." Somehow the conversation had gone in a direction she did not wish.

"Ewan gave it to you, as I remember. During the war."

Ewan again! Was he always to rise up and haunt her even when she least wanted it? "Yes, he did. It's beautiful and rather valuable."

"Does it remind you of him?"

"Why, I don't think so."

Richard pulled her to him, lightly kissing her neck. "I only wondered. What do you think, Celia? I've had an idea in the back of my mind for a long time now. What do you think of selling our house in New Rochelle and building one of our own?"

Celia pulled back, looking into his eyes. "Build a house? Where?"

"I thought perhaps on the property Mother left me on Hudson's River. It's a beautiful spot, completely fallow and high up so that the view of Haverstraw Bay is magnificent. It's near

Elisha's old dock, which would be convenient in floating in materials. And the river is closer to my various interests—as you put it—than our home on the Sound. We could design it ourselves, make it as elegant as you want. A real showplace. What do you think?"

Celia felt a growing excitement. "It's a wonderful idea, Richard. I should love it. Can it be really spacious like Mr. Dyckman's new home, or should it be more like our farmhouse on Myer's Point?"

"No farmhouse. This will be a mansion, even grander than Dyckman's. And with a better view."

"Won't it be difficult to get materials up the hill? Mr. Dyckman's home is very near the water and his wife told me that made it a simple matter to bring in supplies."

"It will be harder, yes, but I believe it can be done. And in the end, the view will compensate. It will be our 'country home' and a splendid one. We'll start the plans tomorrow."

He dropped his arms and turned away, still holding the pearls. Remembering them, he dropped them into her hand.

"I never really liked this thing. Why don't you put it away? I'll get you a newer and better one."

Celia closed her fingers around the velvet ribbon, "Of course, if that is what you want." He was nearly to his door.

"Richard!"

He turned, watching her standing in the golden light of the lamp, the pale shimmering pink silk of her gown outlining her slender figure.

"Stay with me tonight. I . . . I feel lonely, for some reason."

He hesitated while Celia prepared herself for a rebuff. Then he smiled and came toward her.

"Of course, my dear. If that is what you want."

twenty-nine

Renting a horse in the half-built harbor town of Yarmouth, Nova Scotia, Josh turned his back on the wharf where the *Aurora* lay at anchor and rode inland along the coastal road to Annapolis Royal. The directions were not difficult to follow in this hill-lined, verdant island, and he rather enjoyed the feel of a horse under him after so many days on the open sea. The sun, struggling to break through a cloudy, overcast sky, now and then succeeded with a sword thrust of bright gold which quickly faced back to gray, while the smell of the salt air followed him like a lackey down every mile. On an island like this one never got away from the sea. Josh liked that.

The mysterious, wanton, enigmatic sea! How he loved it. Was there anything on earth to compare with the feel of the wind catching the sails to wing you along the water, gliding just above the surface of the waves, like an eagle skimming the Hudson in search of an unwary fish?

All his common sense told him that eventually he would be landlocked, forced by necessity to take up his place in his father's business and carry on what Richard Deveroe had so painstakingly built up. He didn't really mind the thought, though if dreams could be his portion he would prefer to ship out as a common seaman. Well, perhaps not a common seaman, for everyone knew that their lot was probably the worst of any man's on earth. But a captain, commanding a ship like the *Aurora* all the way to China—ah, *there* was a dream! Someday that dream would be laid aside with the rest of youth, but not for now. Now was the time for visions and aspirations. The world was waiting for him to put his hand to the plow. There was so much to learn, to explore, to experience, and he wanted to know it all. He sensed that now was probably the only time in his life when he would be free to search.

The squawking of the gulls drew his eyes to the gray sky.
Even this far inland they accompanied him. He began to notice
fenced and tended fields thick with sheep and herds of goats.
The land began to take on aspects of cultivated farmland,
though still a far cry from the rich fields of West Chester. He
wondered what Cousin Ewan had found here when he first
arrived. What kind of a wilderness had he had to tame? Now
there would be a man's job—taking a wild wilderness and
forcing it under your hand to a state of domesticity. For a
moment he fancied himself arriving with a new wife in such
a place.

But that romantic notion evaporated with the first thought
of what Cousin Ewan had left behind. What it took to bring
this land under cultivation was grueling, bone-exhausting work,
for both man and wife. Besides, he had never yet met a woman
with whom he would wish to share such an adventure. Most
of the young girls at home were frivolous children with a lot
of poetical nonsense in their heads, while their mothers were
either hard or vaporish—eternally manipulating and just as
uninteresting. Not a none of them had the quiet, levelheaded
dignity and warmth of his mother. How he wished he could
meet such a girl.

Plenty of time for that! He was young and the world was
filled with women. He would know when he saw the right one.

On either side of the road long rows of apple trees festooned
in pink and white blossoms lent a fragrance and beauty to the
afternoon which even the dim sun could not discourage. He
turned onto a path that led to a distant white house with an
unmistakable air of comfort and gentility, unlike any he had
seen in Yarmouth or on the road to Round Hill. This would
have to be Ewan's estate. Idly he thought of the letter he had
written, remembering with a twinge of anxiety that he had
received no reply. What kind of reception would he find?
Would Cousin Ewan even be there to greet him?

Tying his mount to a hitching post, Josh stepped up on a
long porch and pulled a bell handle which set up an echo
somewhere inside the house. The upper half of the door creaked
open and in the shadowed interior he could just make out the
indistinct shape of a young boy, his light hair the only brightness in the dark hallway.

"Is Colonel Deveroe to home?" Josh asked.

"Yes. That is . . . I think so. I don't know. Who is it who
wishes to see him?"

"A kinsman from America. Joshua Deveroe by name."

"Oh. Well. Wait just a moment."

The boy was swallowed up by the darkness inside. Josh waited patiently while he heard his youthful voice calling up the stairs.

"Morna! Morna, come quick. Someone is here to see Father."

A girl's voice called down, "If it's Mr. Fowler about the lawsuit tell him Father says he will not talk to him again and he might as well go away."

"No. It's a kinsman from America," the boy whispered loudly.

This brought the girl's quick steps on the stairs and down the hall toward the door. "Jeremy, where are your manners! Leaving a guest standing outside on the porch. Please excuse the boy, mister..."

"Deveroe. Joshua Deveroe from New York State," Josh offered, politely stepping inside. The hallway stretched the length of the house and had several doors opening off it, all of them closed. The girl chatted all the way down the shadowed hall, then threw open a door on a room as shuttered and dark as a cave. Bustling around, she plumped up cushions on a settee and swept back the folding wooden panels at the windows, letting in the gray sunlight.

"Please excuse my brother, Mr. Deveroe. It is not often that we get visitors from America. Jeremy, quick, run to the stable and take Dan to call Father. He is at Mr. Jenson's mill. Hurry, now."

Pulling back the last of the drapes, she moved around to face Josh, who had been standing near the window wondering what to do with himself. As the sudden light fell on her upturned face the mundane pleasantry he was about to offer fled from his mind.

She was the most beautiful creature he had ever seen. Under her white cap wispy tendrils of jet-black hair framed an oval face with the delicate creaminess of the pale apple blossoms he had admired all the way out from Annapolis Royal. Her lips, smiling up at him quizzically, were beautifully sculptured, her nose long and narrow. Her eyes under their arched black brows were heavy with thick dark lashes, and the color was neither blue nor green but a combination of both, like the undulating clear water of the ocean waves. Josh looked down into them and felt as though he was being drawn toward their depths just as he had so often been drawn toward the mysterious tantalizing depths of the sea.

"I . ." he stammered.

"Yes?"

"What did your brother call you?"

"Morna. I am the eldest daughter of the family." She grew self-conscious under his intense scrutiny, and a faint pink blush tinged her cheeks. "I am very sorry, Cousin Joshua, that my mother could not welcome you, but at this moment she is lying ill upstairs with a rheumatoid complaint. In her place may I say how very happy we are to have you visit our home."

"Thank you," Josh answered, wondering why his simple words managed to sound so oafish.

"You are Cousin Richard's son, are you not?"

The mention of his father helped him recover a little. "Yes. And both my mother and father send you their very kindest regards. And Aunt Hester too."

"It's strange," she said in a warm, quiet voice, "I have never met any of our American kinfolk, yet I feel as though I know them all. Father speaks of them so often."

Suddenly remembering they were still standing, she gestured him quickly toward a chair. He sat down feeling as though all his bones had suddenly gone brittle.

"How I long to see America," she said wistfully, sitting down opposite him on the edge of the settee. "I've heard so much of its beauties."

"Perhaps one day you shall," he offered.

"No, I don't think so. Father can never go back, of course, and I would not wish to leave him. But tell me about it," she added, brightening. "I do so want to hear everything. Where do you live? West Farms? Father says Bronxdale is one of the most beautiful places on earth."

"Why, as a matter of fact, I barely know West Farms."

"Oh. Then tell me of the rest of West Chester. And New York town too. You don't mind my curiosity? I don't want to inconvenience you."

Josh brought his gaze back to her sea-green eyes and felt his heart lift. "My dear cousin Morna, nothing in the world would give me greater pleasure. Nothing at all."

"Fancy Ewan with six children!" Hester said, sniffing at her vinaigrette. "I never thought of him as the family type."

"Six of his own and two of his brother's left in his care,"

Josh said, leaning forward in his chair. "It's the most bustling household I've ever seen, though the youngest is now at least nine or ten years of age."

"Fancy it," Hester repeated. "I'm really surprised. Aren't you surprised, Celia? Can you imagine Ewan as patriarch?"

"I suppose not," Celia murmured, concentrating ever more intently on her needlework. It was a nightmare sitting here trying to remain composed while Josh went on exuberantly describing every detail of Ewan's life. How often had she wondered how things were with him, yet now she realized it had been better not knowing. Quickly lifting her eyes, she caught Richard staring at her from across the room. Of course he would see right through her studied composure. She felt a flush on her cheeks as she furiously sorted the silks in her basket.

"I suppose dear Ewan is showing his age by now?" Hester asked almost hopefully.

"I found him one of the most dynamic men I have ever met. It was all I could do to get him talking about his days at the head of the Refugees, but once he started it all came pouring out. Wonderful! Wonderful!"

Richard shifted in his chair. He was nearly as uncomfortable as Celia to see Joshua's near-worship of Ewan's glamorous career as a cavalry officer.

"And you say he has prospered up there in the wilderness?" Hester went on.

"Oh, yes indeed," Josh answered. "He has a vast sheep farm and owns extensive acres of apple orchards. He keeps several slaves and is called 'the Colonel' by everyone. He has even served in the legislature for several years. He's a great man in those parts, no doubt of it."

"Well, that does not surprise me, does it you, Celia?"

"What? Oh, no. People always looked up to Ewan."

"How blasé you and Richard are about it all. If I didn't know better, I would think you were jealous. Here we've heard nothing for years about our favorite cousin and now Josh tells us he has prospered greatly and all you can say is that people always looked up to him!"

"What should I say? I'm happy for him—that he is happy, I mean. And I'm especially thankful that Josh is safely home. There's nothing more to be said."

"Happy? I don't think I'd call Cousin Ewan 'happy,' Mama. Indeed, there is a kind of sadness at his core, as if he never really overcame his grief at leaving America. At least, it seemed that way to me."

"If he has done as well as you say I see no reason why he shouldn't be happy," Hester added petulantly.

Celia smiled at her son. "At least *you* seem happy, Josh. Your adventures did you good."

"I discovered so many new things—not the least of them . . ." He paused, looking between the expectant faces of his parents. "I haven't spoken yet of the most wonderful discovery of all. I met a girl!"

"Oh, la," Hester said, flourishing her handkerchief. "So *that* explains your excellent spirits. I suspected something like that."

"A girl!" Celia exclaimed. "What girl?"

"Cousin Ewan's oldest daughter, Morna." He leaned toward his startled mother. "She is the most beautiful girl I have ever seen—coal-black hair, dark lashes, and eyes the color of sunlight on the waves."

"She cannot be Ewan's oldest daughter with that description," Hester laughed.

Richard said seriously, "She could be if she took after her mother. Remember Mercy? She had black hair."

Josh was still looking intently into his mother's eyes, silently pleading for her acceptance. "I took one look and my heart was lost. Then, as I got to know her better during my stay, I found that her character and sensibilities were just as pleasing as her appearance."

"She sounds a veritable paragon," Hester said.

"I . . . I made up my mind before I left that I would ask her to marry me."

"Josh!" The exclamation escaped Celia's lips before she could catch it back. "What are you saying?"

He reached out and took her hand. "Oh, Mama, you will love her. She is the dearest, sweetest person on earth. She has done me the great honor of accepting my suit and Cousin Ewan has given his consent. It's all arranged."

That brought Richard out of his chair. "You did this without asking us, Josh? Weren't you getting a bit above yourself?"

"But how could I ask you? I had to leave in a few days, perhaps never to return. It had to be decided then or never."

Celia's face was white as the silk in her fingers. She could not seem to find her voice. Ewan's daughter! Mercy Lawrence's daughter!

"It won't happen for at least two years," Josh added, trying to placate his parents. "She's young yet and so am I, for that matter."

"I'm glad you at least recalled that fact."

"But, Papa, in two years I'll be of age. I can go and fetch her then. She has promised to wait for me."

"Oh, Josh," Celia stammered. "In two years you may change your mind completely. Perhaps you will have discovered some other girl by then. It's happened before."

"Not to me," and she recognized the familiar lines on his face. "From the moment I first saw Morna I knew she would always have my heart. If I live to be eighty that will never change—I know it."

"That is a romantic dream," Richard said, not even trying to hide his exasperation.

Hester settled back in her chair, enjoying this domestic scene more than anything in a long time. "Well, Celia," she said archly, "you see what comes of always giving a child everything he wants. He'll just go on taking all his life with no thought at all to your sensibilities."

To her surpise Josh turned on her. "Aunt Hester, Mama and Papa both know I would never do anything to hurt them. If I were not so firmly convinced that once they know Morna they will love her every bit as much as I do, I would never have had the audacity to make these plans without their consent." He looked back to Celia. "You *will* love her, Mama. I'm sure of it."

She tried to smile back at him. "I . . . I shall try to, Josh." A hand on her shoulder steadied her, and she realized Richard was standing behind her.

"Perhaps we can discuss this again later. After all, we have two years to accustom ourselves to the idea of a daughter-in-law. I'm sure your mother would agree with me that neither of us thought to have to face this issue for a long time to come."

"How like a son to spring something like this upon you," Hester added. "A daughter is easily arranged for. Christy was a relief to marry off. But when Dexter ran away with that trollop who wound him around her finger, Mr. Carne all but disowned him. And, for once, I was in complete agreement."

Catching a glimpse of his wife's white face, Richard gave way to a rare burst of temper. "Oh, Hester, will you please keep quiet! Celia, perhaps you would like to lie down?"

"No—no, thank you. It was just a momentary headache. I'm quite well now. In fact, why don't you step out in the hall,

Josh, and tell Lucy to bring in tea. It's nearly time, anyway."

"Of course, Mama."

He left the room feeling a strange sense of disquietude and disappointment. It had never occurred to him that his parents would not share the same happiness that filled his own heart. Especially since Morna was the daughter of a well-loved cousin and thus part of their own family! Their attitude puzzled him and took the edge off the ecstasy he had carried with him since that moment in Ewan Deveroe's parlor.

Behind him he could hear his Aunt Hester's voice. "I declare, I never saw such a fuss. You'd think it was the crown prince himself who had just become engaged."

The next day Celia left with Richard for her first glimpse of the spot where their new house was to be built. It had been many years since she had taken such a leisurely journey through West Chester, and the signs of change and growth that they met at every interval of their journey both surprised and appalled her. Farmlands turned to villages and towns . . . factories and quarries where before she remembered only rolling hills and quiet fields . . . mills and taverns along roads which had once been no more than narrow paths, now filled with the never-ceasing din of carriages to and from Albany and New England. As they moved across the county the land began to change as well, growing upward into low hills surrounding rolling valleys. She had not realized how flat and marshy the land along the Sound was until she found herself admiring the thick-forested hills and valleys that lined the Hudson shore.

It was a steep climb through a track strewn with brittle dried needles and shadowed with a canopy of pines, maples, oaks and tulip trees. But when they broke through the cover near the top of the hill to look out over a vista of the silver Tappan Sea swelling in the distance, and below it the long shining coil of the river all the way as far south as New York itself, Celia felt as though she had been abruptly transported to paradise.

"It's beautiful!" she whispered, more to herself than to her husband.

"Isn't it. I have been here many times these last few years, and never once have I failed to come away with some feeling of a vision renewed."

"I think I could stand here and drink it in forever. What a glorious spot for a home."

Richard dismounted and lightly fastened the reins to a maple branch. Stepping heavily in the loamy earth, ignoring the mud on his polished riding boots, he paced out for her the rough design of the house.

"This plateau at the top is flat enough, I think, to set a house without having to level too much ground. I thought a porch here where we could have the full effect of the view, a wide hall and staircase with rooms to either side, then upstairs a wide center hall with bedrooms grouped around it. If you wish a ballroom we could put one at the rear similar to the Morris house on Harlem Heights."

"I wonder if we would be entertaining that much. Perhaps it would be simpler to build the drawing rooms so that they could be opened onto the hall. But won't it be difficult to get materials up here, Richard? Perhaps we should build closer to the river. Certainly it would cost less."

"Yes, I don't pretend it will be easy. But I am determined to try. The next step is to hire a surveyor and have the place laid out, and if they think it can be done, hang the expense. I want my house on this hill, not down there near the wharfs."

Trying to visualize her new home, Celia caught her first glimmer of excitement at the thought of furnishing its elegant rooms. "There are so many new and beautiful styles coming in now, especially from France. Think what fun it will be to decorate. Can we really afford to hang the expense?"

He smiled at her indulgently. "My dear, for what other reason have I worked these years but to build a fortune? Make it as lovely as you wish. I want the Deveroe house to be known up and down the river as the showplace of the Hudson!"

"Well, perhaps it won't be *that* grand. But it will be beautiful, as beautiful as you and I can make it. What shall we call it?"

"I've already thought that through. I want you to make a garden here,"—he gestured toward the woods to his right—"and line it with rows of that pungent southernwood you always have about you. And that's what we'll call it. 'Southernwood.'"

"Oh, Richard . . ." Did the dismay show in her voice?

"That frothy plant always makes me think of you."

She turned away. How could she tell him that the same plant only made her think of Ewan? Should that memory be carried over right into his home—this house which she and Richard together were to make new? Was she never to be finished with her past? With her old love?

Pretending to admire the vista, she walked to the edge of

the grassy knoll to look out over the river. The past would never go away. It seemed to have a diabolical way of curving around on itself to come back at her—just as it had with Josh's announcement of his intention to marry Ewan's daughter. There was a kind of fatality about it, useless for her to fight.

The heaviness she had felt two days ago when her son first spoke of Morna Deveroe swept over her again. She had tried very hard to put it from her mind, but here it was again, turning the bright day to gray. Two years would pass swiftly and the day would come when she would have to call Morna 'daughter.' The daughter who might have been hers.

A hand on her shoulder startled her and she looked up to see Richard standing beside her, his pale face reflecting the pleasure he was so sure she shared with him.

"You'll come to love this place as much as I already do, I'm sure of it," he said, drawing her to him.

Pulling out a four-inch-long hatpin, she removed her fawn-colored riding hat and tucked her head into the crook of his neck.

"I'm sure I will."

After all, two years. Anything could happen in two years.

Celia paid only indifferent attention to national affairs and so she could not know that behind Richard's determination to build his house now was the very real fear of a move by President Jefferson to restrict trade with England and France. With a kind of urgency he would not have felt in better times, he threw himself into the business of designing and building Southernwood, devising imaginative ways to drag the bricks, timbers, marble and stone it required to the top of the hill. He had Celia spending days in New York purchasing Wilton carpets and Empire furniture long before the rooms were ready for them. Mirrors, sofas, draperies, chairs, hangings, beds— all the elegant accouterments of a fine estate were collected and stored in a warehouse near Dock Street. Artisans created flocked and Chinese wallpapers, before the walls were up to receive them. Pictures, the new fashionably framed Grecian landscapes as well as family portraits, were stored away with only a vague thought as to where they would be hung. A glossy new fortepiano waited for Celia's eager touch. By the time the last of the artisans had executed their Greek key and shell motifs in the mantels, doorways and plasterwork, not a major item which was to go into the house but had been acquired.

The house was finished and furnished before the wide graveled walks were installed or the tiny orchard trees set about in the garden. It was ready to receive its new owners, smelling of fresh paint and plaster and shining like a brightly minted new gold dollar, before the outbuildings of root cellar, springhouse, stables and barn had been full completed. Only one outbuilding was fully ready as the house itself—the brick necessary house with its elaborate Greek-temple façade and four round stools.

Time proved the wisdom of Richard's haste, for it was less than two years from the day Celia stood on the plateau falling in love with the shining river that President Jefferson's embargo became almost a certainty. Panic was already beginning to be felt when, a few months after settling into their new house, Josh left for Nova Scotia to bring back his intended. For Richard, there was still enough security in the local river trade and in building sloops that he was not dismayed yet. Certainly, all the schooner runs would be curtailed and with that the profitable trade with China, not to mention England and France, brought to a standstill. But if the embargo did not drag on too long, Richard's local interest would see him through.

Celia watched her son leave with a sinking heart. The dangers of a ship in open waters were worse now than they had been two years before. The English were more daring than ever about stopping American ships and impressing young men into their navy. Many people now thought a violent confrontation inevitable.

Worse than that, the two years that had passed had done nothing to alter Joshua's obsession with Morna Deveroe. How Celia had connived to parade every attractive girl she could find before him, hoping that one would turn him from this disastrous alliance. But her son, she found, could be as stubborn as she herself, not to mention his father. Nothing would do but that he should marry the black-haired girl with the sea-green eyes who, with one glance, had stolen his heart.

Suppose Morna's mother should accompany her? Or, worse yet, Ewan himself! What would she do? How could she go on living the self-contained, disciplined life she had so painfully built up for herself if her past should suddenly stand before her again? All those feelings she had struggled so hard to curb— what would she do if they violently engulfed her again?

And the girl herself. Could she ever love her as a daughter as he had always imagined she would Josh's wife? She both longed for her son's safe return and dreaded the thought of his walking up their porch steps with this problematical girl on his arm. What was she to do?

For the hundredth time these thoughts were raging through her mind when she was suddenly aware that Richard was calling her.

"Come out here a moment, Celia. You should see this."

Richard stood against one of the colonnades of the porch, looking out over the river.

"What is it?"

"Look down there." He pointed. Out on the middle of the sequined Hudson, dotted with frothy whitecaps, the squat black form of a barge was sliding upriver. From its flat deck a small sail billowed, and in its stern a long brightly painted canopy was just visible. Strangest of all was a tall black chimney in its middle from which a long spiral of black smoke curled.

"It's the *North River* working up to Albany on its first trip."

"It's certainly a peculiar-looking boat."

"It's powered by steam. Robert Fulton designed and built it with old Livingston's money. So far it seems to have been the most successful attempt at steam power yet. I read that it was launched in the city just a few days ago. Gave everyone quite a scare at first when they thought she was going to explode. But Fulton's a clever fellow and he corrected the defect."

"What is that curious business on the sides?" Celia asked, straining to see more clearly.

"Paddles. The steam forces the paddles to rotate to propel the boat. Much more effective than oars. Faster too."

Celia smiled at the intense concentration with which her husband studied the long, squat form on the river sliding along like a water bug.

"Is steam to be your next venture, Richard?"

"I don't know. Elisha thinks it is a sign of the future, but I'm not sure I agree. It's still primitive, and besides, they are coming up with dramatic new improvements in the old sailing ships. I think I'd like to watch a while longer before I leap into anything. Besides, Fulton has a patent on this particular model."

She linked her arm through his affectionately. "Well, I have the feeling that if there's money to be made from it, you'll find a way. As for myself, I should be terrified to set foot on Mr. Fulton's deck. Suppose that boiler blew up!"

"You are not alone. Many fear the same thing. But if it can be made to work, it might just help improve the packet business on our inland waterways, and that would certainly ease some of the hurt we're sure to feel from the loss of foreign markets. Time will tell."

"Yes," she sighed, picturing Josh walking up the steps with a girl of dark hair and blurred features on his arms. *Time will tell so many things*.

Out of a cloudless sky a white tern swooped down at the whitecaps like a falling star. Dipping its prow in the heaving water, the boat slid downward to catch the rhythm of the waves. Morna Deveroe stumbled into the rail, gripping it with the white knuckles of one hand while with the other she clutched at her lurching stomach. All the way from Yarmouth she had struggled vainly to adapt to this ceaseless, monstrous rhythm of the waves. Only by the most flagrant pretense had she kept Josh from knowing just how unseaworthy she was. Thank God they were finally nearing New York and this ghastly trip would soon be over, or she would give up even trying.

The boat stabilized momentarily. Looking away from the white tern triumphantly climbing skyward again, she glanced toward the taffrail where Josh stood talking to the captain at the wheel. Even from this distance she could tell that he was in his element. What a handsome man he is, she thought, her heart swelling. All his concentration and delight were focused on the ship and the ocean as though each were under his power. That confidence, that power, is just what a young man should possess, she thought, and certainly it must be what had brought her too under his spell. Why otherwise would she be here, suffering this dreadful voyage, having left five hundred miles behind her, the best home and family a girl could ever have, moving inexorably toward a strange land, a strange people and an unknown home? She studied his tall form as if to restore her courage. For him she had risked all, for him now was her life.

Leaning over the rail, she looked through the transparently green waters. "Morna Deveroe!" She smiled to herself. No maiden and married names for her. With all the other drastic changes her marriage had brought, how strange that her name should remain the only thing unchanged. Arching her slim fingers, she admired once again the round gold band studded with diamond chips. She still could not believe she was really married to this glorious young man—this Leander from across the sea. For two years she had dreamed of him, pored over every written word, thought and planned for such a marriage without really believing it would happen. Then, there he was to claim her. It seemed only a few days ago, yet it had been the better part of three months. One month to become reacquainted, one to work out the details of their marriage, and one to begin life together. Then—this voyage to a strange planet. If it had not been for her parents' illness . . .

"My love, are you sure you should be up on deck? I thought another hour of resting would do you more good."

She looked quickly up to see her new husband standing beside her, concern in his brown eyes. A lurch of the boat threw her against him, and he steadied her with an arm around her shoulder. The wind, catching her long black hair, blew strands across his cheek. Josh smoothed them back, lost in the beauty of her and still unable to believe that this lovely girl was actually his wife.

"I couldn't bear the closeness of the cabin any longer. Truly, the sky is so blue and the air so clear up here that I think it will do me more good. You don't mind, do you?"

"Of course not. I only want you to be comfortable. Look, over there," he pointed to a thin dark pencil line across the water as she nestled against him. "That's the Jersey shore. We should be entering the Narrows in another hour. It won't be long now before you'll have solid land under your feet again."

How wonderful. "Will we stop in the city? I should like very much to see it. Father told me so much about it."

"What did he tell you?" he asked, smiling down into her radiant face.

"Oh, memories of skating on the Fresh Water Pond, assemblies at Hick's, balls and receptions, plays at the John Street Theatre, the busy wharfs, the promenade at Trinity Walk . . ."

He threw back his head, laughing. "Your picture of the city is sadly behind the times. There is no Hick's any longer. The Park Theatre long ago replaced that John Street relic, and the Fresh Water Pond has become a bog. They talk of filling it in completely, since water comes now from the Bronx River in West Chester."

Morna felt a flush on her cheeks. Not for the first time in her short marriage she felt like a child being reprimanded. It was humiliating and annoying of Josh to be so overbearing.

"Well, surely the shops . . ."

"Yes, my love," he said pulling her to him. "The shops are more grand than ever—or they will be anyway until Mr. Jefferson's embargo closes the harbor to the world. Your father would not recognize New York now. It has been built up, so my mother says, far beyond the boundaries at Corlear's Hook where my grandfather once had his estate. And it is beginning to be overrun with Irish bullies from the Dublin stews who live worse than the pigs that roam its streets. To be sure, it still has its elegant places like the City Hotel and Ranelagh and Vauxhall, and I shall take you there at the first opportunity. But for now I think we shall sail straight upriver to Mount Pleasant. Mama and Papa will be anxious to meet their new daughter."

Morna fought down disappointment. After all, Josh was her husband. How many times had her mother reminded her that a good wife is obedient to her man? But she would have liked to see something of that grand city. He might at least have asked.

Josh completely misread her frown. "You're not anxious about meeting my parents, are you?"

"Well, the truth is, I am a little fearful. Suppose they don't like me?"

"Not like you! How could they not love you? And I'm sure you'll love them. I know it is fashionable to make grandiose claims for one's parents even when one secretly despises them, but in my case the respect is truly earned. They are the finest parents a child could have ever had. Papa is a true gentleman, though a tiger in business, and Mama—well, she is simply the loveliest and most loving lady I have ever known, until I met you, that is."

"They sound like paragons . . ." She looked up into his light-brown eyes, the color of a topaz ring her mother wore. Without warning, the closeness of their bodies triggered the special excitement that set her body shivering. Her lips parted, her arms slid about his neck, and he caught her to him. Then the boat upended again and they lurched forward, losing their balance and tumbling onto the deck.

Tangled in a coil of hemp and skirts, Josh emerged laughing and helped her back up on her feet.

"Damn Poseidon! We'd better save such delights for the cabin."

Morna affected a smile even though her side hurt painfully where she had fallen agains the iron anchor ring. Another lurch of the boat set her stomach heaving and she clutched at Josh's coat.

"Are you sure you won't go below and rest?"

"No. I won't hear of it. I want my first sight of New York as soon as we reach the Narrows. And besides, I'm determined to be as good a sailor as my husband!"

She was rewarded with a look of unabashed admiration.

"That's my brave girl!"

To Morna's enormous relief, when the *Aurora* entered New York Harbor and slid northward up the Hudson, the quieter water was almost like stepping back on land. She hung over the rail devouring with her eyes every spire and tall building— some of them six stories high—which clustered around the end of New York Island. She was enthralled at the crowded rows of houses, warehouses and shops, the sea of masts that jammed the wharfs, the noise of carriage wheels, horses and vendors that could be heard across the water. When they sailed above the city, she found the uneven shoreline of the island, dotted with grand homes and cultivated orchards, as interesting as the lower city had been. On the other side of the river the steep rock walls of the towering Palisades were like nothing she had imagined. The river itself was a crowded highway, the brightly colored sails of sloops and the majestic billowing white sheets of schooners like the *Aurora* herself filling its narrow channel.

The farmland they sailed past looked verdant and rich even from the deck of the ship. Flowers were everywhere, some wild and untended, others in a colorful profusion of gardens surrounding the homes that graced the river's edge. She could see sheep grazing on the green slopes, cattle and horses pastured among fences of hedge or rail. Josh stood at her side calling out all the strange names that meant nothing to her now: Spuyten Duyvil, the Tappan Zee, Dobbs Ferry, Tarry Town. She drank it all in, enjoying it so much she nearly forgot how each sweep of the prow brought her closer to the inevitable homecoming.

The wharf at Mount Pleasant was a shabby affair, something like the ones thrown up at intervals outside Annapolis Royal at home. But the air was warmer than any she had ever known and she began to fear she would appear before her new in-laws in a wilted condition. She went below before stepping into the launch, combed her hair and fastened it in a knot, put on a fresh though wrinkled blue-and-white spotted muslin dress and draped a pleated shoulder cape about her shoulders. Then, tying her straw chip bonnet under her chin and dabbing her cheeks and arms with jasmine water, she went forward, knowing now how the Christians felt as they were led into the arena.

Holding tight to Josh's hand, Morna followed him down the ramp to what looked like a crowd of country people milling around the wharf. The she saw an elegant carriage, all red and gold, standing behind two beautiful matched grays. With a sinking heart she watched a tall, slim man descend from the carriage and approach them. So, she was not even to postpone this meeting until they reached the house.

"Papa." Josh waved and pulled her through the crowd. Timidly Morna followed, keeping her eyes shyly downward.

"Josh! How good to have you back." Father and son embraced while Morna stepped back, wishing with every fiber of her being that she had stayed in Nova Scotia.

"And this must be Morna."

When Morna looked up into the warm gray eyes they smiled a welcome that immediately quieted her fears. Richard Deveroe was the most elegant man she had ever seen. His dark-green morning coat covered a light-colored striped waistcoat and was cut away to reveal buff trousers and gleaming Hessian riding boots. The ruffled shirt below his folded stock and high collar was of the finest cambric. In one hand he held both kid gloves and the rolled rim of a beaver hat, while with the other he reached out to take her hand and raise it to his lips.

Morna curtsied, thinking how unlike his son he was. It was obvious his classical features had sharpened with the passing years, but as a young man he must have made the ladies swoon.

"Welcome to America, my dear cousin," Richard said gently, aware of her discomfort. "I trust the trip was pleasant. Josh is a consummate sailor and this must have been one time when he made the sea obey his voice!"

"I fear Morna will never make a sailor, Papa, though no one can best her at braving the discomforts of a voyage. I see you brought the carriage. Good. And Vestal—good old Vestal. Are you driving today?"

The largest, blackest Negro Morna had ever seen smiled broadly from his place by the horses' heads. "Be welcome, home, Mista Joshua."

"Come along now, children. Your mother is waiting at the house, Josh, and she's anxious to see you and to meet Morna. Help your-bride-to-be into the carriage, why don't you?"

Morna and Josh exchanged glances. "Well, Papa," Josh said hesitantly, deciding on impulse to go ahead and break the news, "as a matter of fact, Morna is my bride, not my bride-to-be."

Richard tried to hide his surprise and dismay. "Why, I don't understand. I thought the wedding was to be at Southernwood."

"That is what we had planned, but circumstances . . . well, things happened at Annapolis Royal that made us change our plans. We were married at Cousin Ewan's a month ago. I hope this does not upset you."

"No, no. But I fear your mother will be sadly disappointed. She was planning on an elaborate affair."

Josh handed Morna up into the carriage. "She can still have her affair—make it the grandest reception to introduce a new daughter-in-law into society that Hudson's Valley has ever seen."

He had one foot on the step when his father stopped him with a hand on his arm. "What circumstances?"

Josh's glance flickered over his wife's white profile against the plush seats inside. "I'll explain it to you both when we reach the house. All right?"

Richard shrugged. He was more distressed by this precipitous wedding than he wanted to admit. The girl seemed pretty and gentle enough, and Josh usually showed good judgment in the things that mattered, but he was anxious to know what on earth could have brought this about.

Morna held tight to her husband's hand all the way up the long, slow, gradually rising ground which led to the house on the hill. The road had been laid out with horses in mind and it seemed to wander and curve incessantly until they finally came to a long stretch of graveled driveway that looped around itself in a small cul-de-sac where a broad veranda opened onto the side of the house. By the time she stepped out all her worst fears had swept over her again. She had known that the Hudson Deveroes were well off, but nothing in Josh's easy manner had prepared her for this luxury. Looking around at the topiary garden and the rows of young trees, at the colonnaded porch of this huge mansion, and then at the lovely vision in yellow jaconet muslin who flew down the steps to embrace Josh, she wished only for the ground to open and swallow her. For a moment mother, father and son seemed joined in a tiny world that excluded her. Then Celia broke away and reached out her hand to her daughter-in-law, and the two women gave each other a close appraisal.

Celia had to stifle a gasp. Before her stood the living, breathing replica of Mercy Lawrence as a young girl, the way Celia had seen her last. The black hair and arched eyebrows, the

clear white skin, the delicately shaped lips—what was there
of Ewan in this girl? She easily hid her dismay at the old-
fashioned straw gypsy hat and the country muslin dress. Perhaps the gentry of Nova Scotia made no effort to keep up with
fashion, but that was easily remedied. So lovely a creature in
homespun would be exquisite in silks and velvet. But how was
she going to ever accustom herself to living with the ghost of
Mercy Lawrence!

Morna's eyes fell under her new mother-in-law's scrutiny.
She was completely unable to read what lay behind Celia's
eyes, but the clear dismay in them made her the more uneasy.
She really knew very little of Josh's mother—Celia had seldom
been spoken of during her growing-up years—but she did know
that she was older than her own mother. Yet the years were
worn gracefully. She had to be in her forties, and Morna was
accustomed to forty-year-old women looking and acting more
like sixty. This lovely woman still had the look of youth in her
creamy skin and beautifully coifed hair. Her buttery-colored
dress, trimmed in corded tucks and scallops and with long
sleeves in puffs, made her look as fashionable as her husband.
Morna wished desperately that she had worn one of the damask
or taffeta gowns her mother had insisted that she bring with
her. But she was so unused to frills and furbelows that it had
seemed pretentious to deck herself in such finery just to make
an impression. Now she appeared before them straight off the
farm. What would Father have thought of her, he who was
always so much the gentleman and in control of every situation?

Celia tried to give the girl her warmest smile. "Come inside,
my dear. You must be weary. We have tea set out in the back
parlor. Vestal will bring your things up later."

It was obvious how impressed Morna was with the elegance
of the house. Trying her hardest to put everyone at ease, Celia
seated them around the cherry-wood table and began pouring
tea into fine china cups, touching on every innocuous subject
she could devise. A hundred times she searched her mind for
the words to ask about Morna's parents but somehow could not
get them past her lips. She looked over to where Richard sat
preoccupied. He was not helping her at all. What she couldn't
know was that he was actually waiting for Josh.

Finally Celia decided to take the indirect approach. "I spoke
to your Aunt Hester, Josh, the last time I was in the city, and
she has agreed to help Morna with the selection of a wedding
dress. She knows all the best mantua-makers and milliners and,

for all her other faults, her taste in fashion is impeccable."

Moving closer to his wife on the sofa, Josh put an arm around her shoulders, with such a tense look on his youthful face that Celia began to feel uneasy.

"Actually, Mother . . ."

Celia was suddenly aware of the velvety cooing of a flock of pigeons which had alighted on the brick terrace outside.

Josh plunged on. "The fact is, Morna and I were married in Annapolis Royal last month."

Uncontrollably her eyes shunted to the previously unnoticed gold band on Morna's finger. "But I don't understand. I thought you were to bring her back here so your father and I could take part in the wedding." Did her voice sound as strained to the others as it did to her?

"I know that was the plan and I fully intended to carry it out. But when I arrived at Annapolis and found Cousin Ewan so ill . . ."

Deliberately Celia set her cup and saucer on the cherry table, noticing in passing that her hand was uncommonly steady. "Ewan was ill?"

"Yes, and Morna's mother too. It was the influenze epidemic. So many died. We didn't know how to tell you—someone you've known since childhood, so long and so well."

Morna's eyes filled with tears. "It meant so much to him, Mrs. Deveroe," she broke in earnestly. "Just to see us married . . . before. . . . It was the last thing he asked of us. We couldn't refuse."

Dead? Ewan dead? Celia stared at them both as though they were total strangers. Then she was on her feet, her voice shrill. "No! He can't have died! He can't!"

"Why, Mama, what's the matter? Let us explain."

Josh reached his arm toward her and she pushed it away, staring wild-eyed into his startled face. "He wouldn't die, not without a word, without ever seeing—"

"Celia!" Richard's sharp voice. She heard the anger, the bitterness, in it just before the grayness clouded over her and she slumped forward into her son's arms.

"My God," Josh cried, jumping up to keep her from crashing into the table. "What's wrong with her?"

Richard took her limp body and laid her down on the brocade couch. "Get some water, quick. And call Betsy or Dorcas—one of the servants. Tell them to bring her sal volatile."

Stunned, Josh hovered over Celia's unconscious body a

second before he could move, unable to believe his eyes. His mother, always so self-possessed, so poised, swooning away like some vaporish matron. As he ran from the room Morna went to kneel beside the couch, feeling Celia's wrist where she lay in Richard's arms. "Is she given to fainting fits?" she asked quietly, looking up at him.

"No, not usually. But she has not been at all well," Richard lied. "It was the news of your father's death. He was such an—an old friend."

She looked up at him, her large eyes full of questions. "But it was not Father who died. It was my mother. He asked us to be married for her sake, because she wanted so much to see me settled and happy. She and I were always very close."

Richard's eyes took on a glazed brightness. "Mercy? It was Mercy who died? Not Ewan?"

"Yes. And since all of you had been close friends in West Farms, all through the war and everything, we thought you would surely understand why we went ahead with the ceremony."

Richard turned away so as to avoid her face. "Yes, of course we understand," he murmured. "You mustn't think this little incident means we don't approve. You did the right thing."

He barely knew what he was saying, so consumed was he with a bitter and unreasoning rage. He was hardly aware when Betsy came waddling behind Josh, carrying a vinaigrette which she waved energetically under Celia's nose, bringing her gasping back to consciousness. Before Celia could do more than turn her startled, wounded eyes on her husband he had her on her feet and out the door.

"I'll see that she lies down for a while. You two wait here."

Upstairs he laid her on her bed. She grasped his hands before he could turn away.

"Richard!"

He couldn't answer her. Look at her.

"I can't believe it," she said, her eyes brimming. "I cannot bear it!"

Pulling his hand from her grasp, he sat down on the edge of the bed. He was tempted to let her grieve, to say nothing. But that would be too cruel.

"If you had not given way to such unreasoning hysteria you might have learned that it was not Ewan who died, but Mercy."

A long pause.

"What are you saying?"

"That your great swell of feeling for Ewan precipitated you into that disgraceful scene. Josh was trying to tell you that it was for Morna's mother's sake they were married earlier than planned, not Ewan's. Evidently he recovered from *his* influenza."

She could not mistake the bitterness in his voice. Covering her face with her hands, she slumped against her pillow. What had she done!

"For God's sake, Celia," he went on remorselessly, "it's been twenty-five years. Twenty-five years without so much as setting eyes on him. How can you still feel..."

The tears came flooding out. "I don't know. Oh, Richard, I'm so ashamed."

He made no move to touch her. The pain within him had caused something to freeze and harden inside. He did not deserve this after all he had done to build her a secure and comfortable life. Everything had been for her. She had borne his son. How was it possible this specter could come between them again? How could she be so faithless!

"Look, I must go down and get those young people settled. Try to rest for now. They believe you've been ill. Might as well let them go on thinking it."

He started to rise, but she clutched at his arms, pulling him back, the tears spilling down her face. "Richard...help me. I can't bear it."

Something in her face swept away all the defenses they had so patiently built up through the years, pulling them back through time. It frightened and appalled him. He wanted to shake her, strike her, force her to remember the years she had shared with him. Instead he pulled his hand away and started to the door.

"I have helped you all I can, Celia. This is your problem. You'll have to help yourself."

Though Richard did not really wish to offer any explanations, he felt that something must be said. He made it sound as neutral as possible. "Your father and mother, Morna, and my wife shared many vicissitudes during the war which brought them close together." *He could only hope Ewan had never told her the truth.* "Although we have not seen each other since that time, I think you can understand what a shock it was when Celia thought you were trying to tell her they had both died.

A small prevarication. You won't usually find Celia so fragile. Tell me what happened."

"She was badly crippled by rheumatism and her health had been failing for some time—in fact, she was never really well. I think the climate was harsh for her in Round Hill. Often, when I was growing up, I stood in for her, helping with the younger children and even hostessing at times for my father. She was always so frail. Father always seemed to have such a strong spirit, towering over hers. Then when the influenza came, they both went down with it. Poor Father had a harsh time, but he recovered. Mama just never seemed to throw it off." Her eyes filled with tears and Richard realized how fond the girl had been of her mother. Perhaps there had been more to Mercy's quiet spirit than any of them realized.

"When it was obvious she had only a short time to live, it seemed very important to Father that we be married for her sake. So we had a quiet wedding at our home, with only my family there to witness. Within the week she was gone."

Her voice broke and her tears brimmed over her blue-green eyes. "All my life I will be grateful to Josh for indulging me in this, Mr. Deveroe. It made Mama so happy in her last days, and so it made me happy, too. I am truly sorry if it distresses you."

"Nonsense, my dear. Josh's mother and I naturally wished to stand up with him on his wedding day, but under the circumstances I feel sure we both would not have wanted him to do anything but what he did."

"I knew you'd feel that way, Papa."

"Celia will no doubt say the same when her health allows her to look at the issue more objectively. Mark my words, in a week she'll be planning you the grandest reception anyone in these parts has ever seen."

"Oh, dear," Morna murmured, looking furtively around the room as though seeking a way out.

"Didn't I tell you?" Josh smiled at her triumphantly.

"Now I'm sure you would like to get settled in and rest. Perhaps later on, Morna, you will walk around the grounds with me. I should like to show you what we've done here."

The look she turned on him was full of gratitude. "I should like that above all things," Mr. Deveroe.

Richard lightly took her arm and led toward the door as a delighted Josh followed. "Come, now, if I am to be your father-in-law you must call me by something less formal than 'Mr. Deveroe.' Will 'Papa' be appropriate?"

"Thank you." Her smile gave an unexpected animation to her cool features. "I should love to call you Papa."

thirty

The Bronx River, still, cold, slate gray, moving sluggishly below the oppressive clouds of a lowering morning. The fields of West Farms, stretching away from the stone bridge into misty nothingness, beckoning her to leave the road and follow, enticing her into their haze. She had to hurry, to reach the Mill House, but her bare feet refused to move. She fought to run and could not. There was a man ahead of her, a shadowy form barely discernible in the murky morning. Arms clutched at her, trying to drag her forward, and in desperation she struck out. There was a cudgel in her hand—how had she not known it was there? She struck her assailant on the temple; spouting blood, he fell in the mud at her feet. She knew his face then. It was Dominie Brec, pale, with the raw, bloody wound stark on his face. But she must go on and she pulled her leaden feet across his body. Then she was standing in the hall of the Mill House surrounded by its flaking plaster and bare boards. And Ewan was coming toward her down the hall, his red military coat gleaming like the blood on Dominie Brec's face. She was in his arms, wild with longing, filled and overflowing with an intensity of passion, and he was pulling her down on the scratched and splintered floor...

Celia woke shuddering, her body on fire. It was a moment before she came back to consciousness and it took even longer to calm the overwhelming sexual longing that consumed her. "God!" she cried aloud, and the tears poured out like fluid from a raw wound. All that was left now was the dimming of Ewan's face, every feature so remembered and loved. Just for a moment in her dream she had seen him clearly again. Hopelessly she fought to keep that picture in her mind.

Impossible to sleep. She might as well sit up and watch the dawn creep in. Perhaps if she thought this through calmly she could make some sensible order of it.

Settling in a chair at the window, she looked with unseeing eyes at the gauzy curtains that draped the blinds. What a dreadful mess she had made of everything. And all the time it was Mercy who had died! That quiet, enigmatic, black-haired vixen who had been fortunate enough to live all those years beside the only man Celia every really wanted. Ewan, Ewan! Had she ever really ceased to grieve over him? Probably not, although she had done a good job of pushing her pain and longing to the back of her mind. That day he sailed away from New York he took part of her with him, and to her own dying day she would feel the loss and the emptiness where part of her heart had been.

Yet it was not the pain and embarrassment which surprised her but the shards it had made of the finely formed shell over the years she had so painstakingly built around her emotions. A shell which she was not, until this very moment, even aware she had made.

It had been easy to lose herself over these last years in the pleasures of creating a home for her son. It had been comfortable to delight in the luxuries and refinements Richard's success had brought her. Friends, matronly concerns, the rhythms of running a busy household—they had filled her days with just enough pleasure and satisfaction that she was able to push down any other less comfortable part of herself.

Even Richard—how she had prided herself on having finally learned to accept his self-contained, unemotional personality. Dwelling on his good points, grateful for his love and concern, she had put from her the memory and longing for the passion she had shared with Ewan. Now when she was nearly forty-eight years old, here it was again, unwanted, unbidden, breaking through the confident façade she presented to the world, to drive and bedevil her like a girl of eighteen again.

And now, too, she must learn to live with the terrible knowledge that Ewan was free and she was not. Nor probably ever would be.

Angrily she pushed aside the white lawn curtains at the windows and snapped up the blinds. Over the black river a somber pewter light touched the tops of the hills on the far shore, rimming them like tarnished silver.

Celia stared at the light with eyes as dark as the river below. How angry she was at Richard—that cold, passionless, imperturbable creature! And how she hated that black-haired girl asleep somewhere in this house. And most of all, how she hated herself—for still caring, for still feeling, for, even after all these years, still loving!

Long ago she had detested Mercy Lawrence, and she detested her still, even in death. There was no way of knowing if Ewan had ever told her of the love they had shared, but if she had known, and hoped someday for revenge, she had it now in full. In one blow she had brought about an estrangement in Celia's placid marriage, severed the strong bond between Celia and her son, and sent the living replica of herself to live in Celia's house as a constant reminder of the past.

She turned her face into the curtain, catching up a handful of the flimsy fabric against her face to stifle the sobs she could not control.

Oh, Ewan. My heart. My only love! Come back to me. Come Back!

Exhausted, she finally fell asleep in the chair before the window, and woke to a sun-dappled world. She almost did not dare look at her face in the elegant gilt mirror over her dressing table, knowing by the burning in her eyes how red and puffy they would be. But there was nothing for it but to put a defiant face to the world, so she splashed a little soothing cold water on her cheeks and wrapped herself in her loveliest silk dishabille. Then, led by the voices on the landing outside her bedroom, she went to join her family at breakfast.

An informal table had been set in the wide foyer between the master bedrooms. Josh and Richard sat on either side of her new daughter-in-law, who looked fresh as the morning in a high-waisted green dimity walking dress. Celia made a determined effort to shrug off her embarrassment over last night's scene in the parlor. After all, how much could this girl really know of the intertwined relationships between her parents and this family? Surely she had not deliberately intended to give the impression that it was Ewan who had died.

It was Josh who rose at once when he saw his mother, pale and dark-eyed, enter the room. "How do you feel?" he asked, giving her a quick kiss on the cheek. "Why didn't you tell me you've been ill? You don't look yourself at all."

"It's nothing, really. I'm fine. Now, don't fuss over me, Josh. Save your concern for Morna. Good morning, Richard."

Her husband drew up a chair at the table, nearly covered with heavy ornate silver dishes and fluted Staffordshire china.

"Feeling better this morning, Celia?" She knew him too well not to miss the edge in his voice, and she noted that though he appeared attentive, he avoided looking directly into her eyes.

"Yes, thank you." Steeling herself, she looked directly at her new daughter and gave her the warmest smile she could muster. "I do so apologize for last night, Morna. I hope Richard saw that you and Josh were well settled. I had everything arranged for you, even an especially intriguing supper. Sometimes things don't go as you plan . . ."

"Of course, madam. I understand. Please don't vex yourself over us, we were quite well taken care of. Frankly, I was so happy to have the floor stand still under my feet that I would have been comfortable in a hay loft." Morna's laugh had a childlike, infectious quality.

Celia made an effort to appear pleasant. "Now, Morna, you must accustom yourself to calling me something less formidable than 'madam.' I haven't been called that except by the servants in all these egalitarian years following the Revolution. And 'Mama' doesn't seem quite right. What about simply 'Celia'?"

"If you wish. But it seems somehow lacking in the proper respect."

"Mama does not care a jot for titles and formalities, Morna, as you will soon learn. And respect comes naturally as you get to know her."

Embarrassed, Morna looked away from the warm glance that mother and son exchanged. She had not been prepared for the strong bond between these two. It gave her a strange feeling of standing on the outside looking in.

"Now, what do you plan to do today?" Celia asked, trying to make it sound as though she really cared.

"Papa is going up to the Dolphin yards in about an hour and I thought I'd ride along. But first we promised Morna a tour of the grounds."

Morna laid a hand on her husband's sleeve. "A promise I intend to hold you to, since I must spend the rest of the day alone. Oh, that is . . ."

Celia's smile was condescending in spite of all she could do. "Not quite alone, although I do admit my company is not the brightest right now. But perhaps later in the day we can have a go at the house. You should get to know the servants, and perhaps you would like to know something of the way it's run."

Josh gulped down the last of his coffee. "And I absolutely

promise to be back by late afternoon when the sun is still high enough to go for a ride. What do you think, Papa? Are we spoiling my new bride too much on her first day? She will begin to think all her days must be full of entertainment."

"She seems far too levelheaded ever to think such a thing," Richard said with what Morna felt was genuine warmth. "Come along, now. If we're going to take that walk we'd better be about it. Josh and I will meet you outside on the front porch, Morna, in, say, ten minutes. That'll give you time to finish your breakfast." Richard's hand hovered over his wife's shoulder without actually touching it. "I'll stop in before I leave for the yards."

There was an uncomfortable silence at the table after the two men left. Morna stared at her plate trying to think of the right thing to say. Without knowing why, she realized she was actually afraid of this formidable lady. Glancing at Celia from under her thick black lashes, she wondered what there was about her that was intimidating. She was elegant and fragile, had a serene, mature beauty about her, and a manner that was aloof but kind. No, there was nothing in her appearance, unless it was that touch of perfect fashion that made Morna feel like a country-bred girl beside her. Absently she tipped her head to one side, toying with her fork. She was intensely curious about that strange little scene of the night before. Nor had she missed the undercurrents that flowed between Josh's mother and father both last night and this morning. Some nerve had been touched here, but she could not fathom what it was. Raising her eyes just in time to catch the withdrawn, saddened expression on Celia's lovely face as she stared vacantly toward the window, Morna was struck all at once by a sense that underneath Mrs. Deveroe's genteel, mannered exterior there was a very complicated person. Was she jealous perhaps because a wife had come between her and her adored son? She had no reason to be. If anyone had cause to be jealous it was Morna herself, for a woman who inspired the kind of love and devotion Josh obviously felt for his mother was going to be a formidable rival indeed.

Celia seemed to become suddenly aware of the silence. "Is there anything you need, Morna? Can Betsy help you put your things away? You'll find she moves slowly and is a little careless, but she's very willing to help. Betsy and Vestal have been with us since I was a young girl," she added almost as an afterthought.

Morna could not remember which one of the shadowy servants was Betsy, but Vestal, she recalled, was that huge man who drove the carriage.

Mrs. Deveroe seemed to have drifted back to those faraway years of her youth, and Morna began to wonder if perhaps Josh's mother suffered from melancholy.

"Thank you, but I can put everything away myself. I'm used to waiting on myself." She emptied the last of her chocolate. "Perhaps I'd better go now."

"Yes, they'll be waiting," Celia said absently. "And don't forget your hat. The sun can damage a fair complexion like yours, and you cannot be used to it."

"Is . . . is there anything I can get you before I leave?"

"No. I think I will go back to bed. I didn't sleep at all well last night." Celia rose regally from the table and pulled the shimmering fabric of her robe around her. "Enjoy your walk."

With a sense of reprieve Morna watched her disappear back into her shadowy bedroom. Then, throwing down her napkin, she darted hurriedly back to her own room for her hat.

"Did you have any trouble on the voyage down?" Richard asked his son as they stood on the porch waiting for Morna.

"We had a close call only once. As we approached Sandy Hook a ship appeared off the coast heading straight for us. Captain Manning crowded on the sail, and thanks to the *Aurora*'s superb speed we were able to outdistance her. I would swear, though, that she was foreign."

"It was probably one of those British warships that have been hovering along the coast. How brazen they are! I didn't want to speak of this in front of Morna, but just a few days ago they fired on an American merchantman coming into New York and took the head right off one of the sailors. The city was up in arms. They had the body on view in City Hall for three days. The mob broke into a warehouse and carried off supplies stored there which the Britishers had purchased for their ships. There were three of these warships right at the mouth of the Narrows and probably some French vessels as well. Something has to be done and soon, but, God knows, I hope it is not an embargo."

"But an embargo might well teach them a lesson."

"And ruin us all in the process. No, Josh, we will feel it very keenly, being so deeply involved in ships and trade. And merchants will feel it even more. There must be another way."

"Well, something has to let the Royal Navy and the Frenchies know that they cannot pirate American ships and men. Had I known about that incident in New York I would have brought Morna back by land. Thank God we did not meet with such unpleasantness."

"Thank God, indeed. Here she is," Richard said, his voice brightening. "And in a very fetching bonnet, too."

He offered Morna his arm. What an uncommonly pretty daughter his son had brought them back.

"It's old fashioned, Papa, but still serviceable. And it will keep off the sun."

"Your bride not only is pretty but has excellent good sense, Josh," Richard said, leading her down the shallow steps. "I think we are going to get on very well indeed."

For nearly an hour the three of them wandered the large plateau on which Southernwood stood before Richard left the newlyweds alone while he went to the stable to see that their horses were saddled.

"What do you think of the place?" Josh asked, sitting his wife on a stone bench at the end of the garden.

"There is almost no place you can go where you cannot see the river. It's like standing on top of the world."

"I hope you will think of it as home. I am beginning to, although for a long time it was difficult to give up my memories of the old farmhouse in New Rochelle where I grew up. This is so . . . grandiose, so formal, so—I don't know. It seems less a home than a palace. But I'm getting used to it now."

"It *is* a palace," Morna said dreamily. "It reminds me of the stories my father used to tell me—romantic tales of princes carrying their sweethearts off to places full of magic."

Leaning one boot on the stone bench, he propped an elbow on his knee and watched her with affection. There was so much he had yet to learn about her. All of her childhood, her dreams, her longings.

"Did your father tell you stories? He struck me as such a practical, active man, not one for dreams."

"Oh, he had his dreams. I think they were all lost when he had to leave this country, and he filled my head with memories. I shall always remember them."

"Tell me about them."

She was suddenly self-conscious. "They would only sound silly."

"No, no. I'm a romantic myself, in case you haven't noticed.

And I think your father is one of the most interesting men I ever met. Please."

She shrugged. "They were only fanciful things about beautiful ladies with hair the color of topaze and men who rode magnificent black horses and swung their sabers like the warriors of ancient Greece." She closed her eyes, remembering. "There were ballrooms, glowing like the golden sun with a hundred candles, powdered wigs and coats so shot with gold thread that their stiffness made it difficult to move. There were graceful ladies playing at the clavichord, rides in the mist across fields touched with magic. And always, a handsome officer who gives his lady-love a fillet of green velvet ribbon laced with gleaming pearls—a symbol of his steadfast devotion." Sighing, she opened her eyes to look back over the verdant rows of vegetables and flowers laid out all around them. "Poor Father. He has never really stopped grieving for this land."

"I fear he is even more a romantic than I. I've heard enough of those old days to know that even though they included all those lovely things, they also involved a great deal of anguish. He forgot to tell you the other side."

"Perhaps that comes with exile. You remember things as you want them to be. Look, your father is calling you."

"Yes, I have to go." Pulling her to her feet, he cupped her hand in his hand. "Away from candles and ballrooms and velvet ribbons with pearls. Back to the banalities of building ships and making money. Have a good day, my love. I'll see you this afternoon." Lightly he kissed her lips.

With quick panic she threw her arms around his neck. "Oh, Josh, what shall I do all day with you gone?"

"Why, sit here and look beautiful and be a lady, of course."

"But I'm accustomed to have a day's list of chores. I'm not used to sitting around tatting. I want to be *useful*."

"My dear, you now have a houseful of servants to do the chores, leaving you free for anything you like. Enjoy it." He nearly left her there, but the dismay in her eyes held him a moment longer. "You are rich now, Morna. You might as well agree to let it make you happy."

thirty-one

The Tammany wigwam was a dilapidated one-story room attached to Martling's Tavern on the city outskirts. So unprepossessing was it, filled with noise, smoke and assorted odors, that the Federalists scathingly dubbed it "the pigpen." For once Jaspar Carne took some comfort in the insult as he stalked out the door and down the steps, kicking at the ever present pigs along the brick walk who refused to make way for him. An old woman with a thick Irish accent shoved an apple into his face and begged him to buy her wares. Roughly he struck her hand away and wiped his own on his coat. Those filthy refugees—you never knew what you might be picking up from anything they had touched.

Yet this afternoon the calls of the vendors, the iron rumble of wheels on the cobbles, the nuisances of the pigs and stray dogs did not really intrude too heavily. His mind was still too full of that conversation in the room he had just left. Little had he realized when he arrived there—a routine political meeting to discuss a candidate for next year's state-senatorial election— what he would hear. Naturally he had never thought of himself as a likely prospect. He knew well enough that he did not possess that popular touch a good candidate needs. It was enough to be behind the scenes planning strategy for the attractive, foolish men who would win the elections. His rewards were more subtle, but he would see that they came nonetheless.

No, he never expected to hear his own name put forward. But to hear that of the one man he detested above all others— it was too much. He could still see that Tammany sachem, Teunis Wortman, waving a seegar like an eleventh fat finger, his crafty mind already made up.

"Richard Deveroe has everything we need. He is attractive, he is wealthy, he has a showplace up there over the Hudson

427

where he can entertain all the important people who must be courted. He has some training in law and, if I remember rightly, was no stranger to the first Congress."

"His name is closely connected with the Loyalists," Carne had offered tentatively. *Someone* must bring facts into this.

"Ah, but go even farther back and remember that his name is also an old and important one in New York politics."

"That was a very long time ago."

"But is he not a Federalist?" John Bingham might raise issues, but in the end he would always go along with Wortman.

"As a matter of fact, he is, yet his sympathies have always verged on the Republican. I think he would go along with us."

"Change parties?"

"Why not? After all, Aaron Burr did it successfully. Besides, I remember him as a young man. He once intended to go into government seriously but gave it up to make money."

"He has certainly been a success at that."

"Exactly. That is why he would be the best man we could run."

Carne tried again, knowing how futile it was. "Are you aware of how he made his fortune?"

"He started with sloops on the Hudson and branched out from there. What of it?"

Carne made a quick decision. "Nothing, I only wondered." Better save his hard facts for someplace where they would do more good.

"The only problem now is to feel him out. I thought to make a trip upriver in the next day or two. How about it, Jaspar? Would you accompany me?"

"I regret that I cannot. Some pressing matters here concerning the outer ward. John, what about you? Could you go along?"

How pompous and important Bingham looked. "Yes, I think I could see my way clear."

And so it was decided. Within a day or two those scheming men, who held in their hands the power to make a state senator, would walk into Deveroe's parlor and offer him the opportunity of his life. It made the bile rise in Carne's throat. And there was nothing he could do. He could and would, of course, see to it that Richard's speculation in securities in '89 became common knowledge. But would that be enough to block his rise? Carne thought not. There was too much in his favor. His money, his looks, his powerful friends, that damned infuriating aristocratic Deveroe name. The electorate would love it. Americans, for all their talk of equality and democracy, were always easy prey to the old sirens of wealth and class. They would adore him for being an aristocrat. And in their admiration they would elect him senator for the Southern District. Merciful heavens, how it galled!"

He became aware of voices in the parlor only as he was handing his hat and coat to Brooke, the black footman Hester had engaged against his wishes. At least, he made her think it was against his wishes.

"Who is there?" Carne asked curtly. He never did Brooke the courtesy of addressing him by any name other than "you."

"Madam is receiving guests." At least the man had learned to speak proper English in place of that incomprehensible dialect so prevalent among Africans.

"What guests?"

"Relatives from up on Hudson's River, I believe, sir."

Oh, God! Was he to be forced to be civil to the very man whose prospects were causing him so much misery? Stalking into the parlor ready to face Richard Deveroe, Carne was relieved to see only Richard's son with a dark-haired young beauty at his side. The new bride, no doubt. Scowling, he quickly took in the other people around the room—Agatha, Hester's mousy daughter, dressed in her usual white muslin and colored sash that made her look thirteen even though she had to be in her twenties; and Dexter Barnett, that wastrel, lounging against the mantel in true *beau-monde* style. What was he doing here wasting his time when he ought to be working? And Hester herself. She was surprised to see him all right.

"Oh, Mr. Carne," Hester cried, jumping up, her pale face suddenly white. "How grand that you have arrived in time to greet Josh and Morna. You remember, I went to Southernwood to their wedding reception last fall . . ."

He silenced her with a look. "Well, Joshua," he managed to say, and extended one limp hand.

"Mr. Carne." Josh had never been able to bring himself to call this imposing man "Uncle." "May I present Morna, my wife. Aunt Hester's husband, Morna. Jaspar Carne."

She curtsied prettily. "So pleased to meet you, Mr. Carne."

Jaspar gave her the briefest of nods and turned his cold eye on Dexter. "You are out early, I see, Dexter. Does the firm give you leave to spend your afternoons at tea parties? If so, then the business world has changed mightily since I was a young man."

Dexter seemed to wilt in the confines of his wide neckerchief. "Mama asked me to drop by . . ."

"That is true, Jaspar," Hester said tentatively. "It is so seldom that Josh is in the city."

"I do not see that the visit of a relative gives one license to neglect their responsibilities. I think you had better get back to your office, young man."

Glaring at his mother, Dexter moved toward the hall. Josh took advantage of his going to bring Morna to her feet and take his leave.

"We do hope to see you again soon, Aunt Hester. Thank you for receiving us so hospitably."

"Do come back, Josh," Hester murmured.

He gave her a light kiss on the cheek. "Mr. Carne, Agatha. Good day to you both."

Agatha nodded as he drew Morna from the room. None of the three made any move to follow them, but Dexter was still waiting in the hall, fury on his face.

"That . . . that. . . . If your young wife was not present, Josh, what I would call him. I hate him, blast his reptilian soul."

"He is certainly a strange man. How does Aunt Hester bear it?"

"She got what she deserved. Look here, you two," he said, brightening. "Why don't you join me at the Park Theatre tonight? You can see my wife, Angelica, in a frothy farce that's quite good fun and afterward I'll take you backstage to meet her. You'd love it."

"What do you say, Morna?"

"No, I don't believe I feel up to the theater tonight. But you go, Josh. You'd enjoy it and I shall be perfectly all right in the hotel with Dorcas."

He could not disguise his delight. "You're sure?"

"Of course. Go ahead."

"All right, then, Dexter. I'll meet you there. When?"

"Eight o'clock. No, a quarter to. In the lobby. Capital."

They left together, discussing the evening's play. In the parlor behind them Hester sat as quiet as her daughter. Jaspar's return had caught her by surprise, since ordinarily he was not home so early. Now she knew what to expect, and he did not disappoint her. The front door had barely been latched shut before he turned to her.

"How dare you bring that woman into this house!"

"But, Jaspar. She's a kinswoman. What could I do?"

"She's the daughter of a notorious outlaw and traitor. That I should be forced to be civil to her, should have to undergo the indignity of a formal introduction! It's outrageous. I told you, Hester, I never wanted to receive your family in my home. Bad enough to have to endure your worthless son and mousy daughters."

She lowered her eyes before the fury in his face. "I'm sorry, Jaspar. It won't happen again. They droppped in without warning."

"See that it does not. I'm going upstairs now to my study. I do not wish to be disturbed until supper."

"Very well."

Hester watched him leave, staring sullenly from under her pale lashes. Then she caught the black look her daughter was turning on them both.

"What are you looking at! Go and get my vinaigrette at once. I feel the migraine coming on. Hurry up, you useless girl."

Agatha rose and walked sedately to the door without a word, leaving her mother to sink on the cushions of the sofa behind her.

Passing up the cabs that filled the streets, Josh decided to walk the three blocks up Pine Street to the Park Theatre. It was a cold but clear night and he was filled with a sense of release—a carefree exuberance. He felt like a student again, out on the town for a night's lark. Certainly it had nothing to do with his feelings for Morna. She was the dearest, most exquisite creature, and he prided himself on the fact that his devotion for her had not wavered from that first moment he set eyes on her. All the same he was glad she had decided to stay home this evening. He himself had a few qualms about spending the night in Dexter's company—it was obvious that dear Dexter had not changed too much from the spoiled, self-indulgent boy he remembered. Morna was better off at the hotel.

Dexter was waiting for him in the lobby, foppishly dressed in a Spanish-blue cloth coat with huge padded shoulders, a brocade waistcoat, kid slippers and the highest collar Josh had ever seen. With his long hair swept forward around his face, he drew all eyes as they moved through the lobby and into their box. Yet once the curtain rose and the stage became a golden nimbus in the candlelit house, he forgot Dexter completely and lost himself in the performance.

Angelica did not appear until the farce following the interval, but one look at that striking beauty heightened by paint and Josh could see how Dexter would have lost his heart. She was a terrible actress, and a more worldly man might have assumed at once that it was not talent that got her onto the boards in Mr. Price's company. He decided his cousin must have some genuine feeling for her by the way he pounded on the rail and cheered wildly after her every speech.

Dexter's enthusiasm grew as he dragged Josh backstage afterward. In the melee of actors, props and paints, Josh was pulled along, trying to see everything at once. The machinery of ropes and pulleys which created arrangements of voluminous clouds, not to mention a real waterfall, particularly intrigued him, but Dexter gave him no time to examine it. He dragged him down a dark, narrow hall, rapped once on a door and threw it open. With a rush he wrapped his arms around the woman who sat at a dressing table illumined with lamps.

"Darling wife, you were magnificent, as always!"

Angelica disentangeled herself from her husband's close embrace. "Why, Dexter. I didn't know you were in the house."

"Come on, now, love. Give us a proper kiss."

"Please, Dexter. There are others present. Who's your handsome friend?"

"She's always a stickler for what's proper, Josh. This is my cousin, Joshua Deveroe. My wife, Angelica, the best little performer in New York—on stage and off."

Josh ignored his cousin's lewd wink. Angelica looked him up and down appraisingly while Josh shifted his weight uncomfortably. Under the heavy paint there was a delicacy of features which showed that she must have been a real beauty in younger days. But a hardness already showed through, as though the makeup had dried on her face permanently. He made her the most politely formal bow he could manage.

"My, my, one of the famous Deveroes," Angelica said coyly, extending her hand. "I knew my husband was related to that illustrious family, but I had about given up hope of ever meeting any of them. How very nice finally to make your acquaintance."

Her smile was a blazing starburst. Josh bent his head over her hand to keep his dismay from showing.

A girl's voice came from the doorway. "Angie, where did

you put the—Oh, I'm sorry. I didn't know you had company."

"That's all right, Grace. Come in."

Turning, Josh saw a blond vision. She was small, barely five foot three, he guessed, with creamy skin and a cascade of long blond hair framing her oval face. Her eyes were large and deep green and her mouth was pert, beautifully shaped, like the petals of a rose. Where had *she* been in the program?

"This is Mr. Joshua Deveroe, Grace. One of my husband's 'rich' relations. You've met Dexter."

With an aplomb that showed how perfectly at home he was backstage Dexter draped one arm about the blond girl's shoulders and kissed her full on the mouth. Surprised, Josh noticed she did not bat an eye. It gave him the uncomfortable sensation of wishing he could do the same.

"Mr. Deveroe," the girl said when she could break free of Dexter's embrace. "So pleased to meet you. I'm Grace O'Malley."

He raised her small hand to his lips. This girl could be no more than sixteen. What was she doing in this libertine world?

"Miss O'Malley. I am trying to remember why I did not notice such a rare face during the performance."

She laughed, the tinkling of crystal. "That's because I was only one of the Muses in the drama. There were four of us, trying to push the others back. They are all bigger than me, so more often than not I find myself hidden by the scenery. It is one of the hazards of the profession."

Angelica draped herself like a queen in the chair before her table. "You won't find Grace O'Malley in the program either. In the small print, however, you'll see one Graciana Overton. That's our Grace." Dipping her hand into a jar of cold cream, she began to wipe at the paint on her face, making steaks of heavy color across her skin. "Yes, Mr. Price thought 'O'Malley' far too prosaic for the theater."

Grace's long lashes fluttered up at Josh. "Do you stay in town, Mr. Deveroe? Surely you must have seen our company before."

"No, I live up the North River in Mount Pleasant. The truth is, I used to visit the Park Theatre regularly, but since I've . . . been involved in my father's business, I do not get down to New York very often. You must have joined the company since my last time here, or . . ."

"Or what, Mr. Deveroe?"

Josh glanced up at Dexter, who was watching him with a

knowing look in his eyes. "Or I would have remembered you," he said, trying to brazen out his embarrassment.

Angelica and Dexter exhanged a long glance. If Cousin Josh was taken with little Grace it might in the long run be to their advantage.

"Grace, my dear, why don't you show Mr. Deveroe around backstage? He might be interested to see all that goes into a production."

"Why, I should love that. Are you interested in the theater, Mr. Deveroe?"

"As a matter of fact, I would like to know how that machinery works. The effect in front was striking. I'd especially like to know how they create that waterfall on the stage."

"It will be my pleasure to show you." She took his hand, and he was suddenly conscious that her slender body was covered only in a loose negligee of clinging silk. Yet willingly he went. It would have been impossible not to.

The door had barely closed behind them before Dexter and his wife fell laughing into each other's arms.

"What a conquest!" Angelica shrieked. "Who would have thought it of little Grace!"

"She didn't seem to mind. She was more congenial to him in those five minutes than she's been to me in all the year I've known her."

"Well, what do you expect, Dexter dear, when you pounce on her every time she walks into a room? I do wish you'd learn to keep your hands off the chorus. It's degrading to me." Picking up a brush, she stroked her hair, still sticky with pomatum.

He stood behind her, his hands on her shoulders. "Now, my love. It's just that you are all so tempting."

She studied his face reflected in the mirror. "Your cousin is very rich, isn't he?"

"Would I were half so!"

"This could be a good thing for us, Dexter. God knows you led me to believe you were an aristocrat with a fortune and I've seen none of it since we married. Now here is our chance to turn some of your family's money our way."

"I would not start counting the shillings yet, my love. The truth is, Cousin Joshua, for all his wide-eyed innocence, is, at heart, as straight and proper a little gentleman as ever turned your stomach. And he has a new wife, to boot. A very pretty one, at that."

Angelica shrugged her white shoulders. "Even with the best of wives a man likes a free and easy romp now and then. It adds spice to his life. Mark my words, the look your strait-laced cousin gave our little Grace had nothing of propriety in it."

"Perhaps so, but I can tell you his conscience is compelling. He won't be so easily led by a pretty face. Even when it comes on such a curvacious body."

"We'll see. If he has so much resistance, then nothing is lost anyway. But if he could be led to . . ."

He slipped his hands around her narrow throat. "Yes?"

"Well, I only was thinking it might be to our advantage . . ."

Dexter did not really care for this sudden interest Angelica was showing in his cousin Josh. How could he convince her this was a hopeless proposition? What would get through the scheming mind? Suddenly she turned in the chair and slipped her arms around his waist. All arguments fled.

It was after midnight when they left the theater. Josh was both pleased and embarrassed that the lovely girl, Grace O'Malley, still hung on his arm. She had changed her negligee for a slim gown of pale-green tabinet, with a sleazy-looking squirrel cape around her shoulders. Her long hair had been thrown up and covered under a wide-brimmed velvet hat with a sweeping brim—the "Lavinia," it was called. In the shadows underneath he could just see her green eyes sparkling with mischief and her provocative smile. He had not really intended to prolong his friendship with the little actress beyond their tour of the theater, but somehow it happened that Dexter and Angelica swept the two of them along as they left the building.

"A late supper at the Shakespere Tavern. Just the thing!" Dexter gave him no time to argue. Then there she was, taking his arm and smiling up at him. He gave the sleeping Morna back at the hotel one quick thought, then shrugged and went along.

They knew something was wrong the minute they came out into Chatham Row. The darkened park and the street were crowded with people, the rumbling noise of their voices like a roar of the ocean. Torches illumined the night like huge fireflies. Strange, Josh thought, how some groups almost gave off the smell of trouble. The four of them stood grouped together looking across the Row and wondering if it was really wise to set off down Chatham Row toward Broad Way.

"Who are they?" Grace asked in a small voice.

"Damned troublemakers," Dexter answered her. "They're out again and at midnight to boot. This is the third time in as many weeks."

Josh had picked up enough of the angry cries from the park to begin to understand. "They're sailors, I think. Demanding work or at least bread."

"Of course they're sailors. Look at those faces. Some of them even still wear that disgusting greased pigtail."

"What are we going to do, Dexter? We can't go through that mob." Angelica clung to her husband's arm.

Dexter started down the Row, pulling his wife after him. "I'll be damned if I'll let such riffraff intimidate me. Come on. They won't hurt us."

Josh caught him back. "Wait a minute, Dexter. You and I might pass by that bunch and get nothing more than a broken head, but I don't think the ladies should go near it."

"The 'ladies' are tougher than we are, Cousin, or haven't you learned anything about city life?"

"No," Angelica cried. "I'm not approaching that mob, Dexter Barnett, if I have to walk all the way to William Street to get to the Shakespere. Don't you know that men in that condition will only be infuriated by your evening clothes? They'll take you for a swell and likely put you in the stocks, if not worse."

"She's right," Josh said, taking Grace's hand and starting back inside the theater. "If you want to, Dexter, go ahead. I'll take the ladies the back way and meet you at the tavern."

Suddenly the mob began to move, spilling out across Chatham Row straight toward them. With dismay Josh realized it was going to head down Beekman Street to the slip, probably to burn a warehouse or a few boats. Hurriedly he pushed the two women back toward the dark alcoves of the unfinished theater entrance. "Quick. Hide in here till they've passed."

To his dismay Grace dropped his hand and began to run. The seamen were milling close enough now that he could see their faces yellow in the torchlight, their bad teeth and angry, distorted mouths as they yelled their protests.

"Hey, look there," one called, glimpsing Grace as she darted toward the doorway. She was nearly in the darkened safety of the entrance when hands grabbed at her cape, tearing it from her shoulders. She screamed once and struck out at the man.

By then Josh had reached her, and he pulled the seaman away by the collar, punching him down to the deck. He stood over the man, sickly aware of how thin and weak he actually was. Leaning down, he pulled him to his feet. "Come on now, mate. Leave the lady alone and go on about burning your warehouse. We've no quarrel with you."

"God-damned swell!" the seaman snarled. His friends were close enough that with only a few calls he could have this dandy tarred and feathered. It was a tempting thought.

"This embargo is hurting me too, in spite of the way I look. I'm likely to go to debtor's prison in the next few days. Go along, now, and tell your troubles to those who can do something about them."

"Ye'd better be glad I didn't bring the others."

"I am glad. Now get on about your business."

Josh watched the man slink away after the larger part of the mob, which was halfway down Beekman Street by now. Just to be sure, he waited until there were no stragglers left, although in the shadows of the Row he could still not be sure that one or two of these desperate men were not hiding, lying in wait to rob them.

In the quiet he was not aware of Grace until she suddenly stood up on her toes, threw her arms around his neck and kissed him.

"Oh, thank you, Mr. Deveroe. You saved my life. That terrible man!"

"We got off lightly, I admit. With angry and desperate men like that you never know what might happen."

Picking up her cape, he arranged it around her shoulders while she, clinging to his arm, laid her head against his chest. How like a child she was.

"Who are they? Why are they so angry?"

"They're sailors forced out of work by Mr. Jefferson's embargo. Haven't you noticed the deserted waterfronts, the grass growing on the wharves, the dismantled ships moored at the slips, no traffic in the harbor? This damned embargo is going to ruin us all."

Quickly Josh ushered the others down the now empty Row to the comparative safety of Broad Way. Not until they turned onto its wide walkway, burnished gold under the street lamps, did he breathe easier.

"Are you really going to debtor's prison?" Grace said, looking up at him from under the provocative brim of her hat.

"No." He smiled mischievously. "At least, not yet. Who knows what might happen before this thing is over?"

"I don't understand embargoes or politics at all." Grace sighed, leaning closer to Josh's tall body. As they turned down the darkened Fair Street, she pictured herself sitting close to this attractive man during supper, the small ways she might entice him, the return to her room at Mrs. Bradley's boardinghouse. Who knows what the night might bring?

Her disappointment was bitter in her mouth when they came to a stop under the lamps above the entrance to the Shakespere Tavern. Josh waited for Dexter and Angelica to catch up with them, then took Grace's hand and put it on Dexter's arm.

"You must forgive me for denying myself the delights of a supper with two such lovely ladies, but I'm afraid I must get back. Morna will worry."

Dexter could barely hide his contempt. "My dear cousin, don't you know it is better for the wife to worry than to think she can drag you home on leading strings? Come on, the evening is not half over."

"No, I have pressing matters to face in the morning and I have enjoyed myself long enough. Dear Miss O'Malley. It has been such a pleasure."

With an actress's aplomb, Grace feigned a sweet smile. "I do hope I will see you again, Mr. Deveroe. You must come back soon to see our company perform. We do a very tolerable La Belle Sauvage."

"I should like that very much. Mrs. Barnett, your servant."

He was gone almost before they could protest. Angelica followed her husband through the doors of the Shakespere, just managing to be heard over the cacophony of the crowded taproom.

"You fool! Why didn't you make him stay?"

Setting off down the street, Josh was filled with a sense of release. It was satisfying to him that he had done what he felt was the sensible thing, even at the cost of the desire. Part of him really wished to stay there with Grace. In fact, he had left more because he wanted to stay than because he did not. Actually, he had no intention of going back to the hotel. Morna was probably sound asleep and would not even know when he returned. No, he thought, striding toward the corner of Fair and Nassau. He was going to Beekman Slip to see what those seamen were up to. Their desperate, starved faces had bothered him more than he wanted anyone to know. They had a just cause. The Congress had taken the bread right out of their mouths, not to mention the mouths of their children. They were a force that would have to be reckoned with.

thirty-two

As Celia entered the side door of her house she heard Richard leading his visitors out onto the broad piazza that faced the vista of river and hills. Thankful to have missed them, she slipped upstairs and began pulling off her riding habit, stained and sweaty from the long, exhuasting gallop she had just endured. Such rides were almost a daily occurrence now as she tried vainly to exorcise the furies of memories and melancholy by driving herself to a state of near-collapse. Throwing the heavy keysermere habit across the bed she slipped on her robe. Then listlessly she sat down to brush at her hair, just as Richard entered the room.

Celia looked up in surprise. It was not often lately that he deliberately sought her out.

"Good morning, my dear," he said, stepping up behind her and placing his hands lightly on her shoulders. Surprised, she looked up to see his shining face in the mirror and realized that something had put him in an excellent humor. It was a welcome change from the polite restraint that had existed between them these last months.

"Have your visitors gone?" she asked.

"Yes. Two gentlemen from the Tammany Society down in the city. Listen to this, Celia," he said, drawing up a chair beside her. "They want me to be a candidate for the April elections next year. Can you believe that?"

"Candidate? For what?"

"They want me to run for state senator from the Southern District on the Democrat-Republican ticket. I confess I'm intrigued."

"And pleased, I can see."

"Yes, that too. There is always a good deal of flattery involved in the making of a candidate."

"But, Richard, I thought you no longer had an interest in politics."

"I thought so, too. But now, given the chance to get back into government, I find myself intrigued more than ever. The business is going well, we have wealth enough for three families—now perhaps it is time for me to go back to my first love. You don't look very happy about it. What's the matter?"

With sudden vigor Celia pulled the brush through her hair, sorry she was not better able to disguise her lack of enthusiasm. The truth was, she did not really care much one way or the other, though she supposed she should be glad for Richard's sake.

"Will the business go on without you? After all, you made it what it is."

Some of his enthusiasm faded. "You won't starve, Celia, if that's what you're worried about. We have enough now to last us quite a few years in the elevated style we've grown accustomed to."

Her eyes flashed. "You don't have to be so sarcastic. I didn't mean to sound worried."

"Look, I can put Josh in charge of the yards—it'll do him good to be completely responsible for some aspect of the business. Elisha still does as much as I to keep the wheels running smoothly, and perhaps we can even move up a couple of younger men to positions of increased responsibility. If I handle it right, I won't even be missed."

Celia laid down her brush. There was something in Richard's face that revealed his old love for the intricacies of government—a love she had forgotten over the years and thought he had, too. Now she was reminded of how he had given it all up once before, for her sake. Turning in her chair, she took his hands.

"You're right. There is not a single aspect of your work which you have not handled well all these years. If you want to run for state senator now, I'm sure you will find the way to manage it."

"And you don't mind?"

"Of course not. I'm not expected to campaign, am I?"

"No, no. I'll see that you don't have to." He was suddenly very serious. "Of course, I am not so naïve as not to know that it is my money and the Deveroe name they are after. The Republican Party is so divided at the moment between the Clintons and the Burrites, each side at the other's throat, that the Federalists could almost walk into office. They are hoping my lack of strong associations will be a unifying factor."

He perched on the arm of a chair, crossing one leg over the other and smoothing the buff trousers over his knee. "And I fancy I might make an attractive candidate, Celia. Moreover, I'll have a platform from which to speak so that by the time the election comes round people will be voting for what I stand for, not just my wealth or my name."

He was even more idealistic than she had thought. "But Richard, aren't there power struggles and compromises—the dark side of politics which you really don't know very much about?"

"Oh, yes. I'm quite aware, for instance, that this is an important election becuase certain selected senators serve on the Council of Appointment, which fills nearly all the civil offices in the state and the city. The spoils are enormous and, naturally, the Martling men hope to keep one of their own on that Council." He grinned a little sheepishly. "I'm already learning, you see."

She had not seem him so enthusiastic about anything in what seemed years. None of the pitfalls that loomed ahead seemed to appear on his horizon. Well, it was her place to encourage him. He'd discover the perils soon enough.

"My dear, I hope you will run, and if you do I'm sure you'll win. If that is what you want and will make you happy, well, then, it will make me happy, too."

He raised her hands to his lips. "Thank you, Celia. Your encouragement is very important to me. Without it I might not take this on. I'm glad you didn't force me to make that kind of a choice."

Predictably it was Josh who was most excited about Richard's prospective candidacy. Leaving on a night boat from the Albany wharf, he and Morna arrived on the flood tide at the dock below Southerwood, and entered the house to find their parents at breakfast in the large upstairs hall.

"Well, I think it is a capital idea," Josh exclaimed as he helped himself to his mother's untouched plate of rum steak, fish and eggs. "In fact, if you were not running, Papa, I'd be tempted to try it myself. Someone has to bring this damned government to its senses."

Richard stifled a laugh. "Come, now, Josh. Assuming I can be elected, I will be such a junior, inexperienced member that my influence will not be felt for a long time. Then, too, the Congress in Washington City is not noted for being swayed by the opinions of State Legislatures."

"All the same, it's a beginning. Your name means something in New York and West Chester, and—gross as the thought is— your money means power. Besides, you have the gift, Papa. I've long thought that your real talents were wasted in trade. I feel certain that once you get started you'll have a great future before you."

"Listen to the boy, Celia. They've only asked me to consider the campaign and already he has me President!"

With a piece of bread Josh mopped up the last of the juices on his plate. "What do you think, Mother? Are you pleased?"

"Of course," Celia said diffidently. "If this is what Richard wants, then I am happy for him. It will put a burden on you, though. I hope you are aware of that."

Josh looked at his father. "Does that mean I'll have to take more responsibility for the business?"

"I intend to give you the full control of the Dolphin yards. You know the work inside out and it will be yours someday, anyway."

Josh hesitated only a moment. "All right, Papa. I think I can handle it and I'm willing to try. But will you really be withdrawing from everything?"

"Pretty much. I remember too well how Mr. Jay's law practice became practically nonexistent while he was devoting his time to the Congress."

Celia, noticing her daughter-in-law's preoccupation, made a halfhearted effort to draw her into the conversation. "How was your trip, Morna?"

The large sea-green eyes abruptly shifted to her face. "It was very nice," Morna answered softly. Actually, she had barely caught the comment, she was so busy studying the table.

"We saw Aunt Hester, Mother," Josh broke in before Morna could elaborate. "Had tea at her fine house and even met her husband as we were leaving. What a grim experience!"

"Dear Hester," Celia replied without enthusiasm. "I haven't seen her since the reception. How was she?"

"Does she ever change? She is extremely put out with you because you haven't visited her. Complained about it the whole time we were there."

"Then she hasn't changed."

Josh turned back to his father. "You should arrange to visit the city very soon, Papa, if you really intend to go into politics. You would not believe what has happened. Mobs in the streets, wharves silent and rotting, ships lying like so many corpses in the harbor. Last month alone the embargo sent two hundred merchant's to debtor's prison."

Morna suddenly brightened. "Oh, yes, Mr. Deveroe. If you were in a position to do something for those poor sailors, what a blessing it would be."

"Are there no other jobs they could fill until shipping is resumed?"

"What else do sailors know, Papa, but ships and the sea?"

"Mobs and riots are never an answer to any problem," Celia started, but Morna interrupted her.

"But it is their wives and children who are starving. You should see their pitiful faces."

Celia vainly fought down a surge of irritation. "Surely you didn't go into the areas where these people live?"

"No, but we saw them at a protest rally in front of the City Hall. My heart was truly moved at the sight of their pinched faces and swollen bellies."

Richard leaned over and gripped Morna's hand where it lay on the table. "My dear, no problem is as simple as it sounds. You must understand that."

"That is easy for you to say sitting here at a table which can barely hold all the food in silver dishes that are set upon it! Does understanding the problem put bread in the mouths of hungry children? Something must be done. Someone must act."

Celia frowned at the girl. "My goodness, you certainly have let yourself be caught up in their cause."

"She really has, Mother," Josh said with pride. "Actually I was the one who first was pulled along on the fringes of a riot one evening after the theater, but when I told Morna about it the next day she became more inflamed with righteous indignation than I. She spent the next two days ladling gruel in a kitchen house for the unfortunate victims of the embargo."

"You didn't!" Celia said angrily, but Morna met her gaze squarely.

"Yes, I did, and it was one of the most moving experiences of my life."

"But did you never consider the kinds of illnesses you were exposing yourself to?"

"Is that what really matters? They were children and they were hungry."

Her righteous stubbornness only increased Celia's annoyance. "It was a foolish thing for you to do!"

Her face white, Morna jumped to her feet. Biting back what she really wanted to say, she turned to her husband. "I think I shall go lie down awhile, Josh. The boat trip was terribly rough. I don't feel at all myself."

"Of course, dear. Go ahead." Josh waited until she had disappeared down the hall before facing his mother. "Really, Mama, you were really quite severe with her. She was only performing an act of charity."

"I shouldn't wonder if her indisposition is the first sign of some disease she picked up in that dreadful place."

Quietly Richard spoke to his son. "Josh, will you please step downstairs to my study and search out last month's ledgers on the Dolphin's yards? We can go over them here before I leave for the day." Though his voice was all politeness, Josh recognized the edge in it.

"Of course, Papa."

He had no more than disappeared down the stairs before Richard threw down his napkin on the table. "There was no need for you to speak to Morna that way, Celia. She has a perfectly understandable and admirable concern for those less fortunate than we are."

Celia fought back the tears that sprang to her eyes. "It is a foolish charity that destroys itself in the process of helping others."

He made a determined effort to be patient. "I seem to recall a time when you braved disease and dirt to help a parcel of orphaned children. Was the concern you felt for the Grovers any different from what Morna feels for these children?"

The image of Hannah's young face was a searing knife. "That was different," she said stubbornly.

"Besides," he went on in his infuriatingly level voice. "Since when have you cared about propriety? I never knew anyone to worry less about the foolish nonsense of convention."

She could not control the words that sprang from her lips. "I don't like her!" There. It was out at last.

Richard looked at his wife as though a stranger had taken her place across the table. "I don't know why not. Morna is a sweet, innocent creature. A daughter anyone would be proud of."

"She is neither sweet nor innocent. She has fooled all of you. I tell you I don't like her!"

"Keep your voice down!" Richard ordered, hearing Josh's steps in the hall below. "I don't understand what has come over you, Celia, but I tell you this. I do not want to hear a word against that girl in my presence or in your son's. Keep your opinions, which are biased and unfounded, to yourself. Is that clear?"

Celia glared at him across the table. How tempting to take her Staffordshire plate and hurl it in his face.

"Confound you," she muttered. "Confound you all." Jumping to her feet, she started toward her room.

Trying to keep a curb on his anger, Richard grabbed at her sleeve. "Celia, listen to me!"

"Let me alone!"

She tore her arm from his grasp and rushed into the sanctuary of her darkened bedroom.

Slamming the door behind her, Morna threw herself into a chair by the round table, pounding her clenched fists on her knees. What a lie it had been to say she needed to lie down! With this fury inside her there was no way she could rest. But one had to say something, anything, to get away from the supercilious, arrogant woman looking down her aristocratic nose and teaching her, her—Ewan Deveroe's daughter—her manners!

She got up to pace furiously around the room. Everything in it reflected what was wrong with this place. Elegance and richness, in the velvet hangings, the embroidered pillow slips, the embossed gold cherubs on the marble mantel, the silver sconces and crystal lamps, the thick Turkey carpet under her feet. Decadence! She wanted to strip it all away and put up simple homespun and indigo-blue resist linen curtains like those that had hung in her room at home.

Southernwood had never been a comfortable place for her, and now that she had seen firsthand how others lived in squalor and hunger while she wallowed in all this richness, she could barely stomach the place. If it were not for Josh—but then if it were not for Josh she would not be here in the first place.

She stopped in front of the round mahogany table, its waxed surface mirroring her features in a blurred copper tone. Above it her gaze was caught by her father's portrait, staring unseeing out toward the window.

She fought down the tears. Dear Papa. How slim and young and handsome he looked in his military uniform. Not at all like the heavy man she had left in Nova Scotia. In this, her favorite picture of him, he was the youthful prince he had told her of so many times. The brave soldier who comes to claim a princess with amber eyes to match her chestnut curls and brings her a green ribbon entwined with glowing pearls as a fillet for her hair.

Her sobs overcame her. What had happened to her dream? Why was reality so unlike the vision? How was she ever going to be able to live the rest of her life here, trying to share a house with a woman she disliked, and who, she was sure, disliked her every bit as much? If only her mother were still alive to come and rescue her.

By the time Josh found her later he was full of ideas for the management of the Dolphin yards. "I was skeptical at first," he told her, stretching the plans out on the bed, "but after talking with Papa I believe I can really do an even better job of it than has been done so far. If we can continue building the sloops long enough to survive this damned embargo, afterwards I intend really to expand. With the way things are on the high seas, surely the government will be authorizing a navy soon, and they'll need ships. Men-of-war as well as tenders and brigantines. I intend to see we get our share of those contracts. And with Papa established in government, that should not be too difficult."

Morna watched him, shyly trying to summon the courage to speak. "Josh, do you think we might have our own house? I mean, well, it would be an advantage for you to live nearer the yards and I would not mind being closer to the village."

He looked at her as though she had lost her senses. "Leave here? Why? There is everything here at Southernwood you could possibly want, more comfort and finery than anywhere else in the world. We could never match this."

"I don't want to match it. I only want a simple house to arrange and run my own way. Don't you see? I'm not accustomed to living in all this luxury. It makes me uncomfortable."

He rolled up the plans, studying her face. "It's Mama, isn't it? I confess I have never seen her as she is now. She has always been the most sweet-tempered of women. I fear she is really ill. If only you could know her as I do . . ."

"It's not your mother," she lied. "Truly, it's just that I would so like to have my own home. A home more like the one I was accustomed to at Round Hill. Is that so terrible?"

Putting his arms around her, he pulled her to him, smelling the freshness of her hair and the faint pungency of rosewater on her white skin. "Of course it isn't. I suppose every woman prefers her own home, even to living in someone else's palace. All right, my love. We'll look around near the yards for a suitable house."

Morna hugged him so hard it hurt her arms. "Oh, thank you, Josh." When she pulled away, her eyes were shining. "I'll go back to New York as soon as we find a house and choose the proper furniture. Can we afford that?"

"Yes, my love, as long as you don't mind American goods. With the ports closed the way they are there won't be much to choose from in English or French."

"I *want* American furnishings—the simpler the better." She threw her arms around his neck. "Oh, Josh, you are so good to me. I love you so very much."

He fell back against the coverlet, pulling her with him. "Keep talking like that and there's nothing I won't give you!"

Part V

*Beyond the
Shining River
1808*

thirty-three

In an uncharacteristic gesture that betrayed his anger, Jaspar Carne crumpled up the *Packet* and threw it on the table. Around him the raucous babble of the coffee room of Dyde's Hotel went on unabated. Waiters carrying platters of fried oysters and terrapin soup weaved their intricate dances among the men going and coming around the crowded tables. He had purposely selected one near the wall to gain a measure of quiet, but now it was unwanted. What use was reflection and reading when he had to digest the galling information that his rival was rising on the crest of success while he stood swamped below? Unseeing, he stared at the checkered cloth stained with gravy spots and soiled with coffee stains. There must be something he could do! To sit back helplessly while Deveroe's star ascended was more than he could bear. Of course, this newspaper carried only the first tentative mention of "Senator Deveroe's" candidacy. The door was now open to praise and agreement, but it was open as well to innuendo, false accusations, damaging suggestions about Deveroe's past. Perhaps in the long run this was what he needed. Once in the open, Deveroe was vulnerable.

A loud burst of laughter made him look up. Only two tables away two young men stood exchanging gossip—and Carne knew it was gossip because he recognized one of them as Jack Trollope, a reporter on the *American Citizen*, a young, snoopy, ambitious and not overly ethical newspaper hound. The man even looked as though he should walk with his nose to the ground, eternally sniffing around for anything that might get him a byline. However, at this moment he was a welcome sight.

Trollope heard Carne call him over. Not hiding his surprise, he weaved around the intervening tables—*Just like the snake he is*, Jaspar thought—and pulled up a chair across from the Alderman. His thick lips wore a quizzical half smile. He knew Alderman Carne, that grim humorless fellow, well enough to realize that if he was inviting him to his table it was in the interest of the story.

"Can I buy you a pint?" Jaspar asked, managing to make the offer sound as though the drink might be poisoned.

"Ordinarily that is a gesture I never refuse, Alderman, but it happens that I have to meet some friends in the back in only a minute or two. What can I do for you?" No sense beating about the bush. Jack Trollope liked good company, and Jaspar Carne was certainly not that.

"I am curious about what the fellows at your place thought of this." One long, carefully manicured finger fell on Richard Deveroe's name.

Trollope shrugged. "The wind was blowing that way, so it was no surprise. Naturally, we shall oppose any candidate you Martling men propose."

"Yes. With your editor, Cheetham, in De Witt Clinton's pocket, what else could you do?"

"At least Mr. Clinton has spent a lifetime in government, which gives him an edge over this fellow who only knows piling up money and boats."

"Does it not strike you as odd that Tammany would back a man with no experience?"

"They probably figure he can win on his money and his looks. It's been done before." Trollope stirred uncomfortably in his chair. Was the Alderman—a known Wigwam man— trying to ferret out which direction the winds of opposition would blow? If so, it would be wise to break this conversation off right now.

"Deveroe, as some men might still remember, belongs to a prominent family of Tories."

Trollope could read nothing in Carne's inscrutable face. "That is certainly one little piece of ancient history which can be used against him."

"Might I suggest it is not so ancient as you young gentlemen believe? There are still a number of us around who felt strongly about our past differences with Great Britain. So strongly that we will carry to our graves the prejudices and ideals of that revered age."

Passing over Carne's rhetoric, Trollope suddenly came alive to what he was saying. Was it possible that the good Alderman *opposed* Deveroe's candidacy? Could that be why he had summoned a Clintonite reporter to his table? What an intriguing idea. Trollope could almost feel his nose quivering.

"Would such men," he said carefully, "still be swayed enough by the label of 'Tory' to turn against a candidate? It all seems such a long time ago."

Carne leaned forward on the table, looking up at Trollope from under his heavy brows. "Mr. Trollope, never underestimate the strength of the hatred good men felt for those who opposed the Revolution. 'Tory' was synonymous with 'traitor.' It still is to those of us who suffered through those dread days. It always shall be."

"But I understood that Richard Deveroe served with the Continental Congress."

Carne sat back suddenly, his long, clawlike hand tapping the checkered cloth. "A vile rumor. Oh, he was there all right, supposedly in the capacity of a clerk or secretary. Actually he was there as a spy. Look at his family, sir. His cousin was a notorious outlaw who laid waste to West Chester County in the name of 'loyalty.' His father, mother, cousin, the whole tribe, had their estates confiscated after the war, and most died in exile in England or Nova Scotia. This man only escaped by passing himself off as a patriot. Can anyone, knowing the whole picture, doubt it was a vile disguise?"

Trollope was beginning to realize he had stumbled on a gold mine. How pleased his editor would be to pull the rug out from under a Tammany candidate, especially using the foul taint of scandal. Old Cheetham would owe him quite a favor for the satisfaction of a good stab at Tammany. Besides, whatever the reasons Alderman Carne opposed Deveroe's candidacy, there was more of feeling than of reason behind them. Trollope almost laughed. He had thought Carne possessed no feelings of any kind.

"It might hurt him, this Tory label, but I doubt it will ruin his chances. As you well know, the Federalist Party is half dead."

"Then there's the business of the securities," Carne went on as though Jack had not spoken.

"What securities?"

Jaspar relaxed and leaned back in his chair, an enigmatic smile on his sharp face. "Look into it. How did Deveroe make his money? Why was it when the rest of the country was suffering from lack of cash and depreciated currency, he was

able to buy mills, factories and yards up and down the North
River? What was his friendship with Mr. Hamilton worth to
him? Did he possibly know—before he went around purchasing
them—that the new goverment of 1789 would redeem all those
state and federal bonds at full value?"

"He was a speculator?"

"I make no accusations." Carne lifted a hand like a priest
bestowing a benediction. "I only suggest it might be worth
your while to examine."

"It strikes me, Alderman, that for a staunch Martling man
you are very generous with your 'suggestions.' Can it be you
do not go along with your party's choice of candidate?"

Up went the hand again. "I only *make* these suggestions.
Anything more is really none of your business."

No, but it would be worth pursuing, Trollope thought. "Very
well, I shall certainly take note of your 'suggestions,' and you
will no doubt be reading of them in the paper!"

"I trust that your source shall be anonymous," Jaspar said,
his cold eye on Trollope's face. "If by any chance my name
should crop up I shall deny this conversation ever took place.
And with my reputation . . ."

"Oh, you needn't worry. I'll keep you anonymous if only
in the hope that further 'suggestions' might be forthcoming.
We'll use anything, Alderman, that you feel might hurt the
prospective candidate."

He rose to leave, looking every inch of the cocky youth
who had discovered a full wallet lying in the street.

Carne watched him disappear into the mob. *If only I had
more*, he thought.

"I'm sorry to bother you, Jaspar . . ."

Looking up over the iron rim of his round spectacles, Carne
was irritated to see his wife's figure framed in the doorway.
In today's pseudo-Grecian, clinging fashions, Hester's plump
body reminded him of nothing so much as a sausage.

"I've asked you not to bother me when I'm in my study."

"I know. And ordinarily I wouldn't, but I've had a letter."

He slammed shut the copy of *Palmer's Principles of Nature*
and pushed his chair back from the desk.

"What letter could you possibly receive that would require
that you interrupt the only quiet time of reflection allowed me
in this house? But what's the use of complaining? Just like any
Deveroe you must have your wishes seen to the instant you
want something. Come in, then."

"You needn't insult my family," Hester muttered, sitting primly down in a chair opposite her husband. "Though why should I be surprised? I've never seen you pass up an opportunity to do so since I came to this house."

"Let me remind you, my dear, that this is *my* house and you are here on sufferance." He pushed his iron-rimmed spectacles up his long nose. "Now, what is this pressing correspondence?"

Hester quickly turned her eyes away lest her anger be too obvious. What was there about this man that so thoroughly cowed her? He did not beat her, he allowed her, within certain limits, a very free use of his money, she fancied he even respected her for the shipshape way she ran his house. He made few demands on her. The infrequent times he visited her bed he became a man consumed by a ravenous lust which left her sore and weary the next day. It left him a little frightened, too, she suspected; for weeks afterward he would act as indifferent to her as if she were a servant.

"Actually, it is about my family that I wished to speak. I've had a letter from Celia."

A shadow fell across Carne's face at her sister's name. The eyes narrowed, the fingers drummed on the arm of his chair. She recognized the symptoms. Her brother's name or that of his wife were just about the only words that could produce a crack in that carapace.

"Well, get on with it or must I wait all evening?"

"Celia tells me her son and his wife have purchased a house and are in the process of furnishing it. Morna wants to visit New York to buy some furniture, but Josh cannot accompany her and Celia is too ill to do so. She asks me to receive the girl as a guest and help her get about the city."

"I told you I never want to see the daughter of that damned traitor in this house!"

The quiet coldness with which he spoke made her want to flee the room. She did rise to her feet, folding the letter in her hand.

"Very well. I shall let her know that it is impossible at this time."

But now that he had been drawn away from his reflections Carne was not willing to see her get away so easily. "Sit down," he said, and Hester quietly backed into her chair. She was now in for the lecture on the ingratitude of the Deveroes and the selfishness of Richard Deveroe in particular.

"Knowing how I felt, why did you even mention this?"

Hester looked up in surprise. "Why, I suppose because I hoped you might let her come. It would be diverting to help her shop and she seemed a very sweet young creature."

She was even more surprised to see him stare thoughtfully at the dark damask curtains. For a long moment he said nothing.

"She might be company for Agatha, too," she added hesitantly. "The child has so few friends and they are not so far apart in age."

Jaspar was not fooled by this sudden concern for Agatha. And yet. . . . An idea took hold in his mind, as compelling as it was repugnant.

"Ordinarily I would never consider such a breach of my honor as to receive that man's daughter here. But circumstances are such that now . . ."

"Circumstances?" They must be compelling circumstances indeed to induce Jaspar to back down from his high-flown principles.

"Did you see the article in the *Packet* on your brother's possible candidacy?"

"Richard? A candidate? For what?"

"How many times have I told you, Hester, your mind would be improved by reading something more than those frivolous romances. If you would open a newspaper once in a while you would know that your brother is being put forward as a possible candidate for state senator next year. He has a a good chance of winning, too."

Hester could not resist. "That must be a difficult pill for you to swallow!"

"And for you, I should hope, as well. After all, he did you out of your rightful inheritance."

"For which I shall never forgive him!"

"And that wife of his. Did she not usurp your position as the only daughter in the family? Have you forgotten *that* old injury?"

To please her husband Hester summoned all her anger against Celia. "No, I shall never forgive her either. They are two of a kind."

"And you are *my* wife. I trust you stand with me in whatever position I see fit to take."

"Of course."

"It does seem an injustice to me that a man who has done you so much wrong should not only reap the rewards of a large fortune but should now have fame and public position as well."

"It is unjust. You are absolutely right."

His quiet voice went on. "And do you not feel that we should take every precaution to prevent this from happening? You and I?"

Hester could not resist a sly smile. He was after something all right, and he was offering her a partnership in finding it. She wanted to laugh in his face, but wisely she held that back.

"My goodness, Jaspar, I confess I simply cannot follow you."

"Don't be coy, Hester. You are much too long in the tooth for coquetry. I want to block this nomination, by whatever means I can."

The silence of the room was broken by the musical pealing of bells as the gilded French clock on the mantel chimed the hour.

"You are thinking that this girl might be of use to you. But how? She seemed such a meek little thing—I can't imagine anything she might do or say that would hurt Richard."

Absently Jaspar picked up a long turkey quill and smoothed the feather along the arm of his chair.

"Talk to her. Be sympathetic. Draw her out. There may be nothing there to learn, but it's worth trying on the chance there is. If you do discover anything that can be used against your brother, be assured I will know how to give it maximum impact."

"Ha!" The laugh escaped. "For all your righteousness, Jaspar Carne, you are no less devious than the rest of us mortals. Oh, don't glare at me. Let's for once be honest with each other. You want to confound Richard's new career and you want me to help you. Very well, I don't mind getting in a few blows at Richard for all the ones he's given me. But you must understand it will be very difficult to earn Morna's confidence with you sulking about the house as though she brought in the plague. You will have to help me."

The quill was slammed onto the pewter tray. "Very well. We are understood. I shall try to be pleasant to the girl when we meet, which I trust will not be too often. Encourage her to be a friend to Agatha. And especially be a friend to her yourself. Anything you can get from her which might be damaging to your brother will make it worthwhile."

Celia pulled out the long hatpin that secured her riding hat to her hair and threw the hat on her bed. Sitting down before her mirror, she began absentmindedly to unbutton the long rows of buttons in the front of her habit.

A tentative knocking at her door brought her back to the present.

"Come," Celia called, and saw Morna's reflection in her mirror.

"Am I disturbing you?" the girl asked. Why must she always apologize!

"No, no. Come in, Morna. I'm just getting out of this tight habit. These infernal fashions are enough to strangle one. They make it very hard to thump around in a saddle. I long sometimes for the loose, easy dresses I wore as a girl."

She noticed with irritation that Morna looked surpassingly pretty in a gown of yellow muslin with stripes of drawnwork. And so young.

"I've had a letter from Aunt Hester," Morna said, sitting primly on the edge of a gilt chair. She was never comfortable in her mother-in-law's fancy pink room, but whether it was the delicate furniture or Celia's attitude she could never tell. Certainly she felt she could do nothing right in the older woman's eyes.

"She has invited me to stay with her for a week or two while I shop for furnishings for the new house."

"Yes, I wrote her about it. I'm pleased she asked you to come, but I warn you it is likely to be an unpleasant experience. Hester is not one to put herself out for other people."

"Oh. Well, at least it means that I shall not have to wait until Josh finds the time to take me down. I am most anxious to begin setting up the house."

"Are you so eager to leave us, then?"

A pink flush crept up Morna's white face. "I didn't mean that."

Celia could have bit her tongue. In some perverse way she must always enjoy hurting this girl. Her fingers tore at unpinning the diamond-studded watch fob she wore on the high waist of her habit.

"Young people always like to be alone," she said, trying to mend the moment. "And furnishing one's first home can be a most exciting experience. I'll never forget the pleasure of building Southernwood, though I must confess that at the time I fancied Josh would be a part of it for years and years to come. Now Richard and I shall rattle around in its empty rooms. Such is life and the ingratitude of children."

She was looking down at the pin and so missed the angry glare her daughter-in-law gave her. Morna was beginning to realize that Celia never missed an opportunity to needle her. She was just starting to admit to herself how very much she disliked Josh's mother and how grateful she was going to be to get out from under her shadow.

With a last tug the pin broke loose. "Morna, would you please put this away for me in the box over there? I must have ridden too hard this morning. I suddenly feel so very tired."

Obediently Morna took the diamond fob and moved across the room to the large mahogany jewel chest that stood on a lowboy. This was the first time she had occasion to see Celia's large collection of necklaces, earrings, bracelets and pins. She knew they must include some very expensive stones, and ordinarily she might have enjoyed examining them and reveling in their beauty. Now she was too annoyed to do much more than give a cursory glance at the neatly arranged shelves.

"Josh was saying to me last night how good he thought it was that you are riding out every day. He fancied you must be feeling better to want so much exercise."

"Sometimes I have to force myself to it," Celia sighed, "but it is excellent for one's health and I like to think it has improved mine. The pin goes on that little shelf near the bottom. Third from the bottom, to be exact."

Morna pulled out the shelf absently and laid the pin on the burgundy velvet where the dazzling chips glimmered against the rich darkness of the lining. She started to push the shelf back into place when her eye was caught by a piece lying against the back of the drawer. She reached in and drew out a wide green velvet ribbon entwined with delicate small creamy pearls.

"Oh, what a beautiful thing . . ."

Celia saw only the hand holding up Ewan's gift reflected in the mirror. She twirled around.

"Put that back!"

"It's lovely." Morna's eyes were radiant. "Just like the one my father used to tell me about."

She was so intent on examining the fillet she failed to notice her mother-in-law's stricken face.

"It is just this kind of thing that the beautiful ladies always wore in their hair in the stories he told me. Where did you get it? Did Mr. Deveroe give it to you?"

Celia turned away, struggling to make her voice matter-of-fact. "It was a gift, given me long ago. It's old now and I never wear it anymore. Put it back, please."

"But..." She was about to ask if perhaps Celia might let her wear it, since she obviously didn't want it. But, looking up, she was shocked at the change that had come over the self-assured woman of a few moments before. White and drawn, shoulders slumped forward, Celia looked as though she had the weight of the world pushing her into the cherry-wood dressing table.

An idea leaped into Morna's mind. It was only a quick thought, but it suddenly reversed their positions, placing the older woman at the advantage of the younger.

"Did Father give you this?" she asked lightly.

"No! Put it back and please leave me. I'm excessively tired and I want to rest."

"Of course." The drawer was shoved into place. "I'm sorry if I've disturbed you, but I thought you would want to know about Aunt Hester's letter. Perhaps when you feel better we might discuss what I should look for in my shopping."

"Of course. Yes, I'll be glad to make suggestions. But later, when... when I feel more rested."

As Morna closed the door behind her she could still see Celia sitting at her dressing table, her bodice half undone, staring at the table. She leaned against the frame a moment, smiling to herself.

"Josh, tell me about when you were young."

"What could possibly interest you about those days?"

"Oh, little things. I wonder what life was like then and how it is different now. Did you ever see General Washington?"

"Yes, at his first inaugural. But since I was only two or three years old at the time, I only know what's been told me about it. Most of my recollections are of Myer's Point in New Rochelle—a very fine place for a boy to grow up."

"Was your mother pretty as a young girl?"

"I thought she was the most beautiful woman in the world."

"What color was her hair?"

"Hmmm. Often it was powdered, of course. I remember that. The damned stuff was always all over shoulders and coats. But the natural color of her hair was the loveliest shade of golden brown. In fact, it was the most striking thing about Mama, that her eyes and her hair were nearly the same color.

That's unusual, you know. Papa has mentioned it often."

"I saw the prettiest piece of jewelry today, stashed away in her chest. It was a lovely thing of pearls twined around a wide green ribbon. A fillet, they call it. She says she never wears it anymore."

"No, I haven't seen her wear it in years. But she used to. I have many memories of her with that piece of finery in her hair. It was a great favorite of hers once."

"I should like one like it someday. I wonder where your father bought it."

"He didn't. It was a gift during the war when contraband was popular. In fact, she has told me many times as a child of how it was buried in a field for nearly four years, along with the topaz my father gave her on her wedding day and all the hard specie they owned. Those were fascinating days—more so for one who did not have to live through them, I suspect, than for those who did."

"A gift? From some love-stricken officer, I surmise, I wonder if he was British or rebel?"

"As a matter of fact, it was a gift from your father. Papa let that slip once a few years back. That was why she stopped wearing it—Papa really didn't like to see it. Actually, I can't imagine why he should feel that way when everyone thought the world of Cousin Ewan."

Morna turned away to keep him from seeing the self-satisfied smile on her lips. So Celia had lied to her. The mosaic was fitting together. If it had not been for those romantic stories her father had told her so often, she would never have paid the slightest attention to that fillet. But she had enough imagination and intuition not to miss the highly powered associations that came alive with it. She was seeing a few things in a new light. How Celia had fainted that first day when she thought it was Ewan who was dead. How it was that her father's name was never mentioned in this house. How, in fact, it was avoided by the people who were supposed to admire him so thoroughly. It was only an idea, of course, but she would be willing to stake a good deal on the guess that there had been some kind of association between Josh's mother and her father before he left for Nova Scotia. Had it been merely a deep friendship or had it been a real love affair? Remembering that series of stricken, remorseful looks on Celia's face, she guessed it was more than platonic. Perhaps it explained as well why her mother-in-law disliked her so much.

Ah, well, at the very least, it certainly put Celia in a different light. She was no longer the formidable matron but a vulnerable woman.

Just like me, Morna thought.

thirty-four

"If I had ever thought we would run into that orange-haired hussy this afternoon, I would certainly never have brought you here!" Grasping Morna's arm, Hester hurriedly pulled her into the refuge of the Roman sculpture room.

"How could you know, Mama?" Agatha replied, quietly following. "There is always a crowd at the Academy of Fine Arts. You can meet half of New York here any afternoon."

Morna looked back wistfully at the gaudy figure of Dexter's actress wife, Angelica, laughing and chatting to friends in the hallway, apparently unaware that she had just missed colliding with her mother-in-law. She was flamboyant and pretty and it might have been amusing to meet a real actress. Yet, glancing around the room they had just entered, Morna found all interest in Angelica quickly driven from her mind. It was like a fairy palace. In fact, the whole Academy was the most fascinating place she had ever visited.

"I deeply regret, my dear," Hester said, patting Morna's gloved hand, "that you should be exposed to that woman. Bad enought that she has no reputation at all, but she can't even act! I never saw a worse Lady Teazle since Charlotte Campbell—who everyone knew was nothing but a draper's daughter—set the crowd jeering at Covent Garden. Disgusting! Celia will never forgive me."

"Please don't distress yourself, Aunt Hester. I am enjoying the display, I truly am. You see, I have never seen anything like it before, certainly not in Annapolis Royal."

"You are too gentle and too kind," Hester gave her another pat. In the two weeks Morna had been living with her she had developed a small fondness for the girl. With her quiet ways she was easy to influence, and Hester had enjoyed directing her shopping excursions.

"Isn't the mechanical panorama in the adjoining room?" Morna asked, peeking around the plaster statues. "Oh, I am dying to see it. Can't we hide in there?"

"I am anxious to see that, too," Agatha said quietly. She was afraid her mother would pull them all back downstairs to the second floor, where stuffed animals along the walls stared at you through sightless eyes. How she hated it, all that rich life dead and indecently perpetuated. Her heart had hurt even over the giant-sized terrapin, the biggest attraction in the Academy. "Won't you come, Mama?"

Hester's eyes stayed on the hallway, where she was prepared to flee at any sign of Angelica's feathered bonnet. "No, I shall stay here and hide behind the statue in case I should meet anyone I know." Her eyes widened as she looked over the gray plaster. "What is this?" A quick glance at the handbill. "Number eight—'The Reclining Hermaphrodite.' Merciful Heavens! Perhaps I'll just stay over here behind 'The Fighting Gladiators.' You two girls go along. Never, never shall I forgive Dexter for making me a mother-in-law to that horrid woman. My own son!"

Morna and Agatha left her still muttering and made their way around the crowd into a smaller room, where a large table in the center under a tasseled canopy held the artificial curiosity of moving parts which represented New York City. They spent a good half hour admiring the replica—the tiny figures moving along the streets, the mechanics at work in the building, carriages sliding along streets and bridges, ships entering and departing from the busy harbor, even tiny wooden waves moving up and down in the wind. By the time they returned to the next room they found Hester well hidden on a bench near the window behind an amply robed Socrates. Morna's face was flushed with excitement as she sat down beside Hester.

"I've had the most wonderful idea, Aunt Hester. While Agatha and I were watching the mechanical panorama we got to talking about Southernwood and it occurred to me that she has never seen it. I would so much like for her to go back with me and stay for a few weeks. She could help me set up my new house and be company for me with Josh away so much. And it would do her a world of good to get away from the city, especially now that the weather is growing warm."

Hester's eyes shifted upward to her quiet daughter standing with downcast eyes, her face half hidden by the taffeta bows of her hat.

"Come, now, Morna. I can't have you taking my daughter away from me. Why, I don't see how I should manage without her."

Morna's enthusiasm was undampened by this expected response. Hester could manage very well without anyone—she simply liked having her daughter there to wait on her, an unpaid servant. Morna's sense of injustice was aroused. She looked up at her cousin, pleading silently for help, but the girl had already turned to stare defeated out the window.

"Of course, we could both go," Hester said, draping her lace mantle in graceful folds over her arm. "I haven't seen Celia for an age."

Morna pulled back as though she had been struck. Bringing Agatha back to Southernwood was one thing—Celia would never object to such a quiet, mousy little creature. But Aunt Hester! It would only create another injustice for Josh's mother to add to the already long list she had collected against her daughter-in-law. "She has been . . . ill, for a long time now," she said lamely. "I'm not sure . . ."

"She probably only needs a little company to cheer her up." Hester was startled, looking up, to catch Morna staring down at her hands, resentment etched in her face.

"Forgive me, my dear," she said laying her hand sympathetically on Morna's arm, "but I have suspected from a few things you have said during our visit that Celia and you do not get along. Would she be so upset that you invited us?"

"It's possible. She keeps mostly to herself these days. And I must admit, she does not seem to like me very much."

"Ah, it is as I suspected." Hester's fingers closed like claws over Morna's sleeve. "Perhaps she fears I am leading you astray down here in the wicked city. Now that Richard has renewed his political ambitions she must be extremely cautious about doing anything which would seem improper."

Morna fought down her irritation. How had Celia come into this? All she wanted was to get this poor girl away from her overbearing mother.

"Mrs. Deveroe is not so proper," she muttered.

"Why, what do you mean? Celia is the soul of respectability. She always has been."

"Only that . . ."

"Yes?"

"Well . . ." the words came stumbling out. She had been dying to tell them to someone for such a long time. "Well, I believe your sister was in love with someone else before she married Mr. Deveroe, and I think that someone was my father!"

Hester's eyes grew very bright. "Did she tell you this?" she asked, leaning forward almost into Morna's face.

"Oh, for heaven's sake, no. She would never tell me such a thing. I learned of it accidentally from some of the things my father told me and from a few mementos I stumbled across in her room."

A loud gentleman in a bottle-green morning coat ushered two giggling ladies out into the hall, leaving the room thinned of viewers. Hester dropped her voice in the sudden quiet.

"My dear girl, you are quite mistaken. I was there when Celia and Richard were married. They were little more than children, and they never even so much as glanced at anyone else. They were as thick as thieves right from the first moment Celia came to my father's house. Besides, I never saw Ewan be anything more than politely friendly to her or she to him. No, I think you are mistaken."

"I know I'm right," Morna said stubbornly. "It was my father she loved, I'm sure of it. There are too many coincidences. If it wasn't before she married Mr. Deveroe, then—then it must have been afterward!" There was a peculiar satisfaction in making this accusation—revenge for a hundred little slights and discourtesies.

"Now, that is nonsense. Celia would never..." Hester fussed with the soft folds of her lace mantle, rearranging it around her shoulders. The light from the window reflected in her pale-blue eyes, turning them almost white. Of course— those war-time years. She was remembering how Richard was gone for months at a time on that preposterous business of the Congress in Philadelphia, while Celia lived at the Manor House at West Farms near Ewan's headquarters. Suppose.... What an interesting idea! Mr. Carne might be very pleased.

Outside, a gray cloud crossed the path of the sun, momentarily darkening the room. The shadowy plaster sentinels suddenly seemed suggestive of a tomb. Abruptly Hester stood up.

"Would you like to accompany Morna to Southernwood, Agatha, my dear?"

Her daughter could barely contain her astonishment. "Yes, Mama. I really would."

"Very well. We'll discuss it further over tea. Perhaps I can join you there after a week or two, and we'll come back together."

Morna and Agatha fell on each other's necks. "Oh, thank you, Mama. Thank you."

Settling the silk crown of her bonnet firmly on her white-gold hair, Hester stared toward the door, immensely pleased. "Don't thank me, my dear. Thank your cousin Morna."

Celia looked with dismay at the list of names Richard handed her. "All these people? I'm not sure we can fit them in, even in this house."

"Oh, we can manage it. Throw open the doors to the parlors and the dining room and with that wide entrance hall we have a good-size reception room. If necessary, we'll use the upstairs foyer. But I'm hoping for good weather so people can spill out onto the porches, and we can even put lanterns up in the gardens. That will solve the problem nicely."

"But this looks like half of West Chester County!"

Richard tried patience. "My dear, this is the real beginning of my candidacy. It *has* to be a spectacular event. One that will make people remember me as an excellent host and an influential man."

"Dyckman's, Tompkinses, Van Cortlandts—I don't mind having *them* here. They're all gentlemen. But Richard, surely some of these people are farmers and tradesmen. Do you really want them tramping through our beautiful home?"

"My dear, they are the electorate. I want their vote." Reaching out, he tipped up her chin and looked into the familiar large brown eyes. "My love, I fear Southernwood is making a snob of you!"

To his relief, she smiled a little shamefacedly. "You're right. Having built this lovely place, I want so much to keep it as beautiful as it is. Even if that means never using it!"

"How you have changed."

"All right, I give up. You must have your fine party to announce your candidacy and I must deal with muddy tracks, seegar ashes, brass spittoons, and broken china. So be it."

"You really don't mind?"

"No, Richard. Didn't we agree this campaign was your dream come true?"

"Good." Crossing his buff-trousered legs he took the list from her hands. "You plan the food—simple if you like, but plenty of it—and alert Lowery to the need for the stables. We'll probably have to run a carriage back and forth to the wharf to bring up guests from the city. Oh, and some will be staying the night. You'd better plan on that."

"How far away is this?"

"Nearly a month and a half. By that time Hester will be gone—I trust."

Celia shrugged. "I trust so, too, but she has not seemed very anxious to get back. She has become very thick with Betsy and Vestal. I think she may still have hopes of luring them away. Perhaps I can drop a subtle hint or two."

"With Hester it had better not be too subtle."

Celia laughed. "Well, if worse comes to worst, I shall simply tell her she has to leave because I need the room."

"On the other hand," Richard added reflectively, "since she is Carne's wife and he is a Republican alderman, it might not hurt to have her here. It might give an appearance of party solidarity which actually is not there. Perhaps you'd really better encourage her to stay."

"If Mr. Carne's mind runs in the same tracks as yours he will no doubt make sure she comes home before this reception. But, we'll see. She can stay or leave, as she wishes." Celia's eyes played for a moment over her husband's face as he bent over the long list. "You are enjoying yourself, aren't you, Richard."

He looked up, pleased at her words. "I've never enjoyed anything more. It's exhausting, of course, but exhilarating too."

"You are becoming a crusader," she said, teasing him a little.

"Yes, perhaps I am. Politics can be such grubby business, Celia, yet where else does one have such a far-reaching effect on other people's lives and fortunes—for good or ill. President Jefferson, for example, and the Congress, by passing into law this detestable embargo, sent innumerable men to their ruin, all to teach France and England a lesson. I'm fascinated by the interaction between nations and powers that reach down to touch the lives of individuals. How exciting to become part of that process!"

"I know you too well, Richard. You think you can influence these decisions for good. I see you every day becoming more and more the flaming zealot for the rights of man. How can you reconcile those ideals with the Tammany men who defraud the city of hundreds of dollars every year?"

He shrugged. "I need them to get my foot in the door. Once established, I have hopes of bringing a little integrity into the business of government. I like to fancy that there should be a morality in politics toward which I can at least point the way."

She shook her head. "Oh, Richard, I hope you will not be disillusioned. They are powerful men with long memories. They will think you owe them the spoils of office in exchange for their support."

But she could say nothing that he had not already thought through himself. He took her words lightly. "They have not yet realized that I am not so easily led. Besides, in four years I may become as big a cynic as they."

She had to go. Her horse would be saddled and waiting at the stables even now. "Not you," she said, rising. For a moment she almost reached down to kiss him lightly in the old way, but something made her turn toward the door instead. Irritation? Anger? With herself and the world in general?

"Have a good ride, dear," he called after her, but she could see he was already deeply absorbed in the sheaf of papers outlining plans for the reception.

Josh had tried very hard not to come to the theater this evening, and once there, he had tried even harder to leave without going backstage. Yet at the last moment his feet had led him there almost against his will. No, unfortunately not really against his will, for the truth was he wanted to see her again, this lovely young girl with the gamin face and the long flaxen hair.

"Why, Mr. Deveroe. I never thought to have the favor of your presence again."

He had to speak over the loud laughter and calls of the people strolling through the hall. "I'm not in town very often." Silently he pushed the door closed behind him. How fortunate to find her alone.

"Is your cousin with you, then? And your wife?" She sat down at a table and picked up a brush, pulling it through her yellow hair.

"No, I'm quite alone." How he longed to run his hands through that golden cascade. "As a matter of fact, I am only here on business which has kept me very involved. I had this one evening free, so I thought to enjoy a play. I . . . I recognized your name on the program."

Grace studied his reflection in the surface of her mirror. She had not quite forgiven this Mr. Deveroe for leaving her in the doorway of the Shakespere Tavern to go running back to his sleeping wife. That kind of peremptory treatment was not what she had come to expect from gentleman friends. She swiveled around in her chair to face him.

"Well, it's been very pleasant seeing you again, Mr. Deveroe. Please give my regards to your cousin when next you see him." The quick turn sent her robe sliding off one shoulder, half exposing her creamy breast. She drew the silk up languidly.

"Are you engaged for supper?" Josh asked, never taking his eyes from her face.

"No." She was, but she could easily get out of it.

"Would you allow me, then, to make up for my former rudeness?"

Her direct gaze never wavered. "It *was* rude, you know."

"It was. I apologize."

Grace brightened. Her smile was infectious. "Very well, then, Mr. Joshua Deveroe. I accept your apology and I would be delighted to take supper with you. I'll only be a moment. Where will you be?"

"Oh, looking around the stage, I suppose."

"Of course, I forgot." Her eyes looked up provocatively from under long golden lashes heavy with paint. "You are so very interested in the machinery."

They had a quiet booth far back in the room, with a degree of privacy. Fascinated, Josh took in every detail of Grace O'Malley—the faded gaudy hat with its wilted feathers, the slightly shabby dress which revealed too much of her small shapely breasts, the delicacy with which she picked at her food, the long, shapely fingers of her hands which she used unconsciously in an actress's flamboyant gestures.

He was enjoying himself hugely, from this quiet thoughtful assessment of the girl to the pleasurable sensation of her silken thigh against his leg. He was interested to discover that she had a quick mind in addition to her other charms.

He was completely unaware that Grace was studying him every bit as closely and coming up completely mystified. Here was a tall, good-looking man, a gentleman of means and breeding, obviously interested in her. Yet he made none of the ordinary advances she had learned to deflect—only an arm around the back of her chair, an occasional movement of thigh against thigh. For once in her young life *she* wished for more!

"How old are you?" he asked suddenly.

Grace set down her fork, wondering if she could afford to be honest. "Eighteen."

Resting his chin on his hands, he frowned at her. "Not possible." He shook his head.

"All right, then, seventeen. Just seventeen."

"That's more believable, anyway. So young to be already an actress!"

"In the chorus, remember. Hopefully by the time I'm twenty I'll be an ingenue, a leading lady at twenty-five, and retire at thirty, terribly, terribly rich."

"What a wonderful scenario. How did you ever come to choose the stage?"

His brown hair fell over his forehead, his eyes were warm, and all in all, Grace thought, he looked like a young Adonis. How to tell this elegant, pampered creature the sordid details of her sixteen-plus years? For a moment she debated producing the usual fictional account of her youth, but decided against it. For all his youthful appearance she suspected he would see clear through a falsehood.

"I grew up on the docks of Baltimore, watching my mother kill herself washing clothes, never knowing my father. I decided when I was ten that I would have something more in my life, and the theater was an easy way to get it. All you need are looks. You can get by with no talent, no money, no particular gifts, as long as you have beauty. That's the only asset I have and as long as it lasts I intend to make the most of it."

His eyes never wavered from her face. "Have you known many men?"

The direct question startled her, but she answered unflinchingly. "More that I would wish."

"I suppose it comes with the . . . the 'career.'"

She shrugged. "To some extent."

"Come on, I'll take you home."

He hailed a passing cab and handed her into its tangy leather interior. Through the dark streets they sat quietly swaying in the cab, listening to the horse's hoofs clacking on the stones, hearing the cries of the watchmen in the distance. Mystified, Grace sat silent while Josh managed to make the small distance that separated them seem larger than it was.

At her door, she rummaged in her reticule for a key. "I'm not supposed to have guests in my rooms, but if you slip up the stairs quietly, I'll make you a cup of tea."

He hesitated. "All right."

They tiptoed up the stairs, trying to keep the creaking wood from announcing their presence. Inside her tiny two rooms, she lit a candle and poked up the half-dead embers in the hearth. Josh threw his cloak and hat on a chair, then went to stand behind her where she knelt. When the coals caught flame she rose, satisfied, to find him looking down into her upturned face.

The dark shadows of the room accentuated the fine planes of her cheeks and sculptured lips. "You are very beautiful, you know," he said, laying his hands upon her shoulders.

When she did not reply he went on. "Look. I have a lovely young wife whom I love very much."

She smiled provocatively. "What do you want with me, then?"

"I never thought to have a mistress . . ."

"Then you are certainly different from most young men in this city."

He hesitated. "I should not like Dexter to know."

"That you are here with me? You needn't worry that I will tell him—or Angelica either. They are both far too preoccupied with his debts to be concerned with my affairs. Or yours either."

Still he hesitated. "I feel that I really should not be here."

Her thin shoulders shrugged imperceptibly under his hands. "Then you must go."

Sensing the struggle, she knew a sense of triumph when it was lost.

"I don't think I can." His hands slipped sensuously over her shoulders, undoing the laces and sending the thin, filmy dress of cheap satinette cascading around her ankles. Grace's laugh came from deep in her throat as her arms slipped around his neck and he lifted her in his arms and carried her to the bed in the dark alcove of the next room.

thirty-five

In spite of the cupola that adorned its roof, the gray stone walls of the three-story New York debtor's jail projected a grim aura of despair. Josh had never been in a prison before. As the barred doors of the second-floor gallery clanged shut behind him he felt his throat close, as though the very air itself was being shut out behind these damp, enclosing walls.

The three wards on each side of the gallery were as cheerless as all the rest, even though the men were thrown together dormitory fashion rather than separated by cells. Dexter saw him coming from the length of the room, and, dodging between the variety of bedding that littered the floor, he bounded almost into Josh's arms, wringing his hand and all but sobbing on his shoulder.

"You look terrible," Josh said, embarrassed at his cousin's embrace.

"Thank God, you've come. Thank God!"

"I got your letter. It took me a while to get back to the city, but as soon as I got a free afternoon I took advantage of it."

"Come over here. There's a corner where we can talk. I know the man whose cot it is and he's walking up on the roof right now."

The dilapidated camp bed creaked as they sat upon it, sending a large rat scurrying into the shadows of the blackened brick walls. Josh winced. This place reminded him of nothing so much as a ship's hold.

"For God's sake, Dexter, how did you come to this? I can barely believe my eyes."

Dexter leaned forward, lowering his head in his hands. "Well might you ask! Some of these poor bastards are here because their business failed, but there are many like me who for the want of a few pounds were thrown like dogs into a cage. See that man over there on the pallet. He owed twenty-four pounds to his estimable creditors but because he couldn't pay it they sent him here. A measly twenty-four pounds!"

"I'd be willing to guess your debts were not so measly."

Dexter was too miserable to smile. "More like three hundred."

"Three hundred pounds! How in God's name..."

"How do I know how? Some of it was just trying to live the life of a young man-about-town. A lot of it was Angelica—she must be kept in style, you know. It simply grew. As I got a little extra I'd pay off the most pressing of the bastards I owed, but the time came when there were too many of them. So, here you find me."

"What about your mother? Wouldn't she help you? Or your stepfather?"

"That tight-fisted bastard! Why, he wouldn't throw me a rope if I was drowning—which is not such a bad description of what's happened. Mama at least sends me enough allowance to purchase a little food, but for anything more she is completely under the thumb of Jaspar Carne, and he thinks I should learn my lesson. 'Good for the soul,' he says—the God-damned self-righteous, Bible-thumping son-of-a-bitch!"

How like Carne, Josh thought. As though Dexter would actually take to heart the fact that he got himself into this mess. He was too busy even now feeling sorry for himself to learn any "lesson" from the situation.

"Look, Josh," his cousin said, and for an instant Josh thought he was going to take his hand. "You've got to help me. Your father's rich. *You're* rich. You won't even miss three hundred pounds, and it would free me of this place forever." Dexter's tongue flicked at his dry lips. "After all, your papa's about to launch himself into politics. He wouldn't like it to get around that his own nephew was in jail because he couldn't pay his debts, would he, now? I mean, after all, it could be used against him."

Josh almost snorted. "My father has as good a reputation as any man in this state. Publicizing your vices could not hurt him as much as it would you." At the strange look Dexter gave him he found himself holding his breath. If he should ever learn about Grace. . . . But his cousin only turned away, more dejected than ever.

"Look," Josh went on, "you don't have to bribe or blackmail me. I'll help you because you need it. Three hundred pounds

had jilted his mistress and moved to Nova Scotia. It even implied, though not directly, that since the son had married the daughter of this Tory, the dreadful scourge of incest was lurking in the Deveroe family closet. Richard sank back in his chair, fighting down the bile in his throat.

"Where did you get this?"

Wortman thought he had never seen a man so in control of himself. "A 'friend' got wind of it and made sure we had a copy before it went public."

"Jaspar Carne?"

"No, as a matter of fact it was our secretary, Carleton."

A vein throbbed painfully in his temple, yet Richard forced himself to read every word of the scurrilous pamphlet. "Lies, lies," he muttered, and indeed some of the outrageous accusations it made, including how Celia had made herself available to half the Westchester Refugees, he knew to be libel. But there was just enough truth . . . especially where Ewan was concerned.

"I hesitate to dignify this filth with a reply, but you gentlemen should know that my son was born a good many years after my cousin Ewan moved to Nova Scotia. If that makes him his son it is certainly a medical first!"

"Of course you don't need to reply," Wortman sputtered. "Why, anyone who knows you or your lady would know this is trash—the desperate scandalmongering of a desperate cause. I think any refutation would give it an importance it does not deserve."

"It won't go away simply because we ignore it," Bingham suggested tentatively.

"That is certainly true." Richard stifled an impulse to tear the thing into shreds and fling it out the window. "Whether I deny or ignore it, it will still drag Celia's name through the mud. And there are those who would be willing to believe what it says."

"Deveroe, as near as I can tell they have not the slightest basis for these accusations. Why, you could take them to court and win easily—if you knew who wrote the thing. It is all based on innuendo, no more."

"That is all it requires." Once more Richard opened the pamphlet wide enough to glimpse that degrading cartoon. "Gentlemen, I very much regret that I must withdraw from the campaign. I hope it won't cause you too much inconvenience to replace me at this late date."

"Mr. Deveroe," Wortman cried, genuinely distraught. "Don't suggest such a thing! You can't withdraw now just when we are on the verge of announcing your candidacy."

"It has yet to be announced formally. You could still bring forth your second choice. After all, there has only been speculation up till now that I would be a candidate at all. You can say the speculation was a smokescreen, no more."

"But, Richard," Bingham broke in, "even if you withdraw, that is no guarantee this scurrilous thing won't hit the streets. You may be sacrificing yourself for nothing."

"I don't think so. Go back to Carleton, Mr. Wortman, and send him back to the person who gave him this in the first place. I think you'll find that without me this would be a waste of time and effort."

"You don't know that."

"No. But I'd stake my life on it. Anyway—" Richard moved easily to the decanter and poured another glass of wine, unable to disguise the trembling of his hand—"be assured, gentlemen, there is no way on earth I will allow my wife's name to be dragged through the gutter. Not for any political office this side of heaven. You must honor my feelings in this matter as I honor hers."

Teunis nearly wrung his hands. "God damn it, Deveroe, you knew when you got into this that it would be difficult. I thought you were prepared to take whatever they could hand out."

"For myself, yes. I really don't care what they choose to say about me. But Celia—no, I will not stand for that."

He gulped down the port, turning away from them. Damn the selfish villain who nosed out this story! There was just enough truth in it to bring it close to home. The cartoon revealed that they even knew of the velvet-and-pearl fillet. Damn the past that he had thought dead forever. Damn the loud mouths who gossiped behind their hands. *Damn, damn, damn!*

Wortman could see weeks of work lying in ruins on the Turkey carpet.

"Well, sir," he almost groaned, "I do not feel this is the right way to handle this thing, no, sir, I do not."

Richard remained intractable. "Perhaps not. But it is the way I choose. Believe me," the words strangled in his throat, "it is a sacrifice for me too."

The quiet, long-faced Bingham understood what this was costing Richard even though Teunis Wortman could not. "Suppose we are not able to stop this after all," he said quietly.

"You must. But either way, I will not run."

Sachem Wortman picked up his hat, sick at heart. "Come along, John. We'd better do what we can about this thing before it gets any later." He could not bring himself to extend his hand to Richard. "I suppose we owe you that much."

"Thank you."

Richard felt Bingham's hand lightly touch his shoulder as he passed. The door closed behind the two men, and for a long moment he stood looking at it, studying the swirl of grain in the polished wood. When he turned away he noticed almost curiously that his stemmed glass was still in his hand, empty. In one motion he sent it crashing against the marble mantel, splintering into shards.

"You've withdrawn from the campaign?"

She knew when he came home unexpectedly that something was terribly wrong. "But, Richard, just when everything is ready for your announcement next week. Why, the work we've done for the reception . . ."

"Store it away. There'll be other occasions when you can use the food."

"But why? Why? It meant so much to you."

He could not bring himself to look into her eyes, for fear she would guess the reason. "I gave it long and considered thought and I simply came to the conclusion that it was not in our best interest. You have not been well since the first day I entered into this—"

"Oh, no!"

"I think the interruption it would bring to our lives and the demands it would make on you are simply too great."

"No! You will not do this to me again."

He looked up, startled. "Do what?"

"Lay the blame for your decision on me!"

He could hardly believe the anger that contorted her face. "Why, Celia, I'm not blaming you. It was for your good."

Furiously her voice rose. "I can't bear any more of your making yourself a martyr in my best interest! I won't carry the burden of guilt that you load on my back every time you are unable to get what you want out of life! I've had all of it I can take. Don't do it to me again!"

Dumbfounded, he could only stare at her, unable to reply.

"You said you wanted this career," she went on, fighting

back the hot tears, "and gladly I agreed to help you. I *will* help you, Richard. Anything you want, I'll do. But don't pull out of it and say it is for me. I cannot bear another sacrifice! I can't!"

"Celia, you are not yourself. We'll discuss this when you are calm. You're tired now. Why don't you go and rest?"

"Rest!" She caught back her hand from flinging right at his head the china figurine standing on the shelf near her shoulder. "Oh, Richard. You don't understand anything, do you? How can a man who is so shrewd in business be so—so *stupid* about everything else!"

Running from the room, she nearly collided with Josh as he was entering.

In the charged atmosphere of the small room her son knew at once that a scene had taken place. "Captain Elisha was at the yards today—" he stopped when he glimpsed his father's white face. "Why, Papa. Are you ill?"

Richard reached for his chair. He did indeed feel ill, more ill than ever before in his life. His son's big, healthy body and the loving concern on his face were too much. The tears felt hot behind his eyes, but he fought them back. Yet he could not keep the truth within himself. It was too tempting, too comforting to tell someone. So, trusting in Josh's maturity and good sense, he spilled out the whole sorry story. He even showed him the pamphlet. Years seemed added to the young man's face as he forced himself to read it.

"Is this true?" Josh asked, his face ashen.

"Only one thing out of it is actually true," Richard said evenly. "While I was away during those years your mother and I were . . . estranged. She fell in love with Ewan and he with her. It was for everyone's good that she stayed with me when he left for Nova Scotia. But, you see, that one thing is just damaging enough that I could not dare to let the rest of this pack of lies go before the public. It would kill your mother. I think she, Ewan, I—we all have suffered enough over that indiscretion without this."

Josh was surprised to realize that he felt so little disappointment and anger at his mother, at least right at this moment. Perhaps that was because all his concern moved toward his father, whom he had never seen so miserable before.

"It must be a grievous disappointment for you."

Richard nodded. "It is, but I would have it no other way under the circumstances."

"What did you tell her?"

"Oh, the usual nonsense about her health and so on. She did not take it very well. It seems I have made a habit of sacrificing myself for her. It never occurred to me what a burden that puts on one."

"Oh, Papa. If she knew—"

"She must *never* know! I shall never forgive you, Josh, if you breathe a word of this to anyone, especially to your mother. She can rage all she likes about my 'sacrifices' as long as she is not aware of the scandal she has so narrowly missed. I count on you to keep that secret."

Underneath Richard's distress Josh could sense his father's usual steely determination. "Of course I won't tell her. But I intend to find out for myself who was behind this."

"Just take it and burn it for me. It was a crazy ambition in the first place."

"No," Josh said angrily. "It was an honest ambition and it is a damned shame that with all you have to offer this state, you must hide your light here at Southernwood. Someone did this on purpose to get at you through Mother, and if it takes the rest of my life I intend to find out who it was and make them pay."

"Oh, Josh. Revenge is a canker on the soul. Forget it. I shall try to. It all turned out as I thought it would, you know. Once the author of that libel knew I had withdrawn, there was no sign of it on the streets. I think they made only one copy, in fact. Its purpose was to get rid of me and it certainly worked."

Joshua studied the sensitive, gentle man he knew his father to be. This was a deep blow, he could tell, and one Richard did not deserve. Neither of his parents deserved it, no matter what their mistakes of years before. A burning anger deep within him took root and grew even as he sat watching his father's bent head. This would be the last try for Richard Deveroe. From now on his life would revolve around quiet attention to his business and his country estate. A door had closed on the world he had reached for so eagerly. He was too old now and too disheartened ever to try to open it again.

But Josh was resolved that someone would be made to pay for closing that door!

thirty-six

Josh stood at the clouded window of the Dolphin office and watched without seeing the work going on in the yards below. He had stayed away from Southernwood about as long as he could, suffering within himself as he knew his parents were suffering up on the hill. How long could he go on brooding over that lewd cartoon and the knowledge it had given him? When you came right down to it, was he any better than his mother, he wondered, thinking of Grace O'Malley. After all, it was not uncommon in today's world for married women to have affairs. But Celia? That lovely, gracious woman he knew so well? The idea of his mother wrapped in a hot embrace with that portly gentleman he had conversed with so prosaically in the parlor at Round Hill brought the blood to his cheeks. He could not drive the caricature from his mind.

He tried to smile. *You idiot! How do you think you got here! Yes, but one's parents . . .*

In a nervous gesture he ran his fingers through his hair. The world had slammed up into his face and now he must pick himself up and put things back in some new arrangement. But how? And how long could he put off facing his mother?

"Well, Cousin. I see you are diligently at work."

Josh turned at the sound of Dexter's voice, to see him standing in the doorway. It was an incongruous sight, his cousin Dexter, that city man personified, there in this cluttered busy shipyard office.

"Just supervising the workers down there," Josh lied. "Come in, have a seat if you find one that isn't covered with books and papers."

Absently he noted that Dexter still showed the signs of his recent ordeal in the yellow pallor of his skin.

"If there is anything I can't stand it's an office that looks as though it is thoroughly used. This one reeks of hard work."

Josh managed a smile as he settled before his desk. "I have never learned any other way to keep a business going."

"All the same," Dexter said, crossing his legs in the best dandy style, "if fate had seen fit to reverse our respective fortunes you would not find *me* cooped up in this dusty cage. I'd be out enjoying myself, spending the income."

"Yes, but how then would you be able to deliver *me* from debtor's prison when I found myself there?"

"Oh, not you, Cousin. You would be a hard-working lawyer's clerk, very upright and honorable, living on your miserable three dollars a week, while I, though I had a veritable fortune as my inheritance, no doubt should still end up in gaol with you to rescue me."

Josh pulled out a beautifully enameled snuffbox and offered it to his cousin. "It is about that debt that I wish to speak."

"I gathered as much when I got your note. Very decent of you to send me the ticket for the boat trip up here, by the way. It made me wonder if you were actually bringing me up to dun me for the first payment."

"No. In fact, I would be willing to forgive the entire three hundred pounds, Dexter, in return for . . . a favor."

This brought Dexter up in his chair. "Forgive it! Why, Cousin, that is most generous of you. What about the 'good of my soul' and all that?"

"Don't be sarcastic."

"Sarcasm is my defense. Actually, I am overcome. And very grateful." Clamping the lid shut on the box, he handed it back to Josh. "I almost fear to ask what the favor is. On the other hand, to erase the debt there is almost nothing I would not do."

"It is nothing so great, though it is very important to me. I want you to get some information for me. You have contacts with all kinds of people in the city . . ."

One eyebrow on Dexter's thin face rose. "Cousin, you are so flattering. Why don't you just say I know some of the lowest as well as the highest?"

"All right. It is the lowest who concern me. Especially the kind who would cause to be printed a libel with which to ruin the reputation of a good man."

"This has the smell of politics."

"Exactly. My father has withdrawn from the campaign for the State Legislature because of the threat of a pamphlet which

would have dragged both his name and his family's through
the gutter."

"Why, that happens to everyone who runs for office."

"I want to know who put together that pamphlet."

"Why should Uncle Richard care what is printed about him?
He sits high enough on his money to be above it all."

Josh became more cautious. In spite of his jaunty attitude,
Dexter's ferrety nose was almost visibly sniffing. He loved
gossip, and this had the smell of a ripping good story.

"My father is a very upright, sensitive man. He underesti-
mated the effect of such scurrilous attacks. Once he realized
what it felt like to have them aimed directly at him, he knew
it was not what he wanted. I resent the fact that this kind of
scandalmongering could drive him away from a career which
would have been of great satisfaction both to him personally
and to the state."

"My, my. Such filial devotion."

"Call it what you will, I intend to find out who was behind
this calumny. I fancy you owe me a favor, Dexter, and I'm
asking you to help me."

"Well, as it happens, I do have several acquaintances among
the newspaper crowd. Perhaps they might know something of
these handbills. Of course, I'm not guaranteeing anything."

"If you find out who wrote that pamphlet—*if*, I say—I am
prepared to write off the three hundred pounds as a bad debt.
Otherwise, I must insist on the first payment plus interest by
next month."

"Cousin, you are a hard man. Give me two months at least."

"All right. Two months. But I warn you, Dexter, I am not
above sending you back to jail."

For the first time Dexter realized that perhaps his cousin
was capable of such a thing. There was a new hardness to him.

"You don't have to threaten me, Josh. I'll find out who
wrote that handbill for you. It's worth more to me than to you."

The steel fell away and his cousin sat there smiling at him
like the handsome, good-natured ass he had always been.

"Good," Josh said. "That's settled."

It was nearly a month before Josh was able to get down to
New York again. During that time he finally forced himself
to Southernwood, where his mother's withdrawn sullenness
and his father's quiet misery awoke only pity for them both.
He kissed Celia on her pale cheek and in a few moments was

able to look directly into her large brown eyes. The desperate sadness there made him realize for the first time that he had never really seen Celia as a woman and not as his mother.

When he finally arrived in the city he had to force himself to stay away from the Park Theatre. Time and again he nearly gave in to the urge to go see the tiny golden-haired girl whose memory made his blood warm. Yet part of him was appalled at the thought. Just a glimpse of the newspapers, full now of the nomination of Robert Williams for state senator and the shrill rhetoric of the campaign, was enough to turn his stomach.

It was a barren visit, bereft of everything but hard work. Even Dexter disappointed him. In all that time he had learned nothing except that one reporter for the *American Citizen* had been involved in tracking down information which could be used against the Martling men. The man's name was Trollope and he was a nosy, gossipy reporter with no compunctions about putting anything in print. Yet he denied vehemently knowing about the Deveroe campaign.

One bright morning he came out of the Merchant's Exchange and walked toward the Battery Walk, too absorbed to notice his surroundings. A panoramic view of the bay lay before him, dotted with vessels at anchor and others in full sail up the North River. The fresh sea breezes off the harbor rustled the Lombardy poplar trees lining the military parade. Suddenly the loud clang of a ship's bell drew his attention to the water, where he could just see the ferry from Jersey pulling into the slip. Curious, he stood watching the flurry of activity the "floating teakettle" still caused among the knot of people on the wharf.

Right now Fulton and Robert Livingston had no competition to speak of. Yet, Josh thought, watching the clumsy boat trying to maneuver into its berth, that would not last. Sooner or later it would be tested in the courts and their virtual monopoly would have to give way to open competition. And then the Dolphin Shipyards would be among the foremost to begin to build steamboats. Steam was not going to replace sail for a long time to come, but it had to be the vanguard of the future. At an amazing seven miles an hour, it was too fast not to.

Staring at the water, he failed to notice a cab that pulled up at the road behind him. A woman leaned out the window, ducking her feathery hatbrim, and waved to the driver to stop.

"Mr. Deveroe!"

Josh turned to see Grace O'Malley framed in the cab window.

"I thought I recognized you." Grace smiled down at him. "I didn't know you were in the city."

"Just a quick trip. On business."

"And you haven't been to see me! For shame."

There was no suggestion of hurt in her teasing, Josh was relieved to notice. "I wanted to, but . . ."

"But your wife is with you."

"No. As a matter of fact she stayed in Mount Pleasant. I really have been involved."

"I shall assume that making money kept you from my presence when you were actually dying to come. Tell me no more."

"You would not be entirely far off the truth."

Her green eyes brightened to turquoise in the reflection of the cloudless sky. Through thick lashes she looked up provocatively from under the feathers of her bonnet. All his resolve began to slip away.

"Come ride with me," she said, opening the door. "We are going back up Broad Way. I'll drop you at your hotel."

He hesitated only a moment before climbing in. The cab smelled musty after the clear salt air of the wharf. He settled next to her, catching a faint whiff of lavender water.

"Now, how do you know where my hotel is?"

"Does it matter?" Her smile was triumphant.

He took her hand. "No."

He was no better than his mother!

Autumn was almost gone when Celia walked up on her porch one afternoon and nearly careened into Captain Yancy. She had just returned, tired and muddied, for one of the long rides she used to exhaust her restless energies.

"Oh, Elisha. I didn't know you were here."

"Hello, Celia. I was up to see Richard and decided to speak to you. How was the ride?"

"Oh, excellent as always. Come, sit down with me in the back while I try to get the mud off these boots. We haven't seen you for an age."

"You haven't, but your son and husband have kept me busy enough."

"All right, then, *I* haven't seen you for an age. Tell me about yourself. Are you still running that boat?"

"When I can find the time." Celia still thought of the Deveroe fleet as the two sloops they had begun with over twenty years before. He was always surprised to realize how little she knew of her husband's business empire.

They sat together on a long bench on the side porch while Celia scraped her riding boots on a boot rack. Elisha, never adept at idle conversation, searched for some innocent remark that might be a prelude to what he really wanted to discuss.

"Do you miss the young people?" he finally asked.

"Oh, yes. Especially Josh. It was always such a pleasure to have him skipping about here, into everything, enjoying everything, wanting to know how everything worked. I shall never get used to his living in another house."

"'For this cause a man must leave his father and mother . . .'"

"Oh, I know. But knowing the Biblical injunction doesn't keep a mother from missing her son."

"His lady wife seems pleasant enough."

"She is, of course."

"And now ye have Richard to look after."

"Richard looks after himself very well."

Yancy leaned his elbows on his knees, working his big hands together nervously. "It's about Richard I wish to speak."

Celia did not even look up from her energetic scraping. Yancy's irritation got the better of him and he grabbed at her knee, holding it still.

"I want to talk to you about your husband, Celia."

Her large eyes were veiled. "What about him? Didn't you see him earlier? He's upstairs, I believe."

"For God's sake, woman. Are ye blind? Don't ye see anything? He's ill."

"Richard ill? I hadn't noticed. He hasn't spoken of it."

With one heavy boot, Yancy pushed the boot rack across the porch. "Do you think he would? When have you ever known the man to complain? He keeps it to himself right enough, but if I can see it, you certainly should have."

"Richard is never ill. As for complaining . . ." Why should he complain when every effort was a sacrifice on her behalf? He was satisfying his martyr complex at her expense. She was the one who should complain!

"I'm trying to tell you he is not well. I don't know what it is, but I've never seen him so gaunt. Does he ever eat? How much does he go out?"

"Captain Yancy, you know my husband is suffering right now from disappointed hopes. Since he gave up that nomination he has done nothing but mope around this estate, starving himself and brooding. If he looks pale or thin, no doubt that is the reason why."

Yancy stood up, pulling down his old-fashioned captain's coat and looking sternly.

"Celia, I've known ye for a long time. You used to be the warmest, gentlest creature a man could ever hope for. But since ye came to live in this great pile of stone, ye're hard and haughty. If this is what riches does for a body, then I'll take my old cabin and bottle on the shore of the North River! I never thought to see the day when you'd be so callous about the welfare of a good man, and him your husband, too."

Celia felt herself stifling a scream. How much of this was she to take? Her loneliness and boredom, and now Elisha telling her how she had changed for the worse. Was Richard ill? She hadn't noticed, but then she had hardly noticed him at all.

"Captain Yancy," she said stiffly, "thank you for your concern. I'll look after my husband's health, you can rest assured. Now, if you will excuse me, I must get out of this uncomfortable habit."

He took her polite formality as a rebuke. "Of course."

"You'll stay and dine with us?"

"No. No, thank you. I have to be getting back to the yards. I'll stop in again next week."

"Perhaps you'll find the time to stay longer then."

"Perhaps."

Troubled and confused, he watched after her as she entered the house. Was this the same woman he had known all these years? Whatever had changed her so? He looked around at the elegant façade of the expensive house, at the manicured grounds. Wisteria climbed the porch railing, bright autumn flowers lined the brick walk that led to a profusion of apple trees heavy with ripe fruit. This ought to be paradise, he thought. Yet all he could feel was a longing for his simple roughhewn cabin near the shores of the river.

Yancy's words were not completely wasted, for Celia did take the time to look more closely at her husband. He certainly was not his old, controlled self, but when she asked him about it he passed it off as merely the struggle to readjust to his old life. Beyond that, he was as fit as could be, he assured her.

"Perhaps Betsy should brew you up a tonic," Celia suggested. "Or I could order a bottle of that Vegetable Pulmonic Detergent from the city. They tell me it has great restorative power for everything from asthma to consumption."

"Good God, Celia. Am I an old woman to be taking tonics! It hasn't come to that, has it?"

"Well, you've pressed enough of them upon me these last months."

"Yes, but you needed them. Give me a little more time. I'll work my way out of this melancholy, you'll see."

"As long as that is all it is."

"Of course that's all it is. Now please, say no more about it."

So be it, then. She would let him alone.

The brilliant colors of autumn gave way to the muddy gray-browns of winter before Josh finally heard again from Dexter. A note from New York, enclosing the amount of the interest on his loan but nothing of the principal, admitted that he had not been able to trace the source of the handbill beyond a hint of association with the *Citizen* reporter, Trollope. Josh was almost as disappointed at this news as Dexter had been to write it. He fought back a charitable urge to send the money back to his cousin and forgive the debt anyway, and decided instead to add a few more months to the time limit he had previously set. After all, that pamphlet had to come from somewhere. If someone in New York knew a secret as carefully guarded as this one had been—for he had never in his entire life so much as heard a hint of an affair between his mother and his cousin Ewan—they must have learned it from a source close to his family. But who? His first suspect was, of course, Aunt Hester—malicious mischief like this would be just her style. Yet Hester had lived in England those years during the war. How would she ever have known what went on in West Chester? Perhaps he should make an effort to talk to her, though, just on the chance something might slip out. Yes, the next time he was in the city he would call on Hester.

"Josh, why don't you talk to me?"

He looked up to see Morna standing over his chair, a frown on her lovely face.

"Oh, I'm sorry, my love. I didn't hear you come in."

"You never hear me lately. You're always so preoccupied. I feel as though I live alone."

He reached up and pulled her down on his lap. She looked especially lovely this evening. Her black hair had been done Grecian style, a high knot on the back with wavy tendrils framing her face. She had on a lime-colored sarsenet dress trimmed with an intricate embroidery of roses. She was all elegance and goodness, not earthy and elfin like Grace, and she was his dearest wife. How strange that you could hold two women in your heart at the same time—yet perhaps not so strange when they were so different.

"Have I been so difficult to live with lately? Forgive me, I do have a lot on my mind, but that is no excuse for ignoring a perfect creature like you."

"Yes, you're heartless," she said, throwing her arm around his neck and kissing him lightly. She sat back in his lap, her eyes gleaming with vivacity. "I have some great news for you, Josh. I think we are going to have a baby."

He was too surprised to speak for a moment, then, engulfed in a wave of pleasure, smiled at her mischievously. "So I have not been completely derelict in my marital duties!"

"Are you pleased?"

"Of course I'm pleased. It is about time, when you come to think of it. Think how delighted Mama and Papa will be. Their first grandchild."

Morna's face went sour. "I don't know about that. Your papa will be happy, but do you really think your mother will care?"

"Not care! She'll be turning cartwheels. It was the sorrow of her life, you know, that she had only one child. Even my adopted sister, Hannah, died as a young girl."

"No, I didn't know. But she doesn't like me, Josh. She never did. I hope she won't let that affect her feelings for the baby."

Baby. The word conjured up for Josh a whole realm of unexpected, mysterious sensations. It would take some getting used to.

"Are you all right? I mean, isn't there some worry or apprehension involved?"

Morna took that lightly. "I'm not worried. My mother had six children with no difficulties and I fancy I'm a lot like her. I helped her to raise them, too, so I'm not exactly a stranger to motherhood. I'm so happy, Josh."

He started to fold her in one of his strong bear hugs, then

held back. She would be more fragile and precious than ever now. The warm embrace he gave her conveyed how much he shared her joy. He wished all the world could share in it. The brooding people in that big, overdone mansion on the hill suddenly seemed very far away.

thirty-seven

Morna went to Celia with the news of the coming grandchild determined to make a special effort to win her friendship. She was pleased that for once her words did away with that constant scowl her mother-in-law wore, allowing some small glimmer of delight to show through. For a brief moment she thought Celia was even going to unbend so far as to embrace her.

"You must take very good care of yourself now," Celia said stiffly instead, fussing with the silks in her sewing table. They were seated in the back parlor with a crackling fire to make the small room cozy as a featherbed. Morna adjusted the fire screen beside her chair to keep the pulsing heat off her face.

"I never felt better. As I told Josh, my mother had six children and . . ."

The scowl returned with a vengeance.

". . . and I am a lot like her. Anyway, I'm so happy to be with child that I shall not allow any fears to dampen my pleasure. Are you all right, Celia?"

"Yes. Of course. Does Richard know yet?"

"No, I shall tell him next."

"He's in his study now. Why don't you go along and give him the news? He'll be so pleased. He's been so melancholy since last fall, it will be sure to cheer him up."

Morna gathered up shawl and gloves. How foolish she had been to think the news of the coming baby would have brought her closer to this difficult, distant woman. "I'll do that."

The girl had barely left the room when Celia heard her son coming in through the outside doors. Throwing down his great-coat and scarf on a hall chair, he brushed his fingers through his hair damp from the snow and hurried in to the fire where she sat.

"Vestal is getting so rheumatic, Mother, you shall soon have to retire him to the rocker in his cabin. He could not handle the cooper's adze for me at all just now."

"He's worked so hard for us all his life, perhaps it is time he rested. We are all of us getting old, Josh. Your father, I, Vestal . . ."

"Nonsense. I've seen you coming in from riding that mare of yours and you look the picture of health and vigor. It's sitting around this house that depresses your spirits. You need to be involved in something besides your own thoughts."

Celia admired her handsome son standing beside the mantel. With his grandfather's big frame he carried something of his father's elegance and grace. It was a nice combination.

"You're probably right. I feel sure that Richard too, had he gone on with his campaign and been elected, would be a far happier man today. His old interests simply don't hold the same attraction."

Josh turned away, unable to look at his mother. Everything she said was true, of course, but she knew nothing of the reason behind it.

"Mother, Vestal tells me there was a man up here last summer asking around about the family. Do you know anything about it?"

Idly Celia picked up her tapestry frame and began working her needle through the canvas. "No, I never saw such a man. What did he want?"

"He was doing some research on the history of the county during the war years and wanted to know about West Farms. Particularly about Uncle Ewan."

Though she never looked up, he saw her color deepen and he realized that but for that scurrilous handbill he would never have noticed it.

"Your Uncle Ewan was a famous man back then. His reputation has been so blackened by the Whigs and patriots, I hope someone is now about to show him in a truer light."

"Vestal says this was a slight man with a large nose and a narrow chin and he wore a plaid coat. You never saw anyone who looked like that hanging about?"

"No, I didn't. Perhaps your father knows who it was."

"I intend to ask him."

"Morna is with him now." She smiled up at him, looking for a moment like the mother he remembered so well. "She told me about the baby. I'm so happy for you both."

His face was a picture of delight. "I suppose between you

and his mother he shall end up being spoiled beyond hope while I have nothing to say about it."

"I'm not worried. Your Aunt Hester thinks you were the most indulged child who ever lived, yet I like to fancy that you turned out very nicely."

He kissed her lightly on the top of her bent head. "Dearest Mama. You were always my greatest admirer."

Uncle Ewan or no, she *had* always been a loving mother to him, and he made up his mind that he was not going to let that memory be ruined by an old scandal. But it was very hard not to remember, not to let that ugly picture fray the edges of the perfect portrait he had carried in his heart for so many years.

For more than a month Josh brooded on the stranger in the plaid coat. He felt in his bones that the man was somehow linked to that pamphlet. How better to learn family secrets than to go about questioning the servants who had lived with them for so long? Had he not himself, as a young child, listened enthralled to the stories Vestal told him of raids and skirmishes, burning barns and houses, and food and money buried in holes out in the fields?

He thought of facing Betsy and demanding to know every word she had spoken to this stranger. But in the end he decided not to. If she had revealed anything damaging to Celia's reputation—and Vestal was insistent that there was nothing to reveal—old Vestal would beat her for sure. What good would it do, anyway? Though they might have suspected an affair, surely even well-established servants would not have known the kind of intimate details contained in that handbill.

Sitting at his desk, he reached up into a hidden drawer and pulled the wretched thing out from under a pile of deeds and letters. He forced himself to open it, smoothing out the loathsome caricature of his mother and uncle in their lust. Who would have known? If only there was some way to find out.

A sudden loud crash from the far end of the hall gave him a start. Josh jumped up, his first thought that Morna had fallen, but he had no more than reached the door when he saw her walking calmly toward him down the hall, a packet of letters in her hand.

"What happened? I thought it was you."

"No, that fellow you sent over from the yards has probably toppled off the chair in the kitchen, where he was trimming the beams. I told him it wouldn't hold, but he insisted on doing it his own way. You'd better go and see if he will listen to you. These letters just arrived, by the way."

"Put them on my desk." Relieved, he went into the kitchen, where the joiner was trying to clean up the clutter of pewter dishes that lay scattered among the remains of the chair. With a few well-chosen words he set the man about his work again, then moved back down the hall to his study. As he entered he saw Morna standing by the desk, the pamphlet in her hand, her face when she looked up at him as white as the snowy cap that covered her hair.

"My God, I did not intend for you to see that!" he muttered, reaching for the handbill.

She snatched it away. "Josh, this is terrible. Where did it come from?"

"I don't know. But what you have in your hand is the real reason my father withdrew from the state-senatorial campaign. They threatened to cover the city with them. He wouldn't expose Mother to that, of course, so he got out." He waited for her to express her indignation and astonishment, hoping he would not have to lie about the accusations involved. Better to let her think it was gossip.

But Morna already knew the truth and she was appalled to see it in print. The familiar waves of nausea began to sweep through her body.

"Aren't you going to ask me if it is true?"

Her stricken face seemed to shrink. "What does it matter? I have suspected that something like this went on between your mother and my father, these many months now. But to have used it against poor Papa Deveroe . . ."

"*You* suspected! What do you mean? How would *you* know anything about it? I've never so much as heard a hint of such a scandal. Where would you have heard it?"

"I didn't. I just put a few things together. The hair fillet, for example. It's right here, described perfectly. I found it in your mother's jewelry case and it was exactly like one my father told me about in his romantic stories. And there were other things—little things, but they fit so perfectly. But I never thought . . ."

An uneasy sensation was creeping up Josh's neck, warming his scalp. "Morna, you didn't say anything about these suspicions? You didn't tell anyone?"

"Yes, yes, I did," she cried in growing anguish.

With a mounting fury he seized her narrow wrist. "Did you talk to that man in the plaid coat? Did you tell him these lies about my mother?"

She shrank from his anger. "What man? What coat? Josh, you're *hurting* me!"

Horrified at himself, he dropped her hand and stepped back. With a determined effort of the kind he had seen his father make so often he forced himself to be calm.

"Whom did you tell, then?"

Morna crumpled the hated paper in her hand. "Only your Aunt Hester!"

Like a shifting of light all the pieces suddenly fell into place. Of course! Who better would know the details of the family with which to flesh out the central core once Morna had supplied it? And who better to see it all transformed into a libelous handbill than Jaspar Carne—a man whose hatred of Richard Deveroe had long been a festering sore. He sank into the chair, heartsick.

"Oh, Morna! You don't know what you've done!"

Morna was crying now. Flinging herself on her knees beside him, she frantically clutched his hand. "Josh, I'm so sorry. I didn't realize they would use my careless remarks this way. I would never, never have said anything if I had known."

A terrible rage was growing within him.

"How could you have said anything anyway? To Aunt Hester, of all people. That envious, gossiping, hateful woman! Don't you have any judgment at all?"

Morna sat back as though he had struck her. "She was very friendly to me."

"I'm *sure* she was. And you were just brainless enough to spill these ruinous suspicions right into her lap so that she and her snake of a husband could use them against my mother and father. You were just the silly chit she needed!"

Tears of chagrin and hurt flowed down Morna's face. "Josh! How can you speak to me this way?"

"Well, it's the truth, isn't it? I ought to beat you. By God, if I were a different kind of man and you were not with child, I'd do it and be glad!"

Morna fell sobbing against his knee. Not as long as she had known him had Josh ever spoken harshly to her. She would almost have preferred the rod. Impatiently he pushed her away and stalked to the door.

"What you have done, Morna, in your ignorance and foolishness, has come close to destroying my mother's reputation and my father's happiness. I don't know if I can ever forgive you."

"Josh! Please, don't be so hard on me. I didn't know."

Crawling on her knees, she tried to get across the room to clutch at his hand again but got tangled in her skirts.

"Well, you know now, don't you?"

Furiously he turned his back on her, slamming the door.

"I can't believe it! I cannot believe she would do such a silly, cruel, senseless thing."

Josh paced the tiny cramped rooms while Grace sat watching him, quietly turning a hem on the velvet dress she was to wear that evening for *The Wanderer*. Since the moment he had appeared at her door without warning he had not ceased this restless pacing. She was astounded at the depth of his anger toward his young wife. Obviously the young woman had innocently blundered into deep water, and her loving husband was prepared to let her drown.

She removed two long pins from between her lips. "Is your wife a silly creature? It never sounded so to me from the things you said about her."

"I never thought of her that way. I thought she was perfect. Wise, gentle, loving. How could such a woman deliberately harm someone who had never done her anything but good? I will never understand it."

"Please, Joshua Deveroe—*sit down*! I'm finding it very difficult to concentrate on my sewing with you plowing the carpet. And I must have this ready by this afternoon's rehearsal."

Josh looked around him, almost surprised to realize where he was. "I don't think I can sit still. I want to thrash her. I'm so . . . disappointed in her."

"Oh, for heaven's sake, Josh, the poor girl probably made an innocent remark or two never dreaming they would be used so maliciously. Give her credit for ignorance, at least."

"No. Ignorance in a case like this is unforgivable. The results are too damaging. I don't know if I can ever find it in my heart to forgive her."

Straightening out the fabric over her lap, Grace looked up at him. "You are being very hard. Did you not say you left her weeping on the floor? It sounds to me as though she has suffered enough remorse already without having to bear your unforgiving anger the rest of her life. I can't believe that of you."

"She *should* weep. Her tears are nothing to those of my poor parents."

Sinking onto a sofa, he realized all at once how utterly weary he was. His anger had carried him away from his home all the way down to New York and borne him in righteous indignation straight to Grace O'Malley's rooms. Why he wasn't even sure. He only knew he must vent his frustration to someone, and he had learned to trust Grace's discretion. How long had he been raging here? By this time his anger was beginning to dissipate itself, leaving him exhausted and depressed.

Grace laid aside her dress and poured him out a glass of claret. Then she deliberately went back to her chair by the window, keeping the length of the small room between them.

"You know, Joshua," she said, carefully weighing her words, "I believe you have put a terrible burden on your wife. From the things you have told me she sounds a perfectly normal young girl, yet you have made her a paragon. No woman can live up to that."

"I only saw her as she was."

"No, you saw her as you wanted her to be. Did you never think she had faults, insecurities, a small streak of meanness perhaps?"

"No. She never displayed them to me."

"Does your mother like her or is there some bad feeling between them?"

"A little coolness perhaps, but nothing to begin to justify this."

Grace laughed, unable to believe his naïveté. "Oh, Josh. Wake up! If there really was an affair beween your mother and Morna's father, how do you think she felt to see you bring home his daughter as your wife? Didn't you say she swooned away the very moment she thought your cousin was dead? Even if she had wanted to love Morna, it must have been difficult for her to do so. Personally I would never have let her come to live in my house. I'd never be able to look into her face without remembering."

Without answering he stared at the slight figure in the plum-colored dress, her feet tucked daintily under her, speaking words that were knives in his soul.

"I have always suspected you were naïve about some things, but I did not think you would be so foolish as to make of both your mother and your wife some kind of ideal. You are angry because you cannot believe that your precious mother could have once fallen in love and given herself to another man outside her marriage, or that your perfect wife would have stooped to gossip and talebearing—very human foibles, I assure you. In my profession I see plenty of both."

It was galling to have to admit there was a great deal of truth to what she said. For the first time it became clear to him how he had clung to that first idealized vision of Morna standing at the window of her father's house, the flecks of light reflected in her sea-green eyes. He had not wanted to let go of that image. He wanted it to stand bright and clear and never changing against all the vicissitudes of this turbulent world. Yet she was a woman, a human being, for whom change, failure and growth were facts of life. His vision of her was shattered beyond repair, but perhaps he could put together a new one, more true to the person she was.

Grace watched the struggle going on in him, hoping she had not gone too far. "Can you learn to love her as a person and not as a goddess?" she asked quietly.

To her relief he gave her something resembling his familiar good-natured smile. "I suppose I'll have to. I suppose I may even want to, once I get over wanting to beat her. Wanting to beat my mother too. At least, one good thing has come of this. I am certain now that it was Jaspar Carne and my Aunt Hester who were responsible for that handbill."

"I know about Mr. Carne. He is eternally attempting to shut down the theater in spite of the fact that ninety-nine percent of the people of New York want it open. He's made no end of trouble for us."

"He would, the cold-blooded, self-righteous hypocrite. Always trying to save other men's souls and stabbing my father in the back every chance he gets—a man worth a hundred of him."

"You would do better to direct your anger toward paying Mr. Carne in kind rather than punishing your poor wife."

Josh glanced up at her sharply. "I have every intention of repaying Mr. Carne, but I've not decided how."

"Well, then, let's think of a way to topple Mr. Alderman Crane from his pedestal. I'll help, if you like."

Josh sipped the claret, absently wondering what on earth Grace could possibly do to help him in such an enterprise.

"I *am* an actress, you know," she said artfully, as though reading his mind.

"Yes, but you don't even know the man. What would you possibly have to gain?"

"It's better that I haven't met him. He won't know me as one of the theater people. And if I could help to get him off the manager's back, who knows—in his gratitude, Mr. Price might even give me the second lead. I'd prefer to earn it that way rather than in bed."

Josh hardly heard her. Already his fertile mind was working. If Carne had never met Grace, there were no end of possibilities. She was so young and still bore such an aura of innocence, she might easily pull the wool over even Jaspar Carne's jaundiced eyes. It was worth a try, anyway.

Impulsively he rose and went to her chair to bend down and kiss her. "Dear Grace, it must have been inspiration that led me here today. I've just had a brilliant idea. You are about to embark on the greatest challenge of your career."

thirty-eight

Celia reached for her dressing gown and slipped it around her shoulders. What was it that had wakened her from her restless dreaming? It was then that she heard the moaning.

Low, agonized groans were barely audible through the door to Richard's room. Startled, she pushed it open and looked in. There was no light in the room, but she could make out the darkened form writhing from side to side on the canopied bed. And now she could clearly hear Richard calling her name in anguished moans that he was trying to stifle under the covers.

Pulling back the coverlet, she saw her husband doubled up on the bed, his arms gripping his stomach, beads of sweat covering his face. Even in the dark she could sense the agony in his eyes as he looked up and saw her bending over him.

"I tried not to wake you," he said haltingly.

"Why, Richard, what is the matter? Are you ill?"

"No. Yes . . . it's some kind of pain. Terrible, terrible."

"What can I do? How can I help you?"

"Nothing. It . . . it will go away in a minute." He turned from side to side as Celia struggled to light the candle by the bedside. When the flame sputtered up she was horrified to see the suffering on his face.

"My dear, my dear. This is terrible. I had no idea . . ."

"Give me your hand."

He clutched tightly at her fingers, but Celia did not feel it. Frantically she cast about for something she might do to help him.

"It's getting better now," he sighed, straightening up a little. "Yes, it's going."

His body seemed to collapse with the relief of lessening pain. Celia wiped at his wet brow with the corner of the bedsheet and waited until the attack was over.

"Can I get you something? Clematis tea, or perhaps a little wine?"

"No, nothing. If I drink anything it makes it worse. It's getting better now."

"Richard, how long has this been going on? Why didn't you tell me?"

"A while. It's just a touch of indisposition, sometimes more intense than others. Tonight was bad, though. The worst yet."

She slipped down beside him, cradling his head in her arms.

"Easy," he breathed, and she knew it had not completely gone.

"Have you seen a doctor? What does he say?"

"I haven't wanted to bother him. It will pass in time, I'm sure. There's no need to make a big thing of it."

"How can you say that? I've never seen you in such agony before. At least let him look at you."

"No, no. There's no need. I'm glad you came in, Celia. I feel so worn out now. Stay with me a while, please."

"Of course. Of course I will. Try to sleep."

"Yes, sleep. You're so good, Celia."

"Oh, Richard . . ."

He was still clutching her hand when he fell asleep.

"What's wrong with my husband, Dr. Singleton?"

Celia sat on the edge of her parlor sofa and motioned the doctor to a chair. The short, dapper little man, who had a home in the nearby village of Sing Sing, had the look of a country practitioner. However, he was all that was available at the moment and she had wasted no time in getting him here. That very morning, still red-eyed from lack of sleep, she had dispatched Vestal into the village to fetch him up the hill.

"Please excuse my thoughtlessness. Would you like a glass of wine or cider?"

"No, no. That's perfectly all right. I know you are worried about your husband, and it grieves me to be the one to tell you that you have good cause."

Celia felt a sinking sensation in her chest. "What do you mean?"

"Mr. Deveroe insists that he has a mild indispostion, but I fear that what ails him is much worse than that. I very much fear that he has either an abscess or a malignant tumor in the bowel.

The room seemed to close around her. "Oh no," she groaned, fighting the urge to sink her head into her hands.

"I'm afraid so."

"But how can you be sure? Perhaps you are wrong?"

"It takes only a cursory examination to detect the presence of even a small growth. All the signs are there. The pain, the loss of appetite, the diminished weight."

She couldn't look at the doctor. So absorbed had she been in her own melancholy that she had never noticed Richard to have any of those things. How could she have been so blind?

"Is there nothing you can do?"

"Only to leave you a good supply of laudanum, which will help ease the pain. I've given him a dose now and he's sleeping peacefully. He must keep to a very strict, bland diet. We don't know much about tumors, you know. Sometimes they go away of themselves, but more often they grow larger and more destructive until . . ."

Celia jumped to her feet. "Thank you for coming, Dr. Singleton. May we call on you again if there is a need?"

"Of course. Anytime." A little miffed at this abrupt dismissal, he gathered up his hat and leather bag. Celia had barely seen him out before she went back to her parlor desk and took out her writing paper. Already her mind was working furiously. First, their old friend Dr. Sayre must see Richard. This Singleton might be an ignorant quack, for all she knew. Let Sayre tell her the truth about Richard's condition, and if he could not help let him tell her where they should go. There was a medical school in Philadelphia and one in New York. She would take Richard anywhere that might help him, even to Europe if she could.

Her hand paused over the quill. But first she must see her son. Josh would have to know about his father, and perhaps Josh could even comfort her. Everything in her suddenly longed for Josh to hold and support her. He would know what to do. Yes, she would get this note off, then look in on her husband just to be sure he was resting quietly as Singleton had said. Then she would ask Vestal to bring out the carriage and drive over to the new house near the Dolphin yards.

The house was quiet as she entered. Too quiet. She had insisted that Vestal drive her first by the yards, so she knew Josh was not there and had not been there for two days. The quiet pall that hung over the white clapboard house gave her the first uneasy indication that she would not find him here either.

The young serving girl who let her in seemed overawed to see the master's mother from the manor house on the hill standing in the hall wrapped in a green silk pelisse.

"The master is not home," she said shyly.

"Where is he, then, girl? It is very important that I speak with him."

"I'm sorry, ma'am, but I don't know."

Celia sighed with exasperation. "Well, your mistress, then. Is she here?"

"Oh, yes," the girl replied, finally looking directly at Celia. "She is upstairs in bed."

"In bed! At this hour?"

"She's been poorly these last days. Very poorly. We taken her meals up, but she don't touch a thing. Just lies there, terrible upset."

"She's ill?" Celia's eyes automatically went up the stairs with their dark-burgundy carpet treads. Had Morna lost her baby? That was all she needed right now!

"I would like to talk with her."

"Oh, no. She won't see nobody. She told us not to—"

"Don't answer me back, girl! Go upstairs and tell your mistress her mother-in-law is here and that if she won't come down I'll come up and talk to her directly in her bed."

The girl cowered before her. "Yes, ma'am," she replied, hurrying up the stairs. Celia watched her disappear into the room at the top of the hall, then, setting aside her pelisse, decided not to wait for Morna's answer. Something was not right in this house.

Quickly she went up the stairs and opened the door to Morna's room. She could hardly believe her eyes. The woman who sat staring at her from the high canopied bed looked like an apparition. Her black hair was disheveled around a white face swollen and blotched from crying. Her nightdress, like the bedcovers, was a heap of crumpled linen, sour and none too clean.

Celia went straight to the bed—where Morna turned away from her, hiding her face in the crumpled pillows—and barked at the cowering servant girl to get out. Then she drew up a chair beside the bed and sat down.

"Morna," she began, trying to make her voice sound gentle,

"what is wrong? Have you lost your baby?"

"No," the muffled cry came from a face buried in the pillows.

Relief came flooding over her. "Thank God for that, at least. But what has upset you so? Are you ill?"

The black head shook no.

Celia waited in silence for the explanation that did not come, her irritation growing with every passing moment. "Morna, it is very important that I talk to Josh. Do you know where he is?"

To her amazement this question brought forth a rush of sobs. "He's in New York," Morna managed to get out.

"New York?" That was not unusual, of course. Josh often made trips to New York. Yet there was something about all this that made her uneasy. "Did you two quarrel?"

Morna was beyond the ability to dissemble. "He left me," she cried, the tears streaming down the swollen face, "and went off to the city. I don't know if he's ever coming back!"

"Now, that *is* nonsense. Of course he'll be back. His life is here, his home, his work. You are his wife. Josh is not the man to throw those things over lightly. For heaven's sake, girl, stop this caterwauling and sit up and talk to me."

Deliberately Celia went over to dip her handkerchief in the washbowl. Pulling Morna up from the crumpled pillows, she put her arm around the girl's shoulders and wiped at her swollen face with the cold cloth. "Nothing can be this bad," she said quietly. "Now tell me what happened."

"He hates me. I did something dreadful and he swore he'd never forgive me for it." Morna's hands went over her face, and the sobbing broke out anew. Celia hugged her to her.

"You may think he feels that way, Morna, but the truth is Josh loves you more than anyone in the world. He certainly is not a man to hold a grudge. Stop this crying now and be sensible. I can think of nothing that you could do that would turn my son away from you."

"You don't know!"

Celia nearly laughed. This naïve little girl—what indiscretion could she possibly have committed that would cause such a scene? It was probably some little thing which had been blown out of all proportion.

"No, I don't. But I do know that if you don't get hold of yourself, you are going to harm your baby. Isn't that the most important consideration right now? Don't let a lover's quarrel damage the child you carry. You'll regret it the rest of your life if you do."

Morna pulled away from her and Celia was dumbfounded at the stricken misery on her face.

"Lover's quarrel! That's what you think? Well, it was a great deal more than that."

In a flash she was off the bed and over to the highboy. Pulling the pamphlet from a drawer, she threw it in Celia's lap, then ran back around to stand by the bedpost, her eyes burning into Celia's face.

A harmless-looking handbill—a political pamphlet of some sort. Yet Celia knew as she picked it up and the words began to register that it was something more. Her hand trembled as she opened it to the inside and the lewd cartoon was spread before her. From deep inside, nausea and revulsion began to grow.

"A lover's quarrel!" Morna went on relentlessly. "Read that, Mrs. Deveroe. Read it as your son did, knowing that I was the one responsible for it!"

Dumb misery like bile in her throat. Hot tears burning behind her closed eyelids. A searing pain in her chest. How sordid this made the love she had shared with Ewan so long ago! How it dragged through the mud some of the most memorable moments of her life.

"Where did you get this?" Her voice was a stranger's.

"Josh says it was printed by Jaspar Carne, from information I gave Aunt Hester. Gossip. Talebearing. Stupid, vicious, idle chatter that destroyed everything!" Breaking into remorseful sobs again, Morna fell against the bedpost and slid to the floor. For a long moment Celia did not move while thoughts and feelings churned inside her. Part of her wanted to choke the brokenhearted girl crying against the coverlet. But what good would that do now?

"But how? How could you know anything about it?"

"I surmised it from some things my father told me and the fillet I saw in your jewelry case. I was so clever! I put everything together, then I unwittingly told my suppositions to Aunt Hester. Josh thinks she took it to her husband, who used it this way."

"Oh, Morna."

It was more a groan than a name. Morna pulled herself up against the side of the bed. "I cannot ask you to forgive me, that would be too much. I only ask you to please try to remember that I never thought anything like this would come of my idle talk. I would have cut out my tongue before saying a word if I had known. Now I don't think my husband will ever forgive me for nearly destroying you and smashing his father's political career. This is my punishment."

Celia's head shot up. "Did Richard see this?"

"He gave it to Josh."

"When?"

"I don't know when."

But Celia did. It was not difficult to figure that out. This libelous handbill had to be the reason Richard had withdrawn from the campaign. He would have given up twenty careers before he would have allowed her good name to be dragged through the mud with this kind of filth. And she had castigated him with her talk of sacrifices!

Through her own tears she was suddenly aware of her daughter-in-law's sobbing on the floor. Sick inside, she was yet able to go to the girl and raise her up, holding her close.

"Oh, Celia, I'm so sorry. So sorry," Morna cried against her.

Celia stroked back the disheveled hair as she used to do Hannah's so long ago. "It's all right. It will be all right."

Morna sat back to look into her face. "Can you forgive me?"

"Yes. Oh, of course I am annoyed and angry with you, but I'm just as angry at myself. I am as much at fault as you. If you had felt I loved you, you could have asked me about Ewan without ever having to resort to gossip. But I found it hard to love you, Morna, not because of you yourself, but because of your father and because I was always jealous of Mercy. I have been angry with you for simply being who you are ever since you came to live with us, and I did not even try to hide it with simple good manners. I should ask *your* forgiveness."

For the first time Morna looked at the older woman and saw the suffering in her eyes. This was not a cold, angry, distant person but a woman in distress. Throwing her arms around Celia's neck, Morna kissed her wet cheek.

"You see," Celia went on in her quiet voice, "you don't know the extent of my sins. I am every bit as much in need of forgiveness as you. I am not talking about Ewan—what we did, wrong as it was, had at least the bond of a deep and a lasting love behind it. No, that was mild indeed compared to . . . to other things."

Mild indeed! How many people had she injured with her self-absorbed longings? Morna, herself, and Richard. Most of all, Richard.

"Do you think Josh will . . . come home?"

"Certainly. But when he does he must not find you in this state. You must wash your face, comb out your hair, straighten up your house and make sure he finds you calm and in control. If he saw you like this he would feel disgust—not pity. Can you pull yourself together now?"

"Yes, I think I can. Oh, Celia. I'm so glad you came today. I am so happy we have got this all out. Perhaps now we can be friends."

Celia kissed her white brow. "Yes, we will be friends now. For a long time Josh has been my only child. Perhaps now I can really believe that I have two children instead of only one."

Morna stood up and looked about her. "Oh my goodness, this room. I did not realize how dreadful it had begun to look."

"Ask that little girl downstairs to straighten it. And, Morna, take this thing and burn it. I think the least ever said about it again, the better."

Morna took the handbill and threw it on the dying coals of the fire. "Good riddance to a troublesome piece of evil," she said vehemently.

"Perhaps some good will come of it," Celia added, watching the charred edges curl into nothingness. "My dear, I came today because Richard is very ill and I want Josh to know. When he returns will you send him up to the house right away?"

"Papa ill? I hope it is nothing serious."

Celia almost shrugged, but thought better of it. If they were to really be friends, then honesty must prevail. "It looks as though it might be. At any rate, I am anxious to talk it over with Josh."

Morna already began to look more her old self. "Please stay and have tea with me," she asked almost hesitantly. "I'll be dressed in a jiffy and we can go downstairs. I'm only beginning to realize how famished I feel. And, who knows, perhaps Josh will come in while you are here."

"I should get back to my husband," Celia started, then saw the girl's hopeful face. "Perhaps I could take the time just for a cup of tea. I'll wait for you downstairs." She smiled at Morna as she moved to the door. How resilient was youth! Dimly she knew that her own strength and inner resources had in the last twenty-four hours taken a battering from which they would not quickly recover.

"Mrs. Favorsham here to see you, sir."

Jaspar Carne closed the ledger in which he had been writing and waved an ink-stained hand at the clerk standing in the doorway to his office.

"By all means, tell her to come in." Hastily he straightened the books on his wide expanse of desk, then slipped on his coat over his shirtsleeves. By the time the diminutive figure wrapped in a threadbare mohair shawl appeared in his doorway he was there to hand her in, self-contained and polite as always.

"My dear Mrs. Favorsham, how very nice to see you again. Do come in and sit with me awhile."

"Dear Mr. Carne. You are so kind to allow me to intrude on your busy schedule this way."

Jaspar pulled up a fan-back Windsor chair in front of the leather wing chair he was accustomed to taking but now relinquished to his visitor.

"No intrusion at all, dear lady. No man is so busy but that he can find the time for a female in distress."

"Oh, la. How gentlemanly you are."

With any other woman Carne would have taken such a coy comment with the contempt it deserved, but with Belinda Favorsham he had long ago accepted the sincerity behind her every word. She was the most fragile, delicate little flower he had ever known, and her very helplessness stirred his heart to protect her. Hardly a client, more a friend, he had come to look forward to these visits as a brief ray of light in the dull grayness of the day.

"I purposely stopped by to return your pamphlets," she said, taking several well-handled folded papers from her threadbare reticule. "I enjoyed them so very much, especially the one of *The Errors and Dangers Inherent in 'The Age of Reason.'* I cannot say I always understood your argument, being only a poor ignorant female, of course, not schooled in the deeper reaches of philosophical thought, but I understood enough of it to conclude with you that Mr. Paine's infamous book should be burned on the altar of every Christian church."

"Indeed, madam, it surely should. That book is an atheistic, heretical document calculated to lead the wavering Christian from his narrow way. I would have Mr. Paine in the pillory did we live in another, more godly time."

Belinda sat back, clutching her shawl across the tight bodice of her cheap homespun dress. "Yes, well . . ."

"Since you enjoyed these so much, dear Mrs. Favorsham, I wonder if you would like to take one or two more with you. I have just come into the possession of a remarkable treatise on the virtues of the preached Gospel. I am sure it would bring you some measure of comfort in your difficult circumstances."

"Oh, Mr. Carne. You are too good to me."

"My only concern is for your welfare."

He was amazed at himself that he took her little hand, criss-crossed by mesh mittens, and raised it to his lips. Poor little thing. She might even be pretty if she was not so mousy and drab and forced by indigence to dress in such appallingly shabby clothes.

"But I am sure you did not stop here today simply to return those tracts. How does it go with you? Has there been any . . . improvement?"

Mrs. Favorsham removed her round iron spectacles and dabbed at her tear-filled eyes. "Unfortunately, no. My husband returned shortly after the last time I saw you, more incensed with strong drink than ever before. The sea seems to return him to me ever that way. Oh, Mr. Carne, if you could but see the welts and bruises on my poor body . . ."

Carne felt an ungentlemanly stirring at the thought while Mrs. Favorsham blushed prettily.

"You must leave the brute. I have told you so many times."

"But I have no place to go. I cannot throw myself out on the sidewalk to live with the stray dogs and pigs."

"You know I have offered to help you find a place. You are only causing yourself more hurt by staying with this man. Why, he may do you real harm one day."

"Alas, I cannot push you in such a dangerous position. I well know that if Lucius ever learned you had been my bene-factor . . ."

Carne jerked back as though she had struck him a blow. "Surely, madam, you know that I would be the soul of honor."

"Oh, of course. *I* would know that, but he would never believe it, not of you or of any man."

"I do have a wife, you know," Carne added lamely.

Her little gloved hand rested deliciously on his arm for a moment. "A woman to be envied indeed," Belinda said, look-ing up at him from under her long darkened lashes.

Jaspar squirmed a little in his chair. "She perhaps, but not I," he muttered.

"Why, Mr. Carne, do I detect that your marital state is not a felicitous one?"

"Madam, it is a great mistake for any man to marry a widow with children of her own. I, for my folly, am now saddled with two great useless leeches that have not a drop of my own blood in their veins."

Belinda Favorsham's round eyes grew larger behind her small iron-rimmed spectacles. "But surely you are a very wealthy man, Mr. Carne."

"You might think so looking around my office here. But the truth is that business has been very slow indeed with all the troubles on the sea, and the public duties which I fulfill, while affording me great satisfaction, are not very remunerative. No, I fear I struggle along with the rest of the population."

Her warm hand grasped his. "I have known poverty, Mr. Carne, and still know it. I can truly feel for you."

"Indeed, your poverty is far greater than mine. But all things are relative, are they not?"

"Oh, relative indeed."

Mrs. Favorsham's dainty face disappeared into the shadows of her ribboned hat brim. For a moment he was afraid she was about to break into tears and he reached for his handkerchief, but when she lifted her eyes there was only the quiet smile he had come to know so well.

"Since you are a man who obviously is concerned for money . . ." she said hesitantly.

"As who among us is not in these difficult times."

"Exactly. I . . . I hesitate to bring this to your notice, yet I feel that I owe you so much goodwill for your kindness to me. And I know you for a man of tender sensibilities."

"Go on," Jaspar said, leaning forward in his chair and not unaware of the light touch of his knee against her skirts.

"Well, sir. As you know, my husband is a sailor, and he has let certain things drop—a hint here and there—that the master of his vessel is bringing in illegal goods from England, very quietly, you understand, and at great profit."

Jaspar rubbed a long finger across his narrow chin. "Smuggling. It is not uncommon in spite of all that the government can do to prevent it."

"Well, my husband says that his ship, the *Aurora*—"

"The *Aurora*!"

Belinda looked up, startled. "Why, yes, that is the name of his ship. And her master—Mr. Yancy..."

"Yancy—Elisha Yancy. The *Aurora* is a Dolphin schooner."

"That is correct. Master Yancy was carrying on a fly-by-night trade with the British all through the embargo days and still is, in spite of the Non-Importation Act. It is enough to make one green with envy to think of the money he has made. You may be sure none of it ever found its ways to the poor *seaman's* pocket."

Jaspar searched her innocent eyes. "But he must have done this with the collusion of the merchants in the city."

"So my husband hints. The *Aurora* is to sail this very week for Halifax. I understand that is where they take on the British cargo and hand over American goods for delivery to England. All of it quite underhanded."

"Your husband revealed all this to you?" Jaspar asked suspiciously.

"Well, he was deep drunk on cheap Barbados rum. Otherwise he would never tell me anything. This time, when he began letting out a few small hints, I thought of you and your high position on the Council and I felt sure you would be interested. So I managed to get a good deal out of him."

Carne was practically licking his lips. "I am more interested than you realize, my dear Mrs. Favorsham." What a plum this would be, to catch Yancy breaking the law so flagrantly. He might even send him to prison! What a delicious thought!

Her liquid eyes were very close to his. "Of course, you cannot know how it hurts me that rich men grow richer by means of their perfidy while the families of the poor and upright suffer in their penury." She flourished her handkerchief. "Sometimes when life is so hard and there is no money..."

A small suspicion touched Carne's consciousness that the conversation was veering toward a request. Well, so be it. For the opportunity to destroy the Dolphin Shipyards he would gladly return a favor. Besides, he was already fond of this gentle lady.

"My dear woman, dry your tears. I feel sure there will be some way I can help you, especially if what you say is true."

She brightened immediately. "You do? Oh, Mr. Carne, it would mean so much. Of course, I would not dream of asking you to do anything not completely upright."

"Nor would I do so," Carne replied, stiffening. "But there are ways I can be of assistance."

"What ways?"

"Well, for example, there is some city property on Barclay Street over which I as alderman have jurisdiction. I suspect that eventually the city will want to purchase it back. I will sell it to you for a nominal sum and then later you can resell it to the city for a fair price.

"And is this quite—legal?"

"To all intents and purposes, yes. It may be stretching a point here and there, but nothing to quibble about. When I think of the thousands of dollars some of my colleagues have defrauded the city of, this is really nothing."

"And you have always managed to stand so far above them, unspotted and untainted."

"I pride myself on that, as you may well imagine."

Impulsively she reached out and squeezed his hand. "Oh, how can I thank you, dear friend!"

Carne allowed himself to be warmly pleased by her touch for all of half a minute, then he carefully withdrew his fingers. "I think the best thing to do would be to let me know when your husband arrives back on the *Aurora*. If he could somehow manage to bring some evidence incriminating both Yancy and the merchants at this end who are involved, it would be very helpful. In the meantime I will have the deeds drawn up."

"I shall see that it is done." Straightening her skirts, she made as to rise. "I, of course, understand none of these things, yet I hope they may be of some little use to you, my dear friend."

"A man who would profit by dealing with the enemies of his country should be hanged as a traitor. I appreciate the motives that led you to mention this matter to me."

"You are always so correct in your sentiments, Mr. Carne. Now," she said, pushing back her chair, "I really must be going. If you would be so good as to give me a copy of the tracts you would like me to read . . ."

"Of course, of course," Carne said, opening the doors of a large black oak secretary behind his desk. Absently he searched out the papers, his thoughts intent on using this interesting bit of information Mrs. Favorsham had just dropped into his lap. As though she could read his mind she laid the pamphlets in her cloth bag, then smiled up at him coyly.

"Of course, I would not wish to bring Captain Yancy to grief—after all, my husband does sail on his ship—but if he is truly an enemy of his country, might you not find some way to expose his treason? I mean, would that not be the patriotic, Christian thing to do?"

Carne rested his long fingers lightly on her elbow to lead her to the door. "It would, yes, but it would require careful investigation. If he knew the game was afoot he would be very careful to cover his tracks."

"Does it not occur to you, dear Mr. Carne, that one way you might gain both his confidence and the information you seek is to pretend to subscribe to the transaction? Or is that too dangerous?"

"Why no. It is possibly the very way to proceed, but one which fills me with distaste all the same. How very clever you are, Mrs. Favorsham."

"La, I'm not a bit clever, Mr. Carne, merely anxious to help a friend. A friend whom I feel I can . . . call upon in my hour of need."

"Certainly I am that. Be very discreet with your husband. I'm sure you can use your womanly ways to good advantage. Try to learn who are the partners among the merchants and, if possible, how it is that Captain Yancy handles the financial transaction. And remember, any kind of signed papers would be incriminating evidence and would help immeasurably to bring him to jail."

Belinda extended her hand. "I shall do everything I can. Good day, Mr. Carne."

"Mrs. Favorsham."

His eyes lingered on her dainty form as she disappeared down the hall. A delightful woman. He had sensed from the first that she was worth helping, and now he knew it. For Elisha Yancy was not the sole owner of the *Aurora*. He was a partner with Richard Deveroe, and it was certain that if he, Carne, could bring down the one, the other would come toppling beside him. He had blocked the political career. He had only to play his cards carefully and he might effect the complete ruin of Deveroe's business empire.

Dear Mrs. Favorsham!

thirty-nine

After exchanging several letters with Dr. Nicholas Romayne, the president of Columbia Medical College, and after much persuasion on her part, Celia finally got Richard to agree to take the boat down to New York. On the first good day the *Caroline* carried them, peaceful as a drifting leaf, past the rolling farmlands and graceful farms lining the Hudson's shore. With the sun on her face, the lilting smoothness of the boat under her, the beauty of the silver river against the emerald green of the countryside, Celia felt a great sense of hope just to be quitting Southernwood. As fond as she was of her home, it had at present too many associations that both shamed and disturbed her. Now that it was receding into the blue haze of the distant shore she could not even understand what was the obsession that had held her brooding there for so long.

Nicholas Romayne was a huge bear of a man with gentle hands on a body that weighed well over three hundred pounds. He and his colleagues gave Richard Deveroe two days of the most careful examination, and in the end all they had to tell Celia was the same thing she had heard from Dr. Sayre. She begged them not to reveal to her husband the true nature of his illness, not knowing that Richard had already asked the same of them for her. Romayne went along with them both, so that when they turned their attention back to seeing New York each knew the truth and was convinced the other did not.

That evening, sitting in the elegant dining room of the hotel, Richard watched longingly at the parade of green turtle steaks, lobster pastries, pigeon pies and marrow puddings that graced the tables around them.

"I'd give a year of my life to sample one of those sweetbread pastries," he said almost licking his lips.

"Given the state of your constitution right now, it would

probably be worth a year of your life."

"No doubt you are right. Very well, I'll grit my teeth and stick to that horrible bland diet Romayne foisted on me. But once this improves, I warn you, I'm going on a gastronomic orgy."

"I'll chef it for you myself," she said, taking his hand across the table. Suddenly her grip tightened as a figure appeared in the wide archway beyond Richard's chair.

"Oh, no," Celia cried. "It's Hester, Richard. Standing right behind you."

Richard stopped himself from swiveling round in his chair. "Devil take her! She's the last person on earth I want to see."

"There! She's recognized us! Are you up to this?"

"Do I have a choice?"

Trailing yards of vermillion gauze, Hester swept over to stand looking down at them, surprise and consternation on her face.

"If I didn't believe my own eyes..."

"Hello, Hester," Celia said, unsmiling, nodding at the ever present Agatha, who hovered behind her mother.

"And how is it that you are in the city without my knowing it?" Hester said, plopping herself into one of the free chairs at their round table. "How long have you been here? Why did you not send round a card?"

Celia made a vain attempt to hide her irritation. "Only a few days."

Hester peered closer into her brother's face. "What's the matter with you, Richard? You look terrible. You've grown thinner and your color is bad. Are you ill?"

"Hester!" Celia cried angrily before she could stop herself.

"I have not been well," Richard said levelly, "but I've had a good diagnosis from the doctor and I expect shortly to be my old self again. You're looking very fit, Hester."

"Well, I'm not at all. I have terrible migraines and more worries than one person should ever have to deal with. And now, as if I didn't have enough to bear, I find that my only brother visits the city and slights me. I'm hurt, Richard, deeply hurt indeed."

Celia turned to the quiet girl by her side. Fleetingly she thought that every time she saw Agatha she was dressed in white dimity with a different-colored sash. Yet the girl had to be well into her twenties. What was the matter with Hester, keeping her in such childish fashions?

"How have you been, Agatha dear?"

The girl murmured a reply barely audible under the clanking of dishes and the chatter of patrons in the dining room.

"Agatha never changes," Hester offered. "Old age has not placed its cold grip on her youthful frame yet, as it has the rest of us. However, I must not stay to chat," Hester said, jumping to her feet, "because I am to meet some friends of Alderman Carne's here and am already late. But I'll be around tomorrow to call, Celia, I presume you're staying at this hotel."

"Yes," Celia mumbled.

"Good evening to you, then."

She was off wending her way around the tables as Richard got to his feet. "If Carne walks into this room I won't answer for my actions. Let's get out of here."

"But your supper . . ."

"I don't want it. Come along."

He nearly stumbled, and Celia quickly took his arm. "I should have told her we were staying at the Union Hotel."

"She'd track us down. You can stay tomorrow and talk to her, but I promise you now I shall be out all afternoon."

"I wish I could go with you."

True to his word, Richard left the hotel the next afternoon, but Celia did not have to entertain Hester alone after all. She was very pleased when about two o'clock Elisha Yancy appeared at the door of the hotel suite, anxious to hear the surgeon's report, and with only a little pleading on her part, he agreed to stay and support her through the coming interview. When three o'clock came without her visitors Celia began to hope they would not come at all. Then only ten minutes later Hester knocked at her door and swept grandly in with Agatha a shadow in tow.

"Captain Yancy," she said, showing him perfunctory attention. "It has been years, hasn't it? Are you still sailing the North River?"

Elisha looked through Hester to her gentle, silent daughter standing behind her. Suddenly he remembered that young face looking up at him that day he had discovered the children stranded on the dockside. He recalled a soft hand in his own, and trusting eyes looking up into his as though assured he could carry them safely home. What an uncommonly pretty girl she had become. Not a bit like her mother.

"What? Oh, aye. I still sail, mostly on the schooner *Aurora* or *Caroline*. And I've graduated from the North River to the

North Atlantic. We make runs between New York and Halifax."

Hester settled primly on the stuffed brocade sofa. "I am surprised you will venture on the open seas at all, these terrible times. Mr. Carne says the British grow daily more daring at boarding our ships and impressing our seamen. They must be taught a lesson."

Yancy replied sardonically, "I don't think the country can afford another lesson like Mr. Jefferson's embargo. It pricked the British while damned near stabbing a mortal wound in our own heart."

"There's no need to be vulgar," Hester said in a voice that showed she expected little else of a common sailor. She had never been able to do more than tolerate this gruff man. How Celia could bear to have him in her sitting room was more than she would ever understand.

"Perhaps the Non-Importation Act will serve us better," Agatha said suddenly. Celia was startled to hear Agatha speak up at all, much less exhibit a knowledge of something that was essentially a political and economic problem.

Elisha's voice was unusually gentle. "I greatly fear that as long as England and France are engaged in this tug-of-war they've carried on for nearly fifteen years there will be no peace for any of us. Our only hope is to somehow force them to respect our rights on the high seas."

"But how do you see that happening short of war?"

"You have a point, Miss Barnett, but—"

"Now, stop all this talk of war at once," Hester broke in. "I did not come here today to discuss politics." She turned on Celia. "I want to know about Richard. How ill is he, Celia? And don't try to foist me off with some silly tale of indisposition. I have never seen him look worse. Is he dying?"

"No!" Celia fought back her irritation, then proceeded glibly to spin a tale that sounded both plausible and reassuring. There was just enough truth in it that Hester seemed to accept it without question.

"I confess that I'm relieved. You and he are all the Deveroe family left and I would not want to lose either of you."

Celia took her words at their worth. Perhaps there was something left of the old closeness they had shared as children, some nostalgic affection which might withstand the battering of the near-enemies they had become. Then she remembered the handbill with its lewd drawing.

"What are you doing this afternoon?" Hester said suddenly. "I have been dying this age to see the new managerie. Why don't you put your hat on and come with me? It might be pleasant to spend some time together again."

"Oh, Mama," Agatha spoke up, startling them all, "you know I can't bear to look at those wretched animals. It breaks my heart. Please don't let's go."

Hester gave her daughter a withering glance. "Dear Agatha is the most fainthearted creature alive. We cannot even have a magpie or a canary in the house that she does not manage to leave the cage open. But you must not be so silly, my dear. You have to learn to steel yourself against such foolish feelings."

Agatha seemed to wilt visibly. Recalling the girl's quiet gentleness when she visited Southernwood away from her mother, Celia took pity on her. "I can go with your mother," she offered, "if you would prefer to return home, Agatha. Hester is right. We have not had a visit for some time."

"Perhaps I could see you home, Miss Agatha," Elisha gently suggested. "I don't especially enjoy looking at caged creatures, either, no matter how exotic."

Agatha turned to him gratefully. "You understand, then, how I feel?"

"Of course. It would be my pleasure to escort you."

"Is it all right with you, Mama?"

Hester waved a hand airly. "Yes, yes. Go ahead. Though I hate to indulge your foolish fancies, I'm sure Celia and I will enjoy the place more without you. I'll see you at home."

With little enthusiasm Celia went into the bedroom to don her hat and shawl. Perhaps before that handbill she might have been able to enjoy this excursion but now she truly doubted if she was going to be able to be civil to her sister-in-law. Ah, well, the afternoon was half gone already. As she reentered the sitting room she saw Captain Yancy shepherding Agatha out the door. An incongruous couple they made, she thought absently—the big, gruff sailor and the dainty, petite childlike Agatha. More like a father and daughter than anything else.

"I'm ready." Celia followed Hester through the door. Captain Yancy was always good company. She rather envied Agatha.

By late evening, though there were still people walking the streets, the house at Hanover Square was already quiet. A light flickered in the study window where Jaspar Carne was poring over bound ledgers. Upstairs, behind the drawn drapes, Hester lay on her bed trying to get involved in the latest romance from London. Across the hall Agatha sat staring at her image in the wavering surface of her mirror, thinking back over the pleasant afternoon. Captain Yancy had proved such a warm and accommodating companion that instead of coming directly home she had taken him by the Charity School and introduced him to the children with whom she worked on odd afternoons. He was interested enough in her good works that he had even agreed to meet her there again the day after next. Of course, he was an old man, yet his kindness to her and his interest in her concerns was like a dim beacon in a long dark tunnel. She smiled to herself, pleased beyond measure that she seemed at last to have found a friend.

Almost without noticing, Jaspar heard the clopping of the carriage horse stop outside his doorway. A hesitant knocking brought him to the hall, where he waved back his black butler whose flapping slippers were already audible coming up the stairs from below. He opened the door just enough to be able to make out the shadowed pock-marked face of a young man in the light of the street lamp, with straggling red hair falling forward over his thin face.

"What do you want?" Carne wasted no time on formalities.

"Alderman Carne?" he said in a whispery voice. "If I might have a word with you. I was sent to fetch you, sir, if you was to be so good as to come. I'm a friend of Mistress Favorsham's."

Carne was about to shut the door in the youth's face, but at this name his hand steadied. "And what would Mistress Favorsham want with me at this ungodly hour? I'm a respectable citizen—"

The young man interrupted him with a raised hand. "I know that, sir, I know that quite rightly. And Mistress Favorsham, she would not of bothered you at this improper time but that she was truly in a bad way. A very bad way."

Carne opened the door wider in order to thrust his head nearer to the young man's low voice. "Has her husband returned? Has he been abusing her?"

"Aye, sir, he's returned all right. I'm a neighbor, you see, and I hear the terrible cries that comes from her rooms when he's in port. Tonight . . ." He shook his head as though unable to continue. "Tonight was like none I ever heard before. Terrible! Terrible!"

Jaspar's sense of propriety struggled with his feeling for Belinda Favorsham. "But why did she not call a magistrate? Or the sheriff? Surely they could be of more practical service than I."

The young man nodded. "Aye, I said the same, I did. The very same. At the least, I says, let me fetch an apothecary, not an alderman. But she seems to rely on you, sir, that she does. And she says it is most urgent, sir, that you come this very night."

"An apothecary! Is she that bad, then?"

"Oh, aye. That bad indeed. I ran out and paid three bob for this here carriage which is waiting here to take you back, and all because my heart was torn just to look at the poor distressed creature."

Carne sniffed at the sight of the black hulk waiting beside the curb. It would be musty and damp and smell of sordid humanity. Yet...

He made a hasty decision, deliberately not examining it too closely. "I'll just put on my coat," he said and closed the door on the young man. Five minutes later he was ensconced inside the carriage, unpleasantly aware that it met his every expectation.

They wandered through the dark streets for what seemed a very long time, and as well as he knew the city he managed to get completely turned about. When the carriage finally stopped he looked around, not believing where he was.

"She asked me to bring you in the back way," the youth whispered conspiratorially, jumping down from the cab. "If it turns out that husband of hers has come back, I'm to turn you right about and slip you away just as you've come. He's been known to go at a man with a knife with no more concern that if he was carving a joint of meat."

The hairs on Carne's neck were suddenly prickly. "I detest violence," he muttered and tried to follow the youth through the dark warrens of a half a dozen backyards. When at length they finally ducked into a dimly lit hallway leading to a steep flight of stairs, he was beginning to wonder if he should have come at all. And yet Belinda needed him.

The shabby hallway at the top of the stairs was as bleak as anyplace Carne had ever stood, but he barely had time to

examine it before a door opened on a lighted room and he was
hurriedly pushed inside. As his eyes adjusted to the bright
lamps he was astounded to see Belinda Favorsham hurrying
toward him, as unlike the little mouse who had visited his
office as a woman could be.

Her black hair was loose and flying about her shoulders.
She wore some flimsy sort of nightdress which barely covered
her white breasts, and which looked to be torn in several places.
One sleeve was in fact hanging away from its seam and halfway
down her arm. That part of her face which was not blotched
with weeping was purple and distorted with ugly bruises. Before he could stop her she had her arms around his neck and
was sobbing into his black merino coat.

"Oh, Mr. Carne, thank God you came. I'm so grateful! So
grateful."

"Please, madam," Carne answered stiffly, pulling her arms
away. "Cover yourself. You are immodest."

Belinda stood back, hanging her lovely head. "You must
forgive me, Mr. Carne, it's just that I have been so distressed.
Please, sit there on the sofa and I will just go and slip on my
dressing gown."

"That would be more in order," Jaspar replied, and he attempted to collect himself while Belinda retrieved her robe.
When she returned she looked much calmer and certainly more
covered. She sat opposite him, making an obvious effort at
composure.

"It has been such a terrible night," she began, then broke
into fresh weeping.

Jaspar allowed himself to take her hand. "Come, now, dear
lady. Calm yourself and tell me all about it. More can be
handled by quiet reflection than by all the hysterics in the
world."

"Ah, you are so wise," Belinda cried, hiding her face with
her long fingers.

"Would you like my handkerchief?"

"No, no. Just having your presence in this room where I
have suffered so many horrors helps me immeasurably."

He patted her hand in what he considered a fatherly manner.
"Tell me about it. I presume the brute misused you."

"The beast! The raging beast! I fought him with all my
strength, yet who am I, a small, fragile woman, against such
force? He had consumed too much rum, you see."

"You must have a doctor to look to those bruises." Hesitantly he reached out to touch the wounded cheek, and in a flash she was sitting beside him, resting her head against his shoulder. Jaspar struggled to move away before the sweet aroma of some heavy scent and the soft touch of her hair against his cheek overcame his scruples. He laid a protective arm around her shoulders.

"You are so strong. So gentle," she murmured against him. "You cannot know how much it means to me to know that there are still men like you in this world."

Carne's crumbling reserve gave way completely and gradually he let down his guard, forgetting that in terms of the strictest propriety he ought not to be sitting with her at all.

Suddenly Belinda sat back, looking at him with her large earnest eyes. "I have forgotten the real reason I wanted you to come," she whispered. "Wait here a moment."

She disappeared briefly into the other room, returning with an old-fashioned man's purse made of some kind of heavy red fabric. Opening it, Carne was dumbfounded to see that it was stuffed thick with British pound notes. It was a moment before he could speak.

"Where did you get this?"

"I found it in my husband's seabag I believe he stole it from Captain Yancy, and I think it is part of the payment due the merchants who sent goods to Halifax. Is that not a great stroke of luck for us?"

"Why, there must be nearly a thousand pounds here."

"Yes. And it's illegal tender. Are you pleased?"

"I am indeed. Was there any kind of receipt enclosed?" Carne asked, digging through the two flap pockets of the purse.

"I could not find one. But it *is* Yancy's purse. See there, his initials embroidered on it. All we need is someone to swear they have seen him carrying this identical one and you'll have him."

"I don't know—that is rather circumstantial."

"For what other reason would he come back from Halifax with a thousand English pounds in his pocket?"

"Hmmm. Yes, that certainly is damaging. Do you think you can find out where and when he was to turn this money over, and to whom?"

Belinda thought for a moment, her eyes darkening almost as if she dreaded facing her husband again. "I can try. Yes, I *will* try—for you. Meanwhile, I want you to take this money and keep it for me."

Jaspar dropped the purse as though it burned his hand. "Me?"

"Please, Mr. Carne. There is no place in these rooms that my husband would not ferret out at once. But if it is not here, I can hold that over his head and bargain with him. He'll *have* to find out more information for me then."

"But he will be in deep trouble with these men who are owed this money. Not to mention Yancy himself. Your husband might come to grief."

She shrugged her white shoulders. "I hope he does." Her eyes narrowed, giving her face a feline cast. "It would serve him right for all the times he has hurt me. There is no other way anyway. If you turn this money over to the Council you will never know who else is involved. This way, you might just catch them all, Yancy included."

It was tempting. But it went against his better judgment. He hesitated.

"Please," she said quietly, placing the purse between his hands and folding her own over them. "Take it. Hide it in your office. No one will know. As soon as I know to whom he is to take it I will send the young man who brought you here tonight. Give the money to him and that will be all. Unless . . . unless you want to be there when it's handed over."

Uneasily Carne felt his control of the situation slipping from his hands. Yet the end result would be well worth any risk. "I think an accurate list of names would suffice, and, of course, your husband would have to testify. Can you convince him, do you think?"

The feline smile returned. "Yes, I think so."

"I am not in the habit of carrying away other people's money. It goes against my scruples."

"That is easily handled," Belinda said, reaching for a battered writing box. "Here, I shall write out a receipt for it, saying that you have received of me this sum of money for safekeeping. Will that satisfy your conscience?"

"Well, that would be more in order." She scratched a few words on the paper, signed her name, then handed it to him. Before he could run his eyes down it she was again sitting beside him, her arms moving silkily around his neck, her lips murmuring thanks against his cheek.

Jaspar's senses were reeling. Hastily he signed the note and edged himself away from her.

"You keep this and I will take the money. And keep your

eyes open for anything in writing which will help us bring this treason to justice."

She dropped her arms to take the note while, reaching into his coat pocket, Carne pulled out a folded page of heavy paper. "Here is the deed to the property I promised you, made over for the sum of one dollar. You do have that much?"

"I think so," she said, slipping the deed smoothly into her writing box. "Oh, dear Mr. Carne, you have no idea what this means to me. Once I get my husband through this ugly business I shall be in a position to care for myself at last. You are practically giving me my life over again."

Before he knew what was happening she had her arms around his neck again, her soft lips close to his. There was the faintest sweetness of jasmine on her skin. Hurriedly he slipped Yancy's purse into his coat pocket and forced himself to pull away.

"I will take care of this until I hear from you, then. And don't forget—anything you can obtain in writing will help us bring these thieves to justice that much more quickly."

"Dear Jaspar," she said demurely. "I will do my best. I'm truly grateful you came to me tonight."

"I did say you could depend on me, did I not?"

"Yes, you did, and you have proved as good as your word. Oh, dear. I'm so very tired. Do you think you might stay beside me awhile as I try to rest?"

Carne looked around panic-stricken. Wild horses were not going to drag him into that bedroom. Yet perhaps he might compromise.

"Why don't you rest here on the sofa and close your eyes? You look exhausted. I'll turn down the lamp."

She grabbed for his hand. "You won't leave me?"

"No, I shall just sit here beside you while you sleep. I promise."

"You will not let go of my hand?"

How tiny, fragile and trusting the little fingers seemed in his. "No, I won't let go."

forty

In some mysterious way the trip to New York seemed to have wrought a miraculous improvement in Richard's condition—this in spite of the fact that the doctors had given him no hope. Celia did not understand it at all, she merely thanked God for it and enjoyed watching him begin to be more his old self. As the summer began, he was able to take renewed interest in his business affairs and to be gone for longer periods of the day either to the Dolphin yards or with Captain Yancy on the river. She kept an anxious watch over his diet, and when the pains came she was ready with the laudanum. Thankfully she had had to offer it to him on only two occasions. In fact, the only discouraging thing about her husband's health that warm, lazy summer was that he grew continually thinner.

The birth of Morna's baby, a fragile, tiny girl they named Emily, brought a lifting of spirits to Richard and Celia both, and for a time she began to hope the physicians might be wrong and nature's healing pwers would take matters into their own hands after all.

It was on a hot August afternoon that she took her embroidery and went into the garden to sit in the cool shade of a tulip tree. The chirping of the insects around her in the high grasses between the hedges droned a sleepy obbligato to the quiet of the afternoon. Far in the distance she could hear the work sounds coming from the stable and the distant calls of the servants near the house. Leaning her head against the tree, she closed her eyes and let herself drift away on the sleepy waves of the warm afternoon.

Crunching sounds on the oyster-shell path roused her from her revery to stare with unbelieving eyes at the two incongruous figures walking toward her. They simply did not belong there—the large graying-bearded Captain Yancy and beside him the slim, demure Agatha. What on earth were they doing at South-ernwood? She had assumed Elisha had spent the better part of the last two months on the high seas, and Agatha—where had Agatha ever appeared without her mother? Yet here they were, approaching her with obvious trepidation, and self-consciously aware of their strange appearance in her garden.

A little while later, as she sat on her parlor sofa and listened to them, Celia's sense of unreality grew.

"Please help us, Aunt Celia," Agatha pleaded, having said more in the last ten minutes than in all the years Celia had known her.

"But married! I mean—"

Yancy did not give her time to elaborate. "We well know how it looks," he said, breaking in. "It's true that I'm old enough to be Agatha's father, but what does that matter? I've been lonely most of my life, and now here's a sweet, good, gentle girl who wants to be my companion. Do you think I care what her age is?"

"I've been lonely, too," Agatha added quietly, looking at the captain with such warmth that Celia's heart was touched.

"But you are so young." She shook her head.

"I'm four years older than Josh. Not so young really."

That old! With some surprise Celia realized that she had always thought of Agatha as a child.

"But your mother. Surely she has not agreed to this."

For the first time the old shyness overcame the girl. "No, she knows nothing of it. We left the city early this morning before light. I left a note, but I did not tell her where we were going. Just that I was going to marry Elisha."

"Oh, my God!" Celia had no trouble imagining the con-sternation this must have caused in the house on Hanover Square. The captain reached for Agatha's hand and gripped it tightly. "We had no hope of Hester's blessing, Celia, so we didn't even try for it. But Agatha is of age. She does not really need her parents' permission to marry me—we are breaking no laws. We came to you because I felt sure you and Richard would help us." He paused, studying her worried face. "You will help us?"

Did she really have a choice? Celia struggled with herself for only a moment, feeling an old sense of duty and propriety which might make her not wish to go behind Hester's back this way. Then she remembered the handbill. Her lips turned up in a wry smile.

"Of course I'll help you. There'll be a terrible scene with Hester when she finds out, but no matter. I'll take her on. However, I would like to keep Richard out of this as much as possible."

"Of course. Can Agatha stay here with you just until we get the banns cried and the service arranged? It won't be long."

"Certainly. But it had better not be too long or Agatha will certainly have her mother up here trying to drag her away."

Elisha enveloped his radiant young intended in a warm hug. "I'm off right now to the village to make arrangements with the parson. Let Celia help you get settled, Agatha, and I'll be back as soon as possible."

The girl's eyes followed him all the way through the door, and when she turned back to Celia it was with such glowing gratitude on her face that Celia felt that whatever Hester's wrath, it would be worth it.

"How can I ever thank you, Aunt Celia?"

"You don't have to. Come along now and let's see if we can't cut down one of my dresses to fit you. If there's one thing I insist on it is that you will not stand up to be married in that childish style of dress your mother has foisted on you all these years!"

Even pulling all the strings Elisha could manage, they were not able to be married for nearly two weeks. Celia lived on pins and needles, expecting at any moment to have Hester descend upon her like an avenging angel. To her great surprise and relief, the outraged mother did not materialize, and on a sunny September morning Agatha, in a stylish pink silk ball dress trimmed with crepe, became the wife of Captain Elisha Yancy. With her hair crimped stylishly and ornamented with dusty-rose ostrich feathers, and her glowing face reflecting her inner happiness, Agatha was actually a handsome young woman. But then, all brides are beautiful, Celia thought wistfully, remembering that day so long ago at West Farms when she had stood, a girl of sixteen, at Richard's side.

He seemed to be remembering that day as well as she. He had been young, too, she thought. Only eighteen. Children, clinging to each other out of fear of the unknown and out of a genuine and old affection. Had it been right? she wondered, looking across at the wan, thin figure of her husband, still elegant in a coat of burgundy velvet, back still straight and proud in spite of the obvious marks of illness.

Would she have been happier if she had waited until she knew more of who and what she was? By every worldly measurement Richard was a successful man, and she had shared in the rewards of that success. Yet no one had caused him greater heartache than she, the person he was closest to in all the world. Was it her weaknesses, her failings, that had turned her from him? No, be fair. She had wanted to be a good wife. She wished that all of her own longings and needs could have been fulfilled by her husband, the man who rightfully should have fulfilled them. Surely some of the blame for her failure had to fall on him.

The ceremony was over and Celia shrugged off her gloomy thoughts. With Agatha radiant at his side, Elisha Yancy had never looked more at peace with the world. She wished them both great happiness.

It was providential that the newlyweds left Southernwood right after the wedding, for the very next day a hired coach drawn by blowing, lathered horses pulled up before the porch to discharge an enraged Hester.

She sailed into Celia's sitting room, shoving aside the servant who would have announced her.

"Where is my daughter? And don't tell me she's not here, because I know better!"

Celia took a moment to recover from her surprise. "Sit down, Hester. Would you like a glass of madeira? Or tea, perhaps?"

Hester's pale eyes blazed. "Don't try to put me off! This is no social call. I know Agatha is here, I know you are secluding her until that beastly scoundrel of a sea crawler can carry her off. I demand you give her up to me. At once!"

"How can you be so sure Agatha is here? You don't see her, do you?" Celia said, gesturing around the room. "Perhaps you would like to look under the sofa, or upstairs beneath the beds?" She had been dreading this interview, but now that it was here she began to enjoy it.

"Don't be coy with me!" Hester screamed. "I want my daughter. If you don't call her down here quietly I am prepared to bring in the sheriff."

"Sit down, Hester," Celia continued quietly. "I refuse to talk to you if you intend to stand there and scream at me."

"Do you deny that Agatha is here?"

"No. That is, she was here. That much is true."

Hester's face grew white. "What do you mean, 'was'?"

"She is gone. She was married yesterday to Captain Elisha Yancy and they have sailed on the sloop *Caroline* for a wedding trip upriver. I don't know where. So you see, it will do you no good at all to rage at me. Sit down and calm yourself, I pray you."

Hester's petite figure deflated at this piece of news. Sinking into a chair, she covered her face with her hands, and for a moment her genuine distress almost awoke a glimmer of pity in Celia's breast. But only for a moment.

"Too late! Too late! Oh, my poor, poor baby!"

"Come, now. I have known Elisha Yancy for nearly thirty years, and a finer man does not exist. Agatha could have done a lot worse."

When Hester lifted her face none of the rage had left it. "He could be her father! And he's far beneath her. An inferior."

"That is nonsense. Captain Yancy is as much a gentleman as your Jaspar Carne, and a far better Christian. He is genuinely fond of Agatha and will treat her wonderfully. I've seen them together, Hester, and they are very happy."

Hester's face contorted. "Don't tell me how happy they are. This unnatural marriage—nothing good will come of it. It's all your fault. Letting that gross drunkard seduce my innocent daughter behind my back! Throwing them together—"

"I never did any such thing!"

"Encouraging them to deceit and fraud, then assisting them in this despicable elopement."

Celia fought to keep her own fury in check. "The first I ever knew of this relationship was when they appeared on my doorstep two weeks ago. How unjust you are, Hester. What of your own suspicions? You must have known something was going on."

"I knew she spent time with him, but it never crossed my mind—never!"

"You never really thought a man would want to marry Agatha, did you?"

"Well, she is such a child and such a plain little thing."

Celia threw up her hands. "Oh, Hester, how can you be so blind? You kept your daughter looking like a child when she has been a woman for a long time now. And when you take her out of those ridiculous frocks and put her in a woman's dress she is a very pretty creature indeed. Why could you not be proud of her the way she is instead of trying to keep her something she is not?"

Hester gripped the arms of her chair. "How dare you! How dare you tell me how to raise my children."

"I am not trying to tell you how to raise your children. I think you made a mistake with Agatha—"

"That is none of your concern. You've not been so perfect that you have the right to tell me how to run my life."

"What do you mean?" Celia said, after an icy pause.

"You know very well what I mean."

With her last strength Celia made one more try. "Hester, please. You have always been a sister to me. For the sake of the affection we once shared, let us not say things we will regret."

"I never bore you any affection," Hester replied with quiet coldness. "You were thrust on me by my mother and father— a dirty urchin suddenly presented as my 'sister.' You took my brother's affection away from me, you stole my patrimony, you insinuated yourself between me and every member of my family I loved, including my dearest cousin, and you dragged the good name of Deveroe through the mud. But then we should have expected nothing less of a ragged foreigner."

Celia felt the room heave around her. "You selfish baggage!" she uttered through clenched teeth. "That's all you've ever been, self-centered and thoroughly egotistical. What would *you* know of affection, you who have never loved anyone but yourself! Even now you won't admit the real truth of why you want Agatha back. It's not because you fear the disgrace or begrudge her the happiness. It's because you are losing an unpaid servant to wait on your every whim."

"How *dare* you speak to me—"

"We have nothing more to say to each other," Celia cried, jumping to her feet. "Get out of my house."

"Do you deny you cuckolded my brother? Do you deny that you wantonly conducted an illicit affair with Ewan while Richard was away during the war, you slut!"

"Whether I did or did not is between Richard and myself alone. It is none of your business, though you and that jackal husband of yours tried to turn it into a slander to destroy Richard. And you came near succeeding, damn you."

The startled look in Hester's eyes betrayed her. She had not realized that Celia would link the handbill to the Carnes.

Celia fought to hold her trembling body in check. "I feel sorry for you, Hester. With all my sins and mistakes I have at least had the sustaining love of my husband. Can you say as much! And Ewan too—what we shared was deep and beautiful. Have you shared as much with a living soul? You don't know *how* to love."

Hester snorted. "Love! Deep, beautiful! Flimsy excuses. They don't change what it makes of you—a whore!"

"Get out of my house!"

Hester pulled her flounces around her and rose with an affected dignity. "Yes, I'll get out. I hope never to set eyes on you again."

"That will be too soon for me."

She stopped by the door and turned briefly. "You can tell Agatha for me, when next you see her, that I have done with her. Not a penny shall she ever get from me and I hope never to see her again."

"I'll give her your loving message."

For a brief moment their eyes met across the room, both too full of rage to allow any regret for the young girls they had once been.

"Goodbye, Hester," Celia said finally.

Hester's only answer was to fling herself out the door and into the waiting coach. Celia listened as the horses thundering down the drive carried her away, then walked, shaking all over, to the decanter by the window. With a trembling hand she poured a glass of wine and gulped it down, heedless of its burning all the way down. It was always painful, cutting away a familiar appendage. Even a malignant one.

When the committee came through the door Jaspar Carne knew by the look of them that something was amiss. Coming hurriedly to his feet, straightening his neckcloth and pulling down his coattails, he searched his mind wildly, wondering what this unexpected visit could be about. Grand Sachem Cowdrey took off his hat and stared down his nose at Jaspar. Beside him Wortman, in a brightly checkered long coat, wore an unaccustomed look of severity. Behind the two committeemen he recognized the pockmarked face of the young man with a shock of red hair falling over his eyes—the young neighbor of Mrs. Favorsham's who had twice taken him to her apartment and who had picked up the money for delivery last month.

"Gentlemen, won't you sit down?" Carne began politely.

Sachem Cowdrey lowered himself into a creaking Windsor chair, while Wortman stood uneasily beside the Franklin stove. The young man hovered in the back of the room, appearing to blend in with the dark paneling of the wall.

Carne settled in a chair opposite Cowdrey and waited. After a brief, uneasy silence, the Grand Sachem reluctantly spoke up.

"Well, Carne. As you see, we've had to pay you a call."

How like Cowdrey to waste time, Jasper thought with irritation. "I confess I am completely at sea, gentlemen, as to what could have brought you here this time of day. I understood we had no plans to meet until next Tuesday at the Belvedere Club."

"Yes, well, that is so. But something has come up. Something of great significance. We thought that as colleagues who have worked together for a long time, we owed it to you to put before you the charges—"

Jaspar gaped. "Charges!"

"—to put them before you before we took them to the Council."

"Why, I cannot imagine what you are talking about. You surely cannot mean to accuse me of wrongdoing."

Wortman broke in, obviously enjoying Jaspar's surprise. "Now, that would be a change, wouldn't it. Customarily it is you who are accusing the rest of us."

Cowdrey glared his fellow committeemen into silence. "No one's accusing you—yet. But there are some questions that we feel deserve an answer."

"What questions?" Wortman noted with pleasure that Jaspar swelled with indignation like one of those frogs who blow up before your eyes.

"You know that these have been—ahem—difficult times, Carne. Tammany has come in for its share of accusations of graft and corruption—"

"Deservedly so."

"Now, let us not be contemptuous. Some few of us have committed—ahem—errors, from time to time. All of us have had to face inquisitions—all except you."

"You gentlemen know that I pride myself on my reputation. If I did not know better I confess I would think this is some sort of a joke you are plaguing me with."

This was too much for Wortman, who had never been able to stomach Jaspar Carne's overbearing piety. "This is no joke,

Jaspar. These are serious charges and we feel compelled to examine them."

Carne glanced uneasily at the young man hovering near the shelves in the back of his office. He did not like the half-concealed smirk on that homely face. Yet what could he have possibly done to warrant an accusation? He settled stiffly back in his chair. "All right, gentlemen. I can see that something has perturbed you. Put it before me and I shall do my best to set your mind at ease."

"Well, to begin with—" Cowdrey looked up at Wortman, hesitating—"it has come to light, Carne, that you have accepted a bribe. And a large one. One thousand British pounds."

There was no perceptible change in Carne's face. "A bribe? Surely you don't believe that."

"We have it on good authority," Wortman broke in, leaning closer, "that such an exact sum of money was placed in your hands in order to obtain your cooperation for the sale of city lots on Barclay Street—property your son-in-law then sold back to the city at exhorbitant prices. How much did you make on that deal, Jaspar?"

"This is a lie! I never accepted a bribe in my life."

"Young Mr. Rose here has the receipt. Show it to him, Rose."

Eagerly the pockfaced young man dug into the pocket of his shabby coat and produced a familiar-looking folded bit of paper covered with a familiar scrawl. Carne felt a prickling sensation on his neck as he recognized his own signature next to Belinda's.

"But—"

"Can you deny this receipt is genuine? Did you not sign it in return for a secret cache of one thousand pounds sterling? Is not Dexter Barnett your son-in-law?"

"Yes, but you don't understand. That money was gotten illegally. I was only holding it for someone. It was to be used to prove an accusation of piracy and smuggling. And I haven't spoken to Dexter in years. I had no idea he was surety for Mrs. Favorsham." He could hear that all his protests sounded like excuses even though they were the gospel truth. Why hadn't he read that paper more thoroughly!

Cowdrey and Wortman exchanged glances. "Yes, she said that would be your story."

"What do you mean? Have you talked with Mrs. Favorsham?"

"You do not deny knowing the lady?"

"Of course not."

"And do you deny that on two occasions you went in the late hours of the night to her rooms and there stayed for several hours?"

"Of course not."

"I think we have heard enough, Cowdrey."

Carne stared unbelieving at the two men as they rose to leave. "But, gentlemen, I've done nothing wrong. Mrs. Favorsham is helping me to construct a charge of smuggling against Elisha Yancy and his ship, the *Aurora*. He has been bringing in English goods for sale in the city in defiance of the Non-Importation Act. I can prove it. I have a bill of sale."

"Pshaw!" Wortman exclaimed. "I don't know where you got such a bill, but it has to be false. There are three inspectors of the port who are willing to swear that the *Aurora* sails to Halifax with regular cargoes of lumber and nails."

"Even more serious, Jaspar, is the fact that you turned over to this woman city property which was then sold back to the city at a huge profit. Can you deny that?"

"But it was a legal sale."

"Oh, *indeed*. And how much did she pay for it? One dollar, I believe, was the precise amount. Do you expect us to believe you did not plan to share in the windfall with her? You would do better to confess, you know. We already have Mrs. Favorsham's word."

Jaspar's mind was working furiously. "And just what did she say?"

"Let the lady speak for herself. Call her in, Rose."

Somehow Jaspar did not feel at all reassured to know that Belinda was waiting outside. When she sailed into his office he could not believe his eyes. It was the same woman but transformed. Gone were the round eyeglasses, the severe hair style, the dowdy clothes. With ringlets framing her rouged face, a French lace shawl barely covering her exposed bosom, a clinging crepe dress emphasizing her figure, this was a gaudy butterfly emerged from the cocoon of the woman he had known. Even her manner was different, provocative and alluring where before she had seemed the picture of timorous, helpless femininity. Jaspar's keen nose was beginnning to smell a ruse.

"Good morning, Mr. Carne." Belinda smiled up at him archly from under the pert brim of her bonnet.

"Mistress Favorsham. What a miraculous transformation."

"Mrs. Favorsham," Wortman said, taking her hand and leading her to the only other chair in the room, "is this not the deed Mr. Carne signed over to you in return for a great deal of money?"

"Indeed it is," Belinda said, glancing at the paper. "The very one."

"But, dear Mistress Favorsham," Carne noted with pointed politeness, "tell these gentlemen the facts. You gave that money to me for safekeeping, did you not? It was a favor on my part, until such time as your husband discovered whom it was actually meant for."

"La, Mr. Carne, these gentlemen know well enough that I have no husband. As for a favor, well, you did say, did you not, that you were stretching the law just a bit—that your colleagues did the same kind of thing all the times? Those were your very words, I believe."

"Well, yes, I did, but—Gentlemen, this is a trick. A vile trick!"

"Come now, Carne," Cowdrey interjected. "If you have the money in safekeeping, produce it. You have only to convince us of your good faith. Bring it out. Let us see it and perhaps we will be more ready to believe you."

Carne's eyes shunted to Rose, but the self-satisfied smirk on that young man's face told him he would get no help from that quarter. "I cannot," he answered lamely. "That is, it is not here in my place of business."

"Why don't you tell them, Mr. Carne?" Belinda smiled sweetly, "You used the money to purchase English goods brought into this country illegally. Oh, not by the *Aurora*, surely, but on some vessel of undetermined origin. That is the truth, is it not?"

Carne looked daggers at Belinda Favorsham. His neck was growing warm inside his high starched neckcloth. "I was trying to discover what merchants were in collusion with Yancy."

Wortman snorted. "Of course you were, you hypocritical prig. Touting your puritanical conscience all over the city when in private you were spending the midnight hours with this lady in her notorious rooms, no better than any other man. I only hope I'm there to gloat when you come before the Common Council."

"Notorious?"

"Now, Jaspar," Belinda cooed, "surely you won't deny that

you did visit me in the late hours of the evening once or twice. Can you have forgotten those delightful occasions?"

"This is a gross lie!" Carne cried, nearly losing control. "Tell these men I went there only to comfort you because you were in distress. My actions were at all times proper."

"You expect us to believe that?" Wortman exclaimed, beginning to enjoy Carne's dismay. "Why, the address itself gives you away."

"What address? I never knew what the address was. I went in the back..."

"Humph. Of course you went in the back. We watched you do it once ourselves, thanks to this gentleman here. Wouldn't do at all for you to be seen at the front door, would it? Surely you are not going to pretend that you don't know that 16 Anthony Street is one of the most notorious brothels of the city."

Jaspar's face turned as white as his collar. "Brothel!" His eyes burned into Belinda's while she sat watching him with a look of pure innocence on her pale face.

"Gentlemen, this has all been a trick, a plot of some kind..."

Cowdrey picked up his hat. "Well, I've heard enough. If I were you, Jaspar Carne, I would consider resigning the cares of office before I was asked to leave by the Council. I don't think we are going to be able to keep these matters from the press, though we shall certainly make an effort."

"The press," Carne muttered weakly.

"Oh, yes," Wortman could not resist turning the screw. "Miss Favorsham has assured us she will not hesitate to stand as a witness against you, and, of course, the papers love a juicy scandal. Especially when the perpetrator has long made himself obnoxious by imposing his so-called high ideals to other men. Sachem Cowdrey's advice is sound. We shall expect to see your resignation by tomorrow at the latest."

Carne watched them leave, amazed at his own coolness. His public career—the only thing that mattered in his life—was in ruins. His private reputation, would be dragged through the papers and soiled. And all because he had let his stiffened spine, for the only time in his life, be softened by a pitiful face and a pair of large tearful eyes.

Grabbing for his hat, he stalked from his office and out through the long hallway. Clerks seated behind high desks on

raised platforms looked up as he stormed by, then went back
to their work, unable to sense behind that frozen exterior the
deep fissures inside the man.

Striding through crowded streets, he saw no one. Not daring
to think, he forced his feet forward until he found himself near
the docks where the long jibs of the ships lying at anchor jutted
out over the near-empty walkways. The harbor was beginning
to show signs of life again now that the embargo was lifted,
yet there were still many ships standing with their masts capped
by empty kegs to protect them from the weather while they sat
out the arguments among the nations. They were like the spirit
within him—drear, empty, void of purpose. He walked past
them to the end of the pier where the stagnant water lapped at
the wooden posts. How comforting to be swallowed up in that
enveloping nothingness. Never to see the newspapers with
one's name blazoned in dishonor!

What were his alternatives? To go home to his complaining,
eternally dissatisfied wife? To take a post stage for Albany,
there to purchase a rifle and a cuckskin shirt and disappear into
the wild reaches of the western Alleghenies? He was too old,
too tired. And life was really not all that pleasant anyway . . .

Of course, many Tammany men had survived this kind of
scandal—survived and come back to thrive on the spoils system
once more. Romaine, Bingham, Jonas Humbert, even the foun-
der of the society, William Mooney. Scandal had never broken
them. Perhaps he could survive it, too. Yet he knew he did not
possess the attractive personality and popularity which would
enable him to live it down. The voters knew him for an honest,
upright man. If that was destroyed he had nothing to win elections with.

And to have to hide his face in shame. To know that other
men were gloating at the loss of his reputation. To have to
resign in ignominy an office that was the most significant thing
in his life. To be branded a thief and a lecher as other men
were, even though he knew in his heart it was a lie.

To have to avoid the shocked and reproving glances of his
Deveroe wife. To know that her detestable Deveroe brother
had beaten him once again.

Looking around, he saw that the pier was for the most part
empty of people, though the street above was still teeming.
Sitting down on the wooden platform, he dangled his legs over
as he had not done since he was a child, a time so long ago

in memory that he could barely recall it. Leaning out over the black water, he stared into its somber depths.

Very slowly he took off his coat and carefully folded it, laying it on the pier beside him. Taking off his shoes, he anchored down his hat on top of his coat. Then, without looking back, he slid off the pier and into the black, welcoming water.

forty-one

"Are you aware, Josh, that we have been driving for at least half an hour and we have discussed every topic except the one most important to us both?"

"Very well, Grace, where do we start?"

It was cool under the canopy of the tree-lined roadway. When they left the houses and streets of the city behind, the rolling fields sprinkled with summer wildflowers gave them the sense of entering another world. Grace reluctantly broke the spell.

"Were you pleased?" she asked quietly.

"Oh yes. You were magnificent. I only hope it was not too unpleasant for you."

"Unpleasant! It was my first leading role. I enjoyed it to the hilt. Furthermore, I was mightily impressed with myself. I think now I may have a real career before me as an actress."

He laughed. "Then it served some good purpose."

"It also served to accomplish your revenge, you know. Isn't that what you wanted—to ruin Jaspar Carne? Surely you must feel some personal satisfaction."

Josh pulled the horses to a stop. Around them insects hummed noisily, and in the trees above the birds kept up an incessant chatter. "I expected to feel a tremendous satisfaction, Grace. Yet you see, my father is still dying without ever having had the career he wanted so badly, and even if Jaspar Carne was paid in full for what he did, it doesn't help to alter that. So, somehow, I could not savor the revenge."

"I must confess, too, Josh, that had I known the man would be so unhinged as to drown himself, I never would have become involved in the thing. I feel like . . . like a murderess."

He reached for her hand. "I suppose we both should feel some degree of remorse. Yet that is foolish. Carne never experienced a moment's remorse over the grief he caused my father. Even his suicide, I believe, was more out of fear of public disgrace than any sense of guilt for wrongdoing."

"But Josh, that is just it. He hadn't really done anything wrong. We just made it look as though he had."

He shook his head. "Yes, but, you see, the things he *had* done wrong—the slander and lies that destroyed my father—those we could not bring before the world. So it had to be this way. In one sense it was only a trick. Some men would have shrugged it off and gone on about their business. Frankly, that is what I thought Carne would do."

"He was a cold man, but I think he felt some little spark of pity or affection for my 'Belinda Favorsham.' Perhaps that is why I feel so rotten about the whole thing."

The coach jerked to a roll as he set the horses down the road again. "What will you do now?" he asked letting the animals drop into a leisurely walk.

"I've had an offer to go on tour with a company Mr. Cooper is putting together. What about you? Are things going any better?"

"Once these maritime problems are settled they should be very good indeed. I expect that if ever trade relations with England are restored both the shipyards and the import business will boom."

"That is not what I meant. What about Morna?"

He smiled across at her. "Since our daughter was born we have become a real family. I think we understand each other better than ever before. She has even become friends with Mama, something I never expected to see."

"Well, Mr. Deveroe, you should be a happy man. Your home life is content, your business is a success and your enemies lie in the dust."

They rolled past the Episcopal burying ground and toward the small homes and cultivated fields that lay on the outskirts of the growing village of Greenwich. Just ahead, they could make out the colorful red sign announcing the popular Campbell's Tavern, where Josh expected to stop. He was a long time answering.

"Happy? Who is ever really happy?"

* * *

While Josh and Grace O'Malley sat in Mr. Campbell's paneled taproom, Celia stood in her herb garden admiring the
tangled profusion of plants. To the uninitiated the large plot
looked like a haphazard collection of seeds sown carelessly by
the wind, but they were each of them her old friends. She knew
them each separately, their healing propensities as well as their
flavors, and she had enjoyed the rare privilege of an afternoon
spent lovingly weeding and spading between their thick rows.

But it was hot now and she was tired. Unfastening the strings
on her wide hat which kept the sun off her complexion, she
walked over to a large apple tree with a circular bench around
its gnarled trunk and sat down, leaning back against its welcome
support.

It was good to be tired physically for a change instead of
emotionally drained. It was comforting to have one's muscles
ache from bending and stretching rather than from sleep interrupted or no sleep at all.

Yet who was she to complain? These last weeks had been
so dreadfully hard for Richard, trying stoically to bear increasing agony and living from one dose of laudanum to the next,
that her own weariness and despair seemed a feeble thing in
comparison. They had long ago stopped pretending that he
would get better. No longer did they discuss plans for the future
or make veiled remarks about what they would do when he
was well. Yet at the same time never once had they faced
together the fact that he was going to die. He knew it, she felt
sure, and he must be aware she did, too. But the words lay
unspoken between them, too terrible to be faced. Neither of
them seemed to want that kind of reality yet. She smiled wryly
to herself. When had they ever wanted that kind of reality
between them?

And yet, the thought of Richard gone forever brought with
it such a pain in her heart that she sat upright, clutching her
breast. With the horrible reality of that night when she had
heard Richard calling out her name in his agony and need, the
doors had opened again on all those years of friendship and
love she had shared with her husband. A different kind of love
perhaps than that she had known with Ewan, but love nevertheless. With Richard's need for her in his illness and her
realization of the sacrifices he had been so willing to make to
protect her good name, she realized almost for the first time
the depth of her feeling for this man. He was a part of her and

had been since she was nine years old. The tragedy of their relationship was that he could not be all to her that she wanted and needed.

She felt the tears fighting to run free and covered her face with her hands. Now when she was about to lose him she finally knew how very much she cared for Richard Deveroe. Too late, she understood the bonds that had held them together through so many long years. It had never been any good trying to make their love something it was not, but never again would she pretend that it was not strong and good as it was.

Suddenly she was consumed with an urgent desire to see him, to touch him, to make sure he was still with her. She had left him asleep in the bed he seldom left these days. She would just look in on him, make sure the opiate had done it work. Starting up the path to the house, her hat in her hand, she realized that even with the dreaded future they faced she was more at peace within herself than she had been in years.

A week later Elisha Yancy appeared again, having sailed the *Aurora* in from her latest voyage. He happened to come on one of Richard's good days and they spent nearly an hour, the captain sitting beside the bed where Richard lay propped up against the pillows, discussing the relaxation of the trade regulations against Great Britain and France and how they had not improved the situation on the high seas. American ships were still being boarded, and nearly one thousand seamen had been impressed this past year alone. Celia sat nearby keeping an anxious eye on her husband, whose obvious enjoyment of the conversation with his old friend seemed to more than make up for the fatigue it brought him.

At length when the gray cast on her husband's thin face was so pronounced she could ignore it no longer she sent Captain Yancy back to his young wife waiting in their new home near Josh and Morna's house close by the Dolphin yards.

"You'll come back tomorrow," Richard asked hoarsely.

"Without fail," Elisha answered, laying his large hand on the shoulder so thin now that the bones were easily felt.

Celia saw him downstairs, then went quickly back to the bedroom, where Richard lay exhausted, without even the strength to watch her as she quietly closed the blinds and removed the tea tray to the hall. For a long time she sat by him, thinking he was asleep and wishing she too could doze for a while. But rest refused to come. She had hoped that Elisha's return would bring him new strength. Instead it had only served to make clearer than ever how few resources he had left.

Outside a light rain began falling, making the darkned room even gloomier. She studied Richard's sharpened profile nearly indistinct in the failing light, the bones now so prominent that it suggested a skull more than the familiar handsome face she had known so long. The tears began to run down her cheeks. She had turned away from him so often in her lifetime, but he had always been there when she turned back. What would she do when there was only emptiness where he had been?

"Oh, my dear, don't cry," he said suddenly, and with a start she realized he had not been asleep after all. "I can stand anything but that."

She tried with all her strength to hold back her tears, but they refused to stop. Then, giving up the struggle, she went thankfully into his arms, sobbing against his shoulder while he held her close. When she finally lifted her head he brushed the tears from her cheeks with this hand.

"Will you be all right without me?"

She pressed his hand against her cheek. "I don't know."

"I've made so many mistakes in my life, Celia, but one thing that was always constant was my love for you. I hope you know that. Perhaps I was not always able to show you what I felt, but it was there nonetheless."

"My mistakes. All mine!" she said brokenly.

"No. That is not true. Don't blame yourself."

"Richard, I saw that terrible handbill. I know why you withdrew from the campaign last year that you wanted so badly. It was all for me, to protect my name. I want you to know how grateful I am to you and how much I love you for doing it."

In the dim light his eyes were huge and burning. "You should not have seen that vile thing. I never meant you to know."

"But, my dearest husband, I *had* to know. I wish you had shown it to me from the first and we could have faced it together. We were never honest enough with each other!"

He was startled at the depth of feeling in her voice as she went on. "There were so many times I wanted to tell you of my needs and my desire for you and I never felt I could speak."

"Many times I wanted to go to you and wouldn't let myself."

"I thought you didn't need the kind of comfort I wanted to give you so badly. So, out of pride and hurt feelings, I wouldn't let myself be the one to reach out."

He pulled her down against him. "Perhaps our mistake was that we fell into the habit of not speaking, and now it is too late."

She curled up beside him, clinging to him like a frightened child. "I've hurt you terribly, Richard. Can you forgive me?"

"What a foolish word," he answered, stroking her hair. "We had many good years, a fine son, a satisfying life. I can die content. But you, Celia, you were always the restless one, always searching for something more than I could give you. I understand that now better than ever. I only hope that what I was able to give you served to make you happy."

How could she answer? How to explain that too late she had learned that there are many kinds of love, and that the love she felt for this man, while not the whole of life, was nevertheless deep and real and abiding, so much a part of herself simply by virtue of the time gone into it that she did not know how she was going to be able to live without it. She kissed the gaunt cheek and clung to the wasted body and hoped that spirit could answer spirit. When he finally slept she too felt drained, wasted, but with a measure of peace in her heart that had never been there before.

Richard clung lingeringly to life until the end of October, when the hills around Southernwood were wrapped in scarlet and gold splendor. The last weeks he was seldom lucid, and finally fell into a coma from which he drifted quietly out of life. Celia buried his body in the cemetery of the village below their hill, overlooking the river and across High Street from the old meeting house. A simple headstone marked the grave, whose raw overturned earth was soon blanketed with a sheaf of leaves in brilliant hues of yellow and orange, russet and green from the thick trees softening the graveyard. She stood looking down at the mingling colors and thought how Richard would have been pleased to have so beautiful a pall for his tomb.

She went there often. Far from welcoming the opportunity now to rest and recuperate its strength, her body seemed unwilling to heal. It was as though a part of her had been amputated and refused to stop bleeding. Time and again she made her way down the hill to sit beside his grave, in some perverse way trying to restore the pieces of her spirit that were buried there.

She continued to go even when the snows began to fall and the bitter cold was painful to her wasted body. What drove her there? she asked herself. Guilt, grief, the shattering sense of loss. If she caught a cold and died it would not matter. In fact, it would serve her right, would be her proper punishment.

She knew how much her family was trying to help her. Morna and Agatha were untiring in their visits to Southernwood and in urging her to come and stay awhile with each of them, yet Celia turned away from them both, unable to become interested in their kind attempts at healing her grief. Josh bore with her patiently, trying now and then to talk common sense to her. Even Captain Yancy gave her a stern bawling out which she easily rebuffed. They were all of them kind, patient and understanding, but all she wanted was to be left alone with her sorrow and guilt.

She herself did not realize how obsessed she had become, until early February when a long spell of winter storms kept her inside. Restlessly she waited for the weather to lift, feeling that she would be whole again only when she could once again kneel beside Richard's snow-covered grave. When a weak sun at length broke through the clouds she was off, driving the sleigh herself down the hill to the cemetery, wrapped in fur-trimmed heavy wool against the bitter cold.

She lost track of time that day, not even feeling the cold and oblivious to the snorting and nodding with which her uncomfortable horse attempted to distract her. She did not know that Josh had entered the cemetery until she felt his hand on her shoulder.

"Get up, Mother," he said in a voice she had not heard for months. "You're coming home with me."

Celia stared at him numbly. Before she could object he had pulled her roughly to her feet and was drawing her cloak tightly around her.

"I don't want—"

"What you want no longer matters. You can't go on like this and it's time someone put a stop to it. Do you have any idea how long you've been here sitting in this freezing cold?"

Celia shook her head. She didn't even care.

"Vestal's son came to the yards and got me. You have the

whole house in an uproar. They know you won't pay any attention to them and they see you killing yourself like this and it breaks their hearts."

"What does it matter?"

Taking her arm, he pulled her roughly along toward the sleigh. "It may not matter to you, but for some reason it is important to everyone else."

"Josh," she cried, stumbling along beside him, "I don't want to go!"

He stopped and looked down into her stricken eyes. His resolve almost melted, yet he felt so sure that his father would not have allowed her to carry on this excessive, self-destroying way. Since Richard was not here, it was up to him.

"Mother, you are killing yourself. Do I have to lose a father and a mother in the same year? I cannot bear that."

Celia leaned against his broad chest and for the first time since Richard's death let herself be comforted a little. "What am I going to do, Josh? I'm so lost. So lost."

He laid his arm around her shoulder and guided her to the sleigh. "Well, to begin with, you're not going back to that empty house. You're going to come and stay with Morna and me for a while and help us raise our baby. That should help take you out of yourself."

For once Celia did not argue. Perhaps it was time to let someone else make decisions for her.

"Then I've been thinking ahead," he went on, helping her into the sleigh and arranging a blanket around her lap. "A war with Great Britain is almost sure to come now—"

"Oh, dear. Not another!" Old specters, old dreams.

He fastened his riderless horse to the back of the sleigh and climbed up into the driver's seat. "No one knows what it will bring, but it is certain that the sea lanes will be closed for as long as it lasts."

Gliding easily over the crusted road, they started on the winding trail toward the village. "If we want to get away at all it has to be soon."

"Get away? What do you mean? Are you going away?"

"Yes. And so are you."

He had her attention now. "You see, I decided that a trip would do us all good. The yards are busy, but Elisha has assured me he can handle everything if I leave for a while. Morna and I have not traveled since we were married—I don't count trips to the city as traveling—and you, well, you especially need to get away. It would go a long way toward helping you through this difficult time of adjusting to life without Papa."

Celia stared at him aghast. "I can't leave here, Josh. Why, it would mean leaving my home—Richard . . ."

"Papa is dead, Mother," he said firmly. "He is buried in that churchyard back there where he will wait for you until you return. Life is for the living and though you may not want to be among them, you are."

"But your daughter? How could you leave her?"

"Agatha has already agreed to keep Emily for us. She'll be in good hands. It's done all the time. Besides, we won't be gone that long."

In spite of herself Celia found she was intrigued. "Where did you think to go?"

"Well, I'd love to go to England, but that, of course, is out of the question. Europe will have to wait for more settled times. Yet there are still many interesting places nearer to home we've never seen. Boston, Philadelphia, perhaps even Charleston. Or there's the West Indies, although possibly it would be too dangerous to go that route."

Celia found herself reacting to the thought with a glimmer of pleasure. She had never been to visit any of those places, although she had heard of them all her life. It would be good to get away for a while, to let her mind and spirit heal.

Josh did not give her time to begin an argument. "Morna is already thinking of what clothes she can buy for the trip, so the two of you must go down to the city soon on a shopping spree."

Celia murmured, "I already have more clothes than I need."

"Surely there is something new you would like. Visit the dressmakers and drapers, the milliners. Make yourself pretty again. You are not an old woman, Mother, and you have to learn to go on living. I think a trip like this will help you do it."

They had pulled up before the porch of his house. When she sat without answering, lost in her thoughts, he began to fear he had said too much. Jumping down, he hurried around to set her on her feet. She clutched at his hand for a moment, then smiled up at him.

"You know, Josh, perhaps you are right. I think I would enjoy a trip."

Because she turned away to hurry into the house she did not see the look that came over his face. He had never expected her to agree so readily. With a sigh of relief he turned his thoughts to some letters which must now be written.

forty-two

By early May all the arrangements had been made. Josh, Morna and Celia, two servants and a large assortment of trunks and portmanteaus were set to sail on the *Caroline* from Beekman's Wharf for Boston in early June. Celia walked around Southernwood like a person in a dream. There was an unreality to it all, as though the trip were being planned for someone else. At fleeting moments she could almost become excited about the prospect of an ocean voyage and a tour of a new city, but quickly she would sink back into that preoccupied withdrawal which had been her normal state since Richard's death. In some far recess of her mind she knew that she should make this trip, that it would perhaps finally and for all time lift her out of that morass of grief and guilt from which she was not able to extract herself. So she made up her mind to allow them to lead her aboard the ship when the time came, but until then she did not really allow it to intrude upon her mourning.

But the time galloped closer with each day until finally she could ignore it no longer. All her planning and packing had been done by others—Morna and her maid, Nettie—and everything stood ready in her bedroom at the house. When she woke on the morning of the third and realized that the very next day they were to take the sloop to New York, suddenly the parting was a reality and she was filled with an unreasoning panic.

Bringing in her morning chocolate, Nettie was brimming with excitement and anticipation. It was all Celia could do to listen to her conversation, full of the next day's trip to New York and the sailing the day after. Finally, unable to bear it any longer, she sent the girl away with directions to send word to the stable to bring around her basket phaeton, then she hopped out of bed and hurriedly dressed. In an hour's time she was sitting behind her gentle speckled gray horse, the reins firmly in her hands, on her way down the hill.

Celia had made a special effort to stay away from Richard's grave through these spring months. Somehow the strong lure that drew her there had loosened its hold a little, and she knew that was for the best. How often had she gone there feeling that in that quiet place she would be with him again, and how often had she arrived there to realize that there was only the sleeping earth and a gray headstone, weathered now from the winter's furies.

But now, now that she was going away, she felt the old compulsion to be near him again. She would just sit there a while, perhaps share aloud her fears and pleasures concerning this voyage, talk to him as though he was there to hear. Surely that couldn't hurt.

The day was glorious—golden sunshine, a bright-blue sky, the last brilliant burst of the flowering white dogwood and lavender lilacs transforming the hills into a garden. She left the phaeton near the road and walked around the quiet cemetery for a while before settling near Richard's grave, now blanketed with emerald green of new grass. There were good sounds of the earth around her—the soft buzz of insects, the chatter of the birds busy among the flowering trees, and far away on the road the dim rattle of a carriage passing toward the village. Leaning back against the shady half-grown maple, she closed her eyes and let the peaceful moments comfort her. Surely there is a place for this, she thought; it cannot be so harmful to be drawn here when it brings such comfort and the nearness of a person you miss so much.

She tried to picture Richard in her mind, seeing his gaunt, tired face as it looked in those last months. No. That would not do. Other images came crowding in, and, by carefully blocking out all reality, she could for a little while see them all. Samuel, fat, kindly, in his powdered wig and old-fashioned satin breeches. And there was Elizabeth, her patrician face lightly dusted with powder, her ruffled sleeve reaching out toward her, her lovely lips saying, "You are our daughter now." And Ewan, in his scarlet jacket and military wig, smiling that tender, knowing smile of his, his hand smoothing back her hair where he twined a twig of fragrant southernwood behind her ear. And Richard, the elegant gentleman holding a crowing Josh on his knee. Or Richard as she remembered him even better, picking himself up at the bottom of the stairs with his wig askew and his dignity in shreds, smiling up at her with the kindest eyes she had ever seen. And Hester, her long white-gold hair flying behind her, as she danced around the garden of the Manor House. Hester, her plump overripe figure in a blue morning pelisse, the thin lips turned down in a scowl, her eyes accusing...

Celia shook herself and opened her eyes. Her parade of images from the past was so real that she was startled to see one of them materialize before her eyes. She gave a short gasp, then realized that this was no ghost but the living, breathing person standing in the flesh before her.

"Hello, Celia."

It was so impossible that Hester Carne should be here in the Presbyterian cemetery of Mount Pleasant that Celia could not for a moment take it in. Yet there she was, quietly standing about ten feet away, blue pelisse, straw feathered hat and all. It had not been an image after all. How long had she been there?

"I went up to your house and they told me you were here. Since I had not visited Richard's grave, I thought to join you. I hope you don't mind."

Celia got hesitantly to her feet. "No, of course not. I'm so surprised to see you. I thought I was dreaming."

Hester moved around to the other side of the green mound. "May I sit with you awhile?"

"Of course. Please do."

Both women settled on the grass on either side of the gray headstone. Uncomfortably Celia searched for something to say. A lot had happened since that day when the bitter words between them sent Hester storming out of her house. She had never really expected to face her again, certainly not here. With a start Celia realized that the months between had made widows of them both.

"You were smiling to yourself," Hester said. "It must have been a pleasant dream."

"I was remembering Richard the very first time I saw him. He had tripped and fallen down the stairs. He was such a comical sight with his wig half over one eye that I couldn't help but laugh."

"That must have been one of the few times Richard lost his dignity."

"It was. But it made us friends."

"You two, you were always thick as thieves. I used to be quite jealous at times." Hester's eyes took on a faraway look.

"We did have some good times, didn't we? How carefree those days were. Nothing to do but work samplers, learn a few lessons and play games. Remember the skating on the Fresh Water Pond in winter? And the sleigh rides?"

"I remember more the summer days at the Manor. How Mama Deveroe would scold us for sneaking away from our embroidery to run on some childish escapade."

"That was almost always Ewan's fault. He was always getting us into trouble."

Remembering, Hester's quick glance took in the way Celia let this pass without a glimmer of self-conscious pain. In fact, she seemed lost in reveries.

"Remember the day we rode Father's horse and Richard fell."

"Oh, yes. I was so angry at him."

"I can see you yet screaming into his face—'I hate you, Ewan Deveroe!' But you didn't, you know."

Celia looked down at her hands. "No, I didn't. I was just afraid poor Richard had been killed. Later I realized Ewan was just as frightened as I."

"He had a warm nature, for all his adventurous ways. Richard did, too, though I admit I often doubted it. I suppose of the whole family I was the one who was most lacking in the ability to care."

Celia looked up, astounded at Hester's words, not really trusting their sincerity.

"You had a warm nature, too," Hester went on, "and they appreciated that. I wanted to love you, Celia, as a sister, but I just couldn't. It isn't in my nature, I suppose, to love people much."

"Why, Hester..."

"Oh, I'm not castigating myself. I've just come to realize a few things more clearly than before. I don't really like people, and I don't trust them. Most of us are pretty self-serving down underneath the charitable posturing we show the world. But some of us do have an ability to care more than others."

Celia did not know how to answer. "There were times we were close, surely."

"Oh, I suppose there were. Remember those days before I married Cortlandt? The balls and parties, the ball gowns. Life was very gay then, in spite of the fact that the war would not go away, and it was nice at that age to have a confidante. I think I truly felt then that you were a sister to me. But when

I went away to London everything changed. And when I returned it seemed as though you had everything and I had nothing. I resented it, Celia, perhaps I still do." She met Celia's direct gaze without swerving. "But I came here today because I want us to be friends again."

Celia could see what this was costing Hester. She sat stiffly, trying to sort out her own emotions, her old anger, sense of betrayal and hurt.

"You see, I realized that you and I are the only family we have left now. All the others are gone. We have no one but each other from those lovely days at Wayside and the Manor House. I don't like the thought of all those years lost in bitterness and anger."

Yet there were things which could not be so easily dismissed.

"Oh, Hester. Do you know the hurt you caused us? For myself it doesn't matter so much. I broke my marriage vows, no matter how much I loved Ewan, and I was prepared to pay the price. But you robbed Richard of the single thing he wanted most in his life. He did not deserve that."

"I don't excuse the handbill, Celia, although it was mainly Mr. Carne's doing. But surely we are both to blame, you and I. Richard had been good to both of us and we both robbed him of his dreams. You as surely as I."

Celia covered her face with her hands. Her voice was strangled. "I know! That is what drives me here. My guilt! My failures! Time and again he forgave me and sacrificed himself for me, and always my sins came back to hurt him. And now it is too late."

Hester made no move to reach out to her in her distress, but her level voice had a calming effect. "It is very hard to live with someone else's sacrifices."

To Celia's surprise, for once the tears did not come. Hester's sensible words seemed to dissipate their strength.

"Perhaps it is time to give up your guilt, Celia. Of the two of us I think perhaps I am better off. I'm too selfish to waste time crying over the past. Your warm heart is robbing you of the life you have left. You have enjoyed your grief and guilt for too long, and Richard himself would not want you to go on this way."

"No. I'm sure he wouldn't. And no one else but you would dare to say those words to me."

Hester looked away so that her face was hidden under the

feathers of her hat. "What is a sister for but to speak hard words when it is time for them?"

Celia watched her raise her small figure from the grass, where she stood reaching out her hand across Richard's grave. "Friends again?"

Rising to stand opposite her, Celia took her hand. "Friends."

Hester's eyes took on as wistful a look as Celia had ever seen in them. "Celia, I want to see Agatha. Do you think ... would she turn me away?"

Hester's struggle with her pride was almost painful to watch.

"You see, Charlotte still lives in England, and Christabel and I are far too much alike to get along. Dexter never bothers with me, nor I with him. But I miss my gentle, quiet daughter. Now that Mr. Carne is gone, I have no one."

"She will never come back, Hester. She and Elisha are happy together in spite of the differences in their ages. She's found a contentment and love she never had before and you are wrong if you think to turn things back to what they were."

Hester winced and dropped Celia's hand. "I know that. It's not that I want her to come back with me but that I want to be part of her life again. I'm not pretending that I approve of what she did or that I ever will. I simply do not wish us to be estranged. Will you help me?"

Was she telling the truth? Celia's old distrust surfaced again and she wondered if this entire attempt at reconciliation was just an elaborate ruse to manipulate them all back into some vulnerable position. Yet, looking at the sadness in those faded blue eyes, she thought not. Perhaps Hester had finally come to grips with the loneliness her selfishness had earned her. Perhaps she had begun to realize how much they all needed one another.

"Of course I'll help you," Celia said. "We'll ride over there this afternoon. You'll have a chance to meet my little Emily, my grandchild, whom Agatha is going to care for while Josh and Morna are away."

Hester looked genuinely pleased. "I'd like that. I never see my own grandchildren. Well, then, shall we go back now up that dreadful hill? Surely you'll give me a cup of good hot chocolate after my coming all this way to see you."

"I'll be happy to," Celia said, picking up her light cloak from the grass. "How did you get here, anyway?"

"Vestal drove me down. I saw your phaeton, so I sent him back."

She was already starting toward the gate. "Hester," Celia called after her, "will you wait for me in the phaeton? I'll be along in just a minute."

"All right. But don't be too long."

Celia smiled to herself as she watched the plump little figure struggle up the grassy knoll and out through the gates between the rough hewn stones of the fence. Then, turning back, she looked down again at the granite slab with the letters of Richard's name and the dates of his life span carved into deep shadows. Reaching up, she broke off a branch of blossoming white dogwood and laid the lovely thing across the green of Richard's grave. Then she turned and walked slowly toward the gates.

When the *Caroline* slipped smoothly through the Narrows on a balmy June morning, Celia knew they were heading north toward Boston, but she soon ceased to care about anything beyond that. For someone who had spent all her life surrounded by water she had never really been on it for any length of time before. By the time the ship went scudding past Sandy Hook she had grown horribly, incurably seasick, and after that the days were spent in a black miasma, lying on the narrow bunk of her cabin, wishing she could die and get it over with. Now and then she ventured up on deck and felt a brief momentary refreshment from the billowing sails and the cornflower-blue sky, the silvery water, its turquoise surface broken by a froth of whitecaps or an occasional school of playful dolphins. But the respite was brief and it seemed to her they never would reach the stillness of the Boston harbor.

One glorious morning, she woke to feel a steady quiet under her and realized the walls of her cabin were not tilting dizzyingly as they had been for what seemed like two years past. Standing on her feet, she was amazed to realize that she felt normal, no giddiness, no nausea. She dressed quickly and went up on deck, delighted to find, as she had suspected, that during the night they had entered the harbor and moored offshore. Standing at the rail, she was enjoying the feel of a brisk, cool breeze on her face when Josh found her there.

"Feeling better?" he said, placing his arm around her shoulder.

"Much better. I think I may actually even live."

"You and Morna are both poor company on a sailing voyage.

I've seen nothing of either of you these past days. She was almost as sick as you."

"Now I know why I was never on a boat for any length of time before. Did we pass through a storm of some kind or was this a routine form of torture?"

Josh laughed. "You both need to develop your sea legs. The weather was choppy. I admit, and we crowded on all the sail we could so as not to linger where a British frigate might discover us. But I would call it routine, yes."

"Oh, delightful." Celia groaned. "I may go back by way of the post stage. Even the terrible roads between Boston and New York would be preferable to another week like this."

He gave her an enigmatic grin. "You will have a difficult time taking the stage from here. We are surrounded by water."

Celia's eyes took more careful note of the collection of yellow houses and spires scattered among the low-lying hills around the harbor. "Is this not Boston, then? It did occur to me that the fort up on the hill looked large for Boston."

He leaned his arms on the rail, clasping his hands and looking out over the horizon. "No, this is not Boston, but Halifax. We had some cargo to deliver before we could turn back and begin our sight-seeing. I hope you don't mind."

"Not at all. There does not seem to be much to see, but since this is our first port of call I hope we will spend a day or so looking it over. Besides, I'm not anxious to get back on the high seas again right away."

He grinned up at her. "Oh, yes, we'll see a little of the town. It will do you and Morna both good to get some solid earth under your feet again, even if it is only for a day or two."

By the time the dory carried them to the dock, Celia was beginning to enjoy the exquisite pleasure of discovering this new and rather exotic little shipping port. They took rooms at a clean inn on the town square where bright-red flowers grew in window boxes. Morna had more than recovered from her seasickness—in fact, Celia had not seen her so animated for ages. They walked the narrow streets awhile, peering into the stores, which were full of fine English silver and furniture, then went back to their inn to take dinner. Celia ran upstairs long enough to comb out her hair and pull it into a simple knot at the base of her neck. Beyond that she refused to fuss. It was enough to feel a small measure of strength returning simply

from being in a new and different place. It helped to lay the
ghosts of the past, just as Josh had said it would.

When she rejoined Josh and Morna downstairs she found
they had hired a private room, so small it was almost filled
with the one square table and assorted chairs. Pewter utensils
and English slipware covered the table. A bottle of madeira,
opened, stood next to a tray of silver cups. It was all very
festive and beckoning, and Celia found herself pleased with
the coziness of it, and with the thought of how good food was
going to taste again.

Morna sat by the table, her eyes bright and spots of high
color on her cheeks. She was very quiet as Josh poured out a
glass of the amber wine and handed it to Celia.

"No, thank you, dear, I don't really—"

"Take it, Mother. You are going to need it."

She looked closer at them both. Something was not right
and she began to wonder what was going on.

Seating himself next to her, he took her hand. "Mother, we
did not come here just to deliver cargo. We had another motive.
You may not be aware of it, but Halifax is in Nova Scotia.
Morna wished to see her father once again."

Morna's father! Nova Scotia! Celia could not find the words
to speak.

"He made the journey from Annapolis Royal and he is here
now—"

"Ewan! Here?"

"Yes, in the next room. He wants to see you again, but he
did not feel he should just walk in after all these years. He
asked me to prepare you first."

She had to stop herself from jumping out of the chair. Her
eyes went instinctively to the door. Panic, confusion, fear...

"Will you see him?"

"Oh, oh..."

Was there any place to run? To hide? She was old now.
Her hair—she had not even made a pretense of prettying it.
What would he think of her? What would he be like? Suddenly
the idea of Ewan as he was now was terrifying. It would destroy
for all time her image of the young, vibrant man she had carried
in her mind all these years. "Oh, Josh..."

Josh motioned to Morna, who rose silently. "You don't need
us. We'll let you know when dinner is ready."

She was hardly aware that they left the room. Ewan! Part
of her wanted to run away and another part wanted just as much

to run into his arms. Unable to do anything, she sat, numb and confused, by the table. Spotting the silver cup, she grabbed it and drank long drafts of the wine. It burned all the way down to her stomach.

A soft knock on the door. Then it opened and Celia looked up to see a stranger standing there. She rose to her feet, clutching the edge of the table for support, and they stood looking into each other's eyes across the tiny room.

"Celia," he said softly. "Is it really you?"

With the sound of his voice time dropped away and she knew him. Curious little details impressed themselves on her consciousness. He wore his own hair now and it was iron gray but still pulled back in a queue. He wore a dignified coat of black superfine, and the figure under it was more portly than before, yet not as heavy as Josh had led her to believe. The face was fuller, lined and darkly tanned. But the eyes were the same and the shape of the lips, the firm chin.

He crossed to her and took both her hands, raising them to his lips. "Celia. My dear."

Her knees went weak at the touch of his hands. She was trembling like an aspen leaf in the wind. "Oh, Ewan. I never thought to see you again." Suddenly her eyes filled, yet she was unable to turn her face away.

Without releasing her hands he sat her down and took the chair opposite. With a passing thought she recognized the old deliberate taking-charge, the strength of that tall figure.

"Josh wrote me asking if I would meet you here. He said you had been so unhappy since Richard's death. He thought perhaps I could help. You don't mind, do you?"

"Mind!" The tears came spilling down her white cheeks. "Mind. It's like a dream come true. I thought we were going to Boston. I never knew Halifax was anywhere near you."

There was the old teasing grin she remembered so well. "For heaven's sake, Celia, don't you know anything about the world outside West Chester? I live about eighty miles across the island, but it is all part of Nova Scotia. You look so pale. Has it been so difficult for you, then?"

"I was terribly sick all the way up. Oh, Ewan." She laid her hand against his cheek. Her joy was beginning to spill over inside. "How very good it is to see you again."

Gripping her hand, he studied her face. She was changed, though not as much as he knew himself to be. Her lovely hair was graying, too, but it still waved prettily away from her pale forehead. Her large eyes were the same as he remembered, though perhaps the flesh of her face was a little fuller. The years that would have made these changes imperceptible as they occurred lay now between them, requiring a shifting of old pictures, old dreams. But the lovely, elegant, sensual woman he knew her to be was still there.

"Celia, so much has happened. So much time has gone by. We will be like two strangers trying to get to know each other again."

"No. You could never be a stranger to me."

"I have changed over the years, and so have you. It would be impossible not to. But I want us to become reacquainted. Perhaps you will find you don't like what I've become, perhaps I will discover you are not the girl I remembered. But I don't think so. I want us to spend some time together and learn whether or not what we felt for each other once still exists."

"But we are sailing in two days."

"That can be altered. Josh and Morna are quite willing to come back to Round Hill with me for a visit. I would like to take you to Grand Pré—your people came from there. Remember that old deed you used to have. We can look up the land where your father and mother lived."

"Acadia? That is near here?"

"Only a little north of Round Hill. I'm anxious to show you my estate too, and all that I've done there. I built a home out of that wilderness, Celia. It was hard, but I did it. Of course, from what Morna tells me it can never match Southernwood, but . . ."

She tried to smile. "Richard built Southernwood for me, Ewan, so that I would never again fear being poor. Yet I was always poor without you. I never knew what really mattered until you left."

A shadow fell between them at Richard's name. Ewan looked away. "Richard was a good man," he said lamely. "And certainly he loved you."

"He gave me everything he had to give," she said, "and I loved him for that. But I never loved him as I love you. No one ever took your place for me, Ewan, in all these years. For so long I have held on to that dream that now I'm afraid. Afraid that reality will destroy it. Afraid it will not be able to adapt to what is now."

"There is only one way to know, my dear. And that is to

spend some time together learning about ourselves all over again. Are you willing?"

At her smile the years fell away. "So willing."

"If at the end of your visit you want to return with Josh and Morna I shall wish you Godspeed. If not, perhaps we can find something together we gave up as lost years ago. There is only one thing you must remember—I can never go back to New York. Perhaps if you are with me I will no longer want to."

On a sudden impulse she leaned forward and kissed him full on the lips. How soft they were, how sweet, how well remembered. How like coming home. Then she was in his arms, clinging to him and laughing and crying all at once, filled with a kind of joy she had never thought to feel again.

A discreet knock at the door drew them apart. After waiting a moment, Josh stuck his head around the doorjamb.

"Dinner is ready if you two are interested," he said, trying to hide his embarrassment under a jaunty air. He was still not sure how his mother was going to take having this surprise sprung on her. One look at her face and he began to relax.

"Well, will you look at this, Morna," he exclaimed, throwing open the door. "I never saw two people look more glowing."

Morna was right behind him, coming to stand beside her father with her arm around his waist. For the first time Celia saw some resemblance between the two of them. "What do you think, Celia?" Morna asked. "Can we go to Round Hill for a visit? I should so much like some time at home again."

"I ought to be annoyed with both of you for deceiving me this way, but I cannot find it in my heart to complain. And Round Hill sounds like a lovely place to visit."

Filling up the glasses on the tray, Josh passed them to the others. He was beginning to feel really ebullient now, convinced that his hunch had been correct. Only time would tell for sure, but there was a light in both his mother's face and his cousin's that he had never seen before. What a strange thing life was.

"A toast, Cousin Ewan," he said, raising his glass. "To what shall we drink?"

Ewan placed his arm around Celia's shoulder, and looked down into her shining face. They were sharing some of the same thoughts in answer to Josh's question: to a war that had brought them together long ago, then separated them . . . to a gentle man who had given them both so much . . . to time lost and a measure of time regained . . . to the memories of the heart that could sometimes be so strong as to overcome the years . . . to longings that finally held the hope of fulfillment.

He touched his silver cup to Celia's.

"To coming home," he said quietly.

MS READ-a-thon—
a simple way to start
youngsters reading

Boys and girls between 6 and 14 can join the MS READ-a-thon and help find a cure for Multiple Sclerosis by reading books. And they get two rewards — the enjoyment of reading, and the great feeling that comes from helping others.

Parents and educators: For complete information call your local MS chapter. Or mail the coupon below.

Kids can help, too!